Also by Carrie Doyle

Writing as Carrie Karasyov
The Infidelity Pact

Writing as Carrie Karasyov with Jill Kargman
The Right Address
Wolves in Chic Clothing
Bittersweet Sixteen
Summer Intern
Jet Set

DEATH
ON
WINDMILL
WAY

CARRIE DOYLE

Poisoned Pen
PRESS

Published by Poisoned Pen Press, an imprint of Sourcebooks
P.O. Box 4410, Naperville, Illinois 60567-4410
(630) 961-3900
sourcebooks.com

Originally published as *Death on Windmill Way* in 2016
in the United States by Dunemere Books.

Library of Congress Cataloging-in-Publication Data
Names: Doyle, Carrie, author.
Title: Death on Windmill Way / Carrie Doyle.
Description: Naperville, Illinois : Poisoned Pen Press, [2020] | Series: A
  Hamptons murder mystery | Originally published in 2016 in the United
  States by Dunemere Books. | Summary: "The scenic stretch of Long
  Island's East End is renowned for beautiful beaches, quaint villages,
  spectacular houses...and murder! In Carrie Doyle's fast-paced mystery,
  Death on Windmill Way, readers are introduced to gourmet chef and
  innkeeper Antonia Bingham as she digs into an active investigation to
  learn who's behind the suspicious deaths of the Windmill Inn's
  innkeepers. Mixing past and present, seriously sumptuous settings, and
  mouth-watering food descriptions keep things cozy and will feel like a
  stay at your favorite country inn!"-- Provided by publisher.
Identifiers: LCCN 2019049446 | (paperback)
Subjects: GSAFD: Mystery fiction.
Classification: LCC PS3604.O95473 D43 2020 | DDC 813/.6--dc23
LC record available at https://lccn.loc.gov/2019049446

Printed and bound in Canada.
MBP 10 9 8 7 6 5 4 3 2 1

Prologue

December

"OH, IT'S YOU," SAID GORDON HASLETT, HIS VOICE tinged with its usual irritation. "You're always sneaking up on me. Drives me nuts. You just appear like a ghost. Trying to scare the hell out of me?"

Gordon propped the rake against the tree and wiped the sweat off his brow with the back of his hand, leaving a smear of dirt along his face. This small dose of physical labor had intensified his breathing, causing his chest to rise and fall dramatically under his vest. After taking a few gulps from a bottle of water, he examined his visitor critically. "So are you going to help me or what? Don't just stand there watching me. We both know this isn't *my* damn job."

He turned and resumed raking the stack of wet leaves that were blocking the door to the garden shed. They were soggy from the rain and stacked together in sad little clumps. The air smelled moldy, of musty earth. Gordon had apparently been out there for a while, as the brick path leading upward to the shed had already been cleared. He turned gruffly when he felt a tap on his shoulder.

"What?" he barked.

His visitor held out a handkerchief, and motioned toward the beading sweat on Gordon's forehead. Gordon grabbed the cloth.

"Thanks."

He pressed the handkerchief firmly to his head and aggressively wiped his entire face.

"What the hell?" yelped Gordon, suddenly dropping the handkerchief and taking a step back. "Damn, something stung me!"

Gordon began furiously slapping his face, then stopped and glanced around in confusion. He held one index finger to the side of his face. His skin was burning hot. Suddenly his entire face began to swell, and his eyes were enveloped in clouds of puffiness.

"What the..." He couldn't finish his sentence. Instead, Gordon clutched his throat and dropped to his knees.

"Go get help," he whispered.

His visitor nodded. And then turned and walked as slowly as possible back to the inn, and waited.

1

October
(Ten months later)

IT WAS A GLORIOUS FALL NIGHT IN EAST HAMPTON. The sky was inky black with thin clouds racing past a full moon, and the ancient trees along the village streets cast long shadows in the silver moonlight. In the distance, the ocean waves murmured, providing a romantic background soundtrack. The air outside was crisp, not too chilly, but with just enough kick to necessitate roaring fires in the Windmill Inn's public rooms. It was a cozy Friday evening, just how innkeeper Antonia Bingham had imagined it would be when she dreamed of her move to the East Coast from California. Combined with the medley of delicious smells wafting from the kitchen, the weather and atmosphere gave Antonia a sense of great satisfaction.

The dining room of the Windmill Inn was by no means filled to capacity, but for the first time in the six weeks since Antonia had opened the restaurant, half of the tables were occupied. She had heard, of course, that it takes a while for new restaurants to gain momentum, particularly when they are replacing old restaurants that had reputations for terrible service and inedible food. But still, those first few nights when the seats remained empty, she had felt completely disheartened. Not to mention embarrassed: the sound of every ice cube clinking in a glass seemed magnified and the busboys were too eager to replace half-eaten rolls, just to have something to do. But gradually—very gradually—reservations had picked up, with locals and weekenders popping by, eager to try a new place, and more guests booking rooms at the inn and venturing down to try Antonia's home-cooked meals.

Finally, in Antonia's mind, the future was beginning to look a little brighter. She hoped she wasn't delusional; she was by nature an optimist who chose to look at the bright side of things. However, Antonia's optimism made her prone to bad judgment calls, resulting in infrequent but spectacular failures. "Older and wiser" was one of her mottos, and with her recent purchase of the inn, Antonia was hoping that she could put some of the knowledge and experience that she had acquired in her thirty-five years (twelve years of catering!) to good use. She just needed to avoid past mistakes.

Now, as Antonia roamed the sleek navy and white dining room, she surveyed it critically. It was a large space that seated sixty-five diners and the decor was comfortable, while also streamlined and uncluttered. Whereas Antonia had chosen to make the rest of the inn feel cozy-formal with antiques, lots of prints, and colored fabrics, she had given the restaurant a bright and crisp interior. The walls were painted eggshell white and held large canvases of modern art, mostly bright abstracts, but a few small, individually lit oil paintings as well. The floors had been stained a dark walnut wood, brushed smoothly and evenly. In the front of the room, by the maître d' station, was a dark-azure lacquered bar. Its eight barstools had button-tufted backs and sides studded with pewter nail-head trim. Beyond that were a dozen freestanding tables set formally with starched white linens, white china, and blue Murano goblets.

When she was decorating the inn, Antonia had sat on dozens of chairs in an effort to find the most comfort-able; one that would encourage diners to linger and order more courses. The winners were softly rounded and upholstered in blue, with gently sloping arms and maple-stained legs. In the back of the room, beyond the swing-ing door to the kitchen, was a nook housing four booths, their banquettes covered in cobalt vinyl with white piping. Antonia had debated whether or not the booths made the place feel too casual, but tonight they had allowed her to successfully accommodate a last-minute party of seven. Smiling benevolently at the happy group, Antonia knew she had made the right decision in adding the booths. They made the restaurant feel complete.

Tonight, Antonia was clad in her best black satin dress, replete with a plunging neckline to both accentuate her ample breasts and move everyone's eyes away from her widening girth. (*Ah, the havoc that working with food wreaks on your waistline,* Antonia often despaired.) She had on the lowest high heels that she could find, as any-thing even a half an inch higher caused major wobbling in the manner of a drunken streetwalker. It was the last thing Antonia would have liked to have been wearing—sweats, elastic-waisted ruffled skirts, soft cardigans, and Crocs were more her speed—but her manager had told her that she needed to "sex it up and work the room" in order to encourage first-time customers to become repeat customers. She hardly thought that her looking all dolled up would entice diners, especially in this small town, but with all of her money on the line with the restaurant and inn, she agreed to do whatever had to be done for the bottom line. As a result, Antonia had pulled out all the stops tonight, blowing dry her glossy black hair until it fell in cascading waves down to her shoulders and even applying makeup. Her Cupid's bow lips were deep red, her porcelain cheeks blushed pink, and her already thick lashes fluttered darkly around her bright-blue eyes.

"Another wonderful dinner, Antonia, thank you," said Joseph Fowler as he signed his check and flipped the leather-bound cardholder closed. He placed it on the table next to the small pumpkin centerpiece. After finishing the last sip of his sherry, he dabbed his mouth with the cloth napkin.

"Thank you, Joseph. You always make my day!" Antonia beamed at her favorite dinner guest.

Joseph was a renowned writer of historical fiction. He had been recently widowed when his wife of thirty-plus years died after a long bout with cancer. Joseph was Antonia's first customer at the restaurant, and for that she was eternally grateful, especially as he had turned out to be a tremendous cheerleader for her. An elegant man, with refined features (aquiline nose, arched eyebrows, chiseled cheekbones, impeccably combed silver hair) he always dressed in custom-fitted monogrammed dress shirts and a bow tie, cords or khakis (depending on the weather), and a beautiful tweed blazer. As he was still only in his early sixties, Antonia fervently hoped he would find romance again. It was too soon for her to play matchmaker but she had already targeted some of the ladies who came to tea at the inn as potential suitors. Should she mind her own business? Probably. But that wasn't really her style.

"Joseph, I'd love your feedback. What did you think of the truffled polenta with Gorgonzola? It's a new recipe I'm trying out. You can tell me honestly."

He smiled. "It was exquisite."

"I'm not fishing for compliments. Are you sure?"

He patted her hand. "My dear, I would have it every night if I could."

"You know how to make a lady happy," she said, wagging her finger at him. "I'll take your word for it, but I still think it needs some tweaking—maybe a different herb. It says rosemary but I have to be honest, I'm not the biggest rosemary fan. It sort of tastes like shampoo, don't you think? I much prefer tarragon or sage. Even chervil. Thyme could work, but it's kind of wimpy. Well, we'll see…"

"My advice to you is don't overthink it. The best thing about your food is that you cook from the heart. And it shows."

"Well, I try."

Antonia motioned for Glen, the maître d', to assist Joseph into his scooter. Joseph had suffered a bout of polio as a child and although he could walk with the assistance of crutches, in recent years he had primarily used a scooter to get around.

"There ya go, Mr. Fowler," said Glen in his strong Long Island accent. "I tell you, I could use one of these things to escape from the ladies."

Glen was attractive but in an unctuous, hair-gelled way, like Guido the Killer Pimp. A failed actor with an inflated ego, he was a high-maintenance employee but very good at charming women and making customers feel at home.

Joseph chuckled. "Well, I don't exactly have that problem."

"All in good time."

"Have a great night," said Antonia cheerily.

Joseph winked. "You too, my lady."

Antonia moved around the room to greet other guests and to solicit any suggestions they might have about the food. She enjoyed meeting people as much as she enjoyed cooking, and it was always an internal debate as to where she should spend more time. It was fun for her to find out where guests were from, and what their story was, but at the same time, she also adored her time in the kitchen, concocting her latest culinary adventure, darting about, plating dishes. If she could slice herself in half and do both she certainly wouldn't hesitate.

After sending off a cute couple that was visiting from New York City (house-hunting), she stopped off at Len and Sylvia Powers's table. Len headed up security at the Dune Club, a very fancy country club on the ocean, and his wife was a teacher. Tonight, they had brought their son in to celebrate his twenty-fifth birthday.

"You've done an amazing job, Antonia. I tell you, just amazing. The inn looks gorgeous and the food is fabulous," said Sylvia Powers, her big cerulean eyes twinkling. She dabbed her mouth with her napkin, leaving a stain of the hot-pink lipstick that was her trademark, then patted her stomach appreciatively. "I tell you, it is so wonderful that you brought this place back to life. And so quickly. What was it, only six months?" She didn't wait for an answer but continued, "I can't tell you how sad it was to see it fall into disrepair all the years Gordon Haslett owned it. What a mean guy! And that made the place mean. We stopped coming here long ago, didn't we, Len?"

"Well, you didn't really have a choice, Mom," said Matt, giving her a sly smile.

She frowned. "Nonsense. We had a choice. That business was all settled. Right, Len?"

Len Powers glanced up from his apple cheddar crisp, and looked around, dazed by the interruption. He was a large man, with a belly that arrived in a room ten seconds before he did. Everything about him was big and fleshy, from his bulbous nose to his ruddy cheeks and giant ears. "I can't talk! I don't want to tear myself away from this incredible dessert."

Sylvia laughed. "I already inhaled my dessert. I tell you, that chocolate caramel cake with the little dots of sea salt was majestic. This is our third time here and every time I sample some new yummies."

"Thank you." Antonia beamed.

"This may seem like a backhanded compliment, but you cook in a very homey style. The way I like to think I can cook, but actually can't. I like that it's not all that fancy new-wave stuff—foams and edible flowers. That just sounds disgusting to me. Some of those cooking shows, I think, yuck! Foie gras ice cream? Come on. When I have ice cream, I don't want meat in it. But I'm not a food snob. I just prefer food that tastes how it's supposed to. Don't mess with what ain't broke."

"Well, I'm so glad you liked it," replied Antonia. "And thank you for your kind words. I say to everyone I know that the biggest compliment they can give me is to spread the news around. I want everyone to know that there's a new sheriff in town, and the Windmill Inn is back in business."

"Oh, everyone knows that already, Antonia," said Sylvia, chattering on. "East Hampton is a small town. Especially when the summer people are gone. Ah, the summer people! Did you know we call the season 'one hundred days of hell'? Oh, they're not all bad, I'm joking. But it's nice to have the town back to ourselves, where we can get up in everybody's business! Ha, I'm joking again. But of course, everyone knows that the inn changed hands when Gordon Haslett died. In fact, Matt was there—he's a paramedic." Sylvia gestured proudly at her son.

Antonia was having a hard time following Sylvia's dramatic stream-of-consciousness rambling. She looked to Matt for clarification.

Matt put down his fork and nodded. He had a pretty boy face composed of dainty features: a small straight nose, plump red lips, and thickly lashed eyes. There was also something morose and gloomy about his temperament that Antonia was certain thrilled girls who were attracted to the dark, broody types. Looking at his jolly, big-boned parents, it was hard to tell where Matt had come from.

"Yes, I was the first responder to the scene," he said solemnly and with an air of authority. "I arrived less than oh-five minutes after the call. But there was nothing I could do. He was already DOA."

"Well, I've no doubt you would have done everything you could have," said Antonia sympathetically. She patted his shoulder warmly. "But obviously there's not a whole lot you *can* do when someone suffers a massive heart attack and dies before you get there."

"Right," said Matt, nodding, his face oddly empty of emotion.

"*If* it was a heart attack," said Sylvia. She nudged her spoon into her husband's crisp and took a huge bite for herself.

"Mom," warned Matt, rolling his eyes. "Let's not go there." Sylvia shrugged and put her hand to her lips to block the view of food while she talked with her mouth full. "Didn't you say, sweetie, that you thought he died of a bee sting?"

Matt squirmed uncomfortably. "Official cause of death was a heart attack."

"Yes, but one that was brought on by a bee sting," prompted Sylvia. She dove into her husband's dessert for another bite.

"Yes, I did suspect that," said Matt officiously. "He had a red welt on his cheek at the two o'clock position, and his face was inflamed concurrent with an allergic reaction. But that idea wasn't pursued."

"Why not?" asked Antonia, vaguely intrigued by this new information, gossip or not. She motioned for a busboy to refill the Powers' water glasses.

Matt rolled his eyes. "The family didn't want to. Didn't want an autopsy. But it was December, and who gets stung by a bee in December?" He was indignant.

Antonia nodded. "I guess that is strange."

"They thought I was an alarmist, being swayed by the whole reputation of the inn..." he continued.

"Um, Matthew..." his mother interrupted. She widened her eyes and shook her head.

Admonished, Matt abruptly stopped speaking. Sylvia shifted uncomfortably in her chair, and Len shoved a large bite of crisp into his mouth. Antonia glanced at each of them quizzically.

"What is the reputation of the inn?" she asked finally.

Matt looked past her at the wall. "Um, nothing, just an old superstition."

"What's the superstition?" pressed Antonia.

Sylvia sighed. "It's nothing, just a silly thing. And we all know that old stories like that are nothing more than stories. Someone wanted to concoct a ghost story and that's all it was."

"But what was it?" asked Antonia again.

"I wouldn't worry about it, dear," said Sylvia in a cool, reassuring voice (one that she probably used on her third graders at the John Marshall School). "I tell you, it's nothing."

"You can't leave me hanging!" Antonia said in a light voice, although underneath, her heart was racing. "Come on, now, help me out. I bought this place sight unseen eight months ago on the advice of my friend Genevieve. I moved all the way from Petaluma to East Hampton, a town that I had never stepped foot in. Then I poured every last penny I could to get it up and running. I have eight guest rooms and a restaurant, and a dozen full-time employees. I need to know every facet of the inn's reputation so I know what I'm up against."

Antonia blinked her long lashes several times and smiled brightly, in an effort to alleviate the panic she was feeling. Ever since she'd bought the inn, she had been experiencing moments of extreme nervousness and self-doubt, basically questioning her impulsivity. Had she made a mistake? Perhaps she should have been more suspicious of how quickly the sister of the deceased had accepted her low-ball offer. She had congratulated herself on a steal, but maybe she had been the one who was swindled? She wished she would have done more research, but she always became completely restless whenever she was in front of a computer. Honestly, she found the internet to be a colossal waste of time in regard to everything excluding searching for recipes or antiques. But perhaps if she had taken time to Google Gordon Haslett's death, she wouldn't be having this conversation.

The Powers family all glanced at each other uneasily. Finally, Len spoke. He held his fork in the air, indicating he would be brief so that he could return to his dessert.

"The story about the Windmill Inn is that the owners die under suspicious circumstances. Now, it's just a story, makes the place more dramatic."

"I actually think one of the previous owners conjured it up just to attract some business," added Sylvia quickly. "I mean, I taught some of the kids of one of the owners, there was nothing there. Oh dear, now wait…"

She stopped speaking, as if remembering something.

"Well, is it true?" Antonia asked. "I mean, before Gordon Haslett, did the other owners die of suspicious circumstances?"

Sylvia and Len exchanged a look.

"Well…" began Sylvia. But she didn't finish her sentence.

Len cocked his head to the side, as if he was thinking, and finally shrugged.

"It's kind of true," said Matt finally.

"Kind of?" asked Antonia. "What does that mean?"

"I guess it means yes. Some of the owners of the inn have died under suspicious circumstances."

"Great," said Antonia weakly. She needed a drink.

2

THE WINDMILL INN WAS FINALLY QUIET AT MIDNIGHT. The diners had almost all left by ten thirty, except for a last lingering couple who, judging from their body language, appeared to be on their third or fourth date. They stayed until eleven, after working out whether or not they would be retreating to their own homes or having a sleepover. Only three of the guest rooms at the inn were occupied and when Connie, the front desk receptionist, confirmed that everyone had retired for the evening, Antonia had locked all of the doors to the inn with the exception of the two in the kitchen.

It was Glen's responsibility to shut down the restaurant for the night, but Antonia usually helped him out, since it was still early days. It was important for her to establish a hands-on approach from the get-go so the staff would know that she was firmly in control. And it was always important to keep track of the money. Other restaurateurs had told her that it was crucial to watch out for skimming, no matter how much you trusted your employees. They advised her to get a sense of how much was coming in so that she could sense if anything was going out that should not be.

Antonia and Glen went over the books, locked up the bar, and looked at the reservations for the following evening. While he ducked in to the office to print out the next day's menu, Antonia went into the kitchen. Juan and Albert, the busboy/dishwashers, were just finishing up when Antonia went into the staff changing room to switch out of her high heels and into her Crocs. When she returned, they were leaving and she shut the back door behind them, pressing firmly to confirm the click of the latch. The staff had been having trouble with that door closing all the way; it was still warped from the summer heat. Often, it would blow wide open and bang loudly against the wall, startling anyone who was standing next to it.

When Antonia went back to the dining room, Glen had returned with a stack of printed menus, which he placed on the maître d' stand. He turned off the lights and shrugged into his soft leather jacket. She walked with him back into the kitchen so he could exit from the side door. When he opened the door, a gust of wind came flooding in.

"Wow, it's picking up out there," said Antonia.

"Yeah. You're lucky you don't have anywhere to drive to get to your bed."

"I know. Living at work does have its plusses."

"Oh, I forgot to mention, Antonia. This guy from a local microbrewery came by tonight. I told him to come during the day since we don't order during dinner hour."

"Good idea. I'll let Marty handle it. Goodnight, now."

Marty was Antonia's sous chef and he was a lot tougher than she; she liked to let him deal with the vendors. Antonia firmly shut the door behind Glen and twisted the lock. She turned and glanced around the kitchen to make sure everything was in place. The glasses were drying on racks on the counter and all of the prep stations were wiped down. The pots and pans were hung neatly on their pegs. It was difficult to believe that just an hour ago this place had been buzzing. Antonia flicked off the big overhead lights and walked toward the pantry to do the same. It was quiet now, with only the hum of the two industrial dishwashers making a fuss. Antonia heard Glen start his car, then watched as his headlights flicked across the darkened ceiling when he drove away.

Antonia walked back through the dimmed dining room for one last proprietary glance. She thought of all of the people who had come through the door of the inn over the last hundred and fifty years. Throughout much of the nineteenth century, the Windmill Inn had housed a tannery in the barn out back; guests stayed in the main building while their saddles were treated. Were any of their ghosts lurking there now? Antonia shuddered. All she needed was a headless horseman! She glanced around at the shadowed tables. Antonia had always thought that empty restaurants looked a little eerie, as if the ghosts of the people who had just dined there somehow dissipated into thin air. She wondered if she was particularly on edge tonight having just heard the news that Gordon Haslett's death was somehow suspicious. Had previous innkeepers really met untimely fates? She pushed the thought out of her mind.

Instead of heading straight across the dining room to

the small staff hallway that led to her apartment, Antonia made a right and walked toward the front door. While she had taken special care to sand down the floors in the dining room, the floors in the rest of the inn had been left more or less in their original state. Over the years they had buckled under the extreme seasonal oscillation between temperatures, and they were squeaky and uneven. Antonia had placed a few Oriental carpet runners along the way, but they did nothing to contain the noise, and tonight it seemed as if the floorboards creaked particularly loudly under her feet. The chandelier in the front hall was lit, but dimly. Its light was the only one that seeped through the other public rooms.

Antonia turned left into the parlor to make sure that the staff had straightened up before they departed. A few glowing embers amid the ashes were all that was left of the fire that had been roaring earlier. Her eyes darted around the room, straining to identify objects in the shadows. Although she knew that there was a seating arrangement with a sofa and two club chairs in the forefront of the room, they looked different in the darkness. Antonia walked over to the backgammon table against the wall and clicked on the bouillotte lamp. There was no need to completely shut down all of the light in the building. What if a guest was restless and came down to read? These things had to be thought through! Being a novice inn owner was challenging and Antonia was going on instinct. She just hoped that she would do a good enough job that the guests would return and would recommend the inn to friends. That was one reason she always solicited advice and impressions from her guests. She pulled the cord to light the bright bulb and all of the furniture in the room came into clear focus. *There*, she thought. *Much better.*

Antonia moved toward the chairs and picked up various pillows to re-fluff them. They didn't really need it, but something was compelling her to remain in the room. She noticed that a book on Hamptons style had been left on the coffee table so she returned it to its place, sliding it into the shelf next to the fireplace. Antonia then straightened the side chairs that leaned against the wall and bent down to touch the soil in the potted plant to make sure that it was damp. They were all minor adjustments, ones that no one but a perfectionist would notice, but that's what made Antonia a natural innkeeper.

Suddenly Antonia stiffened. What was that noise? She thought she heard something scratching. She paused and listened. There it was again! It sounded like fingernails scraping a blackboard. She strained her ear to find which direction it was coming from and waited. Her head jerked toward the back of the room, from where the sound was emanating. Taking a deep breath, she proceeded to the back, where there was another cluster of upholstered furniture with plush cushions that you could sink into underneath the bay windows. Antonia hesitated for a moment when she reached it, her knees bumping into the low coffee table. She glanced around apprehensively. She waited for the sound. Once again, there was the noise. Antonia paused. An image of swarming bees attacking flashed in her mind. Her stomach turned with nervous anticipation. She slowly turned her head, but to her relief, she realized that the noise she was hearing was only the wind slapping a branch from the birch tree against the window. She exhaled, suddenly realizing that she had been holding her breath.

This was so silly, she told herself. *Why am I psyching myself up?* Before she had heard the suspicious deaths rumor, she had been fine. In fact, she had been sleeping in this inn for six months and never felt frightened. She wasn't a scaredy-cat; that wasn't her thing. Hell, she had survived an ex-husband who'd used all of his energy to scare and harass her for years. So why was she freaking herself out *now*? Just because the Powers family had told her that the previous innkeepers had died suspiciously? It was absurd.

Antonia stood up straight and strode firmly out of the parlor. This was her inn. She was the boss! She walked toward reception and gave it a cursory once-over, and also glanced briskly inside the deserted library. No one was awake in the inn. There was nothing to give her pause. She made her way back down the hall toward her apartment, refusing to be disturbed by the shadows along the wall. She walked past the small antique elevator that was used to transport luggage or guests who needed assistance and peered through the glass. No one was hiding there. Antonia promised herself that she would not let this ghost story about the inn haunt her. She would not succumb to hysteria.

3

Saturday

EAST HAMPTON, RENOWNED FOR ITS AWARD-WINNING beaches, picturesque villages, and the ethereal light that had inspired some of the greatest American painters, is nestled on the tip of Long Island's south shore, bordered by the Atlantic Ocean on one side and various bays on the other. Everything about the town is profoundly quaint: from the acres of farmland bursting with abundant crops to the shaded streets lined with windmills, shingled houses, and churches that actually look like churches. The center of the village is composed of two streets—Main Street and Newtown Lane—that meet in an L-shape, and are home to neatly kept and freshly painted one- to two-story storefronts. Since the end of the nineteenth century when the Hamptons became a resort community, summers have attracted the rich and famous, not to mention a chaotic number of tourists. But for all the glitz and fanfare, most of the time East Hampton feels like any other small town in America.

Antonia Bingham had never thought she would leave California. She was born and raised in Petaluma, and she'd assumed she would stay there forever. Why wouldn't she? But Antonia hadn't counted on the relentless abuse of her ex-husband, Philip. During their marriage she had been a virtual prisoner, and after she finally mustered up the nerve to leave him, Philip embarked on a tyranny of terror that made her life a living hell. Her pleas to the police went unheard. And, of course, that would be the case: Philip was one of them, a sergeant in the force beloved by his brothers in arms. Restraining orders, calls to 911, and reason didn't matter. No one believed her and eventually, no one listened. Until one fateful day when Philip showed up at Antonia's house and her frail father tried to intervene on her behalf. A kick to the stomach from Philip sent her father to the hospital where he died two weeks later from complications. Philip escaped jail time with an Academy Award–winning, teary-eyed, and remorseful performance in criminal court, but she won a restraining order and settlement against him in civil court. It was that money that she had used to purchase the inn, and the inheritance from her parents that she used to maintain it.

Her friend Genevieve, who had worked for Antonia's catering business as a waitress after a relationship with a vintner in Sonoma went sour, sold Antonia on East Hampton, the town where Genevieve's family had rented a house every August. She talked of lush seasons, a town as charming as any Norman Rockwell painting, unspoiled vistas, sandy dunes rolling down to the edge of the blue Atlantic, and Antonia was sold. It was impulsive, but something drastic had to be done. She said good-bye to her parents who were buried side-by-side in the Calvary Cemetery, and made the opposite trip that her ancestors had made one hundred years ago when they set out for California. But in both cases, the Binghams were searching for the "promised land."

"You're a diehard too!"

Antonia turned around and then nearly gasped out loud. She couldn't believe her eyes! It was Nick Darrow, the movie star, talking to her, Antonia Bingham, civilian. She knew he lived in East Hampton but she had not seen him until just now. And here he was, standing in front of her at Main Beach in all his handsomeness, two yellow labs frolicking at his heels, talking to *her*. And she was struck dumb.

"Excuse me?" she murmured, at least she thought she murmured, because she was too busy trying to control the blush that she was certain was creeping up over her pale, white cheeks. Damn her English skin! When she was embarrassed it was as if she paraded it on her face like a scarlet letter.

"I said you're a diehard. Not many people are out on the beach at six thirty in the morning in late October. And I know this is not a one-off because I've seen you here the past three weeks."

"You have?" she squeaked.

"Yes. Sorry that sounds creepy. I'm not a stalker. I'm Nick," he said, thrusting out his hand.

Of course he was, she knew *exactly* who he was, but

she also didn't want to appear like a stalker. His hand-shake was firm, and his hands surprisingly warm on this brisk morning.

"I'm Antonia."

He wore a barely perceptible smile on his face, and yet his expression warmly conveyed a feeling that they were both in on the same joke. It was an intimate gaze, one that wholly embraced a person and created a cozy space for just the two of them. Antonia knew intellectually that it was just Nick Darrow's innate charisma, but he had it on a much higher level than most people. *That's why he's so famous,* thought Antonia. *He just has a spectacular, glowing energy.*

Whatever it was, Antonia was totally starstruck. She couldn't believe this was happening; it was surreal. And it was all so casual, as if he were just some guy on the beach. But he wasn't; he was Nick *Friggin'* Darrow! And although Nick was now in his late forties and definitely not the gorgeous poster boy that he once was, age totally agreed with him—he was more smoldering than ever. He still had very thick dark hair, albeit now graying at the temples, a strong jaw, blue eyes, which were amped up by the orange Patagonia that he was wearing, and plump lips. *Kissable lips,* Antonia thought. Yes, every-thing about Nick Darrow was sexy, including the zesty aftershave that she could slightly smell from a few feet away and the way his faded jeans hugged his muscular legs.

"So, are you on vacation? Some people would say you picked the wrong time of year, but I'd say you picked the very best time to be in East Hampton," said Nick with a smile. "I love it when the town clears out."

He bent down and picked up a ball and threw it near the breaking waves. Both of his dogs took off in furious pursuit.

"No, I actually moved here a few months ago."

"And you waited for the worst possible days to take up walking on the beach?"

He motioned to the barren sand around them. The sun had barely peeked out, and the breeze was ripping through the dunes as if getting the hell out of dodge. Even the waves appeared grumpy, lazily smacking the shore like a teenager dragged out of bed too early. The air was chilly, though the weatherman had promised temperatures in the high fifties.

Antonia laughed. "No. I used to walk later in the day. But now for work it's better for me to leave early so I can be there when the guests wake up."

"Where do you work?"

"I bought the Windmill Inn on Main Street."

"Oh, that's *you*."

He said it in a way that made Antonia feel self-conscious. Had he heard about *her*? Was this a practical joke? Antonia peeked around to see if some camera crew would pop out of the bushes. Maybe he was a Nick Darrow impersonator? She studied him with squinted eyes. No, it was definitely him.

"Yes, I bought the inn. I did indeed," said Antonia. *I did indeed*? She didn't really talk like that. What was she, eighty? She wished she could say something really cool right now, but all she could think of adding was, "and I'm the chef at our restaurant."

"*Really?*" he said in a drawn-out, interested manner. "What kind of food?"

"I guess you'd call it American. Just sort of home cooking. Things people like to eat. Or at least, things I like to eat."

He smiled. "And what do you like to eat?"

"Oh, you know, well, to be honest, my favorite food is bread. I could eat that all day long. And I don't discriminate: it can be sourdough, raisin nut, olive, pretzel rolls, you name it..." she realized she was rambling, and about gluten too. "But as I can't serve bread exclusively, I also have things like roast chicken with crispy skin, baked stuffed lobster with bourbon-spiked butter, grilled pork loin, hash browns cooked in duck fat. Butterscotch pudding with whipped cream."

"Wow! Sounds great! You're making me hungry."

"You'll have to come by. I mean...if you're around. Come by. No pressure." She was embarrassed she was so forward, so she quickly added, "You know where the inn is, right?" She felt herself become redder.

"Of course. Everyone knows."

"Yes, it's been there for over a hundred and fifty years."

"I know."

"You do?"

"Sure. It's a small town."

"Right."

Antonia wasn't sure what to add to that. One of Nick's

dogs returned and dropped the slobbery tennis ball at his feet and he, in turn, picked it up and hurled it across the sand. Antonia could sense the strength of his muscles even through his fleece. The dog took off again, bounding across the sand to retrieve it, with Nick watching him. Antonia realized that she was watching Nick watch the dog and instantly felt foolish. Was she supposed to linger or should she keep walking? The uncertainty made her blush deeper. To her relief, Nick returned his attention to her.

"So you're not worried about the curse?"

"The curse?"

"Sure, you have to have heard about it before you bought the inn."

"You mean that the innkeepers there die under suspicious circumstances?"

"Yes, that one."

Whatever red was hovering in Antonia's cheeks now drained. "Well, no one told me before I bought it. In fact, the first time I heard anything about it was last night. Now you're the second person to alert me. So what's the deal? Am I like, the biggest moron in town? Did I make the biggest mistake of my life? Which by the way, by all accounts, now sounds like it will end shortly."

Nick Darrow laughed. He had a big, booming, hearty laugh that made the people who made him laugh feel intensely gratified.

"I don't know. I'm sure it's just local legend. I mean, there was nothing suspicious about the last guy who died. I think it was a heart attack."

"I've heard it might have been a bee sting."

"Bee sting, whatever. A bee sting isn't suspicious, actually."

"A bee sting in August isn't suspicious," replied Antonia. "But a bee sting in December is."

Nick smiled. "True."

"What about the guy before that guy?"

"I don't really know, I just heard maybe he poisoned himself or something and they weren't sure what happened."

"Poisoned himself?" asked Antonia, her voice rising. "Great, just great. How many months do you give me?"

Nick put his hand firmly on Antonia's shoulder. The warmth from his palm trickled down all the way to her toes.

"I have total faith that you'll break the curse."

She looked deep into his eyes and wished desperately that she was another type of woman: the type who could now reel off a coy, flirty little response, but instead she blurted, "I have bad luck."

"You do?"

Antonia instantly began to backtrack. There was nothing tackier than someone unloading all his or her problems on a total stranger. Especially total strangers who happened to be movie stars. "I mean, just kidding. Anyway, how does everyone seem to know about this curse? Is there a library book I could take out to get to the bottom of it?"

"I don't think anyone has written a book about it just yet," said Nick.

"Okay, then how am I going to prepare myself to stave off my potential suspicious death? I need to be ready in case I accidentally pick something poisonous from my garden and make a soup out of it."

"You know what you can do? I've got a friend at the *East Hampton Star*, Larry Lipper, who covers the crime beat. His office is on Main Street. Just stop by and tell him I sent you."

"The *crime* beat?"

Nick laughed again. "Yeah, I know. He mostly writes about DUIs or reports on those 911 calls that people make where they think they heard something but it turned out to be a neighbor. But it doesn't matter. If there was anything to the inn story, Larry will know."

———————————

Antonia was oscillating between two extremes as she made her way back to the inn. On the one hand, she felt extreme elation at the fact that she had just had an entire conversation with *Nick Darrow*. He was handsome, he was nice, and he acted totally normal. It was literally as casual as talking to the guy at the hardware store, total chitchat. And yet this was a guy who had been voted *People* magazine's "Sexiest Man Alive"! But all of that excitement was tempered by the confirmation that the inn had a curse, and if lore proved true, her untimely demise was imminent. Antonia smacked her steering wheel as she headed along Ocean Avenue. Damn, had it been a totally stupid move buying the place? What had Genevieve talked her into? She had wanted a new start, a new adventure, but one that ended in homicide wasn't exactly what she had in mind. She felt duped. Should she call her broker and give him a piece of her mind? Demand her money back? The inn had already given her a fair share of problems in the six months she had owned it.

For one, the rambling three-story Georgian Revival building was built in the late 1840s and required constant maintenance. It was so run down when Antonia purchased it that it had taken a solid five months to update the rooms and bathrooms and renovate the kitchen to a professional chef's kitchen that would accommodate the restaurant. She had totally missed the summer season and had to delay her opening, which was a major loss of potential income. And when one upgrade was finished, something else always needed to be done: the exterior had to be repainted white, the shutters needed a fresh coat of green, the front yard had to be nuked and new sod laid and the brick path needed to be fixed before someone fell down and broke their neck. The to-do list was endless, and the fact that she was a bit of a control freak/ perfectionist didn't help. The one thing Antonia had on her side was naivete, because if she had known what she was getting into, she never would have done it.

But now, to be honest, Antonia was glad that she had been ignorant. She loved her inn. She loved the antiques that she had chosen for the parlor and the crooked floors in the entryway and the unpredictable twists and turns of the hallways. And she loved East Hampton. The fluidity of the place appealed to her; she appreciated the way that the population ebbed and flowed, just like the tides at Georgica Beach. And now she loved everything a bit more because she had just met Nick Darrow and although it was silly, it was so cool that he had even heard of her. Or well, not her, but that he had heard that someone had bought the inn, and that was her. *Did that even make sense?* she wondered.

The interaction had put a spring in her step and even made her a little flaky. She was usually good with names but upon returning to the inn, when she went to greet the couple from Rhode Island who was staying in room 2, their names escaped her. And later, when the farmer came from Pike's to take her order for next week's vegetables, she completely blanked that she needed potatoes, which would require a phone call to amend. In fact, she was so distracted all morning that she didn't even notice when Lucy Corning, the manager of the inn, came to find her in the kitchen. Antonia had been stirring the mix for ricotta doughnuts, dreamily fantasizing about kissing Nick by the dunes on the beach when she felt a tap on her shoulder.

"Antonia, are you okay?"

"Huh?" Antonia jumped, startled back into reality. She blinked several times before realizing where she was, and unfortunately, where she wasn't. "Sorry, I didn't hear you."

"I was calling your name, but you looked like you were a million miles away."

Antonia blushed. "I was just thinking about something."

A slight smile crept across Lucy's face as if she knew *exactly* what Antonia was thinking about, but she immediately dismissed it and got down to business.

"I didn't mean to interrupt you. But we have a situation."

Antonia sighed. She glanced at the small mousy woman in front of her. Lucy was probably in her early-to-mid-forties, waif thin, with one of those nondescript hair colors (Is it brown? Is it dirty blond?) and one of those nondescript hairstyles (Bob? Shoulder length?) She was neither unattractive nor attractive—somehow just neutral. And clearly somewhere along the line, Lucy had been encouraged to go with an eclectic, vintage look because she insisted on wearing quirky black-framed glasses, and either her trademark cashmere sweater set and retro A-line skirts, or dresses that made her look like an aging 1950s schoolgirl. Come to think of it, Lucy had even mentioned once that she worked at a vintage clothing store and found her style there. Antonia had raised her eyebrows, but kept mum.

Antonia didn't mean to be judgmental because Lucy had proven to be a competent employee—so competent, in fact, that Antonia had promoted her to manager from her previous position of bookkeeper. Lucy was amazingly prudent in helping keep Antonia in line with a strict budget. It was like having an in-house system of checks and balances. And it was a bonus that she had been working for the inn under Gordon, because she had the technical hospitality background that Antonia didn't possess yet. Antonia had high hopes for her, except she did notice that Lucy seemed to appear gleeful every time she had to report bad news, like a cancellation or a broken toilet.

"What's up?" Antonia finally asked.

"It's not good," said Lucy gravely.

_____

"Ladies, ladies, be quiet! It's Saturday morning, many of my guests are sleeping in. Please stop, oh geez, stop!"

There was so much yelling that Antonia's voice fell on deaf ears.

After working her way around the bottom of the staircase, with Lucy hot on her heels, Antonia swiftly inserted herself into the middle of the two women who were loudly fighting in the front hall of the inn. On one side was a voluptuous blond woman around the age of forty-five, who wore a jean jacket over a scoop-neck spandex floral dress. On the other side was a wiry, pencil-thin brunette of about sixty, clad in a white zippered windbreaker over blue slacks. Both women were shrieking obscenities at each other, with the brunette desperately trying to seize hold of the small cardboard box that the blond was clutching in her arms.

"Stop this right now!" bellowed Antonia at the top of her lungs.

They momentarily fell silent. From the doorway, Lucy gave Antonia a decisive nod of approval.

"Now, I don't know what is going on, but I know that this is *my* inn, and you ladies can't act like this here. Now tell me, what the heck *is* going on?"

They instantly spoke at once, their words accusing and angry, and the tone rapidly rose from normal speaking voices to a shouting match. Antonia put her thumb and index finger to her mouth and blew a whistle. (She was so proud that she knew how to do that; the lifeguard at the YWCA pool had taught her when she was fourteen.)

"Let's try this again. I'll start with you, Naomi. What is this about?"

The brunette—Naomi Haslett—shook her head with exaggerated dismay. She was the late Gordon Haslett's sister, and had been the co-owner of the inn along with him. Her hair was pitch black—the color of shoe polish— and cut bluntly into a Louise Brooks bob, with razor-straight bangs slicing across her wrinkled forehead. Her face was pale and craggy, and Antonia couldn't help but think that her hair color actually aged her. Naomi would do much better with a softer look across the board, especially since every interaction Antonia had had with Naomi proved that her character was as sharp as her haircut.

Naomi pointed at the other woman, the sexy blond whose name fittingly happened to be Barbie, and who was Gordon's girlfriend at the time of his death. "Antonia, I think you should call the police. She is *trespassing* on your property."

This was interrupted by Barbie's furious rebuttal. "I am not! It's my stuff!"

"Barbie, you will have a chance to talk," said Antonia, silencing her. "Naomi, continue."

Naomi gave Antonia a slight smile while Barbie glowered. "Like I said, Barbie is *stealing*. That box in her hands? It's yours—"

"Is not! It's mine!"

"Barbie!"

"Listen, Antonia," said Naomi. "When I sold you the inn, I sold it lock, stock, and barrel. Everything from the doors to the hinges, right?"

"Yes," concurred Antonia.

"Well, according to our agreement, that included the boxes that were in the storage areas. And now this woman has snuck into your inn and is taking *your* box!"

"It's mine!" protested Barbie.

Antonia turned to Barbie. "Now let's hear from you."

Barbie Fawcett pressed the box firmly to her chest, smashing her ample bosom in the process. "You said, Antonia, that I could take any of my belongings out of the inn. I had forgotten about this box, so I came here to retrieve it." Her voice was flustered and husky, and in the tussle with Naomi, bits of mascara had flaked off her lashes and landed in black dots on her rouged cheeks like measles.

"It's not your box," snapped Naomi.

"Yes, Naomi, it is mine."

"May I ask, what is in the box?" asked Antonia.

From behind Antonia, Lucy spoke. "It's nothing, some old notebooks that Gordon used to jot down to-do lists and things like that."

"Lucy, stay the hell out of it," snapped Barbie, craning her long swan neck in Lucy's direction.

"Barbie, that's not necessary..." said Antonia.

"Does she really need to be here for this?" asked Barbie impatiently. "I'm just wondering when that woman will disappear forever. She's like a tick that just keeps hanging on. Doesn't know when to leave. Lucy, it's over. Go home."

Lucy reddened. "Say what you want, Barbie. But I ran Gordon's office. I went through everything when he died. I'm not sure what you're looking for, but it's just a bunch of office notes."

Barbie tapped her foot impatiently and rolled her eyes to the ceiling. "Is this how you'll get your revenge?"

"I'm telling you the facts," insisted Lucy.

"See, Barbie? You're not going to find anything that you claim is here because it doesn't exist," said Naomi impatiently.

"I'm lost here. What is Barbie looking for in the first place?" asked Antonia.

Naomi shook her head with irritation. "She claims my brother had another will in which she stands to inherit the inn," said Naomi. "But it's all a lie. An exasperating lie. We just came from court where she is still trying to obtain a piece of my inheritance. But Gordon would have never left this...this...person...anything. I'm positive."

"Naomi, you're forgetting that your brother and I lived together for *five* years. I'm not some one-night stand. We were in a committed relationship. I was his common-law wife..."

Naomi scoffed. "Concubine."

"I helped with the inn, day in and day out. It would not look like this if not for me," Barbie said waving her arms around at the polished mahogany staircase, the gleaming wood floors carpeted in Oriental rugs, and the brightly shined brass sconces. Antonia wanted to correct her and tell her it would not look like this if not for *me* and hundreds of thousands of *my* dollars, but she bit her tongue.

"What a joke," scoffed Naomi. She turned to Antonia. "You can ask anyone, my brother was done with her. He was trying desperately to shake her. There are people who will vouch for that."

"I know who you're referring to, and Ronald Meter is hardly a reliable witness," replied Barbie before turning to Antonia. "That guy is a disgruntled former employee who Gordon fired when I told him that he was stealing money from the inn. He's vindictive."

"And so were you," muttered Naomi.

Barbie narrowed her eyes to slits. "You know, Naomi, you were always jealous of me because you knew that Gordon would leave me his share. There is no way he would have left you anything! He thought you were a money-grubbing user who let him do all the work and tried to drain him of any profits. You always undermined him, since you were children."

"I gave him the money to buy the place!" sneered Naomi with exasperation.

"And he paid you back in turn. But you never stopped. You were always shaking him down for money! That's why he quit taking your calls. And that's why he made sure that I would get his share. He showed me the will! I just need to find it."

"You'll never find it because it didn't exist!" Naomi bellowed.

"Yes, it does!"

"Oh, no it doesn't! And now do you realize that it was a mistake to kill my brother?"

Antonia's head shot around. "What did you say?"

"You heard me. This witch killed Gordon!" Naomi's eyes were feverish, and her fists were balled up, ready to pounce.

Barbie snorted with disdain. She turned her head away and looked down. "You're delusional. I wasn't even at the inn when he died."

"Am I? Am I?"

Antonia was beginning to feel dizzy. "Wait, wait. Time out, now. Gordon died of a heart attack, did he not?"

"Yes," said Barbie firmly.

Naomi glared at her.

"Naomi, didn't Gordon die of a heart attack?" prompted Antonia.

"Yeah, right, whatever." Naomi rolled her eyes.

Antonia was exasperated. "No, *not* 'yeah, right, whatever.' Did he or did he not die of a heart attack?"

"Yes," said Lucy from behind. "Heart attack."

Antonia didn't shift her gaze from Naomi's face. "Isn't that so, Naomi?"

Naomi looked down at her tennis sneakers. They were very clean white Reeboks that she had worn every time Antonia had met with her. She took some time to answer, after taking several deep, relaxing breaths that looked more appropriate for a yoga class.

"The official cause of death was…a heart attack," she said at last, glaring at Barbie, who still wouldn't meet her eye.

Antonia felt her heart race. "What was the unofficial cause of death?"

Naomi finally glanced in Antonia's direction. She gave her a small smile, her lips curling enough so that her thin top lip disappeared into the bottom. The look reminded Antonia of a defiant child forced to lie to a teacher.

"Heart attack," Naomi repeated before adding, "but I'd bet my bottom dollar that this tramp here figured out a way to cause it."

Barbie snorted. "Like I said, I wasn't even here when he died. How could I cause a heart attack?"

Antonia kept her eyes on Naomi. "Why didn't you tell the police if you suspected it?" asked Antonia.

Naomi rolled her eyes. "I wanted to make sure I could sell the inn. No one would have bought this place if they thought Gordon was murdered. That's my official story and I'm sticking to it."

4

THE ONLY WAY ANTONIA COULD PERSUADE NAOMI and Barbie to leave was to confiscate the cardboard box that they had been fighting over and promise to review the contents herself. After ascertaining to whom it rightfully belonged, she would personally deliver the box to her. It appeared to temporarily appease both ladies.

"What do you think?" Antonia asked Lucy, as they sat in her cramped office to regroup. Antonia immediately poured herself a cup of Earl Grey tea, which Lucy refused, and brought out a plate of coconut macaroons that were fresh out of the oven. As Antonia popped the third cookie in her mouth, she noticed Lucy watching her with a somewhat disdainful look. She slid the plate in Lucy's direction but received a vehement shake of the head.

"Sorry, but I totally believe in comfort food," said Antonia, wiping her fingers on her napkin before she took a big gulp of her milky tea. She grimaced slightly at the bitterness and spooned another large scoop of honey into her mug. "Anything bad or unpleasant and I dive for the pantry. Break my heart, pass the banana bread. Steal my money, serve me some buttered noodles!"

Antonia smiled but when Lucy did not, she became serious again.

"So, back to business. Can you tell me a little bit more

about the personal history here? Because I am totally confused."

Lucy smoothed her skirt and took a moment to gather her thoughts before answering. Antonia had noticed that she was always very precise. That and she had excellent posture. Even now while Antonia sat flopped in her chair, Lucy was on the edge of her seat, sitting erect. It made Antonia straighten up a little and reminded her of her mother who always used to admonish, "Sit up straight, shoulders back, head up, stomach in!"

"Well, as I'm sure you can tell, there was never any love lost between Naomi and Barbie."

Antonia waited, but when Lucy didn't continue, she probed further. "Okay, so maybe they hate each other. But why would Naomi accuse Barbie of murder?"

"I'm not really sure."

"But was there a suspicion that Gordon had been murdered?"

"I never heard that," said Lucy, stifling a yawn. "Naomi is just being dramatic."

"But she seemed to believe it."

"People can believe what they want if they so choose. I could walk out of this room and say you punched me and even though there was no proof, many people would believe it."

"True," conceded Antonia, momentarily wondering if such a thought had actually crossed Lucy's mind. "Do you think it's because of the whole mythology of the inn?"

Lucy paused. "I only recently heard about that."

"Really? But you've lived in this town your whole life, haven't you?"

"Well, not really. I've been in East Hampton on and off my entire life. We moved away for a while. But yes, I consider myself a native. And I don't really believe in all that gobbledygook. I have better things to worry about."

"That's reassuring," said Antonia. She took another sip of her tea while Lucy waited. She could tell Lucy was eager to return to work and was only humoring her boss, but Antonia wasn't done.

"What do you think is in there?" Antonia motioned toward the disputed box, now sitting on the edge of her desk.

"Like I said to Barbie, nothing. I packed all those boxes myself. It was just scraps of paper that Gordon jotted things down on, flyers, junk mail. I went through absolutely everything twice and I know there was no will in there. I should have dumped it way back when. I'll go through it again this afternoon. But it really should just be thrown out."

"That's okay, I can do it."

"Are you sure? It's no problem."

Antonia shook her head. "I got it. I don't understand, why was Barbie so hostile to you?"

With a tilt of her head, Lucy paused to consider this. "We got along fine when Gordon was alive, pretty much had minimal contact. I think she's just bitter that I'm still working here and she's out on the street."

Antonia thought there must be more to it than that. "But those were some fighting words she threw at you."

Lucy's face quivered slightly, and Antonia thought she might be embarrassed. "Perhaps I wasn't as discreet as I should have been. I clearly came down on the side of Team Naomi whenever there were these kerfuffles."

"Got it. So, what was Gordon like?"

Lucy shrugged. "Well, I knew him for a long time. Gordon was not a popular man. He alienated vendors, he would impulsively fire staff… One could say he was rude, mercurial, and selfish."

"Geez, doesn't sound like the right personality to run an inn! This is a service business after all."

"I know. It didn't suit him. But *sometimes* he could be wonderful and fun. There was something oddly charismatic about him that made people want to please him. Almost mesmerizing."

"Really? That doesn't jibe with everything I've heard about him."

"Well, no one is one-dimensional. I assume there were many layers to Gordon. But I wouldn't really know; I kept my head down and did my work."

"What was his relationship like with Barbie?"

"I tried not to get involved, I'm just an employee, and I do like to keep things professional…"

Antonia felt this last remark was pointed at her and this line of questioning. Once again Antonia didn't let her off the hook. "But…"

"It *was* hard to avoid it sometimes. They fought like cats and dogs, always screaming at each other, breaking up, making up. Very toxic."

"Bad relationship but nothing out of the ordinary, then?"

"Not really."

"You dealt with the finances, the books. Do you think Gordon was going to leave his share to Barbie?"

Lucy hesitated a beat too long. "I don't know…"

Antonia pounced on the opening. "Come on, Lucy. I feel like you're holding back…"

Lucy glanced around the room, avoiding eye contact. Antonia could tell she was wrestling with some sort of internal debate as to whether she would spill what she knew. Antonia was certain she could break her.

Finally, Lucy sighed deeply. Her face was troubled, her eyes distant. "I would prefer to let sleeping dogs lie, Antonia."

"Ah, but they are not asleep. What do you know, Lucy?"

Lucy was quiet for an entire minute, perhaps waiting for an out, but Antonia didn't bite. When she grasped that she was cornered, Lucy conceded defeat.

"I overheard a conversation Gordon had on the telephone. I don't know who was on the other end. But he said that he *was* changing his will. And he wanted to make sure Barbie got nothing. It sounded like he had originally planned to give her everything, but he was so angry at her that he was cutting her out."

"Why was he angry at her?"

She shrugged. "I don't know for sure."

"And *not* for sure?" Antonia prompted.

Antonia could practically see the wheels in Lucy's brain turning. "I think she had another guy on the side."

"Why?"

"I saw her around town a few times in odd places at odd hours with another man."

"Who?"

"I think he may work at a liquor store. I vaguely remember that because of his shirt. I can't remember what it said exactly, but I was left with that impression. Physically, he's tall, handsome. Married."

"Married?" asked Antonia, raising her eyebrows. "How do you know?"

"Gordon. Those last few months, he was trashing her. Said something about the man being married and that she'd end up with nothing if she pursued it."

This reminded Antonia of something. She almost mentioned it to Lucy, but decided to keep it to herself for now. Instead, she shifted directions.

"So you think he'd have left his share to Naomi?"

Lucy met her eyes and leaned in, as if she was revealing something she shouldn't. "What Barbie said was true. Gordon was furious at Naomi. Claimed she was stealing money from him. If I told him she was on the phone, he'd slam it down. He even threw her out of the inn a week before he died."

"So, he was feuding with both women."

Lucy's head bobbed in agreement. "Yes."

"Then they both had motives," announced Antonia with a shiver. "And this so-called tale of innkeepers' untimely deaths might be true after all. I'm doomed."

"I wouldn't go that far."

Antonia had been tempted to drive, but figuring that was *very California* of her, especially since it was only about three blocks, she opted instead to slip out of her Crocs, don her UGGs and amble east down Main Street, also known as Route 27. To be honest, Antonia found any sort of physical activity repellant in general, but since the extra ten pounds she had been carrying around on her five-foot-five frame had now morphed into an extra eighteen pounds, she vowed to make walking her thing. She was half Italian (from her mother) and half English (from her father). But instead of inheriting her mother's beautiful and smooth tanned complexion, she had her father's white skin (she'd call it pasty, others referred to it as "peaches and cream"), and instead of her father's slight, skinny frame, she had her mother's wide hips. Oh well.

Although Antonia's state of mind was frazzled and concerned, it was a glorious fall day and *that* she could appreciate. The leaves on the ubiquitous plane trees were the color of flames, pumpkins, and gold, and when the wind blew, the leaves cascaded to the sidewalk like fireworks. The October sun dappled the various houses along the far side of the road, and Town Pond shimmered in the orangey light. Antonia was almost regaining her high spirits until she glanced at the cemetery, which prominently held court in the center of the village green. She couldn't help but feel as if it were mocking her. *No way, you won't get me now,* thought Antonia as she determinedly swung

open the front door of the two-story shingled building
with a gambrel roof that housed the *East Hampton Star*.

I will not go down because of some stupid curse!

The *Star* was a weekly paper that had existed for over
a hundred years. Like most small-town papers, it covered
local politics, commerce news, business transactions, current events, and sports. A large part of the newspaper was
classifieds and real estate advertisements. The editorials
were opinionated and often incurred spirited "letters to
the editor," and the sports coverage was a bit reverential,
because all the stars were homegrown. Fortunately, the
reviews of local restaurants were usually laudatory, and
Antonia had already been featured in a glowing piece.
Since then, it was the only newspaper she read.

She was directed to a small office in the back, next
door to the restroom that appeared to double for both
men and women. After knocking briskly and being
invited to enter, Antonia found herself in a disorderly
mess of a room with framed posters of Bob Dylan adorn-
ing the walls and a random assortment of globes. At first,
they appeared to have been collected for a decorative
effect but now looked more like a cluttered afterthought.

Larry Lipper had a chiseled jaw, a full head of salt-
and-pepper hair that matched the two days' worth of
stubble on his cheeks, and thickly lashed, piercing gray
eyes. He would have been considered remarkably handsome except for the fact that he was profoundly diminutive. Small in stature, with eyes bordering on beady, and
small hands, small ears, and a small nose, Antonia found

herself wondering if the old adage was true…but then stopped herself.

"Hello," he said, giving her the up-and-down. His voice was remarkably deep for such a little man. "To what do I owe the honor?"

"Hi, is this a bad time?"

"No…"

She didn't need further encouragement but continued on. "You don't know me at all, but Nick Darrow referred me to you. I'm Antonia Bingham. I just bought the Windmill Inn down the street. Can I sit down? I am sorry to bother you, but I really need your help."

"Whoa, hang on a second. Hang on. Did you just come from the city? You are talking way too fast for this town," he said, leaning back in his desk chair and folding his arms behind his head. He threw her a bemused look. "You've got to slow down."

"Sorry. I'm just a little worked up. I'm not from the city. Believe it or not, I've only been there twice, but maybe those three cups of caffeinated tea that I just had didn't help."

"What's going on, Antonia Bingham?" he said in a singsongy voice. "You do seem like a lady who needs a drink."

"That could be true, although I don't like to think of myself as a daytime drinker. I would never refuse if Baileys found itself into my afternoon espresso, but I don't actively seek out booze in daylight."

He glanced around the room and eyed a half-finished

bottle of whiskey on his window shelf. Next to it were two shot glasses that appeared sticky and used. He reached for the bottle but Antonia stopped him.

"No, really, that's okay. I don't need anything."

"You sound like you do."

"Really, I'm fine. I mean, alcohol-wise."

He gave her a skeptical glance but put the bottle back in its place.

"Take a load off and tell me what gives."

Antonia sat down but just as quickly rose and removed the spiral notebook that she had inadvertently sat on, and after glancing around at the mounds of books and stacks of papers on his desk, decided to place it on a bookshelf next to a Yankees mug and a Bart Simpson bobblehead.

"I'll just put this over here," she said.

"Yeah, sorry about that. My work is pretty complicated, and I need a lot of books to keep it all accurate."

"I'm sure."

"So what about you? What can I do you for?"

"Well, as I said, I just bought the Windmill Inn. And now I'm hearing all these stories about it. Scary stuff. So, Nick Darrow suggested that I talk to you, that maybe you would have some ideas?"

"Nick Darrow suggested me?"

"Yes, he thought you could help."

"Huh," he said, scratching his chin idly. "What's going on?"

"Well, you know Gordon Haslett, the previous owner? Was there any sort of 'cloud of suspicion' about his death, as they say? Because his girlfriend and sister were just at my inn and they were pretty angry. One even accused the other of murdering him, and I have reason to believe they both have motive. And, as they were fighting, I remembered something that I found when I first moved into the inn. I didn't think much of it at the time, but now it is haunting me. Here, look at this."

Antonia pulled out a crumpled piece of paper from her pocket and unfolded it. When she had spoken to Lucy earlier it had reminded her of something, a note she had found. She was so happy that she had kept it and now presented it to Larry. He took it from her, scanned it, and then glanced up.

"I don't get it."

"No, of course, let me explain. I had an industrial cleaning service do a *very* thorough cleaning of the inn. But a few weeks ago, I was opening the window, which is one of those old windows—very hard to open, gets stuck all the time. So I was exerting an inordinate amount of energy trying to get it open..."

"Maybe you should work out."

"Thanks, yes, perhaps. And you should read Emily Post, but anyway, all of my pushing and heaving of the window caused the cross to fall off my necklace behind the radiator. When I reached down to retrieve it, I found this sheet of paper. I was distracted so I just glanced at it and tossed it into my bottom drawer. It is written in what I now know from other documents to be Gordon's handwriting. See what it says? *I swear to god that B is trying to kill me.* B is trying to kill me! Gordon's girlfriend is named Barbie. So he might have been referring to her! But then the weird thing is he said 'that B' not just 'B.' So he might have been referring to someone else and meant 'that B' like the word that rhymes with witch, possibly referring to his sister. It seems like both women had something to gain from his death. So there is possible proof that Gordon Haslett knew that someone wanted him dead. So what do you think? I know, I'm rambling, but do you have any thoughts? Should I go to the police? I do try to avoid them at all costs."

Larry leaned back farther in his chair and put his feet on his desk, so now Antonia had worn, dirty black soles staring her in the face. He kept his gaze on her, studying her face as if he were registering her story. Finally he spoke.

"How do you know Nicky?" he asked.

"Excuse me?"

"Nicky Darrow. You said he sent you to me. How do you know him?"

That was his takeaway from my entire story? Antonia thought. *He wants to know how I know Nick Darrow?* "I don't know him actually. I briefly met him today."

Larry put his feet down and shifted in his chair.

"He's a great guy. You should really get to know him."

"I'm sure a lot of people would love to get to know him, as he is one of the most recognizable actors in the world. But I seriously doubt he's on the lookout for new friends."

"We're pretty tight."

"That's great."

"Yeah, Nicky and I have done some serious damage in this town. That guy can outdrink me and you won't find many people who can do that."

"Really," said Antonia flatly.

"Yeah, but it's not all party-party. Did he tell you how we met?"

Antonia shook her head.

"It was intense. He was doing a film where he played a reporter. He wanted it to be authentic, and you know, he was playing someone who covered the grittier stories. Not a big city reporter that's been done a zillion times. But someone like me, who has to straddle being a member of the community and reporting on it when people do bad things. So Nick followed me around for a week when he was researching the part. Did I tell you who his costar was?"

"No, you didn't mention it."

Again, Larry brought his feet back up to the table and nestled in for a chat. Antonia watched as his eyes drifted back down memory lane.

"Kate Winslet. That is one ballsy lady. But you know, she has kids and is busy being a mom when she's not working, so it was really Nicky and I hanging hard…"

Antonia listened impatiently as Larry droned on about his contribution to Nick's acting career. He began describing in detail how his incredible reporting skills were an inspiration for Nick, and how Nick even had some of the script rewritten to include actual anecdotes from Larry's life. Antonia fervently hoped Nick had won an Oscar for the role, because having to tolerate this homunculus was going above and beyond his duty to his craft. Larry Lipper was an arrogant, boastful, self-aggrandizing person, and she couldn't wait to depart from his presence. She finally had to cut short his discourse.

"I'm so sorry to interrupt and I would totally love to hear more about this, but I actually have to return to my inn to start dinner service. I'm gathering from your subsequent rambling that you were not impressed by my story about the note from Gordon about people who wanted to kill him and then the fact that he died. That's fine. But I had hoped that perhaps there was something you might know about Gordon Haslett, or really any of the previous owners. But if not, I won't waste your time anymore."

Larry gave her an unctuous smile. "What? You don't have time for a little get-to-know-you, Bingham?"

Antonia gritted her teeth. "I would like to chat with you, but right now I'm in a rush. I don't mean to be rude, but I just hoped you might have some quick information."

Larry abruptly pulled his feet off the desk and landed them with a thud on the floor. He leaned in toward Antonia, his eyes glued once again to her chest. "You're attractive."

Antonia reddened. "Thank you."

"So what's your damage?"

"My damage?"

"Your damage!" he said again in his singsong voice, spreading out his arms at the same time. "How did you end up in East Hampton? Everyone who moves here has a history."

"I'd argue that everyone has a history."

"Very funny. You know what I mean. A divorce, a layoff, an alcohol problem, financial problems, something that made you move here to get away from it all. Because this place is paradise for *everyone* three months of the year. And everyone else who sticks around beyond that is searching for a year-round paradise that doesn't exist. So, what was your deal?"

"My deal is that I like to keep my so-called history to myself, thank you."

Larry gave a gleeful smirk and banged his fist on the table. "I knew it, divorce!"

Antonia stood up. "I'm sorry if I wasted your time. Thank you for listening."

"You didn't waste my time. And you didn't waste your time either. Because in"—he glanced at the watch clasped around his hairy forearm—"five hours you can seat me in the best table at your restaurant, buy me dinner and a nice bottle of wine, and I will give you all the information you need."

Antonia gave him a curious glance. "What are you talking about?"

"I mean, I can help you. I'll get you information."

She wasn't sure how to respond. "Okay…"

"Don't look so serious, Antonia! I can tell we're going to be good friends."

Antonia didn't have the heart to tell him that she was absolutely sure that would not be the case.

SATURDAY AFTERNOON TEA WAS BEING SERVED IN THE parlor and Antonia did a quick detour to check in before she headed to her office. Quite a few tables were full and Antonia greeted several guests, including Ruth Thompson and Penny Halsey, two older local ladies who had become a fixture every day at 3:00 p.m. Antonia couldn't help but feel proud as she surveyed the well-appointed room, which looked much less foreboding in the daylight than it had the night before. In her fantasies, this was exactly how she had imagined her snug inn would be. There was a roaring fire at one end, a smattering of antique tables, and plush seating that ladies of a certain age could sink into as they tucked into their scones with jam, served on real English china. At least aesthetically, it was a success. She did notice, with chagrin, that one of the bulbs needed replacing in the recessed light above the bay window, but if any of the guests detected it, they didn't say anything. She made a mental note to replace it later.

When Antonia reached reception, Connie told her that she had a friend waiting for her across the hall in the library. Antonia found Genevieve deep in an armchair flipping through the latest issue of *Cosmopolitan*. Of course, the shelves behind her were lined with the classics from Shakespeare to Faulkner and every masterpiece that Antonia could think of when she compiled it, but that was of little interest to Genevieve. As usual, she was dressed to the nines, appearing as if she was straight out of a Ralph Lauren advertisement, which in a sense she was, as she managed the Ralph Lauren store in East Hampton and exclusively wore his label. Today, she had on a camel-colored cashmere poncho over a cream cashmere turtleneck, and brown suede skintight pants tucked into chocolate leather boots. A few Native American–style necklaces in silver and turquoise were draped around her neck, and she wore a very large aquamarine ring that engulfed her entire middle finger. At first blush, Genevieve was absolutely striking; she had olive skin; long, silky chestnut hair; enormous round green eyes, and was what one would call "a stick"—very tall and very thin. But upon closer examination, her features didn't entirely mesh; the eyes were too close together, her forehead too broad; it was as if the spacing was off. She was, however, inherently sexy, which offset her physical shortcomings. Her immaturity was another unfortunate problem.

"So, what gives? I thought you were chained to your inn. All those excuses that you can't do anything, but then I show up on my lunch break to keep you company and find out you're gallivanting around town," said Genevieve, loudly flipping the page. "Ooh, I love these shoes," she added, casting a disparaging glance at Antonia's UGGs.

"I'm sorry. I should be chained to my inn, in fact, I should be in the kitchen right now working on the loin of

pork with the green peppercorns, but I have totally abandoned Marty and Kendra for a wild goose chase."

Antonia sunk into the chair opposite Genevieve. She
promised herself she would relax for five minutes, and
only five minutes, before returning to work.

"Who the hell are Marty and Kendra?"

"My sous chef and station chef? You've met them ten
times."

"Oh yeah," said Genevieve. She blew a large bubble
with her gum before popping it loudly and flipping the
page of the magazine. "So, where were you?"

Antonia filled her in on Naomi and Barbie and the
curse and the trip to Larry Lipper. She chose not to
mention Nick Darrow, knowing that it would lead to an
entirely different conversation where she would have to
field twenty questions just about his outfit.

"The point is this is so not me, running around worried about a curse, or trying to find out if this guy Gordon
was murdered. What do I care?"

"Well, it is *kind of* you, but that's not the point."

"What do you mean?"

Genevieve rolled her eyes. She dropped *Cosmo* on the
coffee table and picked up *Vogue*. "You're kind of nosy. I
mean, didn't your parents nickname you Snoopy because
you were always snooping around?"

"I never should have told you that..."

"Don't get offended, it's not a bad thing. I never would
have known Steve was cheating on me if you hadn't followed him to the bar that day."

"Sorry about that. But I knew the guy was a cad."

"You saved me years of heartache."

"Years?"

"Okay, months."

"More like weeks, judging from your romantic history."

"Hey, watch it."

"How can I watch it when you are calling me nosy?"

"It's not a bad thing. What I mean is that you like to figure stuff out. I remember you used to be obsessed with your ex-husband's cases. You were more of a detective than he was."

"I was better at it than he was. Nothing wrong with that." Antonia sniffed.

"Most of the time, no. But it's not so great when you think that you are the only one who can do everything."

"I do not."

Genevieve cocked her head and raised an eyebrow. "Take the inn. You decorated it all by yourself. You're the innkeeper, the head chef. A cushion rips, you sew it yourself. I've seen you with tools trying to fix the toilet, and pulling weeds out of the flower beds."

"Someone has to take responsibility."

"Okay, but what about trying to be superwoman? You do your own taxes. You try to play local matchmaker. You're lobbying the town of East Hampton to reduce noise from the airport—"

"I just…" Antonia began to protest but then stopped. It was true. "I guess you're right."

"I know I'm right."

"Are you saying it's a bad thing?"

"No. I'm just saying that you're thirty-five years old. Time to know who you are."

Antonia bit her lip. She could say the same thing to Genevieve. "I think I know who I am."

"Great. Then you know that you're the type of person who will absolutely, positively uncover a crime if there was one."

Antonia conceded that it was true. She was about to offer some explanation and psychoanalyze herself, but as usual Genevieve's attention was fleeting and she had already grown bored of the topic. Genevieve turned *Vogue* toward Antonia and held up a picture of an anorexic model leaping across a stream whilst clad in an absurd metallic jumpsuit. "Hey, would this look good on me?"

"Everything looks good on you… It's just a little ridiculous."

"I'm too fancy for this town."

"True. The same cannot be said of me," said Antonia, glancing down at her prairie skirt.

"That's for sure. But you never listen to me. You just insulate yourself in all those damn layers of clothes. I promise you, if you made yourself sexy, you could find a man. You have great boobs."

"Please. Why do you always want to give me a make-over? I'm happy the way I am."

"What about Larry Lipper? Was he hot?"

"God, no! A vile man. And tiny."

"I met the hottest guy the other day. Okay, early twenties so I know that's, like, robbing the cradle for me, but he was so cute..."

Antonia stared out the window as Genevieve droned on. She watched Hector, the gardener, winding the hose by the front porch. It then dawned on her she should ask him about Gordon Haslett. He had been the one that found him, slumped on the ground by the barn. Dead.

"You're not listening," said Genevieve accusingly.

"Huh?" said Antonia, jerking her head back toward her.

Genevieve sighed dramatically. "Are you really so upset about this guy possibly being offed? See? That's why I didn't tell you."

"You knew?"

"Everyone knew. But deep down no one really believes the story because it's totally manufactured. All that bull about the gardener killing him because Gordon had fired his wife for stealing—"

"Wait, what?"

"Yes, it was the old 'the gardener did it in the solarium with the hoe.'"

"I never heard the gardener mentioned."

"Yeah, I don't know. Apparently, his wife worked at the inn as a maid and Gordon fired her for stealing a few weeks before he died."

"Really?"

"Supposedly. Who knows?"

Antonia turned and glanced again at Hector. He was

small in stature, compact but muscular, and she knew for a fact, very strong. She watched as his muscles rippled through his shirt when he bent down. He wore his black hair in a short-cropped buzz cut and was always tidy and meticulously dressed, even when he had been working outside. From the first time they met, Antonia sized him up as hardworking and competent, and to date he had proven reliable and honest. He was a family man, proud and devoted to his wife and small children. Very proud. Would he have murdered someone to defend her honor? She didn't think so. But maybe she didn't know.

"It's just racial profiling," said Genevieve dismissively. "Don't worry about it. And anyway, if someone killed Gordon Haslett, I would like to personally thank him or her. He was a jerk and his dying brought you to East Hampton, so we're all much better off!"

———————————

An hour after Genevieve left, an odd incident occurred that unnerved Antonia and once again gave her pause about her own mortality. She wasn't sure if she was psyching herself up, but she was definitely flustered. She realized that perhaps there was something to the whole notion that innkeepers at the Windmill Inn were an endangered species.

After the completion of tea service, Antonia had grabbed a stepladder and gone into the parlor to replace the bulb that was out above the window. It had been bothering her for an hour. The afternoon sun was drooping and the south-facing room was growing dark. Outside, the yard was already in deep shadow. Antonia had unfolded the ladder and pushed it against the window seat. It was rickety and when she pressed down on the first step, it heaved under her weight. She felt wobbly as she ascended; it was time for a new ladder. She climbed gingerly to the top and reached up to remove the old bulb. The ceilings were high in this room and Antonia had to rise on her tiptoes to unscrew the bulb. She wasn't afraid of heights, but it did feel precarious balancing on the narrow step while she reached skyward. It was a small exercise but it definitely reminded Antonia again how out of shape she was. Her arms felt as heavy as lead as they extended straight up to untwist the bulb. She made a mental note to buy some weights to work on her biceps.

Antonia slowly worked her fingers around the edge of the bulb, turning and turning until the bulb was loose. She pulled it out but with such gusto that she almost lost her balance and the bulb flew up in the air. Fortunately, her quick reflexes worked to her advantage and she caught it with both hands before it smashed to the ground. Antonia's heart was thumping with the near miss and the exertion she had to use in order to complete the small task. She stepped off the ladder and put the bulb down on the console table. She glanced up. Perhaps it might be better if she stood on the window seat instead of the rickety ladder, she decided.

Antonia removed her shoes and wiggled her

stockinged toes. She took a new bulb out of its sleeve.
Holding it in one hand she used the other to hoist herself on top of the upholstered window bench. She stared
upward toward the light. No, this would not do. The distance was too far and she would have to hold her body up
at a forty-five-degree angle in order to replace it. It was
physically impossible. She sighed deeply. Genevieve was
right; she was such a control freak. She should cut her
losses and ask Hector to come in with his large ladder
and do it. But then she felt silly. What, she couldn't even
change a light bulb? It was like a joke, how many innkeepers does it take to replace a light bulb?

She had an idea. The curtain rods were strong, she
knew that. They were thick-brushed brass, and when
they were installed she had asked the contractor to make
sure they were doubly secured because she was hanging
very heavy damask curtains on them. She would step on
the ladder and hang on to the rod while she replaced the
bulb. Easy-peasy.

Antonia held the bulb in her hand and mounted
the ladder. She grabbed on to the curtain rod and then
hooked her arm underneath it so that she was basically
hanging on it. She was aware she would look ridiculous
to anyone who entered, but she didn't care. She was
focused on getting this done. Antonia had the bulb and
she rappelled her weight away from the window so she
was horizontal to the floor and began screwing it in. Her
foot was beginning to slip off the ladder but it didn't
matter because she was so intent on the task at hand. She

slowly twisted the bulb. Her back now was to the room, facing out the window. She heard someone come in, but she didn't want to glance around for fear she would lose her balance.

"Hello? Just putting in a bulb," Antonia said.

Silence. She must have been wrong; there was no one there.

Beads of sweat were forming on Antonia's brow as she finished twisting. Her underarm hurt from the rod pressing into her armpit. She hoped she wouldn't bruise, that would really be an inane injury. She leaned farther, slipping her foot off the top shelf of the ladder completely so that now the only thing holding her was the curtain rod. It would just take a second, she told herself. But she had put it in at an angle so she had to start over. She turned the bulb again, slower now, confirming it was set in place. With the final twist, the light bulb illuminated and Antonia flinched from the blazing brightness that shone directly into her eye. She blinked several times, but all she could see were burning spots. She paused, waiting for the flashes of light to disappear from her retinas.

Keeping her eyes clenched shut, she pointed out her toe in an effort to locate the stepladder. She couldn't find it. She swung her leg back and forth, searching for it with her toe. It was absurd, her fumbling around. Her arm was hurting, but she realized she was flailing around for no reason. She took a deep breath and again tried to locate the ladder with her toe. Still, she was unable to locate it.

She waited again until her eyes finally cleared. When she was not blind anymore, she glanced down. The ladder wasn't there. Antonia blinked several times to make sure her eyes weren't playing a trick on her. But there was no ladder.

Had it fallen down? She craned her neck as far as she could without falling. No, she couldn't see it anywhere from her angle. And besides, wouldn't she have heard it if it had fallen? Antonia's heart raced. Her arm was on fire; it hurt so much from pressing into the rod.

She took a deep breath. She had no choice. She slowly wiggled her arm out from under the rod. That meant that she had to push one hand against the wall to hoist herself up so that she could remove the arm. She counted to three then did so. She quickly grasped the rod with her hand and found herself hanging onto the curtain rod. She felt totally ridiculous, but it was only for a split second because her sweaty hands could no longer hang on to the rod and she slipped off and fell to the floor with a thud.

She froze. She was alive. She wiggled her feet and arms. She could move. Embarrassed, Antonia sat up. She was lucky; she was okay for the most part. Her butt was another story, and she could feel it already turning purple and bruised: a lovely image. She dusted herself off and turned and scanned the room. Fortunately, no one had seen. It was a relief that she was alone. But then suddenly Antonia's eyes locked on something and the blood drained from her face. She felt chills. The ladder was there behind her. But the strange thing was that it was folded and propped against the wall five feet away. It could not have done that itself. Was someone intentionally messing with her?

6

THAT EVENING DURING DINNER PREP, ANTONIA ASKED around about the ladder. Had it been a prank? Had someone thought it was funny to move it? But no one copped to it. And who *would* think that was funny? She could have landed wrong and really hurt herself, and then who would run the inn? After her questions were met with odd looks and sympathetic clucks, she decided to put the ladder out of her mind. It had just been a fluke. Luckily, tonight was a whirlwind of activity, so she didn't even have time to think once dinner service got under way. She kept her head down in the kitchen and focused entirely on the food.

They had never been this busy in the dining room and, as a result, were a bit understaffed and unprepared. Things were tense. For the first time, the timing was a bit off, and surges of orders seemed to arrive at the same time, which made everyone scramble. They actually ran out of salmon, which was completely embarrassing and they had to make last-minute adjustments. A busboy dropped a tray in the kitchen, unleashing a string of obscenities from Glen, who was already cranky from the unpredictable arrival of several walk-ins, messing up the seating chart that he had spent way too much time on.

Marty, the sous chef, had been manning the grill all night, whining commands at everyone in his nasal voice as the flames danced in front of him. He oversaw the kitchen but was primarily in charge of entrées. With his wiry frame, limp gray ponytail, and pockmarked skin, he was an aging hippie, his appearance better suited for someone selling pot at a Phish concert than cooking fine food. But that was where looks can be deceiving; there was nothing laid back or hippie about Marty's personality. A type-A cantankerous perfectionist, he was one hell of a chef. Alternatively, Kendra, Antonia's line cook, appeared as if perhaps she had spent *too* much time in the kitchen. With the exception of her ginger hair and a random assortment of tattoos, everything about her was pale and dense, like a ball of bread dough. She moved slowly and precisely, and had an intuitive approach to food that Antonia appreciated, always seeming to unearth the missing ingredient that would pull a dish together. Kendra was in charge of salads and desserts and spent most of the night composing them, assisted by Liz, the eighteen-year-old intern. (Antonia was attempting to mentor Liz, despite some grumbling from the kitchen staff.)

The activity in the kitchen was relentless from opening until ten o'clock, when things abruptly died down. Marty and Kendra bolted out to have a cigarette. Antonia gave Liz a tutorial on how to plate rare steak without all of the juices dripping into the mashed potatoes. When Marty returned, Antonia took the opportunity to make her way through the dining room to see what remained of her guests.

Antonia was tired, and the stress from the kitchen as well as the day's unpleasant developments suddenly seemed to catch up with her. She felt exhausted. But she brightened when she saw her friend.

"Joseph! How was everything tonight?"

She was happy to see him there for his second night in a row, in his cute little green bow tie. As she stared at him tonight, he reminded her so much of her father, with his calm, thoughtful demeanor and the way his eyes shone behind his glasses. She suddenly felt a pang of sorrow and a crushing sense of loss. She missed her parents. They were wonderful people. And it was obvious Joseph missed his wife as well.

"It was delicious, Antonia. Just fantastic. You're doing a great job. Treasure it. Enjoy these moments. Beginnings are wonderful."

Again, it was something that her father would have said and as soon as the words were out of his mouth, tears filled Antonia's eyes. She was mortified and feigned a coughing fit in order to account for them.

"Excuse me, I had something stuck in my throat."

Joseph raised his eyebrows as if he knew she was not being truthful and invited her to sit with him for a night-cap. Although she felt she had to make the rounds, she accepted.

"How is everything with you?" he inquired.

Once again her eyes filled with tears. What was going on? This was crazy! Antonia glanced around the dining room to make sure no one else could spot her, but the remaining guests were all engrossed in their own conversations. She was profoundly grateful that she had insisted on low-wattage and mostly candlelight to illuminate the dining room or else she would have been discovered.

Joseph put his hand on top of Antonia's and smiled. They sat like that for a minute, Antonia fighting tears, and dabbing her eyes with a napkin. They both waited until she was able to speak.

"I'm so embarrassed, Joseph. You just remind me so much of my father and it hit me like a ton of bricks."

"Don't worry, my dear. I understand."

This made her want to cry harder. There was nothing that makes you cry more than when someone is nice to you when you are crying. She finally exhaled. "Sorry."

"Don't be," said Joseph. "You know, my father died when I was twenty-one and I remember at his wake a friend of my mother's said to me that her father had been dead for twenty years and it didn't seem like a day had gone by since he died. I couldn't fathom it at the time, but now I understand what she means. And there is something oddly reassuring about it. It's nice to think that you feel the loss as much today as when it happened. It's wonderful to love that much."

Antonia nodded. "I like looking at it that way... I didn't know you were twenty-one when your dad died. I was ten when my mom died."

"I'm sorry to hear that."

"Thanks. It was strange because she was much younger than my father, almost twenty years younger.

And they'd always joke how he'd die first and she'd remarry some handsome guy her own age. Then she got cancer and died within six weeks of her diagnosis. My dad never got over it. He was completely heartbroken. Life is strange."

Joseph patted her hand and waited before speaking again. "It must be tough taking on this whole inn and restaurant by yourself. But you wouldn't know it by watching you. It's so nice to see your smiling face and taste your delicious food. I had the truffled macaroni and cheese tonight with a side of sautéed broccoli rabe. My doctor would be apoplectic but I loved every minute of it."

Antonia laughed. "There's a lot of butter in those two dishes!"

"Bring it on, as they say!" he chortled. He took a sip of his sherry and watched Antonia intently.

"I'm sorry for everything, Joseph. I haven't been myself all day. I heard something yesterday that set me off."

Antonia filled him in on all of the talk about the previous innkeepers dying suspicious deaths, including the new revelation about the possible bee sting. She added that it was making her a nervous nelly, and she replayed the stepladder scene from that afternoon, lamenting that she may be next in line.

Joseph looked excited. "No, don't worry! Biddy Robertson is still alive. She only briefly owned the inn before Gordon, way back when, but that still counts!"

"Really?"

"Sure. Lives in a condo near Springy Banks Road."

"Are you friends with her?"

"Not socially. But my wife, Margaret, ran the Ladies Village Improvement Society Fair one summer and worked with Biddy on that. I think Biddy still volunteers at their thrift shop."

"Well, that's reassuring!"

"Quite."

"What about the owner before her?"

Joseph removed his glasses and wiped the lenses with his handkerchief. "Well…I'm afraid that's *not* such a good story."

"Ugh! Okay, now you have to tell me."

"Greg McKenna was his name. He was a nice man, very energetic, some might say a touch too enthusiastic, but he meant well. He had all sorts of plans. In fact, he was the one who originally put the restaurant in the inn. Before that, there was just a hot plate and a coffee maker for guests to self-serve."

"Then I bow to him." Antonia smiled.

"Yes, but his kitchen was nothing like yours. He was big on ideas but short on execution."

"Did he live here alone?"

"No. He owned it with his wife, Charmaine. They'd met in college in Florida. She had some family money, I believe, that was used to purchase the inn, but he was the real self-starter who made it happen."

"So, what went wrong?"

"Well, it's all rumor and conjecture…but, there was

talk around town that Greg was having an affair with his wife's sister, Lois. Lois actually lived here at the inn with Greg and Charmaine, and was one of those gay divorcées who cut a dangerous figure. By all reports she was extremely selfish, only out for number one. Apparently, Charmaine had been trying to force Lois to move out for months, calling her a leech and a mooch, but she refused, and Greg kept leaping to her defense, which caused a tremendous amount of conflict between him and his wife. In fact, some people thought he and Lois were lovers and I am sure Charmaine suspected that. Well, one night they had a family dinner and Charmaine made a carrot cake for dessert. She knew carrot cake was her sister's favorite dessert. And she knew that Greg hated carrot cake. Well, that night it was strange, because Lois refused to eat the cake—said she was on a diet. But Greg decided it looked so good that he would have some. According to Lois, Charmaine tried to talk him out of it, but perhaps he felt bad that no one wanted it, so he tucked in to a large piece. Ate every last bite. Next thing you know, he's violently ill, throwing up all over the place. Charmaine, who also had some, was sick also. Too sick to help him. Greg went to bed and into cardiac arrest, and he died in the night. His daughter discovered him on the floor of the bathroom. The kid found Charmaine in time and called 911. She was saved, but not her husband. They found arsenic in the cake, which Charmaine swore must have gotten in there by accident. She had picked some thyme from the garden to add to the cake and must have mistakenly included it, she claimed. But the theory always was that Charmaine meant to kill her sister and dispose of her. Ate just enough of the cake to not be a suspect, and ended up killing her husband."

He paused, his eyes shining, and awaited Antonia's response.

"Wow." She shivered.

"Yes. Terrible story."

"What ever happened to Charmaine and Lois?"

Joseph paused and shifted in his seat. "Lois became even nuttier. She knew what Charmaine had done and accused her, but as she was a bit of a drunk who'd had a few skirmishes with the law—stole some money from ex-boyfriends and the like—the police didn't believe her. I think she left town. No one really knows where she went, but I fear it did not end well."

"And Charmaine?"

"Not six months later, Charmaine married her high-school sweetheart and was living back in Winter Park, Florida, in one of those mini-mansions, raising her kids with her new husband as if Greg had never existed. Sold the inn to Biddy and never looked back."

"It's an incredible story…"

Before Antonia could finish her sentence, someone behind her interrupted her.

"I made it. I'm sure you were beginning to lose hope, but hell, if you knew the kind of night I had, you would freak out, so make sure you show me some gratitude. I'm friggin' starving. Is this the best table in the house?"

Larry Lipper plopped down on the chair between Joseph and Antonia and dropped his brown leather satchel on the floor next to him. He pulled Antonia's glass of sherry toward him and downed it, then wiped the back of his mouth with his hand. There were bags under his eyes and he was markedly wearier than he had been earlier in the day. All trace of handsomeness was replaced by a worn and weary facade.

"Joseph Fowler." Joseph put out his hand to shake but Larry ignored it.

"Larry Lipper. Can I get a menu? What's good?" asked Larry.

"Well, the kitchen is just about closed…"

"Don't screw with me. I wouldn't have come if you hadn't promised me a great dinner."

Antonia wanted to protest but decided it was futile. This Larry Lipper clearly lived in an alternate reality.

Antonia asked Glen to bring over a menu and she watched Larry pore over it with intensity. He made clucking noises, voicing his disapproval over various items, and seemed at a loss as to what to order. Joseph gave Antonia a quizzical look but she just shook her head in resignation.

"What the hell is this, smoked pork sausage and sweet corn custard? What is corn custard? A pile of mush?"

"I can assure you it's delicious," said Joseph defensively. Antonia loved that he was protecting her.

"Yeah, whatever, give me the flank steak," he said, handing his menu to Glen. "Easy on the onions, and extra shoestring potatoes. I like them crispy, not greasy. And forget the mixed greens that accompany it. I gave that crap up long ago."

Glen threw Antonia a look of disgust and recoiled. She could only imagine the conversation in the kitchen when Marty received the order.

The busboy came and placed a large basket of fresh baked bread in front of Larry and he dove for the sourdough. He smeared a large slab of butter on his piece before shaking on enough salt to cause a heart attack. He shoved it into his mouth with relish.

"God, I need this!" he said with his mouth full.

Antonia summoned all of the niceness in her body to interact with Larry. "So, what happened tonight that kept you? Because I was really waiting with bated breath."

"I knew you were, Antonia. You were like a dog in heat this afternoon."

That was too much for Joseph. He started to protest, but Antonia stopped him.

"I couldn't get any of the information you begged me for today about the former owners of this joint. As soon as you left, I heard a call on my scanner about a possible crime and so I had to cover it."

"Oh, really? What happened?" asked Antonia, hoping to erase the sound of *dog in heat* that was still ringing in her ears.

"It was a total waste of time at the end," Larry said, a large slab of white bread bobbing around his tongue. "But you know how it is here. Someone dies, and if it's

DEATH ON WINDMILL WAY 77

not straightforward like they were dying for months, it's as if it's the first time that anyone has ever died in this town and it gets the 'suspicious' treatment. The police get called. I get called. You know, because I'm the press and they always want the press there."

"Who died?" asked Joseph.

"This old lady." He glanced at Joseph and gave him the up-and-down. "You know, in her seventies. She doesn't show up for breakfast with her friend at John Pappas's Diner, the friend is worried, goes over to her house, sees the lady slumped on the floor. Lo and behold, the woman was dead."

"What really happened?" asked Antonia.

"They think it was late at night, the woman went to make herself a cup of tea. Turned on the gas, it didn't go on all the way, you know, old range, woman was tired, forgot and went to bed. The windows were all shut—you know how old people like it super hot—and then she inhaled all that gas and croaked."

"How awful!" said Antonia.

Joseph's eyebrows furrowed with concern. "Who was this 'old lady' as you call her?"

"I don't know. Some woman named Elizabeth Robertson."

Joseph's mouth dropped. Antonia gave him a curious look.

"What is it, Joseph?"

Antonia could see his Adam's apple bob as he gulped. He took a sip of water and finally spoke. "You mean, *Biddy* Robertson?"

"Yeah, that's the one."

Antonia felt the blood drain from her face. She and Joseph exchanged shocked glances.

"Another innkeeper," whispered Antonia.

"Poor Biddy," said Joseph.

ANTONIA HAD RETREATED AS SOON AS SHE COULD TO her tiny ground-floor apartment and changed into the soft flannel pajamas that had been with her since college. Her apartment was snug and cozy, consisting only of a bedroom, a living room with a kitchenette, and a bathroom. It suited her perfectly as it was low-maintenance and compact and faced the back, which afforded a pretty view of the gardens. She had thrown her heart and soul into decorating the inn—scouring East Hampton and all the neighboring towns for antiques, spending hours on the internet searching for the few things that she didn't find at Ruby Beets, Mecox Gardens, Hildreth's, or Rumrunner—but her own rooms were decorated with less vision, erring more on the side of comfort than style.

The living room consisted of a white, plush, squishy, oversized sofa with matching armchairs, the type that an elderly person might sink so deeply into that they'd need the Jaws of Life to escape. There was an upholstered ottoman that served as a coffee table, a sideboard cluttered with pictures of her parents, grandparents, and since she was an only child, some snaps of her cousins and their children, with close friends thrown in for good measure. A wall of built-in bookshelves was stocked with a variety of tomes as well as miscellaneous objects like a set of crystal candlesticks that had belonged to her parents, a ceramic lion, two floral cachepots that held dried box-wood plants, board games (Scrabble, Clue, and Trivial Pursuit circa 1990), and a box of tissues. The books were an eclectic assortment based on Antonia's whims. She was a phase reader—for a few months she'd read nothing but mysteries, followed by a few months of self-help, then cooking, and then books on angels and near-death experiences. This was all reflected in her personal library. She had also managed to hang onto all of her dog-eared copies of *Saveur*, *Food & Wine*, and *Gourmet* magazines, which held court at the top of the shelves.

The walls of the apartment were all painted a uniform petal pink, Antonia's favorite color, and featured framed posters of Matisse and Van Gogh paintings from the Met and the Pushkin Museum, as well as a few watercolors of East Hampton that she had bought the previous summer at the Clothesline Art Show at Guild Hall. (She'd waited on line patiently a full hour before it opened.) A thick, creamy white, wall-to-wall carpet ran from the living room into Antonia's bedroom, which was also a testament to comfort: its giant king-sized sleigh bed was adorned with an enormous white comforter and a surplus of pillows. Antonia loathed spending money on herself but she had two vices: expensive sheets and beauty products. Expensive sheets not because they were expensive, but because she adored the buttery softness that accompanied high thread count Egyptian sheets. Whatever those Egyptians were doing, she was incredibly grateful. And beauty products because she couldn't resist any cream or solution that promised her fewer wrinkles, eradication of cellulite, softer skin, or any simple solution to battle the signs of aging. Her bathroom cabinets were bursting with jars and bottles of every size, shape, and fragrance.

When she had first purchased the inn, this space had, of course, been where Gordon and Barbie were living. The walls had been dark; leather furniture had been the dominant theme and the kitchen appliances and bathroom fixtures were broken. It was as if Gordon stubbornly resisted making this anything other than a functioning bachelor pad. There was no whisper that a woman had lived here with him. Now that lack of compromise on Gordon's part resonated with Antonia. Had he been done with Barbie?

Antonia had the TV on with the sound muted and was busy sifting through all of the papers in the disputed cardboard box. She was drinking a glass of cabernet and nibbling on pecan toffee squares that her intern Liz had made that afternoon. Antonia was notably impressed with Liz, who had appeared on her doorstep four weeks prior, begging to work her ass off if Antonia taught her the trade. She had reminded Antonia of herself when she was young, possessing that naive dogged determination that makes you bold. Marty thought it was a waste of time and space letting Liz help out, but even he had recently muttered that she was "doing good," which was high praise from him.

Antonia knew it was late and she should retire to bed, but she was absolutely jolted by Larry's revelation about

Biddy Robertson. *Dead.* The only other living Windmill Inn innkeeper was now out of the picture, and under suspicious circumstances to say the least! With everything that was recently revealed about Gordon, this had to be somehow linked. Joseph had reluctantly concurred with her, although Larry was not convinced. He had been insistent that he was on the scene of the crime, and being the crackerjack reporter that he was, would have been able to suss out if there had been any foul play at work. And despite Antonia's protestations that it was too coincidental, especially as all this speculation about Gordon's death was arising this week, Larry held firmly to his belief that there was no motive and therefore no crime.

Antonia focused on the cardboard box, hoping that there might be some answers there. She leafed through a variety of menus for local East Hampton restaurants, a pamphlet for bike rentals, and a few postcards from satisfied guests, who promised to return to the Windmill Inn in the near future. There were some old Post-its with a few phone numbers jotted down, but nothing that piqued Antonia's interest. Lucy was correct, it appeared to be just a pile of random papers that Gordon had shoved into a box rather than thrown away. The only promising thing seemed to be a spiral-bound notebook, the kind that every middle schooler receives, in which Gordon had jotted some notes on an inconsistent basis. If this was where Barbie was hoping to find the will, she would be disappointed.

Antonia flipped through page after page and felt as if she was gathering more information into what sort of person Gordon was and why his inn had not been very successful. He kept a sporadic account of things that he needed to order for the inn that were neatly detailed, as well as lengthy, delineating everything from toilet paper to light bulbs to candles. But on each list, there were only one or two essentials crossed off, implying that the other desired items were still outstanding. It was the same with his to-do lists. He'd written about his plan to fix the leg of a chair in the parlor, or to repair the ripped headboard in room 3, but once again very few of those things had checkmarks against them. It was totally consistent with everything she had heard about Gordon. He was capable of large bursts of activity and enthusiasm but after an initial bold effort, he failed at follow-up.

It wasn't until Antonia reached the last page of the notebook that she felt a rush. There, in Gordon's unmistakable handwriting, was written in all capitals:

LUCY—HAVE RONALD METER'S SEVERANCE PACKAGE READY. I AM FIRING THAT BEAST TODAY.

Antonia ran over to her hall table and picked up the scrap of paper that she had retrieved earlier. She held it up. *I swear to god that B is trying to kill me.* That B. That beast.

Antonia paused, her eyes gliding from one to the other. Finally, she slid the scrap of paper into the notebook and slapped it shut, before replacing it in the cardboard box.

Ronald Meter was the former manager who Gordon had fired. Why had he fired him? She couldn't remember. But things were starting to piece together. It was time to visit Ronald Meter. Her alter ego, Snoopy, had reared his ugly head. It was time to investigate.

Sunday

Nick Darrow was on the beach as usual on Sunday morning but this time he was in conversation with a young couple, so Antonia merely waved. Disappointed, she cut her walk short and had ample time to make breakfast before setting out to Ronald Meter's house, which was situated at the end of a cul-de-sac near Accabonac Harbor in Springs, one of East Hampton's many hamlets. Springs was renowned for the Jackson Pollock–Lee Krasner museum, which was located in their former house, and where they had spent many years painting. The sign that led into Springs read *The Springs* and, as it had become a trendy part of town in recent years—its proximity to the bay and picturesque clammers and fishing boats were a big draw— it had attracted all sorts of hipster New Yorkers who referred to it as "The Springs." But that made the locals snicker. To them it was Springs; no fancy "The" preceding it. The school was Springs School, not "The" Springs School, they'd point out. But it was one more way to differentiate the locals from the interlopers.

Antonia felt somewhat presumptuous dropping in on Ronald Meter unannounced, but her fear of imminent death by a psychopath who hated innkeepers spurred her on. When she pulled into Meter's gravel driveway, she took note of the large *For Sale* sign stuck in the grass. *Hmm*, Antonia wondered. Was there a reason Ronald was moving? Fleeing town, maybe? She filed away the thought as she exited her car. Antonia was quick to assess that Ronald Meter had done the best job possible with what was an ordinary, run-of-the-mill one-story shingled house. The shutters were painted a dark-pearl gray and the front door was a cherry red, with a shiny brass knocker centered on it like a smiley face. A row of neatly manicured boxwoods lined the sides of the house, and there was a well-maintained slate path leading up to the entrance. Beyond the house, she could see the bay in the distance, and the salt marshes, which were the most exquisite mosaic of purples, reds, and greens at this time of the year. It was by far the best-tended house that she had seen in the neighborhood. She glanced around to steal another glimpse of the neighbors' houses and realized with disappointment that theirs were obstructed from view by the large thicket of trees. Unfortunately, Antonia realized that in the event that Ronald Meter did turn out to be a killer who enjoyed killing owners of the Windmill Inn, she was royally screwed. No one would see a thing. She patted herself down, fumbling through the pockets of her barn jacket for something to use as a weapon. Nothing but balled-up Kleenexes and the keys to her trusty Saab were available to her. She clasped the keys in the palm of her hand and tried to visualize stabbing someone in the eye with them. It wasn't ideal. But hopefully it wouldn't come to that.

When she creaked up the front steps, she heard a TV and through the window could make out a shadowy figure seated on the couch next to the door. This was it, Antonia thought. No backing out now. She took a deep breath of the brisk morning air. She was feeling that antsy lack of exercise gnawing at her. She couldn't believe she actually missed exercising. Although was a walk on the beach really exercise? And maybe what she was really missing was the chance to run into Nick Darrow again.

As soon as Antonia rang the doorbell, a dog started barking, and the figure rose and chastened him, before swinging open the screen door. Ronald Meter was a very tall man, at least six foot four, with reddish-gray hair and a matching goatee. His face was broad and expressive, but also friendly. Antonia put him in about his mid-fifties. It appeared to her as if he was either wearing someone else's clothes or had recently lost weight. His ill-fitting khaki pants seemed to bunch up around his crotch area as if the brown braided belt he wore double looped around his waist was strangling them. He had on a light-blue button-down shirt, with a darker blue undershirt peeking through, and wore black leather sneakers. There was something awkward about him and his bulk, and rather than emitting an intimidating aura, he seemed more like a big oaf. Not unlike the dopey-looking golden retriever that sidled up next to him.

Antonia watched him size her up with curiosity, before giving her a warm smile.

"Are you here to look at the house?" he asked brightly. She detected a slight southern lilt to his accent.

"Um, no, actually. Sorry. I'm Antonia Bingham, I own the Windmill Inn. I'm sorry to barge in on you on a Sunday but I was hoping I could talk to you for a minute?"

He seemed momentarily deflated but then he recovered quickly. He started to say something, and Antonia could see the wheels turning but then he abruptly stopped.

"So you're the one who bought the inn," he said neutrally, but it still made Antonia pause. It was the second time in two days that someone had seemed to know more about her than she knew about them. It was a bit disconcerting.

"Yup, that's me. Some may say the 'crazy one who bought the inn.'"

Ronald laughed heartily. "Aw, I wouldn't say that."

He politely invited her inside, with a few disclaimers about how he was watching his morning cooking shows and apologies for the mess. He flicked off the plasma television (Rachael Ray was rolling chicken breasts in panko crumbs) that hung over the mantel and carefully placed the remote next to it.

She accepted his offer of a glass of water, if only to give herself time to assess his living quarters while he retreated to the kitchen. After discovering that everything was immaculate, she wondered what he would think of her apartment if this was his idea of a mess. Sure, there was a newspaper strewn on the waterfall Lucite coffee table, but other than that, everything was in order. His decor was sophisticated and modern. He had two leather armchairs in the style of that famous Swedish furniture designer whose name was always a clue in crossword puzzles, but Antonia could never remember. The chairs faced a contemporary beige sofa that was flanked by two white lacquered side tables holding red gourd lamps. Two built-in bookcases bordered the mantel and Antonia could see that they held an abundance of expensive coffee table books, the oversize glossy kind that people often give as presents but rarely read.

Antonia took the opportunity to tiptoe over to the dining room to get a better look. It was also tastefully decorated. There was an open laptop on the dining table next to a pile of mail. Antonia glanced at the mail, which appeared to be mostly bills. The computer screen was in sleep mode and Antonia was just debating whether or not to "accidentally" press a button to see what Ronald was working on, when her snoop was interrupted.

"Here you go," said Ronald, handing her a tumbler of water with a slice of lemon in it.

Antonia was startled. She turned around abruptly.

"You didn't have to go to so much trouble," said Antonia.

"It's no trouble."

He didn't appear to notice her snooping and invited her to sit down in the living room. He set out two coasters on the coffee table before placing his own glass down. If he was interested in why Antonia was there, his polite manners restrained him from revealing anything. In fact, his graciousness and ease made Antonia feel as if she was an invited guest just over for a cup of tea. She could see why someone had tapped him to be manager of an inn. He was definitely a pro at hospitality.

They engaged in brief pleasantries about the weather before moving toward the topic of the inn. Antonia confided the trials and tribulations of redoing the place and getting it up and running, and Ronald commiserated. He sighed deeply when she delineated the construction woes and nodded encouragement. The fact was, Antonia found him totally pleasant and as mild as a pussycat despite his big size. There was daintiness to his hand gestures, and this coupled with the languid tone of his southern accent relaxed Antonia. She wondered if she was insane to think he might be a killer. She also wondered if she was totally insane to have put herself alone in his house if indeed he was a killer.

"Well, I suppose you're wondering what I am doing here?" Antonia asked finally, after they had exhausted all chitchat.

"I'm happy to talk to you about the inn, but yes, I am curious as to what brings you to my doorstep," Ronald said politely.

"Look, I'll be honest. I know that things ended badly

between you and Gordon. But I also have gleaned from everything I've heard that he was a difficult man."

"To say the least."

"I'm trying to piece together what went wrong, so that I won't make the same mistakes." Antonia had just thought of that pretense, and was pleased with herself for thinking on her feet. The truth was, she didn't really have any idea what she was going to ask him. She was hoping that if he was somehow guilty he would confess, but that seemed both unlikely and absurd.

"Well, it's not that simple, I suppose. You see, Gordon was unstable. I'm not a psychiatrist but I really believe he was bipolar. He would have these fits of manic energy that could last anywhere from a day to a month, during which time he would take on all sorts of projects, and renovations, and be totally enthusiastic and joyful to be around. Then he would abruptly change and become angry, rude, and totally incompetent."

"That seems to jibe with his notes that I found. All these to-do lists that were never completed."

"Exactly. It was maddening."

"So why did he fire you?"

Gordon glanced at his water as if it held the answer before taking a sip. He re-crossed his legs and looked at Antonia. "It was very challenging for me to deal with all of his mood swings, but I am proud that I hung in there for as long as I did. And as I said, he could be very abusive and destructive. When he was manic, he did bad things, that's all I'll say. But then when he came down, after he slept off all of his manic energy, he really didn't seem to remember them. And you felt sorry for him, because he had really no idea what he had done."

"Like what had he done?"

Ronald shifted. "I don't feel comfortable talking about it."

Antonia was surprised. Was he actually protecting Gordon? Even after Gordon fired him? She decided to press.

"Did you know that Barbie was cheating on him?"

Ronald put up his hands as if stopping her. "All of this drama is water under the bridge for me. Look, I just tried to do my best to manage the inn and not make everything go to hell. I was furious that Gordon fired me, and even more furious that he told everyone it was because I was stealing. But I know that all came from Barbie…"

He stopped himself.

"Because you knew Barbie was cheating?"

Ronald sighed deeply. "You got it. Why are you asking me if you know?"

"Because I don't know everything. Please tell me."

Ronald raised his shoulders. "Yes. I saw Barbie. She was all over some guy at Rowdy Hall. I stupidly told Gordon and next thing I know, he's accusing me of stealing, they're back together all lovey-dovey, and I'm fired."

"You must have been furious at Gordon?" prompted Antonia.

"I was more furious at Barbie. I knew she manufactured this whole lie."

"But Gordon was the one who fired you."

"Yes, but as I said, he was all over the place. And he was vulnerable. And for all his faults, he did have a skill at making people he betrayed stick around and feel the need to defend him, as you know. But Barbie is bad news, that cheap bottle-blond prom queen. Sorry, she just gets my goat. Point is, I wouldn't trust her as far as I could throw her."

"Really? Do you think she was using Gordon?"

"I think she has big plans for herself. Gordon was a stepping-stone. And frankly, I think she stole the money that she accused *me* of stealing. It's her nest egg and she's hidden it somewhere."

Antonia nodded. She believed that Ronald was telling her the truth. He didn't seem to have a grudge against Gordon, just Barbie, and as far as Antonia knew, she was still alive.

"Did you know Gordon was allergic to bees?"

"Bees? Why would you ask about bees?"

"Someone had mentioned that to me."

Ronald gave her a quizzical look before he spoke. "I don't know about bees...I knew he had all sorts of allergies and afflictions. But no, I never discussed that with him. Why?"

"I was just wondering if people knew. Wouldn't someone have warned him if there were a hive in the yard?"

"I don't remember ever seeing a hive in the yard. That seems odd. But you'd have to ask Hector."

"Yes, I definitely need to talk to him. He'll be in later, after church."

"May I ask why all the interest in Gordon and bees? I know you said you don't want to make the same mistakes, but it seems we're talking more about his personal life."

Antonia had to think fast. "True. Well, Naomi and Barbie just showed up and were battling over some of his belongings. I just want to know what I'm getting into in the future with those two. I want to be prepared if they somehow drag me into it."

Ronald nodded as if that answered his question. He took a sip of his water before replacing it on his coaster. "Naomi is a tough one."

"Really?"

Ronald nodded. "Mean as a snake. She'd double-cross her own mother."

"I didn't realize that."

"Fortunately, she liked me for some reason. Not sure why. Well, I suppose in general she prefers men to women. She's the type who's threatened by all women. I think I remember hearing she was once married and her husband ran off with her friend."

"That's awful. But I guess that explains it. Do you think she really hated Gordon?"

Ronald cocked his head from side to side as if he were weighing pros and cons. "No. Despite her meanness, she had a soft spot for him. I think he was her baby brother and she loved him. Sure, they fought like cats and dogs but I think there was love there."

"So, you don't think she would kill him?" asked Antonia in a light tone as if she were joking.

"A lot of people wanted that man dead but no, I don't think his sister was one of them."

Antonia took a second to process that. Was he trying to tell her something? She took a sip of her water and watched him over the rim of her glass. He was sitting on the edge of his seat staring at her. His gaze was unblinking, his face stony. The pleasantness had drained from his facade. She decided it wasn't a good idea to proceed with this line of questioning. Sometimes you've got to cut your losses.

"Right. So, where are you moving to?" Antonia asked, changing the topic.

Ronald smiled, breaking the stern demeanor that had seized him. "I'm going back home, South Carolina. There's a small inn there that has the oldest landscaped garden in America. Horticulture is really my true love."

"I noticed your beautiful flower arrangement."

"Thank you. I have a garden out back. I love wildflowers. And it will be nice to start over. I've already planned some big landscaping projects. I've been doing my homework."

He motioned toward the bookshelf. Antonia's eyes zeroed in on the glossy coffee table books. She rose and went over to examine them. Her eyes flicked across tomes entitled *Southern Style Gardening*, *British Gardens*, *Private Newport Gardens*, and *Charleston Gardens*.

"Wow, these are beautiful," she said, sliding out a copy of *The Gardens of Versailles* and flipping through it.

"I know. I adore them all. I spend hours literally poring

over them. I cannot wait to sell this place and head down South and get started!"

A thought occurred to Antonia. "These are very expensive books."

"I know," sighed Ronald. "Thank God for the L.V.I.S. thrift shop. I purchase all of my books there. You wouldn't believe the things people give away! Whenever one of those big old estates is sold, they send everything to thrift! Half of my house is decorated with furniture from there. And you should see the boxes of books that people have donated. No one seems to want books anymore! But I must be a Luddite because I cannot stand to read things on the internet. Oh, I love this one."

He pulled a copy of *Gardens of Eden* out and started flipping through it. "The roses in here are just gorgeous."

Antonia paused. She closed the book in her hands slowly and turned to face Ronald. "The L.V.I.S.?"

He glanced up at her. "Yes, I'm sure you know it? Right on Main Street in the old Gardiner Brown Mansion, down the road from you. The thrift shop is called the Bargain Box. It's a great resource. For everything."

He returned to examine his book.

Antonia felt her pulse quickening. "Biddy Robertson worked there."

She stared at Ronald to watch his reaction. He kept his eyes downward, focused on a close-up of a sunflower that from Antonia's upside-down view, looked a little phallic. "I know Biddy, of course."

"Do you know she died yesterday?" asked Antonia.

She felt as if she had a frog in her voice so the question barely squeaked out.

Ronald kept his eyes on the picture a beat too long in Antonia's opinion. He glanced up. "Sorry, what did you say? I become so carried away when I read these."

"I said Biddy died last night," she repeated, eyeing him carefully.

Ronald's eyebrows shot up. "Oh dear, how awful. She didn't seem that old."

"She wasn't. She left the stove on and died of gas poisoning."

"Oh, how sad," said Ronald. His face remained expressionless.

Antonia watched him carefully. "Did you know her when she owned the inn?"

"That was before my time."

"Oh yes, of course." Antonia closed the book she was looking at and lifted it back to its place on the shelf. "Well, I should be going. Thank you for taking the time."

"My pleasure. I'll try to stop by the inn for dinner before I go. I'd love to see all the changes you made."

"Anytime."

Antonia could feel him walking behind her as she made her way to the door. If he planned on sticking an axe in her back, the time was now. She abruptly stopped and turned around. Ronald didn't appear to be harboring any sinister plans because he smiled. Antonia stuck out her hand.

"It was nice meeting you," she said.

He took her hand into his large paw and shook it firmly. "You too."

She was about to turn for the front door, when something caught her eye. Straight ahead she could see through the kitchen to the backyard. There was a large vegetable patch and the flower garden that he had spoken of, but also something else. Antonia squinted.

"Is that a beehive?" asked Antonia.

Ronald looked flustered. "No…"

Antonia wanted to take a step forward, but she would have had to push Ronald aside. He was staring at her, his chin raised almost defiantly.

Antonia backpedaled. "Sorry, I just thought it was."

"No," said Ronald, quickly opening the door for her. "Thanks so much for coming by!"

Antonia walked back to her car with confusion. She didn't know much about bees, but she was pretty sure that was a beehive she had seen in the backyard. Why would he deny it? Only if he had something to hide, she concluded. As Antonia got into her car, she could swear she saw Ronald watching her through the window. She shuddered slightly. Was he really "a beast" as Gordon had referred to him? And was he "that B" that Gordon thought was out to get him?

8

THE GLAZED STICKY BUNS HAD COME OUT SO BEAUTI-fully that Antonia was mentally high-fiving herself as she pulled the sheet out of the oven and slammed the door closed with her foot. She held them close to her nose and breathed in the fragrant aroma of cinnamon and cooked sugar that never failed to disappoint. She felt no greater joy than when she had baked something scrumptious. Call her simple, but that was what the true meaning of life was all about: sticking your teeth into a chewy slab of sweet bread with icing and having it swirl around your mouth.

She called over her intern and impressed upon her the importance of indulgences.

"Liz, let me give you a word of advice. If you master two dishes in your life, sticky buns should be one of them. See how gooey they are? No one can resist them."

"They smell delicious."

"They are. And what I am trying to revolutionize is that they are not just for breakfast anymore. No siree, sticky buns can be eaten all day. That's why we will serve them for afternoon tea today. They are one of life's most precious gifts."

"I hear you. What's the other dish I should master?"

"Learn how to make a good roast chicken. Always a crowd pleaser. I'll teach you next weekend."

"Thanks, Chef."

Antonia smiled at her apprentice with maternal pride. Liz was mature for her age, but still looked like the seventeen-year-old that she was. She wore her brown hair shoulder length with bangs, and had big chocolate eyes that didn't miss a trick. She had not yet opted to pluck her eyebrows and Antonia hoped that she never would because there was something so cool and Brooke Shields–like about the look of her dark, thick eyebrows. She was definitely striking. And despite her lack of formal training in the kitchen, the girl was proving herself.

"How are the tea sandwiches going?" asked Antonia.

"Very well. I've finished the egg salad, cut off all the crusts, and now I'm working on the tomato."

"Don't forget the mayonnaise on the tomato. That's key."

"I definitely won't."

"Good girl. And cover them with a damp tea towel as you go, so they stay moist."

Antonia helped Liz plate and prepare for afternoon tea. Marty and Kendra only worked dinner service, so it was really up to Antonia to organize everything for the three o'clock crowd. So far, afternoon tea was not a moneymaking venture. It was actually a money-losing venture. But Antonia liked the idea that she was bringing more people into the inn, and she also thought it was important for the visiting guests who were staying at the inn to have somewhere to go during the late hours of the day when they needed a little pick-me-up.

"Antonia, we have a problem."

It was Lucy, wearing a sour face. Today, her skirt was pea green with such a wide A-line that it appeared she had a hula hoop underneath.

"What's up?"

"*Barbie* is here again," retorted Lucy, shaking her head. "Refused to even talk to me when I asked her to leave."

"It's okay," said Antonia, wiping her hands on a dish towel. "I invited her."

A flicker of surprise passed over Lucy's face and she stood up straighter. "Oh..."

"Yes, I just wanted to talk to her about this box and everything so that we can avoid another scene."

Lucy nodded. "Okay. Shall I accompany you?"

"No, I'll be okay. Thanks."

Barbie stood under the chandelier in the entrance, staring at the large nineteenth-century map of Long Island that Antonia had found at an antique store in Quogue. It had been hidden behind a stack of botanical prints and had a thick layer of dust and a tear in the corner, but Antonia had it cleaned up and had it reframed. It was her goal to collect as many antique maps of the region as possible to decorate the various rooms of the inn. She'd also recently purchased a set of architectural plans of early East Hampton homes that she had mounted in frames and hung in the powder room.

Barbie appeared much less frantic today than she had been yesterday. She was wearing tight blue jeans tucked into high-heeled boots and a long black cardigan that went all the way down to her knees. Underneath, she had on a flouncy black-and-orange paisley blouse, the type that was fashionable but could double for maternity wear, especially with breasts as ample as Barbie's. Her hair, as usual, was styled in cascading curls that ended just above her shoulders, her makeup appeared perfect, and her nails were long and painted red.

She was one of those women who fit the bill for classic American beauty: tall, blond, blue-eyed, and buxom. In Antonia's opinion there was no doubt that she was pretty, but she just wasn't *special*. *She'd probably been homecoming queen*, Antonia thought, *and no doubt a cheerleader, and a popular sorority gal too*. But there was just something generic about her face, a vagueness that left you cold, which had nothing to do with the fact that she was now in her mid-forties.

Antonia led her into the parlor, and after briefly waving and saying hellos to guests, they sat down at a table by the window that afforded a view of the side yard. The afternoon wind had picked up and was dragging leaves across the grass, causing them to dance in whirling circles. A lone guest was outside, lounging on a patio chaise underneath a burning heat lamp, idly flipping through a chunky paperback. But the rest of the outdoor tables and chairs were empty. The slanting rays of the sun were spotlighting a patch of grass in front of the white iron bench that stood in the corner of the yard.

The waitress came by and greeted Barbie with familiarity. Barbie was pleasant in return, but a bit standoffish. Antonia ordered a full tea service and watched Barbie while she scanned the menu. She noticed for the first time how much makeup Barbie wore: an entire coat of base topped with powder, blush, bronzer, eye shadow, liner, mascara, and lipstick. It was a thick layer of cosmetics for daytime, in Antonia's opinion, as if suggesting that Barbie had once had bad skin that she got in the habit of covering up. The sides of Barbie's forehead by her temples were full of deep wrinkles but surprisingly the center was smooth as a baby's bottom. Antonia wondered if she had begun a poorly administered course of Botox.

"This place looks great," said Barbie in her husky voice. She glanced around the room. "I love the walls."

"Thanks. I lacquered them green. I like shiny."

"You really went fancy."

"I suppose," admitted Antonia. "I had a clear image of what sort of inn I wanted. I liked the idea of antiques—English Regency and Biedermeier furniture, oil paintings, chandeliers, but I wanted to mix in modern fabrics on all the upholstery, which is why I chose a lot of Ikat and stripes. I feel like stripes are always in style."

"I was always trying to get Gordon to do stuff to spruce this place up. He wouldn't take advice from anyone," said Barbie.

"Yes, I heard he was quite headstrong."

"To say the least. Whenever I tried to urge him to do something, he'd always say, 'Barbie, baby, you do your thing, I do mine,' in that raspy tone of his. Drew out my name so that it was ten syllables long."

"Is Barbie short for Barbara?" asked Antonia.

"No. Carol."

As Antonia was pondering that, the waitress brought the tea and they waited in silence until she had set up the table. Antonia wasn't exactly sure what she wanted from Barbie, or how she should try and interrogate her (because really that's what she was doing) so she decided the best way would be to let Barbie do all the talking. Her mother had told her once to say as little as possible, particularly in a job interview, because people actually want to hear themselves talk more than they want to hear you. Antonia always found it tough to heed her mother's advice on this one (a chatterbox by nature, she couldn't help herself) but on the rare occasions she did, it always proved true. She found that if you stayed silent, people would keep going on and on and "get themselves in soup," as her mom used to say.

Barbie poured two packets of Equal into her tea and swirled it with a spoon. Antonia noticed the ropy veins on her hands and understood that was the one thing that truly gave away Barbie's age. She slipped her long red nails around her teacup and raised it toward her mouth to blow. Antonia watched as her bright red lips puckered causing the dark liquid to ripple like a pond on a windy day. Barbie took a sip, leaving a faint trace of her lipstick on the rim, before putting it down with a clink on the saucer.

"Did you get a look at the box?" she asked, taking a sticky bun off the caddy and putting it on her plate. She licked off the trace of icing that had stuck to her index finger before picking up a butter knife and cutting the bun in half.

"I did. And I didn't see anything that resembled a will at all. Lucy was right. It was just some notes."

Barbie smiled and cut her sticky bun into quarters. "I knew you would say that. Of course."

"Why 'of course'?" asked Antonia before selecting a soft egg salad sandwich that folded completely into her mouth in one bite.

"Because why would you tell me if you found it? It would only cause complications for you, legal issues, et cetera."

"Barbie, if I had found something, I would have told you. Trust me, I'm not out to break the law."

Barbie laughed and shook her head with condescending disbelief. She stabbed a piece of the sticky bun with her fork. "Oh, Antonia. I know you have this whole wide-eyed, good girl from out-of-town thing going. That little, 'Aw, shucks, who me?' But you're a businesswoman. You're shrewd. Hell, you fired most of the staff that had been here for years. Why would I assume that you would be on my side?"

Antonia felt herself becoming mad, but even worse, defensive. It was not how she liked to play things.

"First of all, Barbie, in regard to the staff. Yes, there were several whom I chose not to invite back. And that was because I was not impressed with their work ethic, or frankly the condition of the inn when I purchased it. I invited many of the busboys and waitstaff to return, but as the inn was closed for six months while I refurbished it, understandably, many had to seek other employment and couldn't wait for us to finish.

"I am not sure why you accuse me of playing some sort of 'aw shucks' role, because I am certainly not trying to pretend to be anything that I am not. And as for being on your side, I am not on anyone's side. I have no vested interest in what happens to Gordon's estate. But you, on the other hand, seem determined to benefit from his death."

Barbie put down her fork. "I resent that. I'm not trying to *benefit* from Gordon's death. But I was his common-law wife for five years. I helped him with every aspect of the inn. And for that, I deserve something!" She waved her arms up in the air. "This was my *home*. Without me, this place would have been a dump. I deserve something. I put up with Gordon and all of his craziness. I shouldn't be thrown out on the street like yesterday's trash."

Antonia watched her as she wallowed in self-pity. Her eyes filled with tears as she looked dramatically around the room. She took deep breaths, as if she was trying to stop herself from crying. It was all very moving…and yet, Antonia felt there was something totally inauthentic about it. Especially since she knew that Barbie had been having a relationship on the side with another man.

"I'm sorry that you lost both your boyfriend and your home," replied Antonia, trying another tack. "You are always welcome here."

"Thank you for saying that," said Barbie with satisfaction. She resumed ripping apart the sticky bun, balling up little pieces between her fingers and leaving shreds on the plate. "It's all Naomi's fault. She is *evil*."

"I'm glad you brought her up," said Antonia. "I was wondering why she said that you had murdered Gordon."

Barbie snorted before taking a sip of her tea. More lipstick found itself on the rim of the teacup. "She's delusional. Quite honestly, Antonia, you know what I think?"

She leaned in conspiratorially. Antonia did as well. "What?"

"I think *she* killed Gordon."

With that, Barbie raised her eyebrows and sat back in her chair with the smugness of a cat.

"Why do you think that?"

"Money."

"Huh," said Antonia. "I admit money is a powerful motive. But he was her brother. The inn wasn't doing well. There's been nothing to prove she was homicidal."

"I found a secret account in her name. She had been stealing from the inn. Gordon was so mad he was going to tell the police!"

Before Antonia could respond Barbie continued.

"And," said Barbie, leaning in again. "I know for a fact that Naomi has had problems with her temper. She could get just as angry and crazed as Gordon. I'm sure you saw that the other day. She once got a summons for threatening her neighbor with a baseball bat. She smashed the neighbor's car windows while she was sitting in the car!"

"Really?" asked Antonia with surprise. Naomi was tough, but she was so thin and wiry she couldn't imagine her doing that. But you never know.

Barbie nodded. "Maybe she just snapped one day with Gordon."

"But how did she kill him?" asked Antonia. "He died of a heart attack."

"So they say," said Barbie. She smoothed the tablecloth with her fingers. "If it were me, for instance, maybe I'd give him some poison somehow. Like, slip rat poison into his coffee."

Antonia eyed her. Barbie glanced out the window, possibly daydreaming about murder.

"Don't you think the police would have found that?"

"Remember, *Naomi* didn't want the autopsy. She was the one who said no way."

"True," agreed Antonia. "Then why would she have even brought it up yesterday? If she had committed murder and gotten away with it clean, why would she even suggest it?"

"To deflect attention from herself."

"Aha. But still. No one was on to her. No one had been talking about murder."

"You see?"

"No, not really. See what?"

"It's part of her plan," said Barbie, raising her eyebrows. She cut into her sticky bun.

"What is the plan?"

"To trip people up. Make them think I murdered him."

Antonia became conscious that they were talking in circles. She took the opportunity to inhale another sandwich, this time cucumber. Ah, when butter meets vegetables, it is so lovely, she thought, a marriage made in culinary heaven! She swallowed gently as if reluctant to release the sandwich from her taste buds to her stomach.

She resumed her interrogation. "What about the bee sting?"

"What bee sting?" asked Barbie.

"I heard that some people think Gordon was stung by a bee and that's how he died."

Antonia slid a piece of sticky bun onto her plate. Now that she had gotten through her vegetables and protein, it was time for sweets.

"I never heard that," said Barbie. She bent down over her plate so that Antonia couldn't read her expression, and speared another piece of sticky bun with her fork. "Why would that matter, anyway?"

"He was allergic to bees, wasn't he?" asked Antonia with confusion. Shouldn't Barbie know this? "A sting could have sent him into anaphylactic shock and killed him."

"Oh."

Something in her tone alerted Antonia. She furrowed her brows. "You did know he was allergic to bees, didn't you?"

Barbie shrugged. "I don't know."

"You don't know? But you lived with him for five years."

She waved her hands. "Gordon had a *lot* of ailments. A lot of allergies, too, so sure, maybe I knew. Or maybe not."

Antonia decided to let it pass. She moved forward with another question. "Who do you think, besides Naomi, would have wanted Gordon dead?"

Barbie chortled. "The list is kind of endless."

"Throw me some names. Anyone who pops into your head."

"Well, Naomi."

"We covered her."

"And Ronald Meter. That beast."

"Uh-huh."

"He's really a terrible person."

"I know you didn't get along."

"Oh, you don't believe me? I could tell you stories about how bad that guy was… He robbed us blind. He set up a secret account."

Antonia listened as Barbie delineated all of the offenses that Ronald enacted against her and Gordon, but with an air of skepticism. She didn't really want to waste time on Ronald Meter right now. Although she hadn't ruled him out as a possible suspect, Antonia was aware that Barbie's information would be biased based on personal slights. And for sure she thought that Barbie was an unreliable narrator when it came to Ronald.

When she had finished rehashing everything about

Ronald—which was just as Antonia thought it would be, petty offenses along with the supposed theft of the money—Barbie paused.

"Anyone else who hated Gordon?" Antonia asked.

Barbie cocked her head to the side. "There were all sorts of former employees whom he fired…"

"Right." Antonia thought about Hector, the gardener whose wife had been fired. She had to remember to talk to him.

"I mean, the list is long. Gordon was mad at a lot of people and they in turn hated him. Some of the vendors that he fought with probably hated his guts. The guy at the bank who managed the mortgage. Gordon screamed at him one time, made a huge scene. There was the building inspector who cited the inn for all these infractions. Gordon thought they were imaginary and the guy was just trying to get him to comp him dinners here."

"Wow, popular guy," said Antonia.

"He was tough. Lots of people loved him. Lots hated him. Oh, and Biddy Robertson."

Antonia replaced her teacup on its saucer with surprise.

"Biddy Robertson?"

"Yeah, the woman who owned the inn before Gordon. He bought it in foreclosure for a really cheap price and pushed her out. She was furious, said she was literally on her way to the bank with the money when he pulled a fast one on her. She was always writing him terrible letters, bad-mouthing him around town. Very vindictive."

Antonia put down her sticky bun. "Biddy Robertson died last night."

Barbie stared into Antonia's eyes. A small smile crept across her face. "Pity."

Antonia waited for her to say more but she didn't. The waitress came to ask if everything was all right and that moved the conversation to a different topic, which prevented Antonia from continuing to review Biddy's death. She wasn't sure she would draw more out of Barbie anyway, as Barbie's cell phone started buzzing and then Barbie was tapping away at a response with a silly smile on her face. Shortly, Barbie begged off saying that she had to meet a friend. Antonia was pretty sure her "friend" was her boyfriend. On her way out, Barbie made one last plea for the cardboard box but Antonia resisted and she didn't press. Perhaps she believed Antonia that nothing in it would be of help to her.

After Barbie left, Antonia sat at the table for a few more minutes to process everything. Her head was spinning and she felt as if her quest was leading her in so many different directions. Was it even worth pursuing? Maybe it all just was a coincidence. She wanted to think that, but that was the easy way to look at it. "There are no coincidences," her mother would say.

She sat back in her chair and took one last gulp of her now lukewarm tea. She glanced over at Barbie's plate, and noticed for the first time that after all that cutting, picking, and forking, Barbie had not eaten one bite of the sticky bun. *Oh well,* thought Antonia. *Her loss.*

9

Antonia's shoes crunched along the leafy path as she wended her way through the backyard: a wide expanse of sprawling grass enclosed by a privet hedge and a deer fence. Thickets of trees lined the back edge of the property as well as dozens of bushes that flowered at various times of the year. On the right side of the lawn was a long, fenced patch of vegetable garden, which was currently dominated by cauliflower, spinach, and squash. The other side held wildflowers and a large magnolia tree. The garden shed that had once been used as the tannery was backed against the most recessed part of the yard, in the shadows of some pine trees.

Antonia loved the smell of the East Coast autumn air, which was a revelation for her after all those years in California. The fresh breeze contained a combination of earth, fireplace smoke, musty leaves, and pumpkins. It was hard to explain but she wished one of her vintner friends back in California could bottle it all into a cabernet that she would enjoy with a thick slice of Vermont cheddar and some soppressata. With such a lively and happy aroma, it was strange to think that autumn is the season of death—where all of nature is falling to the ground and dying. Including Biddy Robertson.

Antonia found Hector toward the edge of the yard, planting bulbs in the bare spots between the perennials.

Gardening and flowers and plants were all things that Antonia appreciated but had known very little about until recently. In California, she had lived in a town house and paid dues to have others maintain the grounds. It was a relief to have someone else trim bushes into perfect cones and meticulously color-coordinate flower boxes so that everything was as neatly manicured as Disneyland. But now that she owned an inn with a giant yard, she felt it was crucial for her to learn more. For instance, Hector had just told her that spring and summer flowers need to be planted six weeks before the ground freezes in the fall. So they had spent an afternoon flipping through a catalog, selecting hyacinths, Dutch Master daffodils, and Spanish bluebells to be planted. And now here he was, bent down, pushing them into the earth. He was so focused on his digging that he didn't hear Antonia approach. Although it was chilly, he had taken off his jacket and laid it on the ground next to his tools. The back of his green shirt had sweat marks, which clung to his back while the rest of his shirt rippled in the wind. He wore Carhartt pants and brown work boots, the standard gardener uniform. When Antonia called out his name he stiffened before turning around.

"Yes, Mrs. Antonia?"

"Hi, Hector, sorry to interrupt. Do you have a second?"

"Sure."

He wiped sweat off his brow with the back of his hand and put down his shovel. He looked up at Antonia with an earnest, eager look, and she at once dismissed the idea that he killed Gordon. This was not that type of person. If there was one thing Antonia trusted, it was her gut. This guy didn't read killer. Now there might be some people who questioned her gut when it came to bad decisions like marrying her ex-husband. But if she were truly honest with herself, she would recall that she knew from the beginning that the darkness in Philip's eyes was not a brooding intensity but rather a menacing rage. She was too young to distill the depth of his anger, and optimistically thought she would be able to shake any darkness out of him, like in those romantic comedies where the nice, well-intentioned girl changes the badass thug into a charming suitor (see *Grease*). How wrong she was.

She momentarily lost her nerve. Instead of asking Hector anything about Gordon, she immediately peppered him with questions about the bulbs and what his plans were for their ailing birch tree. He then showed her a hole in the back fence where the deer had broken through, and she gave him permission to buy more wire. Deer were a huge problem in East Hampton; the town was overrun with them. Beside the fact that they ate all of her plants and flowers like candy (she was particularly bitter about the row of yews that used to line the side of the driveway that would now basically be considered a pile of firewood) deer were dangerous. They carried diseases, not just Lyme, which was particularly debilitating, but many others. And they would run out in the road at top speed at dusk and a driver could slam right into them, totaling a car. Ask most people in East Hampton what they thought about deer and you would not receive a response that was warm and fuzzy like Bambi. Deer were vermin.

After exhausting all of the deer conversation, as well as reiterating all of Hector's plans for the grounds, Antonia had run out of dialogue. She could tell Hector was waiting to return to work, but was politely humoring her. She finally had to make a move.

"How is your wife, Hector?"

He nodded and answered in his thick Guatemalan accent. "She's good. She has a new job, only part time, she stays home with the kids a lot."

Antonia nodded. "That's great. Nice people?"

Hector shrugged. "Yeah, nice."

Antonia nodded again. "Well, so, did she like working here at the inn?"

A brief flicker of anxiety flashed across Hector's face. "Yes, she like. But then, you know, Mr. Gordon was not so… Well, it didn't work out."

"I heard what happened, Hector. But I also heard that your wife said it wasn't true. What was her side of the story?"

Hector's eyes darted around and he hesitated. Antonia could see the wheels turning in his mind. She wanted him to trust her, because she could just instinctively tell that he was an honest and decent man, the way she could tell a ripe peach from a mealy one.

"Soyla, that's my wife, she work hard for Mr. Gordon. That's okay. She do the sheets, the bedrooms, the bathrooms, and the living rooms. She work from seven in the morning until eight at night for three years. Then one day a guest say that she missing gold hoop earrings. She say Soyla take them. Soyla didn't take them, I promise you, Mrs. Antonia. We are Christians, we go to church every Sunday, we no drink, no smoke, no drugs. Soyla never took the earrings. But they missing…"

"Gordon accused her of stealing them and fired her?" He nodded. "Yes."

"Were you mad?" asked Antonia.

Hector blew air out of his mouth in a deep sigh. "Yes, but I no quit because I need this job, Mrs. Antonia. It's a good job. I work all year here, not just summer."

"Did you ask him to hire her back?"

"I tried talk to Mr. Gordon but he no listen."

"Did you try to talk to anyone else?"

"Well, Mr. Ronald was already fired, so it was just Barbie who help Mr. Gordon, and she no care."

"She didn't try to help you?"

He shook his head. "She said she would talk to him, but I don't think so. And I didn't want to ask her again."

"Was Barbie nice to you?"

"She fine," he said in a tight voice. Antonia could tell he was holding something back.

"Did she do something to you?"

Hector glanced longingly at his shovel and Antonia could tell he wished he were not having this conversation. She wanted to reassure him, tell him everything would be okay, but of course after a man like Gordon treated you and your wife like that, it was wise to be hesitant.

"I don't know. Maybe she…"

"She what?" prodded Antonia.

"Someone say, maybe *she* took the earrings. After the guest leave, maybe one week later, Barbie wore new gold earrings. She said she got them for her birthday, but I don't know. The woman who lost them say they were gold with little blue stones on the bottom. These were the same."

Pieces were beginning to fall into place for Antonia. She shook her head. "That's bad."

"Yes. And she also…well, I heard she said *she* had some things stolen from her room, and the hotel. She blamed Soyla for that also."

"Barbie did?"

"Yes."

"Like what?"

"She said she no find a red scarf and some shoes. Oh, and she was mad about a pair of small dishes she couldn't find. They had seashells on them, and they were in the parlor."

"She was missing all that?"

"She say."

"Do you think she was telling the truth?"

"I don't think so."

"Do you think she killed Gordon?"

Hector gave her an astonished look. "What? No, Mr. Gordon had a heart attack. I found him over there…" he pointed to the other side of the lawn.

"But maybe it wasn't a heart attack."

Hector was again amazed. "I think it was heart attack."

Antonia didn't want to press it. Instead she changed the subject. "Hector, have Soyla come talk to me. Maybe we can find her a position at the inn again."

Hector's face brightened. "I will, Mrs. Antonia. Thank you!"

This Barbie is tricky, Antonia thought to herself as she made her way back to the inn to prepare for dinner service. *Definitely more to her than meets the eye.*

10

Monday

ANTONIA WAS IN A GRUMPY MOOD WHEN SHE PULLED her weather-beaten Saab into the small parking lot that abutted the L.V.I.S. It was her own darn fault; she had psyched herself up and inevitably was disappointed. This morning she had risen early, a skip in her step, and dressed carefully. She wore a long red-and-blue paisley Ralph Lauren skirt that she had bought using Genevieve's discount, her emerald green turtleneck sweater, and silver earrings that she'd purchased in New Mexico. Her one nod to comfort was her beloved UGGs. Despite the early hour, she'd put on some makeup and taken time to brush her long dark hair. She looked good, maybe too fancy for a walk on the beach, but not inappropriate.

And of course, all for naught, because Nick Darrow was nowhere to be seen on the desolate beach. Antonia felt silly to have expected him; what were the chances? But nonetheless, she had been fantasizing about another exchange with him. She had even planned to invite him to her restaurant if it came up naturally. When she interacted with attractive men, she had a habit of blurting out non sequiturs. She once met a guy in a bar who told her he was an accountant and she immediately asked him if he liked crab cakes. It was as if she couldn't control herself, like Tourette's of the heart. But with Nick, she'd secretly rehearsed a few possible conversations with him in her mind, just so she wouldn't appear needy, celeb-crazed, or talk about how she had bad luck and loved bread. She would stay away from politics, gossip, and murder (so she wouldn't get worked up) and thought a safe topic would be dogs, since he had two and clearly loved them. She had never owned a dog, but she thought they were cute. She had a cat growing up and liked cats, but she refused to have a cat now that she was single and middle-aged. It was just too cliché. Even Genevieve said it would be slamming the door on a future of romance. Not that she was searching for romance exactly, but she didn't want to slam any doors.

So after pacing up and down the beach for half an hour, being humped by an overeager bulldog whose owner was too distracted by her Starbucks venti latte and iPhone to drag him away, and watching two brave surfers take on the roaring waves, Antonia had called it a day and left. She stopped back at the inn to help with the morning service, but when she found herself barking orders at her line cooks, she decided it was better to remove herself from the situation. She wolfed down a chocolate banana muffin and a mug of milky coffee and set off. And now here she was at the L.V.I.S. and she had no idea why but she felt like she needed to learn more about Biddy Robertson.

The Gardiner Brown House, home of the Ladies Village Improvement Society, was built circa 1740 and now listed on the National Registry of Historic Places. It was a large, two-story shingled house (plus attic) with white trim, framed by well-manicured bushes along the front. A giant American flag fluttered in the breeze atop the enormous flagpole in the front yard. The L.V.I.S. was the oldest organization in East Hampton and began in 1895 when twenty-one housewives came together to water down the dusty streets and clean up the railroad station. Since then, the group, composed of volunteers, had maintained and preserved historic landmarks, parks, ponds, greens, and trees as well as done community outreach to better the town. Without these ladies, East Hampton could have ended up looking like the Jersey Shore boardwalks.

Antonia zigzagged up the wheelchair ramp on the side entrance and entered the Bargain Box. She was instantly confronted with the distinct musty smell of old books, worn clothes, and antiques that may have sat in an attic for several decades before someone got hip to the fact that they could receive a tax write-off by donating them. The thrift store was located in a series of small rooms that fed into each other. The ceilings were low, with large rectangular overhead lights emitting unflattering brightness, and the walls were mostly white, with the exception of a few that were the color of faded sunshine. An inordinate number of windows made the place feel less claustrophobic than it could have. The store was extremely well organized, and every attempt was made to market the donations in a user-friendly way. Antonia couldn't help but thinking of the old adage *One man's trash is another man's treasure.*

After walking by shelves filled with a variety of vases, porcelain figurines, Venetian goblets, and decorative china plates, Antonia hooked left into the main room where the register was located. Two women stood behind the counter in front of a bulletin board that reminded people not to talk on their cell phones and gave them all sorts of information about the guidelines to donating. The women were conversing in hushed tones. The first was in her early sixties, with thin white-blond hair that curled in an upward flip above her shoulders. She had pale skin with the faintest hint of rouged cheeks, and thinly arched, light eyebrows. She dressed demurely and had on a pearl choker, pearl earrings, and a white button-down blouse under a black cardigan, over which she wore a green apron, as did her companion. She was a classic faded beauty who, Antonia could tell, had been very pretty as a younger woman. The name tag on her apron said *LINDA*. The second lady, whose name tag said *ANNEMARIE*, was older and wore her white hair in an unstyled pixie cut. She had the husky voice of a smoker and the yellow-stained teeth to confirm it. The green apron fit snugly over her Easter-egg-blue sweater and her low-hanging ample breasts were making an effort to burst out of the front but instead were flopping out to the sides. She had on gold dangling earrings that softened her somewhat harsh, birdlike features. Antonia walked closer and pretended to be perusing the basket of leather gloves that were by the register. She had a feeling from the solemnity of their voices that they might be talking about Biddy, and bingo, she was right.

"It's just odd how one minute you can be discussing sangria recipes and the next minute the person is dead. I mean, I know life is like that, but it is still odd," said Linda.

Annemarie nodded. "I know. There are lots of people where you see it coming, but not with Biddy! Heck, I know she was seventy, but she was a *young* seventy. She swam in the ocean every day this summer."

"And she was sharp as a tack. That's why the whole leaving the kettle on seems strange to me."

Annemarie sighed. "I agree. I didn't even *know* she drank tea. She always had a cup of coffee in her hand. Maybe she drank tea at night? I like an occasional cup of chamomile to put me to bed."

"I suppose."

When they paused, Antonia moved over to another section so as not to incur suspicion. She had noticed other customers when she entered, but it appeared they had filtered into the neighboring rooms.

"Biddy's son is coming down from Boston to make the arrangements."

"He's a wonderful boy. She adored him." They paused. "Those are darling, aren't they?"

Antonia was so busy eavesdropping on their conversation that she didn't even realize they had stopped and directed their attention to her. She was holding a pair of brown suede high heels in her hand that she would never have even thought to buy, but as the shoes were close to the desk where the ladies were gabbing, she had pretended to be totally enamored of them.

"Yes, very nice," she said, turning around and facing the ladies. "I love them in theory, but unfortunately I think I'd fall down flat on my face if I were to wear them."

Linda laughed diffidently. "They do take practice."

"You're still young, you should take advantage," said Annemarie. "Hell, if I didn't have varicose veins all over my legs, I would still be wearing my miniskirts. I loved my miniskirts. Believe it or not, Linda, I had great legs."

"Oh, I believe it, Annemarie. You still have great legs."

Annemarie turned back to Antonia. "Honey, take my advice. Wear what you can, while you can. It doesn't get any better."

She laughed heartily, one of those guttural, contagious laughs, and soon Antonia and Linda had chimed in. And then for no reason at all, they all laughed harder, and couldn't stop.

"Sorry," said Annemarie. "I apologize. We're a little discombobulated here today. One of our colleagues, a friend, died two nights ago."

Linda wiped the tears of laughter that had formed in the corners of her eyes and nodded her head. "Yes, I think Annemarie and I are just in shock. You know that wide range of emotions that has you going from one extreme to the other."

"I understand," said Antonia gently. "I have honestly found myself laughing at funerals. It sounds horrible but it's just so stressful and emotional, you can have a hard time processing it."

"I guess that's why," agreed Linda. "I don't know quite what it is, but since Biddy died, I have felt completely frantic."

Antonia nodded sympathetically. Here was her opening. "You were friends with Biddy Robertson?"

"Yes, did you know her?" asked Linda.

"Not personally. But I actually own the Windmill Inn now. How rude of me, I'm Antonia Bingham."

The women made their introductions and briefly questioned Antonia about how her move to East Hampton was going and what the progress of the inn was. She answered in detail, hoping to make them feel comfortable and cozy with her so that she could eventually pepper them with uncomfortable and uncozy questions. After stretching out the conversation as much as possible and inviting them to dine at the inn, she wiggled the conversation back to Biddy.

"I have to be honest with you, and please don't take this the wrong way because I am very sympathetic to your loss, but I'm a little nervous since all I've heard about for the past few days was how the previous owners of the inn died under suspicious circumstances."

Both women looked at her with astonishment. Antonia reddened, instantly regretting that she had even mentioned the topic. Here they were mourning their friend and she was telling them how she was sad about it because of how it affected *her*. It was very tacky and very rude.

"I'm sorry, I just—"

But Annemarie cut her off before she could finish. "No, it's not you. It's absolutely strange! I had...I forgot all about that. I had heard that long ago and didn't remember until you said it. What are the chances?"

Linda gave Antonia a worried look. "If that was true, I *would* think you would be concerned right now..."

"Well, to be honest, I am," confided Antonia. "I mean, I know that it's just an old rumor, I don't even know what you would call it, folk tale? Lore? Myth? But whatever it is, it seems *awfully* coincidental."

"Wait a second," said Linda. "Biddy's death was an accident. She died of gas poisoning. So when you say 'suspicious' circumstances, you just mean accidents and things that aren't natural causes, right?"

"Right. I'm not implying anything sinister." Antonia didn't want to bring up murder.

"How did the last owner die?" asked Linda. She was twisting her pearl earring nervously. "I don't remember hearing that was suspicious."

"No, you're right," said Annemarie. "He died of a heart attack, I think."

"Wasn't he Naomi Haslett's brother?" asked Linda.

"Yes," interjected Antonia. "Do you know Naomi?"

"Not very well," admitted Linda. "But we've run across each other's paths at ARF events. We're both dog lovers, and we both had Westies."

"I see."

"Linda has the cutest little Westie I ever saw," said Annemarie. "Teddy. Just a doll."

"My baby. I don't know what I would do without him! He is just so wonderful. Sadly, Naomi's dog, Jack, passed. I felt bad for her. She adored her baby as much as I adored mine. She was distraught. And then her brother died…" Her voice trailed off.

"Yes, that's tough… Do they think his death is suspicious because he was so young? I think he was early fifties," asked Annemarie.

"Yes, exactly," said Antonia quickly. She wasn't ready to lay down the whole murder theory with total strangers. "He was so young."

Annemarie nodded. "Just a kid to someone my age."

"Right. That's why some people are thinking that his death was strange."

Antonia watched as both women absorbed the idea. Finally, Linda broke the silence. "Well, I hope it was truly Biddy's time to go. I hate to think that just because she briefly owned the inn, she died earlier than she should have."

Annemarie nodded firmly in agreement. "That's the important fact. She didn't own the inn when she died, so it's just a coincidence."

"Agreed," said Antonia.

Linda continued twisting her earring, staring off into space until Antonia finally saw her eyes focus. "You know what? It's good that you're here. There is actually a box here that is marked for the Windmill Inn."

"Really?" asked Antonia with surprise.

"Oh, you're right," said Annemarie. "In the back."

"Yes, I'll go fetch it," said Linda.

She disappeared into the back room. Annemarie gave her a warm smile. "Don't worry about all this nonsense about the inn. It's just drama."

"I hope you're right."

Linda returned with an old box that had previously held seltzer, judging from the labels around the edge of it. It looked worn and musty and had probably been used to transport some kitchen items, thought Antonia, as it had stains embedded into its sides. Linda placed it down on the counter and before Antonia could glance inside, Annemarie peered down deep into it, sinking her bird-like nose as if she were a pelican grabbing a fish out of the water.

"I'm not sure what it is exactly. Biddy put it together, but she told us that it had to go back to the Windmill Inn," said Linda.

"Go back? To whom?" muffled Annemarie from inside the box.

"I don't know."

When Annemarie emerged, Antonia moved toward the box. She glanced inside and suddenly felt a chill. The contents included a red scarf, a pair of black chunky plat-form boots with worn gold buckles, and two little dishes with seashells on them. Exactly the items that had gone missing, according to Hector.

"Where did she obtain these?" asked Antonia.

"I'm sorry, but I really don't remember. I know she said someone dropped them off but then she realized there must be some mistake and those things belonged to the Windmill Inn."

"Did she say who dropped them off?" asked Antonia. She could tell both Annemarie and Linda were becoming disconcerted with her rising alarm. She had to play it cool.

"No. I don't recall…" said Linda.

"Why? What are you thinking?" asked Annemarie.

"Oh, nothing. It's just…well, someone told me that they thought these items had been…" Antonia didn't want to say *stolen*. Then the police would become involved and it would turn into a bigger thing. "Missing. Someone misplaced these items. They were meant for storage and they were taken, I suppose, here, by mistake."

"Well, I guess Biddy knew that, so that's why she gathered them together," said Linda.

Annemarie gave her a quizzical look. "Who was missing them?"

Antonia took a deep breath. She couldn't lie. "Barbie Fawcett. Gordon Haslett's girlfriend."

"Oh, I know her," said Annemarie in a tone that suggested that she knew her but didn't like her.

"Perhaps it was Ronald Meter who took them by accident," said Linda.

"He comes here a lot, doesn't he?" asked Antonia.

"Yes, now and then. He buys books. He's dropped off things to sell."

"What sort of things?" asked Antonia.

Linda looked down uncomfortably. "Sorry, but I'm not sure we are supposed to disclose…"

"Oh, I'm sorry for asking. I just know he has a great… candlestick collection. I was wondering if he ever let any of those go."

Annemarie gave a disapproving look to Linda. Then Linda responded, abashed. "No, not candlesticks."

"Oh."

There was an uncomfortable silence. Antonia definitely didn't want to end on an awkward note. "Well, thank you for this box. I'll bring it back to the inn and call Barbie."

"Great," said Linda brightly. "Oh, and tell Hector Gonzalez that we have a new shipment of children's clothes, please."

Antonia paused. So Hector was a customer also? "Hector?"

"Yes, isn't he still the gardener?"

"Yes, yes, he is. Okay, will do."

The door closed with a soft bang behind her and Antonia trotted down the steps to her car. It was so hard to narrow down the list of suspects in a small town, where everyone knew everyone and small dislikes could grow and fester! She placed the box in the back seat of her car and wondered what she would do with it.

11

INSTEAD OF HEADING BACK TO THE INN, ANTONIA decided to zip over to one of her favorite stores in East Hampton. Dorothy's Cupboard, situated on North Main Street, was the quintessential artisanal cheese shop. Located in a low-slung building that had formerly housed a barbershop, Dorothy had kept the barber pole and painted it a festive red, yellow, and white. Three brick steps led up to red double doors and inside, the interior walls were also painted a matching bright yellow, with white shelves.

Antonia was feverishly in love with cheese shops. One of her fondest childhood memories was going to town with her father and stopping in the local cheese shop. She remembered perfectly the smell of all the cheese varieties mingling together, the sawdust on the floor, and the little ceramic dishes filled with samples that you just had to stab with a toothpick and pop in your mouth. She always tried the samples, and adored how the cheesemonger would take his slicer from his apron and cut ribbons of buttery and tangy cheese for her to try. They would burst on her tongue and then melt in her mouth. And buying fancy cheese always meant that they were preparing for a party, so to this day, she felt that sense of hopeful expectancy, like something fun is about to happen, whenever she stepped into a cheese store.

Antonia took her time tasting the various new cheeses while she chatted with Dorothy. There were some new luscious triple creams from Northern California, and a nice, sharp, semi-firm Gouda. All of those went well with some apricot and almond biscuits from the North Fork. There was a bluefish spread produced from fish caught off the coast in Montauk that Antonia smeared on an onion cracker. And, of course, there was new smoked soppressata with the faintest hint of truffle that just burst with flavor. Antonia was becoming very content.

Antonia took the time to peruse the other various items on display, and found herself loading up on spicy red pepper jam, oatmeal shortbread cookies, and mango-jalapeño chutney. She was a total sucker for artisanal pantry items and could never have enough. How great was it when she was tired after a long day to just boil some pasta and coat it with a jar of Parmesan artichoke purée? Voilà, instant dinner! As she lifted a packet of caramelized walnuts out of the case, a flash of blond outside the window caught her eye. When she glanced up to take a better look, she realized that it was Barbie.

Barbie pointed her key at her white Toyota Prius and pressed a button to lock it. She slid the keychain into her pocketbook—one of those oversize satchels, made up of calf-hair and pebbled leather, with all sorts of gold zippers and buckles everywhere and the designer's initials prominently displayed in the center, just in case you missed the memo that it was expensive and fashionable. Today, Barbie had on black leggings tucked into low boots, and wore some sort of gray fur vest over a light pink sweater. She strode confidently across the street toward the I.G.A. paying little heed to the traffic, which had the light and the right of way. Just before Barbie disappeared through the electric door into the store, a tall man in a dark blue windbreaker came up behind her and put his hand right on her ass.

Antonia's every sense jolted with excitement. *This must be the boyfriend!* she thought. She watched as they entered the store and then vanished out of sight and into the aisles. Were they already so intimate that they were shopping for toilet paper and detergent together? And if this dude was married, wasn't he acting very boldly by hitting a grocery store with his mistress in the middle of the day? These were things Antonia needed to know. She quickly paid Dorothy for her provisions and beelined across the street.

Antonia made a sharp turn past the eggs into the produce section. She figured she'd go aisle by aisle until she found them. She had a hunch that they wouldn't be stocking up on vegetables, but you never knew what turned people on. This time, her hunch was correct. The only people perusing fruits and vegetables were an older lady in a purple velour sweat suit, who was squeezing lemons, and a small hunched man who was loading an inordinate amount of green peppers into his cart. Antonia walked down the aisle and took a sharp left into the dairy section. Blasts of cold air immediately smacked her in the face. She wished, once again, that they would distribute sweaters on loan in the refrigeration section so that she wouldn't have to sprint down the aisle into the warmth of canned goods.

Finally, she spotted her prey. They were arm in arm, making a left into beverages. Their backs were to her, so they hadn't seen her yet. Even if they had been facing her, their body language was telling Antonia that they were probably too preoccupied to notice her. She was about to approach them when she abruptly stopped by the rack of pretzels. She had no plan. Should she just go say hello? The fact of the matter was, if they were out and about like this, then they had nothing to hide. Was she going to bust them for shopping?

She peeked behind the rack and watched as the guy put a six-pack of Heineken into his basket. *It would make sense that he was after booze*, thought Antonia. *Didn't he work at a liquor store?* For the first time, she had a visual of him. He was handsome, in a bland everyday way. Very tall, broad-shouldered with a full head of brown hair and a face as round as a moon. Her only slight criticism would be that his head appeared to be a bit too small for his body, and he stooped slightly as if he had never become comfortable with his height. He looked to be in his mid-thirties, definitely younger than Barbie, and that fact was illuminated when she snaked her wrinkled, veiny hands around his waist. Barbie was a cougar! Antonia should have smelled that a mile away. They laughed at some inside joke and then walked over to the tortilla chip section, adding a bag and some salsa into their basket.

Oh, they have fun planned for tonight, thought Antonia. As they continued down the aisle, Antonia leaned a bit forward to watch them. Would they stop by the freezer and snag some ice cream? That would really determine the state of their relationship. Scarfing down ice cream in front of a man meant that he had seen you naked. Just as they opened the door and were reaching, Antonia felt a poke in her ribs. She jumped as if a snake had bitten her.

"Ah!" yelled Antonia. She whipped around.

"Scared ya!" laughed Larry Lipper, mischievously.

Antonia thought she would throw up. Her heart was literally in her throat (okay, not literally in the *literally* sense, but literally in the sense how people overuse that word to make strong points). This little rodent had scared the dickens out of her and now he stood there gleefully smirking, his tiny body in his tiny jeans shaking with mirth, and she wanted to strangle him.

"Larry, you shouldn't sneak up on people."

"How could I resist? You were ripe for the picking."

Antonia took a deep breath and vowed she would not throttle him. "Okay, you got me."

"Damn straight. What were you doing? It looked like you were spying on someone." Larry walked around her and stood in the beverage aisle, attempting to bust her. Antonia momentarily held her breath but was relieved to find that fortunately, Barbie and her man had moved on. The aisle was empty with the exception of a young mom pushing a cart while her toddler daughter pushed a mini-cart next to her.

"I was just trying to figure out which pretzels to buy," said Antonia, grabbing two bags from the rack. "Reading the ingredients."

Larry gave her a suspicious look. He wagged his finger at her. "I don't know, I think you were up to something."

Antonia felt herself reddening. She motioned toward the basket he was holding. "I didn't know you had kids."

"What?" he said, and held up his basket as if seeing it for the first time. Inside were two boxes of Kraft macaroni and cheese, a box of Lucky Charms, a small quart of whole milk, and a pack of Jell-O pudding.

"Oh, no," he shrugged. "I just like kid food."

For a second, Antonia could swear he was embarrassed, and she was secretly glad. Let him squirm.

"I can't believe you eat all that garbage. It's really bad for you. All those preservatives…"

"I know, I know. I'm glad you care."

"I don't care," blurted Antonia.

"Yes, you do!"

"Larry, I'm just trying…"

He interrupted her. "Whatever. Listen, I found out a hot tip that you might be interested in."

"Changing the subject, fine. What is it?" asked Antonia.

Larry smiled obnoxiously. "What will you do for me if I tell you?"

"You're kidding me, right?"

"Come on, this is hot stuff."

"I won't do anything. If you want to tell me you will."

"You drive a hard bargain, lady."

"I'm not driving any bargain. I really don't care either way."

What was it about this man that made Antonia behave as if she were in kindergarten? Really, if she had acted this way with anyone else, she would have been mortified. But he brought out this bratty, childish toddler inside of her. She had to seize control of herself.

"All right, since you are so critical of my eating habits, you can make me dinner."

"Larry…"

"Trust me! This is worth it."

Antonia took a deep breath. "Okay, what is it?"

He looked like a kid at the candy store. "Well, as you know, I have friends in law enforcement…"

He paused for Antonia to make suitably impressed exclamations, but she remained silent so he continued. "They tell me that they are actually going to look into Biddy Robertson's death as a possible homicide."

Antonia's heart leaped. "What? Are you kidding me?"

"I knew you'd freak out."

"What changed? Why do they suddenly think something happened?"

Larry shrugged. "I'm not sure. My buddy just said they were taking and I quote, a 'renewed interest.'"

"That's all?"

"The rest you can read about in my column this week."

Antonia felt the blood boil in her veins. She grabbed

Larry's arm and pushed him into the rack of pretzels. If she had to crush every bag of snack food to elicit more information from him, she would do it. "Are you crazy? Larry, I'm not waiting until later this week to read your column! What else did he say?"

"Antonia, I didn't realize you liked to play it rough."

"Larry, come on," said Antonia, flinging his hand down. "Don't do this. What would Nicky Darrow say?"

Larry's lips widened into a large grin. "Oh, you're going to celebrity name drop."

"I'll do what I have to."

He cocked his head to the side and stared at her breasts. "Okay, I'll tell you, but only you."

"Thank you."

She folded her arms and waited.

"Biddy has a nosy neighbor. She's actually the one who called the police when she smelled the gas. Lives in the adjoining town house, condo, whatever you call it. She heard someone leave Biddy's house at about nine o'clock that evening. Heard the door shut and Biddy say goodbye and then a car door shut and drive away."

"So? Maybe Biddy had a friend over."

Larry nodded. "But then two hours later, she heard the car return. Heard the same footsteps, the person walked to the door and quietly let herself in."

"Well did this neighbor have a look at the person?"

"She's blind."

"She's blind?"

"Yeah, that's why she has such good hearing. My

buddy said they gave her a few tests and it was uncanny how she could tell all sorts of differences between foot- steps and everything. She has ears like a hawk."

"Isn't it eyes like a hawk?"

"Antonia, she's blind!"

She let that one slide. "So that's enough for them to think it's a homicide?"

"I'm thinking there must be other reasons, but that's the only one they told me. Probably because this blind neighbor is going to be running her mouth off around town about the mystery guest. Talk to anyone who will listen. I'm heading over to interview her right now."

"I'm coming."

Larry gave her a quizzical look but then smiled again. "I knew you were hot for me. Can't stay away."

12

LARRY HAD WANTED ANTONIA TO ACCOMPANY HIM IN his car and drive over to the neighbor's together but the thought of spending time with him in a confined space made Antonia sick to her stomach so she refused. Not without a battle, though. Forcing him to impart Biddy's address took epic strength. For someone so diminutive he had an enormously inflated sense of self. Antonia had to wonder about his parents. Maybe since they knew he would be vertically challenged they indoctrinated him with messianic beliefs that he was the second coming. She sincerely didn't think that it was a defense mechanism and that he acted out of insecurity. He definitely thought he was God's gift to women and this earth.

After a search for directions on her phone, Antonia found the location of Biddy's condo. As Antonia drove there, she sifted through all of the recent revelations in her mind. The whole situation reminded her of when she would go on camping trips in high school with her friends. One person would inevitably rise in the night to retrieve water from the stream, and they would see or hear something suspicious. Then the next day, others would add in things—mysterious sounds they'd heard, items that they swore had been moved, shadows that they had definitely seen lingering over their tents in the moonlight. They would psych themselves up so they were appropriately terrified, and return home from their adventure with a tale to tell. Everything that Antonia had heard about Gordon's death could be examined through this filter. Maybe he had been stung by a bee; that was very rare for December but not absolutely impossible, especially if the weather had been mild enough.

Gordon had several enemies (and friends) who would want him dead: his sister, Naomi, because she needed money and wanted to sell the inn; his girlfriend, Barbie, because she had a lover and was also possibly pilfering things from guests; Hector, the gardener, who was angry that his wife was fired; Ronald Meter, the former manager, who was angry that he was fired; Biddy Robertson, who was angry that Gordon bought the inn right out from under her. The fact was, they all had motive, but motive was flimsy. You had to have exhibited homicidal tendencies, too, didn't you? This would have to have been an incredibly well-thought-out plan: to procure a bee, smuggle it to the inn, then have it sting Gordon. Were any of these people furious or psychotic enough to do it? Antonia wasn't sure.

And now there was Biddy Robertson. If it turned out that she had indeed been murdered, the only reason to suspect that her death was linked to Gordon's was because they both owned the inn at one point, and there was that strange "curse" on the Windmill Inn owners. There was also the box that Biddy had put aside to return to the inn. Could that be the reason she was killed? It seemed absurd. All of this information just seemed like a miscellaneous collection of facts that couldn't support any theory.

And yet...there had to be something to it all. Why would the police now think Biddy was murdered? Obviously, they had information. Antonia had to agree with Larry and bet her booties that it wasn't just what the blind lady thought she might have heard. And there was something odd about Gordon's death, some sort of fuzziness that she couldn't pinpoint. People who knew him were acting strangely.

Antonia turned right into Treetop Lane and drove down the bumpy road. A scattering of leaves still held firmly green, but the tupelos had turned a fiery red and the swamp maples were an orange-y maroon. The contrast between them and the yellow leaves of the hickories was dazzling. Some of the most impressive species of trees were in this area, with colors that matched those in the Appalachians. The trees were so thick that immediately everything darkened as if someone had turned off the light switch. Only cracked fragments of sun were able to make it through the heavy leaves. Antonia was not a fan of the woods; they made her claustrophobic. Besides, they were filled with roaming wildlife that made life unpleasant for humans. She would be happy to let the ticks have the woods, if she could have the streets, the farmland, and the manicured lawns. It was a fair trade, wasn't it?

When she pulled into number seventeen, she found Larry Lipper leaning against his blue BMW, with a smug look on his face. The condo structure was composed of attached units and painted mustard yellow, with brown roofs, brown doors, and brown trim around the wide un-paned windows. Antonia wondered about the thought process of the person who chose these Howard Johnson colors. When has anyone ever purposely chosen mustard yellow for anything? Something about it said "reject color." And to combine it with brown? She instantly thought of a uniform that a sad diner waitress might wear, in the middle of nowheresville, taking orders from sexist truck drivers. Yes, it was a stereotype.

"That's your car?" Larry sputtered. "You kidding me?"

Antonia glanced back at her beloved blue Saab. "Yes, why?"

"It's a piece of junk. They don't even make them anymore."

"It's a good car."

"No, it's not. If it were a good car, they would still make it. This is a good car," he said, pointing to his own.

"Whatever."

"Do you know how they marketed Saabs? They called them 'near luxuries.' Come buy this 'near luxury.' That's why they are out of business. Who the hell wants to buy 'near' luxury? You want to feel good about your car, like you're getting the best thing out there. Not *nearly* the best. It was idiotic."

"Well, clearly I fell for it."

"We'll need to talk about that," said Larry, trying to put his arm around Antonia. She wiggled away. "I think you have low self-esteem."

She changed the subject. "So this is Biddy's?"

There was a small, unobtrusive sliver of yellow police tape blocking off the doorway. Other than that, there would be no reason to suspect possible foul play had occurred there.

"Yeah. The neighbor lives there, let's go."

"Hold on, I just want to peek in for a second."

"What are you going to see?" asked Larry with exasperation.

"I don't know, but I just need a sense."

The white curtains were drawn shut on the large picture window at the front. Antonia cupped her hands around her eyes and pressed her face to the glass. She was unable to make out anything but shadowy pieces of furniture. She walked off the deck and around to another set of windows, but again, the curtains were shut. Oh well, so much for her sleuthing. She was hardly expecting to find a note from a murderer, but at least she thought she would try.

———————————

Sharon Getz was in her mid-fifties, heavyset with short brown hair and a neck full of wrinkles that splayed out across her chest like chains. Her eyes were big and brown and blinking, and if Antonia and Larry hadn't known she was blind, they would have never guessed. Larry immediately pointed out this fact.

"You don't look blind," he told Sharon as she led them

into her living room. She moved with ease and the same confidence that any seeing person might have.

Sharon laughed. "I know. I'm legally blind, not totally blind."

"What does that mean?" asked Larry.

"It means I have no peripheral vision but can see a small, pinprick-size amount. Shadows, colors, but not anything clearly."

"Have you always been blind?"

"Yes, I was born this way. Please, sit down."

Antonia and Larry sat down on a large white sectional couch in the cavernous living room. The ceiling was extremely high, with a massive skylight cutting through the center. Antonia instantly thought of what a pain in the neck it would be to clean it, and she could see from the filmy layer of dirt that it had been awhile. There were large screen doors along one wall that overlooked a terrace where a table and chairs stood, behind which was a brief strip of yard that led into woods. The living room spilled into a dining area, which then opened into a kitchenette with an island and two stools. The walls were all painted taupe, and the floors were a very blond wood that matched most of Sharon's furniture. It looked to Antonia as if she had bought everything in an Ethan Allen showroom, in one go, as it all seemed to be part of a set. There was very little in the decor that revealed Sharon's personality, which Antonia supposed was understandable seeing as she was blind. There were no books, no framed pictures, and the only artwork was a Van Gogh poster. In the corner on top of a cabinet a television was perched, one of the older ones that had a giant screen but was big and clunky, not like the newer thin plasma or high definition models that everyone seemed to have nowadays. Next to it stood a violin on a music stand.

After they politely refused her offer of water or coffee, Sharon sat down across from them, sinking into the swollen armchair. She wore black crepe pants and an oversized, shiny-red button-down shirt that flounced over the edge of her seat. Around her shoulders was a colorful scarf, more decorative than warm. Round gold hoops swung from her earlobes, and she had several thick gold rings with various semiprecious stones on her fingers.

"Are you married?" asked Larry, glancing around.

"Divorced," said Sharon.

"Really?" exclaimed Larry.

"Yes, why?" asked Sharon with alarm.

Antonia threw him a look. "Yes, why, Larry?"

"It's just odd for me to think blind people get divorced. I would think, you know, you need all the help you can get."

"Larry!" admonished Antonia. She turned to Sharon. "I'm so sorry."

Fortunately, Sharon was a good sport. "I know what you mean. I may turn a blind eye to some faults, but when a man cheats on me, I can't turn a blind eye to that!"

"Good one!" said Larry.

Sharon turned to Antonia and winked. Or at least Antonia thought she did, how could she be sure? Maybe it was a blind twitch.

"See, even blind people have a sense of humor," said Sharon.

"And even short people can be rude," said Antonia before Larry could answer.

"Touché," said Sharon.

"Okay, down to business," said Larry. He whipped out a small, brown leather notebook, the type Antonia had seen reporters and detectives use in movies and not in real life.

"Don't you have a digital recorder or something? It is the twenty-first century after all," asked Antonia.

"I'm old school, Bingham."

"Right."

He ignored her and instead turned to Sharon. "Tell me what you heard the night Biddy Robertson died."

Sharon proceeded to tell them the same story that Larry had repeated earlier. The only embellishments were a few complaints about a dog that lived two units down and barked incessantly, and several gripes about the management company's inability to clear the paths and fix the streetlight that stood in front of her condo, which had been out for several weeks now and was causing problems for Sharon's guests. Larry was incredibly thorough in his questioning and Antonia was impressed, but the story remained the same. Sharon had heard goodbyes, footsteps, a car, then car, footsteps and a car again. She was friendly with Biddy but not very close, more like pleasant neighbors. Biddy rarely had company, except when her son from Boston was visiting with his children. She was also divorced, but she had an active social life that kept her away from home most evenings. She was a zealous volunteer, an avid bridge player, a film enthusiast, a fan of prix-fixe dinners, and a Guild Hall theater regular, according to Sharon.

"How could she afford all that?" asked Larry. "She lost the inn in foreclosure."

Sharon nodded. "Yes, but then her son started doing very well in his work, some sort of finance. He supported her."

After Larry had exhausted all of his questions as to whether Biddy had any enemies (not that Sharon knew of); had been acting suspiciously (not to Sharon); had been unduly stressed (not to Sharon's knowledge); or had been threatened (again, not to Sharon's knowledge), Larry closed his little notebook.

"Why do you think this visitor might have killed her?" he asked finally.

"I can't tell you exactly," confessed Sharon. "It was just something about the footsteps. They didn't seem natural…"

"Could it be that the person was trying to be quiet so as not to wake everyone in the complex?" asked Antonia.

Sharon shook her head. "No. It was almost as if some-one was wearing shoes that didn't fit. They were trying to be quiet but having a hard time walking."

"But don't you think it could have been an accident?" asked Larry. "Say a friend comes over, they have tea, friend leaves, Biddy forgets to turn off the stove, friend comes back because they forgot something…"

"But why didn't the friend ring the doorbell?" asked Sharon.

"Or maybe it was someone else entirely. You said the streetlight was out in the front yard. It's not that easy to see the unit numbers, and probably very difficult in the dark. Maybe someone unfamiliar with the complex was trying to go to another house and went to Biddy's by accident. When they saw her number, they left," said Antonia. She was proud of herself for this one, it was totally probable.

"Could be," agreed Larry.

"But…" said Antonia. She could tell Sharon wasn't convinced.

"It was the same footsteps. Trust me."

"And then the next morning you woke up and smelled gas?" asked Larry.

Sharon nodded. "Yes. I have a good sense of smell."

"That's a nice consolation from the gods," said Larry.

"Larry," reprimanded Antonia.

Sharon smiled. "That's okay. I'm a big girl. I know this one is a tease. How long have you been together?"

"Oh, we're not together," protested Antonia. "No way, no how."

"Sorry, I just assumed," said Sharon.

"It's okay." Antonia wanted to add that maybe if Sharon could see she would know that Antonia would never go for Larry, but she knew that would be rude.

"Although you are right to pick up on the sexual tension," added Larry. "I can't keep this one away."

Antonia rolled her eyes, but declined to engage. "Sharon, is there anything else you can think of that may be important to us? Anything that Biddy had done or said lately that stands out? Any divergence from her usual routine?"

"Hmm…" began Sharon. "I'm straining to think of anything at all. She had started swimming at the rec center…"

"Uh-huh, anything else?" asked Antonia.

Larry swirled his finger around in a motion that meant Antonia should wrap it up but she pressed on.

"I was watering my flower boxes one day and she said she was heading off to Indian Wells for lunch with a former partner."

"Partner? Who?" prompted Antonia.

Sharon shrugged. "I don't know and I didn't ask."

"That's all she said about it?"

Sharon furrowed her brow. "She said something that they'd worked together and I don't know, I got the impression that it didn't work out because when I told her to have a good time she said, 'It will be interesting.'"

"*It will be interesting?*" repeated Antonia.

"Yes."

"What do you think that means?" asked Antonia.

"It means it would be interesting, Bingham. Geez, do we need to waste time on this?" interjected Larry.

Antonia shot him a dirty look. "I think it could be something."

"Like what?" asked Larry.

"Like, I don't know. Who was this person she had lunch with?"

"I couldn't say," answered Sharon.

"Can we move on?" asked Larry impatiently.

"Fine, anything else of importance?"

"I know she recently bought planters for the back patio."

"Can we go now?" Larry whined.

Antonia glared at him. How could he call himself a reporter when he had so little interest in cultivating sources? Unfortunately, she could see it was futile to continue with him around. "Fine."

After they said their goodbyes to Sharon, Antonia and Larry drove their cars to the end of the complex driveway and waited until they were far enough down the road to exit their cars for recon.

"Why did you rush me?" demanded Antonia.

"We were getting nowhere," snapped Larry.

"How do you know? Maybe she would remember something. What do you think of what she said?" asked Antonia.

"I think Bored Blind Lady."

"Larry, you are the least politically correct person I know."

"Thank you."

"That's not a compliment."

"To me, it is."

"Why do you think she's bored?"

"I don't know. Look, I want a murder as much as anyone. I'm dying for it. Do you know how awesome that would be for my byline? I already have the exclusive. It would just be a money machine for me. I'm talking book deals, and more! I could join forces with Nicky Darrow and do a movie. He'd play me, you understand. But this whole footstep thing is flimsy."

"I guess. She did seem convinced, though."

"I'm convinced I make great coffee, doesn't mean it's true."

"Why Larry, that's the first time I've heard you say anything self-deprecating!"

Larry ignored her. "The fact is, there has to be something that's making the police sniff around. But I don't think it's coming from Sharon."

13

ANTONIA WENT TO HER APARTMENT TO DROP OFF HER groceries from Dorothy's Cupboard and the box of rejected items from the L.V.I.S. Bargain Box there. She placed all of her new condiments in her personal kitchenette cabinets, where they joined about one hundred other jars. One day she would have to host some sort of tasting party, appetizers and hors d'oeuvres only, where she could set out the plethora of chutneys, jams, and mustards she had been collecting and open up some crackers and biscuits to sample them. She slid four cheeses out of the bag and noticed that the two triple creams were drooping from being left out of a refrigerator. Ripe cheese, slightly oozing, was like the last temptation of Christ for Antonia, so she unwrapped them and opened a box of Carr's crackers and quickly dug in. Majestic. Cheese and crackers were definitely on her Last Supper menu.

After taking a few nibbles of the harder cheese, she reluctantly rewrapped them all and placed them in her refrigerator. She washed her snack down with a glass of apple cider from the Milk Pail and wiped her hands with a dish towel. Even though Antonia's apartment was in the inn, she actually spent very little time there, choosing instead to retreat to her office when she had a spare moment. For that reason, there was something decidedly unfinished about Antonia's apartment, a little neglected. She glanced at the two potted plants on her windowsill with dismay. It never mattered that she followed the florist's instructions to a T, she always killed plants. It was a personal failure in her opinion. She filled up a glass of water from the tap and poured it into the pots, and just as she did so, three dead leaves fell to the counter in protest. Antonia sighed. What was she doing wrong? Sunlight, check. Water twice a week, check. Loving glances from afar, check. It was not good to kill plants. Antonia believed in feng shui and it was crucial to have plants in your home. They symbolized life, and now she was killing them. She tried not to think of the larger implications, in the whole scheme of things.

Antonia went to her bathroom to freshen up her makeup. She wore little but felt it was necessary to at least maintain what she had on. She carefully reapplied mascara and put on a little blush. Her hands were beginning to crack from the cold so she squirted a shea butter cream into her palms and rubbed her hands together. The smell was pure divinity. She had just picked up the lotion at White's Apothecary along with a new container of bath salts that she planned on soaking herself in as soon as she returned home from work. On her way out of the bathroom, Antonia caught a view of her profile in the full-length mirror and paused. She was instantly depressed. There was a definite thickening around her thighs, no doubt about it. And that little wheel of fat that she referred to as her "bread belt" was growing like an inflatable inner tube.

She turned to eye herself critically. The positives (and she always tried to focus on those) were that her hair was still a shiny, lustrous black. Not a gray had appeared (she hoped it never would) and her mane was thick and wavy. She did have some wrinkles on her face, but so far those were really more character-revealing and not something that should send her to a dermatologist's chair. Her eyes were still a bright blue (her vision still perfect) and her teeth were remaining white due to the Crest Whitestrips that she faithfully applied (she had to battle the coffee and tea stains). Her breasts had not yet drooped, her upper arms didn't have that hanging flab that women incur (no matter how fit), and she had no varicose veins.

But the sad truth was that she was overweight. And at the rate she kept binging on everything bad for her, it was only going to get worse. She sighed and went to her room and sat on the edge of her bed. Yet another full-length mirror on the opposite side of the door didn't allow her to escape her image (why did she have so many mirrors?). She watched as her tummy popped out over her elastic waist. Muffin top, bread belt, cheese gut, whatever you wanted to call it, she had it. Antonia had tried diets from time to time. But they really only lasted a week at most. And forget juicing, that was absurd! She needed to crunch her way through her day and exercise her pituitary gland or else she wouldn't survive. Okay, perhaps she would survive, but the fact was, what fun was life without food? It was her main source of joy. She loved eating it, shopping for it, preparing it, and feeding people. It was her whole life. Her relationship to it was unhealthy, but doesn't everyone have a vice?

Yes, she would like to be ten to fifteen pounds thinner. But she did not want to make sacrifices to do so. And if this hampered the possibility of a romantic life, so be it. Antonia had tried that before and it hadn't worked. She'd had a boyfriend in high school whom she had worshipped, and that had ended on a bad note. And then she had married Philip, and he had turned out to be a monster. She just wasn't good at love. It wasn't her thing. But she *was* good at food. So let that be her thing. It only took a few minutes for Antonia to convince herself of it. Deep down she knew she was taking the easy way out, but she believed that sometimes that was the way you had to take to protect yourself.

After running a brush through her hair and changing into a clean denim shirt, she went back to her kitchenette. The box from the L.V.I.S. was still sitting on the corner, its miscellaneous contents enticing her like a giant question mark. She had to think through what to do with them. If they were indeed Barbie's, had she just donated them to the thrift store and then accused Soyla of stealing them in order to have her fired? If that were the case, why? She probably could have just told Gordon that she thought Soyla was a bad cleaner. Why would she have to ruin her reputation? Or perhaps someone else like Ronald had stolen the goods and donated them to the L.V.I.S.? But then what was the point? There were too many outstanding questions that would have to wait, because right now her services were needed in the inn's kitchen.

But instead of heading straight there, Antonia decided to pass through reception to pick up her messages and swing by her office to make sure everything was running smoothly. The buzz of activity gave her some much-needed adrenaline. When she had first looked at the inn, Antonia had been dismayed by the reception area. She had pictured an old-fashioned nook at the base of the grand staircase, with a wooden counter where a pleasant person would greet guests and offer them tea while their rooms were being set up. She wanted old England, comfortable and inviting. Instead, Gordon had ripped out the original built-ins (and ripped out Antonia's heart when she found out that they had been there for over a hundred years before he did so—did he have no shame?) and put in a modern white Formica desk with sleek silver stools. When she asked the real estate agent what in the world he had been thinking, he said Gordon had tried to modernize the inn. But since when did "modernize" meant "tacky-ize"? Needless to say, those were the first to go. Antonia had scoured the internet and found the contents of an old inn in the Cotswolds that were on sale. She had the glossy walnut reception desk shipped over and then she tucked it in neatly under the staircase, where it fit snugly. Atop it she put a burnished forest green leather blotter and a silver cachepot filled with black felt-tip pens and two brass lamps with green silk shades. There was always a basket of seasonal flowers next to the silver bell that guests would press for service. Today, an orange vase held cherry brandy bi-colored roses, burgundy mini-carnations, butterscotch daisies, and red Asiatic lilies. Next to them, Antonia had placed some small pumpkins and gourds to celebrate the season.

Behind the desk, Antonia had an antique postman's cubby that she individually marked for each room. Guests generally didn't stay long enough to receive mail, but she would have Lucy type up any of the day's activities around town, weather information, and the dinner menu and place copies in each guest's box every morning so that they felt like they had some correspondence. Above the desk, Antonia hung a wooden sign that spelled out in white cursive *Enquiries,* and above that was a vintage brass clock that needed to be constantly wound. Fortunately, ten feet away, Antonia placed a large grandfather clock that ticked grandly and loudly and kept beautiful time.

Connie was chatting away with a middle-aged couple who had arrived two nights prior from Maryland. Sometimes Antonia worried that the loquacious front desk manager spent a little too much time gabbing with guests, but she hadn't had any complaints. And this couple were very relaxed—they were repeat customers who had been guests at a wedding in East Hampton a decade earlier and had fallen in love with the town enough to make an annual pilgrimage. Antonia had been gratified when they told her that they could not believe the remarkable renovations that she had made, and Antonia was giddy with excitement watching their genuine amazement as she toured them around the public rooms. They had noticed every detail, and complimented her on all of her success.

"Hello, Mr. and Mrs. Winslow, how is everything with you?" asked Antonia.

They were a thin, energetic couple who both had the trim sporty physique of long-distance runners. She wore her brown hair in a ponytail and his was short and sparse, but they were youthful and bursting with energy.

"Super, thank you, Antonia," said Mrs. Winslow. "We had a fantastic day. We picked up some goodies from Round Swamp and went out to the lighthouse in Montauk and had a picnic."

"I *love* Round Swamp," exclaimed Antonia. "It takes every single ounce of strength I have to not go there every day! I would weigh four hundred pounds if I did!"

"The cinnamon buns are pretty incredible!" said Mr. Winslow.

"Incredible? They are a narcotic for the soul. I love cinnamon buns. But everything is good there. The peach raspberry pies? The mini berry muffins that you can just pop in your mouth? And the chocolate fudge cake is divine," said Antonia, her mouth beginning to water.

"We love the baked goods but the main courses are pretty super also," said Mrs. Winslow. "I love their grilled shrimp kabobs. We picked up some of those and had some of their pesto pasta with peas and roasted brussels sprouts. It was so tasty."

"I'm jealous! But have you had their Mexican layer dip?" Antonia asked, raising her eyebrows.

"Oh, I've had that," interjected Connie from behind the counter. "That is dangerous."

"We haven't tried that yet," said Mr. Winslow.

"My gosh, you are missing out," said Antonia. "Now I'm not sure if it's five-layer dip or seven-layer dip, but whatever it is—it's a whole new level. There's cheese, sour cream, beans, guacamole, salsa…yum. It's a creamy, gooey mess. You just heat it up so the cheese is all melted and find one of those sturdy tortilla chips—not one of those pale white corn ones that crumble when you try and scoop up some salsa—but one of those thick ones that won't break and can act like a spoon, and you just scoop up the hot dip. It has a little bit of spice, but it all melds so wonderfully together. I tell you, *nirvana*. You have not lived until you tried that!"

Mr. Winslow turned to his wife. "We're trying that tomorrow!"

"For sure!" she agreed. "Wow, Antonia, you should be a food writer. I just ate an hour ago and I'm already hungry."

Antonia laughed. "I'm always hungry!"

They chatted a bit more about food and Antonia reminded them that they could not possibly leave town without trying Pasquale's homemade mozzarella at Red Horse Market, which was fortunately on their way out of town. "Like candy" is how Antonia described it.

Before Mrs. Winslow headed up to her room, she

stopped Antonia. "Oh, and I just want to say it's so nice to see Gordon's girlfriend is still here."

Antonia was momentarily confused. "His girlfriend?"

"Yes, I bumped into her yesterday."

Antonia realized she must mean Barbie. She was just happy that it hadn't been the day prior when Barbie was tussling with Naomi. "Oh, right…"

"I'm glad she's still around. I mean, it doesn't surprise me, because she once told me that her lifelong dream was to own an inn."

Antonia smiled brightly. She did not want to bad-mouth Barbie in front of a guest so she gritted her teeth. "Yes, well, we had tea yesterday."

Mrs. Winslow nodded. "Well, I was worried when I heard the inn was sold that she wouldn't be here, so I'm glad to see her. She was very helpful. Last time I was here, I lost a pair of earrings, I put them down some-where when I was talking on my phone and I couldn't for the life of me find them. I was so distraught, searched everywhere, and at last she found them in the parlor and brought them to me. I'm so grateful."

"How wonderful," said Antonia.

As she made her way into her office, Antonia's mind was filled with Barbie. Was she just a garden-variety kleptomaniac? She had probably stolen Mrs. Winslow's earrings herself and planned on selling them or wearing them but when Mrs. Winslow caused such a scene, she aborted her mission and tried to play the hero, Antonia conjectured. It was all so bizarre. But it was interesting that she had revealed it was her "lifelong dream" to own an inn. To what end would she have gone to fulfill such a dream?

Antonia was planning on sitting down at her computer and Googling everyone from Barbie and Gordon Haslett to Larry Lipper but she noticed with dismay that her inbox was overflowing and demanded immediate attention. She lifted up the pile, flipped through, and was disappointed to see it mostly consisted of bills. It sometimes felt as if her inbox self-generated bills. She'd pay a round of them and then more would magically appear, as if someone had sprinkled a fairy dust that just serviced creditors. Antonia was trying to figure out how the electric company could be demanding so much money from her when Lucy entered her office.

"Ah, finally. I need you to sign off on those so I can pay them," Lucy said, a twinge of reprimand in her voice.

Lucy remained in the threshold of the door, her arms folded. She was wearing a black-and-white mini-polka-dot dress with a cherry-red cardigan on top; she was one red, tied neck scarf away from doing the bunny hop. She wore very peculiar pointy black shoes that made Antonia think if she clicked them together Lucy may end up in Kansas or some far-off Midwestern state.

"Yes, I suppose I've been avoiding them," sighed Antonia. "Why does it seem like the bills keep coming?"

"I have to pay them if we want to keep things moving along here."

Antonia leaned back in her chair, the foam inside the

cushion flattening under her weight. "I know. Ugh, I just hate dealing with this part of it."

"Antonia, can I be frank with you?"

"Of course."

"The inn is losing money."

"What do you mean?"

"I think perhaps, you don't understand the extent of things. I don't mean to speak out of place but as your bookkeeper, and now manager, but I feel it is necessary to warn you that you are in a precarious financial situation. The inn has not yet been fully booked. Yes, we are steadily making progress, but we've never even had guests stay in the upstairs suite—and the restaurant is hemorrhaging money."

"I can't understand how that is happening. I know we're new, we've only been up and running for six weeks, but I thought that we had a bigger cushion than this."

"Your renovation costs were hefty. You had to carry all of your utility costs during that period, and pay the small group of employees that you chose to continue working here. The furniture and decor you chose were most definitely extravagant, as you are well aware. You insist on having the best of everything—soaps, towels, shampoos, food…"

"If I want to be a high-end boutique hotel, I have certain standards that I need to adhere to…"

"I don't disagree. But how will it help you to be that certain type of hotel if you are bankrupt?"

Antonia opened her mouth to protest but snapped

it shut. As her mother always said, "Don't kill the messenger." It was perhaps a conversation that she needed to have. She knew deep down that she had been coasting and trying to avoid the entire financial component of running an inn and restaurant. Ultimately, she had to face the facts. The income from the stocks that her father had left her when he died generated a nice income for her, but it wouldn't last forever if she kept selling them off to make payroll. She would have to figure something out.

"So what are you proposing?" she said finally.

"If we were prudent, we would shut down the restaurant," Lucy said firmly.

Antonia thought she would be sick to her stomach. A wave of nausea came over her. "You're kidding."

Lucy pressed her glasses up closer to her eyes. "I'm not."

Antonia sat in stunned silence. Lucy shifted her weight in the door.

"But…that's my favorite part…" Antonia said weakly.

"I think you need to make some hard decisions."

It would be a total heartbreak for Antonia to have to close her restaurant. During her darkest days, when she was suffering from the tyranny of her ex-husband, she used to imagine owning her own restaurant. It didn't need to be ambitious or fancy, she just wanted to serve homey comfort food, all of her favorite things that she loved. It was the good dream, the dream that kept her going. If she had to shut down the restaurant, it would mean more to Antonia than just a failure. It meant that Philip, her ex, would have won. The money she received from him would be gone; all lost in the failed inn, and all that she would have is the nagging sense of failure. Cooking was the one thing that made Antonia happy. Feeding people. She had always loved it. And now, to close it down?

"There has to be another option. We're just gaining traction with the restaurant."

Antonia gave Lucy an imploring look. She could tell there was one side of Lucy that was sincerely enjoying this masochistic exercise. Lucy was probably one of those people who enjoyed breaking bad news to people. She'd hide behind her numbers, or statistics, or whatever, but she would wear that secret smirk that she was wearing now. She should have been an emergency room doctor next to a race-car track.

"I knew you wouldn't want to take this step just yet so I have a temporary solution. We are heading into winter, and everything will start slowing down. I don't think you should keep the restaurant open seven days a week anymore. Starting next week, we should move to winter hours. Only Thursday through Saturday night. This will save on food costs. We can't offer tea service every day…"

"No!" the word leapt out of Antonia's mouth. Lucy gave her a stern look and continued.

"For now. Only offer it a few days a week. And I have composed a list of alternative vendors we can use for produce, sundries, and laundry. We have to reduce the fresh flowers around the inn, scale back on our waitstaff, and find more partnerships with local businesses who can bring more people into the inn."

She handed Antonia a spreadsheet. Antonia glanced at it with dismay.

"Really?"

"Antonia, I'm sorry but this all has to be done. Again, I don't mean to overstep, but you don't have experience running an inn. I've been in this business longer than you and I know what the costs are. We are struggling."

Antonia stared at the spreadsheet. It was like watching a horror movie; she saw how all of her money was drifting away. "Okay," she said finally.

She knew Lucy was right. It stank, but maybe if they did all this, they could generate some money and stay afloat.

"Is that all?" asked Antonia.

"For now."

14

ANTONIA WAS MOROSE AS SHE PREPPED FOR DINNER service and everyone in the kitchen could sense it. Marty and Kendra made an effort to keep their bickering in check, and Liz assisted Antonia in silence. It was Monday night, and Antonia had instigated a "Fun Monday" prix-fixe, three-course meal, where everyone in the kitchen (including busboys and waiters) could submit an idea for an appetizer, an entrée, and a dessert, and the zaniest would make the menu. That usually led to a rowdier atmosphere in the kitchen, but tonight was subdued.

"Liz, why don't you make the special dessert," said Antonia. She poured a measuring cup of maple syrup over a baked ham and started spreading it evenly with her brush.

"Me?" sputtered Liz.

"Sure. You came up with it."

"But…I'm just an intern."

"That's okay. I think you're up to the task. You probably have some idea how to make Cap'n Crunch cakes with bacon and candy corn ice cream or else you wouldn't have suggested it."

Liz smiled. "I did make it once at home."

"Go on, I'll help you if you need anything."

Liz gleefully went over to the pantry to gather provisions. Antonia couldn't help but crack a smile. Liz reminded her so much of herself it was crazy! There was something so liberating about purely cooking the food you love. Maybe Lucy was right and she should just cut her losses. But instead of the inn, just do the restaurant. Here she was in her happy place, and she was unable to enjoy it because she was worried about money. It seemed absurd!

For the rest of the afternoon, Antonia took on the more laborious and less-rewarding tasks like filleting the fish, butchering the meat, and peeling the shrimp. She knew she was being a little masochistic, but it felt good to get down and dirty and stab things. By the time dinner service commenced, Antonia's hands felt as if they would fall off. If she had to ladle one more scoop of gravy onto the roast chicken and mashed potatoes, she thought she would scream. So it was a relief when Glen came into the kitchen and told her she had a friend who was asking for her. Marty and Kendra were only too eager to have her leave the kitchen, so she realized that her bad mood was rubbing off on everyone. She had to make a note to try to contain her problems and not let them affect everyone around her. That was no way to run a business.

"Hey, girlfriend! So glad you came out. Please come sit with us for a bit!"

Even though she had seen her yesterday, Antonia felt a rush of joy at seeing Genevieve. No one could cheer her up like her old friend. She wasn't sure what made them click, but there was something about Genevieve that was so lighthearted and fun, and it amused Antonia to death. Gen had been there in her darkest days with Philip and was always a source of beaming light. Maybe it was because she was the polar opposite of Antonia, so irresponsible and scattered, that the friendship worked.

Tonight, Genevieve was, as usual, dressed to the nines. She had on a glittery gray sequined blouse underneath a black velvet dinner jacket. Her dark hair was slicked back into a tight ponytail and she wore dramatic eye makeup that quite honestly, looked a little crazy in Antonia's opinion. Antonia never went for that intense eyelinered look that was so popular in fashion magazines. It looked absurd on her. But some people could pull it off. Just like the approximately seven thousand gold bangles running up and down both of Genevieve's arms that reminded Antonia of Egyptian mummies. She worked them as well as she worked the large gold necklace so tightly coiled around her neck that looked to Antonia as if it could strangle her.

Genevieve was seated in the banquette next to a very young-looking blond man (teenager?) who was wildly underdressed in a blue V-neck T-shirt and jeans. His baby face was tanned but smooth, not a wrinkle to be found, and he seemed so young that at first Antonia wondered if Genevieve was babysitting, but when she saw her put her hand on his knee, she prayed that wasn't the case or else Genevieve was headed to the clink. It was all very Lifetime movie, in Antonia's opinion.

"Antonia, this is Ty. Please meet."

Antonia held out her hand to shake but Ty gave her the peace sign instead.

"What's up?" he asked. His teeth were white but a bit crooked and he had the slightest, tiniest, hint of blond mustache under his lip but nothing on his chin. His jawline was weak, which was a shame, because it was as if God himself had sculpted the top of his head but then got tired and quit in the middle, rendering him gorgeous at first blush but then kind of average and pinched when you studied him.

"Nothing, just work."

Antonia sat down across from them. Genevieve gave her one of her "I can't believe how lucky I am" looks and Antonia rolled her eyes.

"Dinner was awesome," said Genevieve. "We had the fun menu. I totally loved the potato chip fried chicken with peas n' cheese mash. That was so yummy."

"I'm glad you liked it. Kendra created that dish."

"Who's Kendra?" asked Genevieve, taking a sip of her Cosmopolitan.

"For the umpteenth time, she's my station chef!"

"Oh, right. Well, she's talented."

"I know."

"That cereal dessert was rocking," said Ty in his slow surfer drawl. He drained the contents of his beer mug. "I could have eaten that all night."

"Thanks," said Antonia. She folded her hands in front of her and tried not to be judgmental. This guy was too easy of a target. "So, Ty, what do you do?"

He swept a piece of blond hair off the side of his face and gave her an earnest look. "What's my job or what's my passion?"

"Both, I guess," said Antonia. She refused to look at Genevieve because she knew Genevieve would be sending her imploring glances.

"Yeah, well, I work in the pool industry in the summer, through the season really."

"Swimming or billiard?" interjected Antonia.

"Swimming," said Ty, nodding his head solemnly. "You know, opening at the beginning of the season, cleaning throughout, closing at the end."

"And how's that for you?"

"Mellow. I can rock it with my headphones on, so it's like, no prob. Pretty straightforward, I would say."

"Ever find anything interesting or unexpected in a pool?"

"Naw, usual crap. Leaves, toys, mice, bugs, nothing sexy."

"Got it. No floating bodies," joked Antonia.

"Naw, not yet," Ty answered with all seriousness.

Antonia smiled. "And in the off-season? What do you do then?"

She could see Genevieve fidgeting out of the corner of her eyes, squirming. Genevieve did not like to engage in any sort of intense exchanges with the men she dated. She preferred to take them all at face value. Ty didn't seem to care; he gave Antonia the smile of a Cheshire cat.

"That's when I live out my passion. I follow the waves."

Of course, thought Antonia. "Where do you follow them to?"

"Wherever they take me. Where the ride is the most badass. Hawaii, South America, wherever."

"That sounds nice."

Antonia wanted to proceed with her line of questioning but Genevieve interrupted. "Okay, enough third degree. Ty and I are here to have fun. Any update on the murder sitch? Shall I be planning your funeral?"

"Ha ha, very funny," said Antonia. She felt the stress creeping back into her body. "Nothing to report."

Genevieve squinted and studied Antonia's face.

"I'm glad. And I hope you dropped it. You have to stop looking for trouble. You're like a pig sniffing for truffles. Life is great, you're happy, but you feel the need to bring problems to yourself. Let it go," advised Genevieve.

"I'll try."

"Don't try. Succeed."

Genevieve definitely had her mantras that Antonia suspected came from feminine hygiene commercials and the like, but actually tended to be prudent. She *should* succeed in making herself happy. Why the heck was she snooping around trying to solve murders that may not really be murders?

"Dude, what murders?" asked Ty.

"Antonia thinks the previous innkeeper was offed."

"Seriously?"

"No, no, Genevieve is just teasing you," insisted Antonia. The last thing she wanted was to perpetuate the inn's reputation as a place of death.

"I never thought of East Hampton as dangerous as South Central, but, dude, this place is seriously sketchy these days."

"What are you talking about?" asked Genevieve incredulously. "There's basically no crime here."

Ty wiped a piece of hair out of his eyes. "Don't you remember that someone stole my phone off the beach when I was riding the *W*s?"

"Okay, but you were practically asking for it. You left it on a rock on the jetty. Someone probably thought it was lost."

"Yeah, well, if they'd have looked out in the ocean, they would have seen me."

"Whatever."

Ty bristled at being blown off. "Okay, and then like, the other night, my sister heard this bang in her backyard. Someone was climbing over her garbage cans."

"And?" asked Genevieve.

"She yelled out and said she had a gun. Saved her own life. The intruder ran away."

Genevieve and Antonia exchanged skeptical looks.

"Maybe it was an animal?" asked Antonia finally. "Where does she live?"

"Northwest Woods. And no, it wasn't an animal because she saw someone running away, and then get in a car and drive off."

"Did she call the police?" asked Genevieve.

"Naw. She's kind of the type who likes to take the law into her own hands. She's waiting for them to come back."

"What did she think they were after?"

"She collects vintage birdhouses. They're super valuable."

Antonia nodded. "Were any stolen?"

"Naw," said Tyler.

"She was lucky," said Antonia. Only Genevieve detected the amusement in her eyes.

"Totally."

Soon Ty grew bored of the inquisition and started to make sounds about going home, which made Genevieve nervous, so Antonia took her leave. She found Joseph finishing up his dinner and went over to join him.

"You weren't here yesterday. I was worried," said Antonia lightheartedly. She sat down across from him and motioned for the waiter to bring her a glass of wine. Time to relax.

Joseph dabbed his chin with his napkin and didn't meet her eye. "Yes, I couldn't make it yesterday."

"I'm just teasing you. Of course you don't have to come every night. I know there are other restaurants out there. I'm not jealous!"

Joseph reached down into a worn brown leather satchel and carefully pulled out a manila folder that he held in his knotted hands. He placed it on the table and slid it toward Antonia.

"What's this?" asked Antonia, flipping it open.

"After we heard about Biddy Robertson, I couldn't shake her from my mind. I was in the library yesterday and decided to do some research."

Antonia scanned the article from the *East Hampton Star* that Joseph had printed out for her. It was the police blotter from six years prior. Underneath an item about a

Friday report of youths smoking in the Waldbaum's parking lot there was the following mention:

The owner of 15 Treetop Lane, Elizabeth Robertson, accused her neighbor Naomi Haslett of placing a dead raccoon on her doormat. Haslett denied the allegations, and as there was no proof, no arrests were made. Police advised the two women to stay away from each other and call them if there were more problems.

"Wait, Naomi and Biddy are neighbors?" asked Antonia with astonishment.

"Were neighbors," Joseph corrected. "According to the Recorded Deeds section of a later issue of the *Star*, Naomi sold her condo four years ago."

"Wow. Was there anything else about this raccoon?"

He shook his head. "No more mentions of their conflict."

"Obviously they hated each other if Biddy would think that Naomi put a dead raccoon on her doormat."

"Agreed."

"That's also pretty disgusting. You'd definitely have to be a certain type of person to use road kill as an act of retaliation."

"Absolutely," said Joseph. He took a sip of his sherry.

"Oh, Joseph, what to do now?" lamented Antonia. "I spent the entire afternoon and evening thinking that I had to stop focusing on this ridiculous theory and return my attention back to my inn and restaurant that are clearly struggling! And just when I want to get out, you pull me back in!"

"I'm sorry, my dear, I did not mean to distract you. I thought it necessary to provide you with all the information I had at hand, but it doesn't mean you have to do anything about it. Remember, the police are already looking into Biddy Robertson's death as a possible homicide. So I am certain that they found this information and are interviewing Naomi Haslett."

"I guess, but for some reason I feel responsible. At least to look into the possible Gordon murder side of things. Clues and weird coincidences keep popping out at me."

Antonia filled him in on all of the recent revelations. There was her discovery of Gordon's note that referred to "firing that B," her meeting with Ronald Meter and the possible beehive in his backyard, the sighting of Barbie and her boyfriend, the box of stolen inn items that she reclaimed at the L.V.I.S., and her interview of Sharon. Did it all add up to something or was it a whole lot of nothing?

"There are definitely a lot of unanswered questions," conceded Joseph.

"That's for sure. But I think at this point, I realize I'm way out of my league. I'm of the mindset 'Don't quit your day job.'"

Antonia sighed deeply and drained her wineglass. Joseph paused and pensively played with the edge of his spoon.

"I also read up on bees yesterday. Fascinating creatures. I didn't know much about them other than what a nuisance they can be when you want to have a beach picnic in early September. But then, I'm not having many of those in my current invalid state."

"Oh, please."

"It's true, dear. But yes, bees are interesting. Did you know there are nearly twenty thousand species of bees? And that's just of the known variety. The actual number is probably higher. Bees are found on every continent in the world except Antarctica."

"That makes sense. Where there are plants, there are bees."

"True. It's actually amazing how much humans rely on them. It's estimated that one third of the human food supply depends on insect pollination, most of which is accomplished by bees, especially the domesticated European honey bee. What is frightening is that over the past four decades we have seen a rapid reduction in the number of bees, especially in the United States."

"Why?"

"It's an accumulation of many different factors. The winter generally knocks off about twenty-five percent of them to begin with. There was a DNA-based virus that scientists discovered in 2010 that when coupled with a particular fungus proved one hundred percent fatal to thousands of colonies. Pesticides have played a great role in their eradication, as well as mites and the reduction of commercial beekeepers. In addition, urbanization is a problem. As we expand, wildflowers decrease and thus eliminate the food bees need to survive."

"Leave it to the humans to mess things up. A pity on so many levels, but especially since I truly appreciate a community where the queen is the bigwig."

"Agreed, my dear. And bees are revered in most societies. In ancient Egypt, the bee symbolized the lands of Lower Egypt, and the Pharaoh was referred to as 'He of Sedge and Bee.'"

"But they are considered pests to a certain extent," added Antonia.

"Well, actually that's sort of a misnomer. It's yellow jackets and hornets that are the ones that mostly bother us. And they are misidentified as bees. In fact, virtually all bee species are nonaggressive if undisturbed and many cannot sting at all. Unless you are allergic to bees, in which case a sting is fatal, it is actually humans who are more dangerous to bees than the other way around."

Joseph paused to sip his drink. Antonia furrowed her brows.

"Would there be any way to know if Gordon was stung? And how would that have happened?"

"If we are proceeding with the theory that someone with knowledge of Gordon's allergy procured a bee to sting him, then I conjecture that it would have been a honeybee. Someone could purchase—or steal—one from many of the commercial hives in the area, or purchase one on the internet, as they are the most popular and easiest to obtain. Or breed them, like that man you mentioned?"

"Ronald Meter."

"Yes. The fact is, a honeybee rarely stings away from her hive, unless mishandled and treated roughly. If the murderer brought one to the garden, aggravated it, then somehow set it on Gordon, it would sting him. And a honeybee leaves a stinger inside the victim."

Antonia considered this. "Then if that's what happened to Gordon, the stinger may still be inside him?"

"I'm not sure what happens when the body begins to decompose."

"Hmm, there's only one way to know. What do you think, we try and exhume the body?"

"Oh dear, I hope it won't come to that."

"Me too," laughed Antonia. "Plus, no one would allow us to do that just on a gut feeling. Especially if one of our major suspects includes the next of kin. Too bad. But how are we going to find out who killed him?"

Joseph took off his glasses and wiped them with his handkerchief. "I think you need to focus on Detective Work 101."

"And what's that?" asked Antonia.

"Who has the most to gain from Gordon being killed?"

15

Tuesday

THE WINTER BIRDS HAD ARRIVED. THE OSPREYS AND the cormorants headed south, but the southern terns, the western kingbird, and the dickcissel had landed to set up residence. Despite the approaching winter months, and the promise of cold to come, the trees and dunes were still bursting with feathered life.

The morning air was brisk. Antonia had set out early for her walk in an effort to clear her head. The waves had thumped the shore violently overnight, and the tide had driven the water all the way up toward the edge of the dunes. The sand was wet and compact, and with every step Antonia took she cracked a piece of it underneath her.

The mansions that lined the coast were weather-beaten but defiant. Most of them had withstood numerous hurricanes, eroding dunes, infestation of the piping plovers, but they remained sturdy and grand, like true Yankee stock. She loved the dichotomy of an old shingled house with a gambrel roof and a wraparound porch that was perched next to a stark-white, modern Charles Gwathmey–style masterpiece with walls of windows and irregular angles. Each had its own personality. Celebrity maps weren't sold in East Hampton but Antonia wished they were because it would be nice to have an idea of whom they belonged to. She knew the CEO of Starbucks lived in one house, and a newspaper magnate lived in another. President Clinton rented one every summer, too, and there was one supposedly in trust for a sixteen-year-old orphan. There were countless billionaires who had their homes on the beach, but others belonged to old East Hampton families whose bank accounts had been depleted and were now house-poor. What they all had in common was this majestic view of the Atlantic Ocean and instant access to one of the most pristine beaches in the country.

"There you are!" boomed Nick Darrow as he trundled toward her. He wore jeans and a black zippered fleece and his hair was damp, as if he had just showered. He carried a white paper bag in one hand and his dogs were heavily in pursuit.

At first, Antonia thought there must be someone standing right behind her but when she remembered the beach was fairly empty, she turned a crimson red and realized he must be talking to her. "Hi," she said shyly.

"I thought you came every day?"

"Me?"

"Yes, you, who do you think I'm talking to, Antonia?" He glanced around dramatically to look for other people. Antonia felt a rush inside her. He remembered her name.

"Yes, I do. I was here yesterday."

"Oh, I had a thing yesterday. But I didn't see you the day before. I thought you said you were always here?"

"Right. I had something also. A thing…"

"Got it. I guess we both have these elusively named things that sometimes keep us away," he said. Then he winked at her. "So I brought us some doughnuts this morning. From Dreesen's."

He held out the bag and offered her one. Antonia was totally and completely touched. He had brought her something? He had thought of her? She was on his radar even? Wow. No matter that she had already wolfed down a pumpkin muffin—nothing was going to stop her from partaking in one of these amazing confections. She chose a cinnamon over a powdered sugar (for fear the powdered sugar would end up all over her face) and she bit into the warm, sugary sweet.

"Delicious, thank you."

"I love Dreesen's doughnuts. I used to buy them when I was a kid. Back when there was still an actual Dreesen's and they weren't sold by Scoop du Jour."

"The town has changed a lot from what I understand."

He shrugged as if it was an old argument. "Look, yes. Some things for worse, a lot worse. But I choose to focus on the positive transformation. East Hampton is now a town that offers everything, all year 'round—there's a great art scene, wonderful beaches, fantastic restaurants, as you well know…"

"You sound like you're running for mayor."

Nick laughed. "No, maybe someday, though." He shook his head. "But the comparisons to the past get old."

"It seems to me that it's the summer people that are the most nostalgic about the way it's changed."

He ran his hand through his thick hair. "True. Because it used to be this fantastic secret and there were wide-open potato fields and no big gates and hedges. And it was easy to do everything. You could park right on Main Street in town on a rainy summer day and go to the movies. Nowadays, good luck trying to find a parking space anywhere in August, even on a sunny day! Everyone has discovered this town and the population has exploded. There's more congestion, more noise, and more attitude. People pay a lot of money to come out here for a short period of time, so the expectations and demands are high. And they can be rude about it."

"I know. Then what are the benefits to this?" asked Antonia with a smile.

"There's more going on during the off-season. It doesn't feel like a ghost town when the summer ends."

"So you live here all year?"

"Yes, except when I'm on location. My son is in school here."

"You have a son?" asked Antonia with her mouth full. She was genuinely surprised.

"Yes, Finn. He's seven."

"I had no idea."

Nick gave her a sideways glance but didn't say anything. Antonia realized he was probably not used to meeting people who didn't know everything about him. But she had purposely avoided Googling him on the internet. She knew if she did, and was ever lucky enough to talk with him again, that she would slip up and mention something that she had read about him and would appear stalker-ish. It was starting to become a big fear of hers that she would come off as a stalker.

Nick's dogs came bounding up toward him. One held a slimy wet ball in his mouth. He dropped it with a thud on the sand in front of Nick. "Oh, you want to play?" asked Nick, before hurling the ball down the beach. The dogs ran after in hot pursuit.

Antonia finished her doughnut and rubbed her hands together in an attempt to rid them of the sugar. She was tempted to rinse them in the water, but then she'd have the salt stuck to her fingers and that was no better. Her hands felt sticky. She tried to discreetly wipe the sugar on the back of her thighs and hope the sugar speckles would not be illuminated on the legs of her dark pants. How did women eat doughnuts elegantly? She supposed that was an oxymoron. Elegant women most certainly did not eat doughnuts.

Antonia and Nick walked down the beach, and he continued his game of throwing the ball to his dogs while they retrieved it. She was dying to ask more about his son but felt as if the topic was too personal. And all of a sudden something dawned on her. If Nick had a son, the son must have a mother and did that mean that Nick Darrow was married? Antonia didn't like that idea at all.

"So are you shooting a movie now?" Antonia asked. She had to break the silence somehow.

"No, not until December. I'll be gone for several months so I made sure I'm around now for Finn."

"Oh." So he didn't say, for Finn and my wife, thought Antonia. That was a plus. Maybe a wife wasn't in the picture.

She tried to think of another question, but Nick announced he should probably head back so they turned around to walk back toward the parking lot and her opportunity for clarification was gone.

———————————

Antonia steered her car into the inn's small parking lot and squeezed it between Lucy's red Mini and the Winslows' blue Audi with white Maryland plates. She turned off her ignition. The radio, that had been warbling a new tune by an aging female country star who had crossed over to pop, went silent, and the hum of the engine clicked off. Antonia was instantly enveloped in silence. She made no motion to move, feeling very content sitting completely still on her warm leather seat staring at the leaves scattering around the backyard through her windshield. She had this strange calmness wash over her as she reflected on her talk with Nick Darrow. She was excited about it, but didn't want to be. But hell, it was hard not to be excited and flattered when a movie star remembers your name, brings you a doughnut, and asks why you missed walking with him the other day! That definitely doesn't happen every day. That happens in fantasies. She wondered again whether he had a wife. If he had a wife, then he was just a friendly guy. But if he didn't have a wife…

A flash of movement across the yard interrupted Antonia's musings. She squinted to see if she could make out anything. Her eyes scanned the cluster of oak and sassafras trees that stood in front of the back privet hedge that bordered the property. The only motion was branches swaying in the breeze. With a deep sigh, Antonia reluctantly pulled the handle of her car door. As she hoisted herself out of her seat, once again something caught her eye. She halted and stared once again, waiting. It had just been a flicker, but it was enough to give her pause. Her eyes danced back and forth until finally settling on the rhododendron bush. She waited, certain that there was something behind it. It could possibly be a deer, there were always tons of them, but they blended so much into the East Hampton landscape that she doubted a deer would even have garnered a second look from her.

Antonia briefly hesitated before crunching over the pebble driveway to the brilliant green of the still-young sod. It held the morning dew and she could feel the suede on her UGGs becoming damp. She wiggled her toes inside, letting the fur nestle between them. She loved her UGGs. There was a cigarette butt on the ground next to the white wrought iron bench and when Antonia bent down to pick it up, she saw a white streak run from behind the rhododendron bush to the safety of the azalea bush.

"Hello?" yelled Antonia.

There was no response. *If it was a guest, then what were they hiding?* she wondered. Antonia moved quickly to the bush.

"Hello?" she repeated.

Antonia pushed aside some branches and rounded the corner to the mulch clearing that stood between the trees and the back fence. She saw a figure in white running the other direction.

"Naomi?" Antonia bellowed.

The figure stopped and froze, then slowly turned around. It was Naomi Haslett. She was once again in her white jogging pants and sneakers, and this time she had a white windbreaker over which she wore a hot pink down vest. Her hair hung straight in limp clumps, giving the impression that she hadn't washed it lately, and her wrinkled face was contorted into a frown. She took a deep breath, as if Antonia's interruption was a huge inconvenience.

"Hi Antonia." Her voice was weary and neutral, as if they were acquaintances who saw one another often, but really had nothing to say to each other.

"Naomi, what in the world are you doing?" Antonia put her hands on her hips and tried to appear authoritarian.

Naomi met her gaze evenly and stood up straighter. "I was jogging."

"Jogging?"

Naomi raised her eyebrows defiantly. "Yes."

"Come on, Naomi, I find that hard to believe."

"It's true," interrupted Naomi.

"Then why in the world were you 'jogging' in my backyard?"

"I was jogging down Windmill Way. Then I saw a

cardinal and I decided to follow it. It happened to fly into your yard."

Antonia gave her a skeptical look, but to humor her, glanced around the bushes. The clearing was dark from the tangled branches hanging overhead, and clotted with leaves. There was no wildlife in evidence, least of all a cardinal.

"I don't see one."

"Flew away," said Naomi.

They stared at one another in silence. Antonia felt as if she was in *West Side Story*; it was a total standoff. If Naomi was embarrassed or remorseful for "jogging" in the backyard of the inn, she did a sensational job hiding it.

"Why are you really here?" asked Antonia.

"I told you. I saw a bird."

Antonia sighed. She decided to change tack. "You're always welcome here, Naomi. You don't have to sneak around the backyard."

Naomi appeared surprised. "Thank you."

"I'm sure this place means something to you."

"There will always be part of my heart buried here."

Antonia nodded. There was a pause and she couldn't resist taking the opportunity. "On another note, did you hear Biddy Robertson died?"

Naomi rolled her eyes back slightly. "Yes."

"I suppose you're not shedding any tears."

"She was a lunatic."

"How so?"

"You know, we were neighbors. Our condos were next door to each other. We were friendly. Not friends, but polite. I had no idea that she owned the Windmill Inn, nor did I suggest to my brother that he buy it in foreclosure. I agreed to lend him the money and become his partner, but as you can see I had very little involvement other than the initial financial backing. It was all his idea. Then one day, Biddy shows up banging and screaming at my door and accuses me of stealing the inn out from under her. I had no idea what she was talking about. I told her to get the hell off my property. She was a raging storm. And then the next thing I know the police arrived and she accused me of throwing some dead animal on her doormat!"

"Why did they think it was you?"

"Hell if I know! The woman was crazy. I didn't see it coming. She thought I was doing all this plotting against her. It was ludicrous. And she never got over it. I finally had to move away."

"What about now? Did the police question you? I heard they think she was murdered."

Naomi's lower eyelid quivered but the rest of her face remained emotionless. "I'm really not at liberty to say. And besides, I don't think it's any of your business."

"True," conceded Antonia. "But come on, Naomi. How does it look to me? After your little tiff with Barbie last week and all those accusations of murder, I'm a wee bit suspicious. Don't you think that's fair?"

"Don't think twice about Barbie. We've almost

finished all the legal issues surrounding Gordon's estate and she will be hightailing it out of town, penniless and with her tail between her legs. Trust me on this one."

"Okay," Antonia replied.

"Gordon had his flaws, but the primary one was his taste in women. He always went for the crazy girls. And they flocked to him like bees in honey. Pardon the expression." Naomi pulled the zipper on her vest all the way to the top so that it strangled her veiny neck. "I'm going to finish my jog now."

"All right," said Antonia.

With that, Naomi turned on her heels and took off. Antonia watched her odd, slow gait and thought to herself if that could be considered a jog, then when Antonia raised a spoon to her mouth it could be considered weight lifting.

Once Naomi was definitely out of sight, Antonia glimpsed around the clearing. What was Naomi really doing back here? She trudged through the damp mulch, stepping over dead wet leaves, clearing them with her foot. She kicked something with her toe, but when she bent down, she saw that it was only a large rock propped in the ground. She peered high and low, but there were no markers, no signs of recent digging or removal of anything. It was very odd.

16

ANTONIA ENTERED BY THE BACK DOOR THAT LED INTO the sunroom. It was empty, but there were signs that a guest or two had recently chosen it as a spot for breakfast. A discarded copy of the *New York Times* lay on the coffee table, with the business section folded on top. Alongside it was an emptied coffee mug and a plate with mixed-berry scone crumbs. Antonia picked them both up and walked them into the pantry area. She handed them to the dishwasher before working her way back toward the front hall.

It was only about eight thirty, but the inn was coming to life. The cleaners had arrived and were currently sweeping out the fireplace. Antonia spotted a few guests having breakfast and reading the paper in the parlor. Connie was talking on the phone, while Lucy stood next to her, leafing through the guest registry. Today, Lucy wore a bright-orange skirt made of a heavy wool and a cream silk blouse with one of those loopy bows that were popular with businesswomen in the eighties. She glanced up and began to say something to Antonia, but Antonia had already started with her Naomi story.

"You cannot believe who I just found in our backyard! Naomi Haslett. I have no idea what she was doing but it was very strange. She was hiding by the back bushes and she tried to run away from me when I saw her! Do you have any idea what's behind there?"

Lucy was surprised. "No, that's so odd. Antonia…"

"She always was a nut," said a male voice behind Antonia.

Antonia turned and was face-to-face (well, more like, face-to-belt-buckle) with Ronald Meter. Today, he wore a tweed blazer over baggy khakis (which he must shop at a Big & Tall store, Antonia thought) and brown loafers. His goatee was neatly trimmed but his face was a bit flushed as if he had just done some strenuous physical activity, or had gotten wind-whipped from sticking it out a car window like a dog.

"Mr. Meter, nice to see you again," said Antonia.

"Thank you," he drawled. "I was hoping for a quick chat if you have a minute."

"Certainly, let's go into my office," said Antonia.

She exchanged glances with Lucy, who gave her a look as if to say *I was about to tell you* before leading him away. Antonia noticed that Lucy gave Ronald a look of disdain as he passed. Clearly no love lost between those two, thought Antonia.

Ronald hunkered uncomfortably into the captain's chair that sat across from Antonia's desk. It was definitely not made for men of tall stature. Ronald looked like toothpaste squeezing out of a tube. He accepted her offer of tea but declined pastry. Antonia ignored his refusal for food, believing that no one could turn down her baked goods once confronted with them, and rang for a waitress in the kitchen to bring them a full breakfast service. "All the bells and whistles," she had instructed, hoping that the kitchen would understand what she meant.

"You really shouldn't go to any trouble," Ronald said.

"No problem at all."

He admired the way she had set up her office, even though Antonia knew he was being polite. The rolltop desk was about to snap in half with all of the paperwork piled on top of it. Her bookshelves were a messy display of someone who does not operate a tidy system of organization. It looked as if someone on acid had just shoved all the paperwork between every book and hoped it would go unnoticed. But now all the loose pieces of paper were spilling out. Ripped envelopes and mounds of junk mail lay in messy heaps that Antonia had abandoned. A sloppy collection of miscellaneous rubber bands was piled on the radiator for no apparent reason.

Oh well, yes, it was a disaster zone, Antonia thought, but at least she had her strong suits. The artwork was nice; Antonia had framed local watercolors of the beach in a beautiful blush gold–painted wood that she felt was both subtle and classy. And her desk chair was an antique that she had painted white and outfitted with a cushion upholstered in a pretty blue batik from Quadrille. On the far wall she had hung a beautiful calendar that featured famous still lifes from MOMA that would be exceptionally classy if it was turned to the correct month (it was currently opened to July.)

The waitress arrived with a tray and Antonia glanced at it and was pleased to find that they had indeed understood what *bells and whistles* meant. She pulled out a tray table that was leaning collapsed by the door and opened it next to Ronald. (No use even attempting to clear off her desk to make room for it.) The waitress placed the tray on top and offered to serve but Antonia declined. When she had left, Antonia moved over to sit in the other guest chair next to Ronald. She poured the steaming tea into the flowered china and glanced up at him.

"Milk or sugar?"

"Just milk, thank you."

Antonia gave him a generous portion before reaching for the other dish on the tray. "Would you like some honey?"

Ronald hesitated. His eyes met Antonia's. "No, thank you."

"There are some mini-muffins in the basket as well."

"I'm all set."

She handed him his cup and gave him a curious look. "I love a good pot of tea. Actually, I also love a good mug of coffee. I'm an equal opportunity caffeine drinker."

"Oh, me too."

"I will take it in virtually any form. I try to lay off the soda, but I've been known to imbibe. It's impossible to go to a movie and eat popcorn without soda. Ditto a slice of pizza. Although red wine will work with that. But soda is better. The only thing I really steer clear of is Red Bull. I've never even tried it; it just sounds disgusting to me. I suppose I have my standards. It's the same with wine. I love wine, but would never drink it out of a box. I think we all know deep down when we have to control our addictions."

Ronald had been holding his cup to his mouth, blowing softly as she spoke. He took a sip and firmly placed it back down in the saucer. It made a clanking noise.

"I apologize," he said.

"No worries."

Ronald twisted uncomfortably in his chair and Antonia made a mental note to entertain tall visitors in the sunroom or parlor.

"Antonia, I came here today because I wasn't truthful with you the other day."

Antonia arched her eyebrows and gave him a quizzical look. He glanced down, as if very uncomfortable with what he was about to confess, and sighed deeply.

"As you were leaving, you asked me if I had a beehive in the backyard."

He peered up at her and waited. She held her breath. Was this going to be a confession? She wished she had one of those buttons underneath her desk that she could press and record everything. She had never assumed she would need one, seeing as this wasn't the Oval Office, but of course you never knew. Now that she was involved in a possible murder case, she was way behind the eight ball. She wondered if one day she'd have to put a little room behind a mirror so that police could watch from the other side, undetected...

"Yes, I did," she prompted.

"Well, I'm sorry I wasn't truthful. The fact is, it *is* a beehive." His eyes gave her an imploring gaze.

"Oh? Well, I'm not sure why you would hide that?" she said, playing dumb.

"I know, it seems silly. They are legal, for Lord's sake. But you see, well, you didn't know me before…"

He trailed off. Antonia stepped in. "No, we just met."

"Right. Well, I used to be a large man. I mean, I am a large man now, but I used to weigh a lot more. I'm not sure if any of the gang here told you, but I lost one hundred and eighty pounds."

"No!"

"It's true. I'm the 'Biggest Loser' at my church. Although I hate that title. Problem was, I always had a sweet tooth, and I ate all the time. I gobbled up everything! I'm from the South, and we liked it fried, breaded, and sugarcoated. But then I found out I had diabetes, and I had to cut back. My doctor warned me, my pastor warned me. So I did. I cut out all sugar and the like. Began to exercise, which is a hoot!"

He paused, evidently conjuring up the image of him exercising in his brain. It didn't seem so absurd to Antonia, but then she didn't know him before. He continued. "Well, then. I do have a vice. I adore honey. Lord, how I adore it. I didn't set out to have a beehive, it just sort of happened. I kind of inherited it. And they make the most delicious honey in the world! I promise you, it is my one vice. I just can't quit it. And sitting here, staring at that sweet little dish of honey that you have on that tray is making me, well, all of my self-control is holding me back from drinking it. So there, that's my dirty little secret. And I am sorry I lied."

He stared at her with a guilty look, more apt for someone who had skinned her cat than someone who told a fib about owning a beehive. *Hey, whatever floats your boat*, thought Antonia.

"Ronald, I appreciate your honesty. Thank you for telling me the truth. But I just wonder why... You didn't lie about anything major. You don't have to answer to me, so why come tell me this?"

He nodded as if he had known she would ask him that. "I mentioned my pastor to you. I've gone through things in recent years, had some issues, and I have turned to my faith more and more. And this was burning on my conscience, so I talked to my pastor who advised me to speak to you. I just want honesty in my life. Clarity. Sobriety. I'm trying to be a good person, not to succumb to any vices or temptations."

"Wow, I think that's great. I should take a page out of your book. Everyone should."

"Oh, I hope I'm not preaching. Different things work for different people, that's what my mama always says."

"She sounds smart. I quote my mom also."

"Mother knows best to this day," laughed Ronald.

Antonia removed the dish of honey as well as the mini-muffin basket and asked Connie to dispose of them somewhere far away. Antonia and Ronald finished their tea without any temptations, and had a pleasant chat about a variety of topical issues. Her impression of him was that he was a nice man, but attempting to live his life in a way that might not be organic to who he was. It was almost as if he had been subjected to an intense amount of therapy recently, the type that started off being very beneficial but then became a little bizarre and self-indulgent. In addition, his pastor seemed to be very influential on him. At least it sounded like he was pushing him toward goodness. It did make Antonia wonder how dark it had been for Ronald before this pastor. Was this religious inclination new, say, post-murder? Had Ronald been an angry enough person to kill Gordon?

After tea, Antonia toured Ronald around the down-stairs of the inn. He was suitably impressed with the changes, and extremely flattering. Antonia was such a sucker for that, especially since she had poured so much time and effort (not to mention money) into every change and upgrade. He particularly appreciated how she had restored the original millwork, most of which had been stripped out. Antonia had scanned through all of the photos and archives of the inn to ascertain what it had originally looked like. She spent hours at the East Hampton Library searching for anything that would be helpful. Then she had worked with an architect to recre-ate the crown moldings on the ceilings, the wainscoting along the walls in the front hall and public rooms, and to reproduce mantels that resembled the originals. Ronald was the first person to articulate how much of an effort it had been.

They were in the sunroom when Liz came to find her. She wore an apron over her white chef's pants, and had her hair back in a ponytail, which made her look younger than her years.

"Sorry to bother you, Antonia, but the vegetable delivery is in and Marty wants me to confirm the mushroom order with you."

"Okay, sure." She turned to Ronald who spoke before her.

"Oh, don't worry about me. I'm on my way anyway. Just will pop out and say hello to Hector. I'm so glad you kept him on."

"Yes, he does a wonderful job."

"Well, thank you so much for the tea and company. You've done beautiful things with the inn."

"Thank you," said Antonia.

They shook hands.

17

Wednesday

IT RAINED ALL DAY WEDNESDAY. NOT JUST RAINED, but teemed. When Antonia's morning alarm sounded, she reached for it with excitement, ready to bound out of bed and prepare for her beach walk with (hopefully) Nick Darrow. But she was dismayed to see the wet drops furiously pounding against the glass panes, forming streams of water that rushed down to the ground. She rose and surveyed the yard from the window, but it was futile. Pools of water had already formed on the lawn and the walkways were slick. No one in his or her right mind would be walking the beach that morning.

With dismay, Antonia returned to her bed and curled up in her cozy comforter. As she stared at her ceiling, she thought to herself that this must be the first time in her entire life that she was disappointed to forgo exercise and remain in bed. Geez, what men can do to you! And of course, once again she had to remind herself that she was being silly. Nick Darrow was probably just a friendly guy who had no interest in her other than in a neighborly fashion. He probably was nice to everyone, perhaps to sell movie tickets. Maybe he took that "one ticket at a time" approach.

After breakfast service, there were enough tasks,

chores, and concerns to keep Antonia busy for the next few hours. These days she felt as if she always needed to be in three different places at once. She knew she had to put in some time for clerical duties, but there was so much to be done in the kitchen with deliveries arriving and prep work to be done. She wished she could hire an extra person to help either in the office or in the kitchen but after Lucy's stern dressing-down about costs, she realized it was not possible. She was also going to have to let the current staff know that starting the first of November, the restaurant would only be open four nights a week. Oh, she dreaded these management duties! If only she could just do the fun parts of owning an inn and a restaurant.

At eleven thirty, Antonia made herself a little lunch and escaped to her office with a tray. She bit into one of her all-time favorite sandwiches—Saint-André cheese on a crusty baguette with sliced cornichons, cherry tomatoes, and Dijon mustard. The cheese had to be soft enough to be gooey and spread evenly on the bread, and the cherry tomatoes had to be chopped so they didn't squirt everywhere when you bit into them. The sandwich also demanded lots of pepper and a hefty sprinkle of truffle salt. A slice of lemon in seltzer along with some vinegar potato chips accompanied it. Antonia was in heaven, practically moaning with satisfaction when her telephone rang. Reluctantly she answered.

"Bingham, it's Lipper."

The hunk of bread dropped down her throat like a ball

of lead. If there was anyone who could ruin the moment, it was Larry Lipper.

"Hi, Larry," said Antonia in her fakest cheery voice. "How are you?"

"Put November twelfth on your calendar," he barked on the other end of the phone.

"What's November twelfth?"

"There's a Ross School benefit at Wölffer Vineyards. Billy Joel is headlining. I know you love him, so you'll go with me."

"Wait, I do love him, but how did you know?"

"You're the type."

"Huh. Well, I'm not sure that date will work for me. It's a Saturday night and the restaurant is open..."

"My boss got a table. It's free. You'll be with me."

"Yes, see, it's not really a great time..."

"I thought you loved kids. Don't you want to support them?"

Antonia did not recall having any sort of conversation about children with Larry Lipper. "I do support kids, and I like kids, it's not that..."

"Blah, blah, blah. Look, enough with playing hard to get. You and I both know where this is going..."

"Excuse me?" bristled Antonia.

"We can play this dance, or we can cut to the chase. I like to cut to the chase..."

"Larry, what are you even implying? Contrary to what you may think, I am not trying to facilitate a romantic relationship with you."

"Who said anything about romance?"

Antonia was instantly embarrassed. "Oh, I thought..."

"I'm thinking *sexual* relationship," said Larry.

"I'm hanging up now."

"I wouldn't do that."

"Why?" asked Antonia. She took a large bite of her sandwich and waited for him to continue his clumsy courtship.

"Because I have more scoop about Biddy Robertson's death."

Antonia tried to speak but her mouth was so full of bread and cheese and pickles that it all came out in a muffled bumble.

"What the hell are you saying, Antonia? Did you swallow your sock?"

Antonia put up her finger as if instructing him to wait, but comprehended that it was useless, as he couldn't see her, so she chewed as quickly as possible and washed down her bite with some seltzer. She drank the seltzer so quickly that the bubbles burned the back of her throat and she proceeded to have a coughing fit.

"Jesus, Bingham. You really turn on all the charm when a man tries to ask you out. I'm loving all the sounds you're making," complained Larry.

"Tell me about Biddy," Antonia garbled as soon as she could speak again.

"Say you will go to the benefit with me."

"Biddy first."

"Benefit first."

It was a standoff. Antonia kicked herself because she

knew she would lose. Curiosity always trumped self-respect in her book.

"All right," she conceded in her most defeated and dejected tone. "I'll go. Now tell me about Biddy."

"And promise you'll wear something hot. Show off your tits."

"Larry!"

"Come on!"

"I promise to dress appropriately. Now tell me about Biddy. And it better be good or else I won't go."

"Fine. My buddy on the force told me that at first, when they went to her house it all seemed pretty status quo, just like a bad accident. She forgot to turn off the stove."

"Old news," interjected Antonia.

"Bingham, let me finish!"

"Sorry."

"Then my buddy noticed something in the kitchen. There was an outlet by the floor against the wall. Nothing was plugged in. Didn't appear as if anything had been there. But then the sun started pouring in and he realized—this guy is good—that there was a dust outline along the wall as if something *had* been plugged in there. Something the shape of a carbon monoxide detector."

"Interesting. But how could they know for sure?"

"This is where it gets good. Biddy had some photos attached to her fridge. Her grandson had taken them. They were shots of Christmas last year. The family cooking in the kitchen—all that irritating junk people do together around holidays before everyone drinks too much and the backstabbing begins."

"You paint a lovely image of the holidays."

"I'm a realist. So sure enough, in one of those photos, Biddy is standing next to the refrigerator, and you can clearly see the outlet and the carbon monoxide detector plugged in. Someone removed it."

Antonia was stunned silent, which didn't happen often. "Wow."

"Yeah. They got confirmation from the son that the old lady was really diligent about that crap. Had all sorts of alarms and everything ready."

"Do the police have any suspects yet?"

"Not that they're telling me about. But it will all come out soon."

"Larry, let me ask you this. Did you mention to your buddy anything about the inn or Gordon Haslett's death? Did they think there was a connection?"

"I sorta threw it out there but he laughed at me. And anyway, I agree, it's a waste of time. But if you're scared of going to bed at night for fear you'll be the next one whacked, I can tell you my bed is warm and I got satin sheets."

"Why do you always have to make these references?"

"You love them! Gotta go."

Antonia resumed munching on her sandwich and thought about what Larry had told her. Why would someone want to kill Biddy Robertson? From all accounts she was just an average, run-of-the-mill woman. The only motive that Antonia could think of was that she had once owned the inn. If the police didn't take the connection seriously then it was up to Antonia to figure out why someone would want every owner of the inn dead, or else she would be next! She picked up her phone and dialed Lucy's extension, but there was no answer and she remembered that Lucy said she was running to the bank to deposit some checks. It was time to compile a list of all the employees who had worked for both Gordon and Biddy. Maybe that was the connection? Antonia jotted down a few names that she could think of, but after getting nowhere she pulled out an old issue of *Cook's Illustrated* to read as she finished her lunch. Then there was a knock on the door.

Hector was standing on the threshold and next to him stood a petite woman that Antonia knew at once must be his wife, Soyla. She was approximately early thirties, thin, and neatly dressed in a jean skirt and a red-and-blue striped long-sleeved shirt with a V-neck. She wore small pearl earrings and a gold cross on a chain. Her black hair was pulled back neatly into a bun, and her eyes were big and prominent on her thin face. She appeared nervous, her hands fidgeting with the brown leather pocketbook that she wore over her shoulder.

After apologizing profusely for interrupting her, Hector asked if it was a good time for Antonia to talk to his wife, Soyla. Antonia did her best to be effusively positive but despite that, Hector and Soyla still exchanged worried glances when he left the office to allow Antonia to talk to her in private.

"Your husband does a wonderful job with the gardens here," said Antonia. She smiled brightly.

Soyla nodded. "Thank you."

Her voice was but a whisper. She sat upright on the edge of the chair that Antonia had offered her with her hands still clasped around her pocketbook as if someone might burst in and try and rip it from her arms.

"I understand you worked at the inn."

Soyla nodded.

"Did you know Biddy Robertson?"

Soyla looked confused. "No."

"How long did you work at the inn?"

"We worked here five years."

"Oh," said Antonia, who made a mental note to scratch Soyla and Hector off the list of crossovers who worked for both Biddy and Gordon. She returned her attention to Soyla.

"From what I have heard from various sources, you were a good worker. Now I know that Gordon Haslett was a tough boss. And I know there were some accusations. But I would like to hear from you what happened exactly."

Soyla began her story. Her English was much better than Hector's but she spoke so softly that Antonia had to crane her neck to hear her. She told how she worked at the inn for three years without problem, but then one day a guest had lost some earrings and accused Soyla of stealing them. Gordon ended up firing her. It was all information that Antonia had heard, but she wanted to watch Soyla carefully as she told it.

"I would never take anything, Mrs. Antonia. I promise you. I am not like that. I saw many things in the rooms
that I could have taken. But I would never. It is not me.
It is not my religion. I just can't believe Mr. Gordon
thought that I took it!"

Antonia could see tears welling in the corners of
Soyla's eyes. She handed her a tissue. Soyla wiped her
eyes fiercely, as if angry that they had betrayed her, and
shook her head. "Most of all I feel shame."

"I'm sorry about that. And I just want you to know, I
do believe you."

"Thank you."

"But do you have an idea of who you think *did* steal
the earrings?"

Soyla hesitated. She glanced at the door and then
quickly back to Antonia. "I don't know…"

Antonia sat up straight. "Please, Soyla. It's important
to me. I need to know."

Soyla looked down at her pocketbook as if it held
the answer. Antonia waited. *Let her do the talking. Don't
speak.* Antonia used all of her self-control to pipe down.
She knew the only way to prompt Soyla to talk was to be
patient. Not one of Antonia's strong suits, but she had to
try. Finally, Soyla broke the silence.

"Some people thought it was Barbie…but…"

"But?"

"One day we were looking for a pair of cuff links. A
guest said they were missing. They were blue with pink
whales on them. I was looking. The ladies I work with

were looking. Ronald, Mr. Gordon, everyone. And I found them…"

"Where?" asked Antonia, breathless.

Soyla spoke very softly. "They were in Ronald's office. In his drawer. I didn't go there to check, but Mr. Gordon needed the stamp for the inn and he asked me to go get it in Ronald's office. I opened his desk drawer and the cuff links were there."

Antonia sighed deeply. She had sort of hoped to rule Ronald out as a thief and now his name was back in the ring. Ugh, would she ever find out the truth?

"Did you ask him about them?"

Soyla shook her head. "I went to Mr. Gordon and I asked him to come with me. I said I wasn't sure which stamp he wanted. He was not happy but he came. When I opened the drawer, he saw the cuff links."

"What did he say?"

"He just looked at me, and said thank you. We both understood."

"And what happened after that?"

"I went home, so I don't know."

"Was that when Ronald was fired?"

"No, because I was fired first. Maybe he gave Ronald one more chance, I don't know."

Antonia twisted a piece of hair between her fingers. Something wasn't adding up. "It's possible that someone else put the cuff links in Ronald's drawer."

Soyla nodded. "Yes."

"Did you ever suspect Ronald of stealing from guests?"

"I don't think so," said Soyla, shaking her head. "He was always so busy. And also, it was mostly ladies' stuff that was stolen, except for the cuff links. Why would he want that?"

"True."

They sat in silence as Antonia considered everything. Did Barbie frame Ronald? This question seemed to keep popping up. The answer was, she didn't know. If only she had a time machine and could zap herself back to see what really happened.

Eventually, Antonia changed the conversation and returned to the topic of Soyla's employment.

"As you know, we currently have a cleaning staff."

"Yes, my cousins Rosita and Angela."

"I didn't realize that! Yes, they do a great job."

"Yes, they are very good."

"The thing is, the inn is struggling right now, to be honest. And I just had a discussion with Lucy, who is now our manager, about ways to cut cost. The sad fact is, I'm not really in the position to hire anyone right now."

"I understand."

Antonia felt horrible. She hated to disappoint everyone. And it made her sad to think that Soyla had gotten all dressed up only to experience rejection. It was awful. "Where are you working now?"

"I'm working at the South Fork Farm. Only part time."

"What do you do there?"

"I do everything. I help with the food stand, I help clean, I help with the beehives…"

"Excuse me?" asked Antonia.

Soyla gave her an alarmed look, clearly terrified by Antonia's new intensity. "I work with the bees…"

"They have a bee farm?"

"Yes," said Soyla, not understanding Antonia's wild interest. "They make honey."

Antonia's mind was racing. Here was another link to bees. Soyla worked at a bee farm, Hector was her husband, his boss was stung by a bee… Was there a connection? Did she have to consider Hector a suspect again? "Soyla do you know who Biddy Robertson is, or was?"

Soyla shook her head. "No."

"Are you sure?"

She nodded. "Sorry, is it important?"

Antonia shrugged. "No, not important. Don't worry."

"Okay."

Antonia took a deep breath. It was time to conclude the meeting. Soyla got the hint and stood up. "Thank you for taking the time to meet me."

"Thank you," said Antonia. "And if something changes, I will definitely call you."

"Yes."

As she was leaving, Antonia watched Soyla eye the issue of *Cook's Illustrated* on her desk. Something about it gave her pause.

"Do you cook?"

Soyla smiled, and for the first time she appeared relaxed. "Yes, I like to cook."

"Are you good?"

"I've never had training, but my family says I'm good. I cook for everyone. I love to cook."

"What do you cook?"

Soyla smiled shyly. "I make my native dishes, but I also make pies and cakes."

Antonia sat back down as Soyla continued. Finally, Soyla resumed sitting, and for the next twenty minutes they compared recipes and cooking notes. She told Antonia her trick of roasting mushrooms before frying them to dry them out so they were not so watery. Antonia asked her what she made out of tomatillos, as Antonia had never had much luck with them. As they continued talking, their mutual excitement grew. Until finally Antonia wrapped up the conversation with the following question:

"Soyla, how'd you like to help me out in the kitchen?"

Soyla beamed. And all Antonia could think was how Lucy was going to kill her.

18

AFTER SOYLA LEFT, PANIC SET IN. ANTONIA WANTED to kick herself. She had acted totally impulsively. One minute, she's regarding Soyla as a potential suspect or at the very least the wife of a potential suspect. Someone who has motive for murder and whom she learns over the course of the interview has access to beehives. Antonia is building the case in her mind, picturing Soyla handing off a purloined bee to Hector who in turn lures Gordon into the backyard and smashes it into his face (okay, the picture was a little fuzzy) and the next minute Antonia *hires* Soyla for a job the woman has zero experience doing, not to mention that Antonia is supposed to be cost cutting, not adding to the overhead she has to carry. Was she insane? Why not double the order for expensive linen napkins while she's at it? Why not narrow the margins on alcohol?

And yet, Antonia trusted her instincts about people. She had a good vibe about Soyla. She didn't truly think she was homicidal, or that her husband was. The motive was way too flimsy. People didn't kill just because they were fired, did they? And Hector probably appreciated his job; there would be no reason for him to put it in jeopardy, because if he killed Gordon, there was no job security. And the fact was, Antonia did need more hands in the kitchen. This would be a trial run; she had only hired Soyla for a probation period, so there was always an out. Antonia did not want to work herself up into a lather. She decided to focus on the positive.

Liz was slicing lemons in the rear of the kitchen when Antonia entered. Lemons were an expensive luxury. People didn't know how much lemons cost, and would toss aside the slices that adorned their diet cokes or their hot tea. That always killed Antonia, even more so now that she was counting every penny. Sometimes she just wanted to yell and say, "People, lemons are not free!" But that would be inane.

"How's everything today?" asked Antonia.

Liz gave her a brief rundown on what was happening. Marty was outside accepting deliveries, his little scale in hand, and no doubt haggling over every gram of fish and meat. The executive chef was usually the one who negotiated with vendors, but Antonia needed someone tough and no-nonsense to make sure that no one was ripping them off, and Marty was better at that than her. The margins are tight at any restaurant. Every ounce of meat counts, because that's where the money comes from. She had been told that it was important early on to be tough with the vendors so they wouldn't cheat her. And because she didn't exactly have a tough personality, she had nominated Marty for the job. He adored arguing, complaining, and grumbling, so he was very well fit for the task.

"You should have heard Marty yelling at the fishmonger," laughed Liz.

"Uh-oh, what'd he do now?"

"He was blasting him about the striped bass. Said he'd get better quality at Petco."

"Oh, dear."

"Yes, and he refused the bluefish. Said it was garbage."

"What is he talking about? I can make a nice smoked dip out of the bluefish and serve it with a little crudité, yum."

"You better tell Marty before he scares them back to Montauk."

"Geez, what have I done?"

"Actually, I wouldn't worry, Antonia. I think that they respect him for it," said Liz.

"See, that's why he is perfect for that job. I can be tough for a minute but then I buckle."

"Yeah, but they probably wouldn't try to cheat you. You're too nice."

"I don't know about that."

Antonia went and peeked out the window at Marty. He was talking to the fishmonger, but another man was standing next to him, a grin on his face.

"Who's that other guy?"

Liz peered over Antonia's shoulder. "That's the guy from the local microbrewery. The one that wants us to sell his Summer Honey Ale."

The guy was in his mid-thirties with scruffy facial hair and greasy dark hair. He had on an army jacket and blue jeans. He was not bad looking but it occurred to Antonia that he might need to be boiled in a hot bath to disinfect. She wondered if Genevieve had caught a glimpse of this guy yet.

"Is Marty giving him a hard time?"

"Not yet."

"He *is* persistent. Maybe we should give him a shot."

"You're a good person."

"I try to give everyone a chance."

Liz smiled. "I meant to mention it to you, Antonia, but friends of my parents are searching for someone to look after their house. It's not a full-time job, but they live in the city and just want someone to open it up when there are deliveries, and basically make sure no one is robbing it. I thought you might know someone who was looking for that sort of work," said Liz.

"Hmm, let me think about that. Where is their house?"

"Lily Pond Lane," said Liz, sheepishly.

Lily Pond Lane was the fanciest street in East Hampton, home to billionaires, rock and movie stars, and an entertainment lifestyle maven who did time in prison. The road, shaded by a promenade of Pollard Plane trees, ran between Georgica and Main Beaches, and half of the houses teetered on the dunes of the ocean. Sweeping lawns, manicured landscapes, and refined mansions were the norm. To Antonia, it was elegance at its greatest.

"Oh, I love Lily Pond Lane," said Antonia. "So gorgeous. Wow, it must be a beautiful house."

"It is," said Liz. "And they're really a nice family. The kids are teenagers, one in his twenties, and the parents— their names are Joan and Robert Masterson—aren't out here as much as they want so they need someone to make sure everything is okay. They used to have a caretaker, but he retired to Florida."

Antonia felt the bristle of an idea. "It's not a full-time thing, is it? I mean, could someone like me do it?"

Liz brightened. "I think so. They just want someone to make sure it's still standing. I don't see why not."

"Hmm…maybe I could talk to them?"

"Of course. I'll set it up."

"Great."

If Antonia was able to supplement her income by looking after houses, she could reduce her current salary from the inn and use the money to pay for Soyla. Then Lucy couldn't complain and everyone would be happy! The more she thought about it, the more excited Antonia became. The fact was, she walked Georgica Beach every morning anyway, so how hard could it be to pop in and check on a house after her walk? And it would be good motivation for her, in the dead of winter when she really had no desire to hit the beach, to force her to make the effort. Yes, this could be a jolly situation all around!

On her break, Antonia practically skipped to the front of the inn to find Lucy. She was perhaps a bit premature in assuming that the friends of Liz's parents would hire her to watch their house and pay her enough money to make even a dent, but she preferred to think positively. Wishful thinking, perhaps, but her mother had always told her to look at the bright side.

While Antonia's office was located behind the reception area, keeping her in the loop on arriving and departing guests, Lucy's was situated across the hall on the other side of the grand staircase. It had been her office since she was the bookkeeper, and although there was another office next to Antonia's that was designated for the manager, Lucy had preferred to remain where she was and Antonia acceded. She'd use the other office for printers and some storage, until she needed it. Lucy's door was usually kept tightly closed, as it was now, so Antonia was never quite sure if Lucy was in or not. Antonia knocked and was greeted by Lucy's invitation to enter.

If one of those shelter magazines decided to do a "before" and "after" shoot of what an office in an inn should look like, Antonia's would certainly be chosen for the before picture and Lucy's for the after. Where Antonia's was bursting with papers, mail, books, magazines, files, and jumbled coffee mugs, all smashed together in a cozy mess on top of her antique desk, Lucy's was absolutely pristine. First off, the entire room was white—including all furniture, shelves, and desk accessories. It reminded Antonia of a science lab in a highly classified biotech company. Not that she had ever been to one, but she had certainly seen them depicted on CBS crime shows. Secondly, there was not an errant paper to be found. One wall had drawers of filing cabinets (all white) that had swallowed every scrap of paper that Lucy had chosen to retain after processing her inbox. And speaking of the inbox, Antonia wasn't sure it could ever be referred to as that because she had never ever seen anything "in" it, as if Lucy had a pathological need to immediately remove the "in" to "out." Another thing that amazed Antonia was the fact that Lucy's desk had no drawers. True, Lucy had a wall of filing cabinets, but even if Antonia had three walls of filing cabinets, she would need desk drawers. Where else would she stuff rubber bands, hole punchers, paper clips, old birthday cards from her mother and father, mailing labels, Chapstick, dental floss, stamps, earrings that she took off when she was on the phone and forgot about, instructions on how to use her camera, fabric samples, extension cords, knobs that had fallen off her antique desk, old key chains with old keys, deposit slips, blank Christmas cards, Pottery Barn catalogs and Paul Simon and Carly Simon CDs that she wanted to download on to her iPod? A desk without drawers was…a table. (Unless, Antonia supposed, you were an architect. But even their workspace was called a drafting *table* not a drafting *desk*.)

However it obviously worked well for Lucy, who was Antonia's most efficient employee. Antonia was thankful for her because she allowed Antonia to run around and do the fun stuff. That's what teamwork was.

Antonia found Lucy seated in her modern swivel chair, staring at her desktop, where an Excel spreadsheet was pulled up on screen. She gave Antonia a terse smile but behind her kooky glasses Antonia could see a flicker of irritation in her eyes, as if she disapproved of being interrupted.

"Lucy, I just wanted to let you know that I am working on a plan that may allow me to reduce my salary."

When Lucy didn't respond, Antonia continued. "Well, it's not definite yet, but I may get another job, just a small job, and anyway, that could supplement my income and I could put more money back into the inn."

Lucy pressed her hands down on her pleated wool skirt. "How much would you reduce?"

"Well, I'm not sure yet..."

Antonia realized she had jumped the gun a bit, by already disclosing this news to Lucy. She hadn't even met Liz's friends yet. What was she thinking? What if it was only an hourly rate, like twenty dollars an hour? That really wouldn't help her very much. So she checked on the house twice a week, two hours, that's...forty dollars? And why did she suddenly feel like she was a lowly kindergartener being called into the principal's office. Wasn't *she* the boss? All of her inflated ideas about teamwork drifted away.

"Okay, just let me know when you will be sure," said Lucy. "Otherwise, I am currently examining more cost-cutting ways. Perhaps we switch to paper napkins in the restaurant."

"Paper napkins?" Antonia wanted to faint. "No, no, no. We can't do that."

"We have to examine all of our options. The money is flying out the door, Antonia. And not coming in."

Antonia felt nauseous. She decided she had to change the subject. "Lucy, on another note, can you tell me who worked here when Biddy Robertson owned the inn?"

Lucy squinted, again with disapproval. Antonia had

a feeling Lucy enjoyed needling her about cutbacks. Bookkeepers could be so humorless. "You want a list of every employee?"

"No, only those employees who worked here for both Biddy and Gordon."

Lucy jumped up with such vigor that Antonia was startled. She hadn't expected that response. Lucy went over to the file cabinets and bent down to the ground so that her entire skirt pooled around her on the floor as if she were a dancer in a Broadway musical. She pulled open a drawer and flicked through various files with mechanical precision. Finally, she pulled out a folder that had one of the longest labels Antonia had ever seen—all broken into subdivisions based on year, month, employee list, etc.—and handed it to Antonia.

"This should help you. It's the list of employees that remained with the inn the first year after Gordon purchased it from Biddy."

Antonia took it and opened it. "Wow, thanks. So thorough."

Lucy gave her a look as if to say, what did you expect? "I believe the only person who is still here is Samuel, the dishwasher."

"Ronald Meter worked for both of them," said Antonia, pointing to the list.

"Yes, he did."

Antonia scanned the rest of the spreadsheet. That was the only name that stood out to her. Samuel, the dishwasher, was for all intents and purposes deaf and made little effort to interact with the rest of the staff, so she could hardly imagine him having any reason to murder anyone.

"Antonia, may I ask, what you are looking for exactly?"

"I have no idea. I just think there has to be a connection. Someone who worked for both Biddy and Gordon killed them."

"Why?"

"I haven't gotten there yet," confessed Antonia.

Lucy gave her a puzzled look. "You are just conjecturing."

"You could say that."

Lucy glanced down but Antonia could still see the amusement in her eyes. She clearly thought Antonia was on an insane bender, wasting her time. *Well,* thought Antonia, *you may be right; but without the creative thinkers in this world, all that would be left would be the number crunchers like you. Take that!* Antonia wanted to snap, but restrained herself. She knew deep down she was being defensive.

"I do have some proof that something happened, but I can't disclose it right now," said Antonia.

Lucy nodded, but again Antonia could decipher skepticism. Antonia realized she was being childish. She didn't have anything to prove to Lucy. Who even cared if Lucy thought she was on a wild goose chase? It was *her* wild goose chase.

"I hope you can figure it out," said Lucy. She reached across her desk and made sure the two sheets of papers on her desk were perfectly aligned. Antonia glanced at one and saw that it was a mortgage form from Bridgehampton National Bank.

"That's not for us, is it?" asked Antonia.

Lucy glanced down at the paper as if seeing it for the first time. "No, they just constantly solicit the inn. Gordon was their best customer. He had it leveraged to the max."

"I guess I'm realizing just how much a money pit an inn is."

Lucy gave her a thin smile.

"Okay, well, time to start dinner service."

"All right now," said Lucy, making no sign that she regretted Antonia taking her leave. She took out a sheet of white paper from under her desk and placed it on top of the letter from the bank. Antonia wondered if her OCD made her hate to look at anything offensive.

————————

Later that evening, another unsettling occurrence transpired. Glen—who was already in one of his moods—came into the kitchen to complain that not only had they run out of bev napkins, but also his key to the storage closet wasn't working. Although he was always prone to histrionics, tonight he was especially dramatic and worked up, due to the fact that he had two last-minute cancellations. Rather than deal with his prima donna behavior, Antonia took off her apron and left the kitchen to retrieve the napkins herself. Glen "protested" a bit, but she had little interest in engaging in a longer dialogue so she ignored him and brushed by him and out the door.

The storage closet was located off the hallway under the staircase. It was actually quite a large walk-in closet that had been used as a waiting area for footmen back in the day. Antonia went into her office first to retrieve her keychain and then backtracked to return to the closet. Her key turned the lock with no problem. She left her key in the lock so that she could secure it easily when she was done and pulled the light cord to illuminate the room. Although early efforts had been made to keep the storage area organized and neat, in the haste to open the inn, items had been thrown inside with little regard to system. Stacks of paper towels, extra blankets, light bulbs, miscellaneous tools, towels, toilet paper, cleaning supplies, copy paper, printing cartridges, and DVDs were stacked up in a jumble. Antonia waded her way forward to the racks by the back, certain that was where she had last seen the napkins.

With a look of dismay at all the clutter, Antonia promised herself that she would make it a priority to neaten up the place. Perhaps she should put Lucy on it. Judging by her office, she knew how to deal with clutter. Antonia saw the napkins on the bottom shelf of a rack in the corner. They were obstructed by three twenty-packs of Bounty paper towels. Antonia heaved the paper towels to the side and then moved deeper into the closet to retrieve the bev napkins. She bent over and grabbed three large packets. Just as she did so, the overhead light went out. Quickly, Antonia popped up and hit her head on the corner of the shelf.

"Ouch," she said, rubbing her head.

The room was now completely black. Great. Antonia moved back toward the door, knocking down random boxes as she did so. She fumbled in the blackness. Her eyes finally adjusted and she could see strips of light from the side of the door. She instantly thought of Sharon Getz and became more sympathetic to her plight. It was unnerving not being able to see, to say the least.

When Antonia finally reached the door, she groped around for the handle, sliding her hands up and down. At last her fingers grasped it. She turned the knob and pressed. The door wouldn't open. Antonia twisted again. But the door would not budge.

Antonia felt a wave of panic. She was not good with small spaces. Nor was she good with small spaces that were pitch black. She instantly felt claustrophobic. Antonia tried the knob again and again, pressing against the door and pulling it toward her, but it would not budge. It was as if it was locked.

Antonia reached up and tried to find the cord for the light, but she couldn't see it in the darkness. She turned back toward the door and began banging on it, smacking it with one hand while trying it with the other.

"Hello? Hello? Anyone out there?"

Antonia was met with no response. She increased her yells, her voice becoming more shrill and desperate.

"Hello? Anyone!"

She banged and banged the door and began kicking it. Then she took a step back and lunged at it, hoping it would unstick. Nothing happened.

Antonia paused. She was sweating. She felt panicky. She had to calm down, as she was starting to hyperventilate. She thought she heard footsteps.

"Hello? Help! I'm locked in the closet!"

But there was no response. Antonia told herself to calm down. She would try again. Someone had to come along. Antonia banged on the door again. Then she took one more step back and did a small run toward the door. Just as she did so, the door opened, and Connie was standing on the threshold. Antonia almost knocked straight into her.

"Antonia! Are you okay?"

Antonia was jubilant to have been released. "The door locked! I thought I was stuck."

"Oh, that's awful," said Connie. "I just turned the key. It must have stuck."

Antonia looked at the knob. Her key was still in there. "I don't even remember closing the door."

"Maybe the wind blew it shut?"

"Maybe."

But Antonia was skeptical. How would the wind blow it shut? She turned around and pulled on the light cord. The light instantly went on. Why had it gone off before? Had someone pulled it off?

"Connie, did you see anyone around here?"

"Like who?"

"I don't know...anyone who would lock me in?"

Connie's face fell in astonishment. "No..."

"Sorry, probably nothing. I just got a little crazy in there."

"Yeah, it's scary to be locked in the dark."

"You're telling me."

Antonia was disturbed for the rest of the night. Was there a ghost at the inn? A mean ghost who folded up her ladder when she changed light bulbs and locked her in the storage closet? Or was it someone else? Could it be someone who liked to kill innkeepers? Antonia shuddered each time she thought about it.

19

Thursday

ALTHOUGH THE WEATHER HAD CLEARED WEDNESDAY afternoon and the sun had peeked out, the following morning the sky was a uniform bluish gray. There wasn't any rain, but it appeared as if a shower was imminent. The air was heavy but still, biding time before it opened up to dump its contents out on the streets, like a balloon about to be pricked with a needle. The birds seemed to have gotten the memo, because there were thick packs of them flying west, squawking en route. Squirrels were dashing into thickets of trees, heading for cover.

Antonia's slumber had been restless. She had nightmares about killers and ghosts and found herself waking up every other hour worried that she had heard something. She finally took her cell phone and pulled it under the covers with her so that she would have a shot at calling the police if someone appeared. As a result of her bad night's sleep, she overslept the next morning and by the time she arrived at the beach, Nick was loading his dogs into his SUV, his walk finished. They had a brief chat over the weather before he politely begged off for a meeting. Antonia's disappointment was so immense that she was tempted to turn around and get back into her car and forego the walk. Curling back up in her bed to catch up on her sleep was a nice temptation. But a glance down at her thighs propelled her onward. She was here; she might as well get some exercise. With her hands thrust into the pockets of her jacket and her jaw locked in defiance, she set out like a reluctant child being dragged by her mother to do something abhorrent. Antonia forced herself to march down to the jetty and then did an abrupt turn-around and marched back. That was sufficient for the day.

When Antonia walked from her car to the back entrance of the inn, she noted with dismay that there was a hole in the fence by the side yard. It couldn't have been done during yesterday's rainstorm and that meant only one thing: deer had breached the fence. She was irritated until she decided her revenge: she would put venison on the menu next week. Served with braised radicchio and red wine sauce, it would be delicious.

She walked out toward the backyard in search of Hector, in order to alert him about the fence in case he hadn't seen it. She hadn't yet had a chance to discuss Soyla's new employment with him, either, although by now he probably knew.

She found Hector standing in the back toward the fence, staring at something he held in his hand. He had dropped his rake next to him, and there were garbage bags full of leaves stacked in a neat row.

"Hey, Hector. Well, the bad news is the deer got in again, as I am sure you know. But I think the good news is that Soyla's going to be joining us here at the inn again!"

Hector glanced up, distracted, his face confused.

Finally he smiled. "Thank you, Mrs. Antonia. Soyla came out to tell me. She's very excited."

"I think it will work out."

As Antonia approached, she peered into his hands. "What have you got there?"

Hector furrowed his brow and glanced down. "I don't know. I was raking in the back and I found it buried under the pile of leaves."

Antonia peered closely. It was a small enamel box, white with a swirling blue font that spelled out mono-grammed initials: *ERV*. Antonia scrutinized it carefully.

"What's this?"

Hector motioned behind him. "I found it over there. I'm not sure how it get there, the fence is so tall. I don't think someone would throw it over."

"Have you seen it before?"

He shook his head. "No. I raked here before the storm and I didn't see it."

"May I?"

Antonia took the box into her hands and studied it. The *R* was bigger than the *E* and the *V*, which meant that it was the last name.

"Hmm…I wonder…" But then Antonia stopped herself. She didn't have to wonder. Things were beginning to click into place. "Was it lying on top of the ground or buried?"

"It had a lot of leaves on top of it, but not buried into the ground."

"Like someone put it there who wanted it to be found. Maybe not right away, but soon."

Hector looked confused. "But why? It's a nice box."

"It *is* a nice box."

And Antonia was ninety-nine percent sure that it was a nice box that had belonged to Biddy Robertson.

"Who would put it there?" Hector asked.

Antonia looked at him. She did not want to tell Hector that she now knew for sure what Naomi Haslett had been doing, lurking around in her backyard the other day. *Bird watching, my ass. Disposing of evidence was more like it,* thought Antonia. *Actually, planting evidence was more like it.*

"I don't know. But do you mind if I hang on to it?"

Antonia returned inside and went to the mudroom off the pantry where the staff changed into their chef's clothes. She put the box down on the bench and stared at it briefly. What was the significance of it? She had to think. Of course, she would have to turn it over to the police. And she'd have to tell them about Naomi. But did she have to do that immediately? No. As of now, there was no proof that it was anything other than a discarded item. She had no legal obligation to report something found on her property. There was no proof it was anything. Right?

Antonia tucked her UGGs underneath the bench where other assorted pairs of dirty shoes stood. She retrieved her Crocs as well as a clean apron from her cubby and sat down to put on the shoes. She stood and looped the apron around her neck before firmly tying the belt around her waist. Finally, she slid the box into the pocket of her apron and debated her next move.

No, she would not tell the police, she decided firmly. They were, in fact, the last people Antonia wanted to deal with at all. Not the East Hampton police (yet) but police in general. When her ex-husband, the cop, was making her life hell, his colleagues did nothing to help her. It had been scary how they all joined together and made her seem like a crazy woman. It was only when that final drastic series of events happened that a woman on the force finally took Antonia seriously. But by then it was too late. So what would propel her to enlist their help now?

It was odd to Antonia that she had been put in this position. She had always thought of herself as a reasonable, law-abiding person, who was not a hysteric by any means. But the contempt of the Petaluma cops had left a bad taste in her mouth, and now she was wary of any interaction with the police. She often found herself driving the exact speed limit so she there would be no reason to be pulled over. She would avoid jaywalking or any other sort of minor infraction that could put her onto their radar. She followed the letter of the law. And yet now, she found herself hunting down a possible killer, working in parallel to the police. She sighed to herself and supposed it made sense. She didn't trust them to do their work, so she'd have to do it *for* them.

———————

That night, dinner service was smooth except for two eventful occurrences: Barbie showed up and made a scene, and Joseph didn't show up at all. Although initially it appeared to Antonia that the Barbie situation was more distressing, it was only later that she revised her opinion. The night itself would have been a total disaster if the restaurant had not made more money than any other evening so far.

The kitchen was busy, frantic really, producing food as fast as possible. But unlike the previous night, where staff grumblings abounded, tonight they were excited. They were finally hitting their stride, the restaurant was gaining momentum and clientele, and they were really getting the hang of it. Even Marty kept his bitching to a minimum, perhaps distracted by how many entrees he had to put out, but his commentary was definitely more of a background noise than a disruptive rant. Kendra was excited about the mushrooms they had procured, and had concocted a variety of salads to showcase them, dishes that were met with enthusiasm by the customers who couldn't order them fast enough. And Liz was pleased with the added responsibility—tonight she was actually plating and cooking vegetables—more than a typical intern.

Glen was back and forth from the dining room, providing a running dialogue about who was there and sitting where, and describing in detail the many challenges a maître d' faces on busy nights. At nine thirty he swung through the kitchen door, flushed and agitated, and announced dramatically to Antonia that a very intoxicated Barbie had shown up with a girlfriend to sit at the bar.

"How drunk do you mean?" asked Antonia, who was placing a sprig of parsley on the striped bass lightly sauced with lemon caper butter.

"Three sheets to the wind," said Glen with obvious disapproval. "And loud as all get out. So is her friend, who laughs like a hyena. They came in and didn't even wait for me to seat them, but proceeded to the bar as if they owned the place and then sat at the stools. I had been saving the stools for the Felds, who had called earlier and very graciously asked me to reserve them. They were going to a play at Guild Hall first, and would be late. So when I asked Barbie to move, she refused, which her girlfriend found hilarious. Now what shall I do with the Felds? They're good people. I don't want to piss them off."

The Felds were lovely people, Antonia agreed. She had met them the previous summer at a wine tasting at Morrell's and they had hit it off. They promised to be her first customers when she opened the restaurant and they lived up to their word. They'd been very supportive to her ever since, sending business her way. She knew that was why Glen liked them, but in addition, she knew they tipped him heavily.

"Let me see what I can do about it," said Antonia. She wiped her hands on a dishrag and took off her apron.

"Look, I can get rid of them myself. I just don't want to cause a scene. I already have a taxi waiting outside."

"No, it's okay. I can do it."

The restaurant was full. Every table was busy, with

a small group waiting to be seated. Through the throng at the bar, Antonia spotted Barbie and her friend swilling glasses of chardonnay, and next to them sat an open bottle on ice. Barbie was clad in a form-fitting Lycra dress, pale blue with silver zigzags running horizontally in an even pattern, except by her cleavage where they went a little haywire and mushed together. Antonia's mother would have described Barbie's friend as "rough." She was a bottle blond with thin hair and dark roots. Her face was hollow with eyebrows plucked into obscurity and sallow skin despite her best efforts with a bronzer, blush, and eye shadow. She had squeezed herself into a sequined top and skintight jeans that only illuminated the fact that she should not be wearing formfitting clothes. Antonia knew the type; everything about her screamed drinker and trouble.

They were talking loudly when Antonia approached, and seemed either oblivious or indifferent (most likely the latter) to the fact that they were the noisiest guests in the dining room. Antonia saw Barbie acknowledge her presence out of the corner of her eye, but she continued to drain her wineglass.

"Hello, Barbie," said Antonia.

Barbie turned and gave her a drunken smile. "Antonia! My successor. Come, I want you to meet my friend Lena. We're having a little 'girls' night out.'" She made fake quotation marks with her fingers to emphasize her point before continuing. "Thought we'd hit the inn to check out the scene but hey, it's not a really rocking place anymore. I feel like I'm in God's waiting room. I mean, the average age is like, dead, you know?"

"This place used to be a blast!" Lena said accusingly. She then hiccupped loudly. This caused a series of hysterical giggles on both her and Barbie's part.

"Come join us!" said Barbie, motioning to the stool next to her, which was currently occupied by an elder gentleman in his fifties, sipping a glass of scotch. "You don't mind moving, do ya?"

The man looked perplexed but before he could respond, Antonia jumped in. "That's okay, no need. I'll stand over here."

"Suit yourself!" said Barbie. She then glared at the man and leaned in to Lena and said in a loud theatrical whisper, "That man is so rude! He should give up his seat to a lady."

The man made a motion to rise, but Antonia stopped him, apologized profusely, and asked the bartender to buy him a drink. She then went to the other side of Barbie and Lena and leaned in. "Ladies, I have to ask you to keep it down. I'm very glad you came here tonight to have a drink, but as you can see it's a quiet crowd, so I would appreciate it if you could respect that and just keep it down a bit."

"What?" asked Barbie.

Now that she was closer, Antonia could see that Barbie's eyes were filmy with that glazed look of someone who has had too much to drink.

"I'm just asking if you could keep it down a little."

Barbie threw her arm around Antonia. "Aw, come on now. Loosen up a bit, will you? This place is so stuffy now! No fun at all. When I was Lady of the Manor, this place was booming! We'd rock out all night!"

"Wasted Wednesdays were the best," concurred Lena.

Antonia extracted herself from Barbie's arm. "I'm sure it was, but we have a different approach now. We're focusing more on fine dining."

"Boo!" said Barbie. She banged her wineglass down on the bar with a thud. Antonia saw Barbie had left about half of her lipstick on the rim.

"Where are all the hotties? I mean, what's up with the cheesy maître d'? How are you going to get ladies to come hang out at the bar with a guy like that?"

Antonia turned around and saw that Glen had hovered close enough to hear, a fact that was confirmed by the color his face turned. He glared at Barbie and stomped away.

"Barbie, please use discretion. That was really rude."

"But true," interjected Lena.

Antonia sighed. This would not be easy. "Look, ladies, I appreciate your business, but I have to say that I'm not hoping the restaurant will eventually turn into a pick-up scene. That's not my goal."

"Clearly!" said Barbie. "All the hard work I put into making this place a smash success has now gone out the window. I've had so many of our old customers say that the place has changed, and not for the better, mind you."

This enraged Antonia. "Barbie, I think you're being awfully rude."

Barbie swiveled around in her chair and gave Antonia a fake smile.

"Rude is nothing compared to the way I've been treated. I devoted my life to this stupid inn—toiled away for the past five years, and then I get nothing, nothing in return! I have to move out. I don't get any money for all my hard work. Did you know that? Today, it was official. I get nada. That bitch Naomi gets it all."

"She's so ugly too," added Lena.

"Ugh, why did that fat bastard Gordon have to die? My life sucks now!"

"You seemed pretty happy with your boyfriend the other day," muttered Antonia.

"Excuse me?" said Barbie in a loud voice. Other patrons at the bar glanced up.

Antonia gave her a defiant look. "I saw you with your boyfriend at the I.G.A. The one I heard you were seeing before Gordon died. So you can shed those crocodile tears all you want, but I'm not buying it."

"How dare you?" said Barbie, she started to lunge for Antonia but instead lost her balance and fell off her barstool. She fell hard on her butt, her legs splayed open. Antonia took a step back while Lena reached down and tried to give Barbie a hand. She was also too drunk to help. Antonia motioned for the busboys to come and assist her. They hoisted Barbie up. Barbie dusted off herself and glanced around the room at the stupefied guests.

"I'm fine, I'm fine. These chairs are too damn rickety! You better watch out, Antonia, or you will have a lawsuit on your hands."

"Follow me, please," said Antonia.

"I'm not done with my bottle."

"Yes, you are."

Barbie appeared about to refuse, but then ran her eyes from Antonia to the two busboys next to her, who were ready to spring into action to defend their boss, if need be.

"Forget it, we're leaving," Barbie said to Lena. She grabbed her purse from the bar, pulled out a fifty and threw it next to her glass.

"I'm ready," said Lena. "Let's go somewhere fun."

"I'll escort you out," said Antonia. "We ordered you a taxi."

"No need," said Barbie.

"Yes, need," replied Antonia.

Most of the guests averted their eyes as the group filed out of the dining room in single file, although some customers made a point to give Barbie and Lena disapproving looks. The two ladies wobbled their way out, with a drunken gait, with Antonia and the busboys holding up the rear. Antonia followed them as far as the front door, which she opened firmly. Barbie took a step to leave before abruptly turning around and pointing at Antonia.

"You are not one to judge me, do you understand?"

"I'm not judging you," protested Antonia calmly, "I am merely asking you to not make a scene at my inn."

The look Barbie gave Antonia was nasty. "Oh, really? Then what was that 'boyfriend' comment all about? You don't know anything about my relationship with Gordon! How dare you say that I wasn't sorry he died? You don't know anything. Gordon was no angel either, but that was between us. So go mind your own business and keep your righteous nose out of mine!"

Antonia was shaken when she returned to the kitchen. She had decided to bypass the dining room to avoid extending the drama with questions and glances. She abhorred it when she felt like she had lost her temper, and she definitely had when she mentioned Barbie's boyfriend. There had been no need to sink to Barbie's level and engage with the drunken woman. She should have stuck on topic and just gotten her out of there. But it did piss her off hearing all of Barbie's little jabs about the inn. The place was low-rent and shabby when Antonia bought it. She had made it a spectacular inn and restaurant. Barbie should shut her trap, as far as she was concerned. Antonia could hear her mother's voice in her head: "Why do you let her bother you?" And it was true; she shouldn't care. From this day forward, she would attempt to have thicker skin.

A situation like this called for knife work. Antonia grabbed her sharpest knife and a bunch of scallions and started chopping them as furiously as she could. It was almost the end of dinner service and lord knew they didn't need chopped scallions, but Antonia needed to cut something and better to attack the onions than a person.

She could always bag them and save them for scallion pancakes in the morning. Or perhaps make a nice beef stew. She'd recently come across a recipe that she wanted to try that included dark beer, Dijon mustard, chunks of potatoes, carrots, and parsnips. It sounded delicious. She let her mind wander over flavor combinations.

The staff knew enough to leave Antonia alone until she calmed down. They were also busy with their dessert orders, and Marty finally had a chance to take a break. Antonia chopped and thought through what Barbie had said. So according to her, Gordon had at least one—or maybe many—lovers. That was interesting. And yet it made sense. Antonia had heard rumors, confirmed by Barbie tonight, that the restaurant at the inn used to be a big party scene. There had even been murmurs that there was a small population of "swingers" in East Hampton, so maybe Gordon and Barbie ran with that crowd?

"Antonia, here are the numbers for tonight," said Glen, interrupting her reverie.

Antonia put down her knife, removed her onion-cutting gloves (no tears for her), and took his paper. She glanced up, a smile on her face. "Wow, this is incredible."

"Yes, I know. We did well tonight," beamed Glen. "If not for the little tiff with that hussy, it would have been a perfect evening."

"I'll say," said Antonia. "And did it work out with the Felds?"

"Yeah, I gave them Joseph Fowler's table. He didn't show up tonight."

"Really?"

"Yes. Didn't call either."

"Hmm, that's odd."

"A lot of people went to Guild Hall tonight. Maybe he did too."

"Could be."

"But come on, Antonia, turn that frown upside down! Let's not focus on the negative, this was a fantastic night," said Glen.

"You're right," agreed Antonia. "Maybe time to open some champagne? I think we all deserve a glass."

20

AFTER SHUTTING DOWN THE RESTAURANT AND returning home, Antonia could tell at once that someone had been in her apartment. Nothing was out of place, nothing was stolen, and there was no rabbit boiling on the stove, but the air was thick with someone else's scent. It wasn't distinct enough that she could place it, but she could identify that the odor wasn't organic to her living quarters. And besides, the energy of her abode had shifted. Antonia would admit that that sounded weird and New Agey, but it was true. She believed you could definitely sense when other people had been in your space and this was one of those moments.

She'd returned to her apartment at about eleven thirty and, as was her norm, flung off her shoes into the coat closet (to be straightened up later) and walked over to the fridge to pull out a bottle of wine before retrieving a glass from the cabinet. (On weekdays she usually put on the kettle for a cup of herbal tea, but as it had been a tough week, she deserved a glass or two of cabernet sauvignon—always from California.) Antonia indulged herself with a steep pour, took a large gulp, and leaned back against the counter to savor the fruity flavor. It was a robust red that contained hints of blackberries, licorice, and cherries, and it was tasty. After a second swig she paused and that was when it hit her. Her home had been violated.

Antonia stood still, the only movement was her eyes gliding along all of her possessions, taking inventory. Her television, laptop, and iPod were all accounted for in their place, and that pretty much was the extent of valuables that she possessed, although once she caught her breath she'd check in the jewelry box on her dresser. She didn't own any expensive jewelry, but she had her mother's diamond engagement ring and a few gold bands that had also belonged to her mother; both were of extreme sentimental importance to Antonia and she'd be distraught to lose them. Fortunately, her jewelry box was something of a tangled mess with all her beaded necklaces and costume jewelry all mashed together, so it was possible that a thief could miss the important stuff, or else be totally repulsed and give up.

She continued her scrutiny of the apartment. The throw pillows on the sofa remained askew in the position she had left them in the previous evening—even the shape of her body was still firmly squashed into her favorite cushion (she was too nervous right now to be dismayed by how large the imprint was.) Stacks of magazines, the cluster of mail on the kitchenette counter, the dirty, tea-stained mug in the sink were all where she left them. There was nothing she could pinpoint at this moment, but she was absolutely certain that someone had been in her apartment.

Suddenly a thought occurred to her. What if the person was still there? She could feel her heart beating through her shirt. What if this was it, she was about to be killed, and the murderer was ready to add another inn-keeper to his or her scorecard? Should she call 911? She slid her body across the counter—never removing her-self from its protective embrace as if that would somehow help her (absurd thoughts for a moment of terror)—and took hold of the phone receiver. She was about to dial, but then she stopped herself. What if it was nothing? What was she going to say to 911? *Hello, I think someone might be in my apartment even though nothing is missing. It just smells different.* It would be wonderful for business to have three squad cars come screeching into the inn's driveway and wake all of the guests because Antonia had a feeling. No, she had to investigate it herself.

She slid a knife out of the block of wood that held a variety of implements of all shapes and sizes and congrat-ulated herself for maintaining their sharpness on a regu-lar basis. A set of good knives is always a great investment for all sorts of purposes, especially if they are in perfect working condition. The one she withdrew could fillet a cow in two minutes, so she was certain if she got the right angle on the intruder she could do major damage.

Summoning her courage, she took a deep breath and a step. She stopped. Perhaps she should give a warning first? Maybe a little shout out, like, "Hey, who's in here?" But that might give an intruder an unfair advantage. And what did she expect, that some voice would call out and say, "Hey, it's just me?" No, surprise was the only thing Antonia had working in her favor right now. She glanced around the room. Fortunately, she had been naive when she arrived home and had whipped open the coat closet, so now she knew for certain that no one was lurking there. She hadn't seen anyone at least, and it was a fairly narrow space, so unless Flat Stanley was alive and well, she could check that off her list. Antonia's eyes moved down to the bottom of the sofa and armchairs. Even though they were skirted she knew the space between the floor and uphol- stered furniture was only about three inches and could only harbor a homicidal mouse. It would be embarrass- ing as all get out if that was the creature who ended up doing her in. That left the bedroom and bathroom.

Antonia clutched the knife close to her side and began gliding across her carpet stealthily. She felt as if she were crossing a river in a jungle, unsure of what would meet her on the other end. Truthfully, right now she would prefer lions and tigers and bears to a killer. She took such baby steps that it was at least a minute for her to cross the entire living room to the threshold of her bedroom. The door was open, as she had left it, and she had a clear view of the mirror that hung over her dresser. In the reflection she saw her bed, the pillows scattered across the headboard, and the cashmere throw neatly folded at the foot. Fortunately, there was no killer lurking in it. Antonia slowly pushed the door so that it hit the wall, just to ensure no one was standing in the miniscule space behind it. She stopped and listened, expecting some- one to protest that they were being smashed, but heard nothing.

At this point she decided to raise her arm to a

forty-five-degree angle, so that the knife was held aloft and all she had to do was start hacking if someone were to jump out at her. She'd seen all those horror movies where young, innocent women stabbed criminals like that. Although it dawned on her that pretty much every one of those women was overpowered and ended up dead anyway. She could still try to beat the odds.

Antonia took a few more steps into her room. She quickly scanned her belongings. At first blush, it appeared that everything was as she left it. Yesterday's clothes lay on the slipper chair in the corner; the shades were still drawn (why bother opening and closing when she was out of the house all day anyway?), and more crispy dead leaves had fallen off of the plant on the window ledge. If she had expected to see drawers left flung open and exploding lingerie from a burglar's hunt through her belongings, she saw nothing of the type. In fact, there wasn't anything immediately obvious that identified the fact that someone had been there. And yet, she knew she was right. Her eyes grazed every surface until they landed on the pile of magazines on the side table next to her bed. They had definitely been disturbed. Antonia always worked on *New York* magazine's crossword puzzle before she drifted off to sleep, and she always put it back on the desk sideways before she clicked off the lamp. Now it was on an angle. It was so subtle that someone could argue with her that she was being insane, but she knew at once that it was not how she left it. You don't all of a sudden change habits thirty-five years into your life.

Antonia took a tentative step into the bedroom. She swallowed hard. She didn't like to think of herself as a scaredy-cat, but she also didn't like to think of herself as dead, the latest on the list of murdered innkeepers. She took one more step and then immediately dropped to the floor and yanked up the bed skirt. She held her knife up high, ready to stab, but fortunately, there was no one lurking underneath. Not wanting to waste time and stay in that compromising Twister position on the floor, she leaped up and ran over to her closet where she flung open the door. Summoning all her courage, she used her knife-less hand to push the clothes from one end of the closet to the other, the hangers scratching out in protest, until she ascertained with confidence that no one was in there. That left only the bathroom.

Once again, Antonia took a deep breath and eyed the bathroom. The door was ajar. Could someone be standing in the tub, hovering behind the shower curtain waiting to reenact a scene from the movie *Psycho*? Possible. Better to find out now rather than later. Antonia walked briskly to the bathroom and flung open the door so that it banged into the toilet. She peered inside, first looking left and right. Nothing. But the pink, floral shower curtain was drawn shut and there was still a possibility of someone there. Antonia said a silent "Hail, Mary" before marching over the chunky pink shag bathroom rug to the tub and ripping open the curtain. She curled her mouth, ready to scream. Her heart was thumping so badly it may has well have jumped out of her body onto the cold porcelain. But she was lucky. No one was there. Her wide array of bath salts and bubbles stood untouched.

Antonia didn't realize she was holding her breath until she exhaled for a solid thirty seconds. Phew. She was lucky she hadn't caught anyone. But now she had to find out who had been there and what they were after. Antonia opened every drawer and cabinet in the bathroom. Finding nothing awry, she retraced her steps into the bedroom. She spent some time going through the magazines next to her bed, searching for some clue. Had the intruder thought that Antonia put something in the magazines? Or had he or she been searching for something but decided to kick back and take a break reading a magazine on her bed before continuing on? Maybe the intruder had poisoned the magazine somehow? Perhaps by placing a giant tarantula in it? If this murderer worked with bees, there was no reason not to assume they worked with other killer insects. With her index finger and her thumb Antonia gently shook each magazine toward the floor. She was semi-expecting some lethal insect to fall out to the floor, but the only results were a floating ticker-tape parade of subscription renewal cards.

Antonia leafed through her jewelry box and was relieved to find all of her heirlooms intact, safely tangled with several Mardi Gras beads. She opened drawers, went back into her closet, and even shook out the insides of her shoes, but found nothing. Then she hit the living room. Although she had adrenaline pumping in her veins, it was now almost midnight and Antonia was getting tired. The day had been long and filled with plenty of drama. Exhausted, she took only a cursory look at her bookshelves, barely flicking open copies of her cooking magazines. She ran her hands through the cushions on all the chairs but found nothing.

Then she spotted it. The cardboard box that Barbie and Naomi had been fighting over! It was resting on the chair in the corner, pretending to look unassuming, but Antonia knew better. She walked over to it and peered inside. This was it! It had definitely been disturbed. Whereas Antonia had left all of the miscellaneous sheets of papers and notes scattered around in the mess she had found them, whoever had been in her house and organized them. It was subtle, very subtle. Everything wasn't exactly lined up evenly, but things were stacked now one on top of the other, and nothing was upside down or haphazardly arranged. The intruder had been interested in this box, for sure.

Antonia picked it up and walked over to the coffee table where she placed it next to the television remotes. She sat down on the sofa and peered in. The musty smell of old cardboard filled her nostrils. She began slowly sifting through the contents again. There was no doubt in her mind that Barbie or Naomi had been the one to break in to her apartment. They both had motive, and she even had proof that Barbie had been at the inn last night. In addition, Antonia had been too lazy to change the locks, so it was possible that both women had the key still, which is why there were no signs of a forced entry. So whoever was in the apartment had searched for something in the box and was disappointed not to find it. When they didn't find it, they thought perhaps Antonia had removed it, so they searched all the obvious places where she may have taken a seat to peruse it further. It all made sense. Now she just had to narrow it down.

Even though she had already dissected the contents of the box and read through everything with a fine-tooth comb, she began pulling things out. Her eyes once again scanned the catalogs and pamphlets, as well as the notebook, which she casually flipped through until the last page where Gordon had written to Lucy about firing Ronald Meter. Nothing jumped out at her as having been displaced. She removed everything from the box and placed it in a Leaning Tower of Pisa stack on her coffee table next to it. She glanced at it idly.

Then something dawned on her. She quickly unstacked the top layer, removing the jumble layer by layer until she was able to extricate the notebook safely. She felt like she was playing Jenga. She flipped open the notebook again to the last page. Nothing was there. She opened the book and shook it, but nothing fell out. She was positive she had put the other note that she had discovered in her office—the one that Gordon had scribbled that he thought "that B" is trying to kill him—next to the note to Lucy about firing Ronald, "that beast." But it wasn't there. Antonia went through the notebook again but didn't find it. Then she started once again, sifting through the contents one by one, opening every page, every catalog. It wasn't there. The intruder must have discovered it and taken it with them. But why?

Antonia leaned back on the sofa to think. Did it mean that Ronald Meter had been in her apartment? It was possible that he had a key; he had been the manager after all. Was he so worried about this note? It didn't really mean anything. Or was it Barbie? Barbie had been upset that her quest to get part of Gordon's estate was definitely over and she lost. Maybe she knew that it was the end of the road once she had snuck into Antonia's apartment to see the will really wasn't in the box? Man, Antonia realized, it could even have been Biddy if she weren't dead. She probably had a key. Ugh, everything was confusing. Antonia felt her eyelids become heavy with sleep. She didn't want to think anymore. She wanted to curl up in her bed and forget about this entire, wretched day. She'd definitely put the chain on her front door tonight, and make sure that she had a locksmith come in the morning.

She trudged to the door feeling violated and dirty. Someone had been leafing around her things. Granted, the box wasn't hers and that's what they were after, presumably, but it still felt awful to have someone come into her apartment uninvited. In fact, Antonia realized, the only person who had ever even been into her apartment was Genevieve. It was weird to think that she had never entertained there. Why would she? She had the inn. And who besides Genevieve would she invite inside? With a sigh, Antonia clicked the top lock and began to pull the chain across the loop when she suddenly stopped, and a wave of worry came over her. Something had just resurfaced in her mind, but she was so tired it had slipped away. Something else had been off about tonight, something other than being "robbed." What was it?

Then it dawned on Antonia: Joseph.

21

JOSEPH'S HOUSE WAS NOT EVEN HALF A MILE AWAY from the inn. In a city, it was walkable. But at midnight in the country, Antonia was going to drive. It was basically two lefts, no stop signs, and voilà. She hoped it was a futile trip, but there was a little nagging voice inside her that told her it wasn't.

When Glen had told Antonia that Joseph had failed to arrive for his dinner reservation, she had been so preoccupied with Barbie and her trashy friend wreaking havoc in the dining room that this news hadn't really registered. And the fact that the Felds took his table and solved the problem of the occupied barstools had seemed like a happy and fortuitous solution to the problem. But now that Antonia had time to dwell on it, she realized that it was highly unusual that Joseph hadn't shown up. First off, no matter what, she was certain Joseph would call to cancel if he couldn't make it. She knew that from the bottom of her bones. It wasn't like him to forget. He wasn't disorganized or absent-minded. He was aware that Antonia was busting her butt to fill those tables, so no way would he ignore his reserved table. Although Glen had thought that Joseph had possibly attended the Guild Hall performance and it ran too late or he forgot dinner, Antonia was positive that wasn't true. They had specifically discussed this performance and Joseph had said he had seen a recent revival of the play in Manhattan and was not going to attend the Guild Hall production. No, it didn't make sense. Antonia hoped she was wrong, but she had a bad feeling that something had happened to Joseph.

She had never been to his house but he had told her where it was, in the middle of Buell Lane, near Most Holy Trinity's parking lot. She prayed he had a name sign because there were a cluster of houses right there, but if not, she would just glide down the block on the hunt for his car, which was an old Volvo station wagon.

The night was very black, with a murky layer of filmy clouds that obscured virtually all the stars. The moon seemed to be half-assing it as well, burning on low wattage, just kind of hanging out in the sky waiting until his shift was over. The air was cold, and Antonia was cranking up the heat as much as possible, but it still took her old Saab several minutes to warm up. In fact, she usually arrived at her destination before the heat actually went on.

A few cars glided along Route 27, mostly going west, but there was no activity whatsoever when she turned on to Buell Lane. She tapped her fingers impatiently on the cracked leather that covered the steering wheel. It was so wrinkled, it felt like chapped lips. The leaves fluttered in the wind, but the houses were mostly shrouded in darkness, except for the outdoor lights that hung over a majority of the front doors. On her left, the whiteness of the Catholic church cut a decisively sharp impression into the inky blackness. Its floodlights made it gleam as brightly as a Broadway theater. Antonia turned her head to the right when she passed the empty parking lot that was across from the church. She slowed her car down considerably.

There were no lights on at the first house past the parking lot and no car in the driveway. Antonia drove slowly to the next driveway, carefully checking the entrances for name signs. She saw only numbers. She peered into the property of the second house and knew at once it was Joseph's, even without spying the Volvo parked deep in the driveway. It just reminded her of him. It was a nineteenth-century traditional Victorian: two stories, shingled, with white trim. The tall and narrow windows were flanked by long black shutters, and there was a wraparound porch with white wicker rocking chairs and tables. Dozens of neatly cut-back hydrangea bushes bordered the house, and through the darkness Antonia could see that the rest of the property featured ancient trees and andromeda bushes.

Antonia pulled in and put her car in park. Although the front rooms were dark, there was a light on in the back that allowed her to see the shadowy furniture through the window. Was Joseph awake? She glanced at her watch. It was late, past midnight. He did say he was a night owl, though. For a second, she wondered if she was being crazy, driving to his house to check on him. But something told her, in absolute terms, that she was not. She exited her car with determination. She crunched over the driveway pebbles and walked up the creaky porch steps to the front door. It was the sort that had a window on top so she peered inside, cupping her hands around her eyes for a better look. In the faint light she could make out a large grandfather clock and a fruitwood table that held a dish of keys and some mail. Antonia took a deep breath and debated whether she should knock or ring the doorbell. She chose the former.

She pounded gently, but then grew bolder and knocked harder. She waited, her breath curling in the cool air. She took a moment to glance behind her, but her view didn't go past the thick hedge that lined Joseph's front yard. There was no response. Emboldened, Antonia pressed the doorbell and was greeted by the sound of an old-fashioned *ding-dong* that was popular in sitcoms. She waited, her eyes glued to the window, expecting to see Joseph glide toward the door in his scooter.

The wind rustled through the trees. In the distance she heard the cars passing along Route 27, but other than that, it was dead quiet. Antonia debated her next move. Was Joseph asleep and she was a nuisance? She was about to leave but she pressed the doorbell again. She waited. But nothing. No movement. Discouraged, Antonia turned and stepped down the porch steps. She stared up at the house. The weather-beaten shingles collected into a wavy pattern at the very top by the roof, with a beautiful diamond paned window centered in the middle. She wondered if Joseph even managed to get upstairs these days. He probably didn't need such a large space.

Undeterred by the lack of response, Antonia decided to walk along the side of the house. She went right, moving along the driveway that ultimately dead-ended into a garage. The side windows of the house were high and obscured by thick green bushes that hadn't surrendered their leaves to fall. As she rounded the corner, she found the source of light, in a back room, presumably the kitchen. There was a metal ramp leading up to the back door, which Antonia walked up. She opened the screen door and peered into the window. She was correct; it was a kitchen, painted custard yellow with red trim along the cabinets. Her eyes scanned the old-fashioned GE refrigerator, past the stove and the sink. All of the appliances were a cherry red, as well as the dish towels that hung neatly on the oven door. Antonia felt a pang for Joseph. She imagined that his late wife, Margaret, had put so much effort into making the kitchen sweet and cute. It was so sad that she had died. Antonia moved her eyes to the left and then suddenly jerked them right. By the door to the kitchen, she could swear she saw Joseph's crutch on the edge of the linoleum floor.

Antonia tried the door. It was open. She walked in the kitchen.

"Joseph?"

"Here!" came his voice, weakly.

Antonia ran through the kitchen and found Joseph on the floor in a narrow hallway that ran off of it. He had obviously fallen. Dried blood was on his head, and his crutches were askew and out of his reach. He attempted to sit up with difficulty.

"Oh my gosh, Joseph, what happened? Are you okay?" Antonia rushed to help him.

Joseph smiled weakly, but instead of sitting up, lay back down. His glasses were smashed on the floor next to him. His bow tie was crooked, but other than that he still appeared unrumpled and dandy in his blazer and cords.

"I'm afraid I took a spill," replied Joseph. "I'm not sure what happened. I was using my crutches and I must have slipped. The floorboards are old and uneven. I often catch myself. I should have been more careful."

"Joseph, how long have you been here?" said Antonia. She took off her scarf and wrapped it up in a ball and gently lifted Joseph's head to put it on.

"I don't quite know," said Joseph. "I think I passed out. What time is it now?"

"After midnight."

"Oh dear, I've been here quite some time. I tried to shout a bit, but I knew that was futile. There's no one about."

"Oh, Joseph. That's horrible. Listen, I think you need to get checked out. I'm not sure you should sit up yourself. I'm going to call an ambulance."

"I don't want to make a scene. But maybe you are right."

Antonia smiled and glanced into Joseph's watery blue eyes. "It would break my heart if something happened to you, so we need to get you fixed up."

Joseph smiled. "Okay."

22

Friday

ANTONIA DID NOT RETURN HOME UNTIL FOUR THIRTY
in the morning. She accompanied Joseph to Southampton
Hospital and waited until his son William arrived from
New York. Fortunately, Joseph was fine and had only
suffered minor bruising on his back and a contusion on
his head that was fixed by two stitches, but the doctors
chose to keep him overnight for observation. Joseph had
tried to make Antonia leave, insisting he would be fine,
but Antonia would have none of that. She hadn't realized
until now how important he had become to her in the
short time she had known him.

Instead of going to bed, Antonia decided to head to
the kitchen at the inn and start preparation for breakfast service. She was tired to the core, and grateful that
baking had become so rote that she could practically
do it with her eyes closed. Today, she experienced none
of the usual joy that sustained her as she measured and
stirred. It was all about getting through it, her bed beckoning her. She waited until her morning team arrived at
six, and then headed to her apartment to collapse. She
was disappointed that there would be no walk on the
beach for her, because she had been collecting amusing
anecdotes to share with Nick Darrow as they walked

along the coast. Now she'd have to wait another day to see him. She allowed herself to wonder if he had brought her coffee this time. She could almost taste the Dreesen's doughnuts they had shared as she drifted off to sleep on her puffy down pillows.

The alarm interrupted her deep sleep at noon. Antonia was disoriented with the confusion that comes when you nap at odd hours. She couldn't even imagine what it would be like to have a night job. There was something so inherently wrong with sleeping during daylight hours. Her body moved slowly today, with reluctance and confusion. She took a long, hot shower, lathering herself with the new shea butter soap that she had picked up at White's Apothecary, and washing her hair with a lavender shampoo that usually perked her up. Today, it did nothing.

After dressing slowly, as if sleep deprivation were an injury, she padded into her kitchenette and made herself a giant pot of coffee. She fortunately had the wherewithal this morning to tuck two freshly baked scones into a paper napkin and bring them back to her apartment, and now she bit into the crumbly confections with gusto. This would only temporarily sate her. She felt as if she had a hangover, and that usually called for one thing: grease. She'd have to download some eggs and bacon into her system and maybe even get her hands on some sausage. Her stomach rumbled loudly at the prospect.

Antonia had a lot on her mind, but she was worried about Joseph first and foremost. When she talked to his son William, he mentioned that he and his brother had agreed that it was time to force their father's hand. Antonia wasn't sure what that meant and the question was on the tip of her tongue, but for once, she kept her mouth shut. She knew better than to meddle in people's family business. That never worked well. Although she hoped that Joseph's sons wouldn't bully him into an arrangement that he wouldn't like. Joseph may be physically weak but he was sharp as a tack and had a very independent disposition.

Of course, she was also concerned about the inn. She was working her butt off and it was getting to her. It had been the right move to hire Soyla. Perhaps if Antonia trained her well enough, she could assume more of the breakfast baking and at least give Antonia some time off to focus on other things. But the money issues were frightening, and made her feel out of control. She'd have to make cutbacks, and that made her stomach turn.

Antonia was also worried about the intruder. As she glanced around her apartment in the daylight, she wondered if there was anything else that had gone missing that she didn't notice. It still made her shudder to think that someone had sifted through her personal belongings. She felt violated. Who had been there? What did they want? Had they been searching for something, or hoping to find her there to kill her?

And last but not least, the murders were haunting Antonia. She had sniffed around, snooped here and there, and yet she had basically come up with nothing. Everyone was a suspect. Although the police did think Biddy had been murdered, that could be entirely unrelated to Gordon's death. So then she was looking at two separate murders. And she had no more answers now than she did three days ago. She was so weary from the tension that she almost believed she should just let the police handle it and forget everything. But that was easier said than done. Especially if she was possibly the next target.

Suddenly, Antonia glanced at her watch, remembering that she had agreed to accompany Liz to meet the Mastersons, the couple looking for a caretaker. She had only fifteen minutes to get ready. She banged down her coffee mug on the counter and rushed to dress. With dismay she realized that there just wasn't enough time in the day.

———————

"The houses around here are gorgeous," said Antonia to Liz, as she steered her old Saab down Ocean Avenue. They were in the estate section of town, referred to in recent years by brokers as "Georgica area" because of Georgica Beach, which was on one end of it. Antonia drove down this street every morning when she went to Main Beach, but she never got enough of this view. Now that the leaves were dropping, the thick bushes were becoming more penetrable, and she could actually see inside the properties and catch a glimpse of the previously hidden houses.

The houses that are "south of the highway" in the Hamptons are among the most coveted in the world. Old Montauk Highway cut through these villages, slicing the property values into two distinct camps: southern properties could run in the multimillions per acre for property value alone, and northern properties went from the hundreds of thousands to the lower millions, depending on size. Southampton had a much larger "south of the highway" area relative to East Hampton so although still very expensive, it was more accommodating to demand. And in addition, unlike East Hampton, the golf clubs in Southampton were north of the highway so they did not eat into the residential availability. East Hampton had a golf club as well as the large Hook Pond eating up much of its "south of the highway" acreage.

"I know, East Hampton is the prettiest town in the world," agreed Liz.

"I mean, look at this house," said Antonia. She pointed to a large, white, three-story Georgian Revival, with black shutters and columns. It was set in the middle of a meticulously landscaped yard, the grass that shade of neon green that it becomes in the fall—morphing from the emerald hue it wears in summer. "I always think of *The Great Gatsby* when I see that house. It is so impressive."

"Yeah," said Liz quietly.

"You don't agree?" asked Antonia.

"I do, but…"

"But?"

"That's actually my house. I mean, um, my parents," admitted Liz sheepishly.

Antonia turned and stared at her intern, her jaw dropping in surprise. "Really?"

"Yes," said Liz, embarrassed. "I mean, they bought it a long time ago, before East Hampton became all trendy. It was a total wreck. They had to fix it up a lot."

"Wow. It's amazing. Smart buy."

"Yes," said Liz.

Antonia could see Liz squirm out of the corner of her eye so she dropped the subject. When Liz came and asked for a job, Antonia had no idea that she was from a fancy background. She was so low-key and quiet and unassuming. Also, there was no pretension or attitude that gave her away. And now it turned out that Liz's country house was worth about twenty million dollars? It was crazy. Here she was with all that money, and yet the girl showed up for work early every day. Not to mention that she didn't parade around in expensive clothes. Antonia had never seen her wear anything with a logo, or carrying a trendy handbag. She was mostly clad in jeans or cords and wore turtlenecks or long-sleeved shirts. Her brown hair had a simple cut—hanging straight to her shoulders with bangs across the top. She wore no visible makeup— not that she needed it, she had that creamy, unblemished skin that young women are blessed with. She was pretty but in that wholesome all-American way. *It just goes to show you,* thought Antonia in amazement. *You never know who's working for you!*

Antonia made a right on Lily Pond Lane.

"This is my favorite street," said Liz, clearly relishing a change of topic.

"I agree. It's spectacular. I love that no two houses are alike. It's the juxtaposition that appeals to me. If it was just all those shingled mansions, it would be monotonous."

"I know. I'm not that into modern houses, but when there are only one or two of them, they definitely jazz up the landscape."

"My antiques would never fit in there, but they are certainly more low-maintenance."

"Agreed," said Liz, before pointing to the right. "It's this one here."

Antonia put on her blinker and turned into the gravel driveway. The Mastersons' house was beautiful. It was a sprawling shingled mansion that appeared to keep unfolding like a hundred-year-old piece of origami. The house was replete with blue shutters, a wraparound porch, a gambrel roof, brick chimneys, and a large solarium attached on the north side. It loomed in the center of what must be at least two sprawling acres, shaded by ancient trees. A gracious circular driveway cut a discreet motor path through the pristine grass, with every pebble restrained by a two-inch metal border. It didn't look unlike most of the traditional houses in East Hampton except that everything was on a giant scale, rendering it larger and grander than any Antonia had been in before.

"Lovely," said Antonia as they exited the car.

"I know," concurred Liz.

23

To her tremendous relief, Joan and Robert Masterson were also lovely. In retrospect, Antonia had to admit she had been nervous. This was her first job interview since she was a teen; she had always been her own boss. She wasn't quite sure how she would handle being questioned about her ability to do anything, and had even prepared defensive answers for the imaginary interrogation that she thought she might face. Fortunately, Joan and Robert abstained from the Spanish Inquisition. They were able to have a very nice chat and reach an agreement quite faster than Antonia had expected.

Antonia did not know many people who came from old money, but the ones that she had met all shared similar qualities. They tended to dance around questions rather than ask them outright, suggest things rather than insist upon them, and there was always a very subtle subtext that Antonia didn't realize until after the conversation had ended. Everything was shrouded in a politeness and an openness that was genuine, and yet she realized that despite the reserved tone, they were always able to get their point across.

The Mastersons had ushered Antonia and Liz into the cavernous living room that was big enough to accommodate three separate seating areas. The decor was tasteful but a bit tired—faded chintz chairs and sofas, skirted round tables covered in enamel-framed pictures of their children on the beach, antique consoles with drawers that were a bit warped from the damp, and large plants set in Chinese pots. The color scheme was pastels— periwinkle, rose, sunshine, and lime. The wallpaper was a bleached-out blue-and-white stripe. The walls were dotted with colorful Impressionist-style oil paintings that hung in thick brushed-gold frames. The beamed ceiling was low enough to make the room feel cozier than it would have with a double-height roof. Antonia felt comfortable at once, and could imagine retiring there after a huge Thanksgiving meal to drink cognac and dazedly watch the flames flicker in the fireplace.

They offered Antonia and Liz hot apple cider accompanied by ginger snaps, which Liz declined but Antonia accepted. After the perfunctory "getting to know you," which was basically where Antonia spoke her business resume out loud, the Mastersons explained their needs. Their caretaker of dozens of years had retired and they were seeking someone to check on the house twice a week, and be available to open it up to any servicemen or deliveries on an as-needed basis. It was fairly straightforward and Antonia knew she was up for the task. *Pretty much a monkey with a lobotomy could do it*, Antonia thought, but of course, didn't say out loud. There was no talk of money, for which Antonia was grateful. It would have been a little awkward to discuss it in front of Liz and besides, she had no idea what a caretaker would make. She'd been dreading that they might ask her to throw out a ballpark figure of what she thought she would deserve, in which case she would be struck dumb. Thankfully, the Mastersons said early on that all of the formalities were run through Robert's office, and it would be a woman named Cindy who she would deal with for all official transactions.

When the business was out of the way, Joan Masterson appeared to visibly relax. She was an attractive woman in her mid to late fifties with fluttery birdlike energy that caused her to constantly move. She'd pop up and down to pass the cookies, retrieve more cider, open the window, and, it seemed to Antonia, seize any excuse to be in motion. Joan wore her wavy brown hair in a stylish short cut, and was chicly dressed in a button-down, pale-blue shantung silk shirt with the collar starched up, and camel-colored cigarette pants that accentuated her thin frame. Her demeanor was perky, her eyes a dancing hazel, and Antonia had a clear image of her standing across the tennis court in ready position, smiling while awaiting a serve, only to hammer back a killer drive.

Robert was tall and lanky and looked every bit the WASP he was. His dark hair was thinning but he still wore it in a cut that would deny the growing presence of a bald spot. He had on tortoiseshell glasses over a face that still held echoes of youth. Antonia knew the type: he was one of those men that had always been handsome and turned heads but then one day suddenly looks old and it's as if not only can he not believe it, but his body can't either. He was a self-described athlete who played golf, tennis, and sailed, and Antonia could imagine him years before on the lacrosse and soccer fields at Yale. He chuckled often, sometimes irrelevantly, and there was an air about him as if he had no idea why he was meeting with Antonia, and was perhaps slightly bored by the proceedings, but overall, appeared to be a decent guy.

"Did Liz tell you that Joan and I celebrated the Millennium at the Windmill Inn?" asked Robert. He had completely interrupted his wife who was discussing the potential deliveries that Antonia might intercept.

Antonia turned toward Robert, who was sitting on the far right of the sofa across from her, his body touching the edge. "No, she didn't."

He nodded. "Yes, we went to…"

Before he could finish Joan interrupted. "It was such fun! They had a costume party! Now we were all a wreck that day, I mean, weren't you? Well, Liz, you were too young, but of course you must have been nervous, Antonia."

Without waiting for a response, she turned to Liz. "They were predicting that all the computers would go off when it hit the year 2000 and that would set off explosions and rockets. It was very doomsday, end of the world. I was in a panic, as were most people…"

"Not most people, just conspiracy theorists and you," said Robert, adding a chuckle at the end.

"Not true. CNN was predicting the worst."

"CNN!" guffawed Robert. "A great source of news," he added sarcastically.

Joan ignored him and continued. "I was very stressed. I thought, this is it! People were storing things in their basements, and ordering gas masks on the internet. Well, finally, we decided, if we were going to go out, we'd go out with a bang! The club was being renovated that winter so we said, what will we do? No one wanted to host. It's too difficult to get a staff to work on New Year's Eve, so we all decided to go to the Windmill Inn. They were having a champagne and caviar costume party and we thought, such fun!"

"That does sound like fun," agreed Antonia. "I would have liked to have seen that."

"You know what?" said Joan, popping up. "I have pictures of the night! Sandy Donaldson had gotten a new camera for Christmas, it was fancy for the time, not a telephone that is also a camera, just a one-off, and she was happy to take pictures. She gave me a whole packet of them, which I put in a book. It might be fun for you to see how it looked back then!"

"Joan, no need…" began Robert before fading off. Antonia supposed after so many years of knowledge, a spouse knows when another one is not going to listen.

Joan went over to the large cabinet that was flanked by the two windows that looked out to the backyard and opened it. On the top shelf, Antonia could see stacks and stacks of CDs and an ancient stereo system that would probably bring twenty dollars at a garage sale. The second shelf held rows of thick, leather-bound, maroon-colored photo albums, with the date monogrammed on the spine in a gold font. Joan ran her finger along the row until she found 1999 and pulled it out. She flipped through the pages as she walked toward Antonia, before settling on a section in the middle and handing it to her.

"Hmm. I guess you can't see much of the inn. It's mostly snaps of people, but you get the idea."

Antonia glanced at the pictures in front of her. A much younger looking Joan was elaborately dressed in a large jeweled ball gown complete with a corset. Next to her stood Robert who was wearing a Harvard football uniform. Just as Antonia suspected, he was ruggedly handsome.

"What were you dressed as, Joan?" asked Liz who had come around to stand behind Antonia and peer at the pictures.

"I'm Madame de Pompadour. I was going to be Marie Antoinette, but Sandy was Marie Antoinette. I know it was a mix-up, but I clearly remember that I told her way in advance I was going to be Marie Antoinette. Oh well, what can you do. Madame de Pompadour is just as dramatic, and actually I had a better costume. Not to be competitive, but she waited until the last minute and I ordered ahead. You'll see her on the next few pages when she finally had Hal take some snaps."

Antonia slowly turned through the pages as Joan pointed out her friends and explained all of their costumes to her, most of which were self-explanatory. Robert took the opportunity to go make a phone call. Antonia moved over to the sofa so that Liz and Joan could sit on either side of her to see the album without leaning in. Joan had been correct; little of the inn was visible. If Antonia didn't know it so well, and hadn't spent so much time studying every single window, she was sure she would not have been able to tell that it was her inn. But it was still fascinating for her to see pictures of it. Almost like one of those magazine "before and after" collages. Now that it was so ingrained in her and she was so invested in it, Antonia felt as if it were a new boyfriend where she wanted to greedily sop up all of the information about life before her.

"Oh look, there's Len and Sylvia Powers," said Antonia, pointing to a picture of her friends. They were dressed as Darth Vader and Princess Leia. They appeared much younger, and thinner, but their faces were flushed either by the heat or the free-flowing booze.

"Look at the cute little Yoda with them," said Liz, pointing to the corner of the picture.

"I didn't even notice him!" said Antonia. "That's their son, Matt. Wow, he looks so little there. He just celebrated his twenty-fifth birthday at the restaurant."

"Right, I remember there were a few children there," said Joan. "It was difficult for most people to find a babysitter that night. We were lucky, our nanny, Sita, came with us from the city. She watched the kids."

Antonia turned the page and scanned the pictures. "Wait," said Antonia. She pointed to a picture on the lower corner of the right page. "Is that Gordon Haslett?"

"Who?" asked Joan.

"The former owner of the inn?"

"Yes, yes, it is. I didn't remember his name, I'm sorry to say, but that's him. He was the host that evening. A very exuberant man. That was actually a good thing for the occasion, he made it more festive. Almost made me forget that the end of the world was at hand."

Antonia carefully studied the photograph, which was close cropped so that it only featured the subjects from the waist up. Gordon was dressed as a gladiator. His helmet was open so you could see his face, and he wore printed armor over a red tunic. In one hand he held a sword and shield, and the other arm was draped over a woman in a mascot bunny costume. At least Antonia assumed it was a woman, judging from size and frame. She was about a foot shorter than Gordon, who Antonia knew had been over six feet, and the bunny was slight like a woman. But her face was totally hidden by her mask. On the other side of Gordon was Joan's friend Sandy, with Joan next to her.

"Who's the bunny?" asked Antonia.

Joan stared at the picture. "Good lord, I can't remember. I must confess I had a lot of champagne that night. The next day was a total blur. But in my defense, I didn't think there would be a next day. But here, keep flipping through and maybe the bunny ultimately took her mask off."

"Oh my gosh," said Antonia when she turned the page. "There's Larry Lipper."

"Who?" asked Liz.

"He works at the *Star*. And of course he's dressed as a cop. The guy covers the crime beat, fancies himself as a law enforcement adjunct. But I bet the real reason is he wants to carry a gun."

"He's pretty short," said Liz. "Or are the two mermaids next to him giants?"

"No, he's tiny."

Antonia squinted. Larry looked like a pig in you-know-what. His head was approximately the same height as the girls' breasts and he wore a giant Cheshire cat grin on his face. *Probably the closest he ever got to a woman,* thought Antonia.

On another page, there was a group shot with Naomi peeking out of the background. It was impossible to see her costume because someone dressed as a pirate was standing in front of her, but her distinctive black bob set her out against the crowd. She appeared younger, but still just as severe.

Antonia turned the page and found more pictures of Gordon. It appeared he enjoyed mugging for the camera and wasn't shy. There were pictures of him with other guests, more of him with Joan and Sandy, as well as pictures of him with a glass of champagne and a microphone, no doubt ushering in the New Year, Antonia assumed. Antonia continued casually flipping through the pages as Joan gave a running commentary about every detail she remembered about the night. She was half listening and half staring at the photos, leaving Liz to make interjections on her behalf. As Antonia flipped further along, she realized something: the bunny was in every picture that Gordon was in.

"Sorry, do you mind if I go back a page or two? I went too quickly." Antonia asked.

"Of course," said Joan.

Antonia turned back the pages and once again studied the pictures of Gordon. Sure enough, even in the pictures where Gordon was in the forefront, the bunny was off on the side or in the corner, her body turned toward his. It was as if she didn't want to lose sight of him. *There was something creepy about the bunny stalking the gladiator,* thought Antonia with a shudder. *Was it Barbie?* she wondered. She didn't think so. First off, Barbie said that she had been with Gordon for five years, and this was over a decade ago. In addition, Barbie was tall and busty. That would come through even in a bunny suit. And Antonia was certain that Barbie would never wear what was basically a mascot outfit for a costume party. Barbie was the type who would shop in the "sexy" costume department. She'd show up as a "sexy witch" or "sexy vampire" or "sexy kitty," and so on. That was a woman who loved her body and her looks; no way would she conceal herself.

Was there a reason that the bunny was hiding in her costume? Antonia wondered. Because when Antonia reached the end of the album, there were still no pictures of the bunny without the top of her costume.

"Was it hot at the party?" asked Antonia.

"Hot?" repeated Joan.

"Yes. There were so many people in there, and

Gordon looks a bit sweaty in some of the later pictures. I was wondering if you could recall if it was hot in there."

Joan folded her hands on her lap. She shrugged. "I'm not really sure. I suppose it was. I just don't remember. Sorry. The old brain is not what it used to be. My memory is mush."

"That's okay, not important," said Antonia.

Liz eyed her carefully. "There's that picture of the two girls dressed as mermaids in the front. They're only wearing bikinis so probably it was fairly warm."

"Good point," said Antonia.

Antonia wanted to ask Joan if she could borrow one of the pictures but she decided against it. First off, she'd have to explain why and what would she say? That she was hoping to track down a possible murderer and the bunny might have a clue? Also, judging from the stacks of neatly arranged photo albums in the cabinet, it was evident that Joan took particular pride in her scrapbooking efforts and Antonia didn't want to appall her by suggesting she take one apart. No, better not ask. Antonia and Liz remained at Joan's for another ten minutes before taking their leave. Joan gave Antonia a warm handshake and said they'd be in touch with specifics shortly and Robert reemerged to bid them goodbye. Antonia felt good about the Mastersons. They were nice people. If the money were worthwhile (and it probably would be; her standards were low), then she would definitely work for them. And Liz seemed to like them, so that was a good recommendation. Antonia trusted her.

"Were you wondering why the bunny didn't take off

her bunny head?" asked Liz, after they had finished all of their chitchat regarding the Mastersons.

Antonia turned to her in astonishment. "How did you know?"

Liz shrugged. "Just a guess. I thought it was weird too."

"Yes," said Antonia. "It was weird."

24

ANTONIA MADE A BEELINE TO HER OFFICE TO MAKE some phone calls. She could have done them from the privacy of her apartment as well, but she wanted to avoid it after yesterday's intruder. It was silly and she'd have to figure out a way to get over it, but right now, she still felt violated. And she had to figure out what to do about it. Maybe a call to the locksmith should have been her first plan of attack. She added that to her list of things to do.

She checked in with Joseph to see how he was doing. His son William answered his cell and said Joseph was sleeping and resting comfortably. The doctors had not found anything to cause alarm, and the MRI had come back clear, so he would be home tomorrow at the latest. Antonia breathed a sigh of relief at Joseph's clean bill of health. It had been nagging at her all day and she was thrilled that he was okay. The phone call was an overall success, until the conclusion when William announced his news.

"I think the only good news to come out of this is that dad agrees with me he can't stay at the house anymore alone. It's just too much," said William. He had a deep baritone voice. Antonia knew he was a lawyer and could imagine that it worked well on his clients.

"I could get you the name of some home care workers to help him. In fact, Rosalie, our cleaner has a sister…"

Before she could finish William interrupted her.

"That's very nice of you, but I think we've convinced Dad to move into the city."

"What?"

"My brother and I are both there and actually the timing is perfect because there's a studio apartment that's come up for rent in our building. It's great. My wife went to look at it. It's on the fortieth floor and looks out at the river. We have all the amenities in our building, pool, gym, and concierge service. It's brand new, so everything is in fantastic shape."

Antonia swallowed hard. It was wrong on so many levels. Take away the part that she would be devastated if Joseph moved in the first place, the concept of Joseph in a brand-new high-rise building in New York City was repugnant to her. She couldn't imagine him in his bow tie and glasses zipping along the carpeted halls of a Trump Tower. All those soulless, cookie-cutter apartments that were interchangeable and lacked character were so not Joseph.

"Oh? What does your dad think about this?" Antonia finally asked when she could speak again.

She could sense William's hesitation on the other end of the phone. "Well, it's still new to him. But he understands the situation has to change. It's just not safe for him to be alone anymore."

"Right," said Antonia.

"This wasn't the first time he fell, you know."

"It wasn't?"

"No, just a few nights ago he was on his way out to

dinner and took a spill. Fortunately, he was near the phone and we were able to send a friend over to help him."

Antonia remembered she had asked Joseph where he had been a few nights prior and he said he couldn't make it. He didn't have a reservation that time so she wasn't worried, but he had become such a regular fixture that his absence was noticeable. She should have known then that he was in trouble.

"Is there anything I can do?" asked Antonia.

"You've been great so far. My family and I really appreciate your help."

"Please, anytime. I stand ready, willing, and able. I adore your father."

She hung up feeling anxious. There was something about Joseph moving to New York that upset the universe. *Why do we have to get old?* Antonia wondered. But then again, the alternative was worse.

Since Antonia knew the next phone call would no doubt elicit the same sensation, she quickly dialed to get it over with. She waited as the phone rang, before it immediately went to Larry Lipper's voicemail.

"Hi Larry, it's Antonia Bingham. I'd love to talk with you when you have a chance. You can call me back at the inn, or if you are in the neighborhood, pop by..."

She let her voice trail off. Larry was so hard to take, but she wanted to find out more about that New Year's Eve party. Since it seemed impossible for Larry to exist without hitting on women, he must have tried his luck

with the bunny. Maybe he would be able to give Antonia
an idea of who she was.

Antonia returned a few more calls, and also arranged
for the locksmith to come by that afternoon and change
the locks to her apartment. She was about to return to
the kitchen when Lucy knocked on her door. She held
some papers pressed against her chest.

"Hi," said Antonia. "I thought you were off today."

Lucy smiled wanly. "I decided to come in and slog
through some paperwork. Also, my office was a mess, so
I had to tidy it up."

Antonia glanced around at her mess and swallowed.
Lucy must be repelled by it. "Well, feel free to tidy up
mine if you want…just kidding."

Lucy actually laughed, if you could call it that. It was
absent any mirth. "I wouldn't know where to start!"

"I know, pretty grim."

"I mean, I'm sure you have your own system of
organization."

"Not really."

"Oh," said Lucy.

"Have a seat. I was just about to crack open my mini
fridge and indulge in some Cracker Barrel and Triscuits,
any interest?"

"No thanks," said Lucy, declining the food, but taking
the seat. As Antonia reached open the door of her fridge
and removed the bright-orange cheese (not the most
appetizing color), she noticed that Lucy was wearing
her "day-off" outfit—one that Antonia had seen before.

It consisted of a red-and-white-checked shirt (with a matching checked scarf that she wore around her pony-tail) and crisp blue overalls. As was her norm, it had a retro fifties feeling to it, and Antonia felt at once that she was sitting with Maryanne from Gilligan's Island. Antonia took a plastic knife out of her drawer and sliced off several thick wedges of the cheese. She took crackers out of the box that was perched on her window ledge and placed them on each one. She again offered Lucy one, but she recoiled.

"I just saw all these pictures of the Millennium party that Gordon hosted at the inn," said Antonia, popping a cracker in her mouth.

"Where'd you find those?" asked Lucy with surprise. "In that box Naomi and Barbie were fighting over?"

"No, these friends of Liz's had them. It was interesting."

"In what sense?"

"Well, you know. Seeing Gordon in action. Old pictures of the inn."

"Right."

"And looking at all the costumes. People went all out. There was this one…"

Lucy cut her off. "I'm not a big fan of costume parties myself."

"Oh. I guess I know what you mean. They're kind of a hassle."

"Agreed. I did dress up one Halloween as Jayne Mansfield. I like that old Hollywood glamour look."

"Jayne Mansfield?" asked Antonia, inadvertently

glancing at Lucy's chest. "No offense, but how'd you pull that off? She was known for her rather, well, large attributes."

"There is such a thing as a padded bra, Antonia!"

"You're right. I just can't imagine you as Jayne Mansfield."

Lucy looked offended. Antonia immediately back-tracked. "I mean, she was just sort of cheap. I think of you as a little more elegant. Maybe Lana Turner."

Lucy shrugged, probably still offended. "I wanted to make a statement. Anyway, the reason I came in was after you came in the other day and asked for the employee forms well, that's when I noticed I needed to clean out my files ASAP."

Their brief banter had been broken and Lucy returned to being all business.

"Yeah, I hate that," said Antonia.

"I went through everything, moved some boxes downstairs into the basement. But then I saw these and thought you might be interested."

She handed Antonia the papers. "What's this?"

"It's the corporate credit card statements from when Gordon owned the inn. It's from the last two years only, because my system is to shred everything after two years of safekeeping. I thought it might be of interest to you."

Antonia glanced at the MasterCard spreadsheet. A quick scan revealed charges to True Value Hardware, Warren's Nursery, King Kullen, and Riverhead Lumber. There were various other costs mixed in as well, but those were the ones that appeared regularly. "Thanks, Lucy. Were there any red flags that stood out to you?"

"Not when I originally did the payments. But look how many charges there are to Warren's Nursery."

"Why is that strange? I feel like I spend most of my money on landscaping costs."

Lucy gave her a small smile. "But Warren's wasn't handling our landscaping. Hector did most of it. So these were not purchases for the inn."

"Are you sure?"

"Fairly sure. It's something I should have caught earlier, but I'd only just become the bookkeeper and it was all new to me."

"Who had access to the corporate card?"

"Gordon, of course, and Ronald Meter. He was the manager at the time."

"And you think Ronald was buying something at Warren's?"

Lucy nodded. "Horticulture is his passion. As you know, Gordon fired him when he suspected him of siphoning money. These credit card receipts could prove that."

Antonia's mind raced. Of course she knew that there was a cloud of suspicion regarding Ronald's dismissal, but would he have been so stupid as to blatantly charge things to the corporate card? "Wouldn't Gordon have been hip to these expenses? I can't imagine they would go unnoticed."

"You would think so, but the bulk of the charges are

from January to May. That's when Gordon was in one of his dark moods, not really focused on anything. I think it's possible they could have passed him by."

Something didn't seem right to Antonia. It all felt very sloppy and unbelievable that Ronald would do something like that. There must be an explanation.

As if reading her skepticism, Lucy stood up. "Anyway, just thought you might like to see them. Not sure if they can help you at all."

"Thanks," said Antonia, who was already scanning the pages. Lucy stood up to make her exit.

"No problem."

Antonia studied the row of charges. The fees to the nursery were substantial. "So it was just Ronald and Gordon who had these cards?"

Lucy paused on her way out. "Yes. Gordon and Ronald…and, of course, Barbie."

Antonia looked up. "Barbie?"

"Well, yes, she was Gordon's girlfriend. She had access to that as well," said Lucy in a tone that conveyed her perception that the question was inane.

"Interesting," said Antonia.

When Lucy had left, Antonia went through the expenses line by line. She almost missed it. On the last page, there was a charge on November 29 to South Fork Farm for twenty dollars. That was the honey farm where Soyla worked. And where they had the beehives. It was worth taking a visit.

ALTHOUGH IT WAS THE LAST THING THAT ANTONIA should be doing on a Friday night when she was needed in the kitchen to start dinner service, Antonia decided to take a ride out to the farm stand. She promised herself it would be a quick trip; it would just be half an hour of her time and then she'd be back in her apron, grilling entrees. The farm was located on Town Lane, a long road in Amagansett that ran parallel to Route 27 and cut through farmland into the woods, before running into Old Stone Highway which led to the bay. It still amazed Antonia how East Hampton had such a disparate number of neighborhoods that all felt worlds apart. One could live by the beach or by the woods, by farmland or in town. And every locale had its own rhythm and vibe, quite different from the others. Many neighborhoods that had once been unfashionable were now being cannibalized by weekend folk, due to the demand, and the fact that people were priced out of the traditional second home area—which would be "south of the highway." Now, it was trendy to live in the un-trendy parts of town, like this.

The South Fork Farm was only about twelve minutes from the inn. Antonia often visited the collective farm down the road, but mostly in the summer, and hadn't been out this way in a few months. The sun was beginning to cast its shadow across the rippling grass and as dusk was approaching, Antonia slowed her car. Late afternoon and early evening were the time when deer chose to run in a pack into the middle of the street and get hit by oncoming traffic. Antonia wanted to avoid that.

When she paused at a stop sign, she glanced at the houses to her right. They were modest and close together, shaded by thick trees. She glanced into the driveway in one and saw Ronald Meter standing next to his Mini talking to a guy, gesticulating wildly as if they were in a heated discussion. She squinted. The guy looked familiar; where had she seen him before? She craned her neck to get a better look and then suddenly the car behind her honked. She jolted. Ronald and the guy turned their heads in her direction. As soon as she locked eyes with Ronald, fear flashed across his face and he quickly turned away from her. *That was odd*, thought Antonia. *Was he trying to hide from me?*

After cruising some time, she saw South Fork Farm's stand up ahead and turned on her blinker. There were three cars parked in the makeshift lot; weekenders, no doubt, stocking up on produce on their way out from the city. Antonia pulled in next to a dusty Lexus SUV and turned off her ignition. She glanced at her reflection in the mirror and saw that the lack of sleep and stress were definitely catching up with her. There were light red rims on her eyelids and puffy bags gathering under her eyes. Lovely. She whipped out a lip gloss from her bag and spread some on, plumping up her lips with a shade that L'Oréal called "Luscious" before exiting her car.

A man and woman in their late thirties, dressed head to toe in black athletic gear (her tiny frame coated in spandex lululemon; his wiry body clad in Prada, judging by the abundant logos) were frantically heaping bunches of kale into their basket while their two young children haggled for their attention. Antonia watched them as they squeezed, sniffed, and scrutinized every vegetable in the various bins. The intensity they displayed making their selections instantly gave her anxiety, but she found herself fascinated by their exchange.

"Bruce, these eggplants are good. Not too much bruising," said the woman.

Her husband came and held up the eggplant to the light.

"Right here, there's a dent," he said, dumping it back into the bin.

"What about this one?" asked the wife, holding up another.

The man looked at it, then shrugged. "What are you going to make with it?"

"Caponata?"

"Too much sugar."

"I can puree it. I saw an eggplant puree recipe in the *Times*."

He nodded. "Okay, but I'm doing a butternut squash puree also."

"We can puree them both. Maybe do a puree cleanse this week instead of a juicing?" she asked.

"I'm juicing this week. You can puree. I need to juice. It's all about the cleanse."

And so on…

Antonia realized she was staring and moved toward the counter. New Yorkers were a funny breed, in her opinion. They were so tightly wound and usually in a rush. She admired their energy but sometimes found it too much to take. East Hampton was "the country" to them, and yet many were unable to shake their city attitude when they came out here. You'd see them zipping around the curvy roads in their SUVs, clamoring to get to wherever they needed to go *as fast as possible*. This bothered many of her local friends. She'd heard that one of the latest "tricks" the locals were pulling on the weekenders/summer people was to drive the speed limit, which was twenty-five miles per hour. This (pardon the pun) drove the summer people crazy. They'd start flashing lights and honking, desperate to force the cars in front of them to speed up, to no avail.

The farm stand was so charming and quintessential that it could be the set of a movie, thought Antonia. On a long wooden table shielded by a roof overhang were various baskets of glistening (and yes, some bruised) produce, "spilling" out of bins. As it was October, that consisted of many root vegetables and squashes—shiny purple onions, dusty beets, butternut squash, waxy yellow-and-blue fingerling potatoes. Alongside them were rows of apples in every varietal—Macoun, Granny Smith, McIntosh, Gala, and Fuji. On the far end of the table were bunches of wildflowers in rich colors arranged in vases, already carefully assembled in a manner that made it appear as if they had just been picked. The owners of farm stands had long become hip to the fact that it was all about marketing, so they also repackaged berries and imported plums and other fruits that were unavailable and blended them in with local wares by putting them in their own rustic packaging. (Most people didn't even realize that strawberries were no longer in season here after mid-June.) Artisanal maple syrups, jams, and chocolates lined the shelves behind the counter, and off to the side of the stand was an entire wheelbarrow filled with pumpkins and gourds of various sizes.

And where would a farm stand be without baked goods? Many farmers didn't bake their own; instead they offered pies from the Blue Duck Bakery and Tate's chocolate chip cookies. But at South Fork they had a stack of lemon and poppy seed bread tied up in white parchment paper with a blue ribbon and bags of homemade oatmeal raisin cookies and cinnamon drops in cute gingham wrapping.

A middle-aged woman stood behind the counter ringing up an older man. Black roots were bleeding into her yellow-blond hair, and Antonia sensed it had been quite some time since she had visited a beauty parlor, judging by the color and her frayed ends, which splayed out across the edge of her ears in a jagged cut. She wore thick black eyeliner under her pale blue eyes, and most of her face was freckled and blotchy from sun damage. She wore a heavy Irish sweater under a puffy vest, and shapeless Lee jeans. Her manner was perfunctory and she emitted that "end of the day" vibe when all you want to do is get home and take a hot bath. Antonia waited for the man to collect his change and goods before she approached. Another quick scan of the premises revealed the jars of honey next to the register.

"Can I help you?" asked the woman after the man in front of Antonia had paid. She had a strong Long Island accent.

"Yes, I'd love two jars of honey, please."

"What size?"

"Oh, let's go for the big ones," said Antonia with a smile.

While not rude, the woman was definitely all business. Antonia watched as she scooped up two jars with her rough, callused hands and put them in a brown paper bag. She punched numbers into the ancient register before glancing up at Antonia.

"Twenty-two dollars."

Antonia gulped. "Wow, who knew honey was so expensive?"

The woman's expression didn't change as she took Antonia's money. "It's organic."

"Now what does that mean, organic? I keep hearing that, but I would assume all honey is organic, right?"

"Not so. A lot goes through China and they add sugar to it. We have our own bees here so we make it ourselves."

Antonia's heart sung with the opening. "You have your own hives?" she asked, playing dumb.

"Yup," said the woman. She handed Antonia her bag,

and gave her a farewell expression. But this was Antonia's chance.

"So, where do you keep your hives?"

"By the farm, down there."

She motioned behind her, and Antonia glanced through the field to the farmhouse in the distance. A tractor stood idle next to it.

"Interesting. I've never seen a beehive."

Before the woman could respond, a young woman, wearing tight jeans tucked into camel-colored boots and a long gray sweater over a concert T-shirt came from the back and stood behind the counter.

"Mom, do we need more turnips?" asked the young woman.

Even if she hadn't addressed the woman as mom, Antonia could see the family resemblance at once. The girl was still young and fresh and carried that rosiness that youth possess, but she was a carbon copy of her mother. The skin on her face was gently freckled and had none of her mother's sun damage, and her blue eyes were animated, her features still sharp and not slackened. She wore her flaxen hair straight to her shoulders, and had on a striped hat like the one Antonia had recently seen on the cover of a J. Crew catalog, and couldn't believe it was back in fashion.

"No, but we do need more carrots," said the woman.

"All right, I'll go in a minute," said the daughter.

Antonia wanted to return the topic to the beehives but at that moment the New York couple came up with their multiple baskets and placed them with a thump on the counter.

"All ready?" asked the woman behind the counter.

"We think so," said the New York woman. "Although give us some of that honey, also."

The woman turned her attention to them and Antonia was left standing idle with her brown bag of honey. She waited a minute, but the New Yorkers were firing a million questions at the woman so she knew it would be awhile. Instead, she walked over the dirt path to the edge of the field and stared at the farm, which was about three hundred yards away. The farmhouse was white, clapboard, shutterless, and definitely due for a paint job. Smoke was trickling out of the redbrick chimney and lights were on in the downstairs rooms. Next to the house was a large barn, unpainted and sagging, with the big doors flung open. A tractor and other farm equipment were scattered around the entrance. Antonia could see beyond there was a low building that almost looked like a greenhouse. Maybe that's where the hives were? She'd have to ask Soyla to give her more details on what went on there.

Antonia was at a loss now as to what she should do. Just as she was debating her next move, she saw the daughter leave the shed and start to walk in the direction of the farmhouse. This was Antonia's chance.

"Excuse me?" asked Antonia.

The girl stopped and turned. "Yes?"

"Um, I just bought some of your honey. I heard it's

delicious, and I was wondering if there was anything I should know about it?" She was grasping.

The girl looked confused. She sunk her hands into the deep pockets of her long cardigan. "What do you mean?"

"I mean, um, well, it's organic, right?"

"Yeah."

"So, anything special about the methods in which you make it?"

"I wouldn't really know about that. My uncle, Frank, is the beekeeper but he's not here now."

"Does he ever have seminars? Or you know, classes on how to make it?"

The girl smiled at the ridiculousness of Antonia's question. "No, not really."

"Oh. You see, I had a friend who was trying to buy a beehive. Do you ever sell yours?"

She shook her head. "Naw. In fact, my uncle buys beehives. It's a good business these days. Then he rents them to some of the other farms and lets his bees pollinate their fields."

Antonia could tell the girl was being polite but really trying to get on with her carrot errand, but Antonia didn't want her to go.

"I guess honey is more popular than ever. Must be a demand."

"Yeah, you're not the first to ask."

"I'm not?"

"No," said the girl. She gave Antonia a look as if to say, *Can I go now?* but Antonia pressed forward.

"Who has asked?"

"I don't know, other farmers."

"Oh, anyone else?"

She shook her head. "I don't really know. We don't keep track."

"Oh," said Antonia. "Sorry, I'm really nosy, I know. I just had a friend who had a bee and I thought she bought it here."

"Bought one bee? No, we don't do that."

"Okay, all right. Sorry to waste your time."

The girl turned away, but then seemingly remembering something, turned back to Antonia.

"You know, there was one thing…" she began.

"What?"

"Well, and this was like last year, or maybe longer, this one woman came and asked if she could buy a bee. She was really weird. We said no, so she just bought some honey."

"Do you remember at all when this was? Could it have been December of last year?"

The girl pulled out her bottom lip and began chewing on it. She tapped her chin with her fingers as she did so. Antonia supposed this was her way of thinking hard. Finally, she spoke.

"Yeah could be. We shut down the stand after Thanksgiving so I remember it was closed, and she came to the door of the house. Yeah, now that I think of it, I remember she kind of commented on our lawn decorations. We go all out at Christmas. We have one of those blow-up nativity scenes, really cool."

"Oh, that's awesome," said Antonia, trying to humor the girl. "And she liked it?"

"Um, actually no. I think she was kind of snotty or whatever, because she sort of mentioned it without saying she liked it."

"Maybe she's the Grinch."

The girl laughed. "Yeah."

"So, then what happened?"

"So, I let her buy the honey…"

"She paid with a credit card?"

"Yeah, she did. We used to take cash only but these days cash is like an endangered species. We had to switch over. My uncle was pretty steamed about that. All the taxes, etc."

"I know. Killer. So then what?"

"I rang her up and then, like, way later, I went to the farmhouse to get more of something, and she was, like, there, hanging around the beehives. She said she was just looking, and I told her she couldn't be there. But then, like, the next day, my uncle said he could swear one of his girls was missing—he calls them his girls. The bees I mean. I don't know if they're girls or not, but that's what he calls them."

Antonia felt her heart fill with excitement. "Do you think she stole it?"

The girls shrugged. "Dunno. But it was weird."

"What did she look like?"

"Kind of average."

"Blond? Brunette?"

"Blond, I think…"

"Thin? Fat?"

The girl looked at the sky as if there was a picture of the bee thief in it. "She wasn't fat. But she wasn't thin… you know, she was kind of stacked."

"You mean big boobs?" said Antonia with a smile.

The girl giggled and held the back of her hand to cover her mouth. "Yeah. I only noticed because my brother was there and he was like 'Wow, that woman has huge you-know-whats.' They were so big, they looked kinda fake."

"That's funny," said Antonia, feigning laughter. "Very funny."

But Antonia didn't think it was funny at all. Humor was not what she was feeling. Antonia's alarm bells were going off big time. Because the girl's description matched Barbie to a tee.

"Do you think you have a copy of her credit card receipt?"

The girl looked suddenly suspicious. "Wait, why do you want it again? I thought you were asking about your friend…"

"I was, I was. Just want to make sure it's her."

The girl had lost all confidence in Antonia. She glanced worriedly at the barn then back at the farm stand. "I should go."

"Right, right. I'm just trying to get the honey for my friend who was here. I'm not crazy, but she's very partic-ular and I wanted to make sure it's the right place. Here's my card, please take it. If you find her receipt, please let me know. I think she paid with a credit card from the Windmill Inn. I own it now. I just want to make sure."

Antonia pushed her card into the girl's face. She stared at it, before shoving it into her back pocket. "Okay," she said. "Gotta run."

"Thanks, you've been really helpful!" said Antonia.

The girl scurried away. With sadness, Antonia realized she'd never hear from her. Antonia needed to tighten up her cover stories in advance. There was no way she'd make a good undercover spy at this point.

26

Despite the conversation ending in failure Antonia was buzzing over the fact that Barbie had most likely taken the bee from the farm stand. This girl was basically an eyewitness placing her there. So now all Antonia had to do was prove that Barbie had stolen the bee and used it to kill Gordon. Ha! Easier said than done. Even if Barbie was at the farm stand that day, it was so long ago that it was unlikely the girl or her Uncle Frank, the beekeeper, would be able to say for sure that Barbie had stolen a bee. Antonia had to think. There had to be a better way. Another problem was that if it were Barbie who killed Gordon, why would she kill Biddy too? There was no motive between those two.

The sky had already gathered into darkness by the time Antonia returned to the inn, and the lights were twinkling inside in an inviting manner. The outside air was fresh and brimming with an autumn medley that consisted of fireplace smoke, grilled steak, apple cider, and ocean mist. Antonia stopped by her office to collect any messages before rushing to change for dinner service. There was a small scribbled note in Lucy's handwriting on top of her desk.

Antonia—

Turns out we were using Warren's Nursery back then. We purchased all of our trees and bushes from them. I was wrong to think the charges were frivolous. Sorry about the false alarm.

Lucy

Antonia crumpled it up and pitched it in her trash can. So Ronald hadn't been siphoning money from the inn. *That confirmation doesn't really change anything because Ronald as the main suspect was so three hours ago*, thought Antonia with a smile.

Marty and Kendra were buzzing about the kitchen and Antonia felt a tinge of joy and dismay that everything had proceeded smoothly without her. Here it was Friday night and they didn't miss a beat. Oh well, she supposed that was a good thing, and she joined in the kitchen rhythm. As she plated a Gorgonzola-stuffed hamburger on a brioche bun, Glen popped into the kitchen to tell her (with an eye roll) that Larry Lipper was asking for her. She scooped some pickle chips onto the plate before heading out to meet him.

The restaurant was noisy and loud, and the crowd at the bar was two-people deep. None of that seemed to bother Larry, though. His tiny body was perched on a barstool and he was tapping away on his laptop, ignoring the women who were standing next to him ogling his stool. A tumbler of bourbon was in front of him. He wore brown corduroys and a blue fleece over a blue-checked button-down. He was totally absorbed in his work and didn't notice Antonia at first. He was so much more pleasant this way, she thought, when he was focused and not trying to be a wise guy.

"Hey," said Antonia.

Larry glanced up. He had about a day or two's worth of beard growth on his chin and his eyes were tired, with little wrinkles creasing around the sides. He snapped down the cover of his laptop.

"Bingham."

"Lipper."

He gave her a smile and for the first time she noticed that he actually had nice teeth. Very white, very straight. *Oh well, you win some you lose some,* thought Antonia.

"You beckoned me here?" he said finally. "Just can't stay away, huh?"

He still had his playful tone but he sounded wearier than usual.

"I did?" asked Antonia with confusion.

"Yes, you left me a message?"

"Oh right! Wow, that seems like it was so long ago."

"What did you want?"

"What's wrong, Larry. You have a late night last night? You look half dead."

"Ha, well, yes, I did have a late night last night. Hot date. But that's not the reason I'm tired."

"What is then?"

"You're not going to believe what happened, Bingham," he said. "This is so up your alley."

Antonia tried to get closer to Larry but couldn't elbow her way through the crowd. "You know what? Let's go into the sunroom and talk. Much quieter."

"I want to eat, though," whined Larry. "You promised."

"I'll tell Glen to send a waiter in to take our order."

"Fine."

Larry packed up his laptop and followed Antonia out through the front door. She greeted some customers along the way and grabbed two menus from the maître d' stand. Glen was busy chatting with the guests at table four, so she mouthed *Sunroom* and pointed and hoped that he would get that she wanted a waiter to find her there.

The sunroom was occupied by a couple having drinks. They were leaning closely together in an intimate conversation. As soon as Antonia entered, they abruptly pulled apart.

"Sorry to interrupt," said Antonia.

The man rose quickly. "It's okay, we were just leaving."

"We can go somewhere else," Antonia protested.

"That's okay. We're done here," said the man with finality.

Antonia glanced at the woman who winced at his words. She put down her glass and stood up reluctantly. Antonia could discern the slightest remnants of tears in her eyes and wondered if she had just stumbled upon a breakup. Both of them left wordlessly.

Larry plopped down on the sofa. "Thank God we got rid of them."

"You are too kind, Larry," said Antonia. She sat in the armchair next to him.

"Yeah, yeah. I'm just happy to sit in a comfortable sofa. I've had a long day."

"Yes, please tell me all about it. I'm dying of curiosity," said Antonia with sarcasm.

"Ha ha, I know you are putting on airs, but do you know where I've been all day?"

"Larry, I really have no idea."

He gave her a wicked smile. "I was at the police station. They brought Naomi Haslett in for questioning in the murder of Biddy Robertson."

Antonia was stunned. "You're kidding me."

He shook his head. "I kid you not. It's big news. They think she offed her."

"Why would she kill her?"

"Oh, Bingham, you know the ways of women! You're all crazy!"

"Ha ha. Seriously."

"Cat fight gone bad. Apparently, the two gals were friends way back when, neighbors, bosom buddies, thick as thieves, probably having slumber parties in their PJs, topless pillow fights, the works."

Antonia rolled her eyes. Larry was clearly enjoying this. He continued with relish.

"Then the inevitable falling-out, who knows why—maybe Biddy stole Naomi's lipstick and she got her panties in a bunch. So when Biddy confided that she was having financial issues and facing foreclosure, Naomi joined with Gordon to screw her out of the inn. After that, it was *on*. And I mean capital ON. Remember that item in the paper about the dead animal?"

Antonia nodded. "But why now? Why wait all those years to kill her?"

Larry took a large gulp, nearly finishing the bourbon

he had brought in with him. The ice cubes clanked down in the glass when he replaced it on the table. He wiped his mouth with the back of his hand and gave Antonia a mischievous look.

"You'll have to read it in my column."

"Larry, not this again!" snapped Antonia in frustration. She was about to grab him by the collar and shake it out of him but he put his hands up to surrender.

"Now, now, Bingham, don't get all wild. Of course I'm kidding. I just wanted to see your face. I love how it gets all puckered up when you are pissed off."

"Stop jerking me around and tell me."

"Okay," said Larry, pausing to take another chug of his drink, finishing it off.

Antonia waited with impatience. She folded her arms like a school marm and tapped her foot. "Larry, just be normal for once," she commanded.

"I'm offended!" he began to protest, but then sensing Antonia's acute aggravation, he backed down. "How about another drink first?"

Antonia remained silent. All this back-and-forth banter made Antonia feel like she was on a sitcom.

"Okay, Okay. Wow, lady, you drive a hard bargain. Biddy Robertson told her son she thought that Gordon Haslett had been killed. She actually even implied that she knew who did it. She didn't tell him, but she did refer to the killer as a 'she.'"

Antonia's pulse raced. "And the police think the 'she' in question is Naomi?"

Larry nodded. "Yes."

"But why Naomi? What about Barbie?"

"Okay, this has to be kept on the down-low," said Larry, for once serious.

"Obviously."

Larry leaned in closer. "When the police searched Biddy's house, they found a letter that Naomi had written Gordon. It was full of nasty stuff like 'I hate you,' 'I hate your girlfriend,' 'You're screwing me'…"

"Why would she put that in writing?"

"It was on the back of some bill for a party that Gordon had. He had rented all these tables and chairs and linens from Bermuda Party Rentals. He expensed it all to the hotel, but the police confirmed it was a birthday party he had for Barbie. Naomi owned half of the hotel, so he was essentially taking money away from her. And I think the kicker was she wasn't even invited."

"How did Biddy get the letter?"

"They think she was investigating Naomi. Trying to find anything she could to get back at her. Somehow got a hold of the letter. I dunno, maybe went through her garbage?"

Antonia had never met Biddy, but she wondered at the idea of her going through Gordon and Barbie's garbage to find incriminating evidence. Biddy was in her sixties, would she really go dumpster diving? Something didn't seem right, but probably the police knew more than they were telling Larry.

"Why would she be investigating Naomi *now*? They 'stole the inn out from under' Biddy twelve years ago."

"The son said that his mother never got over it and always hated Naomi. She had finally stopped talking about it until recently when she was passed over for a position in the Garden Club. She felt Naomi was the one responsible because she trashed her to another member. And Biddy really, really wanted that job. Don't quite know why, because it was voluntary, not even paid, but supposedly prestigious for some reason or other. Not sure why weeding local public gardens is prestigious."

Antonia gave Larry a look. "They do more than that."

"Whatever. I hear the words 'women's' and 'club' in the same sentence and I run for the hills."

"We can talk about your mother issues later," said Antonia. "In the meantime, what about Gordon? Now do the police believe he was murdered?"

"They didn't tell me if they do or not but I get the impression they're not exactly trying to add any more murders to their load. Not good for the local economy."

"Good for you and your paper though," said Antonia.

"You're getting it now."

"Is there anything else? Any other details that you are 'forgetting' that I might read about in your newspaper this week?"

"Hey, come on. I told you everything I know."

"How did they get to Naomi in the first place? They must have had some cause to search her house. Don't you need a warrant for that?"

Larry scorned. "I'm working on that angle. No one is talking. Yet. It's very frustrating, but I'll wait. I'm like a cat stalking my prey. Now you gotta buy me dinner. Isn't that why you called?"

"I actually had another question, but yes, I will buy you dinner," said Antonia. "And I may actually do you the honor of joining you. I haven't eaten either."

Larry gave her a long, leering look. "I know you want me."

"Larry, please."

"Don't deny it."

The waiter entered the room and Larry and Antonia put in orders for dinner. They both wanted the burger, and Larry made a big show out of asking for whole grain mustard to accompany his burger and insisting that his fries should be extra crispy. He made a big deal about excluding tomatoes and lettuce on his bun as if they were toxic. Antonia gave the waiter an eye roll as he patiently took down Larry's requests. Antonia added a glass of cabernet, another drink for Larry, and an order of fried calamari, as well as a small mixed-green salad that she planned to take at least one bite of in an effort to balance out all of the grease and carbs. It really wasn't easy for a carnivore to incorporate leafy green vegetables into her diet. When the waiter left, Antonia returned her attention to Larry, who had grabbed a handful of mixed nuts from the dish the waiter had brought in and was picking out all of the peanuts and throwing them back into the dish.

"Don't do that, please. It's gross," Antonia admonished.

"I don't like peanuts."

"So don't eat the nuts. It's disgusting that you touch every single one and then put them back in."

"Everyone does it. Did you know they did a study and found that there is a ton of urine on bar nuts?"

"Larry. Oh my God, stop."

"It's true. People drink beer, go to the bathroom, and 'forget' to wash their hands, then come back and dig into the nuts. They're like the foulest things on the planet."

"And you're contributing to it."

"I would hope that you would throw out the dish after each person eats some. If you don't, that's a major health code violation. I should write an article on this place."

"Okay, now you are bugging me," said Antonia with exasperation.

"Babe, I don't like to see you upset. Forget the health code thing and talk to me. What made you call in Double L tonight if not for some loving?"

"You refer to yourself as 'Double L'?"

"I do."

Antonia sighed deeply. This man needed help, he was so confused. But that wasn't her problem right now. She decided to drop the subject and move on.

"I wanted to ask you about the Millennium New Year's Eve party that was here at the inn. I met a woman, Joan Masterson, who showed me some photos from that night."

"Man, that was some night! We partied like it was 1999."

"I can imagine. I saw pictures of you ogling ladies. But

what I want to know is if you remember who was dressed as a bunny that night."

"A bunny? A Playboy bunny?"

"No, just like a real bunny. An Easter bunny."

"Geez, Antonia, I have no idea! I was out of my mind that night. The booze was flowing, everyone was giddy, it was like the sixties, or what I imagine the sixties were like. I wasn't alive then."

"Well, do you remember who Gordon was dating at the time?"

"No, I didn't even know the guy."

Antonia was dismayed. "You're a reporter, Larry. Come on, did you take notes on the evening? Could you remember any of the people who were there? You seem to have some capacity for observation."

"Now, now," said Larry. "No need to be nasty. It's true. I wasn't paying much attention that evening. But I can find out."

"That would be great."

"What do I get in return?"

"Larry, I am so tired of this."

"Come on, I'm just kidding you," said Larry. He punched her arm. "Have a sense of humor."

"I'll try."

Antonia and Larry were deep into their burgers when Genevieve arrived in a dramatic flurry, stomping her way into the sunroom like an angry child. Her outfit was a bit more subdued today, Antonia noted. She wore black leggings tucked into black leather motorcycle boots, and a long green-gray asymmetrical wool top with sleeves that flared at her elbows. Her hair was pulled back into a messy bun by a black elastic band, and the only makeup she had on was lip gloss.

"I've been looking for you everywhere!" she said accusingly.

"And now you found me," said Antonia brightly.

"You're not going to believe this," Genevieve said, flinging her leather satchel purse down onto the coffee table and plopping in an armchair. "Ty has a girlfriend."

She said it as if she had just announced the Academy Award for Best Actor or the winner of the Nobel Peace Prize. She waited for Antonia's reaction, but when Antonia didn't comment she continued.

"It's just bizarre that he wouldn't mention it. There were plenty of opportunities. And do you know how I found out? We're watching TV, he's sitting on the couch and I'm lying down, my head on his lap. He picks up his phone and starts texting. I don't really pay attention, but then he's, like, laughing, so I say, 'Who are you texting?' and he says Sarah. And I'm like, 'Who's Sarah?' and he says, 'My girlfriend.' Can you believe it? Does he have no respect?"

Antonia barely had time to react before Larry Lipper jumped in.

"Sounds like a loser."

Genevieve turned, noticing Larry for the first time, despite the fact that he was seated directly next to Antonia. "Yes, he is a loser. You're right."

"Men are jerks," added Larry.

Genevieve nodded. "I agree. Total jerks."

Her eyes went back and forth between Larry and Antonia but finally settled on the latter with a quizzical gaze.

"Sorry, do you two know each other?" Antonia said, making the introduction. "Larry, this is Genevieve."

A small smile crept across Genevieve's lips. She thrust out her hand. "Nice to meet you."

"You too. Not every night I meet a damsel in distress."

Genevieve gave Antonia a wide-eyed look and took a step back. "Well, I'm sorry to interrupt. I should go."

She stood up and began to retreat. Antonia belatedly realized that Genevieve erroneously thought she and Larry were on a date.

"Wait, don't go, it's not what you think," said Antonia.

Genevieve shook her head. "No, no, I gotta run. Just wanted to stop by."

"Larry and I are just talking murder. Don't you want to join us? Please don't go!"

But Genevieve was already out the door. Antonia stood up to go after her but Larry stopped her.

"Aw, let her go and lick her wounds."

"No, she wants to talk. She just probably thought we were on a date so she hightailed it out of here."

"Then she's very astute," said Larry. "No tits, though."

"Larry, you are really very irritating."

"Thank you," he said smugly.

27

Saturday

THE WEATHER REPORT HAD PROMISED TEMPERATURES would hit the mid-sixties, and it was already warm and sunny by the time Antonia arrived at the beach at six thirty in the morning. After living most of her life in Northern California where the weather was even and predictable, a steady hum of overcast and dry and never too cold, New York was a complete conundrum for Antonia. There was a schizophrenic element to the New York climate where one day would be frigid and cold and then the next positively balmy. Last year, she'd made the mistake of putting away her summer clothes too early—for once, making a huge effort to be so clever and organized, she had meticulously folded everything in tissue paper and neatly packed it in a plastic under-the-bed container in late September only to reopen it again a few weeks later when the heat reemerged in full force. Nowadays, Antonia took her mother's old "layering is key" advice and piled on layers of soft fabrics, starting with cotton short-sleeved shirts and moving to loose cardigans, scarves, fleeces, and so forth until she was in a cocoon of clothing that could be unwrapped one item at a time.

She wasn't sure if she should expect to run into Nick Darrow; after all, she had skipped a few days, but she took extra care in her dress nonetheless. It was silly and overly optimistic, but thinking about Nick Darrow gave her a buzz. It was like being in a real-life romantic comedy with someone who often starred in romantic comedies. Antonia had also brought with her two fresh out-of-the-oven banana chocolate chip muffins to present him with. She had tucked them into a white paper bag that was now smeared with grease stains, but if he didn't show she could always eat them herself.

Antonia headed west against the wind. Georgica Beach had suffered immense damage in recent years by two big hurricanes—first Irene, then Sandy. Much of the beach was eroded and most of the jetty there was submerged underwater. The dunes had been hit so hard it looked as if a digger had come in and tried to excavate them. They were cut open, raw like a wound, with darker sand spilling out like a burst bloodline and vine roots tangled in knots like veins.

Antonia glanced at the mansions teetering on the edge of the dunes, with their long wooden staircases that dead-ended into the sand. This expanse was mostly desolate as it was about a mile between public beach entrances. She spotted a few lone dog walkers in the distance, and strained to identify them, but unfortunately, there was no one who looked like Nick, which she supposed was just as well. It was silly of her to think about him or get excited over whether he may or may not appear. It made her feel young and immature, like a child. She decided to push thoughts of him out of her mind. Instead, she busied herself examining the patches of shells that had washed up on the shore. Some days were better than others for finding sea glass, and this was one of the good ones. Antonia loved sifting through all the vacant mussel shells, shiny rocks, cracked seashells, and discarded bunches of seaweed to catch that glimmer of light that was reflected in even the smallest piece of sea glass. There was always so much white glass to be found, seconded by brown, so finding a green or cobalt piece of glass was a bonanza. Antonia pocketed several pieces along her walk, rubbing their smooth surfaces between her fingers, and tried to make a mental note to remember to place them in the glass jar she had on her bookshelf. It displayed a year's worth of collecting and yet the jar was only filled halfway so far.

Every time Antonia made it to the beach for her morning walk, she resolved to come every day. The smell of the salty ocean, the clean breeze, the vast expanse of openness from the water to the sky, made her feel cleansed. It was like mental floss. It made everything in her life fall into place and gave her perspective. The fact that the previous innkeepers at her inn were being whacked off? No problem. With a sea this blue and a beach this vast, what did it matter?

The foamy waves were slobbering along the shores, dragging more bounty with them. They would unfurl their rocks and shells, then recoil lazily. Antonia was so engrossed in her hunt for a piece of sea glass by the break that she didn't notice that Nick Darrow had approached.

It was only after one of his dogs came bounding over and put his wet paws on her knees that she glanced up.

"You made it today," said Nick with a smile. His hair was damp and neatly combed, and he wore a black turtleneck sweater over khakis and brown boots.

"I made it," said Antonia, rising.

They stared at each other for a beat, smiling. Antonia felt instantly awkward and remembered that she was clutching the white bag in her left hand. She thrust it toward him. "Here, I made you some muffins. But if you already ate, that's okay, we can just chuck them, it's no problem…"

"You made them for me? Thank you," said Nick. He took the bag from her and opened it, pulling out an over-sized chunk. "They look delicious."

"No nuts, wasn't sure if you were allergic…"

"I'm not."

"Banana chocolate chip."

"Great," he said, staring at the muffin. "I like the way all the sugar crystallized on top."

"Me too," said Antonia with perhaps too much enthusiasm.

Nick took a big bite. His eyes rolled back dramatically and he moaned loudly. "Oh my God, these are fabulous!"

Antonia flushed with excitement. "It's okay if you don't like them. Please don't feel the need to humor me."

"Stop it! They're great," he said through his full mouth.

Yes, he was an actor, and maybe he was just acting, but

Antonia was thrilled by his reception of her food. There was no better high in her mind than feeding people well. Forget drugs, this was a better buzz.

They started walking along the beach, following the paw print path that Nick's dogs had etched in the sand. The conversation was mostly topical, about food and wine, new restaurants in town, and local politics. There were moments of silence where they watched the dogs or the surfers bobbing in the waves, but nothing felt awkward or stilted. Antonia was both relaxed and energized when she was with Nick. She felt frisson, as if two electrical wires were rubbing together to make a buzz. She was sure he viewed her platonically, but that was okay. Somehow it was enough for her alone to experience the jolt that he gave her, the little fluttering heartbeats that sustained her through the day.

When they had finished their walk and were leaning against the split-rail fence shaking the sand out of their shoes, Nick dropped a bomb.

"I'll miss this beach."

"Miss it?" asked Antonia, replacing her shoe. "What do you mean?"

Nick scanned the shoreline. In the distance a fishing boat was drifting along the water, miles away. "I'm leaving town tomorrow to go film a movie."

Antonia felt her stomach drop. "You are?"

"Yeah," he said, turning toward her. "It's always so hard to leave."

"I can imagine. How long are you going for?" She

hoped she sounded more casual than she felt and that there was no panic creeping into her voice.

"Four months."

"Four months?" asked Antonia. "Wow! That's a long time."

"I know. I hope I can get back for a break in between but it's not looking good. We're filming in Australia."

"Australia? Wow. You really couldn't go much farther than that."

"I know."

A thought suddenly occurred to Antonia. "What about your son? Doesn't he have school?"

Nick nodded. "He's coming. We'll put him in school there and have him tutored."

Antonia's stomach dropped again. She noticed he had said *we*. All her fears suddenly converged. It was clear that this son of his had a mother, and this mother was still in the picture. It was silly that she hadn't looked it up on one of those celebrity websites, but it was as if she had blocked it from her mind. She truly had not wanted to know for sure if he was married. She knew the confirmation would upset her, and now it did, but she had been wrong—it would have been better to be prepared. Because right now it would be very difficult to pretend that she was not upset. Disappointment was running wild all over her face.

Antonia took a deep breath. "Well, I think it sounds like an adventure…"

"Yes, it will be. We'll do some traveling, and I think it's a great experience for a kid to see the rest of the world."

Antonia placed a frozen smile on her face. "Absolutely. Australia's on my bucket list."

"It's great."

Before the conversation became protracted, Antonia had to take action. She needed to get away from Nick now, or she would definitely start looking like even more of an idiot. She started touching her pocket and pulled out her cell phone, glancing at the screen.

"Oh my, so sorry, I have a call from the inn. I should dash."

"Okay, well it's been great walking…"

But Antonia cut him off. She didn't want to hear his pleasantries. She smiled and spoke into the receiver. He had no idea that no one was there.

"Hold on one second," she said before turning to Nick and giving him her biggest grin. "Bon voyage, have a terrific trip!"

And without waiting for his response, she walked away, forcing herself not to look back.

———————————

As soon as she pulled out of the parking lot, Antonia allowed herself to cry. Bitter tears came flooding out of her eyes, dripping down her cheeks, and pooling around her chin. The nose lost it as well, and she could feel it running. She was a hot mess. The obvious and traditional path that Antonia's mind would take would be recriminations and repetitions of "I told you so." But today she didn't want to criticize herself for having a crush, for suffering from disappointment and heartache. Because somewhere deep down, she was actually happy that she felt this way. However absurd it was, however much of a long shot, she was still glad that she had put her tiny little heart out there. She had cocooned it so well under all her layers of fat and fleece these past few years, insulating herself from any opportunity for romance. Every pound she gained was another layer to her shield, used to cover herself. It was as if she didn't want to be *seen* by men anymore. She couldn't bear it.

And yet she had inadvertently fallen for one of the biggest film stars on the planet. And they had formed a friendship. It was the stuff of movies, but then life was weirder than movies. Genevieve often told Antonia that she was too hard on herself, so here she was being indulgent. Now as she drove around the quiet streets of the estate section of East Hampton, she let the floodgates open. She heaved, she scream-cried, she blasted Alanis Morissette on her car stereo (fortunately, she kept the CD handy). She was shedding tears for everything, wallowing in self-pity. And then just like a tropical storm that suddenly stops pounding its raindrops, so did Antonia. She felt better. The clouds cleared. She turned her car around and headed toward Joseph's house.

28

JOSEPH WAS SEATED ON ONE OF THE PAIR OF MATCHING chintz armchairs in his living room with his feet resting on the accompanying ottoman. A blue blanket draped across his knees and was firmly tucked in at the sides. The fabric on the cushions was various shades of pink and blush and featured giant cabbage roses unfurling their petals across the linen tableau. Antonia sat across from Joseph on the slipcovered sofa, in front of the windows. The room was pleasant. As the house was very old, there was no distinction between the entrance hall and the living room; they folded into each other with a large banistered mahogany staircase running against the wall bisecting the formal area from the sun porch. A sizeable oval hook rug was beneath the seating area, and the walls were a cool blue. The furnishings had a woman's touch— consoles covered with an abundance of framed pictures; a corner cabinet displaying blue-and-white china; an antique quilt mounted on the wall; a vase of dried flowers on the coffee table—and yet there was a masculine vibe as well. The oil paintings were of horses and hunters, the books on the small shelf under the side window were historical fiction and biographies of war heroes, and the bar cart in the alcove beneath the staircase exclusively featured hard liquor like scotch and bourbon.

Joseph had been pleased to see Antonia, immediately

putting down his book on his lap and removing his glasses. It also appeared that his son William was even more pleased. As soon as Antonia arrived, the quite serious-looking William begged off to go to the grocery store and Joseph barely bid him adieu.

"How's it going?" asked Antonia.

Joseph shrugged. "I despise being at the mercy of others."

"I hear you. But he is your son."

"And I love him. However, he's very highly strung. He's always been that way. Margaret and I never knew where that came from. I suppose it was good, in a way. He was always the one to put pressure on himself and push. He was a straight A student, a champion soccer and tennis player, captain of the debate team. We never had a bit of trouble with him."

"Sounds like a dream child."

"He was, he still is, and I don't mean to complain. But he was always so rigid. I just wish he would loosen up a bit. Everything is very black and white with him. And he's headstrong as hell!"

"Gee, I wonder where he gets that from."

"Oh no, I'm nothing like him. There is no reasoning with him. He has decided that I am to move to New York and that is that. No more discussion. Last I checked it was a free country."

Antonia smiled. "He's probably very worried about you and wants to make sure you're okay. Sounds like he's the type of guy that hates being out of control. Humor him for a while. I don't mean move to New York, but just let him think he's in control until he leaves. Then you can do what you want."

Joseph smiled. "Very good advice, my dear."

"I can sometimes brainstorm helpful nuggets," said Antonia with a grin.

"Now, I am way behind on everything. Please tell me what is going on with all the murders. I was thinking a lot about it in the hospital and it was the one thing that gave me energy. That sounds absurd and callous, and my sympathies go to the victims, but I do like a good puzzler."

Once again, Antonia filled him in on everything, the big news being that Naomi had been brought in for questioning in regard to Biddy's murder. After downloading everything she knew, Antonia waited as Joseph digested the information.

He finally spoke. "You know, I think it's time to take some notes here. Do you mind handing me my yellow legal pad? It's on the desk by the phone over there."

Antonia retrieved the pad and handed it to Joseph along with a pen. She watched as he wrote a head-line in big bold letters—SUSPECTS IN GORDON'S MURDER—before she sat back down.

"You really think he was murdered?"

"Don't you?" asked Joseph. "And anyway, it doesn't matter. Even if it's just conjecture, let's look at it as a parlor game. We're playing Clue now. Barbie did it in the garden with the bee…"

"Sounds good. Will we discuss each suspect one by one?"

"I think that's the best idea. All of this information is leading us somewhere, and perhaps if we outline it, we will see the connections."

"Good idea. Let's write down each suspect and list their possible motive."

"As well as their accessibility," added Joseph.

"Whom should we start with?"

"Let's start with Barbie. Don't they say that eighty percent of the time the wife did it? I suppose in this case, the 'common-law wife'?"

"Right."

Antonia watched as Joseph wrote Barbie's names in large caps on the pad before underlining it. He looked up at her. "Motive?"

"I think we have to do bullet points on this one. She had the most motive. She had a boyfriend so she didn't need Gordon anymore."

"Then why not just dump him?" asked Joseph. "PS: I'll be playing devil's advocate to sharpen your theories. Actually, now I think it might be a pity William left. He is very good at cross-examination and making people second-guess themselves."

"You're terrible."

"Go on."

"Okay. Barbie had a boyfriend. She had moved on. But she didn't break up with Gordon because she wanted money. She believed he had written her into the will, and at the very least, legally, because she was his common-law wife, she would get something and be his beneficiary. Maybe she had dreams of moving her boyfriend into the inn with her. And that's why she was frantically searching for the will and was so upset she couldn't find it."

"Don't you think she would have kept herself a copy of this supposed will before she killed him? Some sort of insurance?"

"You would think that, but maybe she's stupid. Killers can be dumb."

"Good point. What else?"

"Well, maybe she was getting desperate. She had accused other people of stealing, but it looks like she was the one who had been stealing. And, with Soyla and Ronald both fired, maybe her jig was up and she was about to get caught. Biddy confiscated the box of alleged stolen goods at the L.V.I.S. with intent to return it to the inn, so maybe she implicated Barbie, and maybe Barbie killed her…"

Joseph cleared his throat. "Ahem. Let's get to Biddy's killer later. How do we think Barbie committed the crime?"

"Well, credit card receipts show that she was at South Fork Farm around the time of Gordon's death. Someone fitting her description inquired about purchasing a bee, and then stole a bee. Maybe."

Joseph glanced at Antonia over his glasses. "Seems flimsy. If she were planning on procuring a bee, why would she place herself at the farm stand by charging a purchase with her credit card? That's putting her directly in the line of fire, so to speak."

Antonia sighed with disappointment. "I agree. It's weak. It doesn't make sense why she would pay by credit card when she could have paid cash. And there are other ways to obtain a bee."

Joseph scribbled something down and circled it.

"What are you writing?" asked Antonia.

"I'm writing that the 'How' is unconvincing. As in the 'who, what, where, when, and how?' It's very obvious, and there are other elements to this plan that appear very well thought out. Therefore, this bee from the farm doesn't make sense."

"Maybe she didn't have a plan at that point. Maybe that part was impulsive. And she didn't think that we would put two and two together."

"It's possible. We did decide the killer may be dumb."

Antonia thought back to her conversation with the girl at the farm stand. "Possibly, but what does bother me is that she was so obvious. I mean, I know that's Barbie's character, she's a little flashy, but to hunt down the owner at their farmhouse? The stand wasn't even open, and then to lurk around and steal a bee. It's as if she *wanted* to be seen. Wouldn't she have at least tried to go a little incognito?"

Antonia and Joseph both paused to contemplate that. After some moments, Joseph restored his line of questioning.

"Do we have any other evidence of past criminal behavior on Barbie's part?"

"Only that she was a thief. Possibly."

"What about anything violent?"

Antonia shook her head. "I would love to say yes, but I don't think so. I know she and Gordon fought, but no one mentioned physical violence. There was no police report on her. I saw her when she was pretty much obliterated, and she wasn't throwing punches. So, no. Now, where are we? Everything fits and yet doesn't."

"Let's move on for now. How about the gardener?"

"Hector? Well, yes, he had some motive, but I don't really think he did it. I mean, he was angry that his wife was fired, and Gordon sounds like a really annoying boss, but why would he kill him?"

"I'm writing down, 'weak motive.' But as a gardener, he probably knew something about bees."

"True."

"And Gordon was found in the garden. By Hector."

"Yes. And Hector's wife, Soyla, worked at the South Fork Farm, which has the beehives. He had access," acknowledged Antonia. "But then so does anyone."

"You really don't like the gardener for this one."

"I know," conceded Antonia. "I just don't see it."

"All right. Who's next?"

"Ronald Meter. The manager. He was fired by Gordon and he keeps a beehive, which he at first hid from me, but then told me it was because he was ashamed he ate honey as he was diabetic."

"That's a bit bizarre."

"I agree. But the thing is, Ronald seemed angrier with

Barbie than he was at Gordon. He felt she manipulated him."

"Perhaps he set her up?" asked Joseph.

"It all seems very elaborate. Why bother? Everyone thought Gordon had a heart attack. If he wanted to set her up, he could have framed her. Maybe snuck into their apartment and poisoned the toothpaste…"

Suddenly Antonia shivered. What if that's what the intruder in her home had done? Had she brushed her teeth since then? Of course. But what if it was in her shampoo? Ugh, was she going to have to throw out all of her beauty products? There was no way! She would risk death. Antonia desperately wanted to tell Joseph about the break-in, but didn't want to upset him in his precarious state, so she bit her tongue. Joseph broke the silence.

"Maybe Ronald wanted it to be known that Gordon was stung?"

"The problem is that I only heard that tangentially. The Powerses were eating at the restaurant and their son was the first responder to the scene. If he hadn't mentioned it, it would have died with Gordon."

Joseph gazed off into the distance, deep in thought.

"What?" asked Antonia.

"I wonder if you should talk to him again."

"Ronald?"

"No, the Powerses' son."

"Matt?"

"Yes, Matt. Maybe you should find out a little more about what happened when he first arrived at the inn to try to revive Gordon. Who exactly was there? What transpired?"

"You know, that's not a bad idea. I'll try to follow up with him today."

"It might be worth it. Okay, let's move on to Naomi."

"I can't see her killing her own brother," Antonia confessed. "I mean, I know they fought, but at the end of the day, he's her *brother*."

"Wouldn't be the first. Reread the bible."

"I know, but while they had their differences, from all accounts their relationship was always up and down and very volatile. Frankly, it seems that's how all of Gordon's relationships were. He was bipolar. I just think that a sister, no matter how frustrated, would have empathy for that. Especially since they were apparently very close."

"Didn't you say that she was the one who brought up murder in the first place?" asked Joseph.

"Yes, she alluded to it, then denied it. But all the more reason to question why would she spotlight it if she had gotten away with it."

"True. But she wanted a quick burial, no autopsy, and she stood to inherit everything."

Joseph was right. There was something wrong with the whole scenario. "You have a point," Antonia conceded.

"Let's talk about the suspects in Biddy's murder," said Joseph, writing her name down in big letters and underlining it twice. "And let's go backward because it seems like the police already believe Naomi had a hand in it."

"The motive is clear. Naomi and Biddy hated each other. They had a long-standing feud. There was enough acrimony to cause Naomi to move across town. She bought the inn out from under Biddy and Biddy never forgave her. Naomi threw a dead raccoon on her doormat. And the most recent blowup was that Biddy wanted to become a bigwig at the Garden Club and Naomi was blocking her. Naomi did not want Biddy encroaching on her territory. I wonder actually, now that I think of it, why Naomi and Biddy hated each other so much? What was the genesis of their falling-out?"

"Good question," said Joseph. "Either love or money is my supposition. It's usually one or the other with women, no offense."

"I agree. I've heard nothing about another man, so it must be money. Or they were just totally competitive."

"And why do you think Naomi killed her now?"

"That I don't know," sighed Antonia. "Why now after all these years? And why would she kill her and then steal Biddy's enamel box and drop it in the backyard of the inn so that it could be found?"

"How do you know Naomi did that?"

"Because she was lurking around the backyard one day. Acting all suspicious. And then the next day we found the box."

"Who found it?"

"Hector…"

Joseph shifted in his chair. "Hector seems to be quite the expert in finding things in the backyard."

"Well, he is the gardener," Antonia pointed out.

"Yes, it's just interesting. I'm putting that down under his name."

"Okay, but I don't think it's unusual."

"Not unusual, maybe, but it needs to be noted."

"Okay."

"Anyone else have access to the backyard?"

"Everyone does, you know that. But I didn't see anyone else other than Naomi there..." suddenly Antonia trailed off. She remembered something.

"What is it?" prompted Joseph.

"I just remembered that Ronald Meter came to visit me at the inn the day before it was found. He came to apologize for his behavior, which in and of itself was a little strange, but then I toured him around. I left him in the sunroom and he said he was going to say hi to Hector in the backyard..."

Joseph raised his eyebrows. "The plot thickens."

"But again why?"

"Planting evidence, perhaps. We don't really know what goes on in a killer's mind. Did Ronald have any connection to Biddy?"

"He knew her through the L.V.I.S. And he didn't really react when I said she was dead, now that I think of it..."

"Do you think the box of things Biddy put together from the inn contained things that Ronald stole? We've been assuming it was Barbie but it could have been him."

"You're right. But say he did, was that really motive to go kill Biddy? She could tell the inn that he stole some things and tried to donate it to get a tax write-off? Why would she tell anyone at the inn? It was all done before my time, when Gordon was in charge, and she hated Gordon and Naomi. This could actually work to her advantage, because she could bad-mouth them to potential customers and guests."

"Indeed."

"What about Hector?"

"Hector is a frequent customer of the L.V.I.S. thrift shop. Their paths have crossed, but I'm not sure that matters. I don't see him having a strong motive to kill Biddy. Let's cross him off."

"If we are assuming the same person killed both Gordon and Biddy."

"Are you kidding? Of course we are assuming that! I'd hate to think there were two murderers out there!"

"Agreed. What about Barbie?"

"Again, maybe she dropped off the stolen items to the L.V.I.S. and Biddy called her out on it. Seems like a weak reason to kill Biddy. Although maybe it would unravel her whole plan."

"Possibly."

Joseph and Antonia became quiet and wallowed in their thoughts. Antonia felt dismay; they were no closer to an answer than when they had started. She sighed deeply.

"It all comes down to 'that B.' Who was the B in the note Gordon wrote, where he said 'that B is trying to kill me'? Barbie? Biddy? That 'beast,' Ronald Meter? That B could also be the word that rhymes with witch, maybe used to describe his sister? I don't know..."

"It will come. We just have to keep thinking, my dear. It will come to us, I'm sure of it," said Joseph.

"I really hope you're right."

Gosh, Antonia was really going to miss Joseph if he moved away.

29

IN ADDITION TO VOLUNTEERING AS AN EMT, MATT Powers worked as a physical therapist for East Hampton Sports Medicine (EHSP), which was located on a cul-de-sac near the airport, just off Route 114, which led to Sag Harbor. Whereas vast farmland sprawled on one side of the road, dense trees, intermittent houses, and small clusters of industrial one-story buildings muddled the other side. Antonia pulled into a designated parking spot in the lot in front of the large, windowless, aluminum-sided building. It looked more like a giant storage unit than a place of business or rehabilitation. The sign on the door alerted her that she was in the correct place and instructed her to enter rather than ring the bell. She pulled open the heavy steel door, a feat that took both hands and an extra dose of strength and nearly shocked all of her usually dormant muscles. She wondered if the door ever deterred patients suffering from arm or shoulder pain from proceeding with therapy at this location.

Immediately, the smell of feet, dried sweat, and the sickly sweet air freshener used to conceal their stench smacked Antonia in the face, invading her nostrils like a hostile marching band. She glanced around the room. The center was set up on one side like a gym, with assorted sports equipment including a treadmill, two elliptical machines, a StairMaster, and a metal rack that held a panoply of weights and barbells of varying sizes. There was a stack of blue mats against the wall next to a basket of weighted balls, and pegs that held different colored bands and jump ropes. The entire wall on the gym side was mirrored, and currently there was a rather obese, gray-haired woman in spandex and a white collared shirt staring intently at her own reflection as she attempted to lift a five-pound weight aloft with her right arm. She was assisted in this endeavor by a peppy ponytailed blond in a Juicy Couture sweat suit who was murmuring encouraging words and prattling on endlessly about how the old lady could "do it." To Antonia's left, there were six different stations divided by curtains, mostly ajar, featuring long tables that one would find in a massage parlor or doctor's office. A rather large man was lying facedown on one, moaning loudly, as Matt Powers leaned against his bent leg, pushing down his knee and attempting to get the man's foot as close to his buttock as possible.

Antonia felt a wave of nausea, which was always the case when she was confronted by anything that represented athletic endeavors. Gyms, in particular, made Antonia tense up because they reminded her of her P.E. classes in high school. Those were routinely the worst forty minutes of her day, exercises in humiliation and embarrassment. She was perhaps the least coordinated person she had ever met, and even jumping rope had been a display of ineptitude.

Matt glanced up at Antonia and she gave him a slight

wave. He acknowledged her with a nod. Just as she did so, the receptionist seated at the desk that Antonia hadn't even noticed, spoke.

"Can I help you?" she asked. The girl was young, probably very early twenties, with light brown hair and a rash of acne on her forehead. She wore a blue hooded sweatshirt, lots of eye shadow, and was chewing her gum so aggressively Antonia thought it might pop out of her mouth. A worn copy of *Fifty Shades of Grey* was propped open next to her computer with a purple bookmark peeking out. Beside it was a movie theater concession stand–sized bag of Skittles that was half full.

"Hi, I was wondering if Matt had a moment that I could ask him a question."

The girl glanced over at Matt. "He's with a patient now, but he should be done in about ten minutes. You want to wait?"

"Sure."

"You can sit there."

She pointed to two wooden chairs that were pressed closely together against the wall. On one, sat an older Asian man who was listening to something on his iPad. Antonia sat down next to him, taking care not to crowd him, which was difficult considering how tightly jammed together the chairs were. She stood and tried to move her chair away from his, but once she noticed that the chairs were entwined at the legs and the man would have to get up to facilitate extrication, she abandoned her effort. The man didn't seem to notice her; he was nodding along to whatever he was listening to, which Antonia couldn't make out despite their proximity. It sounded like someone speaking a foreign language, but she couldn't be sure.

Antonia reached over and took one of the dog-eared copies of *Self* magazine off the coffee table and began reading an article about the ten most fat-burning foods. She ingested the information the way one might read about someone else's trip to Antarctica. All very interesting but she knew she would never attempt it.

The clock slowly ticked by, and finally Matt's patient left and he approached Antonia.

"Hi, I hear you'd like to see me?"

"Yes, I was wondering if you had a minute?" asked Antonia.

"Sure, I got fifteen before my next patient. Let's go to my office."

Antonia walked through the gym, dodging the older lady who was now attempting to walk and lift weights at the same time, an exercise that was currently proving elusive and demoralizing despite her enthusiastic therapist who had kept up with chanting. "Yes, yes! You can do it!"

Matt closed the door to the office and motioned for Antonia to have a seat in the chair across from the desk. Antonia declined his offer of a vitaminwater, but watched as he bent down and pulled one out of the mini-fridge. She noticed how well he fit into his tight sports pants and form-fitting T-shirt, his muscles rippling through like a male model in an advertisement for grooming products.

Matt popped the cap and downed practically the

entire bottle before sitting in the leather swivel chair behind the desk.

"Sorry, it gets really hot in there. I get parched easily."

"No prob," said Antonia.

"So what can I do for you? Are you injured?"

"No, thankfully. I'm actually not here for that."

He nodded and she watched as his eyes scanned her body. Antonia felt a wave of self-consciousness and inadvertently wrapped herself further in her coat before rambling on.

"I'm here because I wanted to ask you again about when you found Gordon Haslett, the previous owner of the inn. I know you didn't want your mom to mention that you thought it was a bee sting, but I have reason to believe it was and I would just love to hear from you, blow-by-blow, what happened when you got there."

Matt's face didn't show any expression as he took another sip of his vitaminwater, finishing off the bottle before pitching it in the trash can next to him. He folded his hands neatly on the desk and leaned forward. Antonia noticed how perfectly his nails were filed and wondered if he was one of those guys who like to get manicures.

"You get that I have to be careful with what I say. I don't want any lawsuits for libel coming out of this."

"No, I totally understand," said Antonia. "This is just for my purposes only. Let's just say that I became a little freaked out with all the stories about past innkeepers dying under mysterious circumstances, so I'm doing everything I can to prevent that."

He nodded. "Why don't you just move?"

"Move?"

"Yes."

"Well, it's not that easy."

He gave her a solemn look. "I get it. You have to make choices."

Antonia's face didn't register the surprise with the direction this conversation was taking. Instead, she smiled sweetly. "Yes, choices. That's why I need your help. Could you tell me what happened?"

"Okay. Well, at approximately 4:17, I received a distress call coming from 241 Main Street, the location of the inn. I happened to be nearby at Hampton Market buying my lunch. I was able to immediately respond to the scene, within approximately four minutes."

"Wow, I hope you paid for your lunch," said Antonia, jokingly.

"I did," said Matt.

Antonia could tell that all attempts at lightheartedness or humor would fall on deaf ears, so she decided to keep those comments to a minimum.

"Right, sorry. Please continue. I won't interrupt."

"When I arrived, I found the victim lying on the ground in the backyard. He was unconscious, and his vitals were alarming…"

Antonia waited as Matt continued describing all of the technical features of Gordon's condition, as well as all of the efforts he made to attempt resuscitation. This part of the story was not the purpose of her visit, but she could tell that it gave Matt a certain amount of pleasure to pedantically delineate the procedural aspects of the case, so she patiently waited for him to finish. When he had done so, she proceeded with the line of questioning that interested her.

"Let's start with when you entered the inn. How did you know where to find Gordon?"

Matt furrowed his brow and didn't speak.

"Matt?"

"Yes, I just want to reconstruct the scene in my mind."

"Okay."

They sat in silence for what seemed like a minute while Matt reconstructed the scene in his mind. His forehead finally cleared, and he spoke at last.

"There was a woman at the front desk who told me he was out back."

"Can you describe this woman?"

Again, a lengthy pause. Antonia's patience was wearing thin.

"She had brown curly hair. Middle aged."

"Okay, you must mean Connie. Although she's only about thirty-eight, not really middle aged," laughed Antonia, attempting to lighten the mood.

Matt remained unmoved. "The average life expectancy for a woman in the United States is anywhere from 73.5 to 81 years of age. So technically she is middle-aged, assuming she lives to the median of the average."

"Really? I didn't know that. Good point but not fun to think about."

"As an EMT, I have to think about that all the time."

"Right, I'm sure. Okay, well, when you found Gordon in the yard, who was with him?"

Matt puckered his lips and squinted his eyes, again thinking hard. It was funny to Antonia because she knew that these looks must please the hoards of girls who found him attractive, and she could even hear them describing him as smart and impressive. But there was something so contrived and self-conscious about everything he did that put Antonia off. Sure, he was a nice guy, but a little too humorless. She found him to be nothing like his parents and again wondered if he was adopted.

"The gardener was there, the one who found him."

"Right. And how did he seem?"

"Upset. But not emotional."

"Guilty?"

"Why would he be guilty?" asked Matt.

"Sorry, wrong word choice. I meant concerned. Concerned that his boss died."

Matt shrugged. "I guess."

"Anyone else there?"

"Nope."

"So you only talked to the gardener and Connie the entire time you were there."

"Yes. But on the way out, when we were loading him into the wagon, his girlfriend showed up."

"His girlfriend was there?" asked Antonia, perking up.

He nodded. "Yes."

"Barbie?"

"I don't know that I ever heard her name."

"Are you sure it was his girlfriend?"

"I mean, I used to see them together all the time. I always assumed it was his girlfriend."

Antonia nodded. "And how was she reacting?"

He tilted his head as if it helped him to recall the scene. "I think kind of in shock, because she was keeping it together. She wasn't crying or anything. She just kept asking me if I thought he would make it, and what did I think happened."

Antonia perked up. "Did it sound like she was worried he wouldn't make it? Wait, I know that sounds absurd. I'm sure she was. I just mean, was she acting suspiciously?"

Again a long pause while Matt thought. "I don't think so, but then I wasn't focused on her. I did mention that I thought it was a bee sting…"

Antonia lunged forward to the edge of her chair. "And what did she say?"

"You know, this I remember. She said, 'No, no, no.' Like really strong, as if I didn't know what I was talking about. She said it was December and there were no bees out in the garden. Then my colleague said, 'Let's roll,' so we left. She didn't come with us. En route we performed…"

His mouth kept moving but Antonia was no longer listening. So Barbie had wanted to shoot down the bee theory from the get-go. Very interesting.

———————————

When Antonia walked out to the parking lot, she noticed that a thick layer of clouds had spread out against the sky, erasing any evidence of the sun. It had become a gray day that looked as if it would melt into a gloomy night, and the air was chilly and ripe with moisture and dampness. Antonia got in her car and turned it on to get the heat going. She put down Matt's business card on the seat next to her (*Matthew Powers: Physical Therapy Expert, EMT, CPR Instruction, Notary, Life Coach, Motivational Speaker*, it read) and dialed her cell phone.

Antonia's first choice would be to visit Barbie in person and confront her with this recent revelation, but she didn't know where she lived or even how to attain her address. She was certain that Barbie was too angry with her to agree to meet in person, so a phone call was her only option. Antonia scrolled through her phone for Barbie's contact info, which Barbie had given to her when they were on friendlier terms when Antonia first purchased the inn.

"Hello?"

"Barbie?"

"Yes?"

"Hi, it's Antonia Bingham. Please don't hang up," she added quickly.

There was silence on the other side and Antonia wasn't sure Barbie had adhered to her request.

"Hello?" asked Antonia again.

"Yeah, I'm here. What do you want?"

Antonia was uncertain how to phrase it. If she were

accusatory or hostile, Barbie would just hang up. She had to make up something.

"I had a question for you. It's of a delicate nature, but it's important."

Antonia waited. Barbie didn't respond.

"Okay?" asked Antonia.

"Look, I don't have all day. I gotta get to work. Just spit it out," she commanded.

"Okay, when you found Gordon in the backyard, after his heart attack…"

"I didn't find Gordon," she interrupted.

"Right. I mean, I know Hector found him, but then when you came out to see him…"

"What are you talking about? I wasn't there."

"What do you mean?"

"I wasn't at the inn that day. I had…a meeting elsewhere."

Antonia was confused. "But Matt, the EMT worker, said you were there."

"He was mistaken. I wasn't there."

"Are you sure?"

"Are you friggin' kidding me? I told you I wasn't there. Now is that all? 'Cause I have to go."

"Yes, that's all."

After her call Antonia exited her car again and went back inside the Physical Therapy center to confirm with Matt. He was working with a new patient but Antonia strode past the receptionist and approached him. He was massaging his female patient's thigh but answered Antonia's question.

"Sorry to bother you again, but I just want to confirm with you one last time. I just spoke to Gordon's girlfriend and she says she wasn't there when he collapsed, or any time after that. Are you sure you saw her?"

Matt shrugged, as his fingers kept kneading the woman's muscle. "Some woman was there. I know I saw her at the inn a bunch of times. I remember she was at the New Year's Eve party I went to one year."

Antonia was utterly confused when she drove back to the inn. It wasn't until she pulled back into the parking lot that something dawned on her. Naomi had also been at the New Year's Eve party. Naomi was often seen with her brother. It was probably Naomi at Gordon's side when he died. And it was now possible once again that Naomi had killed him.

30

WHEN ANTONIA ENTERED THE INN, SHE DISCOVERED that all hell had broken loose. Both Glen and Lucy were waiting outside of her office, both vying to be the first to get her attention. They immediately spoke in unison, bombarding her with their urgent news. Antonia could only decipher the words *accident, hospital, ghost,* and *haunted* before she threw the card down on her desk and threw up her hands in surrender.

"What's going on?"

Again, they began to speak at the same time, and she silenced them.

"Lucy, you first."

Glen sniffed that he was not chosen and instantly began pouting, while Lucy began her story. Antonia noticed that the front of Lucy's beige dress was covered in a dark stain, almost the color of Hawaiian Punch.

"About an hour ago, I came to your office to go over some of the latest bills. I knocked on the door, of course, and I thought I heard you say to come in. When I open the door an entire bucket of red dye fell on top of me! Someone had propped it to the door so that when I opened it, it spilled. Nearly missed bonking me on the head!"

"Are you okay?"

"I'm fine, but my dress is destroyed."

"I'm so sorry."

"It's not your fault," said Lucy tersely. "Obviously, you didn't rig your own door."

"Do we know who did?" asked Antonia.

Lucy shook her head. "No. Connie didn't see anyone come in, and neither did the cleaners."

"And no one fessed up? Thought it was a fun prank?"

"No," said Lucy. "But I think—"

Glen interrupted her. "Can I talk now? My situation is freakin' *urgent*."

Lucy bristled and folded her arms with impatience. She refused to look at Glen while he spoke, instead focusing her eyes on Antonia's desk in an act of defiance as if to convey that whatever Glen had to say was of little meaning to her.

Glen's eyes moved from Lucy to Antonia with importance. He lifted his chin as if he was about to recite a church eulogy. "Kendra is in the *hospital*," he announced dramatically. He paused to let the words sink in, before continuing. "The kitchen is a serious *disaster*. We have a full house booked tonight, and it's lookin' like nothing is going to get done."

He folded his arms and raised his eyebrow.

"What happened to Kendra?" asked Antonia.

"It went down like this: she went in the changing area to put on an apron, but she couldn't find any. She came back and started complaining that they were still missing. I admit at this point I just thought she was being a prima donna, especially when I found Rosita, who said she had put them all there. Kendra went back *again* and said there were none. So then we *all* went and looked, and sure as sugar she was right. There weren't any. Rosita started opening the lockers, like, where could they be? Then we all pitched in, and when Kendra opened your locker, this giant hammer smashed her on the head."

"What? A *hammer*? Is she okay?"

"There was a lot of blood," said Glen, waiting for the words to sink in.

"Is she going to be okay?"

"I had Hector take her to the emergency room in Southampton. She's gonna be laid up for the night, but I think she'll be okay. But the big news is, someone is setting booby traps here at the inn. And I gotta say, I think they're trying to take *you* down."

Both Lucy and Glen stared at Antonia as she grasped what they were saying. Someone was playing mischief… or someone was playing murder. It was not good. No, not good at all.

"And we have no idea in either case who did it?"

They shook their heads. "No one saw anything," said Lucy.

"Let's call a spade a spade," said Glen. "Either someone is messing with you, or the joint is haunted."

"Haunted?" asked Antonia.

Glen shrugged. "Those are your two options. Take 'em or leave 'em."

"There must be a third." Antonia sighed. "What do you think, Lucy?"

Lucy's answer surprised her. "I don't usually subscribe to the belief that paranormal activity exists but... all these things are very, very strange. And with the coincidence of Biddy dying this week...maybe there's something to it."

"I didn't expect that from you."

"Well, regardless of what it is, we have decisions to make. Shall we cancel dinner service? I think we also need to consider shutting down the inn."

"Shut down the inn? Right now? Are you crazy?" asked Antonia.

"We can't do that..." agreed Glen.

"We need to seriously consider it," said Lucy sternly. "Think about the liability. It would cost the inn a ton of money if more of these things happened. What if a customer got hurt? Then we're to blame."

Antonia sighed deeply. Her head was spinning; it was all too much to absorb.

"No, we're not shutting down anything. Give me ten minutes to check my messages in my office then I'm heading to the kitchen STAT. Marty and I will get it under control. Dinner is on."

"But what about all these...accidents? What if they are some kind of warning?" asked Lucy.

Antonia grimaced, before nodding authoritatively. "Then let them warn me. I'm not going anywhere. And I have Chubb insurance."

After they left, Antonia eyed the bills that Lucy had left for her on her desk, and did a quick flip through. There were the usual utility bills, which honestly seemed particularly high, and vendors' bills, which appeared to be growing with every installment. Wasn't Marty supposed to be haggling with those guys? It clearly wasn't working. The good news was a notice from the Town of East Hampton regarding her building inspection, which stated the inspector didn't think she had any violations. She smiled when she read the signature at the bottom, confirming it. At least something was going her way.

Antonia had several voicemails, including one from a travel agent who wanted to book three rooms at the inn for the entire week of Christmas, which pleased Antonia to no end, and another from a woman inquiring about room rates for Martin Luther King Jr. weekend. A British man named Jonathan had called back to confirm that she had received his resume, which she had not, so she made note of that. There was a message from some bank that was clearly left in error, and one from the vendor who was still trying to entice Antonia into buying his beer. The last and most important message was from Larry Lipper, which she listened to twice.

"Hi, Bingham, it's me, making your day yet again. I found out how they nailed Naomi. Anonymous call to the police. Apparently, that missing carbon monoxide detector was found in Naomi's neighbor's garbage bin. Got that? Cops have been all over. They're fine-tuning the case against Naomi. She's going down for this."

Antonia leaned back in her chair and glanced out the window. Her mind drifted to the picture of Naomi standing in the backyard of the inn. She had been following a cardinal, she said. She was watching birds. Something clicked in Antonia's brain.

31

Sunday

CLARITY STRIKES AT THE MOST PECULIAR TIMES, BUT when it does, ah, the joy it brings. It's like a sudden pin-prick in the brain that releases the juice of revelation that washes over the entire body. It's a cleansing bath of lucidity that transports the newly sober recipient to an alternate level of wisdom. It's the moment that you reprimand yourself for not seeing it earlier, but also experience the full euphoria at having reached your destination at last.

Saturday night had been challenging, frantic and exhausting for Antonia, but she and Marty, with the help of Glen, Liz, and Soyla (whom she had called in for reinforcement and who had performed beautifully) had pulled it off. Antonia pushed aside all thoughts of murder and ghosts and poured every bit of passion she had into the kitchen, producing meal after meal and putting her whole self into it. She sustained this momentum from the second she entered the kitchen until she helped shut down the restaurant at eleven thirty. The evening was busy, not without flaws, but overall a success. The rib eye with cauliflower gratin and caramelized carrots as well as the fettuccine with lamb ragout sold particularly well.

Afterward, Antonia had carefully entered her apartment, slowly opening the door to ascertain if there were any hammers or buckets of ink waiting to clock her. When she was certain that the coast was clear, she congratulated herself on having changed her locks. She was pretty sure that's why she was still okay. Despite that fact, she still crept around her apartment in the dark; slyly checking under every piece of furniture and behind every door and curtain to make sure that nothing awaited her. She basically did a full cavity search of her apartment, which took about ten minutes, before she allowed herself to collapse into bed and sink into slumber.

She slept deeply but had strange dreams. Flashes of everything and everyone that she had come into contact with over the past week appeared in odd places. But what was even more bizarre was that the secondary players seemed to take prominence in her sleep. Gordon and Biddy hovered in the background of her mind, limiting themselves to the shadows, but random people like the girl from the farm stand, and Biddy's neighbor, Sharon Getz, and the Winslows—the couple who had just stayed at the inn—were center stage. Antonia's dreams were like a kaleidoscope where she would turn her head and everything and everyone in her mind would shake out in a different way, tumbling forward in different directions, but all somehow inextricably linked.

Antonia woke rested, despite the chaos of her dreams. She preceded her alarm, and rose to find a glint of light streaming through her shades, curling its way around the room. The day would be bright and sunny. A soft breeze slid through the open window, ripe with freshness and the salty lick of the ocean. Birds were chirping, their song an optimistic soundtrack to the morning. The day held promise. (The only bummer was that she wished she could go see Nick Darrow at the beach, but he would definitely be gone by now.) And as soon as Antonia sat up in bed, she experienced the moment of clarity that had eluded her.

"Of course," she said aloud, running her burgeoning theory through her mind. "It all makes sense."

She knew what she had to do. She gently unfolded herself from her thick comforter and padded across the carpet to her bathroom to wash her face. With each splash of cool water that hit her cheeks, her plan began to form. After quickly dressing, she went to the kitchen and began mixing scones and muffins, pouring in streams of chocolate chips and raisins depending on which baked item she was making. With each swirl of her wooden spoon, her plan further took shape. After closing the oven door and wiping her hands on her apron, she walked out into the cloudless day and across the bouncy green lawn to the back corner of the yard. She used her foot to slide through the leaves until her toe knocked into a rock. She had found what she was looking for.

At nine o'clock, Antonia made her phone calls. A few didn't answer, and she assumed they were at church or still sleeping, but she left enticing messages that would ensure they did as she instructed. The rest of the day was spent planning. Joseph came over in the afternoon to help her. There were still a few kinks but they both agreed that the plan could work.

"Humans are weak," Joseph had reminded her. "They can be broken."

Antonia had to hope that was true. It was the only way she could prove that Gordon Haslett and Biddy Robertson were murdered and that she had solved the crimes.

―――――――――――

"What's all this?" asked Lucy.

She glanced at the round table that Antonia had erected in the parlor and covered with a blue-and-white floral tablecloth that was hemmed with a green fringe. Atop the cloth, matching napkins were folded in a pile next to a box of antique silverware—the heavy kind, actual silver and not plated—and a stack of blue-and-white Herend china dinner plates. The centerpiece was a discreet low bowl of chrysanthemums and white hydrangeas.

"I'm setting the table," said Antonia. "You're just in time, do you mind helping?"

"Of course not," said Lucy, still wearing a quizzical look on her face. "But why are we doing it in here?"

Antonia smiled conspiratorially. She glanced around the room to make sure no one was lurking around to overhear. The room was quiet and still, an almost foreboding hush hanging over it.

"I'm sort of freaking out a bit, so I'm glad you're here."

"What's going on?" asked Lucy with concern. "Did something else happen?"

"No, it's not that." Antonia leaned in. "I'm shutting down the parlor for the evening. Regular dinner service will take place in the dining room as usual, but I'm having a special dinner party in here tonight. I've invited all of the suspects in Gordon and Biddy's murder over to dinner. I think I have an idea of who did it, I mean, I'm pretty sure, and I think if I get them all here the truth will come out."

Lucy's eyebrows shot up. "Who do you think did it?"

Antonia smiled. "I don't want to say yet. Sorry, it's just that I think the element of surprise will be a real shock and I want to make sure I keep that effect. Hey, do you want to stay? I think it will be very entertaining."

"Do I want to stay? Of course I do," said Lucy eagerly. "I was supposed to go to an independent film in Sag Harbor, but I'll cancel that. This seems way more interesting."

"Great. Actually, I think it will be good to have more people rather than less, especially in case the accused gets aggressive."

Lucy looked worried. "Why haven't you called the police? I mean, what if this murderer goes crazy and decides to attack one of us? I'm not sure that's safe."

"I did think about that, but that may tip the murderer off. I need to make it look like this is a casual dinner to a certain extent. A parlor game, if you will."

"Why don't you just go to the police directly?"

questioned Lucy. "Wouldn't that make more sense? I'm sure this will be more entertaining, but if you know for certain, perhaps it's best to put it into the hands of the professionals."

"I would, but I'm waiting on one more thing… I sort of need it to prove the case."

"What's that?"

Antonia pulled out two silver candelabras from the hutch on the side wall and placed them on the table.

"You'll see! Patience, Lucy, patience. And trust me, it will be worth the wait."

Lucy gave her a skeptical look and shook her head. "Okay…"

An informal white-skirted bar had been set up at one end of the parlor, and a young, dark-haired waiter was standing behind, slicing lemons and limes. A wide array of alcohol was offered this evening, everything from Stolichnaya vodka to Maker's Mark to Baileys. Several bottles of California cabernet had been uncorked as well as a nice 2006 Italian pinot grigio. An open bottle of champagne was chilling in the ice bucket on the edge of the bar.

Antonia decided not to use the overhead lights and instead chose "mood lighting." She illuminated several lamps on the side tables and scattered dozens of candles around the room. She wanted the parlor to appear cozier and more intimate than usual. A fire was already crackling in the fireplace and a young waiter had been assigned the task of feeding it logs for the entire evening. Ambience, Antonia felt, was the key.

Joseph had been the first to arrive after a quick jaunt home to change for dinner. He had on a crisp white shirt and a blue bow tie, and his eyes were twinkling with expectation. Antonia had already plied him with a sherry, and she stood next to him awaiting the assemblage of invited guests. They were both experiencing nervous anticipation coupled with healthy doses of adrenaline. Antonia was twisting her pearl stud earring distractedly, as she always did when she was tense. Her mother had always tried to get her to stop fidgeting when she was uncomfortable, but it had been a futile endeavor. She smoothed down her suede camel skirt and flattened the edges of her black turtleneck. When she ran out of items to perfect on her own body, she had to restrain herself from adjusting Joseph's tie. A passing waiter offered her a breadstick and she took it eagerly, grateful to munch on something crunchy to calm her nerves.

Lucy hadn't gone home to change and was still wearing a blue dress with a white Peter Pan color. She had spent the past few hours by Antonia's side, assisting her in setting up the entire room and overseeing the waitstaff. She had disdainfully removed Antonia's handwritten sign that had indicated that the parlor would be closed for a private event and absconded to her office to print out a neater version, which she had accurately taped on the door in alignment with the wood paneling. She was currently placing coasters on all of the surfaces so that there would be no watermarks left on the antiques from sweating glasses.

"Who do you think will be first?" Antonia inquired.

"I think the guilty party will arrive first," said Joseph with confidence. "How could they contain themselves?"

"Touché," agreed Antonia with a sly grin. "A very tense moment for the killer."

Joseph smiled back.

Suddenly the door slid open and Ronald Meter strode into the parlor. His eyes flickered around the room quickly, his unease apparent. Once he settled on Antonia, he strode toward her slowly, his gait awkward. Faint dots of perspiration were breaking out across his forehead like a teenager suffering from an acne blowout. He had worn a corduroy jacket and a plaid tie for the occasion. Once again, his pants appeared to be about three sizes too large and were constrained by the leather belt that had been working overtime since his weight loss.

"Antonia, so nice of you to have me," he said in a halting tone as if he was unsure if that was the truth.

Antonia clasped his hands. "I'm very grateful you came. Do you know Joseph Fowler?"

Ronald glanced down at Joseph quizzically before remembering his manners and smiling. "I don't believe I do. Nice to meet you."

"Likewise."

"Joseph here pointed out that perhaps my invitation could have been misinterpreted…"

"I'll admit it was sort of a head-scratcher. I'm happy to be at the dinner but it did feel like a command performance."

"I think 'performance' is the key word," said Antonia. "And you won't be disappointed."

Ronald gave her a quizzical look before shaking his head slowly. "I'm not quite sure what this is all about."

"You'll find out in due time."

"You're being terribly cryptic. Shall I be nervous here?" asked Ronald, his voice breaking slightly.

Antonia patted him on the shoulder. "Of course not, Ronald. What do you have to be nervous about?"

They locked eyes and Antonia deciphered the tiniest hint of fear in his. He paused but then broke into a wide grin. "Why, nothing of course."

"Wonderful. Why don't you get a drink at the bar? We have sodas and mineral water."

"Thank you."

Ronald glanced over at the bar. He appeared to be about to say something but instead set off toward it. When he was out of earshot, Joseph spoke.

"He's uneasy."

"I'll say."

"How did you lure him here?"

"Told him that we had some things to discuss before he left town and he shouldn't leave without finding them out."

"You didn't leave him much choice."

"That was the point." Antonia took a small sip from the champagne flute that she had picked up from another passing waiter. She was tempted to drink more but knew she had to be completely sober in order to pull this off.

"I must say, I thought Barbie would be first," confessed Joseph.

"I actually staggered the times. I knew if Barbie arrived early and realized that I lured her under false pretenses she would stomp out of here. So I told her to come at seven thirty. I want to make sure everyone else is in place so that her curiosity overrides her anger."

"Very savvy."

Hector and Soyla entered the parlor. It was clear to Antonia that they were wearing their "Sunday best"—for Hector, that was a coat and tie, and for Soyla, a forest-green dress. Antonia had never seen Hector in anything but his work clothes and he cleaned up very nicely. His hair was neatly brushed, parted on the side, and held in place with hair gel. Soyla wore her hair down and curled at the ends. Both looked very ill at ease, and apprehensively glanced around the parlor. Antonia strode up to them.

"Hector, Soyla, thanks so much for coming."

"Yes, miss. You sure you don't want us to help you?" asked Hector. Soyla clung to his arm, her eyes darting around the room.

"I'm sure. I want you both to go get a glass of wine or champagne and get comfortable. It may be a long evening for you."

"Thank you," they agreed.

"You were a wonderful help last night," said Antonia to Soyla, warmly putting her hand over Soyla's. "Thank you. I could not have done dinner service without you."

Soyla looked down with embarrassment. "Thank you for the opportunity."

"Your wife is a natural," Antonia told Hector. "She'll be running the place before I know it."

"Thank you," said Hector, beaming.

"Now go make yourselves comfortable," admonished Antonia.

They scurried to the bar. Antonia eyed them as they placed a drink order. She watched the waiter pour them each a Coca-Cola, which they clasped with paper napkins before heading to the farthest corner of the room to huddle in conversation. Ronald floated over to them. They smiled at him with relief and began a conversation. Antonia walked back to Joseph.

"It's all going beautifully, my dear."

"So far so good."

Naomi Haslett was next. She entered suspiciously, a scowl on her face and her dark bangs cut shorter than usual, slashing her forehead in half. Instead of her usual white sneakers, she wore brown boots over her black pants and a black blouse on top. She marched straight toward Antonia.

"What is all this?"

"Hello, Naomi, how are you?"

"Cut it, Antonia. I want to know what this so-called party is all about? Why the mysterious invitation?"

"I thought you might enjoy a dinner at the inn."

Naomi frowned. "Don't jerk me around."

"Naomi, I realize you are under a tremendous amount of stress right now because of everything with Biddy."

"That's none of your business."

"I agree," concurred Antonia. "But Gordon's murder is my business."

Naomi's eyes shrunk into slits. "This again?"

"We're not done, Naomi. It's time for the guilty to be held accountable."

Naomi rolled her eyes. "And I suppose you have appointed yourself the person to do this?"

Antonia smiled. "It has to be me. *I'm* the innkeeper."

They stared at each other for what seemed like minutes. Finally, Naomi broke her gaze and glanced around the room. "If you're looking for who killed Gordon, how come Barbie's not here?"

"Oh, she'll be here."

Naomi scoffed. "I think I'm going to need a drink."

When Naomi had a glass of vodka firmly in her hand, she studied the other guests with disdain while punching the lime in her drink with a stirrer. Naomi's very being emitted hostility, her mouth curled into a permanent scowl. Antonia wondered if she had always been unhappy or if something had transpired in her life to render her miserable.

Joseph raised an eyebrow at Antonia. "She's tough."

"You think?"

Sylvia and Len Powers entered the parlor excitedly,

bursting with energy and enthusiasm and wearing giant smiles on their faces. Antonia went over to greet them.

"Welcome!"

"Thank you for having us, Antonia. This is such a treat. A private party! We are so excited," boomed Sylvia.

Antonia could smell her heavy perfume and noticed that she had taken particular care in her outfit. She wore a formal pale-pink silk dress with a lace bodice, and had pearls draped around her throat.

"Twice in a month to dine at the inn, very special," agreed Len.

"I'm so glad you could come," said Antonia. She glanced behind them. "How about Matt?"

"Oh, he apologizes, Antonia; he is so upset to miss it. But he got called into work. Apparently, there's a six-alarm fire in Quogue and they needed extra hands. He'll try and make it, of course, but it isn't looking good."

Antonia was momentarily deflated. She had wanted Matt there to help with her plan. Now she would have to bluff her way through some elements of her theory. *Oh well*, she told herself. Nothing she could do about it.

"Let's hope he can make it. But in the meantime, why don't you two get yourselves a drink? Also, we have some hors d'oeuvres set up on a table over there and no one is touching them. I'm about to take it personally. Please help yourself."

"Oh, honey, you don't have to say it twice! We are there in a flash."

Antonia watched as they made their way first to the

buffet, segueing past the bar. It was nice to have at least
some people who were more focused on the food than
the chain of events that were about to transpire. She
watched as they selected small plates and filled them
with glazed mini-meatballs, plump figs wrapped in pro-
sciutto, and seared pepper-crusted tuna skewers.

Suddenly, Antonia felt someone approach her from
behind and wrap his arms around her. The stranger's
hands darted under her armpits and as Antonia gasped,
they tickled her furiously. Her heart began pounding.
She shrieked and whipped around.

"Larry!"

"Got ya!" he giggled mirthfully. He bent over, erupt-
ing in laughter. "You should have seen your face! God,
priceless."

Antonia's blood began to boil. She looked around the
room. Her shriek had unnerved everyone and they all
stood staring at her, their mouths agape.

"Sorry, everyone. Larry startled me."

"She loved it!" he said with confidence.

They continued to stare uneasily, before slowly returning to what they had been doing before. Len and Sylvia
had their mouths full of food and were hovering over their
plates, additional bites already between their fingers ready
to be hoisted once they had swallowed what was in their
mouths. Naomi had taken another lime from the bar and
was squeezing it carefully into her drink. Ronald was sitting
alone on the window seat, staring outside and anxiously

twisting the signet ring he wore on his right hand. Hector and Soyla were huddled in the corner like hunted animals, talking quietly, their eyes darting around the room defensively. Lucy was giving a waiter instruction about dinner service. Joseph was tentatively watching Antonia.

"Larry, don't do that again. It's really inappropriate," warned Antonia.

"Come on, you love it."

"I *do not* love it." Blood started to rise to Antonia's pale cheeks and she realized she had to relax. No use getting worked up. She needed to save her energy for later. "Let's just drop it. Do you have everything?"

"Of course I do, hot stuff. For you, anything."

"Great, thank you."

"Are you really certain you're going to get the fireworks you want? I mean, I've been in the crime biz a long time. Remember, Nicky Darrow modeled his character after me. It's not easy to solve a crime."

"We'll manage, I'm fairly sure."

"All right. But I'm heading over to the bar. I'm just here for the booze." He gave the room one more glance. "Any hotties here?"

"Larry, really."

"Yeah, I didn't think so. But if any come, I've got dibs on sitting next to them."

He swaggered away.

Joseph rolled his scooter up to Antonia. "Odious man," said Joseph simply. "I don't like him one bit."

Antonia laughed. "I agree. He's so annoying. Not to mention juvenile."

"Let's just hope he can assist us. Aha, look who has arrived."

Barbie stood on the threshold of the door, a hostile and confounded expression on her face. Her distaste was palpable, and when she locked eyes with Antonia, she immediately stormed toward her. Antonia's gaze couldn't help but be drawn to her ample bosom, which was attempting to jiggle its way out of Barbie's tight shirt.

"What the hell is this?" she demanded.

"This is a party, Barbie. Have a drink, dinner will be solved shortly. I mean served."

Barbie peered around the room, taking in each of the other guests with her eyes. "Unbelievable. You are one piece of work, Antonia."

"What do you mean?"

"Don't play that innocent game with me. You told me you found the missing will. Was that all a lie to get me here?"

"Everything will be explained, Barbie…"

"Oh, no you don't. I can't believe I fell for it! Do you or don't you have the will?"

Antonia took a deep breath. She knew Barbie was going to be the toughest guest to convince to stay. And the most important. "Barbie, I don't have it at this moment…"

"I'm out of here," said Barbie.

She turned and began thundering toward the door. Antonia trotted after her.

"Please, Barbie. It will be worth your time to stay."

Barbie scoffed. "Yeah, right."

"Trust me," said Antonia with desperation.

Barbie stopped abruptly and turned around. Antonia practically walked right into her.

"Trust you? Tell me why I should trust you."

Antonia's mind raced. "Didn't you care about Gordon at all?"

"What's that got to do with it?"

"Well, tonight all of the outstanding events surrounding his death will be answered."

"I think we all know how Gordon died."

"True, true. But remember, you say you were supposed to inherit everything. What if we can prove that is true?"

"If you can prove that, tell me now."

An elderly couple entered the front door, bringing a gust of wind with them. Antonia paused to greet them and directed them toward the dining room. Connie was at her post and Antonia could tell she was eavesdropping, even though she kept her eyes averted and was pretending to write something down in the message book. The grandfather clock in the front hall ticked softly and the din from the dining room was floating down the hall.

Antonia was stalling. She had to keep Barbie there. She spoke in a hushed tone. "I can't right now, but—"

Barbie rolled her eyes. "Geez, this gets better and better. I am out of here."

Barbie put her hand on the front door knob and slowly pulled it open. Antonia pressed against it and slammed it shut.

"What the—?" asked Barbie.

"You're not leaving," said Antonia sternly.

"Oh really?"

"If you leave now, you will be arrested and thrown in prison. You should stay and at least try and defend yourself."

Barbie glared at Antonia, who in turn glared back.

"You're bluffing," she said finally.

"Am I?" asked Antonia. "When you walk back into that parlor, and you will, look at every waiter in the room. Every single one of them is an undercover officer, carrying a concealed weapon. If you leave now, they'll just come and arrest you. So why not listen to what I have to say, have a wonderful dinner, and give yourself a chance to explain your side of the story."

Barbie hesitated. It was all Antonia needed. She turned and began walking back toward the parlor.

"Let's go," she commanded. Barbie followed.

Antonia glanced at the expectant faces when she entered the parlor. She was met with a full range of expressions ranging from worried to angry to excited.

"Ladies and gentlemen, dinner is served."

32

THE GUESTS WERE JUST SETTLING INTO THEIR CHAIRS when an attractive young woman in her early twenties appeared on the threshold of the door. She wore a diaphanous dress that didn't leave much to the imagination. She scanned the crowd indifferently, her eyes dancing from one person to the next without any sense of recognition or emotion. Antonia immediately rushed over to her and began whispering something. The girl nodded in concurrence before following Antonia to the table.

"I'm not sure if you all know Jennifer, but she will be dining with us tonight," announced Antonia.

"She sits next to me," said Larry, rising and pulling out the empty chair next to him. "Hi, I'm Larry."

Lucy gave Antonia a quizzical look, but she just smiled in return. There were sure to be surprises tonight. Even Joseph didn't know everything. There were some murmured hellos to Jennifer, but mostly curious looks as she slid into a seat between Larry and Antonia. Larry immediately began bending her ear, explaining that he was a hotshot reporter for the *East Hampton Star* and that Nick Darrow was a personal fan who had followed him around for a week to understand the ins and outs of the newspaper industry.

Close up, Jennifer was less pretty than she had appeared at a distance. Her long thin hair was very blond, but overly processed, which rendered the ends brittle and uneven, as if they died on her shoulders and dissolved into a mass of split ends. She had blue eyes and clear skin but her face was slightly puckered as if she had just eaten something sour, and her dainty features were all slightly smashed together in the center of her face. She overcompensated for her small eyes by applying ample makeup in bright blues and pinks, which cheapened her slightly. But she was thin, had youth on her side, and sizeable cleavage.

"Hey, I know you," said Naomi, who had carefully watched Jennifer's progression into the room. She was across the table, unfolding her napkin onto her lap.

Jennifer turned from Larry and gave her a wan smile. "Nice to see you."

Naomi appeared to be about to say something but then stopped herself. Her eyes remained on Jennifer's face and she squinted slightly, before looking down. Antonia and Joseph exchanged glances.

A waiter came and began pouring the water, followed by another waiter who was offering white or red wine. Antonia watched as Barbie studied each waiter suspiciously, her eyes tracing their dinner jackets for any bulging weapons.

"Well, this is just so nice," prattled Sylvia. "I am so happy to be here tonight. Len and I were thrilled to receive an invitation. What is your connection to Antonia?"

She had addressed Hector, who was seated to her right. His look was pained.

"I work here at the inn," he replied.

"Oh, how wonderful! And what is it you do?"

"I'm the gardener."

"I love flowers!" and with that, Sylvia was off on a tangent listing her favorite blooms, describing her beloved rosebushes, and asking questions to Hector which she did not pause to wait for the responses to. Antonia congratulated herself on the seating arrangement. Sylvia would do all the talking, which she adored, and Hector wouldn't have to say a word, which she was certain was preferable to him. Ronald also couldn't resist conversing about horticulture, so he chimed in on the conversation, which appeared to momentarily relax him.

The waiters returned with trays that they rested on the nearby stands. After removing the silver lids, they carefully placed bowls in front of each diner.

"What's this?" asked Naomi with disdain.

She was staring at the small portion of fricassee of mushrooms and chives in front of her.

"It's butternut squash soup," replied Antonia.

"Where's the soup?" sniffed Naomi.

"It's here, Madam," said a waiter. He poured a fragrant stream of creamy butternut squash puree on top of the mushrooms out of a small silver pitcher.

"How wonderful!" said Sylvia, clapping her hands together.

"Hmm, I smell truffle oil," said Ronald.

"Fancy stuff," commented Len, who was sitting next to Antonia.

"I hope you like it."

"Can't wait to dig in."

The servers had placed two baskets of bread on the table and Lucy took one basket and began circling it clockwise. Joseph took the other basket and circled it as well. Guests selected from pretzel, olive, and sourdough rolls. There were dishes of butter dappled with sea salt spread out around the table, which the diners also passed to each other. Soon everyone was busy chewing their bread or slurping up their soup and a temporary hush fell across the table.

Guests began sneaking looks at each other across the table, with some intentionally sending others nasty glances. At one point, Antonia saw Ronald glaring at Barbie, who gave him a defiant look in return. Later, Barbie was seen shooting Naomi a disdainful look. Soyla kept her head down, staring into her soup bowl. Larry continued to monopolize Jennifer with anecdotes about his career, and to Antonia's eye, she didn't appear to mind. She listened attentively as she ate her soup, her face unexpressive. *She was a hard one to read*, Antonia thought. She had a poker face. It had probably served her well.

Joseph began a languid conversation with Barbie about the full moon. He had purposely chosen a neutral topic to coax her out of her fury. Antonia watched as Barbie's body language relaxed, and she became less defensive. Joseph moved on to astrology and it was as if he had hit the conversation jackpot because suddenly

Barbie came alive and began chattering away. Joseph gave Antonia a wink from across the table.

Sylvia was winning the award for group cheerleader. She moaned with pleasure with every bite she took and kept prompting Len to confirm her belief that the food was "out of this world." They both were working their way through the bread baskets at a furious pace.

Lucy snuck peeks at Antonia and raised her eyebrows as if wondering when the accusations would begin. She was experiencing the same impatient anticipation that Antonia and Joseph were feeling. But everything would happen in due time.

"May I?" a waiter asked Barbie, motioning the wine bottle in his hand to her glass.

"Yes, thanks," she said, before returning to Joseph and continuing to lay out why she was a "true Scorpio."

Antonia had made certain to tell the waiters to continuously fill the wineglasses and make sure the diners were fully lubricated. Ronald, Hector, and Soyla were not drinking, but everyone else was imbibing. It was ticking along as planned.

The second course was an option of New York strip steak with fried buttermilk onion rings and creamed spinach or sunchoke risotto with bordelaise sauce and black truffles. Most guests opted for the former, with the exception of Jennifer and Lucy.

"I've chosen a wonderful California cabernet to accompany these dishes, so everyone please have a taste," said Antonia.

Everyone obediently brought their glasses to their lips and took a sip.

Dinner service continued, with the guests warming up a bit more due to alcohol consumption and their lessening fear that something bad was about to happen. It was all warm and snug in the room, with the fire raging and the candles flickering. A perfect autumn evening in East Hampton. Antonia had purposely chosen a particularly rich menu in order to make the guests sleepy and off their guard. Then she would strike.

When the dinner plates were cleared, the waiters brought dessert. Each guest was given a hefty portion of sticky toffee pudding with a rich caramel sauce, accompanied by dulce de leche ice cream. In addition, silver trays with pyramids of petit fours and homemade almond madeleines were placed in the center for guests to select from.

"Antonia, you have outdone yourself!" said Sylvia, raising her glass. "Cheers to a wonderful hostess!"

Everyone raised their glass in Antonia's honor. She took the moment to run her gaze across every face in the room. Eleven sets of eyes stared back at her, and at least one of those eyes had planned murder. She knew it for certain now. She was in the presence of a killer. It was time to begin.

"Thank you all so much for coming. I am so happy to assemble this particular group tonight. It may seem very arbitrary, but there is a reason you are all here."

"Aw, we thought it was because you liked us," joked Len.

"I do like you, Len, and I'm glad you came. But I'm afraid there is a more serious reason that I have assembled this particular group."

Antonia stood up. All of the heads swung in her direction. She began to walk around the table slowly, before pausing behind Joseph.

"We are here tonight because I have solved the murders of Gordon Haslett and Biddy Robertson. Not all of you are going home tonight. Justice will be rendered."

There was a collective gasp.

Then, in a dramatic bold gesture, two waiters shut the parlor doors with a bang and stood in front of them, folding their arms. They looked like soldiers guarding a crypt. No one could escape.

33

"WHAT ARE YOU TALKING ABOUT?" ASKED SYLVIA. HER mouth was full of sticky toffee pudding, but she couldn't resist blurting out her question.

"Antonia, I'm not sure I follow. Why are *we* here?" asked Len. "And if this is murder, what about the police?"

"If you will all bear with me, everything will be explained in due time."

"This is absurd," snorted Naomi.

"Yeah, just tell us," shouted out Barbie. "Why do we have to listen to this fairy tale?"

All at once, the guests started shouting and talking loudly. The crowd was excited and angry. Antonia brought her fingers to her lips and whistled. Everyone froze. Joseph spoke.

"Now, now, let's all calm down. We can eat these wonderful desserts and listen to what Antonia has to say. We at least owe her that after this delicious meal," said Joseph.

"But this is ridiculous!" snapped Barbie. "Antonia is no detective, so why should we listen to her lies?"

"You have no reason not to," said Joseph sternly. "And if you believe that she will tell you lies and fairy tales, then what do you have to worry about? Just sit down and enjoy the show. All of you."

The guests murmured their agreement. This was

it. Antonia had to start. She was nervous, but she had no choice. It was time to bring justice to the dead. She cleared her throat, and put her hands on the back of her chair.

"I'll start at the beginning. A year and a half ago I was living in California and my life was, well, not going anywhere. Then my friend Genevieve told me about this beautiful inn located in East Hampton, New York. It was a historic inn that was over a hundred and fifty years old. It was beloved in the town. But in recent years, it had become a little run down…"

"Hey, not true," interjected Barbie. "This place was fine."

"There will be time for rebuttals after I speak. Please refrain from commenting until I am finished," Antonia admonished.

Barbie was not pleased. Lucy shot her a hostile look. "Antonia's just being honest and calling a spade a spade."

"Shut up, Lucy," said Barbie. "No one wants your opinion."

"You shut up."

"Ladies, may I continue?" asked Antonia. "As you know, I purchased the inn. And things were off to a wonderful start. I was sad to hear about the death of the previous owner, Gordon Haslett, but I had been told he wasn't the fittest man and had battled some health issues, so I thought nothing of his death in his early fifties. It was a sad footnote. But then last week things began to change…"

"Oh, I see why we're here, sweetie," said Sylvia in what she thought was a whisper but was more like a stage whisper. "It's because we told her the place was cursed."

"Shh!" commanded Lucy. She was sitting up stick straight, giving her complete attention to Antonia, like a nerdy teacher's pet trying to incur points.

"Sorry," said Sylvia meekly. She took several petit fours off the tray and put them on her plate, tucking into a cream puff.

"It's true, you and Len were the ones to alert me to the history of the inn," said Antonia. "Then I began my journey to investigate what really happened. And I came across some wildly disturbing revelations. Gordon Haslett did not die of a heart attack. He died from a bee sting. But this was no accidental death. How many bees are out there, braving a frigid December day in Long Island? No, this was a perfectly executed plan. This was a murder, contrived by a cunning killer who had meticulously planned and organized for years. A killer who knew Gordon was allergic to bees, and knew it would bring on sudden death. And this killer is in this room."

Again, the guests gasped. They looked at one another suspiciously. Antonia allowed the words to sink in. Then she continued.

"Biddy Robertson's murder will be solved tonight as well."

"Didn't Naomi kill her?" asked Barbie.

"Hey, watch it," said Naomi.

"But it's true. Naomi's been arrested for it," said Barbie.

"I was questioned, not arrested. Big difference, moron," sneered Naomi.

"Whatever. Antonia, I think you can just stop right now. The killer has been found," said Barbie, pointing at Naomi.

Naomi appeared ready to jump across the table and throttle her.

"Let me run this show, Barbie," said Antonia. "All will be revealed."

Barbie frowned and took a sip of her coffee.

"Len and Sylvia Powers," Antonia said, walking over and standing behind their chairs. They both glanced up, their mouths full of custard cream.

"Yes?" Len asked. But it came out more like "yef."

"You were amongst my first guests at the inn, and I have been so grateful for how appreciative you've been."

"Thank you," said Sylvia.

Antonia hesitated. "You were also the first people to tell me just over a week ago about the history of the inn. I think, and I quote, you said, 'The story about the Windmill Inn is that the owners die under suspicious circumstances.' Isn't that right, Len?"

"Yes," he said, his wary eyes trained on her.

"Yes, it is. At first you were both reluctant to tell me about the inn's history of deceased innkeepers, but then it all came spilling out. The curse, the ghost story, whatever it was. You had your son, Matt, with you. He was, conveniently, the first responder to the scene of Gordon Haslett's death, was he not?"

"Yes, Matty is an EMT," said Sylvia, explaining to the group. "He was supposed to be here tonight, but he had a fire to put out. Literally. He's a good boy."

"He is. A dutiful son, wouldn't you say?" asked Antonia.

Before Sylvia could answer, Len interrupted. "What is that supposed to mean? I'm not sure I'm following here..."

"I'm just saying that Matt adores you and would do anything for you."

"What son wouldn't?" asked Len.

"I agree. Now Len and Sylvia, I'm thinking back to that dinner a week ago. You were so complimentary, and I continue to be so gratified by your support."

"Thank you," said Sylvia.

"I think you said that you had stopped coming to the Windmill Inn when Gordon Haslett ran it because the food was terrible."

"Dog food," concurred Len.

"Hey..." interjected Barbie.

"You'll have your turn," murmured Joseph, temporarily placating her.

"The interesting thing is that you said that you had stopped coming to the inn. But Matt corrected you. He said, and I quote, 'You didn't really have a choice.' I thought nothing of it at the time..."

"What are you suggesting?" asked Len.

Antonia walked around the table so that she was now facing them. She put her arms on the backs of the chairs in front of her and leaned across the table toward Len and Sylvia.

"Len, isn't it true that in addition to being the Head of Security at the Dune Club, you are also a building inspector in the village of East Hampton?"

"I am…"

"I didn't remember that until the other day when I received my certificate from the town, signed by you. And thank you, you gave me a clear pass."

"You're welcome."

"But you didn't give Gordon a clear pass, did you? You cited him for many expensive violations, and in return he banned you from the restaurant? Barbie told me at tea that Gordon had fought with the building inspector, aka you, and that you hated him."

Everyone turned and gave Len an accusatory look. Len, in turn, appeared incredulous. "Are you suggesting that I *murdered* Gordon Haslett because I was *banned* from his crap restaurant? That's absurd."

"He didn't just ban you. He made a huge stink. Brought it to the town board and demanded an investigation. He said that you had given him a bad citation because he wouldn't comp your meals."

"And he lost that claim."

"But it dragged on for months. You were surrounded by a cloud of suspicion. The town started to crack down on allowing inspectors to frequent the restaurants they were auditing. Other inspectors were angry."

Len reddened. "There was absolutely no impropriety…"

"But with Gordon dead, it all ended. The case was thrown out. He was gone and all that fuss was brushed under the table."

"*I* suffered from all this…"

"So you had motive."

The room was so quiet that you could hear a pin drop. Everyone waited on the edge of their seats. Antonia paused. "And your son was the first responder, so he could have covered up…"

Len bolted up and threw down his napkin. "This is garbage. Sylvia, let's go!"

Sylvia was mid-forkful, dishing raspberry parfait into her mouth. For a split second, she debated putting it down, but instead crammed it into her mouth, before making a feeble effort to stand.

"Stop, stop. Len, Sylvia, please sit down."

"I will not."

Antonia went over to them, and put her hands on their shoulders. "Don't worry, Len. No one really thinks you killed Gordon. You may have had motive, but you are not a killer. Everyone knows that."

Len twisted his tie and glanced around the room. The eyes that met his were tentative, and some looked away.

"Then why did you make me out to be one?" he asked accusingly.

"I'm just proving a point. I'm sorry."

"I'm outraged!" blustered Len.

"I understand, but it was necessary. Everything will be explained. Please stay."

"Yes, please do sit down, Len. Coffee and tea are on their way," offered Joseph. "And, if you do, I think you will be amused."

Len glanced around like a defeated man. "Amused? You mean all of this is a joke?"

Sylvia smacked her hand on the table. The china teacups rattled. "I know what this is! It's one of those murder mystery games where people all get dressed up and come in character. How fun! Len, this is a game. Don't worry. This will be a hoot! Let's see who did it."

Everyone began talking at once.

Len turned to Antonia. "I didn't even know Biddy Robertson."

"I know," said Antonia.

"I did nothing wrong. The place *was* a dump. I had no choice but to cite him. Not to mention, when I saw how disgusting the kitchen was, we stopped coming."

"I understand. I saw that kitchen too. It was gross."

The waiters came around and began filling coffee and teacups, setting out pitchers of milk and cream. The conversations were now swirling in a collective buzz, adding a low hum to the room. There was excitement in the air, but also a sense of relief. But then just as suddenly a voice louder than the others spoke.

"This isn't just a game."

34

It was Ronald Meter who spoke. Every head swung in his direction. He sat gloomily in his chair, twiddling his teaspoon between his thumb and index finger. He was agitated, and sweating profusely, with his cheeks appearing more sunken than usual. His heavy lids looked up and he studied the crowd in front of him.

"I mean, right, Antonia? You've got something on all of us. So you may as well start with me now. I want to get it over with."

Antonia met his stare. She hadn't wanted to select Ronald Meter for the next moment in the spotlight, but now she had no choice. Her hand was forced. She couldn't let this happen again. It was to her benefit to be in control and running the inquisition.

"Yes, Ronald. I do have something on you."

Ronald nodded slowly. "All right. Then go. What do you want to say about me? Because I think in terms of Gordon, I'm a pretty easy target. In fact, let me lay it out for you."

He took a sip of water. Antonia noticed his hand was shaking.

"I have the motive. We all know that. Gordon fired me, and a prosecutor will say because of that, I wanted him dead. I had opportunity. I know the ins and outs of this inn like the back of my hand, having worked here for years. It wouldn't be hard for me to hide in a discreet place to find the right moment to kill Gordon. I had the weapon. I keep a beehive in my backyard. So I clearly killed Gordon with a bee because I wanted revenge."

"Is that a confession?" asked Sylvia, her voice shrill.

Ronald gave her a contemptuous look. Before he could answer Antonia interrupted.

"What about Biddy?"

"Biddy? Well, I knew her from the L.V.I.S. and I had actually briefly worked at the inn under her. Of course, I was not the biggest fan. She was a small-minded woman who had no clue as to how to run an inn."

"So you killed her for that?" asked Larry. "Come on," he said to Antonia. "Get real. This guy didn't do it."

"But he's saying he did…" said Jennifer.

"Plus, he's a thief and a liar," said Barbie. "He stole from the inn…"

"Correction, *you* stole from the inn," boomed Ronald.

Barbie shot up. "I did not, and I don't have to take this. I'm out of here."

"Barbie!" said Antonia. She motioned toward the two waiters at the door. Barbie saw them, hesitated, and sat back down.

"You may search my house, but never did I take anything from the inn," said Ronald. "As God is my witness, and you know I would never betray him or the promises I made to my pastor."

Antonia's eyebrows shot up. "Is that true?"

Ronald's expression momentarily wavered. "Yes."

Antonia nodded. "I've heard a few people call on God to be their witness lately."

"What's that supposed to mean?" asked Ronald.

"Well, take Hector and Soyla," said Antonia.

She motioned to the startled couple, whose eyes widened as soon as their names were mentioned.

"But we'll get to them in a second," said Antonia. "I want to finish with you. You have motive, it's true. And access. But what really got me is that you act suspiciously, as if you are hiding something. It was that skittish behavior that made me think it was murder, but now I know it was something else."

Ronald sat very still, waiting.

"What is it?" asked Sylvia.

"The other day I was driving by a house and I saw Ronald and a man talking in the driveway. I recognized the man but couldn't place him. And then I remembered. He's a vendor who is producing a local brew of honey beer. He's been by the restaurant several times to try and entice us into selling it. And Ronald is his partner. That's what the hives are for, are they not?"

Ronald looked stricken. He didn't speak.

"Why would he hide that?" asked Larry. "That's not a crime."

"It's not. Prohibition ended decades ago. But Ronald Meter has a pastor who preaches sobriety. In his mind, producing alcohol is a sin, am I right?"

Ronald slumped in his chair. Sweat was seeping out

of his every pore. He spoke in a defeated tone, so quietly that everyone had to strain to hear him.

"Yes."

Antonia nodded. "I thought so. Ronald Meter may have a guilty conscience, but it's because he's betraying his faith, not because he is a murderer."

Antonia couldn't be sure, but she thought she detected a bit of relief in Ronald's posture at letting the secret go.

"Speaking of God," Antonia said, "I'd like to return to Hector and Soyla."

Again, the couple recoiled at the sound of their names.

"They both said they were God-fearing people who would never commit murder. They are a couple who have come here to East Hampton to make a better life for their family. They work hard, long hours, and do whatever they can to provide for their kids. And then next thing you know, Soyla has been accused of theft and Gordon has fired her. That's a huge shame. A blemish. They have given this man nothing but blood, sweat, and tears and this is how he repays them, by not trusting them. This makes them angry. Very angry."

Hector and Soyla shrunk so far back into their chairs that they had virtually disappeared. If they could have pressed a button to make themselves evaporate, Antonia was certain they would have. She was about to continue but was interrupted.

"Let's get to the point here, Bingham. I'm guessing that everyone here had a motive for killing Gordon," said

Larry, before turning to Jennifer. "Except maybe you, but I don't know. Maybe you're just eye candy."

Jennifer giggled.

"Yes, who are you?" asked Lucy. She looked at Antonia. "Why is she here?"

"No doubt some other woman who Gordon betrayed," said Len.

"It's true, when I look around this room I see so many people who hated Gordon," said Barbie.

Everyone began talking at once about how loathsome Gordon was and how reviled he had been. Suddenly Naomi stood up and shouted.

"Stop! Will you please stop! You are talking about my baby brother here!"

The group fell silent. They all stared at Naomi. Larry singsonged under his breath, "Awk-ward…"

Naomi gave him a withering look. "Antonia, you're right. Everyone here could have killed my brother. But we all know it was Barbie."

Barbie began to stand up and protest but Joseph put out his arm to stop her. "Just wait," he whispered. "Your turn will come."

"Yes, Barbie," said Naomi. "Shocker, right? She was his girlfriend. She's had me in court for months insisting she should inherit part of the inn, that Gordon left it to her. She killed him to get it. Everyone knows she was running around on him, shacking up with some other guy. She's a slut."

Barbie's face was purple and she was shaking with rage. Antonia glanced at her.

"Barbie did have motive."

"Everyone had motive!" screamed Barbie.

"True. But not everyone had access to the corporate credit card," Antonia said firmly.

All heads turned toward Barbie.

"What's that supposed to mean?" asked Barbie.

"During my research, I scanned through past credit statements. There was a corporate card that you had access to. Upon further research, I learned that the card was used to buy honey at a farm stand the same day a blond, buxom woman attempted to buy bees, and when denied, purloined a bee from the hive."

"You're kidding, right?"

"A worker at the farm stand saw the woman lurking around the hives. The beekeeper later confirmed that he thought a bee had been taken."

"This is absurd!" protested Barbie.

"Is it?" asked Antonia. "You have told me a number of times that you *deserved* the inn. That you put up with Gordon for years, so you were *due* a share of the inn. You were cheating on Gordon, and yet although you were not legally married, you didn't leave him. Why? Because you felt that you earned something after years of helping him make the inn somewhat successful. If you left him, you'd get nothing. So you had to stay. But maybe you got tired of waiting?"

Everyone stared at Barbie. She gazed evenly at Antonia. "This is nonsense. I didn't get anything from Gordon's death other than an eviction notice."

Antonia walked over to the side of the room and

removed a piece of paper from a manila envelope. She held it in her fingers and returned to the table. Everyone in the room stared at the paper.

"You were searching for his will. You claimed it existed, and gave you half of the inn."

Antonia held up the paper. There were audible gasps in the room.

Barbie shot up. "Let me see that!"

Naomi also stood. "This is absurd! I don't believe it."

Antonia pressed the paper to her chest. "All in good time."

"Stop saying that and give me the will!" yelled Barbie, lunging at Antonia.

She reached across the table and knocked over a glass of wine, which began trickling down the table toward Jennifer. Soyla immediately grabbed her napkin and began blotting it out. Other people popped up to help, and another glass was inadvertently tipped over. It was momentary chaos with the crowd talking and giving orders and tossing napkins back and forth.

The two waiters from the door walked over and stood beside Antonia. The crowd glanced at them, and as if sensing something, quieted at once and sat back down. They returned their full attention to Antonia.

"Where did you find that, Antonia?" asked Lucy.

"In one of the old boxes."

"Are you sure it's Gordon's?"

"I'm sure this document is valid," said Antonia.

"It sounds like you got her," said Len. "Maybe you should call the police now."

"What are you talking about?" said Barbie. "This means nothing. There is no proof whatsoever."

"Sounds pretty solid to me," said Sylvia. "And did she kill Biddy too?"

"Oh my God!" said Barbie, rolling her eyes. "Next, you'll say I killed John F. Kennedy."

Antonia stared at her. "Biddy Robertson had put aside a box of items that were dropped off at the L.V.I.S. thrift shop. She recognized some of the items from the inn, ashtrays and such. Those items were later confirmed by Soyla to have been stolen. Perhaps you stole them?"

"Antonia, don't quit your day job," advised Barbie. "I'm not a murderer or a thief."

"What about the fact that gold earrings went missing by a guest at the inn? Soyla was fired for that. Then, a week later, you wear earrings to a meeting with the exact description."

"I got them for my birthday!"

"From who?"

Barbie glanced around the room, nervously. "A friend."

"Your boyfriend?" asked Antonia. "Which one, Gordon or the other guy?"

Barbie gulped. "I'm not sure. There was a box on my desk and it just said *I love you*. I didn't want to ask Gordon if he gave them to me, because he would find out I was cheating. And I felt weird asking my new guy…"

"So you just wore them."

"Yes."

"And you didn't steal them?"

"No!" said Barbie emphatically. "They were a gift. And I didn't steal any of those things from the inn and drop them off at the thrift shop. Why the hell would I do that? I never go into places like that. I had no contact with Biddy."

"Biddy probably had something on her," said Naomi.

"Really, Naomi? Like what?" asked Barbie.

"That you're a thief and a hussy."

"Enough with that," said Barbie. "And enough about me. What about Naomi? I mean, really. She's the one the police think did it!"

"They're wrong," protested Naomi.

Antonia walked around the table again toward Naomi. She gave her a small smile.

"You are the one who has the most evidence against her."

"I'm not even going to engage," said Naomi, shaking her head.

"You inherited the inn when Gordon died. You had a long-term fight with Biddy, going back years where she accused you of taking the inn out from under her, then leaving a dead animal on her porch."

"I'm tired of hearing about it."

"And you were lurking around the backyard of the inn the other day. I couldn't figure out what you were doing there. The next day Hector found this."

Antonia reached atop the bookshelf next to her and pulled down Biddy's monogrammed box. She placed it in front of Naomi.

"I've never seen that in my life," Naomi stated with such derision, it was as if the hotly contested dead raccoon had reappeared in place of the box.

The other guests leaned in. "Whose is it?" asked Larry.

"It was Biddy's. And Hector found it in the backyard."

"Maybe Hector killed her and put it there," said Naomi, folding her arms.

Hector looked like he wanted to throw up.

"I thought of that, but he didn't put it there. The killer did."

"Oh me? Right," said Naomi.

"Actually, Naomi. I know why you were in the backyard."

"This will be good," she sniffed.

"Why *was* she there?" asked Lucy.

Antonia locked eyes with Naomi. "The other day when I was out there, I stumbled on a rock. Didn't think much of it. But then something occurred to me and I went back out to check it out. The rock is a tombstone inscribed with the name Teddy. That was your dog, was it not, Naomi? Your dog is buried there."

Naomi stared at Antonia and her face softened slightly. "Yes," she said flatly.

"It was something you said that gave me pause. You said, 'There will always be part of my heart buried' at the inn."

"He was a wonderful dog," whispered Naomi, her eyes filling with tears.

Antonia was amazed to see Naomi become so emotional. It was as if she had cracked her shell. A tear slid down her cheek and Soyla handed her a cocktail napkin.

"So does that mean she didn't put the box there?" asked Len. "I'm confused."

"Me too," said Sylvia. She motioned for the waiter to refill her wineglass.

"I don't follow at all," said Ronald. "What's the point of all this? Do we know who the killer is?"

Once again the crowd began to argue, debating who the actual murderer was. Antonia watched them, all animated and riled up. She walked over and stood behind Jennifer's chair.

"There's one more thing," Antonia said loudly.

Everyone stopped and turned toward her with expectant faces. Some were shiny with perspiration; others had contented looks after the large dinner and large doses of alcohol, some nervous. But all ready for answers.

Antonia smiled. "I think we are forgetting Gordon's other girlfriend. She is the killer. She killed both Gordon Haslett and Biddy Robertson. And she thought she'd get away with it."

The crowd froze, their eyes moving down from Antonia's face to Jennifer's. They all squinted, attempting to place her, desperately searching their brain to remember her. Jennifer sat solemnly, unmoving. She didn't even glance back at Antonia to confront her. A slow grin slid across her face.

35

"WHO IS SHE?" ASKED NAOMI. "I'VE NEVER SEEN HER before."

Barbie shook her head. "I don't get it. She doesn't look familiar. What's her last name?"

"Jennifer, say it ain't so," said Larry, punching her playfully. "If you're a murderer, you're a sexy one."

Jennifer didn't speak. A sly smile was pursed on her lips.

"Why did she do it?" asked Naomi.

"Yeah, Jennifer, tell us why?" asked Len.

Antonia broke the silence.

"I'm not talking about Jennifer," she said firmly. "I'm talking about Lucy."

Every head in the room whipped toward Lucy in astonishment.

Lucy sat up straighter. "Me?"

Antonia slowly walked around the entire table until she was behind Lucy, the latter of whom now had to twist her neck to glance up at Antonia.

"Yes, you, Lucy. I can't believe it was in front of me all along and it took me so long to see it. It's actually amazing that no one ever considered it, but then Lucy, you have an amazing ability to hover in the background."

"This is ridiculous," she said, before adding in a whisper, "is this part of the plan? To accuse me to shake out the real killer?"

"No, Lucy. It's not part of any plan. In fact, *you* are the master of plans. Not me."

"This is crazy. I should go," said Lucy, standing up.

Antonia firmly pressed her down back into her seat. "You're not going anywhere."

"Lucy did it…it makes sense," said Ronald.

Barbie nodded. "Of course."

Even Naomi added reluctantly. "It does…"

Lucy folded her arms. "This is insane. You have no proof."

"That's where you're wrong, my friend."

"Let's hear the evidence," said Joseph.

Antonia cleared her throat.

"When I first bought the inn a year and a half ago, it was Lucy Corning who assisted me in getting up and running. She had been the bookkeeper for the past several years, and she knew everything about the inn. She was so informative that I promoted her from bookkeeper to manager. I thought, here was a diligent employee. Savvy, too, which was amazing because she had really only worked at the inn for three years. But what I didn't realize is that Lucy had actually been around the inn before that. When she was dating Gordon Haslett."

Lucy shook her head firmly. "That is just not true…"

"It's not? Because if you look at the pictures of the Millennium party that Gordon held at the inn, there you are in the background of every picture with Gordon, dressed as a bunny."

Antonia dumped out the contents of the envelope

that Larry had brought in front of Lucy. There were snapshots of her and Gordon, and in most, like in Joan Masterson's pictures, she had her mask on. But in the last one she held her bunny head in her arms and stared up adoringly at Gordon.

Lucy refused to look at the pictures so Antonia scooped them up and began passing them around the table.

"I don't quite understand why you hung in there with Gordon after he dumped you, but there is a certain tenacity in you. As Barbie said last week, 'I'm just wondering when that woman will disappear forever. She's like a tick that keeps hanging on.'"

"Ouch!" said Larry.

Lucy gave him a hostile look. "Fine. We dated briefly years ago, but so what?"

"I don't think it was brief. We had guests staying with us last week, the Winslows, who told me they were so happy to see Gordon's girlfriend still working at the inn. Barbie had been there that morning, so I assumed they thought she was still working here. But now I know they meant you. And they said that it had always been your dream to own an inn."

"There's the motive," said Ronald.

"That means nothing," said Lucy. "None of this proves anything."

"I think you wanted the inn for yourself. You told me you got into vintage clothes when you worked at a vintage store, and which I realized was the L.V.I.S. thrift shop. You worked there when Biddy was a volunteer. She told you the inn was going into foreclosure. You alerted Gordon and he swooped in to buy it. You thought you would have your dream come true. But Gordon was volatile, unpredictable. He threw you over for Barbie. But you got your revenge. You began siphoning off money from the accounts. You were the bookkeeper; you had access. You put the money into Naomi's accounts or Barbie's accounts to make it look like they were stealing, but *you* are the thief. You also stole from people at the inn. The Winslows said you were so helpful in assisting them in finding something, but that's because you took it! And then you planted those earrings on Barbie's desk, pretending it was from her lover, hoping that she would tell Gordon and he would know she was cheating and throw her out."

"That's not true."

"But it backfired with Gordon. He still stuck by Barbie for some reason. And that enraged you, so you planned his murder. But somehow Gordon knew it. And it is his words from the dead that seized me."

Antonia paused. Everyone was on the edge of their seats.

"I found his note. It said, *I swear to God that B is trying to kill me.* That B. For the longest time I thought it was Ronald Meter, who he called the beast. Or Barbie. Or Biddy. But it was you. That bookkeeper. You were trying to kill him."

"You said yourself the girl at the farm stand saw Barbie!"

Antonia nodded. "You were the one who led me to the farm stand. I was such a dupe. I thought I had discovered it on my own, but you planted the card statements on me, under a false pretense, knowing I would see that purchase. And yes, the girl at the farm stand said that it was a busty blond woman."

"See? Not me."

"Did you forget you told me you went as Jayne Mansfield one Halloween? That meant you had the padded bra and the big shoes and blond wig. I believe you wore that outfit to the farm stand when you stole the bee."

Lucy looked deflated. "I couldn't have…"

"Matt, the first responder, told me he had spoken to Gordon's girlfriend at the scene. I thought it was Barbie, but of course it was you. Matt was at that Millennium party years ago, so of course he could identify you. And by the way, I'm pretty sure you called in that alarm in Quogue just to ensure that he wasn't here tonight."

"Please," she sniffed.

"Just like I'm sure you were the anonymous caller who alerted the police to the carbon monoxide alarm that you threw in Naomi's neighbor's garbage. By the way, Jennifer is here because she is Naomi's neighbor. Her brother Ty dated my friend Genevieve. Albeit briefly."

"So, that's why you're here," said Larry turning to Jennifer. "I'm so happy you're not going to jail so we can go out again."

"I saw a red Mini outside my house one night. I think that's when they put the alarm in my trash," said Jennifer.

"Lucy drives a red Mini!" said Hector, suddenly animated. It was the first time he participated in the conversation.

"So did she kill Biddy too?" asked Len.

"Yes," said Antonia. "Recently, Biddy told her neighbor Sharon that she was going to lunch with an old colleague and it would be interesting. She meant Lucy. I think they had originally schemed together on something to get back at Gordon, but then Lucy changed her mind. Maybe Biddy knew she killed him and was blackmailing her."

"This is absurd," said Lucy under her breath.

"Is it? You've spent the last week playing tricks on me, locking me in closets, taking away stepladders, planting booby traps, all so I would think the inn was haunted and take off. And then you could buy the inn from me at a cheap price. The bank mistakenly called me with your mortgage application—the one you tried to hide from me the other day. I thought it was a wrong number, but something made me call the banker back to make sure. You want the inn and you will do anything to get it. Embezzlement, blackmail, murder."

"But why *this* inn? There are so many," asked Barbie. "It's not *that* special. No offense."

Antonia took a deep breath and let it out slowly. She turned and stared at Lucy, who gazed at her defiantly.

"Because this is her home."

"Okay, sure. But it was my home too, and I moved on," said Barbie.

"You don't understand. Before Lucy was adopted by

her stepfather Walter Corning, she was Lucy McKenna. Her parents Greg and Charmaine owned the inn. Sylvia, didn't you recognize her? Lucy was your student."

Sylvia squinted until a slow smile appeared. "Oh, heavens! Now I remember. So long ago."

"This is the place where Lucy's mother killed her father, shattering her idyllic life. And Lucy wanted it back. Wanted to erase the past, and reclaim it as her future."

There was complete silence. Everyone kept shifting their gaze between Lucy and Antonia, who were staring at each other intently. Slowly Lucy slid back her chair and stood up. She began clapping. Softly at first, but then louder and louder. Tears were running down her face but she was smiling like a madwoman. Her hands began banging against each other so hard it was as if her blood vessels would burst.

"Bravo! Bravo!" she said.

She continued to furiously clap. It became alarming, but she wouldn't stop, or maybe she simply couldn't. Her body started convulsing, and she began some sort of fit, her hands flailing, her eyes rolling. The other diners rushed to her.

"Call an ambulance!" Antonia yelled to the waiters.

"Call the police," said Joseph firmly.

"Aren't those waiters cops?" asked Barbie.

Antonia shook her head. "They're just waiters. I had to tell some little white lies as means to an end."

Barbie scowled. "You tricked me."

"But you got a happy ending, didn't you?"

Hector dialed 911.

36

Early Morning Monday

THE INN WAS QUIET. THE DINERS HAD LEFT. THE PARAmedics had left. The police had left. Lucy had left with them. The black night had spread out against the sky, licking its way into the edges of the horizon. There was no breeze, just a stillness in the brisk air. A comforting hush curled inside the corners of the inn. The dying fire was still doing its best to hang on, its burning embers emitting low flickers. Antonia and Joseph sat in the two armchairs in front of it, glasses of cognac in hand. They were weary and emotionally spent but had that charge of adrenaline coursing through their veins that would not allow them to sleep.

"Well done, my dear," congratulated Joseph.

"Thank you. Couldn't have done it without you."

"That's not true, but I was happy to help."

"I'm so glad it's all over. I mean, it was surreal, but now things can return to normal. I don't need any more drama."

"I hear you. By the way, what was that skirmish with Barbie when she was on her way out?"

"Oh," said Antonia, pausing to take a sip. "She wanted the will. I had to break it to her that I was bluffing. It was a blank sheet of paper. She kind of freaked out when I told her."

Joseph chuckled. "I can imagine."

"I do think there was a will, actually. I think Lucy destroyed it. Why wouldn't she? Barbie was her rival."

"Maybe she'll confess."

"I doubt it," said Antonia. "I doubt she'll confess to any of it. At the end of the day, it's all circumstantial evidence. Not sure it's enough to convict."

"The police will dig up more. You did your part, now you can retire."

"Agreed. I will need a new manager, though."

"You'll find one."

"I'm sure."

Suddenly the front door burst open and Genevieve came rushing in. She was wearing a long black cape, and her hair was done up in a dramatic bun.

"I came as soon as I heard. Is everything okay?" she asked anxiously.

"Everything is fine now. Don't worry."

She walked over to Antonia, bent over her, and gave her a big hug. "I was so worried. Listen, I'm on a date but I can stay if you need me…"

"I'm fine."

Genevieve cocked an eyebrow. "Are you sure?"

"Completely."

"Okay, well, I see you're in good hands. And this guy is hot! He's waiting in the car. He's in a band! They're playing next week at the Talkhouse. Promise you'll come with me."

"Done."

Genevieve went over to the bar and poured herself a shot of vodka, which she downed quickly. "Thanks for the lubricant," she said with a wink. "And now that I know you haven't been murdered or anything, I'm gonna head out."

"She's quite alive," remarked Joseph.

"Take good care of her!" she said to Joseph, flinging the cape over her shoulder and heading for the door. "She's my bestie!"

"I will."

Genevieve left leaving a trail of perfume in her wake. Antonia and Joseph smiled at each other.

"She's a little silly, but she's a good friend," said Antonia.

"I'm grateful to her, knowing she's the reason you're here in East Hampton."

Conversation paused while they sat and simply enjoyed the peace that silence brought. Finally, Joseph spoke.

"Well, my dear, I should call it a night. As much as I'd love to stay, time for me to get home."

Antonia looked at Joseph pensively. "You know, I was thinking something."

"Oh? What's that?"

"Upstairs we have these three little connecting rooms, designed like a mini-apartment. There's a bedroom, a sitting room, and a small, really tiny room that could fit a desk. No one has booked it yet, not even for a night. And I was just thinking, maybe you wanted to move into the inn? I mean, instead of moving to New York City. I would love it if you were here. You've become such a wonderful friend, I don't want you to leave town. And there's the elevator so you wouldn't have to use the stairs. Would you think about it?"

Tears welled in Joseph's eyes. He took out his handkerchief and wiped them away.

"Are you okay? Oh, please don't cry!" She leaned over and patted him on the back.

"That's the nicest offer anyone has given me. I'd love to move in here. Of course, I will pay you market rate…"

"Joseph…"

"I insist. But yes, I would love to, my dear. I was dreading a move into one of those god-awful buildings my son wants to stuff me into."

"Then this is the perfect solution," beamed Antonia.

Joseph clasped her hands and they sat there for a minute, enjoying the moment. Antonia was thrilled she had found someone like Joseph. He was a wonderful friend, and a surrogate father figure. She didn't know why she didn't think of asking him to move in sooner. It had all just dawned on her. Maybe she had been too distracted by murder, but now she was glad to be done with that.

"That's it for me," Antonia said. She was glad to be officially out of the crime-solving business. "Now I won't ever have to deal with any more ghost stories or murders."

"Pity," Joseph said. He sat back in his chair and evaluated her.

Antonia raised an eyebrow.

"It's just that we made such a great team."

About the Author

Photo by Tanya Malott

A fan of mystery and crime novels, a cooking enthusiast, a former employee of Ina Garten's Barefoot Contessa store, and a generally nosy person, Carrie Doyle combined all of her interests to create Antonia Bingham, the foodie innkeeper and reluctant detective who stars in the Hamptons Murder Mystery series. Carrie is the author of several novels and five optioned screenplays (one of which was produced and screened at the Sundance Film Festival.) She was the founding editor-in-chief of the Russian edition of *Marie Claire* and has written for several magazines. Visit Carrie's author site at carriedoyleauthor.com.

PEOPLE ARE TALKING ABOUT
RENEWAL . . .

"While we can't stop the aging process, we can make dramatic changes in the way we age. In his book RENEWAL, Dr. Timothy Smith shows us how."

—New Orleans Times-Picayune

"Smith combines alternative and Western medical approaches, focusing on both physical and mental components in his program that facilitates the body's capacity to regenerate its own vitality."

—Publishers Weekly

"Want to live to 120? Then pick up a copy of RENEWAL by Timothy J. Smith, M.D., and start making diet and lifestyle changes today . . . RENEWAL incorporates the latest longevity research and is packed with terrific information that is a pleasure to read. You'll learn how and why we age and, more important, how to reverse heart disease, destroy cancer cells, erase visible signs of aging, boost brain power, attack aging at the cellular level, and extend your life span by protecting healthy cells and repairing or replacing damaged or dead ones. . . . Follow Dr. Smith's advice and you'll keep each of your body's 100 trillion cells humming for decades to come."

—Amazon.com

"Smith, whose background combines mainstream medicine with ideas from the Far East, is among the increasing number of doctors who make a distinction between the Recommended Daily Allowance first established by the government in the early 1940s and what he calls the Optimum Daily Allowances needed to live longer and better."

—Birmingham (AL) *News*

RENEWAL
THE ANTI-AGING
REVOLUTION

TIMOTHY J. SMITH, M.D.

Timothy J. Smith, M.D.

St. Martin's Paperbacks

Published by arrangement with Rodale Press Inc.

The quotation on page 444 is from *Whatever Gets You Through the Night* by John Lennon. Copyright © Lenono Music. All rights administered by Sony/ATV Music Publishing, 8 Music Square West, Nashville, TN 37203. All rights reserved. Used by permission.

RENEWAL

Library of Congress Catalog Card Number: 98-27507

ISBN: 0-312-97209-1

Printed in the United States of America

Rodale Press hardcover edition published 1998
St. Martin's Paperbacks edition / November 1999

St. Martin's Paperbacks are published by St. Martin's Press, 175 Fifth Avenue, New York, N.Y. 10010.

10 9 8 7 6 5 4 3 2 1

Notice

This book is intended as a reference volume only, not as a medical manual. The information given here is designed to help you make informed decisions about your health. It is not intended as a substitute for any treatment that may have been prescribed by your doctor. If you suspect that you have a medical problem, we urge you to seek competent medical help.

For Dellie, with love

Contents

PART III Supplements: Essential for Maximum Life Span

PART IV The Renewal Anti-Aging Supplement Program

PART V The Anti-Aging Hormones

Acknowledgments

Above all, I want to express my deep, heartfelt gratitude to Patti Breitman, my literary agent, for her positive energy, sage advice, and unflagging support. What do you say when you run out of superlatives? Patti's commitment to healthy living and an enlightened planet is inspiring.

I feel blessed to have been good-naturedly guided by Debora Yost, vice president and editorial director of Rodale Health and Fitness Books, for whose wisdom and caring I am especially grateful.

I owe a debt of gratitude to Susan Berg, editorial tour de force at Rodale. Susan's insight, vision, and sensitivity made her a delight to work with.

I am also grateful to copy editors Kathryn Cressman and Amy Kovalski, whose thoughtfulness and attention to detail ensured the consistency and cohesiveness of the text, and to office manager Roberta Mulliner, who was always ready and willing to lend a helping hand.

Many others at Rodale labored over this book. Their efforts are greatly appreciated.

Lisa Ruffin supplied both editorial and spiritual support early on. She had the foresight to find the perfect organizing principle for my ideas: the word *Renewal*.

Megan Waterman, my delightful friend and office manager, kept my busy medical practice under control, thus freeing up my writing time.

Many thanks go to Richard Carlson, Ph.D., for guiding me toward Patti. His little gem *Don't Sweat the Small Stuff:*

And It's All Small Stuff stood alongside my *I Ching* as a source of spiritual sustenance when the going got rough.

Great thanks also go to my friend Larry Needleman, who created and tested many of the delicious Renewal recipes and provided hugs when I needed them the most.

I'm grateful to my professional friends, colleagues, and teachers for their generous sharing of information and support, especially Stephen Langer, M.D.; Michael Rosenbaum, M.D.; Joseph Helms, M.D.; Stephen Levine, Ph.D.; Fritjof Capra, Ph.D.; Allen Wheelis, M.D.; Ernestine Ward, M.F.C.C.; Carla Dalton, Lic.Ac.; and Elson Haas, M.D.

I thank nutritional pioneers John McDougall, M.D.; Neal Barnard, M.D.; John Robbins; Dean Ornish, M.D.; and Nathan Pritikin for having heightened public awareness of the powerful health benefits of a vegan lifestyle.

I also thank Don Carlson for his indispensable support and guidance, and Gale Young, Ph.D., for her encouragement, for believing, and for being a friend.

Many other friends and patients contributed in various ways to this work. I thank Catherine Connor; Victor Talmadge; Stephen Wooldridge; Janice Diane; Shannon Collins; Mary Jane Soares; Todd Fletcher; Larry Hayden; Margaret Seabury; Hal Cox; Herb Smith, D.D.S.; Jack Einheber, Ph.D.; Annabel Gregory; and Bruce Henderson. I also thank Carole Talpers, who probably doesn't realize how much her encouragement meant to me.

I am grateful beyond measure to my mother, Elizabeth Foote-Smith, who provided love, encouragement, and expert editorial advice all through the writing process. Also, Mom has followed the Renewal Anti-Aging Program longer than anyone. Vital and vigorous at age 85, she is living proof of its effectiveness.

I thank my wonderful daughters, Hana Marijke Kohlsmith and Emma Rose Kohlsmith, who heard "Dad won't be home for dinner tonight—he's working on the book" more times than any daughter should.

And how can I express my love and appreciation for my wife and lifetime companion, Dellie Kohl? She has been truly committed to the creation of this book. During the years I spent writing, she helped me carve out the necessary time; managed our family life, cooking up a cornucopia of incredibly healthful meals and coordinating our children's social calendars; and served as assistant editor, creative consultant, and rejecter of lousy ideas. In her spare time, Dellie also created the menu plan, meal ideas, and many of the recipes for this book.

And finally, I want to thank my patients. Your support for my work has been a continual wellspring of inspiration.

Introduction

Why do we have to die? As a kid, you get nice little white
shoes with white laces and a velvet suit with short pants
and a nice collar. You go to college, you meet a nice girl,
get married, work a few years, and then you have to die.
What is that . . . ?
—MEL BROOKS AS THE 2,000-YEAR-OLD MAN

We live in utterly fantastic times. Groundbreaking
advances in longevity research are giving us the opportunity to add several healthy decades to our lives. And genetic
engineers are poised on the brink of breakthroughs that
could open the door to human life spans lasting several centuries.

As science moves ever closer to unlocking the secrets of
immortality, there is much that we can do *now* to take full
advantage of our maximum life span—the 120 years that
nature has allotted each of us. And that's what this book is
about.

During my 25 years as a medical doctor practicing holistic medicine, I have come to develop a profound respect
for the body's innate ability to heal itself. For this reason, I
have intentionally shied away from the more toxic aspects
of traditional medical practice, such as drugs and surgery,
and instead focused on treatments that support the body's
own healing mechanisms. My "prescriptions" to patients
routinely feature dietary recommendations, nutritional
supplements, acupuncture, herbs, homeopathic remedies,
and other natural, complementary modalities.

This type of practice has been tremendously gratifying to me. But I've drawn even greater inspiration from the deepening realization that nature has provided each of us with a set of built-in mechanisms for continued good health far beyond the days of our youth. I call this Renewal.

Renewal is, literally, nature's gift to us. It is only through Renewal that we continue to exist. Renewal enables the body to constantly protect and repair itself so it can withstand the various kinds of damage—both avoidable and unavoidable—that it is subjected to on a day-to-day basis.

During our younger years, we are more than generously endowed with this Renew-ability. We may sleep too little, eat too much (or subsist on junk food), exercise sporadically, smoke and drink . . . and overall, we feel fine. The payback comes as we approach middle age: We find ourselves slowing down a bit, forgetting things, feeling more aches and pains, getting tired more easily.

Popular culture has drummed into our heads that once we turn 40, it's all downhill. Perhaps we feel a sense of helpless panic as we watch our parents age, then notice our own gray hair and wrinkles. In time, we may be faced with the difficult task of caring for a loved one who has been diagnosed with heart disease or cancer or who has suffered a heart attack or stroke. We look around and realize that far too many people—three in four Americans, in fact—are dying from these debilitating health problems. And we begin to feel vulnerable.

Renewal effectively debunks all of the popular "myth-conceptions" about aging. Our later years need not be a time of prolonged suffering and decrepitude. We can grow old—a lot older than is commonly believed—and remain healthy and vital until the end. We do this through Renewal.

During our youth, we were more or less given a free ride. And thank goodness for that. Had our health depended primarily on our good judgment, we might not have survived for this long. Now we are older and hopefully wiser, and we are being offered the key to continued good health. Whether or not we use the key is for each of us to decide. It does require some effort, some discipline, some changes in lifestyle. But the rewards are manifold, especially when you consider the alternative.

One of the unfortunate consequences of poor nutrition, exposure to toxins, lack of exercise, and emotional stress is that they cause our bodies to wear out prematurely—often decades too soon. They do this by undermining Renewal. We must give our built-in Renewal systems the support they require. As long as we do our job, they'll do theirs, working hard to keep us going strong for a good long time.

The Renewal Anti-Aging Program, which I outline in the pages that follow, can benefit people of all ages. It is based on Renewal Theory, a revolutionary new view of the aging process. Rather than reluctantly accepting the inevitable decline of our bodies, we can welcome the opportunity to participate in their ongoing regeneration.

I've developed the Anti-Aging Program based on extensive analysis of the available longevity research as well as my years of experience as a practicing physician. I follow the program, as do my family and a number of my patients. All of us have been quite pleased with the results. We feel healthier and more alive than ever, and we're on track for achieving maximum life span.

The Anti-Aging Program does recommend some rather strict changes in diet and lifestyle. To make them as easy as possible, I've tried to give you lots of options and choices. Still, if you ever feel overwhelmed or discouraged, remind yourself of these two things: First, meaningful change comes slowly because it must be woven into the fabric of your life. Second—and you'll be seeing this message throughout the book—*the extent to which you follow the Renewal program determines the extent to which you'll benefit from it.*

So when should you start the Anti-Aging Program? Right now. The sooner you begin, the better the results. And never think that you're too old for this sort of thing. Positive changes can produce positive results at any age.

Think of this book as your body's preventive maintenance manual, with specific instructions on what you can do to support your internal Renewal systems and stretch your life span. By putting these instructions to practical use, you can prevent your body from wearing out prematurely or succumbing to the ravages of degenerative disease. And you can guarantee your survival to a truly ripe old age.

If you are in average health now, there is no reason why you can't achieve maximum life span. I sincerely hope that as you read through the following pages, you will become convinced—as I have—that aging is not synonymous with disease and degeneration. May you embrace every one of your years as a time of renewed vitality, enduring well-being, and ongoing discovery.

October 1998

PART 1
Renewal: A Unified Theory of Aging

CHAPTER 1

Renewal Theory and the Aging Process: Hope for the Future

Some people want to achieve immortality through their works or their descendants. I prefer to achieve immortality by not dying.
—WOODY ALLEN

Congratulations! It's the year 2057, and today is your birthday! You blow out all 111 candles in one big puff.

You're in great shape, just as fit now as when you were 80, way back in 2026. You still jog and swim on alternate days. And you've decided to take up windsurfing.

Just last week, your doctor gave you yet another clean bill of health: no heart disease, no cancer, no degenerative illness. Your cholesterol is holding steady at 140, and your arteries are as clean and supple as when you were 20. There's no arthritis in your joints, no osteoporosis in your bones. Your body's chronological age belies its biological age of 62 or so. You're full of pizzazz and right on track to celebrate your 120th birthday—perhaps more.

You've accumulated a wealth of knowledge and experience in your lifetime. Still, you've retained your youthful joie de vivre. These days, your most pressing problem is deciding what to do with all of the extra years that lie ahead. You could start a new career (your third) or travel or spend more time with your great-great-grandchildren.

As you look back over a long and productive life span, your still-sharp mind reviewing the cherished memories of

11 decades, you're thankful that years ago you happened to read a book called *Renewal*. Because you know it changed your life forever.

Impossible? Too good to be true? I don't think so. I'm a physician who specializes in anti-aging medicine, preventive medicine, and natural healing from both Eastern and Western traditions. In recent years, I've seen anti-aging medicine truly come of age, as it were. No longer considered voodoo, the field has gained scientific respectability, as increasingly sophisticated research spawns powerful strategies for slowing—and even reversing—the aging process. This book will empower you to easily understand and implement these medical breakthroughs as a life-extending lifestyle that really works.

IT STARTS WITH THE CELLS

Life is nature's most spectacular accomplishment—an astonishing, extraordinary, unprecedented kind of miracle. As fabulous as it is, however, life would cease abruptly if cells didn't have the ability to renew themselves. To stay alive, your cells need protection from harmful invaders. When protection fails, they need the capacity to heal. When their capacity to heal fails, they die.

Of course, organs and tissues are made up of cells. This means that when too many cells become injured or die, organs and tissues likewise begin to malfunction. For example, cumulative damage to brain cells may cause a person to think or move a tad slower or to lose the car keys more often. Cumulative damage to heart cells may lower a person's exercise tolerance, so that walking a mile or even mowing the lawn demands a little more effort than it used to. Cumulative damage to cells in bones and joints may lead to osteoporosis and arthritis. Ultimately, widespread cumulative damage to cells shortens life.

You can see why the cellular repair process is so important. Surprisingly, despite major advances in cell biology, we still know precious little about how cells heal themselves. The extreme complexity of the process has baffled some of the most brilliant minds of our time.

Fortunately, we do know a great deal about how to stimulate cellular repair, and how to protect cells from becoming damaged in the first place. All you need to do is:

- Eat healthfully
- Take specific nutritional, herbal, and hormonal supplements
- Exercise regularly
- Minimize stress
- Avoid exposure to toxins

These five strategies are the foundation of Renewal Theory, which states that life span can be greatly extended by minimizing cellular damage while optimizing cellular repair and regeneration. The chapters that follow examine these strategies in great detail, explaining why each is important and outlining specific actions you can take to maximize your chances of leading the longest life possible.

HOW AND WHY WE AGE

Just how long is the longest life possible? Modern science offers a number of theories. For the most part, they fall into two general categories: program theories and damage theories. Program theories suggest that human genes are precoded for a specific age of death. Damage theories contend that cumulative wear and tear determines the age of death. Combine the two, and you get a theory of aging that goes something like this: Life span cannot be extended beyond its genetically programmed limit, but it can be shortened by the cumulative effects of a lifetime of excessive cellular damage.

This is kind of a bleak outlook—but don't despair. Both program and damage theorists agree that a human's genetically programmed maximum life expectancy is about 120 years. Most of us fall far short of that mark because we fail to take steps to prevent or repair the cumulative cellular damage that can occur over the course of a lifetime. Cumulative cellular damage, especially after age 30, accelerates aging. Controlling this damage, which is the goal of the Renewal Anti-Aging Program, slows down aging.

Before we move on, let's explore program theories and damage theories in a bit more detail.

PROGRAM THEORIES: LIVING TO THE LIMIT

Central to program theories is the concept of maximum life span, the genetically determined age beyond which a human cannot live. Program theories state that the chromosomes in all animal cells contain a preset biological clock. This clock ticks away throughout life until an internal alarm goes off, triggering death. In effect, aging and death are literally etched into the genetic blueprint.

The age at which death occurs varies from one species to the next. Mice, for instance, have a maximum life span of about two years, while turtles can survive 150 years or longer. For us humans, maximum life span is about 120 years.

If we want to break the 120-year barrier, we first have to figure out how the genetic program for maximum life span works. Solving this puzzle has become the mission of researchers in molecular biology and genetics. Their first step, under way now, is to isolate the genes responsible for aging. Once located, these genes can be reprogrammed for a longer life span, and perhaps someday for immortality.

Of course, this work is still in its infancy, and several decades may pass before it produces definitive answers. But the reality of using genetic reprogramming for longevity is simply a matter of time. In fact, research focusing on the pineal gland, which produces the hormone melatonin, suggests that we may be on the verge of a breakthrough that will enable us to reset our biological clocks. In the meantime, as you will see, you can do a great deal to slow down the aging process.

DAMAGE THEORIES: REPAIRING WEAR AND TEAR

If the human body is genetically programmed to last 120 years, why do we fall so short of that milestone? According to damage theories, it's the cellular wear and tear inflicted by daily life that accelerates aging and does us in much too soon.

The damage referred to in the phrase *damage theory* is caused exclusively by free radicals. Free radicals, the rogues' gallery of biochemistry, are highly charged, rapidly moving molecular fragments that harm healthy cells. The more free radicals present, the more damage they cause, and the more the aging process speeds up as a result.

So where do these free radicals come from? Some occur naturally, as by-products of normal human cellular metabolism (though the optimally healthy body has efficient systems for removing them). Many more result from poor diet, deficiencies of key nutrients, and exposure to toxins. A list of the causes of free radicals would include virtually every toxic substance known. A list of the effects of free radicals would also be long, encompassing all of the common diseases afflicting humans.

This doesn't mean that every disease is caused exclusively by free radicals. Some people inherit genetic predispositions to certain health problems, such as heart disease, cancer, osteoporosis, arthritis, Alzheimer's disease, and Parkinson's disease. So if you possess a "sick gene," are you doomed to illness? Absolutely not. Whether or not such a gene "expresses" itself depends entirely on you. If you minimize free radicals and keep your cells healthy, you can either prevent a disease from occurring or reverse it if it has already begun.

As you'll discover in chapter 2, your greatest allies in the battle against free radicals are nutrients known as antioxidants. Antioxidants neutralize free radicals and, as a result, slow the aging process. They're good guys that you want to have around at all times. You can keep them around by eating lots of antioxidant-rich foods and taking antioxidant supplements.

RENEWAL: THE ANTIDOTE TO AGING

Renewal Theory, the basis for this book, builds on both program and damage theories. I like to think of it as the body's master plan for rejuvenation. It goes something like this: You are genetically programmed to live 120 years. To achieve this maximum life span, you need to do what you can to minimize cellular damage, which precipitates disease and accelerates aging. This means supplying your body with ample quantities of the raw materials that it uses to protect healthy cells, repair damaged cells, and replace irreparable or dead cells.

Protection, repair, and regeneration—these bodily functions are at the heart of Renewal. You can keep them going strong with help from my Anti-Aging Diet, Anti-Aging Supplement Program, and Anti-Aging Exercise Program, which are outlined later in this book.

Remember that the key to longevity is within everyone's reach. The choices you make every day—from what you eat and drink to which supplements you take (or don't take) to whether or not you exercise—exert a profound influence over how long you live. Those 120 years that nature has allotted you are ultimately in your hands.

Since free radicals play such a pivotal role in the aging process, let's take a closer look at these cellular desperadoes. We'll examine how they influence life and death, both on the miniature stage of the individual cell and in the broader theater of the human body.

Defeating Free Radicals: The Key to Longevity

Very few individuals, if any, reach their potential maximum life span; they die instead prematurely of a wide variety of diseases—the vast majority being "free radical" diseases.
—DENHAM HARMAN, M.D., PH.D.,
WHO IN 1954 FIRST PROPOSED THE FREE
RADICAL THEORY OF AGING

"**H**oney, take a look at this. You might find it interesting."

Great moments in human history often begin inauspiciously. Such was the case in December 1945, when the wife of Denham Harman handed him the latest issue of the *Ladies' Home Journal*. It was opened to an article titled "Tomorrow You May Be Younger," written by William L. Laurence, science editor of the *New York Times*. This article, heralding the work of a Russian gerontologist on an "anti-reticular cytotoxic serum," sparked Dr. Harman's interest in finding an answer to the riddle of aging—a subject that scientists of the time knew absolutely nothing about.

For the next nine years, Dr. Harman, a brilliant young organic chemist with a Ph.D. from the University of California, Berkeley, ruminated about the aging process. Because aging is such a universal phenomenon, he reasoned that it might have a single basic cause. But what could it be? The answer eluded him.

Though still obsessed with the question, he had to place it on the back burner while he completed medical school and an internship at Stanford University. Then one morning in November 1954, during a period in which he was simultaneously completing his residency in internal medicine and doing research at Berkeley's Donner Laboratory, Dr. Harman's quest ended. That day, while reading in his office, he had an "aha" experience that would revolutionize medical science: "(It) suddenly occurred to me that free radical reactions, however initiated, could be responsible for the progressive deterioration of biological systems."

Of course, sometimes even the best ideas are slow to be accepted. This one didn't exactly inspire words of praise— not at first, anyway. After thinking it over for a month, Dr. Harman strolled the Berkeley campus, knocking on doors and presenting his newly formulated Free Radical Theory to his colleagues. To say that it was a hard sell would be an understatement. He might have had more success had he been hawking vacuum cleaners.

The scientists whom Dr. Harman approached were singularly unimpressed. In fact, all but two flatly rejected his idea. One after another, they slammed the door in the face of the young upstart, who dared challenge the status quo with the preposterous notion that all degenerative disease—and the aging process itself—could be explained by the presence of free radicals.

Undaunted, Dr. Harman pursued his theory. In subsequent years, he demonstrated how the effects of free radicals are reversed by nutrients known as antioxidants, how antioxidants extend the life spans of laboratory animals, and how antioxidants offer protection against heart disease, cancer, senile brain disease, and all other degenerative conditions associated with aging. Dr. Harman proved that age-related immune deficiency is caused by free radicals and can be reversed by antioxidants.

In terms of scientific significance, Dr. Harman's Free Radical Theory ranks with Galileo's invention of the telescope, Newton's discovery of gravity, and Einstein's theory of relativity. No breakthrough has had more profound implications for human health and longevity.

Now in his mid-eighties and still professionally active, Dr. Harman deserves the Nobel Prize for his revolutionary work.

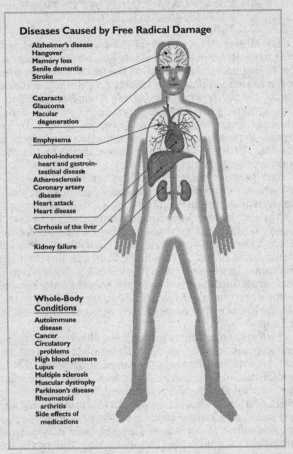

Diseases Caused by Free Radical Damage

Alzheimer's disease
Hangover
Memory loss
Senile dementia
Stroke

Cataracts
Glaucoma
Macular
  degeneration

Emphysema

Alcohol-induced
  heart and gastroin-
  testinal disease
Atherosclerosis
Coronary artery
  disease
Heart attack
Heart disease

Cirrhosis of the liver

Kidney failure

**Whole-Body
Conditions**

Autoimmune
  disease
Cancer
Circulatory
  problems
High blood pressure
Lupus
Multiple sclerosis
Muscular dystrophy
Parkinson's disease
Rheumatoid
  arthritis
Side effects of
  medications

Over time, free radical damage can take a toll on virtually every organ and system in your body. This in turn sets the stage for all sorts of degenerative diseases, as shown here.

FREE RADICALS: LONGEVITY'S MOST FORMIDABLE FOE

Dr. Harman's Free Radical Theory has emerged as the best understood and most widely accepted explanation of the aging process. Having stood the test of time and countless research validations, it has become not just *a* damage theory but *the* damage theory. (You'll recall from chapter 1 that according to damage theories, cumulative cellular damage determines a person's age of death.) In fact, among doctors specializing in anti-aging medicine, Free Radical Theory has transcended mere theory status and is considered a biological fact of life.

Just what are these free radicals, anyway? Understanding where they come from, and why and how they do so much damage, requires a brief lesson in biochemistry.

Molecules are made up of atoms glued together by chemical bonds. Each bond consists of a pair of electrons. When a bond is broken, what's left are two molecular fragments, each of which contains one of the now unpaired electrons. These molecular fragments are highly charged and highly unstable, because they contain only one electron rather than two. These highly charged, highly unstable, highly reactive particles are what we know as free radicals.

Unfortunately for us humans, the biochemical saga of free radicals doesn't end there. Remember, each free radical contains one unpaired electron. And unpaired electrons, like unpaired humans, hate to be alone. They want a partner, and they're not above breaking up another bond to get what they want. Scientists call this process oxidation, and free radicals are masters at it. They're not particularly discriminating about where they get their new partners, either. They'll oxidize just about anything that gets in their way—punching holes in cell membranes, destroying key enzymes, and fracturing DNA.

What's more, free radicals are remarkably prolific. One free radical, unchecked, can cause new ones to form. These free radicals, in turn, give rise to many more. How does this happen?

Because it has so much energy, a free radical zips about until it bangs into a nearby molecule with a stable bond.

The collision splits the stable molecule, releasing one of its two electrons. The free radical nabs the electron as a partner for its own unpaired electron, and the two form a stable bond. All this happens, quite literally, within nanoseconds.

The good news is that the free radical has stabilized itself. The bad news is that in doing so, it may have caused the formation of two more free radicals by breaking a stable bond, leaving the two atoms of the formerly stable molecule to share one unpaired electron. So begins a chain reaction that produces thousands of molecular fragments with unpaired electrons. And every one of these fragments is careening about, looking to swipe an electron from an unsuspecting stable molecule.

To get a clearer understanding of how free radicals multiply, imagine a football stadium filled to the brim with mousetraps, each mousetrap loaded with a Ping-Pong ball. If you drop one Ping-Pong ball into the stadium, it springs one mousetrap, causing it to fling its ball into the air. Then you have two loose Ping-Pong balls, which spring two more mousetraps. Within a matter of seconds, all of the mousetraps are sprung, and all of the balls are loose.

Now if all those mousetraps were stable molecules, and all those Ping-Pong balls were free radicals, you would have just witnessed a free radical free-for-all.

CELLULAR SABOTAGE

In their reckless quest for electrons, free radicals do a lot of structural damage to healthy cells. Injured cells can't function properly and may even die.

Most vulnerable to free radical attack is the cell membrane, which surrounds each cell and guards its jellylike interior. The cell membrane is a sophisticated, highly selective barrier whose all-important job is to guard access to the cell. It decides what gets in, what stays in, and what is expelled (forcibly, if need be). If cells were nightclubs, then cell membranes would be bouncers.

Inside each cell are many subcellular structures called organelles. Each organelle is wrapped in its own protective outer membrane and performs a highly specialized function. Mitochondria, for example, transform oxygen and food into energy, which the cell uses to carry out its tasks.

How Free Radicals Damage Cells

Nuclear membrane

Nucleus (contains DNA)

Mitochondrion

Mitochondrial membrane

Lysosome

Cell membrane

A free radical hit can hamper a cell's ability to function properly, depending on where the hit occurs. Damage to the cell
membrane, for example, impairs the delivery of nutrients to
the cell and the removal of waste products from the cell. Damage to the mitochondria saps the cell's energy supply. When
the lysosomes are injured, the cell can no longer detoxify properly. Most devastating of all is a free radical assault on the
DNA molecules in the cell's nucleus. This can cause a cell to
replicate abnormally or to not replicate at all, leading to its
death.

Lysosomes scarf up and digest cellular garbage, which is
then either recycled or jettisoned. The cell's nucleus is also
an organelle. It houses DNA, the cell's genetic blueprint.

When a cell membrane or an organelle membrane is
damaged by free radicals, it loses its protective properties.
This puts the health of the entire cell at risk.

The cell membrane is a pushover for free radical attack
because it is composed primarily of easily oxidized fatty
acids. Like tiny but powerful bullets, highly charged free
radical particles rip into the cell membrane, literally punc-
turing holes in it. A damaged cell membrane loses its selectivity. When this happens, transportation of nutrients,
oxygen, and water into the cell and removal of waste products from the cell become compromised.

In much the same way, free radical damage to an

organelle's membrane sabotages the organelle's function. When mitochondria are injured, for instance, these submicroscopic power plants can't produce the energy necessary to drive the cell's machinery. If damage to the mitochondrial membrane is extensive, the cell dies.

Free radicals can even bang their way through the protective membrane surrounding the nucleus, gaining access to the DNA molecules housed inside. If free radicals happen to break the DNA molecules in order to snatch electrons, the cell dies, or loses its ability to replicate, or replicates abnormally—a process known as mutation. Mutation can give rise to the collections of abnormal cells that we know as cancer.

But cancer isn't the only health problem for which free radicals are responsible. Cumulative free radical damage contributes to all sorts of organ- and tissue-specific diseases, including allergies, Alzheimer's disease, arthritis, atherosclerosis (hardening and clogging of the arteries), cancer, cataracts, infections, macular degeneration, multiple sclerosis, and Parkinson's disease. In fact, researchers now agree that most common ailments, including virtually all chronic degenerative diseases, are either caused directly by or are closely associated with free radical damage.

IMMUNE CELLS: DEDICATED DEFENDERS

Of all the cells in your body, immune cells are the most likely victims of free radical attack. Ironically, they put themselves at risk just by carrying out their assigned task.

Immune cells scavenge free radicals. If injured, immune cells are less able to do their job. In the short run, their impairment usually doesn't produce symptoms. Over time, persistent fatigue, recurrent infections, and allergies may be among the first signs of immune erosion.

If free radicals continue their attack on immune cells, and if the cells never get a chance to heal, the accumulated damage weakens the immune system even more. Eventually, this opens a potential Pandora's box of disorders caused by altered immune function. Free radical damage to an immune cell's protective outer membrane or DNA can be especially ominous.

Once damaged, an immune cell loses its ability to differentiate between good guys and bad guys. One of two scenarios, neither good, then unfolds. In the first, immune cells mistake friends for foes and begin attacking healthy tissues. This is known as an autoimmune disease, examples of which include lupus, multiple sclerosis, and rheumatoid arthritis. In the second scenario, immune cells mistake foes for friends. For example, they may fail to recognize cancer cells and, rather than annihilating them, ignore them and allow them to multiply.

THE LINK TO AGING

Prolonged exposure to free radicals actually fast-forwards the aging process. One of the clearest manifestations of cumulative free radical damage is a phenomenon known as cross-linking.

Cross-linking affects protein, enzyme, DNA, and RNA molecules. A bit like handcuffing, it hampers the ability of its molecular hostages to perform their assigned tasks. In this way, cross-linking works to the detriment of the entire organism—especially if that organism happens to be your body. Because of cross-linking, the elastic, flexible tissue of youth gives way to the wrinkled skin, stiff joints, and hardened arteries of old age.

What's more, cross-linking worsens with age, as the cellular wear and tear of several decades accumulates and the body becomes less adept at scavenging free radicals. The result is the general, body-wide impairment of function that's synonymous with degenerative disease and aging.

In skin cells, the cross-linking of molecules causes the wrinkles characteristic of aging. In arterial cells, cross-linking reduces flexibility, which in turn raises blood pressure and puts extra strain on the heart as it pumps harder to maintain a continuous flow of blood. In the brain, cross-linking impedes message transmission between nerve cells—not good if you prefer crisp thinking and a rapid flow of ideas. Thought processes slow down, and memory and concentration problems are more likely.

For all of cross-linking's dirty work, its effects on DNA molecules may be most problematic. When these molecules are damaged, they compromise the cell's ability to correctly interpret its DNA-encoded genetic blueprint.

This results in impaired DNA replication and protein assembly. The entire process of Renewal depends on cells being able to replicate themselves exactly. This is why the failure to protect a cell's genetic coding has particularly profound consequences.

MEET THE FREE RADICAL FORMERS

Since free radical damage fosters disease and shortens life, it stands to reason that we need to know not only where these rogues come from but also how to avoid them—or at least limit our exposure.

Unfortunately, free radicals are everywhere. They're in the foods we eat, the water we drink, the air we breathe. Even our bodies produce free radicals.

Our bodies are equipped to rein in and dispose of free radicals. The problem is that we usually have more of these troublemakers floating around than our bodies can manage. And that's when we run into problems.

Any combination of factors that produces excessive free radicals (or suboptimal scavenging) can ultimately cause mass destruction throughout the human body. This destruction has been linked to the development of disease and the acceleration of aging.

True, some sources of free radicals we can't control. But many we can. Here's a rundown of the primary offenders.

THE MOST SURPRISING SOURCE

As you read this sentence, your body is generating humongous quantities of free radicals. And believe it or not, it's quite normal.

You see, these free radicals are a kind of cellular "exhaust"—a by-product of metabolism. They're produced as cells use oxygen to convert food into energy. The only way to avoid these free radicals would be to stop burning oxygen. But then your metabolism would shut down, too.

Because these free radicals are really your body's own doing, your body expects them and is designed to deal with them. It has highly efficient ways of grabbing and neutralizing these renegade particles before they can do harm. So your cells just keep on making them.

THE USUAL SUSPECTS

The free radicals that occur naturally within your body should be no cause for concern. It's the excess free radicals, the ones that your body is not prepared to handle, that cause life-shortening damage. This extra load results from two key factors: an overabundance of toxins and a shortage of antioxidants (more on these later).

A complete list of all the external sources of free radicals would likely run on for pages. So here are a few of the more pernicious offenders.

The standard American diet. The standard American diet is a free radical fiasco just waiting to happen. It's liberally laced with high-fat, processed, preserved, pesticide-laden, chemically treated foods. It's chock-full of known free radical formers such as meat, butter, margarine, sugar, white flour, and alcohol. It emphasizes frying, browning, and other cooking methods that exponentially drive up the free radical count. Most significant of all, it's dangerously deficient in antioxidant-rich, free radical–fighting fruits and vegetables.

A high-fat diet. Consuming more than 10 percent of your calories from fat dramatically increases your body's free radical load. The reason: When bombarded by free radicals, fat molecules split apart easily. The weak bonds that hold together polyunsaturated fat molecules are especially sensitive to and readily broken by heat, light, or oxygen. The more fat you ingest, the more free radicals your body generates. This is why heart disease and cancer, two conditions associated with cumulative free radical damage, are most common in people who consume high-fat diets.

***Trans*-fats.** Also known as funny-fats or ugly fats (because of what they do to the body), *trans*-fats are seething cauldrons of free radical activity. They're created by cooking at high heat and by hydrogenation (the process used to harden liquid vegetable oils). Most people get their *trans*-fats from the margarine they spread on their morning toast, the shortening in most baked goods, and the hydrogenated oil in processed and convenience foods (such as crackers, chips, and nuts). The average American ingests

100 pounds of *trans*-fats annually, a tremendous free radical load.

Chemicals. Some of the nastiest and most pervasive free radicals come from the vast and expanding array of toxic chemicals being released into the environment. Chlorination of water supplies spawns often dangerous levels of chloroform and trihalomethanes, both powerful free radical formers. The air is also saturated with free radical formers: oxides of sulfur and nitrogen, ozone (which is beneficial to humans only if it stays in the upper atmosphere), chlorine, aromatic hydrocarbons (such as benzene and toluene), formaldehyde, carbon monoxide, lead, asbestos, and tobacco smoke. The combustion of tobacco alone creates thousands of different free radical–generating chemicals. Even if you don't smoke, you may have a hard time escaping from secondhand smoke.

Pesticides. Pesticides are notorious free radical formers. They're also very soluble in fat. This means they're found in much larger quantities in foods of animal origin, which are naturally high in fat, than in foods of plant origin. Why? Well, an animal eats pesticide-sprayed feed every day over the course of its lifetime. The pesticide residues become concentrated in the animal's fatty tissues, the result of a vain attempt by the animal's body to remove the toxic substances. Then when you eat food from that animal—be it steak, chicken, milk, cheese, or butter—your body likewise tries to rid itself of the toxins by storing them in fatty tissues. Hidden away, the pesticide molecules eventually initiate free radical chain reactions. This phenomenon helps explain the epidemic of heart disease and cancer among meat-eaters.

Radiation. Ionizing radiation—including medical and dental x-rays, radon gas, and ultraviolet radiation from the sun—fractures stable molecules. In doing so, it creates free radicals. Cells are extremely sensitive to radiation, with the cell membranes and the chromosomes in the nuclei at highest risk for damage. And radiation doesn't have to be strong to do harm: Exposure so weak that it destroys only one molecule in 100 million can nevertheless trigger free radical chain reactions capable of killing an entire cell. And if radiation scores a direct hit on a cell's nucleus, the

Sources of Free Radicals

Avoiding free radical formers may seem like an easy enough task. But the reality is, they're just about everywhere. The following list provides a mere sampling of substances and other factors that can cause a free radical overload. How many of these do you encounter every day?

General Factors
Aging
Metabolism
Stress

Dietary Factors
Additives
Alcohol
Coffee
Foods of animal origin
Foods that have been barbecued, broiled, fried, grilled, or
    otherwise cooked at high temperatures
Foods that have been browned or burned
Herbicides

cell's DNA—the blueprint for cell replication—becomes damaged.

THE STORY OF JOE SIX-PACK

Right about now, you might be thinking that the only way to avoid free radical exposure is to swear off eating, drinking, and even breathing for the rest of your life. Needless to say, the rest of your life would play out mighty quickly. There's no need to do anything so drastic. Remember, your goal is to keep a lid on free radical overload.

To help you put this in perspective, allow me to share the story of Joe Six-Pack. Joe is a fairly typical American guy. On one particular Saturday morning, Joe wakes up a bit hungover as a result of getting a little too happy at happy hour the evening before. He drinks a glass or two of chlorinated tap water to rehydrate himself, then follows

Hydrogenated vegetable oils
Pesticides
Sugar

Chemical Factors
Air pollutants such as asbestos, benzene, carbon monoxide, chlorine, formaldehyde, ozone, tobacco smoke, and toluene
Chemical solvents such as cleaning products, glue, paints, and paint thinners
Over-the-counter and prescribed medications
Perfumes
Pesticides
Water pollutants such as chloroform and other trihalomethanes caused by chlorination

Radiation
Cosmic radiation
Electromagnetic fields
Medical and dental x-rays
Radon gas
Solar radiation

with a cup of coffee (cream and sugar added). His breakfast consists of fried eggs and toast with margarine.

After grabbing a quick shower and splashing on a palmfull of his favorite aftershave (containing alcohol, perfume, and other chemicals), Joe climbs in his car and heads for the beach. It's such a spectacular day that he rolls down all the windows and takes deep breaths of "fresh" air—which has already been contaminated with hefty doses of pollutants. At the beach, Joe buys a bag of chips and a cola at the snack bar, then chats with his buddies (both smokers) before falling asleep in the sun for a couple of hours.

Joe has already set himself up for free radical overload, and it isn't even lunch yet. If Joe maintains this lifestyle, he's headed for serious trouble. By age 60, Joe—a fairly typical American guy—will suffer a fairly typical massive coronary and undergo fairly typical coronary bypass surgery.

ANTIOXIDANTS: OUR NUMBER ONE ALLY

Joe can change many of his free radical–forming ways. And the sooner he does it, the better off he'll be. Because while he can't eradicate every last one of the free radicals in his body, he should make every effort to stay several steps ahead of them for as long as he can. This is the secret of longevity.

Lucky for Joe, he has a powerful weapon in the war on free radicals. Matching these molecular miscreants blow for blow are the body's built-in free radical defense systems. Without these systems, humans would be toast—our lives measured in minutes rather than decades.

The body relies on two particular defense systems to neutralize free radicals: the antioxidant nutrient system and the antioxidant enzyme system. The nutrients can be used as is, straight from the foods and supplements we consume. The enzymes must be synthesized, or manufactured by the body.

What makes the antioxidants so effective against free radicals is their willingness to give up their own electrons for the cause. The free radicals greedily accept the antioxidants' offer, like kids drooling over a piece of candy. Of course, once a free radical finds a partner for its unpaired electron, it immediately loses free radical status. It behaves itself and stays out of trouble from then on. And the best part is, the antioxidants are able to donate their electrons without generating free radicals themselves.

As evidence of the crucial role that antioxidants play in fending off free radicals and prolonging life, consider the findings of one of the earliest experiments conducted by Dr. Harman. In this experiment, one group of rats ate standard rat chow, while another group ate rat chow fortified with antioxidants. The rats in the latter group lived 40 percent longer than the rats in the former. In human terms, this translates to about 40 extra years of life. As Dr. Harman theorized, and as subsequent research has proven, the antioxidants protected the rats from free radical damage, thus extending their life spans.

But just as an abundance of antioxidants can add years to your life, a shortfall can take years away. Free radicals go unscavaged, continuing to roam your system and damage healthy cells. This is why it's so important to eat plenty of antioxidant-rich foods and take appropriate antioxidant supplements. The more antioxidants you have floating around your bloodstream and protecting your cells, the longer you can expect your life span to be.

LAYING THE FOUNDATION FOR RENEWAL

The optimum longevity-promoting lifestyle, then, has two key components: First, it maximizes antioxidant intake from foods and supplements; and second, it minimizes factors that promote the formation of free radicals. We'll cover both of these components in more detail in later chapters. For now, here are the basics.

- Choose organic, pesticide-free, additive-free foods.
- Drink only purified water.
- Avoid exposure to volatile chemicals, including perfume, hair spray, glue, paint, gasoline, solvents, and smoke.
- Limit exposure to air pollution: Keep your windows closed when driving in heavy traffic, and stay off busy streets when exercising.
- When outdoors, limit the amount of time you spend in direct sunlight, especially at midday.
- Check your house for radon gas. (Hardware and home supply stores sell inexpensive testing kits.)
- Get medical and dental x-rays only when absolutely necessary.
- Take medications only when absolutely necessary. (*Note:* Always consult your doctor before you stop taking any medicine that he has prescribed.)

Now that you've been formally introduced to both free radicals and antioxidants, let's explore their respective roles in the grander scheme of Renewal Theory.

Renewal Theory: A New View of Aging

The doctor of the future will give no medicine, but will interest his patients in the care of the human frame, in diet, and in the cause and prevention of disease.
—THOMAS EDISON

"**W**ould you please hold this and take my picture when I'm heading back?"

I handed my camera to my colleague Ellen, then slowly jogged away from our group and up the steep slope. This was the thrill of a lifetime. As I gained confidence, I picked up my pace, weaving past the dense clusters of tourists near the entrance and finally breaking free into the open area beyond. With each step, my excitement grew. I thought back on how Ellen and the others had humored my obsession for weeks: "Don't worry, Tim. You'll get your chance to jog on the Great Wall."

Ellen and I, along with eight others, were touring China as guests of the Chinese government—members of the first delegation of American physicians practicing Chinese Traditional Medicine who had ever been invited to visit the People's Republic. The red carpet had been rolled out for us as we traveled from one city to the next, touring hospitals and universities and clinics, observing firsthand how medical care was provided.

Just the day before, the entire faculty of the Shanghai College of Chinese Traditional Medicine attended my lecture on some acupuncture research I had done. Because I had learned acupuncture in the West, for years I wondered how my skills in this ancient healing art would compare with those of my Chinese peers. I was pleasantly surprised to discover that I had nothing to be ashamed of. I was practicing Chinese medicine the way doctors in China practice it, and I could discuss the finer points of traditional medical theory with ease. In fact, I had something to teach them, which is why they invited me to give that lecture. They had loved it, and now, still flush from that thrill, I thought the excitement would be impossible to top.

Earlier on our tour, I had had the opportunity to scrub in on an open-heart surgery performed only with acupuncture anesthesia. Incredibly, the patient smiled and chatted with me as the surgeons labored inside his chest.

But those emotional highs paled in comparison to this one. Ahead of me lay the Great Wall of China, winding its way across distant mountaintops before disappearing out of sight. It would continue 500 miles east to the Gulf of Chihli, part of the Yellow Sea. Behind me, it carved a 1,000-plus-mile swath westward to the gates of central Asia, deep in Gansu province.

In my lifetime, I had run across the Golden Gate Bridge, to the top of the Eiffel Tower, through the market at Marrakech, through the streets of Tokyo, London, Hong Kong, and Los Angeles. But none of that had prepared me for this.

THE JOURNEY OF A LIFETIME

As I raced along the great stone roadway, my thoughts drifted back 10 years to a night that literally changed my life. At the time, I was a resident physician at San Francisco General Hospital, and on that particular evening, I was on call. As I waited for the next emergency, I picked up a copy of *The Yellow Emperor's Classic of Internal Medicine (Huang Ti Nei Ching Su Wen)* and began reading through it. The book spoke directly to my feelings about the deficiencies of mainstream medicine. It described a system based on health and healing rather than pathology and disease, a system that restored balance and harmony to the body by using natural therapies rather than toxic drugs.

In my mind, Eastern and Western medicines had a lot to

offer one another because they compensated for each other's shortcomings so well. Together they formed a much more perfect system of medicine. That night, I realized that I must learn Chinese medicine so I could offer my patients the best of both worlds.

All my years of preparation during medical school, my internship, and my residency hadn't prepared me for this fundamental shift in my philosophy of health and healing. Still, it came to me effortlessly, as though I could have been a Chinese doctor in a past life. My Chinese teachers presented their medicine as a richly symbolic and powerfully effective system developed to absolute sophistication more than 3,000 years ago. They viewed healing as the body's attempt to correct an imbalance of energy, and they were horrified by the Western practice of treating disease by poisoning the body with drugs. I embraced their teachings, as I, too, had become frustrated with the symptom-masking mentality of Western medicine.

I began prescribing nutritional remedies, herbs, and acupuncture to my patients, and I observed firsthand how these natural medicines stimulated the body to heal itself. Perhaps inevitably, my awe of the body's innate healing powers influenced my research in anti-aging medicine. I took for granted the validity of protecting the body from disease by naturally activating its own defense systems. To this day, I resist any anti-aging therapy that presents the body with unfamiliar chemicals or disturbs its natural balance.

As I ran, it occurred to me that the Great Wall stood as the symbolic destination of my journey into Chinese medicine, which had begun a decade before. My run there had in a way become a personal vindication from those short-sighted critics who had once asked me why I would throw away a bright future in medicine for what they viewed as quackery. Time saw fit to favor my vision and prove my detractors wrong.

AN EVEN GREATER WALL

The Great Wall is an extraordinary sight to behold—a legendary testimonial to the power of protection. The largest manmade structure in the world, and the only one visible from the moon, the wall was built more than two millennia ago to defend the northern border of China against the marauding Huns. It rises 25 feet high and is wide enough to accommodate five horses abreast. In its heyday, it enabled the rapid transport of soldiers and supplies to wherever they were needed. These days, armies of tourists flock to marvel at its magnificence.

Continuing my run, I made my way up a very steep section of the wall to one of the garrison towers that are spaced at 200-yard intervals. Through a small window in the tower, I gazed out at the countryside, imagining myself as a Ch'in dynasty soldier dodging spears and arrows to defend my homeland. What was it like here 22 centuries ago, when the invading nomads from the north menaced the wall?

And then things took a surreal turn. I began to see some compelling parallels between the Great Wall and a cell wall, the tough outer membrane that surrounds every cell in the human body. The Great Wall protected China just as the cell membrane protects a cell.

Of course, the cell membrane is made not of stone but of fat (of all things!). But much like the Great Wall, the membrane serves as a barrier between the inside of the cell and would-be invaders. Swarming in and around the cell membrane are molecular soldiers called antioxidants. These molecules—which are either obtained directly from food or manufactured by the body—stand guard, ready to defend the cell against those enemy particles known as free radicals.

I began to envision the 25-foot-high wall that I was standing on as a giant cell membrane. Hordes of free radical Huns were aiming their spears and arrows in preparation for an attack, only to be turned back by the antioxidant soldiers (such as vitamins C and E, coenzyme Q_{10}, and glutathione) stationed along the wall.

Now if this analogy seems a bit far-fetched, consider this: The total surface area protected by your cell membranes is far greater than the area protected by the Great Wall. And the membrane surrounding just one of your 100 trillion or so cells fends off more free radicals in a single day than all the spears and arrows hurled at the Great Wall since it was built.

The idea of maintaining a strong defense against potential damage, rather than allowing damage to occur and then trying to mop up the mess, made a lot of sense to me. I mulled it over as I ran back toward my group, feigning a dead-heat finish as Ellen snapped my picture. "You look a little dreamy," she said. "Are you okay?"

I just smiled.

WHAT IS RENEWAL?

Even now, whenever I think of the Great Wall, it reminds me of the constant battle being waged within the human body at the cellular level. For me, the wall is a manifestation of the principles of Renewal.

Renewal is your body's master plan for rejuvenation. It consists of three very important functions that give your body the ability to maintain optimum health: protection, repair, and regeneration. Renewal prevents disease by protecting healthy cells and repairing damaged ones. When those options fail, Renewal replaces damaged or dead cells with new ones.

Like an automobile, the human body comes equipped with certain standard features. We each get our allotment of hair, teeth, lungs, and kidneys. We also get a healing system, the mission of which is to achieve and maintain optimum health. This system coordinates the resources that defend, repair, and restore the body. It provides the foundation for Renewal.

Why do we need such an elaborate healing system? In a word, damage. Damage threatens our survival. Any agent that harms the body undermines optimum health. And truth be told, damage can result from almost anything. The body even inflicts damage on itself, as it produces volatile free radicals in the course of carrying out routine tasks.

Fortunately, the body's healing system heads off much of the damage. Injured cells are constantly being repaired or replaced, although we're pretty much oblivious to it. Without this healing system, cells would rapidly succumb. Our life spans would be measured in days rather than decades.

Renewal, in other words, keeps us alive. Remarkably, it works even under the worst conditions, when it is unassisted, ignored, or hamstrung by bad habits. And with some support in the form of optimum diet, nutritional supplements, and regular exercise, Renewal can be your ticket to optimum health and maximum longevity.

The message here is that Renewal is under your control.

You can facilitate it and extend your life span, or you can sabotage it and accelerate aging. What swings the pendulum one way or the other? The lifestyle choices that you make every day.

THE BASIC INGREDIENTS

Prompt, efficient Renewal requires adequate supplies of six types of nutrients, along with a set of plans to coordinate them. When any of the nutrients runs low, Renewal slows. And when Renewal slows, the aging process speeds up.

Before we get into how Renewal works, let's take a closer look at each of its essential elements.

Amino acids. All enzymes are proteins, and all proteins consist of individual building blocks called amino acids. Other useful healing proteins, including antibodies and certain hormones, are synthesized from amino acids as well. To meet your daily protein requirement and give your body the amino acids it needs, without adding harmful fats to your diet, choose whole grains and beans over meats.

Complex carbohydrates. Complex carbohydrates supply the energy that powers a cell's chemical synthesis machinery. Unrefined grains and beans offer the highest quality complex carbs. Please, no sugars—not even natural sugars such as fructose, sucrose, and glucose. They just gum up the works, like fueling your car with kerosene instead of high-octane gasoline.

Essential fatty acids. These "fat vitamins" are irreplaceable in the process of Renewal. They serve as building blocks for cell membranes, as free radical scavengers and immune enhancers, and as anti-inflammatory compounds called prostaglandins. Seeds, beans, and vegetables contain modest amounts of essential fatty acids. But for an optimum intake, you need supplements, the best of which are flaxseed oil and borage oil. (You'll learn more about the essential fatty acids in chapter 8.)

Vitamins. These nutrients serve as catalysts for the astounding array of chemical reactions involved in

Renewal. Certain vitamins—namely A, C, and E—also put in cameo appearances as antioxidants.

Minerals. Minerals play essential roles as cofactors for our enzyme systems. This means that they help enzymes perform certain tasks.

Phytochemicals. These recently discovered, multifaceted healing nutrients bridge the gap between basic nutrition and supernourishment. Research has already shown them to be key players in the prevention of heart disease, cancer, and other degenerative conditions. The various types of phytochemicals number in the thousands, although only a relative handful have been identified so far. What's more, they're found only in plant foods. Examples include the more than 600 carotenoids in orange and yellow vegetables, the quercetin and other flavonoids in citrus fruits, the protease inhibitors in soybean products, and the proanthocyanidins in grape seed extract.

Genetic program. To manage and coordinate the protection, repair, and regeneration of cells, your body's healing system needs, above all else, a set of plans. Your genetic program is the DNA double helix molecule. DNA controls everything a cell does by directing the manufacturing of thousands of different enzymes, each of which catalyzes one of the thousands of chemical reactions that keeps you alive.

A CELLULAR AFFAIR

I never tire of thinking about the miracle of Renewal taking place in each one of the 100 trillion cells that make up the human body. In many respects, a cell is a lot like a miniature human body. It needs food. It generates energy. It eliminates waste. It reproduces. It has a definite life span. Your cells try very hard to stay healthy. And they desperately need your help.

To fully appreciate how Renewal works, you need a basic understanding of what goes on inside a cell. So join me as we take a brief tour of a typical cell to examine its most important components. Throughout the rest of the book, I'll be referring to the structures described here. (You may also want to refer to the illustration on page 14.)

Cell Membranes: A1 Protection

Perhaps the most important cellular structures are the membranes, the protective coverings located both inside and outside each cell. One membrane, called (appropriately enough) the cell membrane, forms the outer surface of the cell. Other membranes surround the organelles, smaller subcellular units that perform specialized functions. Examples of organelles include the mitochondria, which supply the cell's energy; lysosomes, which digest and expel cellular waste; and the nucleus, which houses DNA and chromosomes. You'll learn more about these structures a bit later in this chapter.

The membranes are highly selective two-way barriers that protect a cell and its organelles by functioning as combination security guards/bouncers. Their primary job is to sift through the biochemical soup inside and outside the cell, deciding what gains entry and what gets booted out. Through their selectivity, the membranes control the internal environment not only of the cell as a whole but also of each of the organelles.

Since all of the membranes are made up primarily of fat molecules, optimum membrane health depends on optimum intake of the essential fatty acids. Throughout this book, I will repeatedly emphasize the importance of essential fatty acid supplements. I take them myself, because when undesirable chemical characters come a-knocking on my cells' doors, I want to be sure that my cells' bouncers—their membranes—turn them away. I also make sure that I get plenty of extra vitamin E and coenzyme Q_{10}, because these nutrients hang out in or near the membranes, protecting them from stray free radicals that might do damage.

Mitochondria: Essential for Energy

Mitochondria are teensy powerhouses that generate the energy necessary to drive all of the body's chemical and biological processes, including Renewal. Just as we depend on the local electric company to supply continuous energy to our homes, cells depend on their mitochondria to supply continuous energy for healing and repair.

In the mitochondria, the controlled burning of glucose (a sugar) in the presence of oxygen releases energy. The operative word here is "controlled": The energy must be generated in a smooth, gradual manner. Otherwise, the burning process produces excessive free radicals.

Controlled burning requires adequate supplies of several nutrients, including the B-complex vitamins, vitamin C, and coenzyme Q_{10}. Without enough of these nutrients, energy production, and with it the Renewal process, would fizzle faster than a wet firecracker on the Fourth of July.

The mitochondria also rely on certain nutrients to defend their membranes against the free radicals released during energy production. These protective nutrients include the antioxidant vitamins, A, C, and E; plus the antioxidant phytochemicals—flavonoids, carotenoids, and lycopene. In addition, cells make their own antioxidant enzymes, the most important of which is glutathione. Deficiencies of any of these nutrients can ultimately cause the mitochondria to misfire and lose power like an automobile with lousy spark plugs.

Lysosomes: Waste Disposal Specialists

In some respects, lysosomes are the most remarkable organelles, because they epitomize Renewal on a cellular level. These membrane-bound sacks contain powerful enzymes for digesting large organic molecules. Like teeny garbage disposal units, lysosomes engulf and digest cellular waste material, including proteins, sugars, fats, nucleic acids, pesticides, and food additives.

Lysosomes not only remove unwanted debris but they also help the body recycle its own building blocks by dismantling molecules into their component parts, which can then be reused. Enzymes, for instance, are protein molecules made up of chains of amino acids. Lysosomes can break down these molecules into their constituent amino acids, which are then returned to the body's amino acid pool—a kind of spare parts supply—to make another protein later. Lysosome-assisted cell Renewal is a large-scale operation: A typical human liver cell recycles half of its organic molecules weekly.

To function at top form, lysosomes, like mitochondria, require optimum amounts of all of the essential nutrients. Minerals such as zinc, selenium, and magnesium are especially important because they support a lysosome's digestive enzymes. Essential fatty acids keep the lysosome's protective membranes healthy. And platoons of antioxidants protect those membranes from attack by the toxins that the lysosome is supposed to contain. If a lysosome membrane ruptures, a caustic brew of digestive enzymes spills into the interior of the cell, wreaking havoc.

A diet replete with animal foods, additives, pesticides, pollutants, and other free radical formers is chock-full of the stuff that ends up as garbage in lysosomes. Eating this way places abnormal stresses on the cellular detoxification process and has been shown to shorten life.

Nucleus: The Center of the Action
The protection and repair functions of Renewal are particularly crucial to the nucleus. Located at the center of the cell, the nucleus contains DNA, your genetic blueprint. DNA serves two functions: It manufactures enzymes to help repair damaged cell structures, and it orchestrates replication to replace injured or worn-out cells.

A cell must contain intact, undamaged DNA in order to replicate without error. If the cell's antioxidant supply is depleted, unscavenged free radicals can fracture the DNA, causing faulty protein synthesis (which affects enzyme production) and/or inaccurate cell replication. This can lead either to cell death or to genetic mutation and uncontrolled cell division—the prelude to cancer. So you can see the importance of protecting your DNA with daily antioxidant supplements.

A FEAST FIT FOR A CELL

As you can see, virtually every aspect of cellular function depends on the presence of key nutrients. When even one of these nutrients isn't available, the job performance of the cell's internal structures is compromised.

Unfortunately, the standard American diet, consisting of processed, pesticide-laced, devitalized foods, is not only criminally deficient in essential nutrients but also full of free radicals. It provides little nutritional support to cells and ultimately puts the kibosh on Renewal.

Admittedly, feasting with casual abandon on meat, dairy products, fried foods, fast foods, and convenience foods may feel satisfying in the short run. But in the long run, this practice will tick decades off your life.

On the other hand, following a low-fat, vegetarian diet

and taking broad-spectrum, antioxidant supplements vastly improves your chances of living 100 years or longer. Not coincidentally, these are two of the three pillars of the Renewal Anti-Aging Program (the third being exercise). Sure, building your meals around fruits, veggies, grains, and beans may seem a little unappealing at first. But I'll wager that with time you'll come to love and crave these wholesome foods.

Your cells will appreciate your healthy food choices, too. After all, your cells are the final destination of everything that passes through your lips. And they have very definite preferences in terms of what you eat and drink. If only they could share with you their likes and dislikes, they would naturally guide you to an optimum diet.

In fact, let's suppose for a moment that you've invited five of your cells to your favorite restaurant for dinner. They scan the menu in search of something that suits their very particular appetites. The cells want a vegetarian meal because they crave the protective phytochemicals in produce and fear the free radicals in meat, which could blast their enzymes to smithereens. The meal has to be very low in fat, because an oxidized fat molecule—a free radical—could blow a hole in the cells' protective cell membranes. And the meal's ingredients must be organic, because a pesticide molecule or two could fracture the cells' DNA.

Once everyone has ordered, the cells engage you in a rather enlightening conversation about your nutrition habits. Cell #1, a liver cell, speaks up first: "I appreciate it when you take your supplements. They give me an upper hand on those free radicals, and they make cleaning the toxins from your blood so much easier. By the way, I'd love to get some N-acetylcysteine supplements. I need them to make more glutathione, my main defense against free radicals. The more glutathione I have, the safer and healthier I am."

"For me, more ginkgo, choline, and B vitamins, please," chimes in Cell #2, a zippy and communicative nerve cell. "These supplements help me make more neurotransmitters so I can do a better job of helping you think. And that acetyl-L-carnitine supplement you tried last month . . . excellent! That stuff helped me produce more energy, and it made my membranes more resistant to free radical damage. You could cut out the alcohol, though. The glass of wine you had yesterday really knocked my socks off. I was out for a couple of hours. And two of my sisters died from it! Alcohol really hurts us cells. Mr. Fancy Liver there can handle it—he just clones more cells. But when we nerve cells are knocked off . . . Hey, that's it!"

Cell #3, a kidney cell, also has a request to make: "Would you mind sticking with purified water? Hey, I have a job to do. It's tough enough without you drinking tap water. That stuff is swimming with toxic chemicals, and they make me sick."

"And while we're on the subject," adds Cell #4, a pancreas cell, "I've had about all the sugar I can handle. You've really been pouring it into your system lately, and you don't have to. I can make all the sugar you need if you just feed me whole grains."

Cell #5, an immune cell, throws in its two cents' worth: "We lymphocytes need fewer animal fats and more essential fatty acids to strengthen our membranes so we can protect you better. A virus almost nailed me last week because I had a weak spot in my outer membrane. We'd like more flaxseed oil and borage oil. And skip the margarine and other hydrogenated oils, okay?"

RENEWAL AT WORK

If your cells seem a bit hypersensitive about how you feed them . . . well, they have to be. For them, getting the right nutrients is a matter of life or death. An optimum diet fuels Renewal.

Renewal goes on constantly, just trying to keep up with everyday cellular wear and tear. But sometimes the process kicks into overdrive, as the result of illness or injury. The presence of physical symptoms is a clear message that cells are sustaining damage. Whether the cause of the symptom is an acute, minor ailment (such as a headache or cold) or a chronic degenerative disease (such as arthritis or osteoporosis), Renewal attempts to make the necessary repairs.

Of course, some of the most serious conditions—including heart disease, stroke, and cancer, the ones I call silent killers—develop without obvious symptoms to alert us that the body's healing system has been activated. Nevertheless, Renewal is at work, trying to patch up or replace sick cells. And perhaps more than ever, it needs our support.

When damage occurs on the outside of the body, we can observe the miracle of Renewal as it unfolds. I had the chance to do so a number of years ago, when my mother suffered a mishap. While out for her daily run—a pretty remarkable habit for a woman who was in her seventies at the time—Mom tripped on a bump in the sidewalk, landing flat on her face. Ouch! Her nose was fractured, and her forehead and cheeks were scraped and bruised. She was able to get back on her feet with a helping hand from a Good Samaritan. When Mom reported to a nearby emergency room to get patched up, the doctor on duty told her that she would need at least a month to recover. That doctor didn't figure on Renewal!

Mom had been following the Renewal Anti-Aging Program for several years by then, and her body was revved up for rapid repair. Even I couldn't believe how quickly she healed. The third day after her fall, her scabs were coming off. A couple of days after that, the bruising was virtually gone. Mom recovered completely within about half the amount of time expected for someone her age. The Renewal Program—a combination of diet, supplements, and exercise—had paved the way for rapid healing.

Incidentally, this mishap didn't slow my mother one bit. She's now in her eighties and healthy as a horse. She still follows the Renewal Program, jogging every other day (though she pays a bit more attention to the contours of the sidewalk) and lifting weights on her "off" days. She's on track for maximum life span—120 healthy, vital years.

AN EXTRAORDINARY PROCESS

You now know that in order to extend your life span, you must thwart cellular damage while supercharging your healing system. Accomplishing this requires the three separate but complementary components of Renewal: protection, repair, and regeneration. Each of these components must function optimally. If one falters, the entire Renewal process becomes impaired.

Let's examine the progression of cellular Renewal—from damage through protection, repair, and regeneration—in greater detail.

When Damage Is Done

Since the preceding chapter covered free radicals, I'll assume that you already know more about cellular damage than you bargained for. To summarize, your cells are under a virtually constant state of siege, getting kicked around by free radicals on a more or less nonstop basis. In fact, free radicals are responsible for most cellular damage—the kind of damage that shortens lives and kills people before their time.

A typical cell is hit by approximately 20 billion free radicals per day. By way of comparison, envision an army of 200,000 Hun archers staging an attack on the Great Wall of China. Assuming that each archer has 100 arrows, the amount of damage this army would inflict upon the 1,500-mile stretch of wall would equal roughly one-thousandth of the amount of damage that free radicals inflict upon every cell in your body every day. Viewed another way, each archer would need to shoot 100,000 arrows to match one cell's daily dose of free radical hits.

Amazingly, your cells can withstand this type of punishment, as long as your antioxidant guard is up. Antioxidants neutralize free radicals, preventing them from doing harm. This is why consuming generous amounts of antioxidants from foods and supplements is so important.

When your antioxidant intake falls below par, free radicals gain the upper hand. A few billion hits here, a few billion hits there, and pretty soon you're dealing with major cellular damage. This cumulative damage robs cells of their ability to replicate themselves. It drives the aging process and eventually leads to death.

Protection: The Best Policy

To be sure, free radicals are a persistent, provocative lot. But just as surely, we are not at their mercy. Nature has provided us with a complex and awesome array of weaponry with which to defend ourselves and our cells. Let's take a closer look at these potent protectors.

Antioxidant nutrients. The workhorses of the body's healing system, the antioxidant nutrients fall into one of two subcategories: essential nutrients and phytochemicals. The antioxidant essential nutrients are those that we absolutely must have in order to stay alive. They include the following :

- Vitamins A, C, and E—the nutrients most people think of when they hear the word "antioxidant"
- The antioxidant minerals copper, selenium, and zinc, which support free radical–scavenging enzymes
- Certain essential fatty acids and amino acids that double as an antioxidants (in addition to their other responsibilities)
- Coenzyme Q_{10}, a vitamin-like antioxidant that scavenges free radicals and boosts the immune system

Unlike the antioxidant essential nutrients, antioxidant phytochemicals are not considered necessary for survival. But these plant-derived compounds are just as essential if you want to protect yourself from degenerative disease and achieve the very best health. (We'll discuss these "supernutrients" in more detail in chapter 25.)

In chapter 2, we discussed how antioxidant nutrients donate electrons to free radicals in order to neutralize them. In addition, these nutrients safeguard one another against oxidation (the process by which free radicals snatch electrons from healthy cells) via multiple, overlapping backup systems. For example, beta-carotene recycles vitamins A and E—and even other carotenoids—by replacing their lost electrons so they can rejoin the free radical fray.

In my practice, I evaluate a patient's antioxidant nutrient status using a blood test called an antioxidant profile. This test measures levels of all of the antioxidant essential nutrients as well as several of the antioxidant phytochemicals.

Antioxidant enzymes. The human body has learned that it can't depend entirely on foods for an uninterrupted supply of antioxidants. So cells have developed the ability to produce their own protectants, a trio of special antioxidant enzymes with exotic-sounding names: glutathione peroxidase, superoxide dismutase, and catalase. These "homemade" antioxidants are manufactured by every cell in your body. They work hand-in-hand with antioxidants from your diet, lying in wait to ambush free radicals wherever they might appear.

By far, the most important of the antioxidant enzymes is glutathione, the primary free radical scavenger for a cell's various membranes, including the mitochondrial membranes. The mitochondria, you'll recall, generate a cell's energy supply through the controlled burning of glucose. This process releases high concentrations of free radicals, which proceed to pound the mitochondria's protective membranes.

Since glutathione performs such an important function—if a cell loses its energy supply, it can't do its job—maintaining an optimum level of the enzyme is considered a powerful anti-aging strategy. In fact, glutathione status is closely correlated with vulnerability to life-shortening health problems. The lower a person's glutathione level, the higher his risk for heart disease, cancer, autoimmune disease, and all other degenerative conditions. The opposite is also true: A high glutathione level offers greater protection from illness and increased longevity.

A simple laboratory test called an oxidative stress profile can tell you whether your glutathione level is low and your free radical count is high (excess free radicals deplete glutathione). If so, you can significantly increase your body's glutathione production by taking a supplement that contains the enzyme as well as the enzyme's precursors, N-acetylcysteine and lipoic acid.

The immune system. Your body can also rid itself of free radicals via its immune system, whose cells dispatch the varmint particles in two ways. First, cells called T lymphocytes and macrophages identify, surround, engulf, and digest free radical–forming invaders such as viruses, bacteria, allergens, and pollutants. (This process is known as phagocytosis.) Second, other immune system cells, called B lymphocytes, manufacture antibodies that hunt down the undesirable invaders and zap them before they cause trouble.

Repair: A Cellular Tool Kit
When antioxidants and the immune system fail to protect a cell against damage, the body resorts to its next line of defense: repair. The job can range in magnitude from fixing minor dings in the cell's outer membrane to replacing oxidized strands of DNA in the nucleus.

Before we get into the nitty-gritty of the cellular repair process, allow me to share a short history lesson. In April 1906, San Francisco was shaken to the ground by a devastating earthquake. No amount of precautions could have protected the city from the destruction that ensued. Anything that managed to withstand the temblor was largely consumed by the fires that followed. But the citizens of this marvelous city completely rebuilt it in just a few short years.

Some 150 years earlier, an even more devastating earthquake hit Lisbon, the capital city of Portugal. In six minutes, the city was reduced to rubble. Its harbor dried up momentarily, then flooded when a 55-foot wall of water rushed back in. Fires broke out, and landslides were triggered by aftershocks. By nightfall, 60,000 people had lost their lives. Yet Lisbon rose from its own ashes and these days sports a bustling economy.

By now you may be wondering what any of this has to do with cellular repair. Well, think of your cells as microscopic San Franciscos and Lisbons. For them, the kind of damage that free radicals cause closely resembles that of an earthquake—except it's more severe, and it never stops.

Every single cell in your body sustains 20 billion free radical hits of varying severity every single day of your life. In each instance, repair must occur rapidly and efficiently so the cell's operations can proceed unhindered. You can see why the process never stops.

For Renewal to be effective, the rate of repair must keep up with the rate of damage. Once damage outpaces repair, the aging process accelerates and disease develops. The slower the rate of cellular repair, the faster the rate of aging, and vice versa.

The components of a cell that are most vulnerable to free radical damage are its proteins (especially the enzymes that catalyze essential chemical reactions), its fatty acids (primarily those in the cell's membranes), and its DNA (housed in the cell's nucleus). Fixing damaged enzymes is no big deal. Nor is patching holes in the cell's membranes. Both jobs are simply a matter of synthesizing replacement protein or lipid (fat) molecules, which is done from the genetic program in the cell's DNA. So repairing enzymes and membranes, while important, is more or less an I-can-do-it-blindfolded-with-both-hands-tied-behind-my-back affair. ·

Not so with repairing DNA. Damage to DNA presents a much greater threat to a cell, because its genetic program is in danger. Without an intact genetic program, a cell cannot do its assigned job, repair itself, or replicate itself accurately. Damaged DNA, also known as mutated DNA, is like a damaged floppy disk: The message that's encoded within it comes out scrambled. Failure to repair damaged DNA translates into accelerated aging.

DNA consists of very long chains of pairs of nucleic acids, which are attached to a "backbone" of sugars and phosphates (creating the familiar double helix configuration). Think of the paired nucleic acids as representing letters of the alphabet. Together, they form words that are your genetic code. When the paired nucleic acids are damaged by free radicals, the long chains that make up the DNA are actually fractured, and the words become unintelligible.

Because preserving DNA is so critical to human survival, nature has not left it to chance. Of all of the mind-boggling tasks that the body can perform, I think DNA repair tops the list. It requires a wondrous combination of craftiness and versatility.

Each cell continuously monitors its own DNA for "coding errors"—that is, free radical damage. When such an error is detected, a team of highly specialized DNA repair enzymes (more than 50 have been identified so far) goes to work.

First, an enzyme called DNA nuclease identifies and snips out the damaged DNA segment, which may include several pairs of nucleic acids. Then another enzyme, DNA polymerase, inserts a replacement segment, restoring the correct sequence of nucleic acids. Finally, a third enzyme, DNA ligase, seals any remaining gaps in the DNA chain.

The DNA repair process is kind of like replacing a link in a broken necklace, but it happens much faster. If you could shrink yourself down and watch it, you'd think it was a magic trick.

I can't help but be fascinated by this process—by the free radical "earthquakes" that decimate DNA molecules and the enzymatic construction crews that rebuild them. Why, the mere notion that the human body could repair any molecule, much less a large, complex DNA molecule, was unheard of when I was a medical student.

The process isn't perfect, however. After all, each of your DNA molecules takes about 10,000 free radical hits each day. The DNA repair enzymes do their best to keep up, working nonstop to patch up the damage. But hits come so fast and furious that the repair crew can't help but allow a small amount of damage to slide by unchecked.

A small amount of damage here and there presents no serious problem. But over the course of a lifetime, the damage that the repair enzymes miss begins to pile up. Damaged DNA can still replicate, but it bestows its coding errors on its offspring. Then these new cells malfunction, too.

This always reminds me of that classic *I Love Lucy* episode in which Lucy and Ethel get jobs on the production line in a candy factory. At first, they keep pace just fine. Then the conveyor belt speeds up, and the chocolates glide past faster than the women can pick them up and pack them. They stuff the candy in their mouths, in their clothes—and still they can't catch up. Sure, it makes for hilarious television. But when it happens on a cellular level, the results aren't quite so amusing.

There is a direct relationship between the rate of cumulative damage to DNA and the rate of aging. In fact, species that live longer than humans—turtles, for example—accumulate damage more slowly than we do. The current standard model for aging—the most comprehensive theory to date—asserts that cumulative damage to DNA renders cells unable to replicate correctly, which gradually erodes cellular function and precipitates degenerative disease. What's more, damaged DNA cannot accurately produce the enzymes that drive thousands of chemical reactions throughout the body, which further accelerates aging.

The aging process, then, works something like this: A shortage of antioxidants gives free radicals the upper hand. They assault DNA in such rapid-fire fashion that enzymatic repair crews can't quite keep up. Unrepaired DNA damage accumulates, impairing cell replication and enzyme production—both of which are regulated by DNA. The end result: cellular degeneration.

If DNA repair mechanisms were to fail completely, we'd be in big trouble. In fact, this is what happens to people who have a dermatological disorder called xeroderma pigmentosum. Their skin cells have lost the genetic program to manufacture repair enzymes. As a result, the cells cannot patch up the DNA damage caused by the sun's ultraviolet radiation. (Ultraviolet radiation produces free radicals that are indistinguishable from those produced in the body.) People who have xeroderma pigmentosum invariably experience accelerated skin aging as well as skin cancer.

Because the failure of DNA repair has such catastrophic consequences, you want to do what you can to keep the repair mechanisms in tip-top shape. Above all else, this means maximizing levels of antioxidants while minimizing levels of free radicals. Antioxidants protect DNA molecules against free radical damage. And the fewer free radicals around, the less damage they'll cause in the first place.

This is where the Renewal Anti-Aging Program can help. The program not only provides for optimum antioxidant intake but also reduces free radical exposure. By following the program, you'll ultimately have millions fewer DNA lesions per cell than a person of the same age who does not follow the program.

Regeneration: Nature's Most Amazing Feat
When a cell suffers so much damage that it's beyond repair, it dies. At this point, Renewal offers one final option: regeneration. Your body replaces the dead cell with an exact replica. Since cells are dividing all of the time anyway, this presents no great challenge—provided that cumulative DNA damage is minimal and necessary nutrient building blocks are available.

As I wrote this book, I had a tough time coming up with a story to illustrate Renewal through cell replication. Then fate intervened.

This time, the story involves Emma, my seven-year-old daughter. One day, Emma's preschool teacher burst into my office, visibly upset. "Emma smashed her finger in the door at school," she told me. "Do you think she needs stitches?"

I ran out to the teacher's car, where my daughter was waiting. After the longest 10-second hug ever, Emma carefully unwrapped the loose cloth bandage around her left index finger and bravely held it out for me to see. Her fingertip was just about severed, the bone crushed, the nail nowhere to be found. "Yes, she needs stitches," I said, understating the problem with as much calm as I could muster under the circumstances.

Fortunately, my friend and neighbor, John Canova, M.D., was in his office a few blocks away. For two hours, I held Emma's "good" hand while Dr. John carefully cleaned and anesthetized the injured finger and stitched the severed portion back on—deftly, painstakingly, with superb surgical expertise. I know it hurt a lot, but Emma was a real trouper.

Six weeks later, Emma produced her injured finger for inspection, proudly holding it up beside her other index finger for comparison. "Emma," I said, "you sure did a good job of healing that finger." Except for the nail, which hadn't yet grown back, both fingers appeared identical! Anyone who had seen the "before picture" of Emma's injury would have been amazed at how well her finger healed.

Emma's experience is an ideal example of how cell replication works—though with not so much drama on a day-to-day basis. Your body constantly replaces damaged and worn-out cells in every organ and tissue (with the exception of nerve cells, which can be repaired but not replaced). And this process goes on inside you literally every moment of your life.

In summary, Renewal Theory describes your body's healing system: how it protects your cells from damage, repairs injured cells, and regenerates irreparable cells. The rest of this book will show you how to incorporate Renewal Theory into your everyday life so you can achieve your maximum life span.

But first, chapter 4 will introduce you to the essentials of the Renewal Anti-Aging Program. You'll get a basic idea of the foods to eat, the supplements to take, and the exercise to do, so you can start reaping Renewal's benefits right away.

The Renewal Anti-Aging Program: An Overview

You will observe with concern how long a useful truth may be known and exist, before it is generally received and practiced upon.
—BENJAMIN FRANKLIN

Now that you know a bit about Free Radical Theory and Renewal Theory, allow me to introduce you to the actual Renewal Anti-Aging Program. I'll give you the bottom line first so you know what lies ahead. You can even start the program now, if you like.

The Renewal Anti-Aging Program has three basic components.

- The Anti-Aging Diet
- The Anti-Aging Supplement Program
- The Anti-Aging Exercise Program

Let's preview each of these in turn.

THE ANTI-AGING DIET

To optimize Renewal, you need to eat foods that maximize your antioxidant intake while minimizing your free radical load. You can easily achieve both goals provided you follow a low-fat, vegan diet—one in which the foods come only from plants, not from animals.

The Anti-Aging Diet focuses on organically grown, unprocessed, chemical-free foods selected from the New Four Food Groups: grains, legumes, fruits, and vegetables. (You'll learn more about the New Four Food Groups in chapter 5.) This diet is not only naturally low in fat but also naturally high in desirable complex carbohydrates. In fact, approximately 80 percent of the calories you consume in a day should come from complex carbs such as whole-grain breads, cereals, pastas, brown rice, potatoes, yams, and squash. The other 20 percent of calories should come from protein and fat, in equal portions.

Eating this way automatically eliminates the free radical burden imposed by a high-fat diet. It also sidesteps other known toxins, including pesticides, food additives, alcoholic beverages, and sugar.

By following the Anti-Aging Diet, you can protect your immune and cardiovascular systems from damage, prevent diseases of degeneration, and slow the aging process. In other words, you can facilitate Renewal.

Foods to Choose

When you switch to the Anti-Aging Diet, you'll develop a completely new view of your dinner plate. Gone are the meats, the dairy products, the highly refined and processed fare. In their place is a glorious cornucopia of naturally nutritious, naturally flavorful foods. Tune up your tastebuds for the following foods.

Great grains. As mentioned earlier, the Anti-Aging Diet is high in complex carbohydrates and low in protein and fat. So you'll be getting many of your daily calories from grains such as wheat, rye, oats (oatmeal and oat bran), millet, rice (brown, not white), and corn. For the most nutritional value, stick with organic, whole, minimally processed grains and grain products as much as possible.

Lucious legumes. Legumes are seed pods—beans, peas, lentils, and the like. Stock your pantry with all kinds: adzuki beans, anasazi beans, black beans, brown beans, chickpeas, Great Northern beans, green beans, green peas, kidney beans, lima beans, mung beans, navy beans, pinto beans, and, of course, soybeans and soy products (such as tofu, tempeh, and soy milk).

Fantastic fruits. You can't go wrong in this group, either—simply choose whatever is in season. Fresh fruits are preferable to frozen, since the freezing process can destroy some of the nutrients. As for juices, purchase organic products made from whole fruits or try making your own from organically grown whole fruits. Avoid juices made from concentrate as well as those with added sugar or with preservatives. Unsweetened applesauce and other organic, whole fruit concentrates make excellent spreads and dessert toppings.

Vibrant vegetables. Of all the foods in the Anti-Aging Diet, vegetables are the most nutrient-dense. They're also the best sources of protective phytochemicals. So take your pick in the produce aisle. No matter which veggies you choose, you'll get bountiful amounts of vitamins, minerals, phytochemicals, and even fiber. The following are especially noteworthy nutrition-wise: beets, bok choy, broccoli, brussels sprouts, cabbage, carrots, cauliflower, chard, eggplant, garlic, green beans, kale, leeks, onions, peas, peppers (all kinds), potatoes (sweet and white), scallions, spinach, sprouts (all kinds), squash (all kinds), string beans, Swiss chard, and tomatoes. Of course, buy organic whenever possible.

Foods to Lose

You may be wondering why the Anti-Aging Diet eliminates all foods from animal sources—including red meat, poultry, fish, milk, cheese, and eggs. I address this in more detail in part 2, but suffice it to say that no scientific evidence exists to suggest that these foods promote health, much less slow aging. On the other hand, literally thousands of studies overwhelmingly indict these foods for their role in the current epidemic of heart disease, cancer, and other degenerative conditions. Indulging in foods from animal sources undoubtedly torpedoes Renewal. For longevity, avoid all animal foods.

Similarly, the Anti-Aging Diet steers you away from refined carbohydrates such as white sugar, white flour, and processed foods. Refined carbohydrates have had their vitamins, minerals, and fiber stripped away, so they're of little nutritional value.

In contrast, complex carbohydrates support Renewal because they retain their nutrients and they're converted to blood sugar more slowly. This prevents fluctuations in your blood sugar level, reduces fat storage, and supports weight loss and maintenance. As a bonus, when you eat a lot of complex carbs, your diet automatically becomes low in fat and protein.

If the Anti-Aging Diet seems too restrictive, relax. Sure, you may be eating in a whole new way. But you certainly won't feel deprived. In fact, because the foods have such stellar nutritional profiles, you can eat as much as you like. Nor will you feel bored, thanks to the incredible variety of foods from which to choose.

Of course, most people don't have time to prepare three gourmet vegetarian meals a day. If this describes you, then you'll love the two-week menu plan, meal ideas, and recipes beginning on page 535. Try them, and discover how easy the Anti-Aging Diet can be.

THE ANTI-AGING SUPPLEMENT PROGRAM

I've been taking nutritional supplements since 1946, when my mom stuck a bottle of Unicaps on the kitchen table. Years later, as a student of organic chemistry and biochemistry, I wondered how foods and nutrients work in the body—how optimum intakes create health, and why deficiencies cause disease. To date, I've spent the better part of three decades sifting through the medical literature, using the most recent and most reliable nutritional research to refine and update the Anti-Aging Supplement Program. You can count on its being state-of-the-art.

If you follow the Anti-Aging Diet, why do you need supplements? Because a diet without supplementation, however excellent, cannot optimally protect cells from free radical damage. Cellular repair and regeneration also become compromised. Going through life with your nutritional guard down allows free radicals to relentlessly bombard your cells—definitely a life-shortening experience. This is why I'm such a vociferous advocate of a thorough and balanced supplement regimen.

Nutritional supplements reinforce Renewal by providing protection against free radicals, supporting repair of injured cells, facilitating replacement of dead cells, and boosting production of cellular energy. Each of the supplements listed below promotes Renewal in its own way—guarding against disease, slowing the aging process, improving quality of life.

- Essential nutrients (vitamins and minerals, essential fatty acids, coenzyme Q_{10})
- Antioxidant nutrients (including vitamins A, C, and E, copper, selenium, zinc)
- Antioxidant phytochemicals (including carotenoids, flavonoids, lycopene)
- Anti-aging herbs (including garlic, ginkgo, ginseng)
- Anti-aging hormones: dehydroepiandrosterone (DHEA), pregnenolone, melatonin, natural thyroid hormone, the sex hormones—estrogen, progesterone, and testosterone
- Brain nutrients: acetyl-L-carnitine and phosphatidylserine (ginkgo and pregnenolone also support brain function)
- Internal cleansers: acidophilus and fiber

Yes, this is an awful lot of stuff. But except for the essential nutrients, which are must-haves for everyone, you needn't take every single supplement every single day. It's up to you to determine which ones will have the most benefit for you. In part 4, you'll find more specific information on each supplement so you can decide for yourself whether a particular nutrient, herb, or hormone is right for you. And in chapter 38, you'll get detailed how-to instruction for putting together your own individualized supplement regimen.

THE ANTI-AGING EXERCISE PROGRAM

While diet and supplements get the lion's share of attention in this book, exercise plays just as crucial a role in the Renewal process. Quite simply, a sedentary lifestyle shortens your life span. In fact, it's twice as likely to kill you as a high cholesterol level. Kind of gives that old saw "use it or lose it" a whole new meaning, wouldn't you say?

When you engage in regular physical activity, every cell in your body reaps the benefits. Exercise lowers your heart rate and blood pressure, strengthens your arteries and bones, speeds your reflexes, boosts your brain power, and enhances your immune system. It is also the single most effective method for slimming down. No weight loss program can succeed in the long run unless it has an exercise component.

Besides, being active makes you feel better both physically and emotionally. So for all those extra years, you won't just stay alive. You'll thrive.

The Anti-Aging Exercise Program consists of three types of activity: aerobic exercise, strength training, and stretching. While all three have value, aerobic exercise is by far the most important.

The word *aerobic* refers to any activity that involves repetitive muscle movements and raises your heart rate to 75 to 80 percent of its maximum for at least 20 minutes. (You'll find out how to determine your maximum heart rate and target heart rate range in chapter 37.) For the average person, this translates to a target heart rate of about 120 beats per minute.

Even activities that don't fit this definition of aerobic can help extend your life span if they provide a prolonged cardiovascular workout. Examples include bicycling, dancing, and hiking.

While aerobic exercise burns calories and improves cardiovascular endurance, strength training—that is, lifting weights—builds lean muscle mass and reduces fat mass. This is important for Renewal because the more muscle you have, the more glutathione, growth hormone, and other anti-aging compounds your body will produce. And from a purely aesthetic perspective, strength training rewards you with a trimmed, toned physique.

Stretching, the third pillar of the Anti-Aging Exercise Program, improves strength and flexibility. Both help protect against injury.

A HEART-TO-HEART TALK

So there you have it: the complete Renewal Anti-Aging Program in a nutshell. When you implement the nutrition and lifestyle changes that the program endorses, you'll supercharge your body's Renewal systems and create an internal bulwark that can add decades to your life.

Admittedly, the program requires some effort. Many of the changes that it suggests may challenge your personal views about proper diet, supplementation, and other issues related to health and longevity. But I don't want you to feel overwhelmed or frustrated or to give up in desperation. Rather, I want you to understand why these changes are necessary and why you should incorporate them into your day-to-day routine.

My goal is to help you live a longer, healthier life. Yours is to learn how to do so. If the information I present here serves only to threaten you without nurturing meaningful change, then both of us ultimately fail. This is why I encourage you to adopt the program gradually rather than in one fell swoop. Learning new behaviors—new habits—takes time. You want to weave them into the fabric of your life so they become second nature to you. To accomplish this, you must establish your own natural pace. Make the easy changes first, and save the hard stuff for later. If you commit to the program and work at it, you'll eventually get there.

Keep in mind, too, that you can follow just part of the program rather than the entire regimen. To be honest, very few people could institute every single one of the changes that the program recommends. And frankly, it isn't necessary. As I'll remind you throughout the book: *The extent to which you follow the Renewal Anti-Aging Program determines the extent to which you'll benefit from it.* Positive changes will produce positive results.

One final, important word. Optimum health and maximum life span, the dual goals of Renewal, are inseparable concepts. You cannot have one without the other. When you strive for maximum life span, you're actually striving for optimum health.

Without exception, every recommendation in the pages

that follow is intended to help you live healthier so you can live longer. This is the promise of Renewal.

Now that you have a brief overview of the Renewal Anti-Aging Program, let's examine each of its components in greater detail. We'll start with the foods that promote optimum health and longevity—The Anti-Aging Diet.

PART 2
The Renewal
Anti-Aging Diet

The Anti-Aging Diet for Optimum Health and Longevity

We suggest that people take the food pyramid, cut off the top, and make a healthy trapezoid.
—NEIL BARNARD, M.D.,
  PRESIDENT OF THE PHYSICIANS COMMITTEE
  FOR RESPONSIBLE MEDICINE

Over the past 20 years, a flurry of scientific activity has produced a series of stunning revelations concerning the chemical composition and health effects of foods. Convincing research incriminates some foods for accelerating aging while championing others for slowing it down.

You know that apples and carrots are good for you, while candy bars and potato chips are not. But a whole cornucopia of foods falls somewhere between these two extremes. How do you know which promote health and which undermine it?

Some foods have abundant supplies of cell-damaging free radicals, while others are rich in protective antioxidants. Some foods contain known carcinogens, while others are brimming with cancer-fighting compounds. Some foods promote the hardening and clogging of arteries that so often results in heart attacks and strokes, while others block that deadly process.

As an informed, nutrition-savvy consumer, you have the power to choose only those foods that enhance your body's natural healing powers, reinforce its resistance to disease, and boost your chances of achieving maximum life span. This is why I've created the Renewal Anti-Aging Diet: to serve as your guide to smart, health- and longevity-supporting food choices.

If you're accustomed to following the standard American diet—high in fat and sugar, low in vitamins, minerals, and fiber—you'll find that the Anti-Aging Diet advocates some major changes in your eating habits. But they are by no means an all-or-nothing proposition. Of course, if you can manage them all, great! If not, just remember: *The extent to which you follow the Renewal Anti-Aging Diet determines the extent to which you'll benefit from it.*

DECADES OF DEBATE

Human nature being what it is, and the complexities and uncertainties of optimum nutrition being what they are, the fact that people have long sought guidelines for what they should and shouldn't eat comes as no surprise. In the United States, the pursuit of meaningful dietary guidelines officially began in 1916, with the creation of the Five Food Groups. Numerous revisions and updates have occurred since then, the most recent resulting in the Food Guide Pyramid, introduced in 1992.

Of the guidelines' previous incarnations, perhaps the best-known are the Basic Seven and the Basic Four. The Basic Seven served as the nutrition standard-bearers from 1943 to 1956. They consisted of the following food groups.

- Milk and milk products
- Meat, poultry, fish, eggs, dried beans, peas, and nuts
- Breads, flour, and cereals
- Leafy green or yellow vegetables
- Citrus fruits, tomatoes, cabbage, and salad greens
- Potatoes and other fruits and vegetables
- Butter and fortified margarine

I can still see these posted on the wall of my third-grade classroom in Minnesota, a few miles from the slaughterhouses of St. Paul, in the heart of dairy country. Where I grew up, foods of animal origin were not just accepted. They were a way of life.

In 1956, the U.S. Department of Agriculture (USDA) recommended that the Basic Seven be simplified so that the general public would find them easier to remember and follow. The existing food groups were subsequently reconfigured into four more-general categories. The "new" Basic Four looked like this.

- Milk and dairy products
- Meat, fish, dairy, and eggs
- Bread, flour, and cereals
- Fruits and vegetables

Conspicuously absent from these four groups are the butter and fortified margarine recommended in the Basic Seven. Publicly, USDA officials acknowledged that folks would continue to use these and other fats to flavor their foods. Privately, they had already become privy to information suggesting a link between dietary fat and heart disease.

Apparently, the USDA didn't want to invite criticism by advocating a limit on fat intake. But the agency also didn't want to endorse the consumption of foods that down the road would be implicated in the development of chronic degenerative disease. The USDA's reputation was safe, even if public health was not.

Through the 1960s, nutrition researchers continued to amass evidence of the profound influence of diet on human health. They established that excessive consumption of fat and cholesterol could raise a person's risk of heart disease, stroke, and other debilitating conditions. Still, the Basic Four, featuring high-fat, high-cholesterol, high-sodium meats and dairy products, remained the cornerstone of nutrition education.

By the late 1970s, however, the Basic Four had all but fallen out of favor. They were roundly criticized by experts for failing to keep pace with nutrition research and trends. Studies had already debunked the notion that animal-derived foods were essential to a healthy diet. They had also proven that plant-derived foods—grains, legumes, fruits, and vegetables—supplied all of the nutrients found in animal-derived foods as well as other disease-fighting compounds (which we now know as phytochemicals).

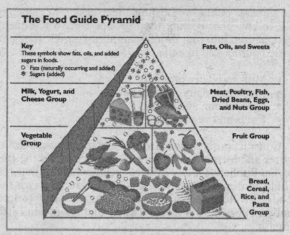

The Food Guide Pyramid devotes its top two tiers to meats, dairy products, and fats, oils, and sweets. By making these foods appear nutritionally acceptable, the pyramid encourages unhealthy eating habits.

BUILDING THE PYRAMID

Despite continued denunciation of the Basic Four, almost 10 years passed before the USDA acknowledged that giving equal status to plant-derived foods and animal-derived foods no longer held scientific water. In 1987, the agency embarked on a project to modify and update the federal dietary guidelines. The goal was not to toss out the Basic Four altogether but to revise them so that they better reflected nutritional reality.

Three years later, USDA officials unveiled their latest handiwork: the Food Guide Pyramid. The familiar four food groups had been reconfigured into six.

- Bread, cereal, rice, and pasta
- Vegetables
- Fruits
- Milk, yogurt, and cheese
- Meat, poultry, fish, dried beans, eggs, and nuts
- Fats, oils, and sweets

Actually, except for the separation of vegetables from fruits and the addition of fats, oils, and sweets, the groups themselves hadn't changed all that much. What had changed was their format.

Whereas the Basic Four had given the groups equal value, the pyramid ranked them from most to least important. Grains held the place of honor at the pyramid's base, with fruits and vegetables receiving runner-up status. Animal proteins—meats and dairy products—and fats, oils, and sweets were assigned the top two tiers of the pyramid, a reflection of their diminished status.

The pyramid won cautious applause from nutrition experts, who hailed it as a step in the right direction. Yes, it still had problems (which I'll discuss a bit later). But at least it shifted the focus away from animal-derived foods to plant-derived foods—something that no previous guidelines had even attempted.

Not everyone greeted the pyramid so warmly. In particular, it drew the ire of the meat and dairy industries, who didn't appreciate the fact that their foods had been made subordinate to grains, fruits, and vegetables. Anticipating a decline in popularity and profits, these groups resisted what they perceived as a demotion.

Their protests did not go unnoticed. Within one day of its release, the Food Guide Pyramid was yanked for what officials described as "further study." It resurfaced in 1992, sporting a few minor modifications intended to keep the meat and dairy industries happy.

THE SAD STATE OF NUTRITION

Unfortunately, even the new, "improved" Food Guide Pyramid fails to embrace the most fundamental truth of modern nutrition: Plant-derived foods heal, animal-derived foods kill. Instead, the pyramid perpetuates a diet that does little to stem the tide of chronic degenerative diseases.

Scientifically accurate and intellectually honest dietary guidelines would emphasize optimum intakes of grains, legumes, fruits, and vegetables, which contain abundant supplies of disease-fighting, Renewal-supporting nutrients. They would not even mention meats, dairy products, fats, oils, and sugars, because these foods have no place in a health- and longevity-promoting diet. They deprive people of essential nutrients, while exposing them to an array of disease-causing substances.

Yet the Food Guide Pyramid, with its meat/dairy and fat/sugar tiers, gives the impression that these foods are not only okay but necessary. It goes so far as to recommend consuming two to three servings of meat, poultry, fish, or eggs and two to three servings of milk, yogurt, or cheese every day.

To reinforce its apparent acceptance of animal-derived foods, the USDA issued a pamphlet about the pyramid that states, "No one food group is more important than another—for good health, you need them all." Not so!

If you buy into this bit of antiquated advice, you're exposing yourself to a nutritional double whammy. First, animal-derived foods raise your risk of chronic degenerative disease. Second, when you eat them, you're forgoing the plant-derived foods that supply the nutrients your body needs. That puts you two steps behind in the Renewal process.

A CHALLENGE TO CHANGE

Outraged by the USDA's apparent willingness to compromise public health in deference to the meat and dairy industries, a group of nutrition-minded doctors launched a campaign to dismantle the Food Guide Pyramid. The Physicians Committee for Responsible Medicine (PCRM) decries the consumption of animal-derived foods as detrimental to both human and animal populations and to the planet as a whole. The organization also opposes animal experimentation as unnecessary, outmoded, and barbaric. I'm proud to count myself among the 6,000 PCRM members.

When the USDA's Dietary Guidelines Committee convened in 1995 to consider changes to the Food Guide Pyramid, PCRM members were on hand to voice their concerns. They criticized the USDA for deliberately watering down the pyramid's recommendations to increase their acceptability, calling the agency's actions "a disservice to individuals seeking accurate dietary advice." They also implored USDA officials to revise the existing dietary guidelines to reflect the latest findings in nutrition research.

Joining PCRM members in demanding a massive restructuring of national priorities and policies on diet and nutrition was a distinguished group of physicians and scientists. They included PCRM president Neal Barnard, M.D.; William Castelli, M.D., director of the famed Framingham Heart Study; Henry Heimlich, M.D., medical innovator and inventor of the Heimlich maneuver; Dean Ornish, M.D., founder and director of the Preventive Medicine Research Institute in Sausalito, California; William Roberts, M.D., editor-in-chief of the *American Journal of Cardiology*; Benjamin Spock, M.D., noted pediatrician and humanitarian; and Peter Wood, M.D., of the Stanford Center for Research in Disease Prevention.

These medical luminaries called for the immediate withdrawal of the Food Guide Pyramid, arguing that it encourages fat and cholesterol intakes far above levels found to be healthful. They also admonished the USDA to refrain from endorsing the consumption of meats and dairy products, saying that such recommendations contradict overwhelming scientific evidence that these foods undermine human health. All of the nutrients that meats and dairy products contain, the experts noted, can be obtained from other, more healthful food sources.

To replace the Food Guide Pyramid, the PCRM proposed new dietary guidelines based exclusively on plant-derived foods: grains, legumes, fruits, and vegetables. PCRM members dubbed these the New Four Food Groups.

IN FAVOR OF THE "NEW FOUR"

By eliminating disease-causing, age-accelerating animal-derived foods, the New Four Food Groups provide for truly optimum nutrition. They encourage maximum dietary intakes of the nutrients known to prevent disease, support health, and maximize life span. Plus, the New Four are easy to understand and follow—an unexpected bonus for those who find the Food Guide Pyramid's multi-tiered recommendations complicated and confusing.

In a news conference supporting the PCRM's New Four Food Groups, Dr. Spock called for everyone—adults and children alike—to give up meat and milk and embrace vegetarianism. He emphasized the importance of teaching children healthy eating patterns at an early age.

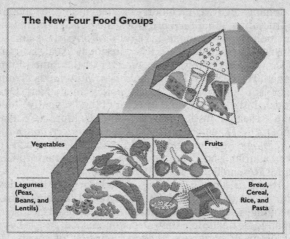

The New Four Food Groups

Vegetables

Fruits

Legumes
(Peas,
Beans, and
Lentils)

Bread,
Cereal,
Rice, and
Pasta

For optimum nutrition, the Physicians Committee for Responsible Medicine (PCRM) suggests simply removing the top two tiers of the existing Food Guide Pyramid. The remaining two tiers represent the PCRM-endorsed New Four Food Groups. By building your meals from these foods, your diet will be naturally low in fat and sugar. (Note that legumes have been removed from the meat group—where they didn't belong anyway—and given their own "block" in the New Four trapezoid.)

As might be expected, the meat and dairy industries pounced on Dr. Spock's comments almost immediately. Meat industry representatives denounced Dr. Spock for making an "extreme" and "unrealistic" proposal, noting that 75 million Americans eat beef every day. A dairy industry spokesman simply stated, "Children need milk to grow on, and that's that."

Of course, neither group offered any scientific evidence to support its position. Why? Because no such evidence exists. On the other hand, thousands of scientific studies have proven beyond any reasonable doubt that people who eat animal-derived foods are much more susceptible to heart attacks, cancers, and strokes than people who don't.

INTRODUCING THE ANTI-AGING DIET

The New Four Food Groups provide the foundation for the Renewal Anti-Aging Diet. They are the only foods that you need to survive and thrive. The farther you stray from them, the closer you move toward suboptimum nutrition, poor health, and a shorter life span.

Because it emphasizes plant-derived foods, the Anti-Aging Diet is naturally high in carbohydrates, fiber, vitamins, and minerals but low in fat and protein. It also seeks to eliminate consumption of pesticides, additives, preservatives, antibiotics, hormones, and other known toxins.

Chapter 18 provides more specific information about the Anti-Aging Diet. Plus you'll find a two-week menu plan and recipes beginning on page 535. In the meantime, let's explore the diet's key principles.

AVOID FOODS OF ANIMAL ORIGIN

Well, this one may be obvious, but I can't stress it enough. If you want a longer, healthier life, giving up your carnivorous ways and becoming a vegetarian is vitally important.

As a nation, we remain wedded to the notion that we aren't feeding ourselves properly unless we eat meat and dairy products every day. Because the health problems associated with these foods usually don't show up until later in life, we're convinced that our diet is harmless. In fact, it is slowly and silently killing us.

I advocate vegetarianism not just because it supports longevity but also because it prevents the debilitating diseases that can make our later years extremely unpleasant. Heart attack, cancer, stroke, diabetes, arthritis, circulatory problems, and other conditions significantly diminish quality of life. They are much more closely related to poor diet than to aging per se.

If you are not already vegetarian, I urge you to make the switch. Phasing out animal-derived foods and replacing them with grains, legumes, fruits, and vegetables is *the* most important dietary change that you can make. You'll take a giant step toward optimum health and a longer life.

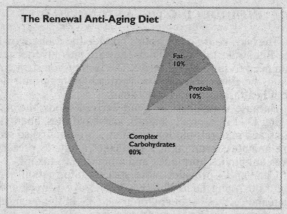

On the Renewal Anti-Aging Diet, roughly 80 percent of your calories come from complex carbohydrates. Protein and fat share the remaining 20 percent of calories.

CHOOSE COMPLEX CARBOHYDRATES

As I mentioned earlier, a diet built around plant-derived foods is naturally high in complex carbohydrates. Ideally, 80 percent of your calories should come from complex carbs—foods such as whole-grain breads, cereals, pasta, rice, potatoes, yams, and squash. The remaining 20 percent of calories should be equally divided between protein and fat.

Incidentally, complex carbohydrates do not encourage weight gain, as conventional wisdom would have you believe. But you do need to distinguish them from *refined* carbohydrates—white sugar, white flour, and other processed foods.

Once ingested, refined carbs are quickly absorbed into the bloodstream because they don't need to be broken down. This sends blood sugar levels on a roller coaster ride, precipitating food cravings and ultimately leading to weight gain. As if that weren't bad enough, refined carbs are quickly converted to fat by the body.

Because complex carbohydrates must be broken down before they're absorbed, they enter the bloodstream much more slowly and steadily. This helps prevent fluctuations in blood sugar levels as well as the food cravings that normally follow. What's more, complex carbs actually discourage weight gain by satisfying your appetite with fewer calories.

ELEVATE YOUR FIBER INTAKE

Plant-derived foods have another distinct nutritional advantage: abundant supplies of fiber. Animal-derived foods contain no fiber at all, while processed foods have had theirs removed.

There are actually several different types of fiber, each of which performs a unique set of tasks within the body. Perhaps fiber's best-known role is as a bulking agent, keeping stools soft and easy to pass. But fiber also promotes intestinal health by sopping up toxins and escorting them out of the body. And it has proven to be a key player in the prevention of an array of ailments, from constipation and hemorrhoids to heart disease and cancer.

To ensure that your body has continuous supplies of the various types of fiber, I recommend augmenting the Anti-Aging Diet with a fiber supplement. You'll learn more about the importance of fiber in chapter 30.

CUT WAY BACK ON FAT

Now here's an interesting bit of information: The typical diets of Western populations are responsible for more premature deaths than all of the wars in human history. What makes these diets so deadly? Excessive fat.

When you follow the Anti-Aging Diet, your fat intake naturally drops to a healthful 10 percent of calories. This is because the plant-derived foods on which the diet is based are naturally low in fat.

Just be careful not to fall into the vegetable fat trap. Many people mistakenly believe that they're doing their bodies a favor simply by switching from animal fats to vegetable fats—oils, nuts, seeds, and the like. Although consuming too much fat is far easier on a carnivorous diet, it's just as possible on a vegetarian diet.

As a Renewal-seeker, you must choose your fats carefully. Because the truth is, virtually all types of fat in some way contribute to the development of life-shortening chronic degenerative diseases. The sole exceptions are the essential fatty acids, which safeguard health and slow the aging process. (You'll learn more about good fats and bad fats in chapters 7 and 8.)

FAVOR FRESH FOODS

The Anti-Aging Diet recommends choosing fresh, whole foods as often as possible. They retain their vitamins and minerals—unlike many packaged foods, which are not only stripped of their nutrients but also pumped with additives and other toxins during processing.

Packaged foods may undergo any of a number of devitalizing procedures, including frying and hydrogenation (which produce disease-causing free radicals), radiation (which sacrifices nutrients to increase shelf life), defatting (which removes all fats, including the essential fatty acids), defibering (which removes fiber), and emulsification, enrichment, and fortification (which attempt to restore the vitamins and minerals depleted during processing). Such high-tech tampering can turn even normally healthful foods such as fruits and vegetables into shadows of their former selves, at least in terms of their nutritional profiles.

To you, these mechanically altered foods may look, smell, and taste just fine. But to your body, they bear only a faint resemblance to the real thing. Your body isn't getting the high-quality nutrients that only fresh, whole foods can provide. Ultimately, this has a devastating impact on cellular health.

BE WARY OF PESTICIDES

Unfortunately, even fresh foods can pose health risks. Many of the fruits and vegetables on display in supermarkets and even farmers' markets have been treated with pesticides and other chemicals. When you consume these foods, your body absorbs the toxins. In effect, you're slowly being poisoned by what's on your plate.

In this country, the use of chemicals in farming remains widespread. Take pesticides as an example: Upwards of 1,000 different products are routinely applied to crops.

Most of these products went to market with minimal testing, especially concerning their long-term effects. Of the few that have undergone adequate testing, virtually all are toxic.

The government hasn't done a lot to regulate these extremely hazardous substances. Nor has it moved to yank them off the market. So the chemicals continue to silently sicken us, making us vulnerable to cancer and myriad other health problems.

Until the government decides to take a more aggressive stance against these toxins, the surest way to protect yourself from them is to go organic. The Anti-Aging Diet advocates consumption of organically grown foods.

There was a time when organics were available only in health food stores. But thanks to public demand, you can now find them even in regular supermarkets.

By spending your grocery dollars on organically grown foods, you do more than improve your own health. You're sending the message that you disapprove of the use of pesticides and other chemicals in the public food supply. In the long run, this improves the health of the planet as well.

MAKE IT A HABIT

If the Anti-Aging Diet seems to ask a lot of you ... well, it does. After all, it has a rather lofty goal: to make your body last a good, long time. You can help by making the diet a habit. By that I mean you should use it to guide all of your food choices—every meal, every day.

There was a time in my life when I believed that an occasional "junk meal" wouldn't do me any harm. Whenever I indulged, I simply reassured myself that I'd eat better the next day. But I quickly cleaned up my act when I realized that even one bad meal produces a dietary triple whammy from which my body may not recover for several days.

To illustrate what happens, let's suppose I stop by the local fast-food joint for a quick lunch of a cheeseburger, french fries, and a cola. Whammy #1: I'm plying my body with unhealthful doses of fat, cholesterol, sugar, pesticides, and preservatives. Whammy #2: I'm depriving my body of vitamins, minerals, fiber, and other basic substances that it needs to function. Whammy #3 (and the coup de grâce): To process my junk meal and minimize its adverse effects, my body has to tap its nutrient stores. In other words, my junk meal not only fails to supply essential nutrients but also uses up my reserves from previous meals.

Eating this way creates chronic nutrient deficiencies and lays the groundwork for heart disease, cancer, and a host of other debilitating conditions. Are you willing to pay the price of a burger and fries with your life? I certainly hope not.

THE DIET FOR LIFE

The Renewal Anti-Aging Diet has helped me to develop eating habits that put me on the fast track for maximum life span. It can do the same for you. You'll build your meals around whole, fresh, organic plant-derived foods—foods that contain abundant supplies of the nutrients your body requires to engage in Renewal. At the same time, you'll wean yourself from animal-derived foods, which mounting evidence implicates as causative factors behind degenerative disease and premature death.

You can begin your transition to the Anti-Aging Diet right now. At your next meal, simply replace some or all of an animal-derived food with a selection from one of the New Four Food Groups—grains, legumes, fruits, and vegetables. With each subsequent meal, devote a little more of your plate to plant-derived foods, a little less to animal-derived foods. Before you know it, you'll be eating vegetarian—and loving it!

Still not sold on the notion that a diet based on animal-derived foods can make you sick or even kill you? Perhaps the next chapter will convince you.

The Case Against a Carnivorous Diet: Why You Should Switch

Socrates: And there will be animals of many other kinds, if people eat them?
Glaucon: Certainly.
Socrates: And living in this way we shall have much greater need of physicians than before?
Glaucon: Much greater.
—PLATO, *THE REPUBLIC*

When I interview a patient for the first time, I routinely ask, "What's your diet like?"

The response is often "I'm a vegetarian" or "I'm mostly vegetarian."

Prodding further, I ask, "Yes, but what do you eat?"

"Well, Doc, mostly vegetables—and some fish or chicken."

I am frequently amazed at how many people think that a vegetarian diet includes fish, let alone chicken. Something else I've noticed: Even though these "vegetarians" may eat no meat, they're nevertheless packing in oodles of dairy products, eggs, and butter. In fact, this kind of diet has so much saturated fat and cholesterol that, though I wouldn't recommend doing it, switching from milk, cheese, and eggs to lean beef would significantly *decrease* a person's intake of saturated fat and cholesterol.

WHAT IT MEANS TO BE A VEGAN

Before we go any further, let's define exactly what a vegetarian is. Generally, vegetarians fall into one of three categories.

- Ovo-lactovegetarians consume eggs and dairy products.
- Lactovegetarians consume dairy products but not eggs.
- Vegans (pronounced VEE-guns) avoid all foods of animal origin, including meats, poultry, seafood, eggs, and dairy products.

The Anti-Aging Diet, one of the cornerstones of the Renewal program, is a vegan diet, which means that it excludes all foods of animal origin. By "animal origin," I mean not only beef, chicken, turkey, pork, lamb, and seafood but also eggs and all dairy products, including milk, cheese, and butter.

By now you may be thinking, "Egads, there's nothing left! An occasional hamburger won't kill me, will it? Where is the pleasure in life if I can't have some cheese now and then? I take the skin off my chicken—you mean I have to give up chicken altogether? What about fish? If I can't use butter, what am I going to put on my toast?" And, of course, the ultimate question: "Is a life without ice cream really worth living?"

These are reasonable questions. And to be honest, if the trade-off were simply less time on this planet, I, too, might opt to go the burger-and-ice-cream route. Unfortunately—and this is what sold me on veganism—a high-fat, fiberless, phytochemical-deprived, toxin-laden animal-foods diet not only shortens life span but also tends to turn those final years into an extremely unpleasant experience. What should be the golden years instead become a nightmare in which inordinate amounts of time and money are spent traipsing from doctor to doctor seeking solutions to debilitating health problems. These diseases of degeneration— high blood pressure, circulatory problems, coronary artery disease, heart failure, kidney failure, stroke, cancer, diabetes, arthritis, osteoporosis, cataracts, and senile brain disease—keep hospital beds filled and dramatically lower the quality of life for tens of millions of seniors.

As a physician who has treated many of these patients— the unwitting victims of self-inflicted illness—I've witnessed the slow deterioration of health up close, and it is not pretty. It always makes me profoundly sad because with a vegan diet, appropriate nutritional supplements, and regular exercise, most of this human suffering could easily be prevented.

In Good Company

In case you haven't heard, vegetarianism has gone mainstream. It's in! It's cool! It's hot! So the next time carnivorous family members and friends tease you for ordering the veggie plate, dazzle them by dropping the names of some famous vegetarians.

If they're into popular music, mention Paul McCartney, Tina Turner, Johnny Cash, and Chubby Checker. If they're impressed with great scientists, bring up Charles Darwin, Leonardo da Vinci, Isaac Newton, Albert Einstein, and Albert Schweitzer. If they're of a literary bent, try George Bernard Shaw, H. G. Wells, Henry David Thoreau, Leo Tolstoy, and Louisa May Alcott.

If they're interested in philosophy, toss out the likes of Socrates, Plato, Pythagoras, Ovid, and Plutarch. And if sports is their bag, point to Martina Navratilova (tennis champion), Dave Scott (6-time winner of the Ironman Triathlon), Paavo Nurmi (20-time world record holder in distance running), and Bill Pearl (4-time winner of the Mr. Universe bodybuilding championship).

THE FAT FACTOR

As much as we might wish otherwise, the typical American diet—that is, one that's loaded with foods from animal sources—simply doesn't support Renewal. An enormous body of compelling research suggests that foods from animal sources not only cause degenerative disease but also lower general quality of life and shorten life expectancy. As observed by the late Benjamin Spock, M.D., a noted pediatrician, author, and humanitarian, "Death from coronary arteriosclerosis, from cancer, and from stroke keep increasing. There is no question that these diseases are linked to diets high in fat—particularly animal fats."

The typical American diet is 40 to 50 percent fat, most of which comes from meat, poultry, fish, dairy products, and eggs—all animal-derived foods. Studies have linked a high fat intake to a litany of ailments, including high cholesterol, heart disease, and obesity.

Fat fuels cholesterol production. Not all fat is bad. Certain fats, called essential fatty acids, help defend your body against disease. (We'll discuss them in more detail in chapter 8.)

On the other hand, saturated fat, the kind supplied by animal-derived foods, has been universally condemned as detrimental to health. Your body uses saturated fat to make cholesterol. So the more of this type of fat you consume, the higher your total cholesterol level will be.

Animal-derived foods raise your total cholesterol in another way as well. All animals, be they cows, chickens, or fish, manufacture their own cholesterol. So when you eat red meat, poultry, fish, dairy products, or eggs, you're taking in not only saturated fat but cholesterol, too.

This dastardly combination can really do a number on your cholesterol reading. People who eat animal-derived foods get fully one-quarter of their cholesterol from their diets, with their bodies making the rest. By comparison, vegans get no cholesterol from their diets. Remember, vegans eat only plant-derived foods, and plants do not produce cholesterol.

This gives vegans a decided advantage in terms of their cholesterol levels. The body of a vegan makes only as much cholesterol as it needs to support itself, and in the right proportions. Vegetarians have low levels of low-density lipoproteins (LDLs), the "bad" cholesterol, and high levels of high-density lipoproteins (HDLs), the "good" cholesterol. For people who eat animal-derived foods, the opposite is usually true: they have high LDL and low HDL.

Many doctors tell their patients that they don't have to be concerned about their total cholesterol levels so long as they're within the "normal" range, typically defined as anything below 200 mg/dl (that's milligrams of cholesterol per deciliter of blood). This "normal," however, is anything but: It's a statistical artifact, derived by studying people who follow a high-fat, meat- and dairy-centered diet. For people who eat this way, the "normal" total cholesterol level is, on average, 210 mg/dl. For vegetarians, "normal" is 150 mg/dl. This little oversight can have some mighty unfortunate consequences.

I'd like to have a nickel for each time I've heard a patient say, "Thank goodness my cholesterol is in the 'normal' range. At least I don't have to worry about that." People with low total cholesterol readings are easily lulled into a false sense of security, thinking that they are not at risk for heart disease. The truth is that the more cholesterol you consume (that is, the more animal-derived foods you eat), the higher your risk for heart disease—regardless of your total cholesterol reading.

People with low cholesterol levels have heart attacks, too, though not quite as often as those with high levels. In fact, approximately half of all heart attack victims have "normal" cholesterol levels.

And forget the misguided notion that you can lower your total cholesterol—and presumably your risk of heart attack—by replacing the saturated fat in your diet with polyunsaturated fat from vegetable oils (such as canola, corn, peanut, and safflower) or, God forbid, margarine. This trade-off would be great if it worked, but it doesn't. In fact, polyunsaturated fat generates lots of disease-promoting free radicals because this kind of fat molecule is held together by oxidation-sensitive double bonds. (You'll recall that oxidation is the process that produces free radicals.) So in terms of free radical activity, "cholesterol-free" fat is even more dangerous than the saturated fat it presumes to replace.

Fat favors heart disease. Because a high fat intake raises your levels of LDL and total cholesterol, it also raises your risk of heart disease. LDL is the stuff that clings to arterial walls, causing the arteries to become clogged and to harden.

To understand what happens, think of your cardiovascular system as a superhighway. Blood surges along the thoroughfare, delivering nutrients and oxygen to your cells and picking up the cells' waste products. Then LDL sets up a roadblock. Suddenly, essential supplies can't get through to your cells. Waste removal becomes impossible, so garbage builds up and further obstructs passage. The cells not only starve, they're forced to wallow in their own excrement. Not a pretty picture.

When this process, called atherosclerosis, occurs in one of the arteries that serves the heart muscle, it sets the stage for a heart attack. Heart attacks are the number one cause of death in the United States. Every 25 seconds a heart attack strikes, and every 45 seconds one is fatal. The average American male has a 50 percent chance of dying from a heart attack.

The best way to beat the odds? Switch to a low-fat vegan diet. By becoming a low-fat vegan, you can all but eliminate the possibility that heart disease will do you in. Because their diet is naturally low in all fats, strict vegans have just a 4 percent chance of dying from a heart attack.

Fat feeds cancer. Animal-derived foods are high in fat, and a high-fat diet causes cancer. People who consume these foods on a daily basis for several decades have significantly higher rates of cancers of the breasts, stomach, colon, pancreas, bladder, prostate, ovaries, and uterus. A low-fat vegan diet, on the other hand, dramatically reduces the risk of these cancers.

If you're skeptical of the link between fat intake and cancer risk, these facts may convince you.

- Women who eat meat every day are four times as likely to develop breast cancer as women who eat meat less than once a week.
- Women who eat butter or cheese three or more times a week are three times as likely to develop breast cancer as women who eat these foods less than once a week.
- Women who eat eggs every day are three times as likely to develop breast cancer as women who eat eggs less than once a week.
- Women who eat eggs three or more times a week are three times as likely to die from ovarian cancer as women who eat eggs less than once a week.

- Men who eat meat, milk, cheese, or eggs every day are about 3½ times as likely to die from prostate cancer as men who seldom eat these foods or who avoid them completely.

Animal-derived foods contribute to all of the most common cancers. It's not only their high fat content that causes problems. It's also their lack of fiber, their high levels of pesticides, their added hormones, and more. (You'll read more about the relationship between dietary fat and cancer in chapter 12.)

Fat packs on pounds. A high intake of fat is responsible for yet another life-shortening condition: overweight. In fact, exceeding your ideal weight by just 20 percent—roughly 20 to 30 pounds—is an acknowledged risk factor for various health problems, including heart disease and certain types of cancer.

There's no truth to the popular view that complex carbohydrates, the kind found in grains, legumes, fruits, and vegetables, are responsible for weight gain. For the most part, fat is what makes people fat. This is because, gram for gram, fat has more than twice as many calories (nine, to be precise) as carbohydrates (only four). What's more, fat calories are quickly and efficiently converted to and stored as body fat, while complex carbohydrate calories are not. (Calories from refined, simple carbohydrates such as white sugar, refined flour, and honey are metabolized like fat and readily stored as fat.)

Thus, a given amount of a high-fat food contributes more than twice as much flab to a person's physique as the same amount of a food high in complex carbohydrates. And once fat calories are stored in the body's fatty tissues, they're much harder to burn off than complex carbohydrate calories.

So leave the butter and sour cream off the baked potatoes, the gobs of cheese and dressing off the salad, the butter off the toast, the pesto off the pasta, the mayonnaise off the sandwich, and the cream sauces off everything. (And don't be fooled by nonfat foods that are laden with sugar: They behave no differently in your body than full-fat foods.)

THE PROBLEMS WITH PROTEIN

The typical American diet is not just high in fat but high in protein, too. "So what's wrong with protein?" you ask. Plenty. As with fat, your body needs protein for certain basic functions. But consuming too much opens the door to disease and whittles years off your life.

You may be surprised to discover just how little protein is too much. The National Research Council (which sets the Recommended Dietary Allowances for nutrients) advocates a protein intake of no more than 8 percent of calories. The U.S. Department of Agriculture's Food and Nutrition Board (which sets the Daily Values) recommends 6 percent. And the World Health Organization suggests just 4.5 percent. By comparison, the average American gets a whopping 15 percent of calories from protein.

Some people—for instance, women who are pregnant or lactating, endurance athletes in training, and patients recovering from burns or surgery—may require a bit more protein in their diets. Most of us, however, are consuming far more than we need.

Protein saps your skeleton. Among the most serious health problems related to a high protein intake is osteoporosis, a debilitating bone disease that affects tens of millions of people—primarily women—in the United States alone. How does an overabundance of protein make bones brittle and susceptible to fractures?

When you eat too much protein, the excess is broken down by digestive enzymes into its component parts, called amino acids. Each molecule of an amino acid must be neutralized before the kidneys can excrete it. Your body calls on calcium to handle the job. But the calcium gets excreted in the urine, along with the amino acids. This process drains the supply of calcium in your bloodstream, so your body has to tap the stores in your bones.

Medical scientists call this condition protein-induced hypercalciuria. In plain English, it means that lots of valuable calcium is being flushed out in the urine by all that extra, unneeded protein. To give you an idea of the seriousness of this problem, female meat-eaters lose about 35 percent of their bone mass by age 65, while female vegetarians lose only about 18 percent.

This finding challenges the long-held belief that calcium deficiency is the sole cause of osteoporosis. Certainly, calcium deficiency accelerates the loss of bone mass. But an excessive protein intake plays a major role as well.

You may wonder where dairy products fit in all this. After all, they're protein foods that just happen to be high in calcium. Unfortunately, the dairy protein also causes a net loss of calcium. So if you want to boost your intake of the mineral, dairy products are not a good choice. In countries such as China, where people consume few dairy products and get most of their protein and calcium from plant-derived foods, osteoporosis is rare.

Of course, your body uses calcium for many purposes besides building and preserving bone mass. This versatile mineral helps maintain a regular heartbeat, aids blood clotting, and prevents health problems such as high blood pressure and colon cancer. Good stuff to have around!

Because a vegetarian diet has a lower protein content, it protects against calcium loss. This is especially important as we get older, because the ability to absorb calcium (and all essential nutrients) declines with age.

Protein taxes your kidneys. Excessive protein consumption has been linked to another disease of epidemic proportions: chronic renal failure. This silent, gradual erosion of kidney functioning hasn't received much publicity, perhaps because it has no outward signs—unlike osteoporosis, which manifests itself as hunched spines in some people and painful fractures in others. Still, chronic renal failure is disabling and potentially lethal. And it's widespread: There are tens of millions of cases in the United States alone. In studies of animals with chronic renal failure, merely restricting protein intake extended their life spans by up to 50 percent.

PESTICIDES: COVERT POISONS

Beyond their high fat and protein contents, meats and dairy products have another, man-made problem. Collectively, these foods account for more than 75 percent of all pesticides residues ingested by Americans. By comparison, only a small fraction of the pesticides in the American diet come from produce—even from the nonorganic kind.

In fact, animal-derived foods dominate what has come to be known as the "Dirty 15." This list, compiled by the National Academy of Sciences (a fairly persnickety group of scientists not given to exaggeration), identifies the foods that contain the most and the nastiest pesticides.

Now you might think that the worst offenders would be weeded out through the food inspection process. But that's not the case. Take meat, for example: Although the U.S. Department of Agriculture claims to inspect it, only one of every 250,000 animals slaughtered—that's 0.00047 percent—is actually tested for pesticide residues.

So why do meats and dairy products have such high concentrations of pesticide residues? Well, animals ingest the pesticides through their feed. Considering that it takes 16 pounds of soybeans or grain to produce just 1 pound of meat, the average cow or chicken consumes an enormous amount of pesticide-laden feed in its lifetime.

Once ingested, the pesticides, being fat-soluble, are stored in the animal's fatty tissues—an attempt by the animal's body to rid itself of the toxins. But the pesticides linger in these fat cell storage sites and eventually get eaten by humans.

Then the human body does the same thing: It tries to get rid of the health-threatening pesticides by stowing them away in fatty tissues. But the toxins remain, poisoning the immune system, sabotaging cellular structures, and scrambling the processes of Renewal.

The pesticides are even more harmful to humans than to animals because they're so highly concentrated by the time they get into our systems. It's actually a two-step process. First, the toxins from the feed are concentrated in the animal's body. Then when a human eats that meat, the toxins are further concentrated in his own fat cells.

Medical scientists are just beginning to understand what types of damage pesticides can do to the human body. Here are a few examples of what they've discovered so far. (For more on pesticides, see chapter 11.)

Pesticides raise cancer risk. Pesticides are carcinogens. They directly and dramatically increase a person's chances of developing cancer sometime in life.

Eat Low on the Food Chain

The Earth Day 1990 Committee adopted the following resolution: "Eat low on the food chain." Just what is the food chain, and why should you eat low on it?

At the bottom of the food chain are plants, which sustain themselves with sunlight, carbon dioxide, minerals, and water. Herbivores, the next link in the chain, eat plants. And carnivores, the final link, eat not only herbivores but also other carnivores.

This is significant because the farther you move up the food chain, the more concentrated toxins become. For example, livestock eat corn and soybeans that have been sprayed with pesticides. The pesticides become concentrated in the animals' flesh. Pesticides runoff finds its way into both the crop irrigation water and the livestock's drinking water, further adding to the toxic burden. Then when a carnivorous human eats this meat, the pesticides become even more concentrated in the body.

This same process occurs in the oceans, where small fish eat plankton, and larger fish gobble up smaller fish. Our oceans have become toxic waste dumps. Fish are commonly contaminated with a variety of pollutants, including methylmercury and other heavy metals, pesticides runoff, chlorinated hydrocarbons, and radioactivity. These poisons can be found in all fish, but they're most concentrated in larger fish such as swordfish and tuna, which are at the top of the aquatic food chain.

It all boils down to this: The lower you go on the food chain for your foods, the fewer toxins you'll ingest. And since plants are at the very bottom of the chain, they're your best choice. By eating them, you'll be doing yourself—and the earth—a big favor.

Pesticides compromise fertility. Polychlorinated biphenyls, dichlorodiphenyltrichloroethane (DDT), dioxane, and other commonly used pesticides are to blame for declining sperm counts and other indicators of reduced fertility. The sperm count for the average American male is 30 percent lower today than 30 years ago. Plus, more than 25 percent of male college students are considered sterile today, compared with only 0.5 percent in 1950. That's a 5,000 percent increase.

Pesticides contaminate breast milk. This is perhaps the most grim reminder of the pervasiveness of pesticides. In the United States, 99 percent of mother's milk contains levels of DDT above the rather conservative limits set by the Environmental Protection Agency (EPA). Meat-eating mothers have 35 times the breast milk contamination of vegetarian mothers. This means that virtually all nursing babies of meat-eating mothers are being exposed to levels of DDT that the EPA has deemed unsafe for adults. It is generally acknowledged that a baby's developing organs are much more sensitive than an adult's organs to the detrimental effects of these chemicals.

WHERE'S THE FIBER?

While animal-derived foods supply plenty of bad stuff—fat, protein, pesticides—they come up short on one very important substance: fiber. In fact, these foods have no fiber whatsoever. This causes real problems for nonvegetarians, because fiber plays an essential role in good nutrition and supports optimum health. Here are some ways in which fiber helps your body function.

Fiber cleans up cholesterol. Fiber sops up cholesterol and flushes it out of your body. Consuming too little fiber accelerates the development of atherosclerosis, setting the stage for high blood pressure, heart attack, stroke, and other cardiovascular diseases.

Fiber supports waste removal. By absorbing water and adding bulk to stool, fiber encourages waste to move through your digestive tract faster. Without enough fiber in your diet, you're at greater risk for chronic constipation and colon cancer. Consider this: World populations with high rates of meat consumption have high rates of colon cancer, while those with low rates of meat consumption have low rates of colon cancer.

Fiber escorts toxins from your system. Fiber soaks up cancer-causing toxic chemicals, so they can't be absorbed from the large intestine into the bloodstream. One Dutch study found that deaths from all cancers—not just colon cancer—were three times higher among men on a low-fiber diet compared with men on a high-fiber diet.

THE PROS OF PLANT-DERIVED FOODS

Interestingly enough, what's wrong with animal-derived foods is what's right about plant-derived foods. Grains, legumes, vegetables, and fruits are naturally low-fat and cholesterol-free. They're high in phytochemicals and fiber. They supply liberal amounts of the healthful essential fatty acids. Preferably, they are originally grown and so are free of pesticides. But even if they're commercially grown, they harbor far fewer pesticides than meats and dairy products.

Replacing the animal-derived foods in your diet with supernutritious plant-derived foods supports health, prevents disease, and promotes longevity. In short, it nurtures Renewal.

Now you know why you should follow the Anti-Aging Diet, which is a plant-based, vegan diet. The question is, how do you do it?

To help you make the switch, you'll find menu plans and recipes beginning on page 535. But if you don't feel ready to completely give up animal-derived foods, remember: *The extent to which you follow the Renewal Anti-Aging Diet determines the extent to which you'll benefit from it.* Try stepping down to nonfat (non low-fat) dairy products since they're the least problematic. They include nonfat milk, nonfat yogurt (sugar-free, of course), nonfat cottage cheese, and nonfat sour cream. Stick with them until you feel comfortable phasing them out.

You might benefit from having a doctor who supports and encourages your newly acquired healthful eating habits. Unfortunately, most doctors are not very knowledgeable about nutrition and its relationship to health. In fact, they received an average of just 2½ hours of nutrition training in medical school. What's more, if your doctor eats meats and dairy products, he'll most likely defend this unhealthy practice. Finding a doctor who is a vegetarian can be difficult. But it's not impossible—and it's well worth the effort.

I'm convinced that if you try the Anti-Aging Diet, you'll like it because you'll feel better than you ever believed possible. Over time, you'll come to see this eating plan not as an exercise in self-denial but as a cornucopia of delicious, healthful foods that you actually crave. You'll be surprised at how easily you make the transition to veganism, even though right now it may seem impossible. And you'll wonder how you ever could have been enticed by disease-causing foods in the first place.

Now it's time to learn more about fats—in particular, how certain fats literally keep us alive, while others literally do us in.

Fats: The Good, the Bad, and the Downright Ugly

No diet will remove all the fat from your body because the brain is entirely fat. Without a brain you might look good, but all you could do is run for public office.
—COVERT BAILEY, BEST-SELLING NUTRITION
   AND FITNESS AUTHOR

Meet Al.

Al is a patient of mine who has coronary artery disease. The blood vessels that feed his heart muscle are blocked with fatty deposits called plaque. He developed the condition because of something he ate—namely, too much fat. But just as dietary factors can cause coronary artery disease, they can reverse it as well.

On this particular office visit, I've asked Al to describe for me what he usually eats in the course of a day, starting with breakfast.

"Well, most mornings I grab a muffin. If I have time, I sit down for a bowl of granola with 2 percent milk."

"Let's stop right there. Most muffins and most granolas are made with vegetable oil and sugar. And did you know that 2 percent milk is actually 34 percent butterfat?"

"That's news to me."

"How about lunch?"

"Usually a salad and an apple. Maybe some corn chips or potato chips—but I get them at the health food store."

"Well, the salad and apple are fine, assuming you use a nonfat dressing. But the corn chips and potato chips are a real problem. They've been deep-fried in fat, which means they're saturated with the stuff. Think about it: A potato has about 1 percent fat, and corn has about 8 percent fat. After frying, both have about 70 percent fat. Not only that, but they're loaded with carcinogens that they absorbed during the frying process."

"So much for lunch. But I know I do dinner right. I always have fish or chicken—without the skin, of course—plus a vegetable and a salad."

"Sorry, Al. You probably don't want to hear this, but the fat content of fish varies from 30 to 60 percent. Chicken without skin isn't much better: It contains 35 percent fat. The vegetables are excellent, as long as you don't drown them in butter. And again, the salad is okay, provided you use nonfat dressing."

"So you're telling me that I have to stop eating fat. That's the bottom line, isn't it?"

"No, not exactly. Fats perform a variety of vital functions within your body. You literally couldn't live without them. The problem is that you're consuming far too much of the stuff. Based on what you've told me, I would say that you're getting about 40 percent of your calories from fat—an intake that we know promotes heart disease, not to mention other degenerative conditions."

A FATAL ATTRACTION?

We Americans are having a love affair with fatty foods. We crave them on deep physical and perhaps psychological levels—the steak and mashed potatoes (with gravy, of course), the cheeseburger and fries, the bacon and eggs, the cake and ice cream. On any given day, the average American consumes ¼ pound of fat, the equivalent of one full stick of butter.

We know that fatty foods are not good for us. Still, saying "No, thanks" to this unhealthy fare often requires supreme willpower.

For our prehistoric ancestors, who seldom knew when or if they were getting their next meal, fat provided an efficient way for the body to store calories from food. Then when sustenance was scarce, the body could retrieve and burn those calories for energy.

Of course, with the advent of supermarkets and refrigerators to stock a ready supply of food, the body's fat-storing mechanism became virtually obsolete. Yet we humans have not shed the genetic programming that causes us to crave and accumulate fat in preparation for the famine that never comes. As a result, most of us consume far too much fat, and that has serious implications for our health and longevity.

The good news is, of all the factors that prevent us from achieving our maximum life span, fat intake is the one over which we have the most control. Eating lean offers us the greatest potential for optimizing Renewal.

MIXED MESSAGES

Admittedly, cutting back on fat presents its challenges. Part of the problem lies with the glut of conflicting information about which fats are "good," which are "bad," and what a healthy intake should be. In my opinion, no other nutrition issue has generated so much confusion and contradiction.

Another part of the problem is that we've simply become accustomed to fat. We like the taste and texture that it gives to foods. And we have a hard time giving it up.

As a kid, I often wondered how fat, which by itself doesn't seem to have any flavor at all, could make food so darn satisfying. For starters, fat is a very concentrated source of caloric energy. It contains more than twice as many calories per unit weight as carbohydrates and protein: a whopping 9 calories per gram of fat, versus only 4 calories per gram of carbohydrates or protein. Because fat is so dense, a high-fat meal can make you feel fuller than an equal-size high-carbohydrate meal. Unfortunately, it also loads your body with more than double the number of calories.

What's more, fatty foods cause your body to release the hormones enterogastrone and cholecystokinin. Both hormones create a feeling of satiety.

But fat also affects your body in other, less pleasant ways. It injures your heart and blood vessels and weakens your immune system, earning it dubious distinction as the substance most often implicated in heart disease, cancer, and stroke. It also contributes to diabetes, obesity, and other life-shortening health problems.

In fact, a diet that contains too much fat or the wrong

kinds of fat is more closely linked to degenerative disease and premature death than any other single risk factor. Absolutely nothing else in your diet poses such a threat to your health and longevity.

THE MANY FACES OF FAT

For Renewal to work efficiently, you have to make sure that you're getting enough of the right fats while steering clear of the wrong fats. I call them the good, the bad, and the downright ugly. Let's look at each in a bit more detail.

Is Your Diet Making You Sick?

The standard American diet—high in fat, low in fiber and essential nutrients—feeds the development of an array of acute and chronic health problems. Particularly troubling are the so-called fatty degenerative diseases, which are characterized by the appearance of fat in parts of the body where it's not supposed to be. For instance, atherosclerosis occurs when fat is deposited on the walls of arteries, causing the arteries to clog and harden over time. Other examples of fatty degenerative disease include the following:

- Acne
- Allergies
- Arthritis
- Asthma
- Cancer
- Cholecystitis (Inflammation of the gallbladder)
- Chronic or recurrent infection
- Cirrhosis of the liver
- Diabetes
- Eczema
- Gallstones
- Heart attack
- High blood pressure
- Immune dysfunction syndromes
- Kidney stones
- Multiple sclerosis
- Obesity
- Stroke

Good fats. These are the essential fatty acids, which you need to achieve optimum health. Your body uses them to manufacture cell membranes and prostaglandins, hormonelike compounds with anti-inflammatory properties. (You'll learn more about the essential fatty acids in chapter 8.) You'll find essential fatty acids in grains, beans, fruits, and vegetables—the fresh, whole plant-derived foods of the New Four Food Groups—as well as in nuts and seeds. You won't find them in animal-derived foods. So by following a vegetarian diet devoid of added oils, you'll automatically get the good fats, and in just the right amounts.

Bad fats. These fats harm your body by interfering with normal metabolism and generating cell-damaging free radicals in quantities that would have taxed the superlative descriptive powers of the late Carl Sagan. Perhaps the best-known bad fat is saturated fat, found in animal-derived foods such as meats, poultry, fish, dairy products, and eggs.

Ugly fats. Ugly fats, also known as *trans*-fats, have undergone chemical transformation via hydrogenation (which hardens liquid vegetable oils), high-heat cooking (such as frying), or other processing. *Trans*-fats are brimming with free radicals, which easily and readily sabotage cells.

Manufacturers use ugly fats in virtually all commercial baked goods as well as in chips, crackers, frozen dinners, and other convenience foods. Other sources of ugly fats include margarine, processed vegetable oil spreads, shortenings, and anything barbecued, broiled, or fried. The average American consumes 100 pounds of ugly fats—mostly in processed foods, commercial baked goods, and margarine—each year.

UGLY FATS: THE WORST OFFENDERS

Of the three types of fat, the ugly fats do your body the most harm. As mentioned above, ugly fats contain excessive amounts of free radicals, the result of hydrogenation or exposure to heat, light, or air. All it takes is one agent—a photon (light particle) or an oxygen molecule, for instance—to rob a fat molecule of an electron and turn it into a free radical. This free radical creates two more free radicals, and a chain reaction ensues. The renegade particles then go to work, rupturing membranes, fracturing DNA, and otherwise decimating cells.

But free radical formation is the least of the problems with ugly fats. Because truth be told, all fats—even the good fats—gradually decompose into free radicals. This process starts the moment that a fat is synthesized and continues at a steady rate over time.

What sets the ugly fats apart is that their molecular structure has been altered. They're not recognized by cells because they look unusual and behave in strange ways. They confuse the body, which doesn't quite know what to do with them.

In its natural state, a fat molecule has what biochemists call a *cis*, or same-side, configuration. This means the atoms within the molecule lie side by side, joined by double bonds. (In a double bond, two atoms share two electrons between them.) When the fat molecule is subjected to hydrogenation or to high-heat cooking, the atoms twist around their double bonds, so the molecule looks as though it has its head on backwards. This is what biochemists call a *trans*, or opposite-side, configuration. It causes dramatic differences in the way the human body recognizes and uses the fat.

Beware of Hidden Fats

When you look at a piece of steak, you can see the fat right away. If only all fatty foods were so easy to identify. Your best bet is to read labels and ingredients lists to assess the fat content before you take your first bite. Some foods to watch out for include breads, coffee creamers, corn chips, crackers, nuts, pie crusts, whipped toppings, and low-fat dairy products such as cheese, milk (even 1 percent), and yogurt.

To the body, *trans*-fats look similar to but not exactly like *cis*-fats. It persists in trying to use *trans*-fats just as it would *cis*-fats, with no success.

This case of mistaken identity can have disastrous consequences, especially if the *trans*-fats derive from essential fatty acids. In his book *Vitamins in Medicine*, Franklin Bicknell describes what happens: "Not only does (the body) fail to benefit (from the *trans*-fats), but it is deluded by their similarity to normal essential fatty acids and so attempts to use them. It starts incorporating them in biochemical reactions and then finds they are the wrong shape. But the reaction has gone too far to jettison them and begin again with normal essential fatty acids. So (the *trans*-fats) not only are useless but actually prevent the use of normal essential fatty acids. They are, in fact, *anti-essential fatty acids*."

The "fake" essential fatty acids end up obstructing receptor sites on cells, sort of like jamming a lock with the wrong key. In this way, these *trans*-fats prevent the real essential fatty acids from doing their jobs and can even create an essential fatty acid deficiency.

Since essential fatty acids are important components of cell membranes and prostaglandins, blocking their activity strikes a devastating blow against cellular health and immune system performance. Over time, this can lead to atherosclerosis (hardening and clogging of the arteries), cancer, stroke, arthritis, and other degenerative conditions.

SICK OILS: DISEASE IN DISGUISE

Among the top dietary sources of corrupted essential fatty acids are what I call sick oils—the vegetable oils that we buy in supermarkets and use in cooking and as salad dressings. Why "sick oils"? Because they cause disease, accelerate the aging process, and thwart Renewal.

On the shelf, these supermarket oils may appear pure and natural. But excessive processing has rendered them damaged merchandise nutrition-wise. Besides having their health- and life-supporting essential fatty acids mangled into *trans*-fats, they've acquired a hefty load of free radicals. And they tend to be saturated with pesticides because their raw materials come from crops (such as corn, safflower, and soy) that are usually sprayed.

As if that weren't bad enough, these raw materials must also endure an array of nutrient-depleting procedures before they're ready for bottling as oils. This processing may include any or all of the following: cleaning and hulling; cooking, rolling, or pressing; solvent extraction, to remove proteins, fiber, vitamins, and minerals; distillation;

filtration; degumming, to remove calcium, chlorophyll, copper, iron, and magnesium; refining; bleaching; steam and/or vacuum deodorizing; defoaming; and the addition of preservatives such as butylated hydroxyanisole and butylated hydroxytoluene.

And all the while, the oils-in-progress are being exposed to heat, light, and air—elements that foster the formation of free radicals. We're talking not random, one-here-and-one-there occurrences but torrential cascades. And once the free radical chain reaction begins, it can go on for a relatively long time. Thousands of free radicals (but only a few milliseconds) later, the chain reaction flames out, leaving a great many toxic by-products in its wake—hydroperoxides, hydroxyperoxyaldehydes, ketones, ozonides, peroxides, and polymers. These compounds weaken the immune system and damage DNA, which causes the cell mutations that lead to cancer.

Incredibly, despite all the evidence to the contrary, the sick oils are still marketed as healthy. Manufacturers label these oils with catch-phrases such as "cholesterol-free" and "high in polyunsaturated," which imply at least some degree of nutritional value.

My advice to you is to shun the sick supermarket oils. Instead, shop health food stores for organic, minimally processed oils. For cooking, use soy or olive oil, both of which are relatively heat stable. For salad dressings and other uses, choose from walnut, pumpkin, flax, soy, and olive oils.

Remember, though, that all oils gradually turn rancid as they age. Light and air accelerate this process. Steer clear of oils in clear glass or plastic containers. Store oils in the refrigerator, and discard them once they're more than three months old.

FROM THE FRYER INTO THE FIRE

Something else to keep in mind: Whenever you raise the temperature of any type of oil—or any type of fat, for that matter—you dramatically accelerate its rate of transformation into an ugly fat. This is why barbecuing, broiling, frying, and other high-heat cooking methods are so unhealthy. Using any of these methods to prepare fatty foods leaves the foods oozing with free radicals and *trans-*

fats. A grilled hamburger or a piece of fried chicken, for example, contains about as many free radicals as one cigarette.

Deep-frying is a particularly noxious practice. The higher heats generate a seething cauldron of free radicals and *trans*-fats. These then get absorbed into your food—be it chicken nuggets, fish sticks, or french fries.

What about stir-frying? It can be healthy, provided that it's done the right way. This means keeping the temperature low and using just a very small amount of oil. Here's how we do it at my house: We coat a pan with olive or soy oil or nonstick cooking spray—just enough to coat the pan's surface. Then we add the vegetables, followed by a little water. The water helps to hold the temperature at 212°F so the oil doesn't break down.

With the exception of these stir-fries, I avoid all fried foods—not only because they have outrageous quantities of free radicals and ugly fats but also because they have way too much fat in general. The bottom line: If you must eat fatty foods (which I hope you won't), refrain from subjecting them to high heats.

BAD FATS: BETTER, BUT ...

One of the lingering "myth-conceptions" about ugly fats is that no matter how bad they are, they're still better than the bad fats. One reason: Hydrogenated oils and sick oils—both ugly fats—are primarily polyunsaturated, while animal-derived fats—the bad fats—are saturated.

It is true that unsaturated and saturated fats have crucial differences in their molecular structures. But polyunsaturated fat molecules contain double bonds, which means they're easily oxidized into free radicals or *trans*-fats. Saturated fat molecules, on the other hand, contain no double bonds and so are more stable. They can still be oxidized into free radicals, but not nearly as easily.

THE SCOOP ON BREAD SPREADS

I can think of no better forum for comparing unsaturated and saturated fats than the great margarine-versus-butter debate. For years margarine, a polyunsaturated fat, has been touted as a healthy alternative to butter, a saturated fat. But new research challenges this view.

Not so long ago, my friend Charlie and I got into a discussion about this very subject. Charlie informed me that he had finally decided to trade in butter for margarine, convinced that the latter would endow him with Teflon-coated arteries. I responded by telling him that if he must have one or the other, he'd be a bit better off if he went back to butter.

Of course, Charlie was appalled, so I explained to him that all fat molecules consist of chains of carbon atoms linked to one another by chemical bonds. The degree to which a fat is saturated depends on the types of bonds that connect the carbon atoms along the "backbone" of the molecule.

In saturated fats (the kind found in butter, dairy products, and other animal-derived foods), all of the atoms are connected by single bonds. In unsaturated fats (the kind that come from plants), some of the atoms are connected by single bonds, while others are connected by double bonds. Monounsaturated fats have just one double bond per fat molecule, while polyunsaturated fats have multiple double bonds per fat molecule.

Double bonds are much more vulnerable to oxidation (the process that produces free radicals) than single bonds, mainly because they're weaker. This means polyunsaturated fats, which have multiple double bonds, are most likely to generate free radicals as well as *trans*-fats when processed or exposed to heat, light, or air. Saturated fats, meanwhile, are less vulnerable to oxidation since they have no double bonds.

So as bad as butter (a saturated fat) is, it's no match for margarine (a polyunsaturated fat) when it comes to generating free radicals. And these free radicals contribute to atherosclerosis, along with scores of other degenerative diseases.

By now, Charlie was looking positively desolate. "I can't believe it," he muttered. "After using butter all my life, I finally switched to margarine because I thought it was better for me. Now you're telling me that it's worse. How much damage have I done?"

"Well, probably not much, considering that you've been eating margarine for only a short time," I replied. "You can thank your own body for that. It's so resilient and so resourceful that it's able to slow the progression of athero-sclerosis and other degenerative diseases. That's why you won't notice symptoms for a few decades.

Choose Your Fats Wisely

If you want to improve your overall health—as well as your prospects for achieving maximum life span—your number one priority is to improve your dietary fat profile. Here's how to do it.

- Reduce your total fat intake.
- Increase your essential fatty acid intake.
- Eliminate saturated fat.
- Eliminate processed vegetable oils.
- Eliminate hydrogenated vegetable oils.
- Avoid fats that have been subjected to high heat.

"But just because you don't notice symptoms doesn't mean that everything is fine," I cautioned. "At this very moment, about three-fourths of all Americans—almost the entire meat-eating population over 30 years of age—are in the earliest stages of degenerative disease. Worse, they don't even realize what's going on inside their bodies. They're prime candidates for heart attacks or strokes or cancers sometime down the road."

"That settles it," Charlie announced. "I'm giving up margarine . . ."

"Wait a minute," I interrupted. "I'm not saying that you *should* eat butter. Butter is solid fat, just like margarine. Both are bad. What I am saying is that if you must have one or the other, butter is probably the lesser of two evils. It contains fewer free radicals and no *trans*-fats."

WHAT ABOUT CHOLESTEROL?

Unfortunately—and here's where the whole butter-ver-sus-margarine debate takes an ugly turn—butter also con-tains cholesterol, while margarine does not. You'll recall from chapter 6 that all animals are genetically pro-grammed to make cholesterol. So any food that comes from animals or is made from animal products—including butter as well as meat, cheese, and eggs—naturally supplies cholesterol.

Plant-derived foods, on the other hand, are naturally cholesterol-free. No matter how hard you try, you can't get cholesterol from a vegetable.

Does this mean that vegetable oils and vegetable oil products are better for you? Absolutely not. These foods are still fats, and eating too much fat—no matter what its source—causes atherosclerosis and heart disease.

Still, people have a tendency to equate "cholesterol-free" with "protection from heart disease," a fact that isn't lost on the companies that manufacture and market vegetable oils, margarines, and spreads. Don't be lulled into a false sense of security by what a product's label claims. The only way to create a safe haven for your heart is to cut back on all dietary fats.

MINIMUM FAT, MAXIMUM HEALTH

How low must you go? If your goal is to optimize Renewal and live as long as possible, you should aim for just 10 percent of calories from fat. Research has shown this low fat intake to be most effective in preventing and even reversing atherosclerosis.

Conveniently enough, the Anti-Aging Diet adheres to this 10 percent fat guideline. It also eliminates your expo-sure to both bad fats and ugly fats. If you follow the diet to the letter, you can actually reverse atherosclerosis and reclaim a younger, healthier cardiovascular system.

But if 10 percent of calories from fat seems too austere for you, remember: *The extent to which you follow the Renewal Anti-Aging Diet determines the extent to which you'll benefit from it.* Even minor changes in your eating habits—like giving up margarine and butter—can make a big difference in your health.

Now that you know all about bad fats and ugly fats, let's explore the good fats: the health-enhancing, anti-aging essential fatty acids.

Fat Power: The Essential Fatty Acids

It started to disappear from our diet about 75 years ago and now is almost gone. Only about 20 percent of the amount needed for human health and well-being remains. The nutrient is a fatty acid so important and so little understood that I call it the nutritional missing link.
—DONALD O. RUDIN, M.D., *THE OMEGA-3 PHE-NOMENON*

She had tried the best therapies that mainstream medicine has to offer. Still, Edna Hampton's arthritis continued to worsen, leaving her with unbearable swelling and pain. But when her internist suggested going on prescription steroids, Edna balked.

She had heard about alternative medicine and figured that she'd give it a shot. She had nothing to lose. If alternative therapies didn't help, she reasoned, the steroids would still be there for her. A friend of Edna's referred her to me.

"Dr. Smith, I worked hard until I was 65," Edna told me. "Now I want to travel and enjoy my retirement. But my joints ache so much that I can't even get out of bed most days, much less go to a foreign country. My internist says I need steroids. But my mother had osteoporosis, and I know that prednisone (a corticosteroid used to treat arthritis) can cause osteoporosis. A friend of mine is on prednisone, and her bones got so weak that she fractured her hip in a minor fall. Can you help me?"

After a thorough workup, I prescribed the following nutritional regimen: a low-fat, vegetarian diet that eliminated dairy products, sugar, and wheat; a multivitamin/mineral supplement; antioxidant supplements; anti-arthritis herbs; and glucosamine, a supplement that nourishes joint and other connective tissues and speeds their healing. I also started Edna on essential fatty acids.

Within just a month of starting this regimen, Edna reported that her arthritis pain had almost completely subsided and that she had cut back her use of anti-inflammatory drugs. Within two months, her arthritis was in complete remission, and she no longer needed her medication.

That was three years ago. Edna still has an occasional flare-up, but arthritis no longer slows her down. In fact, she's more active than ever. She has even begun to realize her dream of traveling the world, with trips to London, the Netherlands, Singapore, and Africa (where she went on safari). And she's loving every pain-free minute of it.

The secret behind Edna's remarkable recovery? She tapped into Fat Power.

IMPROBABLE ALLIES

The "fat" in Fat Power refers to the essential fatty acids (EFAs), nutrients that play leading roles in the drama of health and healing. Essential fatty acids support the production of anti-inflammatory prostaglandins, strengthen immune cells, and minimize autoimmune reactions (in which immune cells attack healthy tissues).

Fat Power can prevent and help cure cancer, heart disease, immune deficiencies, infections, and—as in Edna's case—even arthritis. It can relieve depression and fatigue. It can improve your complexion. And most important for us Renewal seekers, it can slow and even reverse the aging process.

Fat Power doesn't come from the greasy, dastardly fats found in abundance in the standard American diet. In fact, you can't get optimum amounts of the EFAs from foods alone, which is why I recommend supplementation. Otherwise, you put yourself at risk for an EFA deficiency, a condition that predisposes you to an amazing array of life-shortening health problems.

WHY ARE THEY SO DARNED IMPORTANT?

EFAs are essential nutrients, just like vitamins and minerals. They were first identified back in the 1950s, when they were dubbed vitamin F. Researchers at the time didn't understand the exact chemical nature of the EFAs, but they did realize that the nutrients are necessary to sustain human life.

It took researchers years to substantiate the significance of the EFAs in human health. But by the 1970s and 1980s, they had amassed compelling evidence to support the theory that we humans cannot survive without these "fat vitamins." They also discovered that EFA deficiencies abound in the general population, but that the symptoms often go undiagnosed.

Why do so many of us—80 percent of us, by one estimate—come up short? The problem is that EFAs are impossible to obtain in optimum amounts from common food sources. Because they are such an important piece of the nutritional puzzle, a deficiency of essential fatty acids can lead to an astonishing array of ailments, including arthritis, atherosclerosis (hardening and clogging of the arteries), cancer, diabetes, immune dysfunction, and other diseases intimately associated with accelerated aging.

But EFA research is relatively new, and the chemistry behind it is relatively complex. For this reason, most people, including most health care providers, have no knowledge of the EFAs or of their crucial roles in health and longevity.

MAKING CELL MEMBRANES

Your body uses the EFAs to manufacture cell membranes and prostaglandins. Both components perform very important, though very different, functions in the grand scheme of human health. Without optimum cell membrane repair and prostaglandin synthesis, Renewal would become an exercise in futility.

Cell membranes act as protective coverings for the whole cell as well as for the individual structures (or organelles) within it. These membranes are constantly surveying the goings-on both inside and outside the cell, granting access to select substances, turning away the shady characters, and booting out the rowdies.

In the line of duty, cell membranes endure continuous free radical attack and suffer injuries on a regular basis. Damaged membranes have trouble letting in nutrients and expelling waste. They develop leaks. Their receptor sites malfunction, so enzymes can't "dock" on the cell and perform essential tasks. Cumulative damage to cell membranes erodes cell health and accelerates aging.

When Good Fats Fall Short

A deficiency of the good fats—the essential fatty acids (EFAs)—can affect your body in myriad and unexpected ways. Consider the following list of health problems, each of which can be caused or aggravated by a shortage of EFAs.

- Acne
- Allergies
- Angina
- Arteriosclerosis (hardening of the arteries)
- Arthritis
- Asthma
- Autoimmune disease
- Cancer
- Crohn's disease (an inflammatory disorder of the intestines)
- Diabetes
- Diarrhea
- Dry hair
- Eczema
- Fibrocystic breast disease
- Gallstones
- Hair loss
- Heart attack
- High blood pressure
- High cholesterol
- Inflammatory disorders
- Kidney failure
- Multiple sclerosis
- Obesity
- Poor wound healing
- Premenstrual syndrome
- Reproductive failure
- Scleroderma (an autoimmune disease of the skin)
- Stroke
- Varicose veins

Cells can repair or replace their own damaged membranes. But to do it, they need adequate supplies of the right raw materials—that is, the EFAs.

With this in mind, you can just imagine the devastating effects of an EFA deficiency on cellular health. Weaker, less selective cell membranes have trouble regulating the comings and goings of "good" substances and "bad" substances. The result is unhealthy cells and, eventually, an unhealthy body.

When EFAs are in short supply, your immune system suffers most. That's because the immune cells can no longer do their jobs. Many common health problems, including allergies, autoimmune diseases, infections, and even cancer, are actually manifestations of the immune damage that results from chronic EFA depletion.

On the other hand, optimum EFA intake ensures that immune cells not only survive but thrive. With strong membranes, the cells can fearlessly wage war against free radicals, allergens, microbes, and toxins. They fight inflammation better, so they're more effective against conditions such as allergic bronchitis, allergic sinusitis, arthritis, and asthma.

The bottom line: To keep all cells functioning as they should, you need to make sure that your EFA intake is up to par. Damaged cell membranes weaken cells and open the door to serious health problems.

PRODUCING PROSTAGLANDINS

Your body also uses EFAs to manufacture powerful, hormonelike chemicals called prostaglandins (sometimes called eicosanoids). Structurally, prostaglandins look just like EFAs, except that each prostaglandin has a small knot in the chain of carbon atoms that form its "backbone."

Even though they are present in extremely minute amounts, prostaglandins exert tremendous control over a broad spectrum of fundamental physical processes, including heart rate, blood pressure, blood clotting, fertility, and conception. And they work in pairs: One prostaglandin facilitates a particular function, while another inhibits it.

In terms of fighting disease and promoting Renewal, prostaglandins are important because they regulate inflammation. Inflammation is a principal characteristic of virtually all immune disorders, whether infectious, allergic, or autoimmune. Pro-inflammatory prostaglandins encourage "healthy" inflammation, the kind that the body uses to heal an infection or to stop an allergic reaction. Their partners, the anti-inflammatory prostaglandins, prevent the inflammatory response from getting out of control.

To make the pro-inflammatory prostaglandins, your body uses arachidonic acid, an EFA that is readily available in even the most dismal of diets. Unfortunately, the same cannot be said of alpha-linolenic acid and gamma-linolenic acid, the EFAs needed to make the all-important anti-inflammatory prostaglandins. They're relatively hard to come by in foods.

The upshot is that without enough of the necessary EFAs, your body tends to make more of the pro-inflammatory prostaglandins. As a result, inflammation is more severe, which translates into more severe allergies and asthma, more painful arthritis, more rapid atherosclerosis—and, of course, more rapid aging.

The Can-Do Chemicals

Prostaglandins carry out a variety of essential tasks within your body, influencing virtually every aspect of your health. To give you an idea of how important these hormonelike chemicals are, consider their to-do list.

- Trigger cell division
- Regulate message transmission between nerve cells
- Direct endocrine hormones to their target cells
- Stimulate production of steroid hormones
- Control body temperature
- Dilate and constrict blood vessels
- Alter clot formation
- Affect allergic reactions
- Affect arthritic reactions
- Regulate gastric secretions
- Control evaporation of water from the skin
- Control smooth muscle and other involuntary reflexes
- Control tissue swelling
- Turn pain responses on and off
- Regulate menstrual cramps
- Induce labor

ARE YOU GETTING ENOUGH?

By keeping cell membranes healthy and prostaglandins in abundant (and balanced) supply, EFAs facilitate the Renewal process. But as mentioned earlier, as many as 80 percent of Americans don't get enough EFAs through their diets. In fact, a high percentage of these folks are experiencing symptoms as a result of EFA deficiencies.

Why are so many people running so low on EFAs? Blame the poor nutritional state of our food supply. For starters, many crops are grown in nutrient-depleted soil and treated with artificial fertilizers, pesticides, and assorted other chemicals—factors that dramatically alter a food's nutritional profile. Then while some foods go directly to market, others are shipped to processing plants. There, thanks to technological "advances," they're stripped clean of the few nutrients they have left—not only EFAs but also vitamins, minerals, fiber, and phytochemicals.

Many of the foods we buy look more or less the same as they always have. But nutrition-wise, they're shadows of their former selves—like wax fruit compared with the real thing. In the case of EFAs, this situation is particularly troubling. A century ago, the standard American diet had borderline EFA content. These days, our diet is way below that line. There is no question that EFA depletion is a factor in our modern epidemics of heart disease, cancer, stroke, diabetes, and other debilitating conditions.

THE SYMPTOMS OF DEFICIENCY

Because an EFA deficiency undermines immune system function and inflammation regulation, symptoms can appear just about anywhere. If it manifests itself in your intestinal tract, for example, you may experience bloating, constipation, indigestion, inflammatory bowel disease, or food allergies. If it affects your nervous system, you may feel apathetic, depressed, or forgetful. You may even notice external, cosmetic symptoms such as dry skin, lifeless hair, and cracked nails.

Of course, these same symptoms can be caused by any number of underlying health problems, which is one reason why an EFA deficiency is very difficult to diagnose.

What's more, the symptoms are usually very subtle and low-grade and vary from one person to the next.

Physicians, who in general have very little training in nutrition, seldom suspect an EFA deficiency, much less test for it. Until more doctors become aware of the problem, millions of patients whose illnesses are either caused or aggravated by EFA deficiency will continue to slip through the cracks and be deprived of effective, inexpensive, and safe therapy.

MAXIMUM INTAKE, MAXIMUM HEALTH

My patients have taught me a great deal about the many ways in which EFA deficiencies can undermine health. They've also allowed me to witness firsthand the dramatic healing powers of EFA supplements.

Take Angela O'Day. A hairstylist, Angela was cutting a client's hair when she suddenly developed a blinding migraine. She tried lying down, hoping the pain would subside. But it lingered—for several days.

After seeing several neurologists and undergoing an MRI, Angela was diagnosed with multiple sclerosis. Multiple sclerosis is an autoimmune disease in which the immune system goes berserk, attacking nerve cells in the brain or spinal cord.

When Angela came to see me, I recommended a low-fat, vegetarian diet and a broad-based supplement regimen that included flaxseed oil and borage oil, two important sources of EFAs. (You'll learn more about these oils later in the chapter.) The EFAs would coax her immune system to behave itself and to stop attacking her nerve cells.

Angela's multiple sclerosis is now in complete remission. We expect it to stay that way, as long as she adheres to her diet and supplement program.

Another patient, Judy DiMaio, complained of premenstrual symptoms so severe that she could not function for two weeks of every month. "I think I'm losing it," she told me. "When my period is coming on, my personality completely changes. I'm not myself. I get severely depressed and anxious. Just about anything sets me off. My husband threatens to leave me, and my teenage daughter won't talk to me. I'm at my wits' end."

After conducting a thorough workup and systematically

ruling out other possible causes of her symptoms, I diagnosed Judy with an EFA deficiency. At first, she had a hard time believing that taking EFA supplements—again, capsules of borage oil and flaxseed oil—could make her better. But she was desperate, so she agreed to give the supplements a try. Her program also included a low-fat diet without sugar or processed foods and a high-quality multivitamin/mineral supplement.

When Judy came back to my office the next month, she reported some improvement in her symptoms: "Well, at least I made it through my period without tearing my hair out. That's progress." Six months later, she bounced into my office and proclaimed, "I'm a new person!"

In my mind, I was doing my own little victory dance. I knew that Judy was feeling better because the EFAs had restored her pro-inflammatory and anti-inflammatory prostaglandins to proper balance.

The Breast Cancer Connection

Numerous studies have shown that women who consume high levels of essential fatty acids (EFAs) are at much lower risk for developing cancer, especially breast cancer. In women who have already developed breast cancer, low levels of EFAs in the biopsied tissue are the strongest predictor of whether the cancer will metastasize, or spread.

German biochemist Johanna Budwig, a seven-time Nobel Prize nominee and a recognized authority on EFA nutrition, suggested that EFA deficiencies may be at least partly responsible for the development of cancer. Budwig has earned an international reputation for successfully treating an array of degenerative diseases, including cancer, with flaxseed oil supplements.

Then there's my daughter Hana. At age three, Hana contracted a bronchial infection that simply would not go away. Every day, my wife and I gave her a children's multivitamin and chewable vitamin C, but her low-grade cough proved very persistent. Finally, we realized that the vitamins were not enough to push her immune system over the hump.

To soup up her immune system and get rid of her bronchitis for good, Hana would have to take EFAs. Since she was too young to swallow capsules, we came up with what we thought was an ingenious solution: We stirred flaxseed oil into one of her favorite puddings. She ate it, but not without giving us an occasional "I know you put something in here and I don't like it" look. Within a week, Hana's cough—and the infection—were completely gone.

GETTING THE NUTRIENTS YOU NEED

As you can see, correcting an EFA deficiency makes a world of difference in your health. Every cell, every tissue, every organ in your body stands to benefit.

What if you don't have an EFA deficiency? Well, count yourself among the lucky few—and consider EFA supplementation anyway. Scientific studies have shown that supplementation can increase your energy and stamina, lower your blood pressure and cholesterol, and enhance your resistance to allergies, infections, and other illness.

The two most important EFAs are alpha-linolenic acid and gamma-linolenic acid. If you follow the standard American diet, you're getting these nutrients in only minute, survival-level amounts. To achieve and maintain the optimum daily amounts, you'll need both a vegetarian diet and supplements.

FIRST-RATE FOOD SOURCES

An EFA-supporting diet has two key features. First, it emphasizes plant-derived foods, which are the best sources of EFAs. Second, it eliminates animal-derived foods, which supply no EFAs but do contain unhealthy amounts of EFA-depleting saturated fat and *trans*-fats.

The single best food source of alpha-linolenic acid and gamma-linolenic acid is flaxseed. But you'd have to consume pounds of the seeds to meet your daily requirements for these EFAs. This is why I recommend flaxseed oil supplements, which I'll discuss in more detail a bit later on.

Other good sources of alpha-linolenic acid and gamma-linolenic acid include pumpkin seeds, sesame seeds, and walnuts. And don't forget to check out soy foods—tofu, soyburgers, soy milk, and the like.

Produce contains small amounts of very high quality, EFA-rich fats. Fruits and vegetables in general are very low in fat, but the fat they do have is of the highest quality. For instance, dark green, leafy vegetables supply roughly half of their fat as alpha-linolenic acid and most of the remainder as gamma-linolenic acid. Plus, produce is loaded with vitamins, minerals, phytochemicals—all the nutrients your body needs.

SUPPLEMENTS, NATURALLY

Even if you filled yourself to the gills with EFA-rich foods, you'd still fall short of the optimum intake. This is why you need supplements. Not megadoses, but enough to guarantee that you're never even temporarily deficient. It's insurance against disease and premature aging.

To boost your intake of alpha-linolenic acid and gamma-linolenic acid, your best choices among supplements are flaxseed oil and borage oil, respectively. In fact, I prescribe these supplements to all of my patients as an integral part of their individual wellness programs, whether the goal is to treat or prevent disease.

For alpha-linolenic acid, take one to five 1,000-milligram capsules of flaxseed oil twice a day. (If you have any of the conditions listed in "When Good Fats Fall Short" on page 98, aim for the high end of the range.) If that dosage is a bit much for you to swallow, then try one tablespoon of liquid flaxseed oil once a day. For gamma-linolenic acid, I suggest taking one 250-milligram capsule of borage oil once or twice a day.

Many health food stores carry flaxseed oil and borage oil capsules, along with combination products in liquid or capsule form. I use a liquid flaxseed/borage combination, and I drizzle two tablespoons of it on my toast every morning.

Both flaxseed oil and borage oil are harmless food products. Neither has produced any signs of toxicity in doses several times higher than what I recommend.

Expect to see results gradually. After all, the EFAs are

effectively rebuilding your cells from the ground up. So give the supplements at least a few months to work.

Increasing your intake of EFAs—the good fats—is important. So is reducing your intake of the bad fats and ugly fats. The next chapter can show you how to do just that.

The Path to a Low-Fat, Health-Supporting Diet

"But wait a bit," the Oysters cried,
"Before we have our chat;
For some of us are out of breath,
And all of us are fat!"
—LEWIS CARROLL,
  THE WALRUS AND THE CARPENTER

For years now, nutrition experts have been extolling the virtues of a low-fat diet. While some folks have heeded the message, many others persist in their high-fat ways. The average American consumes a whopping 40 to 50 percent of calories from fat, a blubbery burden that explains the current epidemic of heart disease and cancer in this country.

Lowering fat intake to 30 percent of calories, as some experts (and even the American Heart Association) recommend, can slow the epidemic. But it won't help to extend life span. Extensive research indicates that a much greater reduction—to 10 percent of calories—is necessary to prevent the so-called fatty degenerative diseases. You can easily achieve this low fat intake simply by following the Anti-Aging Diet.

BAD, BETTER, BEST

Let's be cynical for a moment. Suppose you wanted to encourage heart disease, cancer, and the other degenerative diseases that thwart longevity and impede Renewal. What sorts of foods would you choose?

Well, you'd likely start your day with eggs, bacon, buttered toast, a croissant or a sweet roll, and a glass of whole milk or a cup of coffee with cream. For lunch, you might have a hamburger, french fries, and a chocolate milkshake, or a cheese sandwich, potato chips, and a cola. Around 3:00 in the afternoon, you'd grab a candy bar or a bag of corn chips to tide you over until dinner. Then a few hours later, you'd sit down to a meal of steak, chicken, or pork chops, a baked potato with sour cream, buttered vegetables, and salad with dressings. Round out your repast with ice cream, cake, or pie, and your fat intake for the day would hover at around 50 percent of calories.

Talk about a diet that's headed for disaster. Eating this way for 10 to 20 years would put you squarely in the group at highest risk not only for heart disease and cancer but also for stroke, diabetes, kidney disease, osteoporosis, arthritis, and high blood pressure. Even more disturbing, this malevolent menu closely parallels the standard American diet.

Now let's suppose you decide to go low-fat. Your breakfast might consist of granola, which often has added fat, and 2 percent milk. For lunch, you might have a turkey sandwich, a salad with vinaigrette dressing, and perhaps a low-fat yogurt. Dinner might feature fish or chicken (without the skin, of course), a plain potato or rice, and another low-fat yogurt for dessert.

On a meal plan like this, you're getting about 30 percent of calories from fat—certainly an improvement, but still too high for Renewal. Surprised? Consider that these "low-fat" foods supply, on average, 33 percent of their calories as fat.

If even low-fat foods don't go low enough, what's left for a diet that gets just 10 percent of its calories from fat? Plenty. But—and this is important—you do have to pay close attention to your food choices.

For breakfast, help yourself to hot or cold whole-grain cereal, topped with low-fat soy milk, rice milk, or juice; whole-grain bread or a bagel, very lightly toasted and topped with almond butter or fruit concentrate; and as much fresh fruit as you wish. For lunch, have a veggie burger, a bean and rice burrito, or a vegetable sub on a whole-wheat roll (hold the cheese and mayonnaise), with carrots and an apple as accompaniments. And for dinner, choose whole-grain pasta with spicy tomato sauce, steamed vegetables, and a salad, or a vegetable teriyaki stir-fry with brown rice (use nonstick cooking spray or just a touch of olive or soybean oil). Don't forget to save room for dessert: low-fat, fruit- or juice-sweetened cookies.

A meal plan like this pares your fat intake to just 10 percent of calories. It satisfies your appetite, too. Hmmm . . . that's not so bad after all.

GREASY VEGETARIANISM

A diet that gets just 10 percent of its calories from fat, such as the Anti-Aging Diet, has two very important features. First, it's vegan, meaning that it allows only foods of plant origin. Second, it eliminates all sources of fat, save for the smallest amounts of certain oils (more about them later).

Unfortunately, many people who decide to "go vegetarian" continue to cook with gobs of vegetable oil, slather high-fat dressings on salads, and nibble on high-fat snack foods. Any one of these factors can convert a naturally low-fat, life-extending vegetarian meal into a greasy, life-shortening meal that has more fat than a cheeseburger with mayonnaise.

I refer to this style of eating as greasy vegetarianism. Its adherents espouse this philosophy: "If I avoid all high-fat, high-cholesterol animal foods, then I'll be eating healthfully." These people avoid all animal-derived fats like the plague, as well they should. But they also buy into the idea that canola oil, olive oil, soy oil, and other plant-derived fats are okay, so they slather them on.

Certainly, the quality of a fat—whether it is saturated (as in meats) or unsaturated (as in vegetable oils)—is important. But it's only part of the issue. For people who want to achieve maximum life span, quantity of fat is actually far more important than quality of fat. If you replace an animal-derived fat with an equal amount of a plant-derived fat, the detrimental effects on health and the aging process are no different.

Here's an example of greasy vegetarianism at work. My friend Alice and I paid a visit to a local salad bar. Alice bypassed the meats and cheeses, opting instead for the grains, beans, fruits, and vegetables. She piled her plate high with a luscious assortment: lettuce, spinach, green peppers, broccoli, carrots, kidney beans, pasta, and a sprinkling of sunflower seeds. Just as I was thinking, "Wow, Alice really knows how to put together a healthy salad," we reached the fat-laden dressings. With three ladles of creamy blue cheese, Alice transformed what had been a 300-calorie, low-fat beauty into a 1,000-calorie, blubbery beast.

On another occasion, I met a friend for lunch at a nearby restaurant famous for its salads and fine vegetarian fare. As described on the menu, the spinach salad seemed innocuous enough—except for the bacon bits, which I asked to have left off. I was appalled at what I was served: a plateful of spinach leaves thickly coated with a creamy, high-fat dressing. I had estimated the calorie content of the salad at about 150 calories, but with the dressing, that figure shot up to around 750. Worse yet, the fat content was about 75 percent of calories, certainly not what you'd expect from a salad. The dressing had transformed my healthful lunch into an unhealthful fat trap.

BE WARY OF DAIRY

Dairy products also contain high amounts of fat. Yet many people who switch to vegetarianism continue to eat these foods, thinking that they're somehow better than meats. They aren't. Like meats, dairy products come from animals. With the notable exception of nonfat items, most dairy products have much more fat than red meat, chicken, or fish.

If I had a nickel for every patient who described himself as a vegetarian but who ate lots of full-fat dairy products . . . well, perhaps I wouldn't be wealthy, but I would have plenty of parking meter money! If these folks replaced the milk, cheese, and yogurt in their diets with lean beef or chicken without skin, their fat intakes would plummet. (Not that I'm recommending this, mind you.)

The bottom line is this: If you want to prevent disease and slow the aging process, you must reduce all fats. This means not only eliminating animal-derived foods but also going easy on vegetable oils and other plant-derived foods. And certain high-fat habits must come to a screeching halt: no cooking with more than a smidgen of oil, no slathering butter or margarine on bread and toast, no drowning salads in high-fat dressing, no melting cheese in or over anything.

FIND THE FATTY FOODS

Occasionally consuming very small amounts of high-fat foods won't harm you. But if you want to stick with an overall fat intake of just 10 percent of calories, you need to be very selective about your foods, and you need to know exactly where the fat is coming from.

To make the task easier, here's a rundown of the fattiest offenders. Avoid them as much as you can. If you're not ready to give them up yet, just remember: *The extent to which you follow the Renewal Anti-Aging Diet determines the extent to which you'll benefit from it.*

Meats. These foods top the off-limits list because they are high in total fat, saturated fat, and cholesterol; they contain hormones, antibiotics, and pesticides; and they have no fiber or phytochemicals. I recommend eliminating all meats—including beef, veal, pork, lamb, chicken, turkey, duck, fish, shellfish, and processed meats and lunchmeats.

The Scoop on Sugar

If you want to lower your fat intake, you need to lower your sugar intake, too. The reason: To your body, fat and sugar are interchangeable. It readily converts sugar—all kinds of sugar—into fat, which is then stored in your belly, hips, buttocks, or thighs for later use.

So if the label on a packaged food screams "No Fat! No Cholesterol!" be sure to check the nutrition information. Odds are, the food suffers from serious sugar overload. (We'll discuss sugar in more detail in chapter 17.)

Dairy products. Like other animal-derived foods, dairy products are high in total fat, saturated fat, and cholesterol. Whole milk, for instance, gets almost 50 percent of its calories from fat. Even 2 percent "low-fat" milk gets 37 percent of its calories from fat. (The 2 percent refers to proportion of fat by total weight, and most of milk's weight is water.)

My recommendation is to eliminate all dairy products: whole milk, 2 percent milk, 1 percent milk (which gets 23 percent of its calories from fat), cheese, butter, and yogurt. If you want to continue eating dairy products, then at least choose the nonfat varieties.

Eggs. One egg has about six grams of fat, which translates to about 65 percent of calories. It also has 250 to 300 milligrams of cholesterol, which is a lot. Make do without, if you can.

All fried foods. From chicken nuggets and french fries to Mexican chimichangas and Japanese tempura, fried foods have a bad reputation, and for good reason. They're laced with *trans*-fats and free radicals, which impair cellular function and discombobulate your immune system.

Steer clear of fried foods as much as possible. When you eat out, be sure to ask how menu items are prepared—many seemingly healthful choices may in fact be fried. When you eat at home, try microwaving thinly sliced potatoes for fat-free "home fries."

Hydrogenated fats. Food manufacturers have developed a bewildering array of margarines and spreads as "healthy" alternatives to butter. Unfortunately, these products are actually more unhealthy than the stuff that they're supposed to replace.

Thanks to hydrogenation, which transforms vegetable oil from liquid to solid at room temperature, margarines and spreads contain a caustic brew of *trans*-fats, free radicals, and other toxic by-products. What they don't contain is essential fatty acids, which are destroyed when the oil is processed. (You'll recall from chapter 8 that your body needs essential fatty acids to manufacture cell membranes and anti-inflammatory prostaglandins.)

For these reasons, margarines, spreads, and other hydrogenated fats have no place in the Anti-Aging Diet. You're a bit better off with butter—and even better off with none of the above.

Salad dressings. We've already discussed what a nutritional land mine salad dressings can be. The good news is that you can now choose from among dozens of nonfat and low-fat varieties. Some do contain additives, so be sure to read the ingredients lists on their labels. As an alternative, you can easily make your own dressing by combining vinegar, olive or soy oil, lemon juice, herbs, and spices. And add a little flaxseed oil, which consists almost entirely of Renewal-supporting essential fatty acids.

Nuts, seeds, and nut butters. All of these foods are loaded with fat. Peanuts and peanut butter have particularly high levels of total fat and saturated fat—plus they contain aflatoxins, potent carcinogens produced by the aspergillus fungus, which grows on peanuts.

Among nuts and seeds, your best choices are walnuts, almonds, sesame seeds, pumpkin seeds, flaxseed, and sunflower seeds. All are rich in essential fatty acids. Just make sure the nuts and seeds you buy are fresh and haven't been boiled in oil. And when you eat them, don't go overboard. Remember, they're still high-fat foods.

Snack foods. Potato chips, corn chips, buttered popcorn, cheese-flavored popcorn, processed nuts, and the like are junk foods. I mention them only to condemn them. For starters, they get 50 to 80 percent of their calories from fat. On top of that, they're made with hydrogenated oils, which means that they're brimming with *trans*-fats and free radicals.

For those times when you have the munchies, many health food stores and grocery stores stock low-fat, baked potato chips and corn chips as well as rice cakes and fat-free wheat crackers. Even better, nibble on fresh fruits such as apples, bananas, grapes, oranges, and pears. My personal favorite snacks are fruit smoothies, which I make by blending together a banana, organic fruit (usually blueberries, mango, oranges, pineapple, raspberries, or strawberries), and rice milk, soy milk, and/or apple juice.

OILS: THE EXCEPTION OR THE RULE?

Cooking oils deserve special mention here. Unlike the foods mentioned above, oils are a very gray area. Some you want to consume because they supply healthy doses of essential fatty acids. Others you want to avoid because of the fats, free radicals, and toxins they contain. Still others straddle the line between good and bad.

As a general rule, I strongly advise against buying liquid oils in supermarkets. Because of the way in which they're processed, these oils have been stripped of their essential fatty acids and flooded with free radicals, *trans*-fats, and other oxidized fats. These oils cause disease.

That said, here's a breakdown of which oils are which, to help you get a firmer grasp on this slippery subject.

NO MORE GREASY KIDS' STUFF

The so-called tropical oils—coconut, palm, and cocoa butter (as in chocolate)—land squarely in the bad category. They're very high in saturated fat, very low in essential fatty acids, and loaded with free radicals. They're joined by peanut oil, which not only has an abundance of saturated fat but also contains those cancer-causing aflatoxins.

The baddest of the bad is cottonseed oil, which is often used in deep-fried snack foods. It supplies a beastly burden of free radicals as well as an unhealthy dose of cyclopropene fatty acid. Not to be confused with beneficial essential fatty acids, cyclopropene fatty acid has a laundry list of malevolent effects. It destroys the enzyme system responsible for converting essential fatty acids to prostagladins, poisons liver and gallbladder cells, undermines female reproductive functioning, and has a high level of pesticide residues.

My advice is to avoid all of these oils at all costs. They're often used in packaged foods, so be sure to read ingredients lists before buying.

OILS OF OLÉ

For an oil to be considered good, it should meet all of the following criteria.

- Organically grown
- Mechanically processed, with no exposure to heat, light, or air
- High in essential fatty acids
- Very low in saturated fat
- Not hydrogenated
- Cholesterol-free
- Free of pesticides and other toxins
- Less than three months old

Fats and Figures

Many packaged foods contain way too much fat. You can identify the worst offenders by learning how to calculate a food's fat content. Take a look at the nutrition label on the package: You'll see figures for "calories from fat" and "total calories per serving." Simply divide fat calories by total calories, then multiply that number by 100. This gives you the percentage of calories from fat. If the food gets more than 20 percent of its calories from fat, put it back on the shelf. It has no place in a low-fat, Anti-Aging Diet.

Of the oils on the market, only four meet all of these criteria: organic flaxseed oil, organic pumpkin seed oil, organic soybean oil, and organic walnut oil. While all four have superior nutritional profiles, organic flaxseed oil is the healthiest hands-down. It delivers more of the all-important essential fatty acids than any other oil. Its remarkable health benefits qualify it as one of the most powerful preventive medicines around.

Flaxseed oil does come with one caveat: It should not be used in cooking. Its essential fatty acids are extremely sensitive to heat and are quickly destroyed during the cooking process. I like to put flaxseed oil on toast, as a substitute for butter. You can try it in salad dressings, too.

Hemp oil also has very admirable levels of essential fatty acids, rivaling even flaxseed oil in desirability. It's not included in the list above because it's illegal in some states. (The hemp plant, *Cannabis sativa*, also happens to be the source of marijuana.)

What about olive oil? Well, it is rich in monounsaturated fat. On the downside, it has very low levels of essential fatty acids. Still, if you need an oil for cooking, olive is an acceptable choice because it withstands heat well. Other cooking oils in this okay-but-less-than-ideal category include corn, safflower, sesame, and sunflower.

One final note: All oils—especially flaxseed—gradually oxidize or turn rancid, the result of age as well as repeated exposure to light and air. Rancid oils contain free radicals galore. By the time an oil actually smells bad, the quantity of free radicals has become astronomical. So rather than using your nose to judge freshness, purchase oils in small quantities, keep them refrigerated, and toss out any unused portion after three months.

A GOOD PLACE TO START

Right now, this may seem like a lot of information to digest (no pun intended). But use it as the basis for your daily food choices and, over time, eating low-fat will become second nature to you.

To reduce your fat intake to 10 percent of calories and maintain optimum levels of the essential fatty acids, start by following these simple rules.

- Eliminate all animal-derived fats.
- Sharply reduce all vegetable-derived fats, with the exception of flaxseed, pumpkin seed, soy, and walnut oils (organic, of course).
- Eliminate all foods that contain hydrogenated or partially hydrogenated oils.
- Increase your essential fatty acid intake by eating walnuts and soybean products.
- Take 2,000 to 10,000 milligrams of flaxseed oil per day, in capsule or liquid form. (Flaxseed oil supplies alpha-linolenic acid, an essential fatty acid.)
- Take 250 to 500 milligrams of borage oil per day, in capsule form. (Borage oil supplies gamma-linolenic acid, an essential fatty acid.)
- Read the labels on packaged foods and learn how to calculate fat content (see "Fats and Figures" on page 115).
- Learn low-fat cooking techniques. (You'll get some pointers in chapter 18.)

Now that you know how to de-fat your diet, let's turn our attention to protein. Like fat, protein is essential to the human body. But when consumed in excess, as it is in most Americans' diets, it causes problems all its own.

CHAPTER 10

Protein: More Is
Not Better

Eating excessive amounts of protein can seriously damage our health.
—JOHN A. MCDOUGALL, M.D.,
    THE MCDOUGALL PLAN

Think of proteins as the Swiss Army knives of nutrients. They're major players in all sorts of bodily processes, including growth, maintenance, healing, and repair. Without them, the very process of Renewal couldn't take place.

Proteins serve as the primary building blocks of connective tissues such as ligaments and tendons. They shuttle oxygen, nutrients, and other vital substances to wherever they're needed in the body. Many proteins function as hormones, which regulate cellular activity; as antibodies, which defend the body against disease; and as enzymes, which digest food and facilitate all of the body's chemical reactions.

Since proteins do so much for us, the more protein-rich foods we consume, the better off we'll be ... right? Well, it's a logical assumption. But unfortunately, it's wrong.

Yes, we do need modest amounts of proteins in our diets. But more definitely is not better. In fact, most of us eat too much rather than too little. And our health is suffering as a result.

BUILT FROM SCRATCH

Proteins consist of various configurations of substances called amino acids. The task of assembling the correct combination of amino acids in the proper sequence falls to cell structures known as ribosomes. The process works something like this: The DNA in a cell's nucleus issues a blueprint that shows how a particular protein should look. A ribosome reads this blueprint, then amasses the appropriate amino acids and links them in the proper order to form a complete protein molecule.

Each type of protein has a unique amino acid sequence, or chain. Amazingly, the body needs just 20 amino acids to manufacture the thousands of different proteins it needs. Even more amazing, the body can make 12 of these amino acids on its own (with the assistance of enzymes made from—you guessed it—proteins). The remaining 8 amino acids must come directly from foods and therefore are essential nutrients in the adult diet.

Any diet consistently lacking in one or more of the eight essential amino acids will cause protein deficiency malnutrition, a condition that affects many people worldwide but is extremely rare in the United States. In this country, our problem is protein overconsumption. The average American eats roughly twice as much protein as he needs.

THE IDEAL INTAKE

So how much protein do you need? In general, the average adult male or female should consume about 0.3 gram of protein per pound of body weight per day. For a person who weighs 150 pounds, this translates to 45 grams, a bit less than 2 ounces, per day.

Certain segments of the population have slightly higher requirements. Pregnant and lactating women, for instance, need more protein because they are literally eating for two. Athletes in training need more protein because their bodies must work harder to repair damaged tissues (protein, you'll recall, is the basic structural component of muscle and connective tissue). For similar reasons, people recovering from surgery, injury, or illness need more protein while their bodies are on the mend.

In addition, some people have difficulty breaking down proteins into their component amino acids. Their bodies no longer produce enough hydrochloric acid and proteolytic enzymes, the substances responsible for digesting proteins. (Hydrochloric acid is secreted by the stomach, and proteolytic enzymes, by the pancreas.) This condition is quite common, especially in older people, and can cause digestive symptoms as well as food allergies.

For people with this condition, eating extra protein can actually make matters worse. You're better off trying supplements to correct any deficiencies. I recommend hydrochloric acid capsules (in the form of betaine hydrochloride) and a plant-based digestive enzyme product. You'll find both supplements in health food stores. If you're not sure which brands to choose, ask the salesclerk for assistance. Follow the dosage recommendations on the labels.

ENOUGH IS ENOUGH

If you follow the standard American diet, complete with generous amounts of meats and dairy products, chances are that you're taking in a lot more protein than you need. Consider that a single six-ounce serving of steak, hamburger, chicken, or fish supplies more than 100 grams of protein—more than double your protein quota for an entire day. That doesn't even account for the cheese, eggs, milk, and other protein-rich foods you may also be consuming.

Overdoing protein in this way, as so many of us do, robs us of good health and long life. Population studies have established an indisputable link between protein consumption and longevity. Quite simply, people who follow high-protein diets have shorter average life expectancies than people who follow low-protein diets. Animal studies produce similar results: Comparing groups fed the same number of calories, those on high-protein diets die younger than those on low-protein diets.

PROBLEMS WITH PROTEIN OVERLOAD

Remember, your body needs some protein to function. It's the excess that gums up the works. How?

For starters, too much protein depletes your body's calcium supply, causing loss of bone mass and eventually osteoporosis. Here's what happens: Breaking down large quantities of protein produces a virtual deluge of amino acids. Your body can't possibly use all of the available amino acids. So to neutralize the excess, it enlists the assistance of calcium, pulling the mineral from your bones. (Antacids such as Tums work on the same principle, except that they use their own calcium supply to neutralize stomach acid.) The "spent" calcium is then excreted in the urine.

When this process repeats itself over and over again, as is necessary for a protein-laden diet, the resulting calcium shortage causes bones to become brittle and gradually disintegrate. This leads to osteoporosis, a condition characterized by bones that break easily and vertebrae that collapse under the weight of the body they were intended to support.

We're Number One

We Americans have earned the dubious distinction of eating more protein—especially animal protein—than any other population in the world. Not so coincidentally, we also have the highest rate of osteoporosis-related hip fractures. Here's how we measure up.

Country	Hip Fractures (Per 100,000 People)	Protein Intake (G./Day)
United States	98	106	72
Sweden	59	105	57
Finland	44	93	61
United Kingdom	43	90	54
Hong Kong	32	82	50
Singapore	20	82	39
South Africa	6	55	11

Of course, there are other risk factors for osteoporosis—some that you can't control (gender, age, genetic predisposition), others that you can (low calcium intake, lack of regular exercise, drug and alcohol use). Add a high-protein diet to the mix, and you make yourself an odds-on favorite for an osteoporosis-related fracture.

If you want to increase your calcium intake, by the way, forget about milk, cheese, yogurt, and other dairy products. These foods have high protein contents. So any calcium they provide, plus a bit more, gets eaten up by the amino acid–neutralizing process described above.

A high-protein diet stresses not only your skeleton but also your kidneys. When you consume too much protein, your kidneys have to put in lots of overtime to flush the excess out of your system. As a result, they wear out sooner than they should—a condition called renal failure.

THE MEAT MYTH

Meats have long had a reputation as the best protein sources around. This is because they're rich in complete proteins—in other words, they supply all of the amino acids that the body can't make on its own.

Unfortunately, when you eat meats, you're getting not only complete proteins but also saturated fat, cholesterol, and pesticides—substances that aren't quite so kind to the body. Saturated fat and cholesterol clog and harden arteries, paving the way for heart disease. And pesticides and other toxins weaken the immune system and stress the organs of elimination.

Plus, meats are completely devoid of the all-important essential fatty acids and fiber. In chapter 8, we saw how essential fatty acid deficiencies can cause or aggravate scores of health problems. When fiber is in short supply, toxins aren't being swept out of the digestive tract efficiently. This increases the workload for the liver, kidneys, and colon, the three organs responsible for cleansing.

The bottom line is that meats frustrate the Renewal process in a variety of ways. You can get all the protein you need from other, healthier sources—sources that won't overburden your body and undermine your health.

PLANT PROTEINS: BETTER FOR YOUR BODY

Grains, beans, fruits, and vegetables—the four main "ingredients" in the Anti-Aging Diet—are naturally low in protein. By eating them in a variety of combinations, you get a balanced supply of all the amino acids that your body needs, without risking protein overload.

Plant proteins treat your body much more kindly than animal proteins do. While animal proteins raise cholesterol, vegetable proteins—especially soy protein—have been shown to lower cholesterol. In fact, the Italian national health service provides free soy protein to physicians for the treatment of patients with high cholesterol.

What's more, the ratio of calcium to protein is much higher in plant-derived foods than in animal-derived foods. The "extra" calcium gets shipped to your bones for storage rather than being spent to neutralize amino acids. So plant proteins support skeletal health—unlike animal proteins, which contribute to osteoporosis.

COMPLETE WITHOUT MEAT

With the exception of soy, no single plant-derived food supplies a complete protein. In other words, no plant-derived food provides all eight essential amino acids. A deficiency of even one amino acid is enough to prevent cells from assembling the proteins your body needs to heal and grow. (You'll recall that cells build proteins by joining amino acids to form chains.)

To avoid a deficiency, you'll need to consume plant-derived foods in combinations that supply all the necessary amino acids. Such foods are often referred to as complementary plant proteins. For example, grains and beans function as complementary plant proteins. Grains in general are rich in the amino acids tryptophan and methionine but come up short in the amino acids lysine and isoleucine. For beans, the opposite is true: They generally contain little tryptophan and methionine but plenty of lysine and isoleucine. (A notable exception is soybeans, in which all four amino acids are abundant.) So by combining any grain and any bean, you get your full complement of these essential amino acids. Your body then has all the raw materials it needs to manufacture complete proteins.

And contrary to popular belief, you don't need to eat complementary plant proteins at the same meal. Research has shown that the body recycles amino acids quite efficiently. So as long as you feed your body a variety of complementary plant proteins on a regular basis, it will have optimum quantities of all the amino acids it needs.

Plant-derived foods are shaping up to be Renewal's greatest allies. As we've seen so far, they're not only low in fat and protein but also high in vitamins, minerals, phytochemicals, and fiber. But even plant-derived foods aren't immune to the corrupting effects of pesticides, additives, and other chemicals. The next chapter explains how you can safeguard your food supply against these manmade toxins.

CHAPTER 11

Avoiding Pesticides and Food Additives: The Organic Solution

Demand safe food.
—FRANCES M. LAPPÉ, *DIET FOR A SMALL PLANET*

Would you choose to sprinkle ¼ ounce of pesticides over your food every day? Or to ingest 150 pounds of assorted additives annually? Of course not. But in effect, that's what the average American—however unwittingly—is doing. As a nation, our annual dose of these seriously life-threatening chemicals is a staggering 2.6 billion pounds, or more than 1 million tons.

Because they are colorless, odorless, and tasteless, and because they don't make you sick (at least not right away), these substances are pretty much overlooked. The slowness with which they wreak havoc inside our bodies lulls us into denial. The insidious diseases spawned by these contaminants surface slowly—we're talking decades here—and only after irreparable damage has been done. Any serious anti-aging regimen must include a commitment to curtail exposure to these life-shortening agents.

First, let's take a look at the baddest of these bad guys: pesticides. Then we'll move on to the omnipresent additives. Finally, we'll discuss what we can do to protect ourselves and our environment—which is a lot!

PESTICIDES: POISONS ON YOUR PLATE

Suppose you're having dinner in a fancy restaurant. You're starved, so when the waiter finally brings your food, you can't wait to dig in. As you lift your fork, the waiter motions toward your plate and looks at you with that familiar "May I . . . ?" expression that waiters get when they're holding a pepper grinder over your salad. Except this isn't pepper.

"What is it?" you ask.

"Our special blend of PCBs, EDB, and dieldrin, with a dollop of DDT, a dash of dioxin, and some other assorted pesticides," he casually replies.

"No, thanks," you say, shaking your head.

"But, sir, I insist," he says.

"No, thanks!" you repeat firmly.

Undaunted, he sprinkles a layer of the lethal blend over your entire meal. Then he turns and walks away before you regain your composure enough to give him a piece of your mind.

Now, you may be thinking that this scenario, while scary, would never play out in real life. And you're probably right. The trouble is, these toxins are showing up in your food anyway—and no one has ever asked your permission.

More than one billion pounds of pesticides—or about five pounds per person—is applied to our nation's food supply each year. Yet the scientific evidence condemning this practice is unequivocal.

Pesticides (including herbicides, insecticides, and fungicides) are not inert, innocuous substances, as those in big agribusiness would have you believe. Rather, they are chemicals specially designed to destroy life by disrupting biological systems. The human body happens to be a complex, intricate set of biological systems, so to even suggest that pesticides don't have a destructive effect inside the body is foolish.

Pesticides kill weeds, insects, fungi, and other "undesirable" life forms by interfering with various aspects of their metabolism. Humans are fundamentally similar to these organisms in that all are complex conglomerations of cells. At the cellular level, there is no real difference in how the poison works. Our size is what saves us. We are larger and more diversified, so we resist the toxic effects of pesticides much longer than a tiny plant or bug. If humans were the size of bugs, we'd perish as fast as they do.

Pesticides accumulate in our bodies, gradually weakening our most sensitive cellular components—especially those of the endocrine (hormone), reproductive, circulatory, immune, and central nervous systems. Over time, they increase the likelihood of heart disease, cancer, and allergies; undermine resistance to infectious organisms; impair fertility; and contribute to miscarriages and birth defects. That they make longevity nosedive goes without saying.

In the presence of pesticides, the Renewal process falters and eventually falls apart. No wonder Rachel Carson, in her seminal 1962 book, *Silent Spring*, dubbed these chemicals elixirs of death.

THEY'RE EVERYWHERE

Thanks to the overzealous application of pesticides to U.S. agricultural products, our food supply is largely contaminated. As Frances Moore Lappé notes in her book *Diet for a Small Planet*, "Pesticides have made fresh produce, the very symbol of health, into a health hazard."

But if produce has become a health hazard, then animal-derived foods might be considered downright lethal. Because the chemicals sprayed onto feed are concentrated in animals' bodies, they're found in much greater quantity in beef, poultry, and dairy products. Whereas fruits, vegetables, and grains account for 11 percent of pesticide exposures, meat and dairy account for 78 percent.

But food isn't the only source of these toxic time bombs (so called because of the delayed onset of the diseases they trigger). Pesticides poison our air and water as well as our home, work, vacation, and entertainment environments. In fact, while many people equate farming with pesticide use, the average concentration of pesticides is actually 10 times higher in the typical American home than on the farm. These toxins are also used extensively in hospitals, schools, and offices.

Outdoors, pesticides are sprayed on lawns, lakes, forests, parks, and playing fields. Through storm drains, sewers, creeks, and rivers, pesticides find their way to the ocean, where they account for more than 90 percent of the water's pollution. A nationwide survey conducted by the Environmental Protection Agency (EPA) found that 100 million Americans are drinking water from pesticide-contaminated water supplies. Of drinking water samples tested in intensely farmed regions of the country, 82 percent contained two or more pesticides. A U.S. Geological Service survey of water from the Mississippi River and its tributaries found herbicide contamination in nearly every sample collected.

Pesticides are not just around you but inside of you as well. All of your tissues are tainted. You—like all other Americans—have measurable levels of dichlorodiphenyltrichloroethane (DDT), polychlorinated biphenyls (PCBs), dioxin, heptachlor, chlordane, aldrin, dieldrin, and other pesticides in your bloodstream. The frightening fact is that these poisons have saturated your internal environment as well as your external environment.

Many—perhaps most—pesticides are carcinogens. Yet only a handful (about 10 percent) have been adequately tested for human health risks before being approved for use on food. Shamefully, governmental regulation of these extremely hazardous substances is virtually nonexistent. The EPA evaluates pesticides as if the rules of democracy apply. Pesticides are not people: They should be assumed guilty until proven innocent, not the other way around.

Pesticide tolerance limits are not set with the health of human consumers in mind. Instead, they reflect the highest residue concentrations under normal use in the field, not on the plate. Richard Jackson, M.D., a California pediatrician and co-author of the 1993 National Academy of Science study "Pesticides in the Diets of Infants and Children," compares these lax tolerance levels with "setting the speed limit at 7,000 miles per hour and then congratulating yourself when no one exceeds it."

The only effective solution to the problem of toxic foods is protective action on an individual level. This means eating only organically grown, pesticide-free foods. (More on this at the end of the chapter.)

IS WHAT YOU'RE EATING MAKING YOU SICK?

For most humans, short-term pesticide exposure won't cause noticeable health problems. It is the cumulative effect of these diabolical agents that really does the damage. Because the body cannot efficiently remove them, they build up in tissues to levels capable of really bollixing things up.

The following is a sampling of commonly encountered pesticides and their adverse health effects.

- Dioxin has been banned from use on food crops, but it is nevertheless widely distributed in the environment. A by-product of paper production, it can leach into foods from cartons. It can also leach into the skin as a result of contact with bleached paper. Dioxin is a potent immune suppressant and also causes cancer.
- Carbaryl also acts as an immune suppressant. It depletes B lymphocytes (the cells that manufacture antibodies).
- Methyl parathion impairs immunity, allowing bacteria to become more virulent.
- Dieldrin blocks macrophages, the immune cells that devour invaders, and reduces immunity to the hepatitis virus. It is banned in the United States but is still used abroad.
- Chlordane causes lifetime immune suppression in animals exposed while still in the womb. It has long been banned from use on food crops in the United States. But it's still applied to crops grown in Mexico and other countries, and so it persists in our environment.
- Aldicarb (Temik) is used on potatoes, beans, soybeans, citrus, peanuts, pecans, bananas, and coffee. It's also a frequent contaminant of drinking water. A potent immune modulator, aldicarb can decrease ratios of helper and suppressor T lymphocytes at concentrations as low as a few parts per billion.
- Carbofuran, a broad-spectrum pesticide used on corn and other crops, suppresses bone marrow. This causes white blood cell counts to plummet.
- Ethyl carbamate is also toxic to bone marrow. It reduces the number of antibody-producing B lymphocytes and blocks the action of killer lymphocytes, which kill tumor cells, bacteria, and other invaders.

When the immune system becomes impaired, the body cannot fight cancer effectively. All five of the most commonly used pesticides—atrazine, alachlor, metolachlor, 1,3-dichloropropene, and 2,4-D—are associated with increased risk of cancer. They're also associated with reproductive damage and birth defects.

In the reproductive system, many pesticides can harm the fetus directly, causing miscarriages, stillbirths, birth defects, and genetic mutations. Pesticide-induced mutations can be passed to the next generation and so can potentially affect the grandchildren or great-grandchildren of the person who has been exposed.

Another grim reminder of the pervasiveness of these chemicals is the fact that 99 percent of mothers' milk in the United States contains dangerous levels of DDT. Meat-eating mothers have 35 times the breast milk contamination of vegetarian mothers.

EXPOSING THE HORMONE IMPOSTORS

A great many of the most widely used pesticides—including the pervasive, hard-to-break-down old-timers (DDT, PCBs, and dioxin) as well as their newer cousins (whose toxicity remains largely a matter of speculation)—are now known to mimic naturally produced estrogenic hormones. They do this by tightly binding to hormone receptor sites in the body, thus discombobulating the highly choreographed ballet that leading progesterone researcher John Lee, M.D., of Sebastopol, California, has aptly dubbed the Dance of the Steroids. At least 50 of these hormone receptor–blocking synthetic chemicals have now been identified, and scads more are waiting in the wings.

For a long time, pesticide-watchers have known that strange things were happening, endocrinologically speaking. But only recently has the connection between pesticides and hormone receptor site contamination been clarified.

Nature designed hormones to act as triggers for cascades of biochemical reactions, so they are effective in unbelievably small quantities. Likewise, the hormone impostors are effective in minute doses, causing abnormal functioning of the immune, reproductive, and central nervous systems. Researchers have linked a diverse array of reproductive system and developmental disorders—including endometriosis, prostate cancer, and smaller brain size—to these hormone impostors. Some examples:

- PCBs, which are widely distributed in the environment, act like thyroid hormone, for which every cell in the body has receptors. Several studies have shown that mothers-to-be who are exposed to PCBs and other hormone mimics are more likely to bear children with physical, behavioral, and cognitive defects.
- Dioxin, which contaminates all bleached paper products, mimics estrogen. It has also been shown to slash the sperm production of laboratory rats in half.
- Bisphenol-A, another estrogen mimic, readily leaches out of the plastic resin used to line food cans and into the food. Those polycarbonate five-gallon water bottles—the ones that we were told were safe—also leach bisphenol-A, contaminating their contents.
- Nonylphenols, which are added to certain plastics (like the kind used in all modern non-iron water pipes), also mimic estrogen.

Perhaps most ominous are the bizarre reproductive effects of the hormone impostors, which have been amply documented in both laboratory animals and human population studies. Among American men, for example, the incidence of testicular cancer is rising. Fertility, meanwhile, is sagging. More than 25 percent of male college students in the United States are sterile, compared with only 0.5 percent in 1950. And the average sperm count has dropped by 30 percent over three decades.

Women, who have more estrogen and more estrogenic receptors than men, are also more vulnerable to the hormone impostors. Breast cancer, a genuine epidemic, is a hormonally dependent disease affecting 1 in 10 women in the United States. Hormone-mimicking pesticides are found in high concentrations in breast tissue that has become cancerous. A study conducted at Hartford Hospital in Connecticut found higher concentrations of DDT and PCBs in cancerous breast tissue than in tissue samples from benign breast tumors.

It's important to note that unlike their natural counterparts, hormone impostors are not broken down and excreted. Instead, these structurally stable scoundrels hang out in the fatty tissues of the animals that consume them. So when you eat an animal-derived food, the hormone impostors get passed along to you—and then establish permanent residence in your fatty tissues.

THE CHEMICAL COCKTAIL SYNDROME

Individually, hormone-mimicking pesticides are hazardous enough. Now there's evidence that their effects multiply when they occur together.

When John A. McLachlan, a toxicologist at the Center for Bioenvironmental Research at Tulane and Xavier Universities in New Orleans, combined the pesticides endosulfan and dieldrin, the estrogenic activity of endosulfan was 160 times greater, and that of dieldrin was 1,600 times greater. When McLachlan combined endosulfan with chlordane, endosulfan's estrogenic activity increased by 100 times. This finding is even more remarkable when you consider that chlordane by itself has no estrogenic activity whatsoever.

This so-called chemical cocktail syndrome is of more than academic interest. In real life, we are continually being bombarded by an array of combinations of pesticides. Multiple pairings may produce exponentially compounded estrogenic activity.

AN APPLE A DAY ... ?

The EPA and the Food and Drug Administration (FDA) share responsibility for protecting the public from pesticides. Though mandated to monitor our food supply for pesticide residues, the FDA samples less than 1 percent of our food. What's more, 60 percent of the pesticides cannot be detected by the FDA's current testing procedures. Newer, non-routine laboratory methods are required to identify about half of the pesticides commonly used today. In effect, fewer than half of the pesticides potentially present in foods are even tested for.

Even so, the FDA has discovered pesticide residues in 48 percent of the most frequently consumed fruits and vegetables. Ninety-nine percent of commercial apples, for example, are treated with pesticides. (Will these apples keep the doctor away, or will they eventually necessitate a visit to one?) More than 95 percent of corn crops are dusted with herbicides.

Remember, since the FDA's testing procedures can't detect more than half of the pesticides potentially present in foods, the true percentages of contamination must be substantially higher. Consider, too, that there is a cumulative effect going on here, since we eat several servings of these foods every day.

THE POLITICS OF POISONS

In her book *Silent Spring*, Rachel Carson raised "a question that is not only scientific but moral. The question is whether any civilization can wage relentless war on life without destroying itself, and without losing the right to be called civilized."

If our war on weeds, bugs, and fungi is slowly destroying us, too, we must ask "Why are we doing this to ourselves?" The answer can be found by surveying the political landscape.

Way back in 1987, the prestigious National Academy of Sciences issued a report estimating that pesticides in our nation's food supply would be responsible for one million cancers in the United States over the course of our lifetimes. Yet since then, the government has steadfastly refused to make protecting Americans from pesticides a national priority.

Meanwhile, we're being treated like human guinea pigs, as most pesticides are being applied to our foods without any testing whatsoever. In fact, many pesticides were approved by the EPA before they had undergone the requisite health and safety analyses. Of the few that have been adequately evaluated, virtually all have shown some degree of toxicity. Still, weak government standards allow these pesticides to remain on the market. The outcome of this diabolical experiment is already visible around us: thousands of cancer cases now, and thousands more to come.

Even the EPA acknowledges that 30 percent of all insecticides and 60 to 90 percent of all other pesticides could cause cancer. Yet of the approximately 400 pesticide products now in use, about 85 percent have not been tested for carcinogenicity.

For one of the most egregious examples of how politics influences public policy on pesticides, you need only look back to the Alar debacle. Alar (also known as diaminozide) is a plant growth regulator that's sprayed on certain fruits and vegetables to give them a deep red color. In the mid-1970s, research revealed that Alar on apples causes cancer. The EPA didn't propose a ban until 1985—and even then, the agency's Science Advisory Panel rejected the proposal. Then two U.S. senators revealed that seven of the eight panel members were serving as consultants to the chemical industry at the same time that they ruled to continue using Alar.

This outrageous behavior underscores a huge, ongoing problem: There is a giant revolving door through which top chemical industry executives get appointed to government regulatory positions, do a stint, and then return to industry. Who speaks for the people who want to stop being poisoned?

Politicians possess the power to stop the carnage. But without a grassroots movement that's determined to institute change, the rich and powerful chemical, agricultural, and food-processing companies will continue to get their way.

A DEADLY EXPORT

More than four billion pounds of pesticides are produced in the United States each year. One-fifth of this amount is exported to Third World countries, where indiscriminate use has had consequences of disastrous proportions. Acute and chronic toxic reactions to pesticides occur with alarming regularity.

According to the World Health Organization, 500,000 acute pesticide poisonings and 5,000 pesticide-related deaths occur worldwide each year. The reasons for this are manifold. For example, pesticide products are often misused. The governments of developing countries seldom have regulations in place to control the application of pesticides. And what good are warning labels to people who can't read?

Another inherent danger of exported pesticides is that

we often end up eating them ourselves. In a shocking scandal of global proportions, pesticides such as DDT—which have been banned as too hazardous for use in this country—are being exported on a large scale to Third World countries. There they're applied to crops such as coffee, bananas, and beef, which we then import and consume. This vicious circle has been dubbed the Circle of Poison by journalists David Weir and Mark Schapiro in their book of the same name.

Several years ago, while on a trip to China as a guest of that country's government, I visited a communal farm near Suchow. Our hosts served us an elaborate lunch in the commune's guest hall, whose windows supplied a panoramic view of very flat farmland stretching off as far as the eye could see. As we ate and the various speakers spoke, I gazed out at the fields. Off in the distance, I noticed several workers dipping large wooden ladles into buckets, then spreading a white, lumpy powder onto the crops. Whatever the stuff was, it was not being applied evenly. Some plants got large clumps of it, while others got none.

This piqued my curiosity. I waited for an opportune moment, then asked the speaker (who was now taking questions about the commune) what the people out in the field were up to. The answer came back through an interpreter: "They are applying a pesticide—DDT—to the crops." Adroitly sidestepping any embarrassing follow-up questions, the speaker quickly moved to another topic.

I was first stunned, then outraged. But my sense of decorum prevented me from making a big deal out of the fact that the workers were clearly poisoning themselves. Didn't they know that DDT was extremely toxic and carcinogenic—that it had been banned in my country? (I didn't realize it then, but their DDT had almost certainly come from the United States.)

Feeling a desperate need to discuss this with someone, I cornered our guide after the meeting and asked him why this barbaric procedure hadn't been stopped. He was well aware of the dangers of DDT. But as he explained, the communes had quotas to meet, and the central government imposed penalties for not meeting them. Using DDT boosted production.

I was horrified—and depressed. Clearly, the dangers of DDT were being downplayed by government officials, and the peasants were being kept in the dark about the true risks to their health.

Sound familiar?

THE FOOD ADDITIVES SCANDAL

The average American consumes approximately 1,500 pounds of food each year. Of this, 10 percent—about 150 pounds—is additives.

The FDA has approved more than 3,000 types of additives for use in our nation's food supply. The vast majority of these compounds have health-eroding and life-shortening properties. This widespread poisoning of the American public constitutes nothing less than a national calamity.

Virtually all of the packaged foods sold in supermarkets contain additives. Some of these foods have so many artificial ingredients—stuff like emulsifiers, preservatives, and stabilizers—that their labels read like chemistry textbooks. They're so corrupted that they don't even look real.

Why do manufacturers insist on putting these literally sickening substances into what may otherwise be wholesome foods? For primarily three reasons: to facilitate processing; to enhance color, texture, and taste; and—perhaps most important—to extend shelf life.

Getting fresh, whole foods to market and stocking them without spoilage costs a bundle. By pumping their products full of preservatives and other additives, food manufacturers and suppliers save billions of dollars a year just on storage and shipping. They can stockpile their products in warehouses and on grocery store shelves for weeks, even months. And they don't have to worry that the foods will decompose.

To be sure, extending a food's shelf life translates into huge financial savings for the food industry. But the consumer pays a high price in terms of health and longevity.

EXCEPTIONS TO THE RULE

Given the proven long-term toxicity of many food additives, you have to wonder why the FDA continues to sanction their use. In 1959, the FDA released what has come to be known as the GRAS list—GRAS meaning generally recognized as safe. The list exempts certain additives from

FDA regulations. One such regulation is the Delaney clause, which prohibits the addition or application of known carcinogens to foods.

According to the FDA, each of the additives on the GRAS list either has a clean record historically or has been proven safe scientifically. Yet at the time of the list's inception, a good number of substances were awarded GRAS status without adequate testing. (They had received government approval prior to 1959 and so were grandfathered onto the list.)

The FDA does reevaluate its GRAS list from time to time, adding and purging substances as more information becomes available. Still, many additives linger on the list long after their toxicity has been proven. Nitrites and saccharin, for example, retain their GRAS status even though ample evidence exists of their cancer-causing properties. Further study will undoubtedly expose even more "safe" additives as poisons.

For its part, the FDA seems to have taken the position that a substance remains innocent until proven guilty—well beyond a reasonable doubt. And so the GRAS list has come to epitomize what former U.S. Senator George McGovern once described as "the never-never land of nonregulation."

Of course, food manufacturers themselves have no interest in finding a substance harmful. They may wind up spending a lot of money to phase out the noxious additive and switch to something safe.

Reading labels won't necessarily protect you from "tainted" foods, either. The regulations governing the disclosure of ingredients are loaded with loopholes. For instance, a given additive may be identified on some labels but not on others. Canned vegetables that contain monosodium glutamate (MSG) must say so in the ingredients list. This requirement does not apply to mayonnaise, salad dressings, and a host of other foods. Go figure.

What's more, the ingredients in packaged foods may themselves have additives among *their* ingredients. The preservative butylated hydroxytoluene (BHT), for example, is often added to vegetable oil to prevent it from turning rancid. The oil may show up in salad dressings, baked goods, and other prepared, processed foods. And you'd never know that they contain BHT, because it won't be mentioned on the labels.

EXTENDING SHELF LIFE, SHORTENING HUMAN LIFE

Additive-laced foods have no place in a Renewal-supporting diet. The toxins that these foods contain disrupt the Renewal process, undermining health and longevity at the cellular level.

Research has shown that additives have especially disturbing effects on mental performance, mood, and behavior. Scientists know that the toxins harm healthy brain cells and scramble the messages transmitted between the cells.

When the New York City board of education decided to cut from its school lunch program all foods containing certain food colorings, they made a remarkable discovery. Students' test scores on a national standardized achievement test rose from the dismal 39th percentile (meaning that 61 percent of the nation's public school students had higher scores) to the 47th percentile. Intrigued, the board moved to eliminate all synthetic colorings and flavorings from school lunches. This time, students' test scores shot up to the 51st percentile.

Figuring that they must be on to something, board members agreed that any foods containing BHT or its "sister" preservative butylated hydroxyanisole (BHA) should no longer be served in city schools. Once again, students' test scores skyrocketed, this time to the 55th percentile. (Prior to the board's experiment, scores had never changed by more than 1 percent from one year to the next.)

Clearly, food additives had some role in suppressing the students' mental processes. Just imagine how much their test scores might have improved if their parents had instituted a similar additive ban at home.

AMERICA'S LEAST WANTED

By sticking with the fresh, organically grown foods of the Anti-Aging Diet, you never have to worry about additives. Only when you eat processed, packaged foods do you expose yourself to these toxins.

Of the additives used by food manufacturers, the following have proven toxic effects within the human body.

At the very least, you should steer clear of these sub-stances as much as you can.

Aluminum. Manufacturers use aluminum as an anti-caking agent in cake mixes, baking powder, salt, and similar items. (Most antacids and underarm deodorants also contain aluminum.) The additive has been implicated as a causative factor in Alzheimer's disease.

Artificial color. When you see "FD&C" in an ingredients list, you can assume that the food contains some sort of artificial color. (Appropriately enough, the abbreviation stands for food dye and color.) Of these appearance-enhancers, the following have the most devastating health effects.

- Blue #1 damages the chromosomes in a cell's nucleus, contributing to the uncontrolled cell mutation and division that eventually leads to cancer. The dye has been banned in Finland and France.
- Blue #2, found in baked goods, candy, and soft drinks, may cause brain tumors. It has been banned in Norway.
- Citrus Red #1 is sprayed on green oranges to make them look ripe. Like Blue #1, this dye fractures the chromosomes in a cell's nucleus, which sets the stage for cancer. The FDA has proposed a ban on Citrus Red #1.
- Citrus Red #2, used to color the skins of citrus fruits, acts as a weak carcinogen.
- Green #3 has been implicated as a cause of bladder tumors.
- Red #3 is often added to canned cherry pie filling, maraschino cherries, baked goods, ice cream, and an array of other foods. Studies have linked this dye to nerve damage and to thyroid cancer.
- Red #40 is a suspected carcinogen.
- Yellow #5 contributes to behavioral disturbances in children.
- Yellow #6 causes tumors in the adrenal glands and kidneys. It has been banned in Norway and Sweden.

Aspartame. Sold under brand names such as Equal and NutraSweet, aspartame enjoys the dubious distinction of having spawned more complaints to the FDA than any other single substance. The artificial sweetener contains phenylalanine, which serves as a precursor to the brain chemical norepinephrine. As such, phenylalanine can alter brain chemistry and cause behavioral changes.

In studies conducted before aspartame won FDA approval, the additive caused brain tumors and epileptic seizures in laboratory rats. Humans have reported a wide variety of symptoms after consuming aspartame, including headaches, fatigue, constipation, menstrual irregularities, and depression.

Occasional small doses of aspartame probably won't cause problems for most people. But consuming large quantities of the sweetener on a daily basis, as folks who are trying to lose weight tend to do, can produce symptoms such as those mentioned above. Ironically, research suggests that aspartame and other sugar substitutes make little difference in the "battle of the bulge." Despite the widespread consumption of artificial sweeteners in the United States, the nation's epidemic of obesity continues unabated.

Mothers-to-be should avoid aspartame for the duration of their pregnancies, as the effects of the sweetener on developing fetuses are uncertain. Also, aspartame should not be exposed to heat or used in cooking. High temperatures cause the sweetener to break down into methyl alcohol, which may contribute to blindness and brain damage.

Benzoic acid and sodium benzoate. These preservatives have been used for more than 70 years to inhibit the growth of microorganisms in fruit juices, pickles, and soft drinks. Though widely believed to be benign, both substances displayed carcinogenic properties in Russian studies. What's more, sodium benzoate inhibited neurological development, stunted growth, and shortened life span in laboratory rats. And in a study published in the British medical journal *Lancet*, benzoic acid produced profound hyperactivity in 79 percent of children who ate it.

BHA and BHT. Oils and other fats turn rancid with age and repeated exposure to air. Both BHA and BHT block this process by scavenging free radicals as they form.

But don't confuse these preservatives with antioxidant

nutrients such as vitamins A, C, and E. In animal studies, BHA and BHT have caused liver damage, baldness, fetal abnormalities, and growth retardation. They also seem to affect sleep, appetite, and other behaviors.

Researchers who fed BHA to pregnant rats noted changes in the brain enzymes of the rats' offspring. In particular, the preservative decreased production of cholinesterase, which is responsible for recycling the brain chemical acetylcholine. (In humans, acetylcholine plays a role in concentration and short-term memory.) Other researchers have found that BHT promotes the formation of cancerous tumors in mice.

Persistent questions about the safety of BHA and BHT have convinced Australia and Sweden to ban the additives and the United Kingdom to severely restrict them. In this country, however, both preservatives retain their GRAS status. And because they're usually added to foods that are then used as ingredients in other foods, BHA and BHT seldom show up on labels.

Much to my amazement, some anti-aging "experts" actually advocate high doses of BHA and BHT because of the preservatives' antioxidant properties. We have access to plenty of safe, natural antioxidants that act in harmony with our bodies. So why should we risk cancer and other life-shortening health problems by ingesting manmade toxins such as BHA and BHT?

Brominated vegetable oil. Manufacturers use brominated vegetable oil as an anti-clouding agent and emulsifier. The additive also shows up in some bottled soft drinks because it prevents the formation of rings where liquid meets air.

As its name suggests, brominated vegetable oil is produced via a process known as bromination. Bromination is quite similar to hydrogenation. One crucial difference: Bromination utilizes the poisonous element bromine rather than the relatively innocuous hydrogen.

Studies have shown that just three ounces of a 2 percent brominated vegetable oil solution could poison children. In adults, the additive reduces immune defenses and depletes histamine, thus encouraging allergic reactions. Yet for reasons that must be clearer to the FDA than to me, manufacturers are not required to list brominated vegetable oil on food labels.

Calcium propionate and sodium propionate. Both of these additives appear to be relatively nontoxic. Still, they can cause migraines and other allergic reactions in people who are sensitive to them.

Carrageenan. Derived from seaweed, carrageenan (also known as Irish moss) serves as a stabilizer and thickening agent. It is often added to low-calorie foods to give them bulk (so they're more filling) and to mask the aftertaste of artificial sweeteners. It thickens and improves the mouth-feel of gravies, ketchup, mustard, pie fillings, puddings, relishes, salad dressings, sauces, soft drinks, and soups. It keeps the chocolate from settling in chocolate milk and other beverages. It minimizes surface hardening and improves the spreadability of cream cheese, processed cheeses, and soft cheeses.

Carrageenan is also used to enhance the texture of a variety of commercial baked goods, including breads, cakes, and doughnuts. And it's a common ingredient in candy, marshmallows, and jellies, because it prevents sugar from crystalizing.

Despite its extensive résumé in the food preparation business, carrageenan seldom gets mentioned on food labels. Better that it would. In laboratory animals, the additive produced pinhead-size lesions in the large intestine, along with bloody, mucus-filled stools. Both symptoms are typical of a human condition known as ulcerative colitis. Other animals developed tumors, ulcers, and cirrhosis-like lesions on their livers.

Ethylenediaminetetraacetic acid (EDTA). In nutrition circles, EDTA has something of a Jekyll-and-Hyde reputation. A binding agent, it latches onto heavy metal ions such as cadmium, cobalt, and lead and disarms these potential toxins. But in the process, it robs foods of essential minerals such as chromium, copper, iron, and zinc. You'll find EDTA in margarine, mayonnaise, salad dressings, and sandwich spreads.

Fluoride. The consumption of fluoridated water plays a role in more than 10,000 cancer deaths in the United States per year. Fluoride is a known carcinogen. It also weakens the immune system, contributes to birth defects, and robs the body of vitamin C.

In the United States, many communities fluoridate water as a means of preventing cavities. In Europe, however, 10 countries now prohibit any use of fluoride. My advice: If your community's water supply contains fluoride, drink purified water—either bottled or run through your own purifier—instead.

Gum arabic and gum tragacanth. Both additives can cause allergic reactions in people who are sensitive to them.

Heptylparaben. Heptylparaben inhibits the formation of mold in jams and frozen desserts. Research has linked the additive to birth defects.

Hydrolyzed vegetable protein. "Vegetable protein" may sound benign enough. In fact, this additive stunts children's growth. It also contains MSG, which I'll discuss in just a bit.

Modified food starch. In and of itself, food starch isn't so bad. It's the modification that causes problems. The process may involve the use of chemicals such as aluminum sulfate, propylene oxide, and 1-octyl succinic anhydride, toxins that linger in the additive and so get passed along into foods.

Monoglycerides and diglycerides. These additives block the absorption of essential fatty acids, which are necessary for well-developed cells and a healthy immune system. In animal studies, monoglycerides and diglycerides are associated with enlarged livers and kidneys, diseased reproductive organs, and high mortality.

MSG. About 50 million pounds of MSG infiltrate our nation's food supply each year. Without question, the flavor enhancer is the most ubiquitous of all food additives.

Most people associate MSG with Chinese cuisine. But you'll also find the additive in the majority of packaged foods, including frozen dinners, frozen and canned vegetables, processed seafood, processed lunchmeats, most soups and soup mixes, salad dressings, condiments and seasonings, baked goods, and candy. Even commercially prepared baby foods used to contain MSG, until public outcry forced the manufacturers to discontinue the practice.

In people who are sensitive to it, MSG causes the symptoms of what has been dubbed Chinese restaurant syndrome: headache, a burning sensation in the back of the neck and forearms, tightness in the chest, heart palpitations, sweating, weakness, and numbness. The FDA has recommended further investigation of the additive's potential adverse effects on the human reproductive system and its role in human cell mutation.

In the meantime, MSG retains its GRAS status. And as with so many other additives, MSG isn't always listed on food labels. To limit your exposure to the stuff, prepare your own meals—using only fresh ingredients—as often as possible.

When you do dine out, be especially careful with your meal selection in Chinese and other Asian establishments. The servers don't always know whether MSG is added to particular dishes. You may need to ask the chef or even the owner. Don't feel uncomfortable about doing so. After all, your health is at stake.

My wife, Dellie, and I had a horrific experience at a local Thai restaurant. Dellie was four months pregnant at the time, and we were having dinner with another couple. When the waiter came to our table, we realized that he spoke minimal English. All I said was "no MSG." The waiter gave some vague response, so I repeated "no MSG." At that point, the waiter called over the head waiter. Again I repeated my request, to which the head waiter replied, "No problem."

About a half-hour after we left the restaurant, all four of us began to experience symptoms of Chinese restaurant syndrome. Needless to say, we were infuriated—and Dellie and I were afraid that our unborn child might be harmed. We later confronted the restaurant's owner, who acknowledged that our food had been tainted with MSG.

Nitrates and nitrites. Both preservatives are routinely added to processed meat products such as bacon, corned beef, ham, hot dogs, lunchmeats, and sausage. They prevent the growth of bacteria and, as a "bonus," give the meat a deceptively healthful-looking pink hue.

But once they reach the stomach, these compounds transform into cancer-causing agents called nitrosamines. So to help avoid cancer, forgo all foods containing these preservatives.

Phosphoric acid. Colas have no nutritional value whatsoever. What they do have is phosphoric acid, a flavoring and acidifying agent that causes serious health problems.

Once in the body, phosphoric acid binds with and removes magnesium. The resulting magnesium deficiency is considered a risk factor for high blood pressure and heart disease.

What's more, phosphoric acid dissolves the aluminum inside soda cans. The aluminum then gets mixed in with the soda and ingested. As I mentioned earlier, scientific evidence implicates aluminum as a contributing factor in the development of Alzheimer's disease.

Other foods—including baked goods, cereals, cheeses, and evaporated milk—contain phosphates, which are forms of phosphoric acid. Excessive consumption of phosphates blocks calcium absorption and flushes the mineral out of bones, laying the groundwork for the brittle-bone disease osteoporosis.

Propyl gallate. An antioxidant like BHA and BHT, propyl gallate retards the spoilage of oils and other fats. It's a common ingredient in chewing gum, chicken soup stock, and meat products. At least one long-term study has suggested that propyl gallate has cancer-causing properties.

Saccharin. In 1977, the FDA considered prohibiting the use of saccharin, because numerous animal studies had shown the artificial sweetener to be a potent carcinogen. But when subsequent studies failed to establish a relationship between saccharin and human cancers, the proposed ban fell through.

To this day, many nutrition-minded experts question saccharin's safety. The sugar substitute remains a common ingredient in processed foods, particularly low-calorie "diet" foods.

Salt. Small amounts of salt (or sodium chloride, as some labels say) seldom cause problems. On the other hand, a high intake of the stuff—as supplied by a steady diet of processed foods—may cause high blood pressure. And high blood pressure paves the way for heart attack and stroke.

If you like the taste of salt, try adding a dash of sea salt or soy sauce to your meal. By all means steer clear of highly salted processed foods.

Sugar. Sugar—an umbrella term that encompasses refined white sugar as well as brown sugar, corn syrup, fructose, honey, molasses, and most other sweeteners—literally saturates the standard American diet. The average American consumes 130 pounds of sugar annually, or more than ⅓ pound per day. As a nation, we eat our collective weight in sugar every year.

By itself, sugar completely lacks nutritional value. And because it takes the place of nutrients in the diet, it contributes to deficiencies. Worse yet, excess amounts of sugar in the body are converted into saturated fat for storage.

For all of these reasons (as well as a few others), a high sugar intake is considered a key player in heart disease, cancer, diabetes, osteoporosis, obesity, and numerous other life-shortening conditions. (You'll learn more about the health implications of sugar in chapter 17.)

Sulfites. On packaged foods, sulfites may go by names such as potassium bisulfite, potassium metabisulfite, sodium bisulfite, sodium metabisulfite, and sulfur dioxide. They're used as preservatives in grape juice, vinegars, and wines. In restaurants, they may be applied to the sliced fruits and vegetables in salads and at salad bars to prevent discoloration.

Sulfites have caused fatal allergic reactions, including anaphylactic shock and asthma attacks, in people who are sensitive to them. Though not cancer-causing themselves, they encourage viruses, bacteria, and fungi to mutate into carcinogens. Sulfites also destroy thiamin in foods.

THE FRIENDLY FEW

In fairness to the FDA, some of the food additives on its GRAS list are safe. A relative handful are even good for you. These substances, by virtue of their molecular structures, work with human biochemistry rather than against it. In doing so, they foster good health rather than destroying it.

For example, some processed foods contain extra doses of the antioxidant nutrients beta-carotene, vitamin C (in the form of ascorbic acid), and vitamin E (in the form of mixed tocopherols). Other foods contain citrate, citric acid, glycerin, lactic acid, and lecithin—substances that your body makes on its own. Still other foods contain innocuous additives such as casein, ferrous gluconate, fumaric acid, and guar gum.

The idea that additives are okay can be misleading, however. Take bread as an example. Most of the loaves that you see in your supermarket have been made with enriched flour, a refined flour that has been stripped clean of fiber, protein, vitamins, and minerals. Enrichment with niacin, thiamin, and other B-complex vitamins gives the bread some nutritional value. These nutrients then show up in the bread's ingredients list, creating a false impression of healthfulness.

When you see vitamins listed in a bread's ingredients list, they're your clue that the bread lacks authentic wholesomeness. Put the loaf back and look for a whole-grain variety instead.

THE ORGANIC ALTERNATIVE

Of course, you can generally avoid such supermarket minefields by choosing only foods labeled "organic" (or "biodynamic"). This shopping rule of thumb applies to processed products as well as fresh fare.

Most people think of organic foods as those grown without the aid of synthetic pesticides, synthetic fertilizers, or other potentially toxic chemicals. But organic, at least as it applies to processed foods, also means that the foods contain no additives or other artificial ingredients.

Going organic greatly reduces your exposure to foodborne toxins of all kinds. A growing number of people are making the switch. Americans spend an estimated $1.5 billion per year on organic produce alone. And in a Louis Harris poll, 84 percent of Americans said that they would prefer to buy organic foods over chemically altered varieties.

EMBRACING THE ORGANIC LIFESTYLE

To be sure, going organic can make a world of difference in terms of your health and longevity. At the same time, it shouldn't turn your world upside down. Here are a few pointers to help ease the transition—and to support the organic movement.

Tell your supermarket to stock up. As the organic movement has gained momentum, organic foods have become more widely available. Several major supermarket chains have added organic sections. If your grocery store has yet to pick up on the trend, drop a note in the store's suggestion box or—even better—speak with the manager. (And if your store already stocks organic foods, nudge the manager to offer even more.)

Remember, supermarkets vie with each other for your business. They understand that customers can quickly change loyalties. And they pass along the word to their wholesalers, growers, and other suppliers that customers want better selections of organic foods.

If you're concerned about the costs of organic foods, you'll be pleased to know that they're much less expensive than they used to be. Improved growing and processing techniques, combined with greater competition among growers and manufacturers, have driven down prices. And they should continue to drop over time. Cheaper organic produce can also be found at your local farmers' market.

Read labels. As I mentioned earlier, federal regulations don't require full disclosure on product labels. So you can never be sure that a packaged food is 100 percent additive-free. Still, you can learn a lot about the food's desirability—or lack thereof—just by perusing the ingredients list.

Even if the label says "organic" or "biodynamic," read the ingredients list anyway. Some foods identified as organic may actually contain artificial ingredients. According to the Organic Foods Production Act, a processed food must meet two criteria in order to wear the organic label: At least 50 percent of the food's ingredients must be organically grown or organically produced, and at least 95 percent of the food itself must be organically produced. So by definition, an organic food may still contain additives and other undesirable chemicals, even if in trace amounts.

Think twice about natural foods. Since the federal government established official guidelines for the use of "organic" on labels, some manufacturers have resorted to identifying their foods as "natural." They want to create an image of healthfulness that consumers equate with organic. Be forewarned: Natural doesn't necessarily mean nutritious or pesticide- and additive-free.

"Natural" breads, for instance, may be made with white flour, sugar, hydrogenated oils, and preservatives. "Natural" cereals may contain more sugar than processed varieties. "Natural" ice cream may be loaded with artificial colors, vegetable gums, monoglycerides, and diglycerides. "Natural" beef may contain pesticides, antibiotics, and hormones.

In addition, beware of produce that flaunts that look of perfection. Flawless fruits and vegetables usually mean that pesticides were used solely for the purpose of enhancing appearance. More than 50 percent of the pesticides used on tomatoes and more than 70 percent of the pesticides used on citrus fruits are applied purely for cosmetic purposes.

Be wary of waxing. When browsing the produce aisle, you may have noticed that certain fruits and vegetables look much shinier than others. The sheen comes from waxes such as palm oil derivatives, paraffins, shellacs, and synthetic resins, the same ingredients in the products that you use to polish your car and your furniture.

Like other additives, waxes enhance the visual appeal of produce. They seal in moisture, which keeps a fruit or vegetable looking fresh and prolongs its shelf life. Unfortunately, they also lock in any pesticides that have been sprayed on the food. (Some waxes contain fungicides, too.)

No matter how hard you scrub, you cannot remove the wax coating from produce. Inside your body, the wax coats your intestinal tract, effectively blocking nutrient absorption. Peeling a fruit or vegetable before eating it helps, but you're still getting unhealthy doses of those sealed-in pesticides and other toxins.

You can usually spot the wax coating on certain produce, such as apples, cucumbers, and green and sweet red and yellow peppers. Other fruits and vegetables to be wary of include avocado, cantaloupe, eggplant, grapefruit, lemons, limes, melons, oranges, parsnips, passion fruit, peaches, pumpkins, rutabaga, squash, sweet potatoes, tomatoes, and turnips. (Of course, if you buy only organic produce, you never have to worry about waxing.)

Plant an organic garden. If organic produce is hard to come by in your area, you can always try your hand at growing your own. All it takes is a small plot of ground and a little bit of time. Lettuce, tomatoes, and zucchini make good starter crops—they are quite hardy and usually thrive with minimal maintenance.

If you suspect that the soil in your garden has been contaminated by pesticides, scrape away the top 12 inches and replace it with organic soil, compost, and fertilizer. A local nursery can provide all the necessary supplies and answer any questions you may have.

Petition government officials. Contact your congressman to voice your concerns about the state of our nation's food supply. Encourage them to introduce and pass legislation that imposes tougher standards for the use of pesticides, additives, and other toxins in foods. Ask them to support the research and development of new food production technologies that could eliminate the need for toxins altogether. Tell them that you oppose the notion of "acceptable risk"—that you feel no amount of a noxious substance is "safe."

Join consumer and environmental groups. Without grassroots political action, the general public doesn't stand a fighting chance against the industries responsible for poisoning our foods and our planet. A number of consumer and environmental groups have taken the fight for safe foods all the way to Capitol Hill. They include the following:

- Food and Water, R.R. 1, Box 114, Marshfield, VT 06568
- Mothers and Others for a Livable Planet, 40 West 20th Street, New York, NY 10011
- Natural Resources Defense Council, 90 New Montgomery Street, San Francisco, CA 94105
- Public Citizen, 2000 Paul Street NW, Suite 300, Washington, DC 20077-6488

You can show your support for any or all of these organizations simply by becoming a member. (Note: Some of these groups may charge annual membership fees.)

LIVING TOXIN-FREE

Switching to organic foods may require some time and effort up front. But these small investments promise huge payoffs. You'll feel better, you'll stay healthier, and you'll earn extra "quality time" on this planet.

And when you spend your dollars on organic foods, you send the message that you want a clean, safe food supply. In this way, you nurture the development of new growing and processing techniques that protect rather than poison foods of all kinds.

Nature gives you only one body. How you take care of it determines how long it will last. Feed your body only organic, toxin-free foods, and it has the best chance of staying youthful and disease-free for a lifetime.

Food-borne toxins play a prominent role in the development of cancer. But they're not the only causative factors. In the next chapter, we'll examine just how this insidious disease begins its slow and silent destruction of the human body—and what we can do to stop it.

CHAPTER 12

How to Prevent Cancer

We have poured vast amounts of money into the search for cancer cures over a very long period of time. We've brought some of our best research minds to bear on these problems, and it just hasn't worked.
—JOHN BAILAR, M.D., PH.D.,
  FORMER EDITOR-IN-CHIEF OF THE
  JOURNAL OF THE NATIONAL CANCER INSTITUTE

I had difficulty writing this chapter. Draft after draft seemed lifeless. I knew something was wrong, but what?

Then it came to me: My father, with whom I had been very close, died of lung cancer in 1977. The profound sense of loss still lingers—so much so that writing about the disease that had torn my family apart was next to impossible.

I miss my dad terribly. Had it not been for the scourge of cancer, we would have had several more years together. I know he would agree that if the information presented here helps even one person avoid cancer, the effort will have been worthwhile. I dedicate this chapter to him.

In the pages that follow, you'll find out what causes cancer and why. Along the way, you'll learn what you need to do to protect yourself against this insidious disease.

Some of what you're about to read may seem boring or discouraging. But I want you to have all of the facts. Becoming informed is your best weapon in the war against cancer—a war that you have the power to win.

Assessing Your Cancer Risk

Scientists have identified the following factors as potential causes of or contributors to cancer. Some you cannot control, but many you can. These are the keys to prevention.

Lifestyle Factors
Age
Family history
Lack of exercise
Obesity
Smoking
Stress

Health Factors
Chronic viral infections (such as Epstein-Barr virus, hepatitis, and herpes)

Immunological disorders (such as rheumatoid arthritis and systemic lupus erythematosus)
Parasites

Dietary Factors
Additives
Aflatoxin (a mold-borne carcinogen)
Alcohol
Animal-derived foods

CANCER IS NOT INEVITABLE

You are not alone if you feel that, like Benjamin Franklin's proverbial death and taxes, cancer is inescapable. That's just not true.

When the topic turns to cancer, many a frustrated soul has said, "Hey, everything causes cancer—the water we drink, the food we eat, the air we breathe. Why should I give up all my favorite stuff when the so-called experts can't even agree on what causes cancer and what doesn't?"

I used to bristle when I heard people say such things. I told myself that they were misinformed or trying to rationalize their own self-destructive behaviors (as in "Everything causes cancer, so I may as well order the bacon cheeseburger"). I'd indulge in long-winded tirades about how it just isn't so, then trundle out my litanies about what actually does and doesn't cause cancer. (Now I can just hand folks a copy of this book.)

Another argument that I often hear goes something like this: "I've read about cancer genes, and I have them. My

	Environmental Factors
Antioxidant deficiencies	Air pollution
Caffeine	Asbestos
Contaminated drinking water	Electromagnetic fields
Essential fatty acid deficiencies	Formaldehyde
Essential nutrient deficiencies	Household chemicals (such as cleaners, glues, lubricants, paints, paint strippers, and solvents)
Excessive fat	Ionizing radiation
Excessive sugar	Lead
Fiber deficiencies	Pesticides
Irradiated foods	Radon gas
Pesticides	Smoking and secondhand smoke
Phytochemical deficiencies	Ultraviolet radiation
Processed foods	Water pollution
Trans-fats	X-rays

mother, father, and grandfather all died of cancer. So if I'm genetically programmed to get cancer anyway, why should I make sacrifices and change my lifestyle?"

These are reasonable questions. True, we can't change our genetic makeup. But by the same token, heredity isn't everything. Lifestyle choices determine whether cancer genes actually express themselves. So even if cancer does "run in the family," prevention works. You control the outcome. Indeed, a fatalistic attitude could prove fatal if it persuades you to throw caution to the wind.

Trust me when I say that almost all cancers are preventable. This is why it's so important to know what causes the disease and what prevents it.

THE COLD, HARD FACTS

The United States is in the midst of a cancer epidemic. One in every three Americans will develop the disease. An astounding 1.2 million cancer cases are diagnosed every year in this country—and that number is going up, not down. Of these, 6 in 10 people will die within five years. One in every four deaths—about 500,000 annually—is attributable to cancer, and the rate is rising.

Now for the good news: The National Cancer Institute estimates that 80 percent of all cancer cases can be prevented. The same percentage of cases are linked to lifestyle and/or environmental factors, according to Margaret Heckler, former U.S. Secretary of Health and Human Services. The most significant causes of cancer are the ones that you can control or influence. You can voluntarily lower your cancer risk from 35 percent to 5 percent through lifestyle changes alone.

In 1980, the National Cancer Institute commissioned the National Research Council to investigate the relationship between diet and cancer. The list of panelists, all selected from the National Academy of Sciences, reads like a veritable who's who of nutrition. Their report, *Diet, Nutrition, and Cancer*, states: "The evidence reviewed by the committee suggests that cancers of most major sites are influenced by dietary patterns." In the years since that report was released, more research results have poured in, and the diet-cancer connection has grown even stronger.

Diet causes more cancers than any other single risk factor, including smoking. Take away cancers from smoking, and diet accounts for more than 50 percent of the remaining cancer cases. Remove the other known risk factors—excessive sun exposure, alcohol consumption, occupational exposure, environmental pollution, viral infection, medicine, and medical procedures—and diet accounts for at least 70 percent of the remaining cancer cases.

A CHANGING FOCUS

By the year 2000, cancer will reign as the leading cause of death in the United States. For the vast sums of money devoted to cancer research over the past quarter-century, we've not seen commensurate improvements in cure rates. "The degree of improvement in death rates in general for the common cancers of adults is really pretty discouraging. It has not been for lack of effort," according to John Bailar, M.D., Ph.D., a researcher at the National Cancer Institute and former editor-in-chief of the *Journal of the National Cancer Institute*.

We've been losing the war against cancer because we've

been fighting on the wrong battlefield. We need to move our front line to prevention. This requires public education.

Unfortunately, the medical research establishment and the government's funding agencies are more enamored with fancy new drugs and other high-tech therapeutic adventures than with teaching preventive lifestyles. For a variety of pernicious political and economic reasons, government-supported efforts have chosen to emphasize early detection and aggressive treatment rather than the true cure offered by prevention. Agribusiness doesn't want to stop placing fat-laden animal foods on the American table. Chemical manufacturers are loath to lose their profits on pesticides and preservatives. Drug companies make a bundle on ever more potent chemotherapeutic weapons.

Government will not reject any industry's powerful, money-driven influence until an enlightened, fed-up populace sends clear messages that the jig is up. Until then, there will be no public education about preventive lifestyles. And even more time will be lost while cancer, a formidable foe, continues its advance.

Of course, when cancer does strike, early detection is absolutely critical. Superlative diagnostic techniques such as mammographies, Pap tests, prostate-specific antigen screening, sigmoidoscopy (for colon cancer), and magnetic resonance imaging (MRI) are capable of identifying tumors long before they have a chance to grow and spread.

On the treatment side, drugs, radiation, and surgery—despite their great value—will never amount to more than too little, too late. Remember, fewer than half of newly diagnosed patients survive for five years.

Prevention is the ultimate solution to the puzzle of cancer. No chemotherapeutic regimen or screening program can save as many lives as some simple preemptive changes in diet and lifestyle.

HOW CANCER HAPPENS

Cancer is a group of diseases characterized by the uncontrolled growth of abnormal cells. It results from massive immune collapse and is the ultimate degenerative disease. Left unchecked, it can kill you.

Cancer begins when a healthy cell—minding its own

business, performing its assigned tasks—encounters one of those renegade molecules called free radicals. The free radical literally attacks the cell's DNA and damages it, initiating the cell's transformation into a neoplastic (tumor-forming) cell. The carcinogenic intruder literally reprograms the cell's DNA. Unless the DNA is promptly repaired, the cell will never again be the same.

Cancer cells break the rules that govern normal cells. For example, normal cells are programmed to die on cue by virtue of a process called apoptosis, which is necessary to make room for new cells. Cancer cells have the audacity to refuse to die. They become immortal, living as long as the host stays alive. And they become greedy, grabbing much more than their share of food, water, and oxygen.

Cancer cells ignore another natural dictum: the universal biological law of contact inhibition. This is nature's protection against encroachment. Normal cells stop dividing when they bump up against neighboring cells. Cancer cells have no more respect for this law than for any of the others. They just push neighboring cells aside and keep on growing.

Even so, cancer doesn't happen overnight. Cancer is a multi-step process, consisting of first initiation; then promotion, then progression. The cumulative outcome of multiple exposures to carcinogens, the average cancer takes one to four decades to develop.

By the time a tumor has reached clinical detectability, it's about 75 percent of the way to being lethal. It has undergone at least 30 doublings, contains about a billion cells, weighs about one gram, and occupies a volume of about 1 cubic centimeter. If it hasn't already metastasized, the risk is high. Only 10 further doublings will produce a clearly lethal tumor of a trillion cells, one kilogram (2.2 pounds), and 1,000 cubic centimeters.

FREE RADICALS RUN AMOK

Cancer cells are continuously being created and (hopefully) destroyed in your body. The combination of intense prolonged oxidative stress—that is, too many free radicals and not enough antioxidants—and the failure of protection and repair mechanisms creates an internal milieu that allows cancer cells to proliferate to the point at which they generate a detectable mass. By the time cancer is discovered, it has worn down and broken through several levels of protection.

Testing can determine whether your free radicals are beating up on your antioxidants, leaving you vulnerable to cancer (as well as other degenerative diseases). I routinely order an oxidative stress panel and an antioxidant profile for patients who are at higher risk for cancer (see "Assessing Your Cancer Risk" on page 152) or who have already been diagnosed with cancer, whether they're undergoing treatment or in remission.

The oxidative stress panel provides three measures of free radical activity. The first is the level of hydroxyl radicals, one of the nastiest of the free radicals. The second is the level of oxidized fats (or serum lipid peroxides, scientifically speaking). Free radicals oxidize fats, so the more oxidized fats, the more free radical activity. The third is the level of glutathione, the principal membrane-protecting antioxidant. If hydroxyl radicals and oxidized fats are high and glutathione is low, I know the patient is in big trouble, oxidatively speaking.

The antioxidant profile assesses levels of the major protective antioxidants, including vitamin A, vitamin C, vitamin E (alpha- and gamma-tocopherol), coenzyme Q_{10}, alpha-carotene, beta-carotene, and lycopene. This test identifies the exact biochemical locations of the holes in the patient's antioxidant armor. For example, a patient's results might indicate adequate vitamin C, vitamin E, and beta-carotene but deficient vitamin A, coenzyme Q_{10}, and alpha-carotene. This tells me where the free radicals are slipping past the antioxidant defenders and causing disease. I then design a targeted supplement program to replace the deficient nutrients. Follow-up testing within a month or two determines whether the levels are within their normal ranges. (This kind of testing can also be used by anyone interested in using optimum nutrition to reduce the risk of degenerative disease and reverse aging.)

YOUR ANTI-CANCER ARSENAL

Your body's cancer safeguard systems protect you in two ways: They help prevent renegade cancer cells from forming in the first place, and they remove those that slip past the front-line defenses. In effect, your cancer safe-guard systems are an obstacle course that your body places in the path of a wannabe cancer cell. These systems include antioxidant defenses, DNA repair enzymes, and immune surveillance. Let's take a brief look at each.

Antioxidant Defenses

We've already discussed the antioxidant defense systems—the nutrients, enzymes, and immune cells that protect you against free radicals. Mutant (precancerous) cells are created when the cells' DNA is overwhelmed by intense oxidative stress. It isn't as though one exposure to fried chicken or pesticide residues causes cancer: Rather, it's the relentless pounding taken by your DNA day in and day out over long periods of time.

Keeping your defenses strong means consuming lots of antioxidants and phytochemicals, those plant-derived anti-cancer compounds. A deficiency can be caused by not consuming enough of these nutrients or by using them up too quickly. Either way, if your antioxidant defense systems are undermined, they lose their ability to contain the growth of cancer cells.

DNA Repair Enzymes

Even if DNA is damaged, it can be repaired. In chapter 3, I explained that Renewal depends on DNA repair enzymes, which restore health to DNA molecules that have been damaged by free radical attack. Each DNA molecule in every single one of your 100 trillion cells sustains this damage at a fantastic rate: about 10,000 free radical hits per day. Most, but not all, of these lesions are fixed by your DNA repair enzymes. If these enzymes have been damaged by excessive free radicals, however, they can't do their jobs effectively. Impaired repair enzymes can thus increase vulnerability to cancer.

If damaged DNA is repaired before the affected cell divides, the DNA passed on to the daughter cells is normal, and the healthy cell line continues. But if a cell containing damaged DNA replicates before the enzymes can repair the damage, the daughter cells carry forward the altered genetic code as a mutation, initiating a line of mutant cells.

On some level, your body's healing systems are acutely aware of what a disaster it would be to pass on a mutant gene. So you have special proteins that are actually programmed to stop cells with defective DNA from dividing. These molecular traffic cops temporarily arrest cell division by sending a message to a defective cell, telling it to suspend replication until the DNA is repaired (sort of like being told to stay home from work until you get well) or to self-destruct. In effect, these special protein messengers give the compromised cell a time-out so that the DNA repair enzymes can do their thing.

Immune Surveillance

Above all else, cancer—regardless of location or type—is a disease in which the immune system falters under the weight of excess free radicals. For cancer to start and then continue growing, it must outmaneuver the many long arms of your immune defenses.

The immune system is both your first and last defense against cancer. As the principal cancer defender in your cells, it plays multiple roles. It tracks down, identifies, and destroys carcinogenic free radicals before they can alter DNA. It also protects its own cells from free radical attack. That's just what it must do before cancer cells appear.

Free radical scavenging and DNA repair are not perfect, so cancer cells are being formed more or less continuously. Your immune system is programmed to locate and destroy them, and it has a multiplicity of weapons for doing this. B lymphocytes manufacture tumor-specific antibodies, which attack and destroy cancer cells. Several types of T lymphocytes (natural killer cells, cytotoxic lymphocytes, and others) are programmed to kill tumor cells. Lymphocytes also manufacture anti-tumor chemicals called cytokines, including interferon, interleukin, and tumor necrosis factor.

Given the multilayered arsenal at your body's disposal, the fact that cancer happens at all is quite amazing. People with impaired immune responsiveness, regardless of cause, are more susceptible to cancer because their arsenals are depleted. Maintaining immune health is so crucial to cancer prevention and longevity that throughout this book I stress the importance of minimizing exposure to immune-suppressing factors such as a high-fat diet, pesticides and other toxic chemicals, air and water pollutants, radiation, synthetic hormones, antibiotics, and immunosuppressive drugs (prednisone is one). If you protect your immune system, it will protect you.

STOPPING CANCER BEFORE IT STARTS

The term *dysplasia* applies to any precancerous growth that has outwitted and outmaneuvered all of the protective defense mechanisms described above and that has become large enough to actually detect. Dysplasia is a group of precancerous cells that can be seen by a pathologist in a biopsy but that have not invaded local tissues or metastasized to a distant location. At this stage of development, changing the internal environment (with diet and supplementation) can often give the immune system the boost it needs in order to reverse the condition.

The experience of one of my patients, Alice Dobson, illustrates this point perfectly. Alice, a family therapist, called me with the news that a routine Pap test administered by her gynecologist had revealed cervical dysplasia—often a prelude to cervical cancer. She asked me what she should do. I told her that many studies had shown that nutritional medicine could reverse a high percentage of cervical dysplasias. She agreed to give it a try.

I started her on moderate doses of vitamin A, B-complex vitamins (including folic acid), essential fatty acids, amino acids, beta-carotene, phytochemicals, and other antioxidants. She eliminated all dietary carcinogens, including the chicken, fish, and cheese she consumed on a daily basis. She switched to a low-fat, additive-free, organic vegetarian diet emphasizing cancer-protective foods (which I present in the next chapter). I urged her to give up sugar and alcohol—which, after some minor resistance, she agreed to do.

After four months on this program, Alice's follow-up Pap test came back negative. With the immune system boost and the extra antioxidants, Renewal had reversed the incipient cancer. Alice was delighted, as was I. Suppressing my elation, I cautioned her not to go back to her old diet now that the scare was over.

THE DIET-CANCER CONNECTION

Diet and cancer are linked in three fundamental ways. First, many foods and food products contain carcinogens. Some, like fats and aflatoxins (produced by a mold that grows on certain crops), are naturally there. Others, like hydrogenated oils, pesticides, and dyes, are added. Still others, like browning and burning, are created through cooking. The good news is that you can easily avoid these food-borne carcinogens. You need only know what they are and where to find them.

Second, certain foods are chock-full of cancer-fighting substances. Therefore, specific food choices, properly made, can help prevent cancer.

Third, cancer-protective nutrients are deficient in the standard American diet. But when taken as supplements, they reduce cancer risk.

This information leads to three powerful preventive options.

- Know which foods contain carcinogens and avoid them.
- Increase consumption of cancer-preventive foods.
- Take cancer-preventive nutritional supplements.

The rest of this chapter focuses on the first of these anti-cancer strategies. The other two are covered in chapter 13.

CARCINOGENIC CUISINE

It is a tragic irony that the foods we find most attractive are the ones least likely to improve our health. This line of thinking, tempered with a dash of cynicism, raises the question: What kind of diet would a person choose if he were attempting to cause cancer? (As you read along, note the similarity between this diet and the standard American diet.)

This person—let's call him Norm—would prefer fried, burned, toasted, barbecued, and smoked foods such as steaks, ribs, hamburgers, pork, fried chicken, fried fish, sausage, bacon, fried potatoes, eggs, and toast. He'd indiscriminately devour other high-fat foods such as cheese,

Fats to Forget

In the fight against cancer, the smartest strategy of all is to reduce your fat intake. Dietary fat has been implicated in even more cases of cancer than smoking. To slim down your diet, steer clear of the following foods.

Fried foods. Frying and fat are a toxic mix: Together they cook up a cascade of carcinogens. Eliminate all fried foods, from the common french fry to the exotic falafel.

Meats. Like all animal-derived foods, meats are high in fat. Women who eat meat daily have 4 times the breast cancer rate of women who eat meat less than once a week. And men who consume meat or any other animal-derived food daily are 3.6 times more likely to develop fatal prostate cancer than men who consume these foods sparingly, if at all. Excise all meats from your diet, including bacon, chicken, duck, ham, hamburger, lamb, pork, processed lunchmeats, salami, sausage, steak, turkey, and veal.

Dairy foods. They come from animals, so they're loaded with fat, pesticides, and other toxins. On the list of offenders are all types of butter, cheese, milk, and yogurt, including nonfat and low-fat varieties.

Skip the butter substitutes, too. Margarine and other partially hydrogenated spreads contain large quantities of *trans*-fats, or "ugly fats."

Eggs. They're not only high in saturated fat but also loaded with cholesterol.

Cooking oils. Use the smallest amounts possible. For stove-top cooking, olive and soybean oils can tolerate higher heats best. For baking, olive, soybean, and walnut oils are good choices.

butter, salad dressings, and cooking oils. Rather than sticking with unprocessed whole grains, legumes, fresh vegetables, and fresh fruits, he'd steer clear of these vital foods as much as possible. They'd be relegated to supporting-role status, while fleshy main dishes, dairy products, and convenience foods would take center stage.

Norm's cancer-causing diet is processed, preserved, and

Salad dressings. Standard dressings, even the "lite" varieties, are usually very high in fat. Several tasty nonfat dressings are now available. Better yet, make your own. Start with vinegar (I like balsamic or the flavored gourmet kinds) or lemon juice, herbs, and spices. For extra flavor (and extra anti-cancer essential fatty acids), add some flaxseed, soybean, or walnut oils. To make a creamy dressing, use soy yogurt or tofu that has been processed in a blender or food processor.

Nuts and nut butters. A tablespoon of peanut butter contains 100 calories, 90 of which come from fat. A 2,000-calorie, 10 percent fat diet allows for only 200 calories from fat per day. So after just 2 tablespoons of peanut butter, you've just about reached your daily fat quota.

Because of their fat content, nuts and nut butters should be consumed in very small amounts. Almond butter is preferable over peanut. If you use peanut butter at all, make sure that it's organic and certified aflatoxin-free. (Aflatoxin is a mold-borne carcinogen that's especially common in peanuts.) Pour the oil off the top when you open it.

Snack foods. Nutritionally, they're junk—not only high in fat but also made with partially hydrogenated cottonseed, palm, or peanut oil. Because these oils are bursting with saturated fats and "ugly fats," they belong in the realm of the truly toxic.

For snacks, choose from fresh fruits such as apples, grapes, oranges, and pears; applesauce; almonds and walnuts (just a few, though); popcorn (without any butter); fat-free corn chips; and rice crackers and other fat-free crackers.

doused with pesticides. It features conventionally grown foods rather than chemical-free organically grown foods. It is deficient in cancer-protective fiber. It includes hot dogs, sausage, cold cuts, and other nitrate-laden processed meats. To wash it all down, Norm swills copious amounts of alcohol, coffee, and sugary soft drinks.

Obviously, this killer diet is low in cancer-protective

nutrients—the vitamins, minerals, essential fatty acids, phytonutrients, and fiber necessary to thwart cancer. Of course, Norm wouldn't think of taking supplements.

YOUR TOP PRIORITY: REDUCE DIETARY FAT

For carcinogenic potential, nothing in your diet comes anywhere close to fat. As has been discussed at length in previous chapters, a high-fat diet dramatically increases cancer risk. This is not speculation: Animal studies and human population studies alike have established this truth beyond any question. In the medical and cancer research communities, "Fat causes cancer" is accepted as fact.

In animal studies, researchers have consistently found that a high-fat diet accelerates the frequency and growth rate of cancers. And in human studies, three of the four most common cancers—breast, colon, and prostate—are closely linked to high fat intakes. Even lung cancer, the fourth most common type, is more likely to occur in smokers who also have high fat intakes. Cancers of the uterus, ovaries, and pancreas are also on the list of those associated with a high-fat diet.

Fat causes cancer in a variety of insidious ways.

Fat breeds free radicals. Rancidification is just another word for oxidation, which is just another word for free radical attack. All fats, including those that your own body manufactures, eventually go rancid.

When fat molecules are oxidized, the resulting chain reactions produce cascades of free radicals. These free radicals can destroy any cell in your body by blasting a hole in its outer wall, or cell membrane. The cell's contents leak out, and it dies.

We can afford to lose a few cells here and there. The truly serious problems begin when free radicals bang into a cell's DNA molecules, mutating them so that they reproduce incorrectly. Or when free radicals damage immune cells, interfering with their cancer-protective powers. (I know that I've already explained all this, but I just want to remind you that excess dietary fats enhance the carcinogenic load.)

Trans-fats are especially aggressive free radicals that get a kick out of fracturing DNA and sabotaging the immune system's delicate cancer surveillance mechanisms, increasing the likelihood of tumor development. *Trans*-fats are fat molecules that have been altered by hydrogenation, processing, or high-heat cooking. They are present in vegetable shortenings, processed vegetable oils, and margarine.

Fat depletes antioxidant nutrients. The health of the immune system is exquisitely sensitive to diet and to the availability of nutrients. Improper diet weakens the immune system's ability to ward off cancer. Conversely, maintaining consistently high levels of antioxidant nutrients provides incredibly powerful cancer protection.

The antioxidant nutrient heroes that valiantly defend the body are vitamins A, C, and E, the minerals selenium and zinc, the essential fatty acids, glutathione, carnitine, N-acetyl-cysteine, beta-carotene, and the multiplicity of phytochemicals. If your supply of these all-important immune-enhancing nutrients is depleted, fewer free radicals can be scavenged, and cancer is encouraged.

Fat-Fighting Guidelines

Not all fats cause cancer. In fact, some can even help prevent it. Want to maximize these beneficial fats while minimizing the harmful fats? Here are six rules to live by.

1. Eliminate all foods of animal origin.
2. Avoid all foods that contain partially hydrogenated vegetable oils.
3. Cook fats and oils at the lowest possible temperature. Bake, boil, microwave, or steam foods—never fry.
4. Cut back on all vegetable fats and oils except those high in essential fatty acids (flaxseed, pumpkin seed, soy, and walnut oils).
5. Take 2,000 to 10,000 milligrams of supplemental flaxseed oil, an omega-3 fatty acid, each day.
6. Take 250 to 500 milligrams of supplemental borage oil, an omega-6 fatty acid, each day.

A high-fat diet not only uses up these protective nutrients at an unusually rapid rate but also fails to replace them. Plus, the very nutrients that we need to break down dietary fat—the B-complex vitamins, especially B_{12}, biotin, niacin, pantothenic acid, and riboflavin—are not sufficiently available in a high-fat animal foods diet, resulting in nutrient deficiencies.

Fat elevates hormone levels. A high-fat diet contains high levels of xenoestrogens (that is, estrogens that are different from the ones the body makes) and induces production of estradiol and estrone, the pro-cancer types of estrogen. High levels of these hormones can trigger cancer in the hormonally sensitive tissues of the breasts and other reproductive organs (the uterus, ovaries, and prostate). Nonvegetarians also ingest the growth-stimulating hormones fed to cows and chickens. These substances confuse and disrupt the body's own hormone-producing equipment (the endocrine system), opening the door to cancer and other diseases.

Fat stimulates bile acid production. All fats, but especially saturated fats, increase bile acid production in the liver. Bile acids are released via the bile ducts into the intestinal tract, where they stimulate intestinal bacteria to produce cancer-causing chemicals. Fewer dietary fats means less bile acid, which in turn means a lower cancer risk.

Excess bile acids can also directly irritate the intestinal wall, eventually initiating tumor cell growth. A high-fiber diet protects against this by sopping up the bile acids and the carcinogens they generate, flushing them out before they cause damage.

Fat packs on pounds. Carrying excess body weight is carcinogenic. Why? The more fat molecules in the body, the more free radicals that are generated, and the greater the potential for cancer. These are persuasive reasons to minimize fat intake and to lose weight. And since excess calories from all sources can be transformed into and stored as fat, these are compelling reasons to reduce total calorie intake as well.

THE BIOACCUMULATION BOOMERANG

The American food supply is pervasively contaminated. Since the 1950s, the Food and Drug Administration and other government agencies have allowed the multibillion-dollar food industry to lace the food supply with hundreds of substances whose safety is questionable. The consequences of prolonged exposure to these chemicals, many of which are known carcinogens, is uncertain. But many experts now believe that long-term ingestion plays a major causative role in compromised immunity and cancer.

In a desperate attempt to protect itself from these toxins, your body stores them in its fatty tissues. This is tantamount to attempting to get rid of a poison by eating it. If this approach seems foolish, remember that toxins are fat-soluble rather than water-soluble, so they can't simply be dumped into the urine. This noxious brew doesn't just hang out harmlessly in fat cells, either: It disrupts local DNA, slowly causing changes that can ultimately lead to cancer.

Polychlorinated biphenyls (PCBs), dichlorodiphenyl-trichloroethane (DDT), and other pesticides stored in women's breast tissues have been linked to breast cancer. Researchers looked at the amounts of two carcinogens in 40 breast tissue samples—20 benign, 20 malignant. Their findings were crystal clear: The malignant samples contained twice as many PCBs and twice as much dichlorodiphenyldichloroethylene (a breakdown product of DDT) as the benign samples.

For carnivores, bioaccumulation—that is, the movement of pesticides and other fat-soluble toxins up the food chain—provides a carcinogenic double whammy. Here's how it works: Just as in humans, the bodies of cows and chickens stow pesticides (which are routinely sprayed on animal feed) in fatty tissues in an attempt to get rid of them. When you eat a burger or a drumstick, you get a dose of pesticide that has already gone through one concentration. Then your body stores the toxin, so it is doubly concentrated.

SUBTRACTING ADDITIVES

Additives create some serious problems for the cancer-conscious eater: Thousands of additives are used in our nation's food supply, most of which are risky for one reason or another, but only a sprinkling of them are listed on the labels. The only systematic way to avoid them is to eat fresh, whole (unprocessed) foods, preferably purchased in health food stores.

Here's a sampling of some of the most commonly encountered carcinogenic food additives.

- Artificial sweeteners such as cyclamates, saccharin, and xylitol
- Emulsifiers and stabilizers such as carrageenan and carboxymethylcellulose
- Flavoring agents such as cinnyamyl anthranilate, oil of calamus, and safrole
- Food dyes such as Blue #2, Citrus Red #2, Green #3, and Red #3. Though widely used in processed foods, these coloring agents are not required to be listed on labels and rarely appear there
- Preservatives such as butylated hydroxyanisole, butylated hydroxytoluene, propyl gallate, and sodium nitrite

THE FUNGUS AMONG US

The fungus *Aspergillus flavus*—which grows on a variety of crops—produces aflatoxin, one of the most powerful known carcinogens. Animal studies have shown aflatoxin to be carcinogenic at remarkably low levels.

When researchers fed rats aflatoxin-contaminated food at the incredibly minute concentration of 15 parts per billion (equivalent to 15 pennies in $10 million worth), every single rat developed cancer. By comparison, the "safe limit" of aflatoxin established by the Food and Drug Administration is 20 parts per billion.

Aflatoxin is the most potent liver carcinogen known. Studies conducted in Mozambique, where aflatoxin contamination and liver cancer are both rampant, strongly suggest a connection between the two. In China, Taiwan, and Thailand, studies have linked aflatoxin-contaminated food with liver cancer.

Aflatoxin-producing mold grows on many crops. It especially favors those that are improperly stored or have been weakened by drought or insects. Among the crops hardest hit are almonds, corn, peanuts, pecans, and pistachios. Many other crops—primarily grains and seeds—are affected, but usually at lower levels.

Here in the United States, the Food and Drug Administration and the food industry consider aflatoxin a significant but unavoidable risk. Monitoring is difficult, poorly controlled, and spotty at best.

To minimize personal aflatoxin exposure, I recommend the following:

- Never eat any food that you suspect may have become moldy either before or after you purchased it.
- Avoid peanuts and peanut butter altogether. In addition to their aflatoxin risk, they're high in fat, and they contain the wrong kinds of fat.
- If you must indulge in peanuts, keep quantities small and use brands labeled "certified aflatoxin-free" (such as Westbrae, Arrowhead, and Walnut Acres).
- Steer clear of dairy products altogether. Dairy farmers can feed their cows moldy, uninspected corn grown on their own farms, then market the aflatoxin-contaminated milk.

COOKING UP CARCINOGENS

Remember the wonderful odor of frying bacon wafting into your bedroom, enticing you to get up in the morning? Or the rich, smoky smell of a backyard barbecue, complete with steaks, ribs, and burgers?

Unfortunately, these foods are among the most toxic known. High-heat cooking (above 240°F) generates huge quantities of highly concentrated, DNA-ravaging carcinogens, while destroying essential nutrients and phytochemicals.

High heat applied to the fats in meats changes them into carcinogenic chemicals such as benzoapyrenes and other polynuclear aromatic hydrocarbons. Those browned and blackened surface residues you see are pure concentrated carcinogens. The fattier the meat and the higher the heat, the more toxins formed. That we humans are enticed by the flavor and aroma of these carcinogens seems a perverse twist of nature indeed.

In a similar way, the essential fatty acids in scorched oils are transformed into chemically similar but physically destructive "ugly fats," or *trans*-fats. The process brews up countless free radicals.

These various physiological insults won't kill you outright. But they do fracture DNA, stress the immune system, and accelerate aging.

Eating foods that have been burned is not a good idea for the same reasons that inhaling burned tobacco is not a good idea. Physiologically speaking, there is no real difference between smearing burned carcinogens onto the surface of your respiratory tract and smearing them onto the surface of your intestinal tract. Either will mutate local DNA before being absorbed into the bloodstream, distributed throughout the body, and finally passed by the excretory organs. In fact, regular consumption of fried and broiled foods can entail an intake of greater amounts of carcinogenic material than heavy cigarette smoking. Researchers have found the same kinds of highly carcinogenic substances in the urine of people who eat fried bacon and pork as in the urine of smokers.

Solving the life-shortening problems caused by high-heat cooking is simple enough.

- Avoid fried, browned, and burned foods. And if you do eat such foods, be sure to load up on antioxidant protection beforehand with supplements of vitamins C and E, coenzyme Q_{10}, N-acetylcysteine, and beta-carotene.

  Note: People who are taking blood thinners should consult their doctors before taking supplemental vitamin E.

- Cook at the lowest possible temperature. The safest temperature is at or below the boiling point of water. Acceptable cooking methods include boiling, microwaving, poaching, steaming, stewing, and low-heat baking (less than 240°F). Recipes that require baking at higher temperatures are acceptable as long as they don't call for large amounts of fat. Adding water to stir-fries keeps the heat down to a safe 212°F.

- Steer clear of high-heat cooking methods such as barbecuing, browning, burning, charcoal-broiling, charring, deep-frying, frying, grilling, smoking, and toasting. The longer the cooking and the higher the temperature, the more carcinogens formed and the more nutrients destroyed.

Should you toss out your toaster? No. Just turn the temperature way down and remove your toast before it begins to turn brown.

OTHER EDIBLE OFFENDERS

Other foods have carcinogenic properties as well. You can significantly reduce your chances of developing cancer by steering clear of the following.

Alcoholic beverages. All alcoholic beverages, including wine, beer, and hard liquor, weaken the immune system. Ethanol, the stuff that gives booze its punch, is a potent carcinogen. It has been directly linked to cancers of the mouth, pharynx, larynx, esophagus, breasts, stomach, pancreas, liver, colon, and rectum. Alcoholic beverages contain three other fairly nasty chemical carcinogens as well: acetaldehyde, nitrosamines, and urethanes.

Alcohol also irritates and inflames the lining of the digestive tract. This can lead to "leaky gut syndrome," in which large molecules of incompletely digested food seep through the weakened intestinal wall and directly into the bloodstream. The immune system identifies these food particles as foreign invaders and launches an attack on them.

The bottom line on booze: If you wish to live to a ripe old age, sip lightly. Or better yet, stay away altogether.

Caffeinated beverages. In varying degrees, all caffeinated beverages nudge cancer along. Coffee, made from roasted beans, contains scads of highly carcinogenic burned material. Drinking more than four cups of coffee a day is associated with an increased incidence of cancer. Cutting back presumably decreases cancer risk, but not as much as if you give up java for good.

What about decaffeinated coffee? It may contain residues of methylene chloride, a powerful carcinogen used to remove the caffeine from coffee. The Consumer Product Safety Commission has designated methylene chloride a hazardous chemical, deeming the cancer risk associated with the compound "among the highest ever calculated for chemicals from consumer products." If you drink decaf, make sure the caffeine has been removed using the chemical-free water process.

My suggestion: Switch to tea. Black tea has about half the caffeine and is not scorched. Caffeine-free herbal teas are even better. Black and green teas contain polyphenols, which protect against cancer. A former double-cappuccino addict, I still enjoy an occasional cup of coffee, but I have now become a red zinger aficionado.

Fish. Fish, especially shellfish, are frequently contaminated with carcinogens that they pick up from the water they live in. They should be avoided. (You'll read more about fish in chapter 16.)

Mushrooms. Certain mushrooms—most notably the common white variety sold in most supermarkets—contain an array of naturally occurring carcinogens and other toxins. Most notably, they're rich in hydrazines, powerful, naturally occurring compounds that—believe it or not—have been used as rocket fuel. These mushrooms should be omitted from any health-supporting diet.

On the other hand, oriental mushrooms such as enoki, oyster, shiitake, and tree ear are assets to an anti-cancer diet. They possess pro-immunity and antiviral properties and have been used to treat cancer, infections, and arthritis, lupus, and other autoimmune diseases.

Potatoes. An exceptional nutritionally complete food, the potato is a staple of any vegetarian diet. Note, however, that any bruises and eyes contain harmful chemicals. Remove these areas prior to cooking.

Processed meats. Nitrite, a potent carcinogen, is used as a preservative in bacon, beef jerky, hot dogs, lunchmeat, sausage, and other processed meat products. You should eliminate these foods anyway because they're so high in fat. If you have a hankering for a frank, try a tofu dog as a tasty, nitrite-free substitute.

Soft drinks. Many popular carbonated beverages contain ingredients that are associated with cancer: brominated oils, caffeine, caramel color, and phosphoric acid. Read labels and steer clear of products that list these substances as ingredients.

All sugar-sweetened beverages should be eliminated. Fruit juice–sweetened varieties are okay. Just make sure that they're made with real fruit juice—not with fructose or "from concentrate," a euphemism for fructose.

As an alternative to soft drinks, try fruit-flavored herbal iced tea. Or make your own "soda" by mixing one part seltzer water with one part organic juice. Some of my favorites are apple, apricot, berry, grape, grapefruit, guava, and strawberry.

Sugar. All excess sugar that you consume is transformed into saturated fat, which adds to your body's burden of carcinogens. Sugar contributes to cancer another way as well: It suppresses immune response by hampering antibody production, impairing lymphocyte effectiveness, and decreasing phagocytosis (the ability of white blood cells to engulf and kill cancer cells).

In one study, healthy volunteers consumed a variety of sugars, including fructose, glucose, honey, orange juice, and sucrose. The ability of their phagocytic cells to engulf bacteria (a measure of immune function) was significantly impaired for several hours afterward. Starches—corn, potatoes, and rice—did not have the same effect.

In another study, rats fed a high-sugar diet had a much higher rate of breast cancer than rats fed a starchy diet.

A CANCER-FREE FUTURE

By adhering to the dietary suggestions outlined above, you can dramatically reduce your risk of cancer. Admittedly, not all of these changes will come easily. But think of them this way: You're making a conscious decision to live healthfully and cancer-free. That's a whole lot better than having to choose between chemotherapy, radiation, or surgery sometime down the road.

As the misdirection and futility of an after-the-fact approach to cancer becomes increasingly evident, government-sponsored research efforts will shift their focus to prevention. More information will become available about specific cancer-fighting nutrients and food components.

Now that you know which foods can cause cancer, the next chapter profiles the foods (and supplements) that can prevent it. Your Anti-Aging Diet has to serve up hefty amounts of these cancer-fighters in order to be optimally protective.

CHAPTER 13

Fighting Cancer with Your Fork: The Cancer Prevention Diet

The preservation of health is a duty. Few seem conscious that there is such a thing as physical morality.
—HERBERT SPENCER (1820–1903), ENGLISH PHILOSOPHER

It should come as no surprise that the Cancer Prevention Diet and the Anti-Aging Diet are identical. Both emphasize the New Four Food Groups: grains, legumes, fruits, and vegetables. These plant-derived foods furnish copious quantities of cancer-fighting nutrients. Plus, both diets are fiber-rich, low-fat, and sugar-free, with most of their calories coming from unprocessed starchy foods such as beans, corn, pasta, potatoes, rice, squash, wheat, and whole oats.

As I explained in the previous chapter, some foods promote cancer while other foods prevent it. By embracing the former and avoiding the latter, as well as taking supplements, you can dramatically reduce your risk of cancer. And you have an abundance of incredibly delectable foods to choose from—foods that embellish your table while souping up your cancer defenses.

ATTACKING ON ALL FRONTS

Of the many thousands of chemical molecules in foods, certain ones go to bat for us against cancer. They include the essential nutrients (vitamins, minerals, essential fatty acids, and amino acids), plus a vast array of nonessential nutrients called phytochemicals. These anti-cancer compounds can be divided into three categories, based on where they interrupt the cancer formation process. Many belong to more than one group.

The Anti-Cancer Arsenal

Among the essential nutrients, the following stand out for their potent anti-cancer properties. Together with the plant-based compounds known as phytochemicals, these nutrients provide almost invincible cancer protection.

Vitamins	Selenium
Folic acid	Zinc
Vitamin A	
Vitamin B_6	**Amino Acids**
Vitamin C	Acetyl-L-carnitine
Vitamin E	N-acetylcysteine
Minerals	**Other**
Calcium	Coenzyme Q_{10}
Magnesium	Glutathione

The first group prevents the formation of carcinogens from precursor molecules. For example, vitamin C stops nitrates from becoming carcinogenic nitrosamines.

The second group, called blocking agents, stops carcinogens from getting to the target site where they would initiate cancer. These compounds activate enzymes that chew up carcinogens and spit them out in harmless pieces. Flavonoids, glutathione, indoles, phenols, terpenes, and thiols are examples of blocking agents.

The third group, suppressing agents, blocks the progression of a cancer after it has begun. Suppressing agents include retinoids (vitamin A and its derivatives), beta-carotene, protease inhibitors, selenium, calcium, flavonoids, plant sterols, and dehydroepiandrosterone (DHEA).

Despite the abundance of research demonstrating that

these and other plant-derived compounds certainly do protect against cancer, nutrition researchers are just now beginning to unlock the secrets of how they do it. Studies have shown that anti-cancer nutrients can do the following:

- Block metastasis-promoting enzymes produced by cancer cells (metastasis refers to the spread of cancer from one body part to another)
- Detoxify or inactivate carcinogenic molecules by scavenging free radicals and/or preventing oxidation
- Encourage DNA repair
- Inhibit tumor growth factors
- Interfere with the binding of carcinogens to cells
- Nourish the immune system, enhancing its anti-cancer surveillance function
- Provide mechanical protection for the body from exposure to carcinogens (for example, fiber sops up carcinogens like a sponge and removes them, preventing irritation of the intestinal wall and absorption)
- Strengthen natural barriers to carcinogens (for example, vitamin B_6 strengthens the mucous membranes)

PHYTOCHEMICALS: PLANT-BORNE PREVENTION

You won't find phytochemicals listed on food labels. Actually, that may be a good thing. With names like "anthocyanidins," "glucosinates," and "isoflavones," these compounds sound kind of scary. But as scientific research unfolds, hundreds of these naturally occurring nutrients are being shown to protect us not only from cancer but also from most of the other diseases associated with aging.

One reason scientists are so excited about phytochemicals is their apparent ability to stop a cell's conversion from healthy to cancerous. Although we still have a lot to learn about these compounds (like what all of them are and exactly how they work), the compelling fact remains that people who eat large quantities of fruits and vegetables experience tremendous reductions in cancer risk.

What is the difference between phytochemicals and other nutrients? From the dawn of the age of nutritional science (which I rather arbitrarily define as the turn of the twentieth century, when Casimir Funk discovered the first vitamin) through the 1980s, researchers made a clear distinction between essential nutrients and nonessential nutrients. We need essential nutrients to survive. We may get some health benefits from nonessential nutrients, but we can stay alive without them.

As researchers discovered more plant-derived compounds that straddled the two definitions, the essential/nonessential logic got more and more tortured. For example, some phytochemicals were classified as vitamins: Flavonoids were named vitamin P, while the glucosinolates and indoles in cabbage were dubbed vitamin U (because they cured ulcers). If a nutrient had no clearly defined deficiency syndrome associated with it, it lost its vitamin designation and was relegated to the lesser ranks of the nonessential.

Certain nutrients with a spectrum of molecular types—such as the tocopherols (vitamin E) and carotenoids—escaped this fate. They retained their essential status because one of their components appeared necessary for life. For example, of hundreds of carotenoids, beta-carotene—the one that most closely resembles vitamin A—was inappropriately singled out for special attention because it fit the model.

MEET THE CANCER "PHYTERS"

With the advent of the phytochemical revolution, the boundary lines between essential and nonessential nutrients have become forever blurred. Although phytochemicals do not have deficiency syndromes associated with them, they nevertheless are absolutely indispensable to slowing aging and preventing chronic degenerative diseases, of which cancer is the prototypical example.

Scientists now realize that foods contain a broad spectrum of nutrients, each of which makes a unique contribution to healing. Some are essential, others are not—unless you want to avoid cancer (or extend your life span), in which case they're all essential.

That said, let's take a closer look at some of the major categories of the known anti-cancer phytochemicals, in order of importance.

Phenols. The red, blue, and violet colors that you see in eggplant, grapes, raspberries, and strawberries are phenols.

These compounds protect the DNA in our cells from damage by carcinogens.

Phenolic compounds in the spice turmeric inhibit both cancer development and tumor promotion. Likewise, the catechins in green tea are tumor-inhibiting phenols.

Isoflavones. Tofu, tempeh, soy milk, and other soy products are rich in isoflavones, a subclass of phenols that can switch off the growth of cancer cells. The amazing soy isoflavone genistein has been found to suppress the growth of most types of cancer cells, including breast, lung, prostate, colon, skin, and leukemia. And by inhibiting angiogenesis (the growth of new capillaries in tumors), genistein blocks the progression of malignant tumors that have already formed. (The effectiveness of shark cartilage in treating cancer is likewise attributed to its antiangiogenesis effect.)

Thiols. Members of the *Allium* family (chives, leeks, garlic, onions, and shallots) and cruciferous vegetables (broccoli, cabbage, cauliflower, and turnips) contain thiols. This collection of sulfur-containing compounds possesses anticarcinogenic and antimutagenic properties. Thiols also inhibit tumor growth and bolster immune responsiveness.

Anthocyanidins. These compounds—a subgroup of flavonoids—serve as antioxidants, neutralizing free radicals and blocking cancer initiators and promoters. Anthocyanidins from pine bark and grape seeds are reputed to be the most effective naturally occurring free radical scavengers known. They can scarf up free radicals 50 times faster than vitamin E. Other food sources of anthocyanidins include apples, beans, blueberries, cranberries, grapes, peaches, plums, raspberries, rhubarb, and strawberries.

Glucosinolates. These phytochemical heavy-hitters, found in cruciferous vegetables such as broccoli, cabbage, and cauliflower, regulate and coordinate the activities of immune cells. Glucosinolates are transformed into other cancer-protective compounds—most notably sulforaphane, which blocks tumor-promoting enzymes.

Genistein and daidzein, another soy isoflavone, are powerful free radical squelchers. Studies have shown that regular soy-eaters are less likely to develop cancers of the breasts, lungs, stomach, uterus, prostate, colon, and rectum.

For these reasons, soy foods are staples for my family. By putting soy milk on our breakfast cereal, eating tempeh sandwiches and soy burgers for lunch, and scarfing delectable vegetable and tofu stir-fries for dinner, we're reaping the unparalleled health benefits of the magical soybean.

Terpenes. Widely dispersed throughout the plant kingdom, terpenes (of which the 600-plus member carotenoid family is just one example) are powerful antioxidant compounds. They protect against the free radical damage that initiates and promotes cancer. You'll find terpenes in grains, green vegetables, and soy.

THE TOP PHYTO FOODS

All plant-derived foods supply phytochemicals. But some foods have exceptionally high concentrations of these anti-cancer compounds. The following figure prominently in the Cancer Prevention Diet. They're listed in order of importance.

Garlic

Garlic's health-giving properties are unsurpassed by any other single food. So step aside, broccoli, carrots, soybeans, and tomatoes: You're special indeed, but the "stinking rose" is not only a food but also a potent natural medicine. Garlic helps prevent cancer, strengthens the cardiovascular system, supports the immune system, and is a powerful natural antibiotic.

Garlic contains a veritable arsenal of potent sulfur compounds that scavenge free radicals, increase the enzymes that break down carcinogens, and provide extra pizzazz to cancer-fighting immune cells. One of these compounds, diallyl disulfide, is among the most potent tumor growth suppressors known. (Chives, leeks, onions, scallions, and shallots contain similar but less potent versions of garlic's anti-cancer constituents.)

Make garlic a daily ritual. Eat it raw, steamed, or microwaved. Use it to spiff up almost any dish containing vegetables or beans. Chop it or mince it, then toss it into salads and stir-fries.

You needn't be put off by garlic's pungency or the hassle of removing its outer skin. I've discovered that popping a few unshelled cloves (or an entire flower) into the microwave for 5 to 10 seconds per clove solves both problems: The garlic easily slides out of the shell, and it tastes milder. My eight-year-old daughter won't touch the raw herb, but she really likes it this way—and she has had fewer winter colds since she started eating it.

If you really don't like the odor or the taste of garlic, you can opt for enteric-coated capsules instead. For more information about garlic, including dosage recommendations, refer to chapter 28.

Cruciferous Vegetables

Almost all vegetables have anti-cancer effects. But the crucifers, having repeatedly proven their powerful cancer-fighting properties, are simply the best. The most familiar members of the crucifer family are broccoli, brussels sprouts, cabbage, and cauliflower. Lesser known but equally important are bok choy, Chinese cabbage, collards, kale, kohlrabi, mustard greens, rutabaga, turnip greens, turnips, and watercress.

So called because their flowers are shaped like crosses, the cruciferous vegetables contain loads of vitamins A and C, beta-carotene, and fiber. They're also rich in indoles, isothiocyanates, and sulforaphane, all powerful cancer-blocking phytochemicals.

Although their mechanisms remain something of a mystery, these compounds apparently employ several means of thwarting tumor growth. In mice experiments, indoles blocked the growth of experimentally induced cancers of the lungs and stomach. Numerous other research studies have convincingly demonstrated the cancer-preventive properties of the crucifer family.

The most potent crucifer is broccoli, the florets of which are concentrated sources of the anti-cancer compound sulforaphane. Sulforaphane is sensitive to heat: Microwaving removes about half of the phytochemical from the vegetable; boiling or steaming removes even more. Frozen broccoli has no sulforaphane at all. Your best bet is to eat your broccoli raw.

As for the other crucifers, you can steam or microwave them. Serve them with rice or beans or all by themselves.

Soy Foods

The soybean, a staple in Asian countries, was discovered in the West only around the turn of the twentieth century. Soy is the only bean—and the only plant-derived food—that sports a complete protein.

Soy foods offer what is arguably the most powerful cancer protection available. This legume contains several categories of anti-cancer compounds, including isoflavones, phytates, and protease inhibitors.

The isoflavones, of which genistein is the best known, can prevent just about every kind of cancer. Even more amazing, they can actually instruct cancer cells to return to normal.

Another group of isoflavones, the phytoestrogens, block estrogen receptor sites on cells. This prevents cancer-causing hormones from "docking" on the cells, where they do their dirty work.

Soybeans, soybean oil, and tofu are also excellent sources of the immune-enhancing, cancer-preventing omega-3 and omega-6 essential fatty acids.

All of this information suggests that hefty servings of soy should be incorporated into any cancer treatment program. Though soy conjures up images of tofu in most people's minds, this very old bean takes literally dozens of forms. There are so many interesting soybean products on health food store shelves these days that it's fairly easy to include soy in your daily diet. Tofu burgers, tofu hot dogs, and tofu enchiladas and tamales come frozen, so they're perfect for quick microwavable meals. And don't forget soy cheese, soy milk, and soy nuts.

Then, of course, there's just plain tofu, whose healthfulness is matched by its versatility. Use it straight out of the carton or marinate it in soy sauce with ginger and/or garlic. Toss it into salads, stir-fries, and soups. Steam it with vegetables. Put it in sandwiches. The possibilities are endless.

Other ways to experience the bountiful health benefits of soy are via tempeh, miso, tamari, and even whole soybeans, which can be cooked into soups and casseroles.

Like their soybean brethren, chickpeas and lima beans contain cancer-preventive isoflavones, phytates, and protease inhibitors. You can buy them dry, but canned versions cook up faster and easier. Mix them with kidney beans and green beans for a bean salad. Or make hummus, a chickpea spread that's delicious as a sandwich filling or with just about any vegetable in a pita pocket. Spread hummus on a warm whole-wheat tortilla, add some diced vegetables (such as broccoli, lettuce, and tomatoes), roll it up, and voilà—you have a quick, nutritious meal.

An Anti-Cancer Cornucopia

On your next visit to the supermarket or health food store, be sure to stock up on the following foods—the staples of the Cancer Prevention Diet. They supply a healthy mix of nutrients for broad-spectrum cancer protection.

- Apples
- Bok choy
- Broccoli
- Brussels sprouts
- Cabbage
- Carrots
- Cauliflower
- Chinese cabbage
- Collards
- Eggplant
- Flaxseed and flaxseed oil
- Garlic
- Kale

- Kohlrabi
- Lettuce
- Mint leaves
- Mustard greens
- Pineapple
- Rutabaga
- Shallots
- Soybeans
- Spinach
- Turnip greens
- Turnips
- Watercress
- Wheat sprouts

Apples

Corny as it may seem, an apple a day really does keep the doctor away. Or, to modernize this old saw, an apple a day keeps the oncologist away.

Apples contain an abundance of anti-cancer phytochemicals: anthocyanidins, biflavans, catechins, flavanones, flavones, and flavonols (including quercetin). They also contain hefty doses of pectin and other fibers, which are cancer-preventive as well.

I am a doctor who eats an apple almost every day. I live in Sonoma County, California, near Gravenstein (as in

Gravenstein apple) Highway, where apples have been a way of farming life for many years. Many of my neighbors are apple farmers, and every spring we attend the local Apple Blossom Festival.

Besides eating fresh whole apples, I snack on applesauce. I sometimes pour apple juice on my cereal, as an alternative to soy milk and rice milk. Two of my favorite desserts are Sebastopol Apple Crisp and Cinnamon-Baked Apples (see the recipes on pages 587 and 590).

Tomatoes

Of the more than 700 carotenoids found in fruits and vegetables, the three most abundant in the human body are alpha-carotene, beta-carotene, and lycopene. Though all three are powerful free radical scavengers, lycopene weighs in as one of the most important anti-cancer phytochemicals. It's twice as effective as beta-carotene at neutralizing singlet oxygen, the nastiest cancer-causing free radical around.

Lycopene is the pigment that makes tomatoes and watermelon red and pink grapefruit pink. It is also found in small amounts in apricots and guava. In fact, relatively few plant species contain significant quantities of this powerful anti-cancer nutritional weapon. Tomatoes are the best source because they have by far the highest concentrations and are the most consistently available.

First harvested in the Andes by the Incas, tomatoes now come in more than 2,000 varieties. You have to wonder whether the French, in dubbing tomatoes *pommes d'amours* ("love apples"), had any inkling of the fact that the highest lycopene concentrations in the human body are found in the male prostate gland. Indeed, lycopene provides powerful protection against prostate cancer. (Men over age 50, who face a 30 percent chance of developing prostate cancer, would do well to include a tomato or two in their daily diets.)

A test called an antioxidant profile assesses blood levels of lycopene as well as the other main antioxidant nutrients (vitamin C, vitamin E, coenzyme Q_{10}, alpha-carotene, and beta-carotene). The results of the test indicate how well your antioxidant defenses are protecting you against free radicals. This, in turn, serves as an important measure of your rate of aging. (For more information about the antioxidant profile, see chapter 12.)

A big bonus with lycopene is that it is relatively heat-stable. Whereas most other phytochemicals (such as the sulforaphane in broccoli) must be consumed with as little cooking as possible, lycopene stands up well to heat. So you can enjoy tomato sauce and paste in pastas, casseroles, soups, stews, and even pizza.

The wisdom of increasing tomato consumption as an anti-cancer strategy is reinforced by numerous studies showing that people who eat lots of tomatoes have half the cancer risk of people who don't.

PROTECTION YOU CAN'T LIVE WITHOUT

Beyond the phytochemicals, other nutrients figure prominently in the Cancer Prevention Diet. You'll want to make sure that you're getting optimum amounts of the following vitamins and minerals from foods as well as supplements.

Vitamin A and Beta-Carotene

Vitamin A and beta-carotene are the best known and most important members of the retinoid family. The retinoids—active forms of vitamin A—were the first nutrients to cause a stir of excitement among cancer researchers. They protect against most cancers, including the most common ones: breast, prostate, colon, rectum, skin, bladder, larynx, and esophagus. The carotenoids are especially potent protectors against lung, stomach, and cervical cancers.

Retinoids appear to have the ability not only to slow the growth of existing tumors but also to reverse cancer in its early stages. Coupled with vitamins C and E, their synergistic free radical–scavenging buddies, carotenoids can trap and destroy cancer-causing chemicals with extreme efficiency.

Study after study has corroborated beyond any doubt the link between low carotenoid levels and high cancer rates. Researchers examining populations of people with low intakes and low blood levels of vitamin A and beta-carotene found dramatically high cancer rates. Likewise, depriving laboratory animals of these nutrients drives up their cancer rates.

Fortunately, carotenoids are widespread within the plant world, where they protect plants' delicate tissues from free radical damage from the sun's rays. Some of the beta-carotene in the plant-derived foods that you consume is transformed into retinol, or vitamin A—the form we humans need. A beta-carotene molecule looks like two vitamin A molecules stuck together. Your body cleaves the bond, converting the beta-carotene (also known as pro-vitamin A) into vitamin A. Your body, in its wisdom, knows exactly how much vitamin A you need. It makes that amount and no more. The remaining beta-carotene is added to the body's roving pool of antioxidant phytochemicals.

The health of your immune system depends on adequate supplies of vitamin A and the other retinoids. How does vitamin A boost immune function? As a free radical scavenger par excellence, it neutralizes carcinogenic chemicals before they can do harm. Both vitamin A and beta-carotene help keep the antibody levels and T lymphocyte count high. This is crucial because antibodies deactivate carcinogens and T lymphocytes kill cancer cells as they are formed.

Vitamin A is also essential for the proper growth and health of all of the body's epithelial tissues—its skin and organ linings. Most cancers begin in these structures. With chronic exposure to carcinogens and underprotection by antioxidants, they're exceptionally vulnerable to damage.

As mentioned above, any beta-carotene left over after the body's vitamin A requirements are met is absorbed unchanged into the bloodstream. There, the molecules circulate throughout the body like millions of miniature *Star Wars* weapons, seeking out and neutralizing free radicals by the trillions. Beta-carotene is extremely proficient at this, squelching even the nastiest species of radicals (singlet oxygen) with ease.

Considering the overwhelming amount of published, peer-reviewed scientific evidence in support of carotenoids—not to mention the nutrients' total safety—you'd think that supplementation would be officially recommended. But it isn't.

Vitamin A and beta-carotene have similar but not identical effects in the body, so both are necessary. Unfortunately, the best food sources of vitamin A—red meats, liver, poultry, fish, and milk—are at cross-purposes with cancer prevention. (All are high in fat and protein, low in fiber.) Therefore, I recommend taking a relatively small amount (5,000 to 10,000 international units) of supplemental vitamin A per day, coupled with beta-carotene and mixed carotenoids. Again, your body can use the beta-carotene to make extra vitamin A, if it needs to. At doses above 50,000 international units per day, vitamin A can cause reversible toxicity in some people. So always keep your daily dose well below that number.

Your Best Betas

Beta-carotene is a potent free radical scavenger. Once inside your body, it's converted to vitamin A, a powerful immune system protector. Together, these nutrients deliver a one-two punch against carcinogens. To maximize your beta-carotene (and vitamin A) intake, pile your plate with the following foods.

- Apricots
- Asparagus
- Broccoli
- Cantaloupes
- Carrots
- Chard
- Cherries
- Collard greens
- Dandelion greens
- Endive
- Kale
- Mangoes
- Mustard greens
- Papayas
- Parsley
- Peaches
- Persimmons
- Prunes
- Pumpkins
- Romaine lettuce
- Soybeans
- Spinach
- Sweet potatoes
- Sweet red peppers
- Tomatoes
- Turnip greens
- Turnips
- Watercress
- Winter squash
- Yams

As for beta-carotene, green and yellow vegetables—leafy greens, carrots, and sweet potatoes—are top-notch food sources. But because dietary shortfalls of the nutrient are common, you should consider supplementation, too. Beta-carotene supplements are quite safe and extremely well-tolerated, even in very high dosages.

For more than 10 years, I took 100,000 international

units of beta-carotene every day. With recent research
highlighting the added benefits of a spectrum of antioxidants, specifically carotenoids, I still take 50,000 international units of beta-carotene and 10,000 international units
of vitamin A every day. I also eat a salad made with leafy
greens, carrots, and tomatoes.

B-Complex Vitamins

All of the B-complex vitamins—including thiamin, riboflavin,
niacin, folic acid, pantothenic acid, B_6, and B_{12}—play major
roles in keeping the immune system strong and healthy. Most
of the research to date has focused on B_6 and folic acid.

Vitamin B_6, found in apples, bananas, beans, carrots,
grains, leafy greens, and sweet potatoes, plays a vital role in
maintaining optimum immunity. A B_6 deficiency creates a
predisposition to cancer by crippling both arms of the
immune system: the humoral (B lymphocytes, which make
antibodies) and the cell-mediated (T lymphocytes, which
round up and destroy cancer cells).

B_6 also helps maintain immune health by strengthening
the mucous membranes that line the respiratory and gastrointestinal tracts. Bolstering the integrity of these natural
barriers between us and the carcinogens in the outside
world pays huge immune dividends.

Vitamin B_6 appears to be especially proficient at protecting against, and even reversing, cervical cancer. To reap
the nutrient's anti-cancer benefits, you need between 25
and 250 milligrams a day.

Folic acid, another B-complex vitamin, is involved in
cell division and maturation as well as the synthesis of
RNA and DNA. A folic acid deficiency can cause cervical
dysplasia (an early sign of cervical cancer) in women. In
studies, supplements of 10 milligrams daily caused abnormal cervical cells to stop spreading and, in some women,
even return to normal.

Folic acid is found in citrus fruits, dark leafy greens,
spinach, broccoli, brussels sprouts, alfalfa, soybeans, chickpeas, lentils, wheat, oats, barley, brown rice, and walnuts.
Aim for 800 to 2,000 micrograms a day.

Vitamin C

Vitamin C works on several levels to prevent and even
help cure cancer. Dozens of studies have documented the

connection between increased consumption of vitamin C and reduced risk of most cancers, including those of the mouth, esophagus, larynx, lung, stomach, pancreas, rectum, breast, cervix, and skin.

C for Yourself

Few other nutrients can match vitamin C for its versatility in the fight against cancer. It labors on all fronts, neutralizing free radicals and stimulating immunity. You can boost your vitamin C intake with the following fruits and vegetables.

- Broccoli
- Brussels sprouts
- Cantaloupes
- Collards
- Grapefruit
- Honeydew melons
- Kale
- Oranges
- Strawberries
- Turnip greens

Many researchers have studied vitamin C's potent anticancer effect. Perhaps the best known among them is two-time Nobel laureate Linus Pauling, Ph.D. His 1979 book *Cancer and Vitamin C* focused on the nutrient's therapeutic and preventive properties.

Vitamin C fends off cancer through several different mechanisms. First, the vitamin is a top-notch antioxidant. It neutralizes a broad range of carcinogens, including nitrites and nitrosamines, hydrocarbons, pesticides, industrial chemicals, and air pollutants.

Second, vitamin C strengthens the "intercellular cement"—the network of collagen and fiber that literally glues cells together. In fact, the body uses vitamin C to manufacture collagen, which protects the body from cancer by walling it off.

Third, vitamin C helps prevent cancer from spreading by neutralizing hyaluronidase, an enzyme made by cancer cells to help them metastasize.

Fourth, vitamin C improves immune system functioning by enhancing T lymphocytes, the immune cells that kill cancer cells. A strong immune system is one of your best defenses against cancer.

To do all this, vitamin C is necessary in larger doses than are available from diet alone. I recommend supplements— 675 to 3,000 milligrams daily in the form of ester-C.

Vitamin E

Also known as tocopherol, vitamin E is a potent antioxidant that helps prevent cancer by blocking lipid peroxidation, the oxidation of polyunsaturated fats into free radicals. Lipid peroxidation is potentially important in all cancers but is especially significant as a cause of breast and colon cancers.

Vitamin E also serves a crucial role in immune system function. A low level of the vitamin leads to impaired antibody production, inability to manufacture T and B lymphocytes, and reduced resistance to cancer and infection.

Vitamin E works synergistically with vitamins A and C and the mineral selenium, with which it has a special affinity. Selenium and vitamin E combined constitute a one-two punch against cancer. Since it is not possible to obtain optimally protective quantities of E from diet alone, I recommend supplements of 400 to 1,600 international units daily.

Note: People who are taking blood thinners should consult their doctors before taking supplemental vitamin E.

Selenium

Selenium is an essential trace mineral that plays an invaluable role in cancer prevention. Dietary selenium deficiency has been shown to increase cancer risk. Blood levels of the mineral are much lower in people with cancer than in healthy people.

Studies correlating low selenium intake with cancer abound. People who eat crops grown in selenium-deficient soil have higher cancer rates. Rapid City, North Dakota, for example, enjoys the lowest incidence of cancer among U.S. cities. Its residents also sport the highest blood selenium levels. At the other end of the spectrum, Lima, Ohio, has double Rapid City's cancer rate. Its citizens have only 60 percent as much selenium coursing through their veins.

In a survey of 27 countries, death rates for the most common cancers (those of the breasts, ovaries, prostate, colon, and rectum, and leukemia) were inversely proportional to dietary selenium intake. In other words, the lower the selenium intake, the higher the cancer death rate, and vice versa.

A close examination of selenium's properties reveals quite a few reasons for the mineral's cancer-preventive powers. For starters, selenium is an essential component of glutathione peroxidase, a very important cancer-fighting enzyme. What's more, selenium maximizes the effects of vitamin E, an antioxidant that, as we have discussed, has anti-cancer properties of its own.

Selenium protects us from the poisonous effects of a variety of pollutants, including the heavy metals arsenic, cadmium, and mercury. It detoxifies environmental mutagens and carcinogens, defends against free radicals and radiation, protects the liver, and supports fat metabolism. It defuses cancer-causing chemicals such as naturally occurring carcinogens, pesticides, and toxins concentrated in fat tissues.

Obtaining an optimum amount of selenium from diet alone is difficult, if not impossible. You'd have to eat 20 ounces of fish, the best source of the mineral, every day to get enough. Supplements are preferable anyway, because all of that fish would put you at very high risk for an excessive intake of saturated fat, microorganism contamination, mercury poisoning, and other chemical toxicity. My advice: Take 100 to 300 micrograms of selenium per day in supplement form.

OPTIMUM ANTI-CANCER NUTRITION

While the nutrients profiled above may be anti-cancer superstars, many more play indispensable supporting roles. These include the minerals calcium and zinc, the amino acids cysteine and methionine, and the essential fatty acids. Though technically not a nutrient, fiber helps rid your body of carcinogens before they do harm.

Providing your cells with optimum amounts of all of these substances will maximize your protection against cancer. But you can't get optimum amounts from diet alone—even the highly healthful Anti-Aging Diet. Eating enough foods to supply enough of even one nutrient would entail a huge caloric consumption. To get just 1,000 milligrams of vitamin C, for instance, you'd have to eat a bushel of oranges—the equivalent of a five-day supply of calories.

I discuss supplementation in a lot more depth in parts 3 and 4 of this book. For now, simply remember that foods and supplements must be equal partners in your personal anti-cancer, anti-aging program.

The Anti-Cancer Stir-Fry

Makes 4 servings

Here's an easy-to-make dish with dynamite flavor. Its ingredients give it a powerful anti-cancer punch.

1 teaspoon soy oil
1 clove garlic, sliced
¼ cup water
1 pound tofu, diced into ½-inch cubes
2 cups mixed vegetables (such as bok choy, broccoli, cabbage, and cauliflower)
1 teaspoon soy sauce or tamari
    Curry and ginger (optional)

Coat the surface of a large skillet with the oil and warm over high heat. Sauté the garlic in about 2 tablespoons of the water until soft. Add the tofu, mixed vegetables, and soy sauce or tamari. Cover and cook, stirring occasionally, for 5 minutes, or until crisp-tender. Add the remaining 2 tablespoons water, if necessary, to keep the vegetables from sticking. Add the curry or ginger (if using). Serve over steamed brown rice.

Per serving: 186 calories, 11.1 g. fat, 19.1 g. protein, 7.3 g. carbohydrates, 2.5 g. fiber, 0 mg. cholesterol, 111 mg. sodium

---

WHAT'S IN, WHAT'S OUT

No single food contains all (or even a small fraction) of the anti-cancer nutrients. In order to reap the health benefits of this vast nutritional treasure trove, you must vary your food choices. Diversity is the cornerstone of both the Cancer Prevention Diet and the Anti-Aging Diet.

To reduce your exposure to carcinogenic pesticides and other chemical additives, choose organically grown foods whenever possible. Recent studies have shown that these foods are best not only because they have no carcinogens but also because they contain significantly higher levels of cancer-preventive nutrients than conventionally grown foods.

The Cancer Prevention Diet excludes all of the foods, chemicals, and additives known to foster malignancies. In particular, it contains no foods of animal origin. These foods supply no phytochemicals or other anti-cancer nutrients, and they displace the foods that do. They pack a hefty dose of carcinogens to boot.

FOOD FOR THOUGHT

To help you capitalize on the anti-cancer nutrients while steering clear of the dietary undesirables, I've developed the following short list of food substitutions and suggestions. For more ideas, refer to the menu plan and recipes beginning on page 535.

• Shop for meat substitutes. Health food stores carry a great selection these days. Vegetarian burgers and soy burgers replace hamburgers. Tofu dogs fill in for one of the scariest foods of all: the hot dog. Seitan, also known as meatless meat, is made from wheat gluten. Because it has the texture of chicken or beef, it makes a healthy stand-in for these carcinogenic foods. You'll also find soy bacon, soy sausage, and even soy chili as well as frozen low-fat meatless tostadas, burritos, and tamales.

• Use soy milk, rice milk, or almond milk as a substitute for cow's milk on cereals and as a beverage.

• For breakfast, make scrambled tofu instead of scrambled eggs.

• Try this delicious cancer-fighting pizza: Spread a whole-wheat crust with tomato sauce (which supplies lycopene). Sprinkle with a small amount of soy cheese (genistein). Then add generous amounts of any of the following toppings: diced tomatoes (more lycopene), tofu (genistein), spinach (folic acid, vitamin A, lutein), parboiled broccoli (sulforaphane), green peppers (vitamin C), onions (diallyl disulfide), mushrooms (lentinan), and even pineapple (manganese).

- In a blender, mix 10 ounces of soft tofu, 10 ounces of berries (fresh or frozen), and one ripe banana for an anticancer berry-banana shake.

- Choose Chinese, Indian, Mexican, and Middle Eastern cuisines when eating out. Be sure to tell your server— or, better yet, the chef—that you're a vegetarian and to please go easy on the oil.

If you're like a lot of people, you may have already reduced your consumption of red meat because of its high fat content. That's good. Because as the next chapter explains, red meat and Renewal don't mix.

Risky Red Meat: Big Beef on the Run

If I had to tell people just one thing to lower their risk of heart disease, it would be to reduce their intake of foods of animal origin, specifically animal fat, and to replace those fats with complex carbohydrates—grains, fruits, and vegetables.
—ERNST SCHAEFER, M.D., JEAN MAYER USDA
   HUMAN NUTRITION RESEARCH CENTER ON
   AGING, TUFTS UNIVERSITY IN BOSTON

If you want to foster Renewal and achieve maximum life span, you may have to change your attitude toward meat. But maybe not for the reasons you'd expect.

True, meat has way too much fat (particularly saturated fat) and cholesterol, which is enough to earn it a dishonorable discharge from the Anti-Aging Diet. But it also harbors antibiotics, hormones, pesticides, preservatives, and coloring agents—toxins that sabotage cells, poison the immune system, and otherwise thwart Renewal.

Technology deserves at least part of the blame for meat's nutritional pitfalls. The days when cattle wandered open fields, grazing on natural grasses and grains, have all but vanished. Instead, the animals are raised on so-called factory farms—bred and fed for the express purpose of winding up on someone's dinner plate. Under such conditions, the meat does get to market more quickly. But both the animals that provide it and the humans who eat it pay a tremendous price in terms of their health.

NOT YOUR GRANDFATHER'S FARM

Many modern farms rely on so-called high-efficiency confinement systems, which house animals in close quarters, then deliver their food and remove their waste with minimal human effort. Such systems are intended to make raising cattle cheaper and more efficient. Indeed, by confining and feeding the animals rather than allowing them to roam and graze, farmers can use valuable pastures to plant and harvest crops.

Even livestock feed has been "engineered" to cut costs and make animals fatter faster. Among its more creative ingredients: waste paper, paper grocery bags, old phone books, newspapers, computer paper, corrugated cardboard, and plastic hay (a kind of artificial roughage). The obvious problem is that this stuff is nutritionally vacant garbage. Beyond that, inks on the recycled paper materials contain cancer-causing polychlorinated biphenyls and other petroleum-based compounds, which cannot be separated out. These toxins are stored in the animal's fatty tissues, and when you eat the meat, they get passed along to you.

If that doesn't spoil your appetite, perhaps this will: Some livestock feed contains poultry litter, a bizarre combination of manure, feathers, and old hen-house bedding that's glued together with molasses and grain. According to the manufacturer, "Cows love it." Of course, the cows may be enticed by the artificial flavors and aromas that are often added.

ANTIBIOTICS: ARTIFICIAL HEALTH

For the farmer, confining cattle and controlling their feed has definite financial advantages. But it also creates problems. Most notably, the combination of overcrowding, poor nutrition, and lack of exercise encourages the spread of disease among the animals.

These days, antibiotics are used to keep herds—and profits—healthy. In fact, more than 5,000 tons of antibiotics, fully half of the amount manufactured in the United States, are added to livestock feed each year. More than 70 percent of beef cattle and beef calves receive daily doses of the drugs over the course of their lifetimes.

Malevolent Medicine

The often-excessive use of antibiotics in cattle-raising has serious consequences for human health. Among the side effects that people may experience:

- The appearance of antibiotic-resistant strains of bacteria
- Reduced effectiveness of antibiotics in treating infections
- Increased risk of epidemics caused by antibiotic-resistant microorganisms
- Lower levels of beneficial intestinal bacteria, which increase susceptibility to intestinal infections (such as acute gastroenteritis with fever, pain, and diarrhea)
- A weakened immune system, which reduces resistance to infections and increases allergic reactions

The antibiotics given to animals are identical to the antibiotics given to humans. Still, farmers don't need prescriptions to get them. While many farmers scrupulously adhere to the recommended dosage levels and withdrawal times (they're required to discontinue antibiotic use a certain number of days before taking their livestock to market), others overdose their cattle in an attempt to compensate for the unhealthful conditions created by overcrowding, filth, poorly heated and poorly lit barns, and lack of fresh air and activity. Sick animals may be given even larger doses of antibiotics and perhaps illegal drugs in a desperate attempt to keep them alive for delivery to the slaughterhouse.

BEEFED-UP PRODUCTION

Fighting disease isn't the only reason for using antibiotics. In 1949, Thomas Jukes, then the director of nutrition and physiology research for the pharmaceutical company Lederle Laboratories, made a discovery that would change the meat industry forever. He found that all farm animals, including cows, grew much faster when they ate antibiotic-laced feed.

Folks in the meat industry picked up on the financial significance of Jukes's discovery almost immediately. With antibiotics, they could get meat to market quickly. The drugs would not only keep the cattle disease-free but also have them ready for slaughter in a relatively short amount of time. As a result, farmers could raise more cattle and earn more money.

Many scientists feared that such widespread use of antibiotics would have a tremendous biological impact down the road. They speculated that bacteria would develop immunity to antibiotics, rendering the drugs useless.

Of course, time has proven the scientists right. You've probably heard news reports about the emergence of "superbugs"—antibiotic-resistant strains of bacteria. Should one of these superbugs find its way into your body, the resulting infection can be very difficult to treat.

When you eat meat that contains antibiotics, you're dosing yourself with the drugs. This reduces the effectiveness of antibiotics in general.

Because of the frightening rise in antibiotic-resistant bacteria and the rapid decline in antibiotic effectiveness, the countries of the European Economic Community—including France, Germany, Greece, Italy, Spain, and the United Kingdom—have agreed to ban the routine use of antibiotics in livestock feed. Will similar action be taken in the United States? Probably not, if the powerful pharmaceutical- and meat-industry lobbies have their way.

STEROIDS: CATTLE ON THE FAST TRACK

In addition to antibiotics, meat often contains an array of natural and synthetic hormones. These compounds, which have received the Food and Drug Administration's stamp of approval, are given to cattle and other livestock to make them grow faster. For example, diethylstilbestrol (DES), a sex steroid hormone banned from use in humans, reportedly produces a 15 to 19 percent increase in weight (mostly fat) and a 7 to 10 percent improvement in feed efficiency (that is, weight gained per pound of feed) in beef cattle. These figures translate to more money for farmers, as they're spending less to fatten up the animals over a shorter amount of time.

When we eat meat that contains hormone residues, we upset the delicate balance within our endocrine systems. The endocrine system produces its own hormones to regulate numerous bodily functions, including metabolic rate, sexual and reproductive activity, growth, and even mood. When the system is out of kilter, it opens the door to disease.

Even seemingly minuscule amounts of the hormones fed to cattle can upset the human endocrine system. Consider that these compounds produce measurable effects on living cells when present in parts per trillion. That's like one grain in a ton of sand or one drop in 7,000 gallons of water.

Scientists and government officials now acknowledge that any amount of hormone over and above what is normally present in a healthy person has the potential to cause cancer and other serious health problems. In women, for example, elevated levels of the hormone estrogen have been linked to cancers of the breasts, ovaries, cervix, and endometrium (the lining of the uterus). They've also been implicated in high blood pressure, heart attack, and stroke.

THE DES DEBACLE

Despite their proven health risks to humans, hormones are still being given to livestock. As is so often the case, a public health crisis may be necessary before any substantive action is taken to ban these compounds.

An incident involving the sex steroid hormone DES illustrates this point perfectly. In 1966, Arthur L. Herbst, M.D., then a gynecologist at Massachusetts General Hospital in Boston, discovered a very rare cancerous tumor in the vagina of a 15-year-old girl. This particular type of cancer, called clear cell adenocarcinoma, has a 50 percent mortality rate. Over the next three years, six more cases turned up—all in girls of about the same age.

Dr. Herbst and his colleagues determined that the mothers of all but one of the girls had been taking DES while pregnant to prevent miscarriage. Subsequent investigation revealed that other sex steroid hormones were causing the same problem. By 1980, the doctors had identified 429 cases of clear cell adenocarcinoma. In 243 cases, the patients' mothers had received DES during pregnancy. In another 57 cases, the patients' mothers had taken some other form of hormone therapy.

Despite mounting evidence implicating DES and other sex steroid hormones in the development of cancer, DES remained a staple ingredient in livestock feed. In fact, prior to 1979, the hormone was being consumed by 85 percent of all livestock in the United States. That year, the Food and Drug Administration finally outlawed the use of DES in feed. But the hormone was never recalled, so farmers continued to use the remaining supply. Few were penalized for violating the ban—a clear message that the government wasn't taking it all that seriously.

As the general public caught wind of the effects of DES, farmers gradually switched to other hormones. Unfortunately, the alternative compounds caused similar problems, including imbalance of the endocrine system and increased risk of cancer.

Treating animals with hormones remains a widely accepted practice within the U.S. meat industry. Hormone pellets are routinely implanted in virtually all cattle, their cost offset by the increase in pounds of beef produced. Still, no one can say for certain that we won't have another hormone-induced public health disaster 20 to 30 years down the road.

Why hasn't the federal government taken a more aggressive stand against the widespread use of sex steroid hormones? The answer involves a dangerous combination of bureaucratic red tape, powerful pharmaceutical- and meat-industry lobbies, and an uninformed public.

Perhaps we could learn a lesson from the countries of the European Economic Community, which prohibit the use of all sex steroid hormones in meat production. These countries recognize their obligation to protect the public food supply. The United States needs to do the same—or risk the proliferation of hormone-related illness in the general population as well as tens of thousands of hormone-related cancer deaths each year.

INEFFECTIVE INSPECTION

The U.S. Department of Agriculture (USDA) does administer an inspection program that—ostensibly, at least—safeguards consumers against drug-tainted meat.

But an inspector's stamp of approval (which, incidentally, was a toxic blue dye until a few years ago) doesn't mean that a particular carcass is absolutely, 100 percent antibiotic- and hormone-free. Remember, both antibiotics and hormones are perfectly legal for use in raising cattle. The inspector simply checks to make sure that residues of these substances are within USDA limits.

The inspection program has its problems. For starters, staffing is woefully inadequate: One inspector per large plant is the norm. Suppose a plant processes 500 head of cattle per hour. To keep pace, the inspector can devote only about seven seconds to each carcass. It's not humanly possible to perform adequate testing in that amount of time.

For this reason, only about 1 percent of all carcasses undergo testing for excessive antibiotic and hormone residues. Of course, by the time the tests are sent to a laboratory, analyzed, and returned to the inspector, the carcass is long gone—processed, packed, and perhaps even eaten. A questionable carcass may be impounded, but trying to trace it back to a particular herd or farmer is virtually impossible.

Then, too, concerns have been raised about the objectivity of the inspection process. While inspectors are USDA employees, they work side-by-side with slaughterhouse and packing-house employees. Critics contend that this arrangement compromises an inspector's ability to make decisions that could have a negative impact on his "co-workers." Rejecting the number of carcasses required to truly protect public health and safety would adversely affect the economic status of the plant as a whole.

In fact, inspectors reject only 0.5 percent of beef carcasses each year. If inadequacies in the inspection process were addressed, that number would likely rise much higher—say, 10 to 15 percent.

Until this happens, consumers have no guarantee that the meat they're eating is truly safe. It's like playing Russian roulette each time you step up to the supermarket meat display: You have no way of knowing how much antibiotic or hormone a particular cut contains.

ALL THAT, PLUS FAT

With all this talk about antibiotics and hormones, we must not overlook the fact that most meat supplies a mother lode of saturated fat and cholesterol. Both substances have been identified as causes of atherosclerosis (hardening and clogging of the arteries), heart attack, high blood pressure, cancer, and other life-shortening degenerative diseases.

Remember, only foods of animal origin contain cholesterol. Foods of plant origin do not. So a person who eschews all meats and dairy products and instead builds his meals around grains, legumes, fruits, and vegetables effectively eliminates cholesterol from his diet.

Scholarly studies have shown that this eating style, called veganism, can dramatically reduce your risk of developing the sorts of diseases described above. It can also improve your odds for living a long, healthy life. I've used veganism as the basis for my Anti-Aging Diet for these and many other reasons.

CHANGING YOUR MEAT-EATING WAYS

Going meatless has definite advantages in terms of health and longevity. But if you're accustomed to having meat on your plate at most meals, you may be wondering: "Can I really give it up for good?"

In a word, "Yes." I, and millions of vegans like me, can tell you that going meatless is not just okay, but great. We get to have our cake (longer, healthier lives) and eat it (fabulous foods), too.

Admittedly, the transition to veganism may take time and effort—but perhaps not as much as you think. Making the switch took me a while. But I did it, and I'm glad. You can do it, too.

I can honestly say that I don't miss meat. And I feel good about feeding my body nutritious foods that support Renewal. Knowing that I'm gaining extra decades with my grandchildren means a whole lot more to me than missing out on a few steaks and burgers.

If you're not quite ready to say goodbye to beef, then please keep your intake to a minimum. Eat only very small portions of the leanest cuts, preferably from organically raised cattle. In fact, I suggest that you relegate all animal-derived foods to condiment status. That way, you can gradually wean yourself from them until you finally give them up altogether.

HEALTHIER BODY, HEALTHIER PLANET

In this chapter, I've encouraged you to eliminate meat from your diet for some very personal reasons—namely, your own health and longevity. But going meatless has more global implications as well.

Raising livestock to feed a meat-hungry populace is a large-scale anti-environmental activity. It consumes vast amounts of land—in fact, 85 percent of this country's agricultural land supports the livestock industry in some capacity—and erodes soil. It pollutes water and air with the pesticides and fertilizers used to grow feed. It even depletes the ozone layer.

With the soybeans that we raise for livestock feed, we could provide meals for starving people around the world. No human would have to go hungry. Instead, we're exporting our dangerous dietary habits, including our penchant for meat and fast food, to developing African, Asian, and South American countries.

The carnage has even spread to the tropical rain forests, where approximately 200,000 square kilometers of trees, an area about the size of Pennsylvania, are destroyed each year to make room for grazing livestock. And as the rain forests shrink, so, too, do the populations of animals, birds, insects, and other creatures that reside there. One species becomes extinct every hour, decimated for no other reason than to feed our appetite for steaks and burgers.

We can persist with our short-sighted, wasteful, environmentally dangerous dietary habits, or we can do our world a world of good. The choice is ours—and yours—to make.

Many folks have substituted chicken for beef in their diets, thinking that they're doing their hearts (and the rest of their bodies) a favor. Sorry to say, that's not the case. Sure, chicken looks healthier than beef. But as the next chapter explains, it has nutrition problems all its own.

CHAPTER 15

Chicken Is Not a Health Food

Chickens are just rats with a good reputation.
—FROM THE MOVIE *STAYING TOGETHER* (1989)

Chicken consumption has been on the rise in this country, thanks in large part to the bird's carefully nurtured reputation as a healthy alternative to beef. We Americans have gotten the message that for nutritious, low-fat eating, white meat is far superior to red.

But like those car ads with the fine print, this message should come with a disclaimer. It is true that certain cuts of chicken may hold an ever-so-slight nutrition advantage over certain cuts of beef. But chicken hardly qualifies as health food, as the poultry industry would like you to believe.

In fact, chicken in general has just as much fat and cholesterol as beef. And it is contaminated with the same Pandora's box of pesticides, antibiotics, hormones, and preservatives. Hardly what you'd expect to find in a health food.

FOWL? FOUL!

The neatly packaged breasts, thighs, and drumsticks that you see in your supermarket's poultry case belie the torturous process that got them there. These parts usually come from stressed-out, diseased animals whose short lives played out as unnatural nightmares.

Commercial (that is, nonorganic) chickens are raised on so-called factory farms, where they're crowded into close quarters and deprived of fresh air and exercise. Of course, the goal of factory farms is not to make the birds comfortable but to fatten them up and get them to market as soon as possible.

Because of their squalid, disease-breeding living conditions, commercial chickens are routinely given antibiotics and other drugs to keep them "healthy." The Food and Drug Administration has approved some 2,000 chemicals, including medicines, for use in chicken feed. But that's not necessarily all the feed contains: Mixed in with the corn and soybeans may be cardboard, sawdust, used newspapers, and even recycled animal feces.

Even medication can't protect the birds from the devastating effects of a nutrient-poor diet and an unnatural, stressful "lifestyle." A high percentage of commercial chickens suffer from a variety of health problems, including cancerous tumors, brain damage, kidney damage, anemia, blindness, stunted growth, physical deformities, muscle weakness, impaired sexual development, and lethargy.

Each year an unbelievable 14,000 tons of poultry must be condemned, primarily because of cancerous tumors. What happens to meat that doesn't make the grade? It's processed into animal feed.

POISONS ON YOUR PLATE

As for the chicken that does make the U.S. Department of Agriculture grade, it retains residues of all the toxic and nontoxic garbage that the bird ate over the course of its lifetime. And those residues get passed along to you.

When you eat chicken, you unwittingly take in unhealthy doses of antibiotics and growth-stimulating hormones. Both of these substances are known to suppress the human immune system. And a weakened immune system, as you know, accelerates the aging process.

Eating chicken also exposes you to pesticides and fungicides, which are sprayed on the grains that eventually wind up in chicken feed. As you'll recall from chapter 6, these chemicals become concentrated in an animal's fatty tissues—a vain if valiant attempt by the animal's body to protect itself from their toxic effects. The poisons eventually find their way into your body via the grilled chicken sandwich you have for lunch or the chicken and noodles you have for dinner. There they become even more concentrated, as your body stores them in its own fatty tissues.

Once stowed away in your body, pesticides and herbicides wreak all sorts of havoc. These chemicals are toxic to all human cells and bodily systems, with the central nervous system, cardiovascular system, endocrine (hormone) system, and immune system taking the hardest hits. In fact, by suppressing immune function, the poisons increase your risk of a host of health problems, ranging from allergies to cancer. They also accelerate the aging process and stymie Renewal.

UNDER SUSPICION

As if all that weren't bad enough, brace yourself for some more foul news about fowl: Despite ingesting high doses of antibiotics, commercially raised chickens have a disturbingly high rate of bacterial contamination. Some experts estimate that as many as one-third of all birds are tainted, creating ideal conditions for an epidemic of food poisoning and perhaps thousands of deaths annually.

According to a report by the consumer watchdog group Americans for Safe Food, scientists contend that contaminated poultry is responsible for a large percentage of the estimated four billion cases of salmonella and *Helicobacter pylori* infections that occur each year. Salmonella poisoning produces symptoms such as fever, diarrhea, and vomiting, while *H. pylori* causes gastritis—an inflammation of the stomach lining—and ulcers. The group also cites a report from the Centers for Disease Control and Prevention in Atlanta linking food-borne illness to approximately 9,000 deaths per year.

THE SAD FAT FACTS

"Okay, so fowl has its flaws," you say. "Isn't it better for me than beef?"

Well, it certainly has been promoted that way. Clever,

captivating ad campaigns suggest that because chicken is lighter in color than beef, it naturally has less fat and cholesterol. Seems logical enough. Unfortunately, it just isn't true.

Compare the numbers: A well-marbled T-bone steak gets 42 percent of its calories from fat, while a chicken thigh with skin gets 56 percent of its calories from fat. Removing the skin lowers the fat content a bit, to 47 percent of calories. (Most of the bird's fat is concentrated in the muscle, which is why removing the skin doesn't make more of a difference.) Still, chicken qualifies as high-fat food. And turkey, in case you were wondering, contains only slightly less fat than chicken.

What's more, the fat in chicken—like the fat in all animal-derived foods—is almost exclusively the saturated kind, which does the most harm to our arteries. In fact, an average chicken supplies more saturated fat than the very leanest cuts of beef. And chicken has just as much cholesterol as beef and pork: about 25 milligrams per ounce.

To round out its poor nutritional profile, chicken has lots of protein but no carbohydrates or fiber. If you were to remove all the fat from chicken (which, incidentally, is impossible to do), you'd be left with almost pure protein. And protein, as you know from chapter 10, depletes bone mass—a precursor to osteoporosis—and overtaxes the kidneys.

Need I say more?

THE BOTTOM LINE

The message is clear: If you want to be healthier and live longer, if you want to support Renewal rather than stymie it, you should make every effort to give up chicken for good. No, you don't have to go cold turkey (pardon the pun). Instead, gradually shrink the portion of poultry on your dinner plate, allowing more room for legumes, which are a healthful protein, and the other members of the New Four Food Groups (grains, fruits, and vegetables).

If you simply can't imagine life without chicken, remember: *The extent to which you follow the Renewal Anti-Aging Diet determines the extent to which you'll benefit from it.* Choose organic poultry over commercially raised birds (the label should say "organic" or "free range"). Rather than featuring chicken as the main event in your meal, try dicing it up into stir-fries and other dishes. Or switch from chicken to turkey. Of all bird meats, turkey breast is lowest in fat.

Now that chicken has "fowled" out of the Anti-Aging Diet, how will fish fare? The next chapter puts seafood in the Renewal spotlight.

The Fish Quandary: Where Has It Been?

Fish die belly upward and rise to the surface; it is their way of failing.
—ANDRÉ GIDE, FRENCH NOVELIST (1869–1951), *JOURNALS*

Fish presents a unique dilemma to us Renewal seekers. It's packed with vitamins (A, B_{12}, D, choline, niacin, and pyridoxine), minerals (iron, magnesium, selenium, and zinc), and heart-healthy omega-3 fatty acids. With so many important nutrients, it ought to be a highly desirable food.

But that's not the case. On closer examination, fish begins to lose its nutritional luster. In fact, it poses such serious problems that the risks of eating it can far outweigh the benefits.

OCEAN ROULETTE

Fish might fare better if only they weren't so mobile. Terrestrial foods—grains, legumes, produce, even beef and chicken—stay in one place, where we can easily keep an eye on them. Fish, on the other hand, swim around a lot. We can't control their environment, nor can we know for certain where they've been.

In the course of their travels, fish ingest a host of toxic substances that are commonly flushed into their watery environment. As a result, they're often contaminated with a sickening soup of industrial waste, sewerage, pesticides, and insecticides. Polychlorinated biphenyls (PCBs), dichlorodiphenyl-trichloroethane (DDT), dioxin, chlordane, lead, and methylmercury routinely show up in inland freshwater fish as well as in fish from the uniformly polluted bays near large coastal cities. Although PCBs and methylmercury are among the most persistent and troublesome of these contaminants, the others are just as likely to turn up on your plate.

The patterns of contamination are totally unpredictable, so you have no way of knowing which fish have been poisoned and which are clean. But scientific research has demonstrated beyond any reasonable doubt that contamination is extensive, with perhaps as much as half of the world's fish population affected in one way or another.

Just like cattle and chickens (and even humans), fish accumulate toxins in their fatty tissues throughout their lifetimes. Large fish are most vulnerable: Because they ingest small fish, their toxin concentrations may be up to 10,000 times greater than those of the water in which they swim.

But fish aren't just carriers of chemicals. They can harbor disease-causing microorganisms, too. In fact, they're responsible for a disproportionate number of cases of food-borne illness—about seven times as many cases as beef and chicken.

The only way to be absolutely sure that your fish is microbe- and chemical-free is to have it tested. Of course, sending a fillet to a laboratory for analysis requires time and money. The alternative is to simply take your chances that the fish you're eating is safe.

You've heard of Russian roulette? I call this ocean roulette. And you play every time you put fish on your plate.

SWIMMING IN TOXINS

As I mentioned earlier, coastal waters, especially those near large cities, have disturbingly high toxin concentrations. They receive the bulk of the billions of tons of chemicals that are dumped into our nation's waterways each year, primarily from the polluted rivers that drain into them. Among the U.S. coastal "hot spots" where toxin concentrations have reached dangerous levels are the Boston and New York harbors and Chesapeake Bay in the east, and San Francisco and Santa Monica Bays in the west.

The fish that reside in these waters are routinely exposed to chemicals, particularly from industrial waste. These chemicals then get passed along to us humans, with potentially devastating consequences. Dioxin from pulp and paper mills, for instance, has been linked to birth defects in children and to nerve disorders in adults. Chromium from metal-plating operations can damage the kidneys. Lead, found in paint and gasoline, can interfere with mental development in children and with neurological functioning in adults.

While coastal fish may face the greatest threat from toxins, other fish are at risk as well. Farm-raised fish, for instance, have a reputation for being safe because they live in a more controlled environment. Unfortunately, their ponds are often contaminated by pesticide and herbicide runoff from nearby fields.

The safest fish, relatively speaking, are cold-water species such as cod, haddock, perch, and salmon. They live in the open sea, far away from polluted coastal waters. They also tend to be more expensive, since fishermen have to travel farther to catch them. But even a higher price tag doesn't guarantee where a fish came from or how safe it is.

METHYLMERCURY: WILL HISTORY REPEAT ITSELF?

One of the most tragic episodes of human poisoning by toxin-laden fish occurred in Japan in the 1950s, when a mysterious epidemic infiltrated the population around Minimata Bay. Autopsies on 100 victims of the epidemic, which has claimed 1,500 lives to date, revealed extensive damage to the brains and central nervous systems. The diagnosis: chronic methylmercury poisoning.

As officials later discovered, local industries had been dumping methylmercury into the bay. Fish ingested the toxin, then local residents ate the contaminated fish. The methylmercury slowly accumulated in people's bodies, causing serious illness and even death.

Similar incidents in Iraq and in Niigata, Japan, confirmed the calamitous effects of chronic methylmercury poisoning. And because bodies of water around the world continue to be polluted with the compound, low-grade poisoning remains a very real risk, particularly among frequent fish-eaters.

Chronic methylmercury poisoning is an insidious affair, affecting not only the brain and central nervous system but also the reproductive system and other organs. Both the extent of internal damage and the severity of symptoms depend on how much methylmercury a person ingests and how long the toxin is present in the body. In fact, internal damage can progress for some time without being detected.

The earliest symptoms of poisoning include numbness and tingling in the extremities, difficulty walking and talking, poor concentration, weakness, and fatigue. Over time, these symptoms can give way to spasms, tremors, and eventually coma and death.

SAFETY IN NUMBERS

People who eat fish no more than once a week are not at risk for chronic methylmercury poisoning. More frequent consumption can cause problems. Scientists know without question that methylmercury produces toxic effects in doses as low as 150 micrograms per day (an amount barely visible to the human eye) if ingested over several months.

Various countries, including Finland, Sweden, and Japan, have set safe limits for methylmercury in fish ranging from 0.5 to 1.0 part per million (or 0.5 to 1.0 microgram per gram of fish). In the United States, the safe limit is at the low end of the scale: 0.5 microgram per gram of fish, as established by the Food and Drug Administration (FDA).

Having a standard sure seems like a great idea. Unfortunately, we have no practical way of measuring the amount of methylmercury in the fish we eat. As a result, tallying a day's intake is virtually impossible.

In areas of the country where acid rain is a problem, larger lake fish such as bass, pike, and lake trout often have methylmercury levels that substantially exceed the official safe limit. The acid rain dissolves deposits of mercury in rocks and soil and washes the substance into lakes and streams. There, bacterial action converts mercury into methylmercury.

Because chronic methylmercury poisoning does so much internal damage, it dramatically accelerates the aging process. Its symptoms become evident only after substantial cellular breakdown has occurred. Rather than waiting until you reach that point, you're better off doing what you can to minimize methylmercury exposure in the first place.

SUPPLEMENTAL PROTECTION

If you've been eating fish more than once a week for a long time, or if you'd rather not give up fish for good, certain supplements can defend your body against the effects of methylmercury. Vitamin C and the amino acid cysteine, for example, help detoxify methylmercury and remove it from your system. Vitamin E and selenium, both scavengers of cell-damaging free radicals, protect your brain and central nervous system.

All of these nutrients have been included in the Anti-Aging Supplement Program outlined in parts 3 and 4 of this book. You'll find dosage recommendations there as well. Be aware, though, that while these supplements minimize damage from methylmercury exposure, they don't offer complete protection. For that, you should seriously consider eliminating fish from your diet.

DOWN IN THE DUMPS

There's another kind of industrial waste that makes eating fish a crapshoot. Radioactive materials routinely show up in waters surrounding nuclear dump sites. Fish harvested near these sites can have radioactive contamination.

Windscale, a nuclear reprocessing plant in England, has released more than one-quarter ton of plutonium—a radioactive substance so deadly that even microscopic doses can induce cancer—into the Irish Sea. Today, the Irish Sea is believed to be the most radioactively contaminated body of water in the world. Among children who live in the area, the death rate from leukemia is five times higher than normal.

Closer to home, the Farallon Islands, located in the Pacific about 40 miles west of the San Francisco Bay, once served as a nuclear dump site. Fish in the area pick up radioactivity from the water, then are caught and sold for human consumption.

As with methylmercury, radioactivity cannot easily be measured—unless you happen to have a Geiger counter handy. So you really can't be sure that the fish on your plate hasn't been contaminated.

POISONED BY PRESERVATIVES

Even if a fish is fortunate enough to live out its life in pristine, toxin-free waters, it still may not escape chemical assault.

Once caught, fish may lie aboard a boat for up to two weeks before being taken into port. They can rapidly rot while awaiting their final journey, because they're so high in polyunsaturated fatty acids.

To retard spoilage and preserve freshness, fishermen often spray their catch with preservatives such as polyphosphates and sulfites (to control mold and yeast), sodium benzoate (to kill bacteria), and polytrisorbate (to keep fish from becoming slimy). Fish flown in from far-away places are especially likely to be treated. That way, they won't decompose before they reach their destination.

All of these preservatives appear on the FDA's "generally recognized as safe" list. The FDA doesn't monitor the amounts used, nor does it require the preservatives to be mentioned on food labels.

Still, preservatives are foreign chemicals. As such, they have the potential to be at least mildly toxic. At this point, we can't predict their long-term effects.

THE LOWDOWN ON OMEGA-3'S

For all its weaknesses, fish has one undeniable nutritional strength: It's a top-notch source of omega-3 fatty acids. In fact, many folks have forsaken red meat in favor of cold-water fish—such as herring, mackerel, salmon, and tuna—so that they can increase their intakes of omega-3's.

These fatty acids have gotten a lot of attention for their ability to protect against heart disease. Indeed, research has suggested that they not only prevent blood clots but also reduce levels of heart-harming blood fats called triglycerides.

And that's not all. Omega-3's help relieve arthritis by suppressing production of interleukin-1 and tumor necrosis factor, two inflammation-promoting chemicals manufactured by white blood cells. Omega-3's also strengthen the immune system and boost production of pain- and inflammation-fighting prostaglandins.

The trouble is, when you eat fish, you're ingesting a lot more than omega-3 fatty acids—not just all those toxins I mentioned earlier but also gobs of saturated fat and cholesterol. In fact, fish has just as much saturated fat as beef and chicken, and it raises cholesterol levels just like other animal-derived foods. Not exactly what you'd call heart-healthy.

In fact, when Harvard University researchers tracked more than 44,000 male health professionals for six years, they made a surprising discovery. The men who most often ate fish were more likely to develop heart problems than the men who seldom ate fish.

Fortunately, you don't have to eat potentially toxic, fat- and cholesterol-laden fish to reap the benefits of omega-3's. You can get these fatty acids from other, more nutritious sources.

Flaxseed oil, for instance, supplies even more omega-3 fatty acids than the best cold-water fish. If you're concerned about getting enough omega-3's, then I suggest taking flaxseed oil supplements—2,000 to 10,000 milligrams per day. Pumpkin seed, soybean, and walnut oils also contain omega-3's, though at lower levels than flaxseed oil.

SHELLFISH: UNFIT FOR HUMAN CONSUMPTION

While finfish have their problems, shellfish—clams, crab, lobster, oysters, scallops, shrimp, and the like—fare even worse. These seafoods have already weathered a storm of criticism, thanks to much-publicized reports of their high cholesterol contents. But you may not believe what else is lurking beneath their shells.

Shellfish are scavengers. They sit on the ocean floor, often in coastal waters, and eat whatever settles there. Their regular diets may include not only industrial waste but also sewerage and fish excrement, both of which carry viruses and bacteria. Contaminated shellfish have been blamed for outbreaks of gastroenteritis (inflammation of the stomach and intestinal lining), hepatitis, and typhoid fever.

Between May and October, shellfish living in the waters of the Northern Hemisphere also face contamination during a curious phenomenon known as red tide. Microscopic red sea creatures rapidly multiply at this time of year, making the water appear an eerie crimson. In the process, these microorganisms produce toxins that are then ingested by shellfish and eventually passed along to humans, causing an alarming and potentially fatal illness known as paralytic shellfish poisoning.

Symptoms of paralytic shellfish poisoning usually show up within a half-hour of eating contaminated seafood—most likely clams, mussels, oysters, or scallops. Mild cases may cause numbness and tingling in the head and extremities, accompanied by nausea, vomiting, and diarrhea. In more severe cases, there may be muscular paralysis, characterized by difficulty breathing, swallowing, and talking. Extreme cases of paralytic shellfish poisoning may lead to suffocation and death.

Clearly, shellfish can be hazardous to your health. Because they are so frequently contaminated, and because they cause some very nasty diseases, all are off-limits in the Anti-Aging Diet.

EATING FISH SAFELY

As for finfish, I personally don't eat it. It's just too much of a crapshoot. Short of testing each and every fillet for contaminants, there's no way to be sure that fish is safe. And besides, it's loaded with saturated fat and cholesterol.

My advice to you is avoid fish altogether. Short of that, you can at least minimize the risks of eating fish by adhering to the following guidelines.

• Limit your consumption of fish to one modest portion (about two to three ounces) per week.
• Eat only fresh fish—and the fresher, the better. Avoid frozen, canned, and packaged products, including frozen fish dinners and fish sticks.
• Stick with cold-water species of fish. They spend their lives at sea, far away from contaminated coastal waters. Fresh salmon and tuna are good choices, as are cod,

haddock, herring, perch, and snapper. (Look for tuna labeled "dolphin-safe.")

• Bypass species that live in coastal waters as well as those that eat near the top of the food chain (and so ingest toxins from small fish). These include bluefish, carp, catfish, striped bass, and trout.

• Make sure that your fish is thoroughly cooked before eating it. The high heat kills any viruses, bacteria, and parasites (such as tapeworms and roundworms).

• Refrain from eating sushi, or raw fish. It often contains bacteria and parasites, which can infect a person's intestinal tract and cause cramping, diarrhea, and vomiting.

• Steer clear of fast-food fish sandwiches. Deep-frying destroys a fillet's delicate omega-3 fatty acids while generating scads of disease-causing free radicals. Plus, a typical fast-food sandwich supplies more than 50 percent of its calories as fat.

And finally, if you continue to eat fish, be sure to take supplements of vitamins C and E, selenium, and the amino acid cysteine. Your cells will need the extra antioxidants and detoxifiers to protect themselves against any chemicals in the fish.

So far you've read a lot about the best and worst food choices for preventing disease and promoting Renewal. But not everything in the Anti-Aging Diet is quite so cut-and-dried. Take alcohol, caffeine, and sugar, the topics of the next chapter. Expert opinion is sharply divided on whether these substances are good, bad, or a little bit of both. Join me as we venture into this nutritional gray area.

The Habits: Alcohol, Caffeine, and Sugar

Only Irish coffee provides in a single glass all four essential food groups: caffeine, alcohol, sugar, and fat.
—ALEX LEVINE, AS QUOTED IN THE *SAN FRANCISCO CHRONICLE*

Unless you've been stranded on a deserted island for the past few years, you've probably read and heard all the "good news" about booze—especially red wine. First came several studies suggesting that wine can lower your total cholesterol, raise your "good" high-density lipoprotein (HDL) cholesterol, and dissolve any plaques in your arteries. Then *60 Minutes* treated us to the so-called French paradox: The fat-loving French have a low rate of heart disease, presumably because they drink wine with their meals. And finally, scientists revealed the discovery of resveratrol, a heavily hyped phytochemical in wine that might help protect against heart disease.

Waves of ecstasy sloshed through the wine industry. Its bread and butter was not only chic and trendy but healthy, too. Suddenly, moderate to heavy drinkers of every ilk had a good reason to engage in a bad habit. Guilt became a thing of the past. It was all too good to be true.

Doctors, zeroing in on one small feature of a very broad landscape, seemed to forget all of the toxicology and pharmacology they had learned. Seduced by statistical artifact and in defiance of all common sense (not to mention cold, hard scientific fact), many physicians began prescribing wine—*Spiritus medicamentosum*—to head off heart disease.

There was no shortage of support for the notion that wine protects the heart. Media reports told us that regular wine drinking reduces heart attack risk by up to 50 percent, while protecting us from other scary stuff like bad oysters and flabby abs. One (industry-supported) Boston University wine and heart disease researcher, apparently intoxicated with the idea of healthy hooch, broke the credibility barrier when he proclaimed that alcohol abstention constitutes a "major risk factor for coronary heart disease."

This was heady stuff. It was almost enough—if we suspend the grisly realities of widespread alcohol-related disease—to temporarily lull us into believing that drinking might actually be a good idea.

But you'd be hard-pressed to find a substance that causes as much sheer human tragedy as alcohol. According to an estimate by the federal Office of Technology Assessment, alcoholism and alcohol abuse cost the United States up to $120 billion annually in lost productivity, law enforcement, property damage, health care, and alcoholism treatment programs. This sum doesn't reflect the immeasurable losses from human pain and suffering. More than 100,000 deaths per year are directly attributable to alcohol. After cigarettes, alcohol is the second most avoidable cause of death in the United States.

Clearly, alcohol abuse causes grave problems. But what about "moderate" drinking? How does a glass or two of wine or a couple of beers affect your life span?

BOOZE AS HEALTH FOOD

Though drinkers would love to feel that their habit is healthy (and the redefinition of wine as health food has helped grape growers to harvest nifty profits), the very notion of "booze for health" is clearly flawed.

First, alcohol is a toxin. If you don't believe me, ask any first-year medical student who has watched through a microscope as vigorous, healthy cells shrivel up and die when slipped a drop of ethanol.

Ethanol is a cardiotoxin, meaning that it adversely affects the heart. Alcohol consumption causes fat accumulation in the heart muscle, heart rhythm irregularities, heart failure, and other damage to the heart and circulatory system. When matching drinking habits and health records of more than 4,000 Framingham Heart Study participants, epidemiologist Teri A. Manolio, M.D., of the National Institutes of Health, discovered that even a little alcohol contributes to the enlargement of the heart's main pump. (The landmark Framingham Heart Study, under the auspices of the National Institutes of Health, monitored the health status of the residents of Framingham, Massachusetts, over the course of several decades.)

Alcohol impacts the entire body, not just the heart. Its most dramatic effects are on the brain and the liver, which is responsible for detoxifying the blood. None of the body's systems escapes alcohol's adverse effects: It causes an array of diseases from cancer to cirrhosis. So even if it did somehow confer heart protection (which it doesn't), moderate drinking would still raise your risk of many other diseases.

Moderate drinking also generates age-accelerating free radicals, causing massive oxidative stress. If you drink more than two glasses of wine a day, have some blood drawn for an oxidative stress panel. (This test measures the extent of free radical damage in the body.) You will be surprised to discover that alcohol has effectively depleted your antioxidants by virtue of adding to your body's free radical load. The small amount of antioxidant (resveratrol) that alcohol supplies has no net benefit.

But perhaps most telling is the fact that the studies that have supposedly shown that alcohol protects the heart have looked only at people gorging themselves on the typical high-fat Western diet, which is low in antioxidants and phytochemicals. These are malnourished individuals under extreme oxidative stress, who are already on the road to heart attacks. Three-quarters of them will eventually die of atherosclerotic heart disease. They are so in need of nutritional support that in their case, a little resveratrol will make a huge statistical difference—even if it comes dissolved in a cellular toxin (ethanol).

If anyone ever gets around to studying the effects of alcohol consumption on the health of low-fat vegans—whose antioxidant intakes are naturally high and whose arteries are clean and clear—we'll see that booze does nothing to benefit the heart. Drink and get healthy? I don't think so.

DEBUNKING THE FRENCH PARADOX

What gives red wine its supposed protective effects—and what's responsible for the French paradox—are substances called phenols. These antioxidant phytochemicals actually do protect against heart disease and other degenerative diseases by neutralizing free radicals and inhibiting the oxidation of "bad" low-density lipoprotein cholesterol.

But why would you want to ingest antioxidants dissolved in ethanol when you can get them in a much more potent form from nontoxic sources? Fruits and vegetables abound in phenol antioxidants. And supplemental grape seed extract (containing proanthocyanidins) and pine bark extract (containing pycnogenol) are the most potent phenols of all.

At some point in the debate, proponents of moderate drinking invariably trundle out the major study (reported in the *British Medical Journal*) that showed that ethanol itself—not red wine per se—exerts a protective effect. They contend that ethanol raises levels of HDL cholesterol, which whisks fatty deposits from arteries and reduces the stickiness of blood platelets, the tiny blood cells that can adhere to fatty deposits in the arteries and form clots. This means that all types of alcohol can help keep arteries clear, although red wine may do it best because it has the most antioxidant phytochemicals.

Well, this is all well and good. But again, I must remind you that all these studies have focused on developed nations, where high-fat, highly processed, coronary-causing diets are the rule. People in these countries are most likely to benefit from a "morning-after" antidote to the destructive effects of their eating habits.

If you are already well on the way to a coronary, booze might help dilute the fat in your blood and prevent that life-threatening clot from forming. But if you are following the Anti-Aging Diet, with plenty of antioxidants, phytochemicals, and natural artery cleansers and clot-busters, imbibing will do more harm than good.

An 11-year Harvard University study of 22,000 men determined that the ideal rate of alcohol consumption to reap cardiovascular benefits is two to four drinks per week.

For those consuming more than one drink per day, the heart-protective effects disappeared and the risk of other alcohol-induced problems skyrocketed. For those consuming two or more drinks per day, the death rate was 63 percent higher than for teetotalers.

Advocates of "healthy drinking" ignore the well-documented fact that alcohol impacts other body systems besides the heart. It is a tissue toxin and a known carcinogen. And it affects the brain by poisoning nerve cells.

More than two glasses of wine (or any other alcoholic beverage) daily dramatically increases the risk of death from several other diseases, such as cirrhosis of the liver, cancer, and stroke, according to Eric Rim, M.D., a Harvard University researcher who is considered one of the leading experts on the relationship between alcohol and health. When the drinking habits and death rates in 21 countries were compared, premature deaths from these other alcohol-related diseases outnumbered the coronary deaths prevented by the drinking.

To correctly interpret the data that makes alcoholic beverages look like they protect the heart, we must look closely at the makeup of the populations studied. Were these people at low risk for heart disease in the first place? Decidedly not. The statistical benefits that wine appears to confer were derived exclusively from studies of populations at significant risk for heart disease. Sadly, this includes more than 90 percent of the adults in Western industrialized nations. Three-quarters of these people will die of heart disease because they eat a high-fat, highly processed, fiber-depleted, chemically poisoned diet composed primarily of unnatural cardio-toxic foods. I'm talking about animal-derived foods, sugar, white flour, and hydrogenated oils. For individuals who undermine their health with this diet, wine is a fantastic "morning-after" drug.

No one has ever looked at the effects of alcohol on people who eat a health-supporting diet and have minimal heart disease risk, like those who espouse veganism. It's no accident that the only groups shown to get significant coronary benefits from alcohol are those at high risk of heart disease.

So drink if you will, but don't delude yourself into believing it will prevent or cure anything. It won't.

A TOXIC PRESCRIPTION

The idea of doctors prescribing "a few glasses of wine to protect the heart" is especially inappropriate. Consider Alphonso, a 48-year-old with early-stage coronary heart disease and elevated cholesterol. He eats few fruits and vegetables, exercises rarely, and is under high job stress. His doctor's advice was fairly typical: "Watch your diet, get more exercise, and have a glass or two of red wine with your dinner."

Alphonso needed to hear from his doctor that his diet of burgers and fries and chicken and cheese is deadly, and that he could benefit from an exercise program. But he didn't need to hear that it's okay to drink.

Previously an occasional drinker, Alphonso—with the green light from his doctor—has started imbibing every night. By following his doctor's prescription for two glasses of wine per night, Alphonso is shortening his life and increasing his risk of virtually every single major degenerative disease. What's wrong with this picture?

The booze he drinks is toxic to his brain and central nervous system. In low doses, it blurs his consciousness. In large doses, it causes confusion and delirium. Alcohol destroys about 1,000 brain cells per drink, hastening the onset of age-related cognitive decline.

Seething with free radicals, Alphonso's nightly glasses of wine deplete his already deficient supply of antioxidants and damage his immune system. Compromised immunity not only shortens Alphonso's life but also increases his risk of cancer in every tissue and organ the alcohol contacts on its way through his body. At two drinks a day, Alphonso's drinking increases his risk of cancers of the mouth, throat, esophagus, stomach, liver, pancreas, colon, and rectum.

Phenolic protective content and Teflon-coated blood platelets notwithstanding, alcohol is an artery-hardening agent par excellence. It not only accelerates the progression of Alphonso's coronary heart disease but also increases his risk for high blood pressure, heart rhythm abnormalities, cardiomyopathy (damage to the heart muscle), and heart failure.

His doctor's advice might have been particularly tragic if Alphonso and his wife, Allison, were trying to have another child. According to the National Institute on Alcohol Abuse and Alcoholism, alcohol is directly toxic to the testes, causing impaired sperm motility, reduced testosterone levels, impotence, and testicular atrophy.

And if Allison joins her husband in his nightly medically approved drinking ritual, she'll experience some particularly nasty consequences. In addition to all of the diseases that alcohol causes in men, women also risk infertility, reduced sexual responsiveness, and significantly higher risks of breast cancer. Alcohol increases circulating levels of estradiol, the hormone implicated in the induction of breast cancer. If Allison happens to be one of the 25 percent of women on postmenopausal estrogen replacement therapy, her estradiol level will shoot up as high as 300 percent of baseline within an hour or so of drinking. And it will stay at that abnormally high level for several hours. One study revealed that just one drink per day can increase a woman's breast cancer risk by 50 percent.

As a nutritional doctor, I'm concerned about the wholesale depletion of essential nutrients and antioxidant nutrients. Drinking destroys vitamins, especially the B-complex vitamins, while flushing out minerals and blocking essential fatty acids from doing their vital work.

Should doctors be prescribing alcohol? Is this really the message we ought to be giving? Have we lost our senses?

In a letter to the *New York Times* a few years ago, Nicholas Pace, M.D., assistant professor of clinical medicine at New York University School of Medicine, expressed the outrage felt by many doctors: "It is dangerous in the extreme to promulgate the notion that alcohol consumption is a healthy practice. . . . One should keep in mind the tremendous number of medical complications that alcohol, even in meager amounts, can cause. For example, one of the leading causes of arrhythmias is alcohol; the worst thing one can prescribe for a failing heart is alcohol in any amount. . . . With 24,000 killed and 500,000 injured each year on the highways due to drunken driving, to suggest that we should be drinking for our health is ludicrous."

THE TRUTH ABOUT RESVERATROL

What about resveratrol, the antioxidant phenolic phytochemical in red wine that has been hoisted onto a makeshift pedestal (mostly by researchers on the wine industry payroll)? In test tubes, resveratrol protects bad cholesterol from oxidation and prevents clots. But serious doubts remain about its effectiveness. Is it absorbed in significant quantities in humans? We don't know. Wine contains only minute quantities of resveratrol. You would have to quaff dangerously copious quantities of wine, according to Dr. Rim, to equal the antioxidant protection you get from a few daily servings of fruits and vegetables.

"The past several years have witnessed intense research devoted to (resveratrol's) measurement in wine and the factors likely to promote its enrichment in this beverage. Up to the present, conclusive evidence for its absorption by human subjects in biologically significant amounts is lacking, and it is questionable (but not yet excluded) that its powerful and beneficial in vitro activities are reproduced as a consequence of sustained moderate red wine consumption," wrote researchers at the University of Toronto, reporting in the *Journal of Biochemistry*.

We do know that when resveratrol is given to rabbits with high cholesterol levels, it accelerates atherosclerosis rather than reversing it. You do need potent antioxidants like resveratrol, but in a broad spectrum. And you don't need to drink alcohol to get them. One colorful salad, with a variety of vegetables in it, provides many times more phytochemicals than a glass of wine. And if you just can't live without a little resveratrol, douse your salad with red wine vinegar salad dressing.

And just for the record: Purple grape juice contains more resveratrol than an equal amount of red wine. (Although if you're following the Anti-Aging Diet, you really don't need the grape juice, either.)

THE BOTTOM LINE

Before you write me off as a reincarnation of temperance advocate Carry Nation, let me assure you that I'm not opposed to drinking. I live in the heart of California's picturesque wine country, surrounded by world-class wine producers. For many years, I drank a glass or two (usually two) of cabernet sauvignon with dinner. But in recent years, as I've discovered the importance of reducing free radicals and oxidative stress, I've limited my consumption to special events. At home, we never drink with dinner. When my wife and I eat out, we sometimes share an exquisite glass of Sonoma County cabernet. When we have dinner with friends or family, as often as not some wine will be on the table.

An occasional glass of wine at social events is no cause for concern. Although I'd suggest a maximum intake of three glasses per week, even a glass a day probably won't hurt you. Heavier consumption, however, is inconsistent with achieving optimum health and maximum life span.

CAFFEINE: STIMULATION BY THE SIP

Talk about dilemmas. I love the taste of coffee and the zippy effect caffeine has on my brain. Most adults are familiar with the wonderful sense of well-being brought on by a steaming cup of java. On the other hand, I can certainly do without the elevated cholesterol, brittle bones, anemia, and adrenal gland exhaustion associated with caffeine consumption. Though I know I'd be healthier if I gave up coffee altogether, I enjoy it too much to quit.

THE CAUSE OF THE KICK

Caffeine is a stimulant (chemically, a methylxanthine) with powerful effects on the central nervous system and adrenal glands. On the upside, it produces mental clarity and temporarily relieves fatigue. On the downside, it triggers the release of adrenaline, increases the metabolic rate, causes nervousness, increases stomach acid production, and boosts both cholesterol and blood pressure.

Most caffeine consumed in the United States comes from coffee—either *Coffea arabica* beans from Central or South America or *Coffea robusta* beans from Africa or Indonesia. The kola nut is the caffeine source in colas, while the cocoa bean supplies the caffeine in chocolate. Caffeine is also found in tea as well as in weight-loss products, pain relievers, and cold remedies.

The American appetite for coffee is ravenous. Upward of 500 million cups are consumed each day. The average person drinks 25 gallons a year.

WOMEN AND CAFFEINE DON'T MIX

Women seem to be more at risk for health problems associated with caffeine consumption. Research has shown that caffeine exacerbates premenstrual syndrome and causes fibrocystic breast disease, a painful, potentially precancerous condition. (Interestingly, fibrocystic breast disease usually goes away on its own when caffeine and other methylxanthine compounds are eliminated from a woman's diet.)

Caffeine has also been linked to an increased incidence of birth defects, premature births, and miscarriages. It can cross the protective placenta to reach the fetus and, in animals, has been shown to cause malformed fetuses. According to one study, women who drank more than the equivalent of one cup of coffee per day were half as likely to become pregnant as women who drank less. For these reasons, women who are pregnant or who are trying to become pregnant should avoid all caffeine-containing products.

THE HEART DISEASE DEBATE

Does coffee promote arteriosclerosis? Probably only in heavy users. A review of eight studies of people who imbibed more than five cups of coffee per day indicated that they were 60 percent more likely to develop heart disease. Several other studies have shown that those who consume more than five cups of coffee per day have an increased risk of death from heart disease. There's also a correlation between a high coffee intake and high levels of total cholesterol and low-density lipoprotein cholesterol. When people with elevated cholesterol stop drinking coffee, their cholesterol drops by about 10 percent.

Interestingly, drinkers of boiled coffee have higher cholesterol levels than drinkers of filtered coffee. The filters may help remove cholesterol-raising culprits, several of which have been identified.

THE BOTTOM LINE

Caffeine clearly places extra stress on your body. But a low intake—say, 100 to 200 milligrams of caffeine or one to two cups of coffee a day—has no proven link to disease. Many studies have put caffeine and coffee under the microscope. If there were a significant increase in risk of disease, we'd know by now.

With a higher intake—500 milligrams of caffeine or five or more cups of coffee a day—all bets are off. At this level, there is no question of increased risk of many serious diseases.

Some people should avoid coffee and caffeine altogether. You should abstain if you have a heart rhythm disorder, high blood pressure, panic disorder, or fibrocystic breast disease. Same goes if you're a woman who is pregnant or trying to become pregnant.

For the rest of us, quitting caffeine is also a good idea. But if you—like me—can't fathom saying goodbye to good ol' joe, just remember to keep your total daily caffeine intake below 200 milligrams. (That equals about one to two cups of drip coffee or two shots of espresso.) Do that, and you should be fine. I'm confident that as long as I keep my intake low, caffeine won't compromise my good health or shorten my life.

If you drink more than three cups of coffee a day, you're addicted to caffeine. You should cut back until you can enjoy just an occasional cup. Going cold turkey may cause severe headaches, so you're better off gradually tapering your consumption. For adrenal support, take B-complex vitamins, especially pantothenic acid (500 milligrams twice daily); vitamin C (1,000 milligrams four times daily); and ginseng. Following the nutrient-rich Anti-Aging Diet can help, too.

If you're thinking of just switching to decaf, you may want to reconsider. When coffee is decaffeinated, some of the chemicals used to extract the caffeine are left behind. Trichloroethylene is a particularly nasty cancer-causing agent (the Food and Drug Administration allows up to 10 parts per million in instant coffee and 25 parts per million in ground, roasted decaffeinated coffee). But other commonly used chemicals—trichloroethane, ethyl acetate, and methylene chloride—are also potent carcinogens. Drink only water-extracted decaf.

SUGAR: STEER CLEAR OF
THE SWEET STUFF

The average American consumes 130 pounds of sugar each year—an astounding 40 teaspoons (more than ⅓ pound) each day. As a nation, we eat our collective weight in sugar every year. That's a lot of sugar.

Where does all this sweetness come from? Most of it, about 75 percent, is tucked away in processed foods. In fact, sugar is the most commonly used food additive.

The top two sugar sources are soft drinks and cereals, which also happen to be the two best-selling foods in America (beef is third). Other major sugar sources include candy, ice cream, baked goods, and similar desserts.

The nine teaspoons of sugar in just one can of soda supplies 180 calories, almost 10 percent of the daily calorie requirement for an average adult. Sugar accounts for an average of 640 calories per day, or 24 percent of total calories, more than half of the carbohydrate content of the standard American diet.

Many cereals contain more sugar than grains. Even seemingly healthful granolas can be as much as one-third sugar (and are usually high in fat).

ONE NAME, MANY FACES

Sugar takes many forms. Sucrose, which includes brown sugar, raw sugar, and white sugar, is a disaccharide (that is, two sugar molecules connected by a chemical bond) derived from sugarcane and beets. Enzymes in the digestive tract break down sucrose into equal parts glucose and fructose. These simple sugars can then be absorbed into the bloodstream.

Brown, confectioners', invert, raw, and turbinado sugars are slightly less refined than white sugar. Otherwise, they're identical.

Fructose is fruit sugar. It occurs naturally in fruit but can also be manmade from corn and other grains. Honey is a combination of sugars: fructose, glucose, maltose (a simple sugar), and sucrose.

Foods labeled "sugarless" often contain sorbitol, mannitol, or xylitol. These naturally occurring sugar alcohols have the same number of calories as table sugar. They are absorbed a little more slowly than glucose or sucrose. While they don't cause cavities, they do cause diarrhea in some people. As little as 10 grams of sorbitol, the amount in about five pieces of hard candy, can cause problems.

A NUTRITIONAL WASTELAND

Unlike real foods, sugar provides only empty calories. It has no fiber, no vitamins, no minerals, no essential fatty acids (EFAs), no antioxidants, no phytochemicals. All sugars are devoid of nutritional value.

A Sweet Gone Sour

Sugar sure seems innocent enough. Yet research has implicated excessive sugar consumption in a host of ailments, including the following:

- Atherosclerosis (hardening and clogging of the arteries)
- Cancer
- Coronary heart disease
- Depression
- Diabetes
- Diverticulosis
- Gout
- High blood pressure
- Hormonal disorders
- Hypoglycemia
- Impaired immunity
- Indigestion
- Kidney Stones
- Mental and nervous disorders
- Migraine headaches
- Nutrient deficiencies
- Obesity
- Osteoporosis
- Periodontal disease
- Tooth decay
- Urinary tract infections

To make matters worse, your body must tap into its precious supply of essential nutrients in order to process sugar. In effect, sugar's empty calories double your nutrient deficit.

Sugar poses a particularly serious health hazard for children. Because kids consume large quantities of soda, cereals, and other sweets, they aren't getting the vitamins and minerals they so desperately need to grow up healthy.

Given the role of sugar in malnutrition and the quantities of sugar that we Americans eat, the proliferation of health problems linked to excessive sugar consumption comes as no surprise. Heart and blood vessel disease, high blood pressure, cancer, diabetes, obesity, osteoporosis, diverticulosis, and impaired immunity are just some of the conditions that have reached epidemic proportions thanks in part to sugar overload.

In laboratory experiments, animals fed sugar die significantly sooner than animals fed the same number of calories as complex carbohydrates such as whole grains and beans.

PULLING INSULIN'S TRIGGER

It's not as if you don't need sugar. Your body depends on a constant supply, in the form of glucose, to fuel cellular energy production. (Your cells generate energy by burning glucose in the presence of the oxygen we get from air.) Glucose is made from dietary carbohydrates, proteins, and fats. We are burning glucose day and night, so we need a constant supply. A set of finely tuned mechanisms keeps blood glucose levels very stable.

Eating sugary foods triggers excess insulin production. This sabotages your blood sugar–regulating machinery, placing inordinate stress on the pancreas (which has to make a lot of extra insulin to clear the extra sugar from the bloodstream), on the liver (which must transform sugar to glycogen in order to store it), and on the adrenal glands (which are stimulated to increase their output of adrenaline).

A BIG, FAT FIASCO

All sugars are rapidly digested, absorbed, and—unless you immediately burn them off through exercise—converted to fat. You already know the difference between good fats and bad fats. Wouldn't it be handy if sugar gave rise to the good fats, the EFAs? No such luck.

Unfortunately, sugars generate the saturated, killer kinds of fat molecules. Here's how it works: In the process of generating energy, the body breaks down sugar molecules into acetates, fragments containing two carbon atoms. Acetates are the basic building blocks from which both cholesterol and saturated fatty acids are made. The more sugar (or white flour or other refined carbohydrates) you consume, the more acetate molecules you'll have in your system. This pushes the body's chemistry in the direction of making extra saturated fat and cholesterol. Sugar literally becomes fat. How much this sugar-generated fat contributes to hardening of the arteries and to heart attacks is not widely appreciated. (More on this in a moment.)

Interestingly, because they are burned much more slowly, complex carbohydrates do not trigger fat production.

UNDERMINING IMMUNITY

Renewal depends on a healthy immune system. Sweets impair your ability to resist infectious diseases, allergies, and even cancer. They are immunosuppressive, that is, they impair the normal functioning of the immune system. Specifically, they hamper phagocytosis, the capacity of white blood cells to engulf bacteria and other invaders.

In one study, healthy volunteers developed a significantly decreased phagocytic index (a measure of the ability of white cells to engulf foreign invaders) after ingesting various types of sugar, such as glucose, fructose, sucrose, honey, and orange and other sweetened juices. The maximum decrease in phagocytic activity occurred between 1 and 2 hours after ingestion, and levels remained below normal for 15 hours. Starch ingestion did not have the same effect.

Another study vividly demonstrated that sugar impairs the production of antibodies, the immune proteins that attack invaders. The diets of mice were progressively diluted with sugar (which is exactly what happens when humans ingest foods containing sugar). As the sugar content of the diet went up and nutritional quality went down, the production of antibodies decreased proportionately.

NO FRIEND OF EFAs

Sugar disrupts the EFA production in two ways. First, it blocks the release of the EFA linoleic acid from tissue storage areas, causing a deficiency. Second, it destroys delta-6-desaturase, the delicate enzyme system necessary for transforming EFAs into prostaglandins and cell membranes.

STEALING PRECIOUS METALS

As mentioned earlier, sugar's empty calories induce across-the-board malnourishment. Certain nutrients are particularly hard-hit.

Excess sugar consumption depletes the essential mineral chromium, which has been shown to extend life span in laboratory animals. Because of its importance in sugar metabolism, chromium is also known as glucose tolerance factor. Of the 43 essential nutrients, chromium is the one most likely to be deficient in people consuming the typical, sugar-laden American diet. Chromium deficiency is a risk factor for atherosclerotic heart disease: Heart attack victims are virtually always deficient in chromium.

People who find it difficult or impossible to eliminate the sweet stuff from their diets can get a modicum of protection from chromium depletion (and the shorter life span associated with it) by increasing their chromium intakes to 400 to 800 micrograms per day. (This range exceeds the 200 micrograms recommended in the Anti-Aging Supplement Program, outlined in chapter 23.) Chromium supplementation will actually decrease sugar cravings and assist in weight loss.

In addition, sugar depletes calcium and other minerals necessary for strong bones. In this way, it increases the risk of osteoporosis.

Sugar also has a profound, though indirect, effect on dietary fiber. We need fiber in order to prevent a massive array of diseases. Whenever sugary, processed foods replace whole, unprocessed foods, fiber intake goes down.

BREAKING HEARTS

In 1953, a high correlation between fat consumption and coronary heart disease was discovered and publicized by Ancel Keys, Ph.D., emeritus professor of public health at the University of Minnesota in Minneapolis. This revelation precipitated a ton of research about cholesterol, fat, and heart disease and led to millions of people changing their eating habits in the direction of less cholesterol and fat.

More recently, a somewhat different view has been propounded by John Yudkin, M.D., professor emeritus of nutrition at Queen Elizabeth College of London University. He concluded that dietary fat may not be nearly as responsible for the cholesterol problem as sugar. He argued that a much stronger correlation exists between sugar consumption and heart disease rate than between fat consumption and heart disease rate. Noting that "no one has ever shown any difference in fat consumption between people with and people without coronary diseases," Dr. Yudkin found that people who had been ingesting a lot of sugar were much more likely to have developed heart disease.

More evidence incriminating sugar as an artery-hardener par excellence comes from a 15-country study. It revealed that death rates from heart disease were five times higher among people who consume 120 pounds of sugar per year (less than our national average) compared with people who consume only 20 pounds of sugar per year (still a hefty load if you are interested in living longer).

And fructose sweeteners, which seem to be showing up in everything these days, are even harder on the arteries than white sugar (which is only 50 percent fructose). When the amount of fructose in their subjects' diets was increased, researchers noted significant elevations in LDL cholesterol, triglycerides, and other blood fats associated with increased risk of hardened arteries.

You might reasonably ask how sucrose (white sugar) and fructose raise fat and cholesterol levels, thereby encouraging heart disease. Sucrose is a disaccharide that the body breaks down into two components: glucose and fructose. The glucose fraction is used by the body to produce energy for cellular metabolism. The fructose fraction is transformed into acetates, those two-carbon units that are used as raw material for the assembly of the cholesterol and saturated fat molecules. In this way, fructose increases levels of the bad types of cholesterol, which are known to promote arterial hardening, heart disease, stroke, and high blood pressure.

Because fructose is a monosaccharide—in other words, it contains no glucose—it generates twice as much acetate as sucrose does. For this reason, fructose sweeteners have an even greater ability to provoke heart disease. Unfortunately, even larger amounts of fructose are finding their way into the American diet, as manufacturers increase their use of pure fructose sweeteners in packaged and processed foods and beverages. This means our bodies are getting more raw material from which to make cholesterol and saturated fat.

Almost all soft drinks, for example, now use fructose sweeteners exclusively (nine teaspoons in every 12-ounce Coke or Pepsi). Millions of tons of these sweeteners are consumed annually around the world.

Whether it's caused by fat or sugar or both, no expert questions the connection between elevated blood cholesterol and increased risk of heart disease. Lowering blood cholesterol by reducing sucrose and fructose (as well as fat) is guaranteed to reduce your risk of heart disease and promote longevity.

WHAT GALL

A study conducted at the University of Auckland in New Zealand correlated gallstone formation in young people with a high sugar intake (through soft drinks and sweets) as well as a high fat intake. Since sugar increases cholesterol synthesis, it is not surprising that it also increases the probability of cholesterol gallstones.

GIVING RISE TO YEAST

Candida, or yeast, normally inhabit the skin and the mucous membranes that line the respiratory, digestive, and (in women) vaginal tracts. Yeast overgrowth is a common condition in which the immune system, for a variety of reasons, has been weakened and can no longer keep the organisms under control.

Millions of individuals, mostly women, suffer from yeast syndrome (also known as candidiasis or Candida hypersensitivity syndrome). The symptoms of this disease are caused not by the infection per se but rather by a systemic allergic reaction to the absorbed products of billions of yeast organisms, which live and die in the digestive tract.

Sugar causes and/or exacerbates yeast overgrowth by serving as food for yeast organisms, thus encouraging them to aggressively colonize the digestive tract. Symptoms of candidiasis include fatigue, weakness, depression, headache, sugar cravings, gastrointestinal dysfunction (indigestion, cramps, gas, constipation, diarrhea, foul-smelling stools), inability to concentrate, poor memory, sleep problems, premenstrual syndrome, aches and pains, heightened allergic reactions, recurring infections, and low body temperature.

Although all sugars cause yeast overgrowth, other factors play roles as well. Antibiotics destroy intestinal bacteria, yeast's main competitors for food and living space. Oral contraceptives and other steroid hormones create a more hospitable environment for candida by weakening immune response. Additional predisposing factors include a diet of refined and processed foods, vitamin and mineral deficiencies, EFA deficiency, recurrent infections, allergies, smoking, and exposure to drugs and other chemicals.

Yeast thrive in a warm, moist environment. Though they can survive on other foods, they love sugar. Eating sweet things causes them to flourish. People suffering from yeast syndrome typically crave sugar and sweets. In fact, sugar addiction is often a symptom of candidiasis.

Periodically eating sweets temporarily relieves the symptoms of yeast syndrome because it allows the yeast organisms to grow and stops (at least temporarily) the release of symptom-causing toxins into the bloodstream. Unfortunately, the longer-term outcome of sugar consumption is more yeast and a bigger problem.

A Roadblock to Renewal

Yes, sugar may taste good. But once the sweet stuff starts working its way through your system, it disrupts the Renewal process—and reduces your chances of achieving optimum health and maximum life span. Its methods are subtle, but as the following list suggests, its consequences are severe.

- Causes excessive insulin production and release
- Converts to saturated fat
- Depletes stores of essential nutrients
- Generates free radicals and creates oxidative stress
- Impairs the immune system
- Induces deficiencies of chromium, calcium, and fiber
- Interferes with the metabolism of essential fatty acids

Curing candidiasis requires following a strict regimen for several months. Most important, all foods containing sugar and white flour must be removed from the diet. No treatment program will succeed unless this is done. Starchy complex carbohydrates—brown rice and other whole grains, and potatoes, squash, and beans—are acceptable, so eat as much of these as you wish.

The combination of a high complex-carbohydrate diet and long-term administration of antifungal medications, such as citrus seed extract, caprylic acid, fluconazole, or nystatin, gradually suppresses yeast growth. Garlic, with its potent antifungal properties, can help to suppress its growth as well. I usually include the herb in yeast treatment programs for my patients. Repopulating the intestinal tract with an acidophilus supplement and sweeping out toxins with a fiber supplement are important adjunct therapies.

Mainstream physicians frequently misunderstand yeast problems. They remember only what they were taught in medical school: that *Candida albicans*, the responsible organism, proliferates in people with severely compromised immune systems, such as patients with terminal cancer: These doctors mistakenly think of candidiasis as just an infection rather than as evidence that the body's ecological balance has been disrupted, causing symptoms of general immune weakness—including not just infection but multisystem allergic reactions as well. These doctors usually miss the diagnosis, not infrequently suggesting that the symptoms of candidiasis are "all in the head."

Alternative-minded and ecologically oriented physicians understand candidiasis better. They are better equipped to diagnose and treat it.

LEARNING LABEL LINGO

Sugar and its camouflaged equivalents are everywhere. Masquerading as harmless ingredients, they find their way into a variety of processed foods from crackers to ketchup. So reading labels is especially important.

The ingredients in a processed food are listed on the label in order of amount. Manufacturers can sneak more sugar into foods while keeping it low in the ingredients list by using several different forms—such as dextrose, fructose, maltose, sucrose, fruit concentrates, honey, malted barley, molasses, and sorghum—in the same product. I've seen as many as five or six sugar equivalents mentioned on one label. Many products that appear low in sugar actually contain more sugar than all of the other ingredients combined.

As I mentioned earlier, carbonated beverages may disguise sugar as "fructose" or "high-fructose corn sweetener." These sound a lot healthier than "sugar"—almost like you're getting some fruit. Don't be deceived. Your body responds in basically the same way to all of these sugars. They supply empty calories, deplete nutrients, trigger insulin release, raise cholesterol and saturated fat, increase oxidative stress, and weaken your immune system.

ARTIFICIAL SWEETENERS: REAL HEALTH HAZARDS

Switching to artificial sweeteners may do more harm than eating the real thing. Despite popular perception, foods containing these sugar substitutes (as well as those labeled "sugar-free" or "sugarless") are not necessarily lower in calories. Although many people have tried, no one has been able to demonstrate that any artificial sweetener actually makes a difference in weight control.

Artificial sweeteners have other problems as well. Aspartame, sold under the brand names NutraSweet and Equal, is the most widely used artificial sweetener in the United States. It is known to cause the formation of highly carcinogenic nitrosamines. Aspartame may trigger migraines in people who are sensitive to it.

Saccharin—sold under the brand names Sprinkle Sweet, Sweet 10, Sweet 'N Low, and Sugar Twin—is also carcinogenic. Research has shown that the sweetener causes bladder cancer in rats. The fact that saccharin-containing products remain on the market is more a testimonial to the demands of the food industry for artificial sweeteners than to the common sense of the Food and Drug Administration, which approves them.

THE BOTTOM LINE

Most of us have a sweet tooth. To satisfy yours, eat a variety of fresh (preferably organically grown) fruits every day. Choose from apples, bananas, berries, grapefruit, kiwifruit, melons, nectarines, oranges, peaches, pears, tangerines—the possibilities are endless. Because these foods contain such minuscule amounts of fructose (not to mention a bonanza of nutrients), they're 100 percent risk-free.

Some other suggestions: Try unsweetened applesauce. Use fruit purees and conserves on toast and to sweeten desserts. Drink fresh, unadulterated fruit juices, avoiding those labeled "from concentrate." Make fruit smoothies. Snack on dates, dried fruits (unsulphured only), figs, and raisins (organic only). Replace the sugar in recipes with small amounts of honey or fruit concentrate.

Finally—and perhaps most important—learn all of sugar's pseudonyms and watch for them on labels. Steer clear of foods with added sweeteners as much as you can.

Now that you know all the do's and don'ts of eating for Renewal, you can use what you've learned to start reshaping your own dietary habits. To help out, the next chapter profiles the New Four Food Groups—the grains, legumes, fruits, and vegetables that provide the foundation for the Anti-Aging Diet.

CHAPTER 18

Foods That Renew: Switching to the Anti-Aging Diet

One who tastes, knows.
—SUFI SAYING

Although I present the Anti-Aging Diet as a fait accompli, I know that for most people, the kinds of changes that I am recommending won't come easy. They didn't for me. I didn't wake up one morning and decide to eat nothing but organically grown, plant-derived foods. Only after much study and a multitude of false starts (in terms of overcoming my cravings for fat, meat, white flour, and sugar) did I finally make the switch.

My personal evolution from burger-muncher to vegan actually began a long time ago. I was raised in the Midwest on what I now know (but what my parents didn't realize) to be a killer diet. It featured breakfasts of eggs, bacon, buttered toast with jam, and whole milk; lunches of a hamburger or cheese sandwich with french fries; and dinners of chicken, steak, pork chops, or pot roast with gravy—and, of course, ice cream, pie, or cookies for dessert.

I was a healthy kid who didn't give much thought to what I ate. In fact, I saved so much time eating fast foods as an undergraduate and then as a medical student that I sometimes wonder if I would have made it through without them. The possibility that my dietary habits could affect my health never really occurred to me. Nutrition, I'm sad to say, wasn't a facet of my medical education.

I had already graduated from medical school, completed my internship, and established myself as a hospital-based resident physician when I first became aware of the relationship between diet and health. One of my earliest clinical experiences had a profound influence on me. I had accepted a moonlighting job with Michael Lesser, M.D., a pioneer in nutritional medicine who directed a medical clinic in San Francisco specializing in the nutritional treatment of mental disorders. Much to my amazement, patients suffering from a wide range of neuropsychiatric disorders, including psychotic depression, schizophrenia, and neuroses, experienced major improvement when we placed them on special diets supplemented with vitamins, minerals, amino acids, and other nutrients.

Impressed with the apparent power of nutrition to reverse disease, I read voraciously on the subject. Eventually, I began prescribing dietary changes and nutritional supplement programs designed not only to improve my patients' general physical well-being but also to treat their specific symptoms and diseases. I also began to change my own diet and upgrade my supplements.

My training in biochemistry helped me to understand the powerful role of nutrition in health and disease. An initial interest in the essential nutrients soon expanded to exploration of the amino acids, essential fatty acids, nonessential nutrients, and Chinese and Western herbs.

In the 1970s and 1980s, research gradually revealed that dietary factors contribute to a wide variety of health problems—for example, a high-fat diet sets the stage for heart disease and cancer. The more I learned about the damage done by animal-derived foods and the benefits bestowed by vegetarianism, the more I shifted toward the latter.

THE DIET OF A LIFETIME

If you are not yet familiar with vegetarian cooking, be prepared for some surprises. Though some might dismiss it as boring, time-consuming, or difficult, nothing could be further from the truth. In this chapter, you'll discover a way of eating that not only supports your body's healing systems but is simple and tasty as well.

If you're in the habit of building your meals around animal-derived foods, the Anti-Aging Diet may seem like a major departure from eating as you've known it. But don't panic. You certainly won't feel deprived or go hungry. On the contrary, you'll have as much mouth-watering, satisfying food as you want. And after a while, the Anti-Aging Diet will have you feeling so much better that you won't even be tempted to go back to your old carnivorous ways.

If you've read the preceding chapters, you're certainly aware that the food choices you make are crucial to optimum health and longevity. Foods can heal and foods can kill. The line between these two extremes is very clearly drawn. Only foods that heal—grains, legumes, fruits, and vegetables—make up the New Four Food Groups.

The Anti-Aging Diet promotes Renewal by maximizing antioxidant consumption and reducing free radical damage and oxidative stress to lower levels than your body has ever known. By adhering to the New Four Food Groups, you accomplish two goals. First, you boost your intake of disease-fighting essential nutrients, antioxidants, phytochemicals, and fiber—the substances that reinforce your body's healing powers, increase its resistance to disease, and extend life span. Second, you sidestep disease-causing substances—the fats, sugar, white flour, pesticides, antibiotics, hormones, additives, and preservatives that undermine health and shorten life span.

It is no accident that the Anti-Aging Diet incorporates most, if not all, of the dietary changes that I usually prescribe to patients with heart disease, cancer, arthritis, osteoporosis, or a host of other degenerative conditions. It is the world's greatest diet, bar none, and your best shot at achieving optimum health and longevity.

The Anti-Aging Diet assembles an exciting variety of luscious foods that you'll love. This chapter lists them, along with related information about eating healthfully. Then beginning on page 535, you'll find a 14-day menu plan and recipes to get you started on the road to Renewal.

Don't feel that you have to overhaul your eating habits all at once. If you can, great. If you can't, just take your time and make changes gradually. Remember: *The extent to which you follow the Renewal Anti-Aging Diet determines the extent to which you'll benefit from it.*

GRAINS: WHOLLY HEALTHY

Whole grains should fulfill most of your calorie requirement. They're naturally high in fiber and low in fat. Populations consuming large amounts of whole grains have low rates of breast, prostate, and colon cancers as well as diabetes.

Grains assume great importance in the Anti-Aging Diet. All of the following are acceptable.

- Amaranth
- Barley
- Basmati rice
- Brown rice
- Buckwheat
- Bulgur
- Corn
- Couscous
- Millet
- Oat bran, oatmeal, and whole oats
- Quinoa
- Rye
- Spelt
- Wheat
- Wild rice

Use only whole, unprocessed grains and grain products—organic, if available. Avoid products that are refined or processed, with added fat, added sugar, and artificial ingredients. Always read labels on cereals, baked goods, and other grain products.

Breads can be especially tricky. They often contain flours from which the essential nutrients and fiber have been removed and to which preservatives, coloring agents, and other toxins have been added. Just because the label reads "whole-wheat" doesn't automatically make a particular loaf okay. Inferior breads and other baked goods often masquerade behind a cloak of apparent nutritional respectability.

Avoid breads and other grain products made with refined white flour or labeled as "enriched"—a dead giveaway that they have been stripped of their nutrients. They may include whole-wheat, pumpernickel, rye, raisin, and white breads as well as hamburger and hot dog buns, cakes, cookies, pastries, pancake mixes, waffle mixes, and most packaged cereals. Not only are these products nutritional vacuums but they also virtually always contain life-shortening additives, preservatives, and other toxins.

Baked goods often contain hydrogenated or partially

hydrogenated vegetable oils. These oils are seething with free radical–laden "ugly fats," or *trans*-fats. Bypass them altogether.

LEGUMES: MORE THAN A HILL OF BEANS

Legumes are plants with seed pods—primarily beans and peas, but also alfalfa, clover, and peanuts. They supply plenty of disease-preventing fiber. As a bonus, they're chock-full of those essential fatty acids that keep your whole body, especially your immune system and central nervous system, healthy.

According to at least one study, beans may control cholesterol just as effectively as cholesterol-lowering drugs. Researchers at the University of Kentucky in Lexington fed canned beans to 24 men with elevated cholesterol. After three weeks, the men's total cholesterol levels dropped by an average of more than 10 percent. The decline could be attributed to the beans' fiber, their vitamin E, their phytochemicals, their essential fatty acids, or perhaps the combination of these substances.

In the Anti-Aging Diet, all whole legumes and whole legume products are acceptable, including the following ones.

- Adzuki beans
- Anasazi beans
- Black beans
- Black-eyed peas
- Chickpeas
- Great Northern beans
- Green beans
- Green peas
- Kidney beans
- Lentils
- Lima beans
- Mung beans
- Navy beans
- Pinto beans
- Red beans
- Soybeans (and soybean products, including tofu, tempeh, and miso)
- Split peas

Many cultures around the world pair legumes with grains to form complete proteins. The following combinations make perfect substitutes for the complete proteins in meats.

- Rice and beans (from Latin American countries)
- Corn and lima beans, or succotash (from Native Americans)

- Pita bread and hummus, a chickpea spread (from the Middle East)
- Rice and tofu (from Asian countries)

SENSATIONAL SOY

Among legumes, soybeans stand out for their exceptional nutritional profiles. They contain all of the essential amino acids and are loaded with vitamin E, calcium, magnesium, phytochemicals, and essential fatty acids.

Soybeans have demonstrated a very strong protective effect against breast cancer. Asian women—both Chinese and Japanese—have very low breast cancer rates. Fewer than one in 50 women develop the disease, compared with one in 10 American women. Asian women also consume large amounts of soybeans.

Scientists at the University of Alabama in Birmingham fed high-soybean diets to rats that had been injected with breast cancer–causing agents. They found that the rats eating the most soybeans were much less likely to develop breast cancer.

These days, you can buy an array of soybean products, including soy milk and soy burgers. And of course, there's tofu, the Asian staple that is becoming increasingly popular in the West.

Tofu is actually soybean curd. It comes in firm, soft, and silken textures, usually packaged in plastic tubs in the dairy case of your supermarket or health food store. Don't purchase tofu that is stored at room temperature or that is bubbly or bulging—an indication of spoilage from bacterial growth.

Once you've opened the container, store tofu submerged in water in your refrigerator, changing the water every day. If possible, use it within five days of opening. Tofu can be frozen, but its texture will change.

Tofu absorbs and takes on the flavor of any dish, so it's quite versatile. Add it to stir-fries, pasta dishes, soups, sauces, even pizza. Scrambled and served with salsa, it makes an excellent, cholesterol-free replacement for eggs. My wife, Dellie, puts tofu in everything. I like it best when she sautés it over low heat with grated fresh ginger, garlic or onions, and soy sauce and pairs it with steamed vegetables.

Here's an easy recipe for a generic tofu stir-fry that can be varied according to taste and availability of ingredients: Very lightly coat a skillet with olive oil or soybean oil. Add garlic and onions and sauté over low heat (or better yet, pre-sauté in the microwave) until soft. Add diced tofu, a tad of soy sauce or sea salt, paprika, and any other spices that you like (I prefer curry powder). Continue cooking for 2 to 4 minutes, until the tofu is hot. Serve over steamed vegetables, with rice.

USING YOUR BEANS

Dried beans of any kind will keep for up to one year. They don't require refrigeration before cooking.

To prepare dried beans, begin by thoroughly rinsing them and discarding the water. Then soak them for at least three hours (or preferably overnight). Soaking beans helps to remove their raffinose and stachyose, two carbohydrates that, when digested by bacteria in the large intestine, produce gas.

Smaller beans, such as adzukis and baby limas, may not need as much soaking. In fact, you can eliminate soaking and increase the cooking time. Likewise, split peas and lentils need no soaking and cook very quickly.

When the beans are finished soaking, discard the water. Put the beans in a large pot and cover them with up to three times their volume of fresh water. Simmer until soft. Smaller beans need to cook only for an hour or so. The rest require 1½ to 3 hours. Do not add salt until the end, as it will harden the beans and increase cooking time.

You can store cooked beans in the freezer (in well-labeled meal-size portions) for up to three months. If you store them in the refrigerator, they're good for about three days. You should definitely discard them after five days.

If the amount of preparation required discourages you from including dried beans in your diet, canned beans are an acceptable substitute. A few provisos: Make sure they come in seamless, unsoldered cans (solders contain lead), and read the label to make sure that they contain no sugar, lard, preservatives, or additives. Your best bet for buying canned bean products is a health food store.

Fresh frozen green beans and green peas, though not quite as good as fresh, are excellent and easy to make. Buy organic, if possible. And read labels: The only ingredient should be the bean itself.

FRUITS: NATURE'S SWEETS

Rich in nutrients and full of flavor, fruits are naturals for the Anti-Aging Diet. Choose whatever is in season—fresh and organically grown, if possible. Here are some suggestions to whet your appetite.

- Apples
- Apricots
- Bananas
- Blackberries
- Blueberries
- Boysenberries
- Cantaloupes
- Casaba melons
- Cherimoyas
- Cherries
- Cranberries
- Crenshaw melons
- Currants
- Dates
- Figs
- Grapefruit
- Grapes
- Guavas
- Honeydew melons
- Huckleberries
- Kiwifruit
- Lemons
- Limes
- Loganberries
- Loquats
- Lychees
- Mangoes
- Mulberries
- Nectarines
- Oranges
- Papayas
- Passion fruit
- Peaches
- Pears
- Persian melons
- Persimmons
- Pineapples
- Plantains
- Plums
- Pomegranates
- Prunes
- Raisins
- Raspberries
- Strawberries
- Tangelos
- Tangerines
- Watermelons

About the only fresh fruit that doesn't qualify for the Anti-Aging Diet is coconut, which gets 35 percent of its calories from fat—90 percent of which is saturated. Dates are high in sugar and therefore should be consumed in very limited quantities.

When fresh fruits aren't as widely available—during the winter months, for example—frozen fruits make fine substitutes. The freezing process preserves fiber and minerals, although it does take a toll on some phytochemicals. You can microwave frozen fruits and add them to cereals and desserts. At home we make smoothies from frozen and/or fresh fruits—whatever we have on hand.

Dried fruits (such as apples, apricots, bananas, currants, dates, figs, mangoes, papayas, peaches, pears, pineapple, prunes, and raisins) tend to have a lot of sugar. They're okay in modest amounts, though. Try combining them with less sweet fruits to improve their flavor. Steer clear of dried fruits that contain sulfur. Many products are labeled as "unsulfured."

Applesauce and whole-fruit conserves make excellent spreads for whole-grain breads and rolls. They're great for breakfast, too. Again, buy organic products if you can.

Many packaged fruit products, such as canned fruits and fruit juices, leave a little (or a lot) to be desired. They typically contain extra sugar, preservatives, and other additives.

Fruit juices, for example, are for the most part unhealthy foods. Many of these beverages have extra sugar—often disguised as "fructose," "fructose corn syrup," or "fruit sweetener." Manufacturers like listing these ingredients on their labels because they sound healthier than sugar. But fructose, like white sugar, is converted by the body to saturated fat and cholesterol unless it is burned off by exercise immediately after consumption.

Likewise, be wary of juices that say "from concentrate" on their labels. These products—whether bottled, canned, or frozen—are frequently high in pesticides, fungicides, molds, coloring agents, and a multiplicity of other contaminants. Arguably the worst is frozen orange juice from concentrate. The vitamins are long gone. Until adequate safeguards are in place to control their content, avoid all frozen juice concentrates.

Cranberry juice has found a niche as a nutritional medicine for urinary tract infections. The fruit contains a phytochemical compound that prevents *Escherichia coli* bacteria from making itself at home in the urinary tract. Because cranberries are so sour, most bottled and canned juices have added sugar. The sweetener is counterproductive because it adversely affects immunity—not good for someone who is attempting to fight off an infection. Encapsulated cranberry products, which have recently appeared on the market, are a better option.

If you're an avocado fan, be aware that avocados get 90 percent of their calories from fat. Try to limit yourself to one per week. The restriction encompasses guacamole as well, so when you order that bean and rice burrito, ask the server to leave off not only the sour cream and cheese but also the "green sauce."

VEGETABLES: UNPARALLELED GOODNESS

Vegetables are more nutrient-dense than any other food in the Anti-Aging Diet. They're especially good sources of phytochemicals, those plant-derived compounds that protect against disease. As with fruits, opt for organically grown veggies whenever they're available. Choose from among the following vegetables (and, of course, feel free to add your own favorites to the list).

- Artichokes
- Asparagus
- Bamboo shoots
- Beet greens
- Beets
- Bok choy
- Broccoli
- Brussels sprouts
- Cabbage (all types)
- Carrots
- Cauliflower
- Celery
- Chard
- Chili peppers
- Collard greens
- Cucumbers
- Dandelion greens
- Eggplants
- Endive
- Escarole
- Garlic
- Ginger
- Green beans
- Green peppers
- Jerusalem artichokes
- Kale
- Leeks
- Lettuce (all types)
- Mustard greens
- Okra
- Onions
- Oriental mushrooms (enoki, oyster, reishi, shiitake, and tree ear)
- Oyster plant
- Parsley
- Peas
- Potatoes (all types)
- Pumpkins
- Radishes
- Rutabagas
- Scallions
- Spinach
- Sprouts (all types)
- Squash (all types)
- String beans
- Sweet potatoes
- Swiss chard
- Tomatoes
- Turnip greens
- Turnips
- Watercress
- Yams
- Zucchini

Some vegetables can cause problems if eaten excessively or prepared incorrectly. Exercise caution with the following foods.

Mushrooms. The common white variety sold in most supermarkets contains high levels of hydrazines, carcinogens that are used as rocket fuel. By comparison, the oriental mushrooms listed above actually contain an abundance of phytochemicals that prevent cancer and enhance immunity.

Potatoes. The sprouts and buds on potatoes contain harmful chemicals, so these growths should be removed before cooking. Likewise, potatoes that appear bruised are actually diseased and contain carcinogenic substances. Remove bruised areas or, even better, choose only healthy-looking specimens.

NUTS AND SEEDS: OKAY IN MODERATION

Though they don't exactly fit into any of the New Four Food Groups, nuts and seeds are nevertheless plant-derived foods. And they can have their place in the Anti-Aging Diet—provided that they're used wisely.

Because they must contain all of the raw materials necessary to support the growth of a new plant, nuts and seeds are loaded with nutrients: high-quality protein, vitamins, minerals, essential fatty acids, and phytochemicals. They are especially rich in vitamins B_6 and E as well as the minerals calcium, copper, magnesium, manganese, and zinc.

Despite this outstanding nutritional profile, nuts and seeds have one serious flaw: too much fat. Granted, it's vegetable fat, which is nutritionally superior to animal fat. Still, research has shown that excessive vegetable fat consumption can elevate risks of heart disease and cancer. So we reformed carnivores, who tend to replace the meat in our diets with nuts and seeds (along with other high-fat snacks), must learn to control our consumption of these particular plant-derived foods.

As components of the Anti-Aging Diet, the following nuts and seeds are acceptable in modest amounts.

- Almonds
- Brazil nuts
- Cashews
- Chestnuts
- Filberts (hazelnuts)
- Flaxseeds
- Hickory nuts
- Macadamia nuts
- Pecans
- Pine nuts
- Pistachios
- Pumpkin seeds
- Sesame seeds
- Sunflower seeds
- Walnuts

Of these, chestnuts have the lowest fat content, supplying 10 percent of their calories as fat. Next come pumpkin seeds, sesame seeds, and sunflower seeds at 40 to 50 percent of calories from fat. Almonds, pine nuts, pistachios, and walnuts are in the 50 to 60 percent range; Brazil nuts, filberts, and hickory nuts are in the 60 to 70 percent range. Cashews, macadamia nuts, and pecans top the list at more than 70 percent of calories from fat.

With the exception of chestnuts, all of these nuts and seeds must be considered high-fat foods. A person following a 2,000-calorie, 10 percent fat diet can afford only 200 fat calories per day. Scarf up a few handfuls of nuts or seeds, and you'll surpass your fat calorie quota in no time.

Nutrition-wise, flaxseeds and flaxseed oil are your best bets. Flaxseed oil has the highest essential fatty acid content of all oils: 58 percent alpha-linolenic acid (an omega-3 fatty acid) and 14 percent gamma-linolenic acid (an omega-6 fatty acid). For this reason, thousands of nutrition-minded doctors, myself included, recommend taking flaxseed oil as a daily supplement. It will supercharge your immune system and foster optimum health and longevity.

Flaxseed oil is available in both capsule and liquid forms. The liquid is easier to take and cuts down on the number of daily supplement capsules, but some people don't care for the taste. Personally, I like to spread flaxseed oil on my morning toast as a butter substitute and pour it on a salad along with a gourmet vinegar. (On page 575, you'll find a recipe for Dellie's Delicious Dressing, which features flaxseed oil.) You can stir flaxseed oil into bean dishes and soups—but do so after cooking rather than before. Temperatures above boiling shatter the essential fatty acids like a brick on china. If you do choose the liquid form, make sure the label says that it's organic.

Sunflower seeds can't match the essential fatty acid content of flaxseeds (they're 65 percent gamma-linolenic acid but completely devoid of alpha-linolenic acid). Nevertheless, they make a great snack. They're packed with the immune-boosting mineral zinc and rich in dimethyl glycine, an important anti-aging nutrient.

Walnuts vie for top honors among nuts. They offer the best compromise between a high gamma-linolenic acid content and good taste. Their oil sports enviable essential fatty acid levels (5 percent alpha-linolenic acid and 51 percent gamma-linolenic acid). And unlike flaxseed oil, you can cook with walnut oil.

Peanuts definitely don't fare well in the nutrition arena. (Botanically speaking, peanuts are not nuts but legumes. Because everyone tends to think of them as nuts, however, I'll discuss them here.) They're very low in essential fatty acids and high in saturated fat. If they're roasted in oil, they have even more fat. Plus, roasting makes the nuts carcinogenic. Salting them doesn't help any.

When peanuts are stored for long periods of time, they can play host to the fungus *Aspergillus flavus*. This fungus produces aflatoxin, a potent carcinogen and liver toxin.

Peanut oil has few nutritionally redeeming qualities. Low in alpha-linolenic acid and high in saturated fat, it raises cholesterol levels and interferes with essential fatty acid metabolism.

If you absolutely must have peanut butter, look for one that is certified aflatoxin-free (the label will say so). Westbrae Natural is one brand, marketed as "laboratory-tested aflatoxin-free, herbicide-free, and pesticide-free."

As an alternative to peanut butter, try almond butter or walnut butter. Both are high in fat, but at least they're full of essential fatty acids. Just be sure to use them sparingly. Almond butter is one of the staple items in my family's pantry. We use it at breakfast, as a butter substitute on toast. (At our house, toast is bread that is heated in a toaster or toaster oven and removed before browning or burning takes place.) For lunches and snacks, we make almond butter and fruit spread sandwiches.

Sesame butter is made from toasted sesame seeds. Toasting not only produces carcinogens but also destroys the seeds' fragile omega-6 essential fatty acids (which account for 45 percent of sesame oil). Instead of sesame butter, use sesame tahini, which is made from unroasted seeds.

Rather than eating nuts and seeds by the handful, sprinkle them into other foods. For instance, try adding them to your breakfast granola or whole-grain cereal for great flavor and crunch. As a bonus, you'll ratchet up your protein and mineral intake a notch or two.

Without their shells to protect their delicate oils from light and air, nuts and seeds quickly turn rancid. So purchase them in small quantities, preferably in their shells, and store them in sealed containers in the refrigerator or freezer. Toss out unused nuts, nut butters, and liquid oils after three months.

BUT WHAT ABOUT . . . ?

In the course of following the Anti-Aging Diet, you're bound to encounter gray areas—foods that are neither plant-derived nor animal-derived but that nevertheless have a nutritional impact. Here are some of the more common dietary dilemmas, along with my advice for navigating them.

Beverages. Purified water—either bottled or run through your own purifier—is the beverage of choice. Get in the habit of drinking at least eight eight-ounce glasses every day to help keep your innards clean. If you prefer something with a bit more bubble and fizz, try club soda, seltzer water, or mineral water.

Caffeine-free herbal teas make delicious alternatives to coffee. Look for brands such as Celestial Seasonings and Traditional Medicinals, which are sold in supermarkets. Or brew up your own herbal iced tea, then add a little apple juice for extra flavor. Also check out the grain coffee substitutes available in health food stores.

As for soft drinks, read labels and steer clear of products made with sugar, fructose, high-fructose corn sweetener, or glucose syrup. You really don't need sugar for great-tasting soda. Many health food stores now carry sugar-free, fruit juice–sweetened carbonated beverages.

You can easily make your own healthy soft drink by mixing one part seltzer water and one part organic juice such as apple, apricot, berry, grape, or grapefruit. (My personal favorite is strawberry-guava.)

Other beverages that fit the Anti-Aging Diet include

fresh fruit juices, vegetable juices, fruit smoothies and other blender drinks, rice milk, and soy milk.

Salad dressings. You can transform a low-fat, low-calorie salad into a high-fat, high-calorie meal just by slathering dressing all over it. Although many of the dressings currently on the market are acceptable, I prefer to make my own. That way, I know that the oil is fresh and free of free radicals.

As I explained in chapter 7, oils turn rancid and form free radicals as they age. The longer they sit on a shelf unused, the more free radicals they generate. Unfortunately, you can't tell that this is happening just by looking at an oil. By the time an oil actually smells bad, it is already highly toxic. Not that eating one salad with rancid dressing will kill you. But regular consumption of the stuff puts a load on your immune system and speeds up the aging process.

For this reason, I always make an effort to purchase only the freshest oils in small quantities that won't go to waste. If I have an oil for more than three months (which seldom happens at my house), it gets tossed.

Making your own dressing is easy. Just add three or four parts vinegar (balsamic, rice, wine, or one of those fancy gourmet types) to one part oil (flaxseed, olive, or soy). You can replace the vinegar with lemon juice, if you prefer. And if you're not using the dressing right away, add two or three cloves of garlic and put it in the refrigerator to marinate.

When you do purchase bottled dressing, study the label carefully. Avoid any product that contains hydrogenated oils and preservatives or other artificial ingredients. If you can't find a suitable product in your supermarket, then check at your local health food store.

Salt. To make salt pour easily, manufacturers add aluminum-based flowing agents (sodium silicoaluminate is one). Aluminum is a brain toxin that has been implicated in Alzheimer's disease. It has no place in the Anti-Aging Diet.

Unfortunately, most salts that contain aluminum don't list it on the label. Assume that any supermarket salt is made with the additive unless the words "aluminum-free" appear on the label. (Aluminum is also added to biscuit, cake, and cookie mixes to keep them from getting wet and sticky.) If you want to use salt, try sea salt, which is sold in health food stores.

What about salt and blood pressure? If you already have high blood pressure, consult your doctor. If you have normal blood pressure, a little salt shouldn't cause you any problems. Just be careful not to use too much.

Sauces. Sauces make meals interesting. But they can be high in fat (and cholesterol, if made with eggs, cream, or meat gravy) and devoid of fiber. The commercially prepared varieties may also contain extra sugar, additives, pesticides, and other undesirable chemicals. Use them sparingly.

In particular, steer clear of béarnaise, cheese, hollandaise, sour cream, stroganoff, and white sauces. These have way too much fat. Acceptable alternatives include curry, lemon, mustard, soy, sweet-and-sour (made with honey and vinegar), tamari, and teriyaki sauces.

If you make your own sauce, use organic ingredients as much as possible. Replace any fatty thickening agent with arrowroot, cornstarch, potato flour, rice flour, or tapioca.

THE TAO OF CHANGE

The Anti-Aging Diet boils down to two basic principles: Stock up on plant-derived foods—grains, legumes, fruits, and vegetables—and steer clear of animal-derived foods. Follow these guidelines, and you'll be well on your way to optimum health and longevity.

I want to help you become a vegan. Though a bit of persistence may be necessary, the transition needn't be painful. I did it, and I'm certain that you can, too. I am equally certain that once you have made the dietary changes that I'm suggesting, you'll actually feel better and healthier. And when you look back, you won't believe how easy those changes were.

In my 25 years of studying, practicing, and teaching Chinese traditional medicine, I've learned a lot about change. Chinese traditional medicine is based on Taoist ideas, and Taoism, at its core, is the study of change. Yin and yang are the manifestations of change (or, in Chinese, *ching*).

Taoism teaches that the only constant in life is change. Nothing stands still. You are always moving in a certain direction. To go in a different direction—for example, to become a vegan—you should first know how change works.

Taoist doctors have learned a very useful concept: the Great Law of Pu-Hsieh. It states that you can influence change most easily with a gentle push right at the point when change is greatest and always in the same direction of flow. (I'm indulging in a little poetic license here, but this is basically the gist of it.) Exerting force at the wrong time or going against the flow won't work and may even have an effect opposite the one you desire.

Suppose you are pushing someone on a swing. Do you push when the person is coming back toward you? No. Do you push when the person is at the bottom of the arc? No. You push at the point of maximum change, just after the person has switched direction and begun moving forward. And you push just a little, in the same direction that the person is moving. You go with the flow, using many small pushes to make a big swing sail high. Intuitively, you've been practicing the Great Law of Pu-Hsieh all of your life.

Of course, everyone is different. A few stalwart souls can make up their minds to do something and then do it. If this describes you, great. Go with the flow. This is the "yang" approach: the sudden, forceful act of will—going cold turkey.

For others, the slower "yin" approach may work better. Just apply the Great Law of Pu-Hsieh. Start by identifying the points of change in direction—the places in your diet, and in your life, where minimal exertion will effect the greatest change (because you are going with the flow). Then at each of the points of change that you identify, you want to give a little push in the direction of the Anti-Aging Diet. Over and over again, apply the Great Law, gently nudging yourself in the direction you want to go.

To start, make the changes that are easiest. Reduce portion sizes of animal-derived foods. Replace cow's milk with rice or soy milk on your cereal. Put tofu in sandwiches instead of meat or cheese. Learn new recipes—pastas, stir-fries, casseroles, bean dishes—and filter them into your meals. Have fresh fruit for dessert instead of dairy products and sweets.

It's up to you to identify the changes that you are ready and willing to make now and to implement them. Over time, what at first seemed like a big change will be reduced to a bunch of little changes. Before you know it, you'll be a full-time vegan.

THINK SMALL

Becoming a vegetarian should never evolve into a task so impossibly humongous and daunting that you could never do it. My good friend Richard Carlson, Ph.D., wrote a bestseller called *Don't Sweat the Small Stuff: And It's All Small Stuff*. This holds true for becoming a vegetarian: It really is not a big deal. Take it one step at a time, one meal at a time. Don't get discouraged, and don't give up. Realize that you have time. With patience and persistence, you'll get there.

Each time you enjoy another scrumptious vegetarian meal, you'll realize that you really don't need meats and dairy products to feel satisfied. On the other side of fear and reluctance lies a delectable banquet—perhaps a few extra decades of delectable banquets—just for you.

Even an optimum diet like the Anti-Aging Diet needs the support of nutritional supplements. Only supplements can push your nutrient intakes to levels that actually fight disease and slow the aging process. The next chapter explains why supplementation is so important to Renewal.

Supplements: Essential for Maximum Life Span

CHAPTER 19

Why Supplements Are Necessary—And Introducing the Optimum Daily Allowances

It is often necessary to make decisions on the basis of information sufficient for action, but insufficient to satisfy the intellect.
—IMMANUEL KANT (1724–1804), GERMAN
  PHILOSOPHER

I hear it all the time from my patients: "Dr. Smith, I'm eating just like you told me to—lots of grains, beans, fruits, and vegetables, nothing fatty or sugary. Now you're recommending supplements, too? Taking so many pills just doesn't seem natural. If Mother Nature felt I needed extra nutrients, wouldn't she have put them in my food?"

It's a perfectly valid question, and one which you may have wondered about at one time or another. I'll tell you exactly what I tell my patients: If you want to fight disease and achieve maximum life span, you can't do it with diet alone. You need the extra nutritional boost that only supplements can provide.

Lots of folks take supplements nowadays. For as many as 40 percent of American adults—about 100 million of us—these pills have become nutritional staples. They're also the backbone of a thriving, $10-billion-per-year industry.

In many ways, supplements are to humans what fertilizer is to plants. Give a plant adequate amounts of sunlight and water, and it will survive. Add some nutrient-rich fertilizer (organic, of course), and the plant will thrive.

For us humans, the same principle applies. A healthful,

balanced diet supplies the body with sufficient nutrients to carry out routine tasks. Supplements such as vitamins, minerals, essential fatty acids, phytochemicals, and more enrich the body's internal environment to fortify cellular protection, repair, and regeneration and support the Renewal process.

MOTHER NATURE'S ULTERIOR MOTIVE

Of course, supplements, at least as we know them, haven't been around all that long. How did our ancestors survive without them? To be painfully blunt, they didn't.

You see, Mother Nature has never cared about optimum health. Nor has she concerned herself with longevity. Her main objective is survival and propagation of the species. So she programmed us humans to survive on even the crummiest diet, nutrition-wise, into our twenties, when we're old enough to reproduce. Beyond that, we're on our own.

This genetic twist is a throwback to primitive times, when supermarkets and refrigerators didn't exist and food was not always plentiful. Those who could stay alive on very slim pickins had a tremendous survival advantage.

Over thousands of years, one generation has passed its "survival genes" on to the next. So thanks to our ancestors, we are equipped to subsist on minuscule amounts of the essential nutrients, just in case a famine comes along. But as I said before, this insurance policy remains effective only into our twenties—just long enough for us to reproduce. It includes no provision for aging.

By the time we reach our twenties, we have established lifelong eating habits. And because our survival genes have protected us from the adverse effects of our dietary transgressions, we have no reason to believe that what we're eating (or not eating) is doing us any harm. So we continue feeding ourselves nutritionally vacant junk foods, unaware that they're quietly eroding our health. Often we don't see the effects for several decades.

The point here is this: Even with a lousy diet, we can remain fairly healthy through our first 30 to 40 years of life. But if we want to achieve optimum health and maximum life span, the nutritional bare bones just won't cut it. We need to eat nutritious foods, and we need to take supplements.

IN THE RED

In part 2, I introduced you to the Anti-Aging Diet, which is designed to get your dietary habits on track for Renewal. If you're like most Americans, you haven't been eating as healthfully as you could.

The standard American diet gets 45 percent of its calories from fat and another 35 percent from sugar. In other words, 80 percent of the calories we consume provide none of the nutrients that our bodies need. Incredibly, despite our dietary excesses and an epidemic of obesity, as a nation we are underfed.

One interesting study examined the incidence of vitamin deficiencies in a randomly selected group of hospital patients. Using the Recommended Dietary Allowances (RDAs) as the standards, 88 percent of the 120 patients came up short in at least one vitamin. Many showed multiple deficiencies. Only 12 percent tested at "normal" levels.

Diet is not the sole force behind the national plague of nutrient deficiencies. Other factors include the following:

- Alcohol consumption (depletes B vitamins, vitamin C, most minerals, and antioxidants)
- Allergies and infections (deplete vitamins A and C and zinc, among other nutrients)
- Exposure to air pollutants and other toxins (depletes antioxidants)
- Smoking (depletes antioxidants)
- Stress (depletes all nutrients, especially B vitamins and vitamin C)

Some people simply require more of certain nutrients than the general population does. Children and older adults tend to need a bit extra, as do pregnant women. Others with increased nutritional demands include those who diet and those who exercise strenuously.

Then, too, some foods that we eat because we think they're healthful have actually been stripped of their nutrients before they get to our plates. Whole wheat loses 75 percent of its B vitamins, minerals, and fiber when it is milled into flour. Likewise, rice loses most of its vitamins, minerals, and fiber when it's polished to turn it from brown to white. Even the soil that these and other plant-derived foods grow in is often nutrient-depleted.

Short by Any Standard

Nutrient deficiencies have become the norm in the United States. As the following statistics suggest, many of us are having a hard time fulfilling our bodies' most basic nutritional needs. The percentages in this table are based on the Recommended Dietary Allowances, which many experts now say are inadequate. Imagine how poorly we'd fare if the required nutrient intakes were higher.

Nutrient	U.S. Population with Deficiencies
Vitamin B_6	90
Magnesium	75
Calcium	68
Iron	57
Vitamin A	50
Thiamin	45
Vitamin C	41
Riboflavin	34
Vitamin B_{12}	34
Niacin	33

THE PRICE OF POOR NUTRITION

Initially, the body hints of a nutrient shortfall with any of a hodgepodge of minor symptoms: fatigue, weakness, insomnia, irritability, nervousness, depression, poor concentration, memory loss, aches and pains, recurrent infections, allergies, circulatory problems, and just not feeling good. These are the vague symptoms that drive patients to doctors, and drive doctors up a diagnostic tree. Because most conventionally trained physicians have little education or experience in nutrition, they're unable to make the connection between a patient's complaints and a nutrient deficiency. Then when the test results come back normal (as they usually do in such cases), the symptoms tend to be dismissed as "all in your head"—or, even worse, as "a natural part of aging."

If doctors do prescribe treatment, they usually bypass

nutritional supplements in favor of drugs such as anti-inflammatories, antidepressants, tranquilizers, and the like. These not only mask symptoms but also deplete nutrient stores even further. This accelerates the degenerative process, which is the forerunner of disease and aging.

Chronic nutrient deficiencies invariably lead to serious health problems. Data collected from large populations show that as the availability of nutrients declines, the frequency of illness increases. Unfortunately, when heart disease, cancer, diabetes, osteoporosis, arthritis, or some other serious deficiency-driven condition develops, neither doctor nor patient is likely to realize that the symptoms had begun years before.

EXPLAINING THE EXCEPTIONS

Ultimately, nutrient deficiencies deprive us of years of life. The average American survives only into his seventies or, if he's lucky, his eighties. Yes, there's always someone who beats these odds and lives to a ripe old age—a 101-year-old Aunt Edna or Uncle Frank who eats nothing but junk food, swigs coffee all morning and downs a shot of whiskey before bed, smokes two packs of cigarettes a day, and has never swallowed a single multivitamin. The fact that such folks live as long as they do is truly remarkable. Unfortunately, they give the rest of us an opportunity to rationalize our own eating habits and lifestyles.

Very few individuals are so genetically well-endowed that they need only stay out of harm's way to survive to age 90 or beyond. For every one of them, there are thousands of the rest of us. And if they took better care of themselves, they could last even longer. Why, Aunt Edna or Uncle Frank might live to see 120.

SHORING UP WITH SUPPLEMENTS

All of us can take a giant leap toward longevity just by taking supplements. Supplementation not only protects against deficiency but also bridges the gap between average nutrition, which culminates in premature death, and optimum nutrition, which extends life span by decades. The extra nutrients that supplements provide prevent marauding free radicals from harming healthy cells, speed the repair and regeneration of damaged cells, and facilitate Renewal. The upshot of all this is a longer, healthier, more vital life.

Supplements are intended to enhance the nutrient density of your diet. By nutrient density, I mean the ratio of micronutrients (vitamins, minerals, and other essential nutrients) to macronutrients (carbohydrates, protein, and fat). The higher this ratio, the healthier your diet.

The Anti-Aging Diet, for instance, has a naturally top-notch nutrient density. Supplements boost the ratio even higher because they supply nothing but essential nutrients—no carbohydrates, protein, or fat.

The combination of a nutrient-dense diet and supplements creates an environment conducive to peak cellular performance. When your cells thrive, your body thrives—and that translates into extra decades of optimum health.

READING BETWEEN THE (REQUIREMENT) LINES

So which nutrients do you need, and in what amounts? Opinions vary. The Recommended Dietary Allowances have been the accepted standard since the early 1940s. But now nutrition researchers generally agree that the RDAs fall far short when it comes to preventing chronic degenerative diseases, promoting optimum health, and extending life.

The RDAs were first established for the purpose of protecting people against severe nutrient deficiency diseases such as beriberi (thiamin deficiency), pellagra (niacin deficiency), and scurvy (vitamin C deficiency). Even though they've been updated several times over the years, the RDAs still do not acknowledge the link between chronic marginal nutrient deficiencies and chronic degenerative diseases. Yet thousands of studies have shown beyond a reasonable doubt that long-term low-grade malnutrition causes or aggravates virtually all of our deadliest illnesses, including heart disease, cancer, diabetes, osteoporosis, and autoimmune disorders (in which the immune system turns against the body). It also contributes to a host of less-serious health problems that nevertheless erode one's quality of life, including cataracts, hearing loss, insomnia, and rheumatism (pain and inflammation in muscles and joints).

Just as poor nutrition can precipitate disease, peak

nutrition can prevent it. Here again, the RDAs are woefully inadequate. They advocate nutrient intakes well below the levels that overwhelming scientific evidence supports as necessary to protect against heart disease, cancer, and all the other conditions mentioned above.

THE REAL IDEAL INTAKE

Achieving the dual goals of optimum health and maximum life span requires nutrient intakes beyond what the RDAs advocate and what diet alone can supply. I recommend replacing the outmoded RDAs with the Optimum Daily Allowances, or ODAs.

The ODAs are the ranges of nutrient dosages prescribed by nutrition-oriented doctors. Each range represents a consensus of experts and is based on thousands of published peer-reviewed studies that determined the nutrient levels necessary to prevent and treat chronic degenerative diseases.

While the RDAs provide only short-term protection against serious acute nutrient deficiencies, the ODAs are necessary to sustain optimum health and support Renewal. Take vitamin E as an example. The human body can get along just fine on the RDA of 30 international units (IU). But it needs at least 13 times that amount to have a fighting chance at staying disease-free and lasting 120 years.

DIET WON'T DO IT

The ODAs far exceed the nutrient levels that diet alone can supply. Supplementation is absolutely essential.

Again, let's use vitamin E as an example. The RDA of 30 IU—the amount necessary to stave off deficiency-related illness—is difficult to get from even the best food sources. So you can imagine the challenge of meeting the ODA of 400 to 1,600 IU without the aid of supplements.

Sunflower seeds have more vitamin E than any other food. To get 400 IU of the nutrient, which is the amount provided by a typical multivitamin or a vitamin E capsule, you'd have to eat 1½ pounds of seeds every day. Even the most ardent sunflower seed fan would find this a bit hard to swallow.

Other vitamin E–rich foods fare even worse. To meet the ODA, you'd have to eat one of the following every day.

- More than 2 pounds of wheat germ
- More than 3 pounds of almonds
- 10 pounds—about 40 ears—of fresh corn
- More than 33 pounds of spinach
- 50 pounds of broccoli or butter

Hmmm ... hope you're hungry.

You have to admit, getting your vitamin E in pill form seems a lot easier (not to mention a lot less filling). And believe me, E is one nutrient that you don't want to run low on. An antioxidant, it scavenges free radicals, stimulates the immune system, protects against cancer and cardiovascular disease (such as hardening of the arteries, angina, heart attack, and stroke), and inhibits the formation of cataracts. For these and many other reasons, vitamin E is a key player in the Renewal process.

Another key player is vitamin C. Like vitamin E, vitamin C is an antioxidant with proven anti-aging effects. It scavenges free radicals, bolsters the immune system, speeds healing, protects against infection, lowers cholesterol, and helps prevent cancer and atherosclerosis (hardening and clogging of the arteries).

To reap these benefits, you need much more vitamin C than the RDA of 60 milligrams. This amount may prevent scurvy, a nutrient deficiency disease that's virtually unheard of these days, but it won't support Renewal. For this, you need the ODA of 1,000 to 10,000 milligrams.

Suppose you're aiming for the low end of the ODA range. To get 1,000 milligrams of vitamin C from foods alone, you'd have to eat 5 cantaloupes, 10 cups of strawberries, 12 bell peppers, 12 cups of raw broccoli, 13 grapefruit, 15 oranges, 40 baked potatoes, 50 red ripe tomatoes, or 62 cups of raw spinach. Every day. And these are the best food sources of vitamin C.

Personally, I recommend an even higher vitamin C intake—2,000 to 6,000 milligrams a day. I base this dosage on reams of research reports as well as on 20 years of clinical practice, during which I've prescribed a great deal of vitamin C to a great many patients for a great many conditions. With the newer, polyascorbate form of vitamin C (called ester-C), you don't have to worry about gastric upset and diarrhea—even at higher doses. This form has more than twice the bioavailability of ascorbic acid, so you need only half as much—1,000 to 3,000 milligrams a day.

For one final example, let's take a look at the carotenoid clan. More than 600 carotenoids have been identified so far. The best known of the bunch is beta-carotene, which your body converts to vitamin A. In fact, both beta-carotene and vitamin A protect against cancers of the larynx, lungs, esophagus, gastrointestinal tract, colon, rectum, breasts, cervix, bladder, prostate, and skin.

To get even a modest daily dose of beta-carotene—say, 20,000 international units, which is actually less than the ODA— you'd have to consume 2 cups of collard greens, 4 large carrots, 7 cups of spinach, 8 cups of broccoli, 10 apricots, 14 cups of prunes, 15 peaches, 30 cups of yellow squash, or 40 cups of zucchini. You're better off taking a supplement that contains mixed natural carotenoids, not just beta-carotene. This way, you're getting the healthiest combination of carotenoids for superior disease-defying powers.

ELIMINATING WASTE?

Beta-carotene, vitamin C, and vitamin E are just three of the 100 or so nutrients that your body needs every day. Imagine how much food you'd have to eat to meet 100 ODAs. Your daily calorie intake would be astronomical.

Despite claims to the contrary, you simply cannot achieve optimum nutrition through diet alone. Even the healthiest, most balanced diet supplies the essential nutrients in amounts far below what are necessary to prevent life-shortening degenerative diseases.

Frankly, I'm amazed that supplementation still generates as much controversy as it does. To me, as to most nutrition-minded doctors, the real threat to health and to life lies in *not* supplementing.

Detractors often charge that supplements do nothing more than create expensive urine. If you take a multivitamin, for example, you may have noticed that it makes your urine turn bright yellow. This does not mean the nutrients are passing through your body unused.

When you ingest water-soluble vitamins—namely, the B

Getting By Versus Getting Ahead

The Recommended Dietary Allowances (RDAs) have come under fire as being too low to prevent chronic degenerative diseases and slow aging. Nutrition-minded experts advocate the Optimum Daily Allowances (ODAs). Here's how the two intakes compare for key anti-aging vitamins and minerals.

Note: The RDAs are for people ages 25 to 50. The ODAs are appropriate for adult men and for adult women who are not pregnant or lactating. They are not intended for children under age 15.

Nutrient	RDA		ODA
	Men	Women	
Vitamins			
A	1,000 mcg. RE (5,000 IU)	800 mcg. RE (4,000 IU)	1,000–10,000 IU
B₆ (pyridoxine)	2 mg.	1.6 mg.	25–250 mg. (as pyridoxal-5-phosphate)
B₁₂	2 mcg.	2 mcg.	500–2,000 mcg.
Beta-carotene	none	none	25,000–100,000 IU
Biotin	30–100 mcg.*	30–100 mcg.*	200–800 mcg.
C	60 mg.	60 mg.	675–3,000 mg. (as ester-C, the preferable form)
D	5 mcg. (200 IU)	5 mcg. (200 IU)	200–1,000 IU
E	10 mg. alpha-tocopherol equivalents (15 IU)	8 mg. alpha-tocopherol equivalents (12 IU)	400–1,600 IU † (as mixed toco-pherols)
Folic acid	200 mcg.	180 mcg.	800–2,000 mcg.

vitamins and vitamin C—your body stores as much as it can in its tissues. Then when the tissues reach their saturation point, any excess nutrient is excreted via the kidneys. So bright yellow urine doesn't mean that your body is

Nutrient	RDA		ODA
	Men	Women	
Niacin/niacin-amide (B$_3$)	19 mg.	15 mg.	50–250 mg.
Pantothenic acid (B$_5$)	4–7 mg.*	4–7 mg.*	60–2,000 mg.
Riboflavin (B$_2$)	1.7 mg.	1.3 mg.	50–250 mg. (as riboflavin 5'-phosphate)
Thiamin (B$_1$)	1.5 mg.	1.1 mg.	100–250 mg.

Minerals

Boron	none	none	1–3 mg.
Calcium	800 mg.	800 mg.	1,000–2,000 mg.
Chromium	50–200 mcg.*	50–200 mcg.*	100–600 mcg.
Copper	1.5–3 mg.*	1.5–3 mg.*	1–3 mg.
Iodine	150 mcg.	150 mcg.	225 mcg.
Iron	10 mg.	15 mg.	0–40 mg.
Magnesium	350 mg.	280 mg.	500–1,000 mg.††
Manganese	2–5 mg.*	2–5 mg.*	5–15 mg.
Molybdenum	75–250 mcg.*	75–250 mcg.*	75–250 mcg.
Potassium	none	none	100–500 mg.
Selenium	70 mcg.	55 mcg.	100–300 mcg.
Vanadium	none	none	25–100 mcg.
Zinc	15 mg.	12 mg.	15–50 mg.

*The amount listed is the Estimated Safe and Adequate Daily Dietary Intake, as recommended by the Committee on Dietary Allowances of the National Academy of Sciences' Food and Nutrition Board.

†People who are taking blood thinners should consult their doctors before taking supplemental vitamin E.

††Supplemental magnesium may cause diarrhea in some people.

wasting precious nutrients. On the contrary, it tells you that nutrients are in abundant supply and that your nutritional insurance policy is in force.

Frankly, I'm worried when my urine is clear. The absence

of the tell-tale gold color warns me that my nutrient levels may be dangerously low. Consequently, my body isn't able to protect, repair, and replace cells as well as it should. If this nutrient shortage goes on for long, it will shut down the Renewal process, leaving my cells vulnerable to degeneration. What critics refer to as expensive urine, knowledgeable doctors view as a sign of optimum nutrition.

YOUR BEST INVESTMENT

Without optimum nutrition, you cannot achieve optimum health. And without supplements, you cannot achieve optimum nutrition. It's as simple as that.

Look at it this way: For the price of a basic multivitamin, you can protect yourself against heart disease, cancer, and all the other health problems associated with chronic low-grade nutrient deficiencies. In the process, you supercharge Renewal and put the brakes on aging.

Personally, I can't think of any investment that pays higher dividends than that.

In the next chapter, we'll examine the relationship between nutrition and disease a bit more closely. We'll pay special attention to atherosclerosis, which is the most common and most deadly of all deficiency-driven health problems. Atherosclerosis develops silently—that is, its symptoms do not appear until it is far advanced. It's also highly preventable, with a little help from supplements.

Preventing a Silent Epidemic

One should die young as late as possible.
—ASHLEY MONTAGU,
  AMERICAN ANTHROPOLOGIST

Almost any diet, even one that consists of three fast-food meals a day, supplies nutrients in amounts that are adequate to keep the average person alive into his sixties or seventies. But eventually, inevitably, the effects of chronic low-grade malnutrition begin to add up.

A heart attack, stroke, or cancerous tumor may seem like a sudden rude awakening. In reality, these and other deficiency-induced illnesses develop slowly and subtly, a consequence of decades of dietary abuses. Arthritis, cataracts, depression, diverticulosis, hearing loss, high blood pressure, Type II (non-insulin-dependent) diabetes, obesity, osteoporosis, periodontal disease, poor circulation, prostate problems, memory loss, senile brain disease—all of these conditions creep up over time. This is why they're so often written off as a "normal" part of aging. In fact, they do not result from aging. Every one of them can be traced to some nutrient shortfall that has persisted for decades.

In our overfed, undernourished nation, this problem has become so widespread that I call it a silent epidemic. "Silent" because for the first 10 to 20 years, deficiency-induced illness may show no symptoms. "Epidemic" because 80 to 90 percent of the adults in this country are afflicted, whether or not they're aware of it.

A GENETIC GLITCH

If you have a nutrient deficiency (odds are that you do), you won't notice any repercussions immediately—perhaps not for years. The disease process is covert and insidious. But a couple of decades from now, maybe more, the symptoms will emerge.

As I explained in chapter 19, the ability to go for so long on a subpar diet is a genetic "gift" from our prehistoric predecessors. For millions of years, they lived off the land, hunting animals and gathering nuts, seeds, and fruits. The quantity and quality of their food supply varied tremendously. They had to survive not only famine but also extended periods during which a limited variety of foods was available. Their bodies adapted to diets extremely deficient in essential nutrients.

Needless to say, our ancestors endured a great deal of nutrient deprivation in order to propagate and ensure continuation of the species. But the genes they passed on to us are programmed for short-term survival, not for longevity—bad news for those of us who aim to stick around for 120 years.

Possessing the genetic makeup to stay alive in times of famine is of little value when food is abundant. On the contrary, it causes major problems by creating the illusion that we can eat whatever we want and suffer no ill effects. Because disease does not set in until much later on, we see no harm in continuing our poor eating habits. We become oblivious to the fact that a lousy diet erodes health and thwarts Renewal.

DISEASE WITHOUT SYMPTOMS

Make no mistake: Malnutrition is rampant in this country. In a long-term study sponsored by the Food and Drug Administration, half of the 12,000 participants—who represented all ages and walks of life—had nutrient intakes below the skimpy Recommended Dietary Allowances (RDAs). Another study produced even more troubling findings: 95 percent of women between ages 40 and 80 suffered from chronic malnutrition, with nutrient intakes significantly below the RDAs. These people experienced unexplained symptoms such as fatigue, joint pain, and shortness of breath. They also had substantially higher mortality rates.

The bottom line is that hordes of symptom-free but nonetheless malnourished people have already begun to develop degenerative conditions such as arthritis, cancer, diabetes, heart disease, high blood pressure, and osteoporosis. Yet because they feel healthy, they believe that they are healthy.

When Minerals Are Minimal

A deficiency of almost any essential nutrient can undermine heart health. But the stakes seem especially high when certain minerals run low, as the following list suggests.

Nutrient	Effects of Deficiency
Chromium	Increases risk of coronary heart disease (reduced or blocked blood flow in the coronary arteries)
Copper	Raises total cholesterol
Magnesium	Increases risk of coronary heart disease, heart rhythm irregularities, and sudden death from heart attack or heart failure
Selenium	Increases risk of atherosclerosis (hardening and clogging of the arteries) and death from heart attack or stroke

It is possible to be seriously ill yet relatively symptom-free. Who hasn't heard of someone getting a clean bill of health from a doctor, only to be felled by a heart attack on the way home from the doctor's office? Did the person's coronary arteries suddenly harden and clog? Of course not. The plaque lining his arteries simply escaped detection. (An astute physician once observed that the first symptom of heart disease is often sudden death.)

With all of its wonderful technology, modern medicine is

Help for Your Heart

Certain nutrients play vital roles in protecting you against atherosclerosis (hardening and clogging of the arteries). While the following list is not complete, these nutrients can go a long way toward keeping your heart healthy for life. Aim for the Optimum Daily Allowance (ODA) each day.

Note: The ODAs are appropriate for adult men and for adult women who are not pregnant or lactating. They are not intended for children under age 15.

Alpha-linolenic acid (an omega-3 fatty acid)
ODA: 2,000–10,000 mg. (from flaxseed oil capsules)
Benefits: Lowers total cholesterol, low-density lipoprotein (LDL) cholesterol (the bad kind), and triglycerides; raises high-density lipoprotein (HDL) cholesterol (the good kind); minimizes platelet stickiness; reduces angina

Calcium
ODA: 1,000–2,000 mg.
Benefits: Lowers total cholesterol, LDL cholesterol, and triglycerides (a type of blood fat); raises HDL cholesterol; discourages blood platelets from sticking together and forming clots; prevents plaque from depositing on artery walls

Chromium
ODA: 100–600 mcg.
Benefits: Lowers total cholesterol, LDL cholesterol, and triglycerides; raises HDL cholesterol; dissolves plaque deposits

Coenzyme Q$_{10}$
ODA: 50–300 mg.
Benefits: Improves heart function; reduces angina and risk of heart attack

Magnesium
ODA: 500–1,000 mg.*
Benefits: Lowers total cholesterol, LDL cholesterol, and triglycerides; raises HDL cholesterol; discourages blood platelets from sticking together; reduces risk

of heart rhythm abnormalities, angina, and sudden death from heart attack

Pantothenic acid (B₅)

ODA: 60–2,000 mg.

Benefits: Lowers total cholesterol, LDL cholesterol, and triglycerides; raises HDL cholesterol; minimizes platelet stickiness

Phosphatidylcholine (lecithin)

ODA: 600–4,000 mg.

Benefits:: Lowers total cholesterol, LDL cholesterol, and triglycerides; raises HDL cholesterol; dissolves plaque deposits

Vitamin B₆ (pyridoxine)

ODA: 25–250 mg. (as pyridoxal-5-phosphate)

Benefits: Lowers total cholesterol and triglycerides; minimizes platelet stickiness

Vitamin C

ODA: 675–3,000 mg. (as ester-C, the preferable form)

Benefits: Lowers total cholesterol, LDL cholesterol, and triglycerides; raises HDL cholesterol; minimizes platelet stickiness; supports production of the enzymes necessary for the removal of cholesterol and triglycerides; facilitates the synthesis of collagen, which is necessary for healthy arterial walls; enhances fibrinolytic (clot-busting) ability; improves circulation in the extremities; prevents saturated fat from increasing platelet stickiness

Vitamin E

ODA: 400–1,600 IU† (as mixed tocopherols)

Benefits: Lowers total cholesterol, LDL cholesterol, and triglycerides; raises HDL cholesterol; minimizes platelet stickiness; improves circulation in the extremities; protects arterial walls from free radical damage

*Supplemental magnesium may cause diarrhea in some people.

†People who are taking blood thinners should consult their doctors before taking supplemental vitamin E.

usually useful only when symptoms turn catastrophic—when chest pain occurs or brain function fails or a lump appears. Until then, we're told that "all the tests are negative" and "your health is excellent," which only reinforces our denial that a problem exists. We continue to believe that the standard American diet—high in fat and sugar, low in vitamins, minerals, and fiber—hasn't undermined our health. But it has.

FIGHTING BACK AGAINST DEFICIENCY

You can dramatically decrease your chances of being among the 90 percent of people who die prematurely as a consequence of silent, insidious degenerative diseases. How? By following the Renewal Anti-Aging Diet and Anti-Aging Supplement Program. Together they serve as preventive medicine—your preemptive strike against chronic malnutrition and the health problems that it causes.

Only in the past few decades have we come to understand human nutrition well enough to exert intelligent control over it. Researchers have unraveled some of the most fundamental mysteries of human biochemistry, including the discovery of essential nutrients, antioxidant nutrients, phytochemicals, and natural hormones. Their findings have spawned an entire industry that manufactures nutritional products not even dreamed of just two decades ago.

Today, a bounty of healthful foods and supplements is yours for the taking. By taking advantage of what's available, you can biochemically supercharge your metabolism, accelerate Renewal, and create longevity. The choice is yours.

ATHEROSCLEROSIS: A CAUSE, A CURE

Atherosclerosis, a condition characterized by gradual hardening and clogging of the arteries, is the most common of all chronic degenerative diseases. In fact, it is an epidemic: In the United States alone, it's responsible for three-quarters of all deaths.

You can arrest the progression of atherosclerosis by correcting the nutrient deficiencies that lead to cellular degeneration in the first place (see "When Minerals Are Minimal"). Or you can prevent the disease by making sure that you get your ODAs (see "Help for Your Heart" on page 274).

Nutritional therapy has proven successful in improving the symptoms of atherosclerosis even after they become physically apparent. But rather than waiting until the disease establishes itself and then trying to reverse it, why not protect yourself against it by aiming for the ODAs? After all, if Humpty Dumpty had never sat on that wall ...

YOUR BEST DEFENSE

Atherosclerosis is just one of many health problems that can be treated and, even better, prevented with proper nutrition. To me, as a doctor, the plague of chronic malnutrition that afflicts the American population is a senseless, heartbreaking tragedy. Most of the heart attacks, strokes, and cancers—the conditions that diminish quality of life and often end life prematurely—are preventable.

The relatively simple measures that I advocate throughout this book can extend your life span with years of good health and vitality while preventing the miseries of disease and decrepitude. Although the biochemistry behind them can seem quite complex, the principles of this Renewal-supporting lifestyle are yawningly simple.

- Build your diet around foods that are known to reduce your risk of chronic degenerative diseases. This means choosing only foods of plant origin—organically grown, unprocessed, low in fat and protein, high in complex carbohydrates.
- Avoid—or at least limit—exposure to toxins in food, water, and air.
- Take supplements to support cellular health and to boost your nutrient intakes to ODA levels.

The Renewal Anti-Aging Diet and the Renewal Anti-Aging Supplement Program make these principles practical. They can help you dramatically decrease your chances of being among the 90 percent of people who die prematurely as a consequence of chronic degenerative diseases.

Think of these plans as a preemptive strike against illness and aging.

We've seen how nutrient deficiencies set the stage for disease. Now let's examine why taking supplements is such powerful preventive medicine.

CHAPTER 21

Supplements Provide
Nutritional Insurance

*Dying is a very dull, dreary affair. And my advice to you
is to have nothing whatever to do with it.*
—W. SOMERSET MAUGHAM (1874–1966),
 BRITISH AUTHOR

The stresses and strains of everyday life—large and small, physical and emotional—take a continuous toll on your body. Renewal must go on constantly just to keep pace.

If your body's healing system does not have access to the nutritional building blocks it needs precisely when it needs them, the Renewal process breaks down. This, in turn, accelerates aging.

You can see why providing your body with abundant supplies of nutrients is so important. The combination of eating healthful foods—foods of plant origin, which are rich in essential nutrients, antioxidants, and phytochemicals—and taking nutritional supplements guarantees efficient cellular protection, repair, and replacement. This is what you need to slow and reverse aging.

A STATE OF CONSTANT CHANGE

In your body's fragile economy, nutrient supply and demand can fluctuate considerably from one day to the next. For starters, your diet varies, which means that your nutrient intake varies. Then, too, your body's needs change. It may require more of a given nutrient one day, less the next.

I'll use myself as an example. On days when I see patients in my office, I take extra B-complex vitamins, because they are depleted by stress. If I'm planning to write or to give a lecture, I'll scarf extra vitamin B_{12}, ginkgo, ginseng, acetyl-L-carnitine, phosphatidylserine, and pregnenolone to give my brain a boost. (You'll learn more about these and other "neuronutrients" in chapter 29.) When I have to spend time in the smoggy city, I increase my doses of antioxidants, including carotenoids and other phytochemicals, coenzyme Q_{10}, garlic, ginseng, and vitamins C and E. These nutrients scavenge the cell-damaging free radicals produced by air pollution.

It would be wonderful if the human body came equipped with a device that could monitor levels of all of the important nutrients and sound an alarm when any ran dangerously low. Then you could just replenish those that had fallen to suboptimum levels. Unfortunately, even scientists armed with computers have found this task impossible. As yet, you have no way of anticipating what your body's demand for each nutrient might be on any given day, much less correlating this information with an intake. You can only guess.

Because of the daily changes in nutrient supply and demand, your best bet is to err on the side of slight excess. Having a little extra of any nutrient won't harm you. But a brief deficiency can, and a prolonged one will.

Supplementation at Optimum Daily Allowance levels can protect you against deficiencies, even on those days when your body's nutrient demands are high or your nutrient intake is iffy. This way, you can be certain that your body always has enough of the nutritional raw materials it needs to administer the Renewal process.

NUTRITIONAL TEAMWORK

Nutrients are specialists. Each performs a specific set of tasks within your body, sustaining life by supporting cellular protection, repair, and replacement. Running low on any one nutrient is like running your car with a spark plug missing: The internal machinery can function, but not nearly as efficiently as when all of the parts are in place.

This raises an important point. Even though nutrients

have distinct assignments, they very much depend upon one another to do their jobs. One nutrient becomes more effective in the context of others, creating a network of mutually beneficial interactions. Only by working together can nutrients dramatically slow the aging process. In Renewal, the whole is truly greater than the sum of the parts.

Because nutrients work synergistically, a deficiency of even one impairs the functioning not only of the systems dependent on it but of the entire metabolic milieu. It's like an orchestra performing without its cello section: The rest of the musicians play their parts, but somehow the symphony sounds incomplete. Likewise, an undernourished body can carry on, but its performance would amount to the biochemical equivalent of cacophony: accelerated aging.

DISRUPTED PRODUCTION

For Renewal to function efficiently, your body requires a continuous supply of about 50 nutrients—none of which it can make for itself. These nutrients support the synthesis of chemicals that your cells need to survive.

To better understand just what happens, imagine your body as a manufacturing plant with tens of thousands of production lines. Each line is responsible for making a certain chemical. It does this by executing a series of reactions, using nutrients as its raw materials.

If a line doesn't have enough of a certain nutrient, the corresponding reaction cannot proceed. Production grinds to a halt until the nutrient is restocked. Biochemists refer to the interrupted reaction as a rate-limiting step.

If a rate-limiting step is short-lived, it affects only a few cells. That's not so bad. If a nutrient remains out of stock for a long time, or if it repeatedly runs out, however, trillions of cells will be affected. That's very bad.

A chronic nutrient deficiency undermines health and promotes degenerative disease, although the symptoms may not appear for many years. Running low on beta-carotene, for instance, opens the door to most types of cancer. A shortage of calcium depletes bone mass, which eventually leads to osteoporosis. Too little folic acid precipitates heart attacks and, in women, cervical dysplasia (the development of precancerous cervical cells). A depleted supply of selenium weakens the immune system.

AGE IS AN ISSUE

The high price paid for suboptimum nutrition rises with age. As you get older, your body's nutrient needs continue to increase. Yet meeting these needs grows ever more difficult.

Once you hit your forties, your gastrointestinal tract begins losing its absorptive power. Fewer of the nutrients in the foods you eat actually make their way into your bloodstream. This poses a significant problem for people age 50 and over, whose bodies are demanding more nutrients but absorbing less. In fact, it is a chief contributor to the chronic degenerative diseases common in our older population.

Other physical changes associated with aging serve only to aggravate circumstances. For instance, the body's production of digestive enzymes, which are responsible for breaking down food, gradually declines. And cumulative free radical damage to the cells of the intestinal lining further compromises nutrient absorption.

Diminished nutrient absorption means reduced nutrient levels in organs and tissues, which in turn means accelerated degeneration—that is, rapid aging. To bring the problem full circle, when the gastrointestinal tract receives less nourishment, it becomes even less able to absorb nutrients efficiently. It's a vicious circle, and it accelerates each time around.

You want to start protecting your gastrointestinal tract now, so it serves you as well later on in life as it has thus far. Think about it: All of the other organs and systems in your body depend upon the gastrointestinal tract for their nutrient supplies. If your digestive equipment isn't working properly, the rest of your body suffers as well.

Aging brings dietary changes, too. Appetite often declines with advancing years. Eating habits deteriorate as well, as food shopping and meal preparation become more burdensome.

All of these factors conspire to create serious nutrient deficiencies in older people. Faced with ever-decreasing nutrient supplies and ever-increasing nutrient demands, their bodies struggle to continue Renewal. But the deficiencies prove to be too much, causing rapid cellular degeneration and speeding up the aging process.

Of course, just by taking supplements, you can protect yourself against nutrient deficits as you get older. Supplementation helps in two ways. First, it raises your nutrient intakes to Optimum Daily Allowance levels, so you're unlikely to experience any shortages. Second, it keeps your gastrointestinal tract healthy, so nutrients are efficiently absorbed.

A SMART MOVE FOR ANY BODY

You're never too old to start taking supplements. But since they can do your body so much good, why wait?

Diet alone can't satisfy your body's nutrient needs. The standard American diet—high in fat, low in fiber and nutrients—is especially inadequate, leaving cells feeble, flimsy, and fragile. In such a weakened state, they're unable to muster resistance to disease or slow the aging process.

Daily supplementation provides powerful protection against age-accelerating deficiencies by supplying all of the nutritional building blocks that your body requires. It also enriches your internal biochemical soup, increasing nutrient bioavailability and facilitating the complex set of biochemical reactions that we call life. When you sustain this nurturing environment for a long period of time—months, years, even decades—each and every cell in your body becomes healthier. What's more, cells conceived and nourished in this soup make robust replacements for those that are injured or die.

These new, supercharged cells are eager to work, and they can perform their specialized functions at peak efficiency. Nerve cells transmit messages better, intestinal cells digest and transport nutrients better, immune cells protect against cancer, allergies, and infections better. Each of the 100 trillion cells in your body does its job with greater ease and effectiveness. Together, they translate to a healthier, longer-lived you.

Even though supplements have proven themselves effective in protecting health and promoting longevity, they're still viewed with skepticism by many in the medical community. Why the controversy? The next chapter offers some answers.

Should You Trust Your Doctor? Most Physicians Are Not Nutritionists

Our studies at Harvard suggest that the average physician knows a little more about nutrition than the average secretary—unless the secretary has a weight problem. Then she probably knows more than the average physician.
—JEAN MAYER (1920–93), NUTRITION EXPERT AND PRESIDENT OF TUFTS UNIVERSITY IN MEDFORD, MASSACHUSETTS (1976–92)

Authors of health books usually qualify their advice by suggesting that readers check with their physicians before making any dietary changes to improve their health. I can't in good conscience make that recommendation.

Unfortunately, although many physicians consider themselves experts on nutrition, surprisingly (and disappointingly) few are actually knowledgeable about the subject. That's because most are never taught. Of the 125 medical schools in the United States, only 30 have required coursework in nutrition. And that coursework is mighty short: The average medical student receives just 2½ hours of training in nutrition over four years.

Clearly, this isn't enough time to cultivate a thorough understanding of the relationship between nutrition and health. As a result, physicians often disregard diet and supplementation as effective means of treating and preventing disease—especially heart disease and cancer, the number one and number two killers of our time.

SUSPICIONS ABOUT NUTRITION

As I explained in chapter 20, heart disease, cancer, and other chronic degenerative conditions get their start years before they show outward symptoms. These conditions progress silently, as poor nutrition erodes cellular protection, repair, and replacement—the very foundation of Renewal.

This process confounds traditionally educated doctors, who are taught to think in terms of demonstrable pathology. In other words, they rely on physical exams, laboratory tests, x-rays, and other diagnostic procedures to confirm the presence of disease. If there is no pathology, there is no disease.

Within this framework, "health" means merely the absence of illness. It doesn't recognize the broader spectrum of wellness, a continuum that ranges from severe sickness at one end to optimum health at the other.

Such a narrow definition of health has spawned an all-or-nothing mindset in the diagnosis of disease. A patient who does not exhibit symptoms of scurvy, for example, can't possibly have a deficiency of vitamin C. A patient with no symptoms of pellagra obviously has no niacin problem. And if a patient has no symptoms of beriberi, his thiamin level must be okay.

This approach to diagnosis does not take into consideration suboptimum nutrition, which has reached epidemic proportions in this country. Nor does it acknowledge widespread subclinical (present but not yet clinically detectable) malnutrition, which will eventually contribute to the deaths of 80 percent of all Americans.

Perhaps you've been fortunate enough to find a doctor who truly understands the importance of optimum nutrition and who dispenses meaningful advice on diet and supplements. Sadly, such practitioners are a rare breed. Less informed physicians often greet questions about nutrition with inaccurate, knee-jerk responses like "You don't need supplements" or "Eat a well-balanced diet, and you'll get all the nutrients you need." Such statements might carry more weight if these physicians outlived their patients, which, on average, they don't.

LEAVING THE MAINSTREAM

While nutritional therapy is slowly gaining acceptance, it is still viewed as alternative medicine by the mainstream medical community. Like acupuncture, herbal therapy, homeopathy, and other alternative modalities, nutritional therapy emphasizes wellness and prevention of disease rather than the diagnosis and treatment of disease. Mainstream medicine, for all of its science, has yet to come to terms with the concept of wellness, much less with the techniques that encourage it.

To illustrate how mainstream medicine and alternative medicine approach health and healing differently, let's consider a symptom that is frequently reported by my patients: chronic or recurrent fatigue. A traditionally educated doctor may order "the works"—a physical exam, laboratory tests, and x-rays. All of the results come back negative. Since the doctor has no objective evidence of pathology, or an abnormality, he concludes that no disease exists.

A holistically trained doctor, on the other hand, believes that fatigue can result from a multitude of factors rather than just one. He, too, does a physical exam—but he also scrutinizes the patient's family medical history, diet, lifestyle, and behavior patterns. Based on his findings, this doctor may conclude that the patient's fatigue is caused by suboptimum functioning of one or more organs or systems. In other words, something inside the patient's body is out of balance—something that wouldn't show up during a traditional diagnostic workup but that would produce vague symptoms such as fatigue. Correcting the underlying imbalance should restore the patient's energy and vigor.

Of course, the true test of a diagnosis is the patient's response to treatment. In this case, a holistic doctor would likely prescribe a combination of dietary changes, supplements, exercise, herbs, homeopathic remedies, and acupuncture. All of these strategies are directed toward healing the faltering organ or system while supporting recuperation and enhancing overall health.

ATHEROSCLEROSIS: DIET MAKES A DIFFERENCE

In the example above, let's suppose that conventional diagnostic techniques do uncover evidence of disease. A traditionally educated doctor, lacking adequate training in nutrition, would likely recommend treatment with drugs or perhaps even surgery. He would probably not suggest nutritional measures to heal the body, save for the standard admonition to "eat a low-fat diet."

Consider atherosclerosis, a condition characterized by gradual hardening and clogging of the arteries. Traditionally educated doctors are seldom aware of all of the nutritional excesses and deficiencies that precede, sometimes by several decades, heart attack and stroke. Yet research has shown that the arterial degeneration responsible for these events is almost exclusively caused by dietary factors.

The conventional treatment for atherosclerosis consists of cholesterol-lowering drugs and possibly a low-fat diet. By conventional standards, a "low-fat diet" gets 30 percent of its calories from fat and includes, of all things, chicken and fish. Yet research by Dean Ornish, M.D.; Nathan Pritikin; John McDougall, M.D.; and other nutrition-minded experts has shown that a truly low-fat, vegetarian diet—one that derives just 10 percent of its calories from fat—can reverse as well as prevent atherosclerosis. What's more, thousands of published studies support the value of broad-spectrum supplementation in treating the disease.

Nutrition-conscious doctors prescribe customized, comprehensive self-care programs for their patients with atherosclerosis. They routinely recommend cutting fat intake to 10 percent of calories and eliminating saturated fat, cholesterol, and hydrogenated vegetable oils. They advocate eating lots of oats, beans, onions, garlic, and other foods known to benefit hardened, clogged arteries. And they're likely to prescribe supplementation of an array of heart-friendly essential nutrients—including folic acid, vitamin E, calcium, coenzyme Q_{10}, chromium, copper, essential fatty acids, magnesium, niacin, pantothenic acid, potassium, selenium, vitamin B_6, vitamin C, and zinc—at Optimum Daily Allowance levels. A program like this can slow and even reverse the progression of atherosclerosis and dramatically reduce a patient's risk of heart attack and stroke.

HOSPITAL FOOD: SUSTENANCE OR SUBSISTENCE?

Even if a disease has progressed to the point where only surgery can help, optimum nutrition is key to the recovery process. Surprisingly, the meals served to postoperative patients, even in some of the nation's most highly regarded teaching hospitals, supply grossly inadequate amounts of the nutrients most essential to healing.

As an example, consider the case of Art Voll, an advertising executive in his fifties. When Art developed chest pain, his doctor sent him for an angiogram. The test results showed that Art's coronary arteries had narrowed. The doctor recommended coronary bypass surgery. But Art, not one to stand on the sidelines and let others make crucial decisions, began reading all that he could about his condition. This man who had never paid much attention to his diet (or to exercise, for that matter) suddenly became nutritionally enlightened. Unfortunately, the realization that his heart problems had resulted from consuming too much fat, sugar, and alcohol came too late for Art to avoid surgery.

When Art saw his first postoperative meal, he could hardly believe his eyes: chicken (high in fat, pesticides, antibiotics, and hormones), canned peas (depleted of B vitamins during processing and cooking), mashed potatoes with butter, white bread (depleted of B vitamins, minerals, and fiber) with more butter, gelatin (high in sugar but devoid of essential nutrients), and coffee—cream optional. Amazingly, this is typical hospital fare.

Thanks to what he had read prior to surgery, Art knew that eating meals like the one he had been served could produce a coronary blockage, which is what landed him in the hospital in the first place. So he left, discharging himself against medical advice. He figured he'd be better off at home, where he could control his diet.

Art can count himself among the fortunate ones. Studies have shown that most hospital patients are undernourished. And when they're undernourished, they recover more slowly, have a higher incidence of residual disease, are more prone to relapse, and generally have poorer prognoses.

Every hospital patient can benefit from health-supporting meals of fresh, whole foods as well as a broad-spectrum multivitamin/mineral supplement. Other supplements can be prescribed based on the person's specific nutritional requirements. For example, heart patients like Art need extra carotenoids, chromium, coenzyme Q_{10}, essential fatty acids, magnesium, phytochemicals, potassium, vitamin C, and vitamin E. Patients with infections need extra vitamin A, B-complex vitamins, vitamin C, and zinc. Postoperative patients need extra calcium, magnesium, B-complex vitamins, vitamin C, and zinc.

Unfortunately, until more doctors become more knowledgeable about nutrition, the dismal state of the hospital diet probably won't change. Nor will patients receive the supplements that are so vital to their recovery.

PUTTING THINGS IN PERSPECTIVE

Nothing I've said here is meant to diminish the value of mainstream medicine. As a doctor who has studied both Western and Eastern medical traditions, I wholeheartedly believe that the two can—and should—coexist. Frankly, when it comes to evaluating and managing serious illness and injury, mainstream medicine has no peer.

If I'm ever hurt in an automobile accident, I want to be taken to the nearest trauma center. If I develop a malignant tumor, I want to be treated by a cancer surgeon. If I'm diagnosed with diabetes, I want to be under the care of an endocrinologist.

These physicians specialize in managing illness and injury, which is exactly what I want if I'm seriously sick or hurt. Out of necessity, they do not focus on promoting health. If I'm searching for a holistic approach to health that shows me how to prevent disease and how to heal myself using nutrition and other natural medicines, however, then an alternative doctor is often the better choice.

One final word: If your doctor seems evasive or uninformed on the subject of nutrition, you may want to consider shopping around for someone new. It takes time, but in terms of your health, it's worth the effort.

You now know why supplementation is so important to achieving optimum health and maximum life span. With that in mind, let's get into the details of the Renewal Anti-Aging Supplement Program. The next section of the book lays it all out for you.

PART 4
The Renewal Anti-Aging Supplement Program

The Basic Components of Your Personal Supplement Strategy

I believe that you can, by taking some simple and inexpensive measures, extend your life and your years of well-being. My most important recommendation is that you all take vitamins every day in optimum amounts, to supplement the vitamins you receive in your food.
—LINUS PAULING, PH.D. (1901–94), TWO-TIME NOBEL PRIZE LAUREATE

After a quarter-century of practicing alternative medicine and Chinese traditional medicine, I'm more in awe than ever of the human body's remarkable ability to heal itself. Injured cells are repaired and dead cells are replaced with astonishing efficiency in a body that is primed for Renewal.

A combination of sound diet, daily supplementation, and regular exercise creates an internal environment that supports the Renewal process. Occasionally—especially if illness has already set in—Renewal may require some extra assistance in the form of acupuncture, herbal therapy, homeopathy, massage, and other holistic (whole-body) therapies.

Of all of the "ingredients" in the Renewal process, perhaps none is as important as supplementation. Supplements guarantee your body uninterrupted access to optimum amounts of all of the nutrients it needs. In doing so, supplements help to prevent disease, create vibrant health, and slow aging.

The Anti-Aging Supplement Program, which I outline in the following chapters, supplies all of the necessary nutrients in the right dosages. Some of the supplements are recommended for everyone, while others are discretionary—dependent upon individual health, diet, and lifestyle factors. As you decide which of these supplements to take, bear this in mind: *The extent to which you follow the Renewal Anti-Aging Supplement Program determines the extent to which you'll benefit from it.*

WHEN THE PROGRAM BEGAN

To understand why I feel so strongly about the value of supplementation, perhaps you should know a bit more about my background. I was a medical student in the late 1960s, a tumultuous time when my generation questioned and challenged anything that we considered to represent the "establishment." Consistent with the climate of the time, I developed a profound skepticism of conventional medicine and its emphasis on treating only the symptoms of disease.

So in the early 1970s, after completing medical school and my internship, I began exploring nontraditional healing disciplines that offered natural alternatives to powerful drugs and invasive surgical techniques. I studied the principles of Chinese traditional medicine, homeopathy, herbal therapy, and orthomolecular medicine, which teaches that disease can be cured by correcting deficiencies of substances normally present in the body. I found inspiration in classic Chinese medical texts as well as in the works of Linus Pauling, Ph.D., Adelle Davis, Abraham Hoffer, M.D., Ph.D., Roger Williams, Ph.D., Robert Atkins, M.D., and other pioneers of the nutritional medicine movement.

Slowly, I began integrating all that I had learned into my private practice. For each patient, I'd identify and prescribe appropriate vitamins, minerals, herbs, and other natural remedies. Invariably, these healing agents performed better than prescription drugs, with patients showing often dramatic improvement. And because the natural remedies contained no "foreign" molecules unfamiliar to the body, they produced none of the adverse reactions or toxicities so often associated with prescription drugs.

My patients' success stories persuaded me to delve even more deeply into the available literature about alternative disciplines, especially nutritional medicine. As I absorbed the new information and applied it in my practice, I realized that the same nutrients used to treat disease could also stop it from developing in the first place. In other words, supplements were not only therapeutic but preventive, too.

Broad-spectrum supplementation became standard advice for all of my patients, both to speed healing and to safeguard health. At first, my prescriptions included primarily vitamins, minerals, amino acids, and herbs. Later on, as scientific research substantiated the potent medicinal powers of other nutrients—essential fatty acids, coenzyme Q_{10}, glutathione, phytochemicals, brain nutrients, natural hormones, internal cleansers—my list of remedies grew.

Then came the most exciting revelation of all—the one that inspired me to write this book. The broad-spectrum supplementation that I was recommending to my patients not only fought disease but also slowed the aging process. Through my patients, I had my first glimpse of the Renewal process at work.

So which supplements gave my patients a jump start on maximum life span? They fall into seven general categories.

- Essential nutrients
- Antioxidants (including essential nutrients and phytochemicals)
- Phytochemicals
- Anti-aging herbs
- Anti-aging hormones
- Brain nutrients
- Internal cleansers

Each of these categories is summarized below and in the table on page 296. You'll learn a lot more about them in the next several chapters.

ESSENTIAL NUTRIENTS: YOU CAN'T LIVE WITHOUT 'EM

The essential nutrients include vitamins, minerals, essential fatty acids, and amino acids. They are called essential because they're absolutely necessary for human survival. Without them, your body would not be able to manufacture the multitude of chemicals required to sustain life: DNA, RNA, neurotransmitters, enzymes, hormones, antibodies, and more.

Diet alone—even the Anti-Aging Diet—cannot deliver optimum amounts of all the essential nutrients, with the exception of amino acids, all the time. (Remember, if you want to achieve maximum life span, you must aim for nutrient intakes at Optimum Daily Allowance levels.) A temporary deficit of just one of the essential nutrients taxes your body. A prolonged low-grade deficiency causes cells to malfunction or die, precipitates chronic degenerative disease, and thwarts Renewal. In the United States, at least, essential nutrient deficiencies have reached epidemic proportions.

The Program at a Glance

The supplements listed below make·up the Renewal Anti-Aging Supplement Program. Those marked with an asterisk (*) also have antioxidant properties. For optimum nutrition, aim for the middle to upper end of each optimum daily allowance range.

Note: *The Optimum Daily Allowances (ODAs) are appropriate for adult men and for adult women who are not pregnant or lactating. They are not intended·for children under age 15.*

Supplement	ODA
Essential Nutrients	
Vitamins	
A*	1,000–10,000 IU
Beta-carotene*	25,000–100,000 IU
Thiamin (B$_1$)	100–250 mg.
Riboflavin (B$_2$)	50–250 mg. (as riboflavin 5'-phosphate)
Niacin/niacinamide (B$_3$)	50–250 mg.
Pantothenic acid (B$_5$)	60–2,000 mg.
B$_6$ (pyridoxine)	25–250 mg. (as pyridoxal-5-phosphate)
B$_{12}$	500–2,000 mcg.
Folic acid	800–2,000 mcg.
C*	675–3,000 mg. (as ester-C, the preferable form)
Bioflavonoids*	500–4,000 mg.
D	200–1,000 IU
E*	400–1,600 IU[†] (as mixed tocopherols)

Supplement	ODA
Minerals	
Calcium	1,000–2,000 mg.
Magnesium	500–1,000 mg.[††]
Potassium	100–500 mg.
Manganese	5–15 mg.
Iron	0–40 mg.
Chromium	100–600 mcg.
Selenium*	100–300 mcg.
Boron	1–3 mg.
Iodine	100–225 mcg.
Copper*	1–3 mg.
Zinc*	15–50 mg.
Molybdenum	75–250 mcg.
Vanadium	25–100 mcg.
Essential Fatty Acids	
Alpha-linolenic acid* (an omega-3 fatty acid)	2,000–10,000 mg. (from flaxseed oil capsules)
Gamma-linolenic acid* (an omega-6 fatty acid)	250–500 mg. (from borage oil capsules)
Other	
Coenzyme Q_{10}*	50–300 mg.
Anti-Aging Herbs	
Ginseng*	25–75 mg. (as standardized to ginsenoside Rg1)
Ginkgo*	120–240 mg. (as 24% standardized extract)
Garlic*	500–2,000 mg. (as standardized extract)
Anti-Aging Hormones	
Dehydroepiandrosterone (DHEA)*	10–100 mg.
Pregnenolone	25–200 mg.
Melatonin*	0.5–10 mg.
Estrogen	Determined by physician

Supplement	ODA
Anti-Aging Hormones (continued)	
Progesterone	Determined by physician
Testosterone	Determined by physician
Thyroid	Determined by physician
Brain Nutrients [§]	
Phosphatidylserine	100–300 mg.
Acetyl-L-carnitine*	500–3,000 mg.
Internal Cleansers	
Fiber [‖]	2–20 grams
Probiotics[#]	4–40 billion

†*People who are taking blood thinners should consult their doctors before taking supplemental vitamin E.*

††*Supplemental magnesium may cause diarrhea in some people.*

[§]*Pregnenolone and ginkgo are also brain nutrients.*

[‖] *Includes psyllium, oat bran, guar gum, rice bran, and fruit pectin.*

[#]*Includes* Bifidobacterium bifidum, Bifidobacterium longum, Lactobacillus acidophilus, Lactobacillus bulgaricus, Lactobacillus casei, Lactobacillus rhamnosus, Streptococcus faecium, *and related beneficial bacteria.*

Because the essential nutrients are so vital to human health, they form the cornerstone of the Anti-Aging Supplement Program. As part of the program, I recommend the following.

Vitamins and minerals. Of the essential nutrients, vitamins and minerals have the most direct involvement in cellular protection, repair, and replacement—the very essence of Renewal. A high-quality multivitamin/mineral supplement should cover all of your vitamin and mineral needs. I strongly suggest that you take a multivitamin, even if you choose to take nothing else.

Essential fatty acids. These "good fats," which I discussed at length in chapter 8, also qualify as essential nutrients. They are the raw materials from which the body manufactures cell membranes, the highly selective barriers that determine what gets into your cells and what must stay out. They also support the synthesis of hormonelike chemical messengers called prostaglandins, which influence the activity of the immune, nervous, circulatory, endocrine (hormone), excretory, and reproductive systems.

Optimum amounts of the essential fatty acids must be present in the body for Renewal to occur. But as with vitamins and minerals, you cannot obtain optimum amounts from diet alone. In fact, if you follow the standard American diet—which emphasizes processed, preserved foods over fresh, whole foods—you almost certainly have an essential fatty acid deficiency. Such deficiencies affect more than 80 percent of the American population, especially people over age 40. Uncorrected, essential fatty acid deficiencies accelerate the development of chronic degenerative disease and ultimately shorten life.

Optimum intake of the essential fatty acids is so important to Renewal that I consider supplementation absolutely necessary. Accordingly, the Anti-Aging Supplement Program recommends flaxseed oil capsules for alpha-linolenic acid (an omega-3 fatty acid) and borage oil capsules for gamma-linolenic acid (an omega-6 fatty acid).

Coenzyme Q_{10}. Technically, coenzyme Q_{10} fits into none of the above categories. Yet it's vital not only to the Renewal process but to your very survival, which is why I've classified it as an essential nutrient.

A potent antioxidant, coenzyme Q_{10} neutralizes free radicals, especially those generated as cells burn food in oxygen for energy. Your body can make its own coenzyme Q_{10}, but production slumps markedly around age 30 and continues to slow with advancing age. Once you reach your forties, your body makes so little that the nutrient becomes essential. Supplementation of coenzyme Q_{10} is crucial if you want to keep the Renewal process functioning efficiently and minimize the effects of aging.

Amino acids. Amino acids are considered essential because they are the building blocks of protein. A good diet usually provides adequate amounts of aminos. For this reason, I usually don't recommend supplements unless testing reveals a specific deficiency.

ANTIOXIDANTS: FREE RADICAL RAIDERS

Coenzyme Q_{10} is just one example of an antioxidant. Many other nutrients have similar free radical–fighting properties. By protecting cells against free radical damage, antioxidants help to prevent disease and slow the aging process.

The antioxidant segment of the Anti-Aging Supplement Program includes the following.

Essential nutrients. Some essential nutrients—such as the vitamins A, C, and E, the minerals copper, selenium, and zinc, and coenzyme Q_{10}—double as antioxidants.

Phytochemicals. Found only in plant-derived foods, phytochemicals prevent disease and support the body's healing systems. As with the essential nutrients, many—but not all—phytochemicals act as antioxidants. This rather recently discovered group of "supernutrients" includes the carotenoids in carrots, the sulforaphane in broccoli, the proanthocyanidins in red grapes, and the protease inhibitors and phytoestrogens in soy.

ANTI-AGING HERBS: PROTECTION FROM PLANTS

Practitioners of Chinese traditional medicine have long recognized the medicinal value of herbs. Scientific research now shows that these plants draw their potent therapeutic powers from the healing phytochemicals they contain.

From thousands of worthy candidates, I've selected three herbs—ginseng, ginkgo, and garlic—for inclusion in the Anti-Aging Supplement Program. This trio offers the most potent array of anti-aging benefits.

Ginseng. For more than 5,000 years, the Chinese have prized ginseng for its rejuvenating properties. For them, the venerable herb has come to symbolize health, strength, and long life. Now Western scientific research is proving that ginseng can indeed fight aging. Among its many benefits, the herb strengthens the immune system, stimulates the hormone-producing endocrine system, enhances mental function, and staves off the effects of stress.

Ginkgo. By boosting blood flow to all organs and systems within the body, ginkgo puts the brakes on the aging process. Though it offers natural protection against heart attack and stroke, the herb's most remarkable restorative and protective effects are reserved for the brain: Ginkgo sharpens cognitive function, enhances memory, and prevents senile dementia and stroke. In fact, ginkgo may turn out to be one of our most effective weapons against age-related brain disorders.

Garlic. Science has proven folklore right: Garlic does indeed have the power to ward off disease. In studies, the so-called stinking rose has displayed an astonishing array of age-reversing effects on the cardiovascular and immune systems. It helps to prevent atherosclerosis (hardening and clogging of the arteries) and cancer, two chronic degenerative diseases that together shorten the lives of more than 90 percent of all Americans.

ANTI-AGING HORMONES: RESTORING YOUTH

As we get older, our bodies begin to slow their production of certain hormones. This decline makes us age even faster.

Through supplementation, we can maintain hormones at optimum levels and so stop the aging process from shifting into overdrive. Here are the hormone supplements that I recommend.

Dehydroepiandrosterone (DHEA). This superstar hormone promotes health and longevity by fighting degenerative disease and slowing aging. In studies, people who took DHEA supplements to restore the hormone to levels found in young adults experienced improvements in several biomarkers of aging, including enhanced immunity, increased resistance to stress, and reduced risk of heart disease, cancer, and diabetes. They also reported improvements in their physical and psychological well-being.

Pregnenolone. The biochemical precursor of DHEA and a rising hormonal superstar in its own right, pregnenolone has formidable anti-aging effects of its own. Beyond slowing degenerative disease, the hormone is the most powerful intelligence- and memory-enhancing agent discovered to date. It also improves mood, boosts energy, and increases alertness and awareness. People who take pregnenolone report a heightened sense of overall well-being.

Melatonin. It may be best known as a remedy for insomnia and jet lag, but melatonin also has impressive anti-aging properties. In fact, the hormone is believed to control your body's aging clock, located within the brain's pineal gland. The most potent known natural antioxidant, melatonin combats the effects of stress and fights disease.

Estrogen. Estrogen replacement is the only type of anti-aging hormone therapy that has been embraced by mainstream medicine. Unfortunately, mainstream doctors prescribe synthetic estrogen rather than the real thing. The biochemical mismatch between fake and real estrogen molecules is almost certainly responsible for the increased cancer risk and other adverse effects associated with estrogen replacement therapy. I advise my female patients who are going through or who are past menopause to take only natural estrogen, which exactly matches the hormone produced by the body.

Progesterone. Like estrogen, progesterone sharply declines in women who are at or past menopause. Replacing progesterone—with natural supplements, of course—keeps levels of both hormones in balance. Progesterone also eases menopausal symptoms, reverses osteoporosis, and retards aging.

Testosterone. Since production of this hormone declines with age, testosterone replacement therapy makes as much sense for men as estrogen replacement therapy does for women. Testosterone protects against heart disease, fights osteoporosis (men get it, too), increases lean muscle mass, reverses age-related accumulation of fat, and energizes the entire body. The hormone also enhances libido for both men and women.

Thyroid hormone. Tens of millions of Americans suffer from undiagnosed subclinical hypothyroidism, or impaired function of the thyroid gland. Symptoms of this condition can vary greatly, from low energy and difficulty losing weight to low immunity, anemia, and heart disease. Fortunately, hypothyroidism is easily corrected with natural thyroid hormone replacement.

BRAIN NUTRIENTS: PRESERVING
MENTAL AGILITY

Halting and reversing mental decline is the highest priority of anti-aging medicine. The fact is, you can be no younger than your brain. Brain nutrients—or neuronutrients, as I sometimes call them—reverse age-related mental changes. In doing so, they improve your memory, raise your IQ, and age-proof your brain.

Two of the most potent brain nutrients, the herb ginkgo and the hormone pregnenolone, were discussed earlier in this chapter. Here are two more that you should be aware of.

Acetyl-L-carnitine (ALC). This compound prevents the loss of nerve cells and maximizes the production of neurotransmitters, the chemical messengers that enable nerve cells to communicate with one another. By enhancing the brain's composition, ALC sharpens memory, alertness, and learning ability. Replenishing depleted supplies of ALC slows—and actually reverses—brain aging.

Phosphatidylserine (PS). Derived from soy, PS supports the renewal of brain cells and improves mental performance. It also assists in the regeneration of damaged nerve cells, ensuring clear and uninterrupted transmission of messages between cells. PS plays important roles in memory, alertness, and brain energy.

INTERNAL CLEANSERS: GOOD FOR YOUR ENTIRE BODY

The internal cleansers keep your digestive system in good working order. This ensures that nutrients—from the foods that you eat as well as the supplements that you take—are efficiently absorbed into the bloodstream.

The following internal cleansers are included in the Anti-Aging Supplement Program.

Fiber. Fiber is not an essential nutrient, because it passes through the body virtually unchanged. Still, it is crucial to efficient gastrointestinal function as well as optimum overall health. Unfortunately, most Americans don't get nearly enough fiber in their diets. Scientific research has linked a low-fiber diet to an array of common and life-shortening health problems, including heart disease and cancer.

Probiotics. About a quadrillion (that's one thousand trillion) microorganisms peacefully coexist in your gastrointestinal tract. Your cells are outnumbered, one thousand to one. If this delicate internal ecosystem is somehow disrupted, disease-causing bacteria and fungi gain the upper hand—and they're just itching to wreak havoc on your body's healing system. Probiotics, or beneficial bacteria, keep the gastrointestinal flora balanced and the bacterial and fungal bad guys in check. You can increase the population of "good bugs" with the help of acidophilus supplements.

WHERE DO YOU GO FROM HERE?

The table on page 296 lists all of the nutrients, herbs, hormones, and internal cleansers in the Anti-Aging Supplement Program, along with their respective Daily Recommended Intakes. Taking every single one of these supplements would be impractical, if not impossible. It also is unnecessary.

To sort through the possibilities and make informed decisions, read through the profiles of the supplements in the following chapters. By the time you conclude part 5 of this book, you should have a good idea of which supplements are most appropriate for you. Chapter 38 offers some strategies for customizing the Anti-Aging Supplement Program to meet your specific needs. For supplement suppliers, refer to Resources and References on page 591.

Now that you know a bit about the Anti-Aging Supplement Program, let's take a closer look at each of its components. We'll start with the antioxidants.

Antioxidants: The Front Line in the Fight Against Free Radicals

The Lord hath created medicines out of the earth: and he that is wise will not abhor them.
—ECCLESIASTICUS 38:4–5

Of all the nutrients that comprise the Anti-Aging Supplement Program, antioxidants have the most direct and profound influence over Renewal. After all, they—and only they—can neutralize those cell-damaging, disease-causing particles known as free radicals.

And the more antioxidants you have in your system, the better the Renewal process works. Cells receive optimum protection from free radical attack, increasing your odds of staying healthy and youthful for a lifetime.

If you've read this book from the beginning, you already know a great deal about antioxidants. So before getting into the specifics of supplementation, this chapter just briefly recaps how antioxidants and free radicals behave in the body. (If you've skipped around the book, I suggest perusing at least chapters 2 and 3 before tackling this one.)

One key point that I want to reiterate up front: Antioxidants are absolutely vital to your long-term survival. Without them, free radicals would quickly decimate your body's cells—all 75 trillion or so of them. Instead of shooting for 120 years, you'd be lucky to last 120 *minutes*. No matter what your current age, antioxidants have gotten you this far—and they'll help keep you around for decades to come.

MOLECULAR MISFITS

You have two ages: your chronological age, which is determined by your year of birth, and your biological age, which reflects the amount of free radical damage that has occurred within your body to date. The total number of free radical "hits" inflicted on your cells so far serves as a measure of the rate at which you are aging.

As you'll recall from chapter 2, a free radical randomly assaults cells in a desperate attempt to find a partner for its unpaired electron. The highly charged, highly unstable molecular fragment may puncture cell membranes, destroy enzymes, and even break down DNA just to steal an electron from another molecule.

Some free radicals occur naturally, as your cells burn food for energy (a process called oxidative metabolism). Other free radicals come from exposure to ultraviolet radiation (sunlight), radon, x-rays, pollutants, pesticides, food additives, alcohol, and other toxins.

To give you an idea of how much damage free radicals can do, consider that these renegade molecules strike and fracture every single one of your DNA molecules 10,000 times a day. About 9,900 of these breaks in the DNA strand are restored to normal by DNA repair enzymes. About 100, or 1 percent, escape the enzymes' notice. This unrepaired damage accumulates over time, setting the stage for atherosclerosis, cancer, and other degenerative diseases. You can see why slowing the damage—by increasing antioxidant protection—translates directly into longer life span.

WHEN FREE RADICALS RUN AMOK

Your body works hard to protect cells against free radical attack. But it can do only so much. Should its antioxidant defenses become too weak, or its free radical exposure become too great, it can suffer a catastrophic breakdown known as oxidative stress. In oxidative stress, free radicals run rampant within the body, corrupting and killing cells.

On a global scale, oxidative stress has claimed more lives than all of the wars and plagues throughout human history. It causes all of the degenerative diseases that go hand in hand with aging. Nothing causes more human misery or ends more lives prematurely.

Oxidative stress commits its greatest offenses at the cellular level. Rampaging free radicals injure the cell's membranes, compromising the delivery of nutrients and the removal of waste. They damage the mitochondria, impairing the production of energy. They break protein molecules, disrupting crucial enzyme systems. And they fracture DNA, causing the genetic mutations and uncontrolled cell divisions that eventually lead to cancer.

Blood fats such as low-density lipoprotein (LDL) cholesterol also suffer the wrath of oxidative stress. Research suggests that, despite its reputation as the "bad" kind of cholesterol, LDL itself is harmless. Only when oxidized—that is, only when it gives up an electron to a free radical—does LDL cause the arterial hardening and clogging that lay the groundwork for heart attack and stroke. This explains why about half of all people with elevated total cholesterol and LDL cholesterol never experience heart attacks: Their LDL has not undergone oxidation.

STALLING OXIDATIVE STRESS

How do some folks manage to avoid oxidative stress? First, they minimize their free radical exposure. Second, they increase their antioxidant protection. Both strategies are necessary to prevent disease and promote Renewal.

You can significantly reduce your free radical exposure by eliminating or at least limiting your consumption of foods of animal origin. Meats, poultry, fish, dairy products, and eggs—although devoid of protective antioxidants—have abundant supplies of free radical–forming fats. They're also likely to contain residues of pesticides, herbicides, and other free radical–producing toxins.

Other environmental poisons, from pollutants in the air you breathe to chemicals in the water you drink, generate free radicals as well. While you have less control over them than over your diet, you should still limit your contact with them as much as you can.

Unseen Destruction

Oxidative stress—when free radicals overrun the body and cause extensive damage—dramatically accelerates the aging process. It's also directly responsible for a host of health problems, some of which I've listed here.

- AIDS
- Alzheimer's disease
- Arrhythmia (abnormal heartbeat)
- Atherosclerosis (hardening and clogging of the arteries)
- Autoimmune disease (destruction of healthy tissues by immune cells)
- Cancer
- Cataracts
- Degenerative retinal damage
- Diabetes
- Emphysema
- Heart attack
- Lupus
- Macular degeneration (cell breakdown in the retina that leads to vision loss)
- Multiple sclerosis
- Pancreatitis (inflammation of the pancreas)
- Parkinson's disease
- Rheumatoid arthritis
- Stroke

To increase your antioxidant protection, start by rebuilding your diet around the New Four Food Groups—grains, legumes, fruits, and vegetables. These foods are naturally rich in antioxidants and virtually devoid of free radical–forming compounds. Then fortify your diet with the supplements prescribed in the Anti-Aging Supplement Program. They'll raise your antioxidant intakes to optimum levels and reinforce your body's natural defenses against free radicals and oxidative stress.

YOUR BEST PROTECTION

An antioxidant can neutralize a free radical by donating one of its electrons without jeopardizing its own chemical stability. (Remember, two electrons are required to form a stable molecular bond.) Once the antioxidant gives up an electron, it remains out of service until it is recharged or replaced. It may be "recycled" by another antioxidant—that is, it may receive a "new" electron—so it can join the free radical fray once again. Antioxidants often cooperate in this way to keep each other operational.

Because free radicals are generated in different areas or compartments of the body, and because antioxidants vary in their ability to penetrate these compartments, an array of antioxidants is necessary to keep free radicals in check. These protective nutrients work synergistically, patrolling different but often overlapping territories within the body.

Vitamin C, for example, is water-soluble. It hangs out primarily in the water compartment, or the blood. Vitamin E is fat-soluble, so it stakes out the cell membrane compartment, which consists primarily of fats. Coenzyme Q_{10} and glutathione position themselves next to the miochondrial membranes, where they field the barrage of free radicals that's released as the mitochondria convert food into energy. Each of the other antioxidants has its favorite hangout, just as these do.

Since different antioxidants have different functions, you want to make sure that you're getting a broad range rather than just one or two. For example, some people take lots of vitamin C, to the exclusion of everything else. Granted, vitamin C is a powerful antioxidant. But it isn't fat-soluble, so it offers little protection to cell membranes and other "fatty" structures. These require vitamin E, essential fatty acids, and carotenoids, all of which are fat-soluble.

THE ANTIOXIDANT ALLIANCE

Your body's antioxidant arsenal consists of three types of weaponry: essential nutrients, phytochemicals, and enzymes. All are equally important, and all work together to defeat free radicals. Let's examine each one.

Antioxidant essential nutrients. As explained in the previous chapter, essential nutrients are those that your body cannot make for itself and cannot survive without. It just so happens that several of these nutrients also have antioxidant properties. These include vitamins A, C, and E as well as the essential fatty acids and certain amino acids. (For a complete listing, with doses, see "Just the Essentials.")

Certain minerals—namely, copper, selenium, and zinc—are often referred to as antioxidants. Technically, that's a misnomer because they lack the ability to neutralize free radicals. They do, however, play key roles in the body's production of antioxidant enzymes (which I will discuss a bit later).

Coenzyme Q_{10} earns essential nutrient status only once you reach age 30. Prior to that, your body makes enough of this potent free radical fighter on its own. But through your thirties and beyond, production declines markedly. Many researchers believe that this genetically programmed coenzyme Q_{10} deficiency shortens human life span considerably by opening the door to chronic oxidative stress.

Antioxidant phytochemicals. Phytochemicals number in the thousands. Though they can act as antioxidants, they have myriad other ways in which they further reduce oxidative stress. For instance, they can block the transformation of precursor molecules into free radicals and carcinogens. And they can enhance the repair of DNA by increasing the activity of antioxidant enzymes such as glutathione.

Only foods of plant origin—grains, legumes, fruits, and vegetables—supply phytochemicals. Foods of animal origin do not. For optimum intake of phytochemicals, nothing beats a low-fat vegan diet. To further boost your intake of these "supernutrients," try capsules containing concentrated fruit/vegetables extracts, such as Juice Plus made by NSA and Phytaloe made by Mannatech. (For more information on supplementation and phytochemicals, see the next chapter.)

Antioxidant enzymes. The human body can manufacture its own antioxidant enzymes. But to do so, it needs proteins, which it synthesizes from the amino acids in foods. This process evolved thousands of years ago, as the body sought to maintain its antioxidant supply during periods when sustenance was scarce. When it wasn't getting enough antioxidants from dietary sources, it could make its own.

Just the Essentials

The essential nutrients listed below are key players in your body's antioxidant defense system. Should any one of these run low, your body will struggle just to function—let alone fend off free radicals. That's why supplementation at optimum levels (the amounts in the right-hand column) is so important. Aim for the middle to upper end of each dosage range.

Note: *The Optimum Daily Allowances (ODAs) are appropriate for adult men and for adult women who are not pregnant or lactating. They are not intended for children under age 15.*

Supplement	ODA
Vitamins	
A	1,000–10,000 IU
Beta-carotene	25,000–100,000 IU
C	675–3,000 mg. (as ester-C, the preferable form)
E	400–1,600 IU* (as mixed tocopherols)
Minerals	
Copper	1–3 mg.
Selenium	100–300 mcg.
Zinc	15–50 mg.
Essential Fatty Acids	
Alpha-linolenic acid (an omega-3 fatty acid)	2,000–10,000 mg. (from flaxseed oil capsules)
Gamma-linolenic acid (an omega-6 fatty acid)	250–500 mg. (from borage oil capsules)
Other	
Coenzyme Q_{10}	50–300 mg.

People who are taking blood thinners should consult their doctors before beginning vitamin E supplementation.

Every cell in your body manufactures a trio of special antioxidant enzymes: glutathione peroxidase, superoxide dimutase, and catalase. These homemade compounds work jointly with other antioxidants, taking on free radicals wherever they might appear.

By far the most important of the three antioxidant enzymes is glutathione. It guards a cell's various membranes, including those all-important mitochondrial membranes.

In my practice, I often run a test called an oxidative stress profile, which measures free radical activity. The test reveals, among other things, the status of a patient's glutathione reserves. If they're low, I recommend a product called ThioDox. It contains glutathione as well as two of the enzyme's precursors: N-acetylcysteine and lipoic acid. This combination is far more effective than glutathione alone. ThioDox is available in health food stores and from alternative doctors.

SIZING UP SUPPLEMENTS

So which antioxidants should you include in your personal anti-aging supplement program? Well, that's really up to you. As I've said before: *The extent to which you follow the Renewal Anti-Aging Supplement Program determines the extent to which you'll benefit from it.*

Of the three types of antioxidants, the essential nutrients are most important. Your body must have these to function, regardless of their free radical–fighting properties. If you take supplements of the essential nutrients, as I recommended in the previous chapter, you'll be getting optimum amounts of the antioxidants, too.

As for the antioxidant phytochemicals, the Anti-Aging Diet—with its emphasis on grains, legumes, fruits, and vegetables—supplies these nutrients in abundance. In fact, foods are still the best sources of phytochemicals. Supplementation won't compensate for a poor diet, but it can afford extra protection.

Supplementation of glutathione (and its precursors, N-acetylcysteine and lipoic acid) may be called for if you have a deficiency of the antioxidant enzyme. A nutrition-minded doctor can evaluate your glutathione level by administering the oxidative stress profile. (For more information about this test, refer to Resources and References on page 591.)

The goal of antioxidant supplementation is to reduce oxidative stress. By pulling the plug on this free radical free-for-all, you can dramatically slow the aging process. But don't think you have to wait until you're in your eighties or nineties to find out if reducing oxidative stress really makes a difference. You see, it's not just an anti-aging strategy but also an optimum health strategy. It will make you feel better right now.

Phytochemicals are probably the least known and least understood of the antioxidants. Yet if the latest research is any indication, these "supernutrients" may turn out to be your greatest anti-aging allies. The next chapter explains why.

CHAPTER 25

The Phytochemical Revolution

Eat your vegetables.
—YOUR MOTHER

Your mother may not have had a degree in nutrition or biochemistry. Still she knew, on some intuitive level, that vegetables—as well as fruits and legumes—are brimming with all sorts of good stuff. And guess what? She was right.

So take your mom's advice and slide your tray past the meat, poultry, fish, dairy products, and eggs in the cafeteria line of life. Instead head straight for the salad bar and thoughtfully fix your gaze on the dazzling display of veggies. Those greens make for a terpene bonanza. The cherry tomatoes ante up a lycopene jackpot. The spinach dishes out lutein, zeaxanthin, and glutathione. The broccoli serves up sulforaphane. The scallions supply allylic sulfides.

The way you view food is about to change forever. Welcome to the exciting, if verbally challenging, new world of phytochemicals.

THE NEW KIDS ON THE BLOCK

Phyto means plant. As their name suggests, phytochemicals (sometimes called phytonutrients) are biologically active plant molecules that promote health and prevent disease. But phytochemicals are more than just interesting new compounds with intimidating names—they are truly the future of food.

Our moms may have suspected the incredible healing power of phytochemicals all along. But it eluded scientists for more than a half-century. Only recently have they gotten interested. What piqued their curiosity is the realization that phytochemicals tune up the molecular orchestra of our cells' biochemistry. In the process, these nutrients offer the best protection we know of against the degenerative diseases that accompany advancing age.

In a research initiative that is still in its infancy—and certain to dominate nutritional news in the twenty-first century—new phytochemicals and even new classes of phytochemicals are being discovered almost on a daily basis. Thanks to what they're learning about these compounds, biochemical supersleuths are now solving age-old questions. For example, what are the ingredients in foods that feed the body's healing systems? How does the structure of a food affect its function in the body's cells?

This research probes the essence of Renewal. In a virtual explosion of new insights, the innermost workings of the body's healing systems are being revealed. On a molecular and even submolecular level, scientists are discovering the nuts and bolts of how food components protect us from damage and nurture our repair mechanisms—literally how food supports Renewal.

Herbalists have long recognized and harnessed the therapeutic power of foods. For many centuries, without the advantage of scientific insight and guided only by their keen powers of observation, herbalists observed the healing effects of herbs and other foods and based their prescriptions on them. They had to rely on subtle clues and empiricism (if it works, it works).

The Phytochemical Revolution has changed all that. Scientific revelations about the relationship between the structure and function of healing nutrients has paved the way to using food components as medicine in ways that herbalists could only dream of in the past. This new understanding of the healing power of phytochemicals validates all of herbal medicine.

Now more than ever, the food choices you make can reward you with a longer life—or snatch precious years away from you. Beyond merely underscoring the importance of eating fresh plant foods, the Phytochemical Revolution has opened the door to preventive nutrition. One of your most powerful anti-aging strategies is to make phytochemical-rich foods the centerpiece of your diet.

Phytochemicals are literally nutritional medicines. They protect, heal, and Renew you. The more phytochemicals you have in your body, the less vulnerable you are to chronic degenerative disease.

BLAZING A NUTRITIONAL TRAIL

Prior to the turn of the twentieth century, all scientists knew about food was that it contained carbohydrates, protein, and fat. Then in the first seven decades of this century, they unraveled the chemistry of vitamins, minerals, amino acids, and essential fatty acids.

With all of the essential nutrients identified, scientists had all the information they needed to keep a person alive on supplements alone. Yet, realistically, they knew this couldn't be done—that the person would succumb to cancer or some other degenerative disease much sooner than a similar person who ate real food. Why? Because foods contained some elusive "mystery nutrient" necessary to prevent disease and sustain life.

All through the 1970s and early 1980s, scientists wondered what this special something could be. Despite a smattering of research forays on various food constituents (like the allicin in garlic, the carotenoids in carrots, the ginsenosides in ginseng, and the tocopherols in grains and nuts), it wasn't until the late 1980s that the enormous number and biological complexity of phytochemicals became evident. The "mystery nutrient" turned out to be not one or two but thousands—possibly tens of thousands—of protective compounds. This was a major breakthrough.

In addition to their specific preventive and curative properties, most of the phytochemicals happen to be antioxidants. As you'll recall from chapter 2, antioxidants protect healthy molecules form oxidation by free radicals. Without antioxidants, we'd be toast (almost literally, since toast is oxidized bread).

When nutritionally blasé molecular biologists realized that phytochemicals could also act as antioxidants, they suddenly got very excited about the compounds. And when those same scientists began seeing the intimate connection between antioxidant phytochemicals and cellular protection, repair, and regeneration (the foundation of Renewal), they suddenly got religion about the benefits of eating plant-derived foods. This paved the road to the Phytochemical Revolution.

CONFRONTING THE DEFICIENCY DISEASE BIAS

With the discovery of antioxidant phytochemicals, the nutritional plot thickened. Earlier research had been based on the supposition that if you remove a specific essential nutrient (such as niacin) from the diet, its corresponding deficiency disease (pellagra) would eventually appear. This logic didn't apply to phytochemicals. Researchers found themselves dealing with "conditionally essential" nutrients—nutrients that wouldn't prevent specific deficiency diseases but the absence of which would promote age-accelerating oxidative damage and contribute to age-related degenerative diseases.

For example, if you don't eat tomatoes, you won't die of a lycopene deficiency. But if you are a middle-aged male, the DNA in your prostate gland cells will sustain much more oxidative damage from free radicals, and you'll be much more likely to develop prostate cancer. Likewise, if you never eat soybeans, you won't die of an isoflavone deficiency. But if you are a woman approaching menopause, your risk of uterine cancer will increase severalfold.

So strong was the bias toward deficiency diseases, however, that the first phytochemicals to be discovered were squeezed into the vitamin category even though they didn't quite fit. The bioflavonoids in citrus fruits, for example, were named vitamin P. The glucosinolates in cabbage were dubbed vitamin U (because they healed ulcers). The tocopherol compounds in nuts and seeds were called vitamin E—and, inexplicably, the entire lot of them has remained in the vitamin category.

The carotenoids are perhaps the most schizophrenic. The best known, most prevalent, and most researched of them—beta-carotene—is still treated as a vitamin, even though it isn't. Meanwhile, the other 599 or so carotenoids have been classified as phytochemicals.

PLANT PROTECTION

Why do plants make these protective compounds? Are they concerned for our health and welfare? No, not really (although that's a pleasant thought). They desperately need to protect themselves.

Plants must cope with all of the same threats to survival as we humans. Considering that they're under continual siege from ultraviolet radiation, soil and air pollutants, oxidation, viruses, bacteria, fungi, insects, animals, and people, the fact that they live as long as they do is a miracle. Their sedentary lifestyle compounds life's dangers. When an insect or a rodent starts gnawing on a plant, the plant can't scurry off to a safer location. When the sun's ultraviolet rays threaten to oxidize the skin of a plant, it can't mosey over to a shady spot or grab a bottle of sunscreen. To stay alive, a plant must stand its ground and "phyte."

Plants make phytochemicals to protect themselves. When we eat them, we become the benefactors of their resourcefulness.

MEET THE PHYTOCHEMICALS

Phytochemical biochemistry is so unbelievably complex that I can't possibly do it justice in just a few pages of this book. In fact, as I mentioned earlier, researchers have only scratched the surface in identifying these compounds and determining what they do in the body.

Phytochemicals are important because they establish a crucial bridge between the complexities of food composition and the complexities of cellular biology and cellular Renewal. By this I mean that the growing understanding of how phytochemicals work is inextricably linked to the unfolding insight about how cells survive assault by free radicals.

Remember the basics of Renewal? Phytochemicals play key roles in protecting cells from damage, in repairing damage that couldn't be prevented, and in regenerating cells that have been injured beyond repair. To give you a general idea of how phytochemicals facilitate Renewal once they get inside your cells, let's take a brief look at the major phytochemical categories. (Don't worry, there won't be a quiz.)

Terpenes

Terpenes are a huge class of phytochemicals found in a diverse array of plant foods, ranging from grains and soy products to citrus fruits and green foods. The carotenoid subclass alone contains more than 600 known compounds.

Terpenes function as antioxidants, protecting plants— and the humans who consume plants—from free radicals. These unusually potent antioxidants shield the sensitive fat molecules in cell membranes, as well as the blood and other bodily fluids, from free radical assault. Terpenes also "spare" other antioxidants such as coenzyme Q_{10}, glutathione, and vitamin E, allowing these antioxidants to be recycled and reused.

Carotenoid terpenes are the plant pigments that give fruits and vegetables such as oranges, pink grapefruit, spinach, and tomatoes their colors. These compounds enhance immune response and protect skin cells against the sun's ultraviolet radiation. Carotenoids are tissue-specific, so they work best when taken together rather than individually.

Limonoids, another subclass of terpenes, protect lung tissues and stimulate the production of liver detoxification enzymes. Limonoids are found in the peels of citrus fruits.

Phytosterols

Phytosterols bear a close resemblance to another sterol: cholesterol. These compounds are able to block cholesterol uptake, thus lowering the risk of heart disease. They also reduce inflammation and block the growth of tumors in the breasts, prostate, and colon.

Most plant species contain phytosterols. Large quantities can be found in pumpkins, rice, soybeans, yams, and all green and yellow vegetables.

Phenols

Researchers have taken quite an interest in the disease-defying properties of phenols, the compounds that give berries, grapes, and eggplant their blue, blue-red, and violet colors.

Phenols are potent antioxidants. But they also have a remarkable ability to modify prostaglandin pathways, block specific enzymes that cause inflammation (relieving inflammatory conditions such as allergies, arthritis, autoimmune disease, and infections), and prevent platelets from clumping (protecting against heart attacks and strokes). What's more, phenols can discourage the development of cancer by blocking the conversion of precursor molecules into carcinogens.

Flavonoids. Also known as bioflavonoids, flavonoids are a very large subclass—more than 5,000 strong—of phenols. Some well-known members of this category include the quercetin in grapefruit, the rutin in buckwheat, the hesperidin in citrus fruits, the silybin in milk thistle, the genistein in soybeans, and the apigenin in chamomile.

Flavonoids may be best known for enhancing the effects of vitamin C. But they have therapeutic properties in their own right. For instance, they serve as enzyme inhibitors. They block the enzymes that produce estrogen, thus reducing the risk of estrogen-induced cancers. They impede angiotensin-converting enzyme, which raises blood pressure. And by blocking the enzyme cyclooxygenase, which breaks down prostaglandins, they reduce platelet stickiness and aggregation.

Flavonoids also protect blood vessels and strengthen the tiny capillaries that deliver oxygen and essential nutrients to all cells. For diabetes, hemorrhoids, varicose veins, and other conditions in which capillaries and smaller blood vessels become weak, I usually prescribe flavonoids and/or quercetin. Though blood vessels can be slow to heal and the therapy may last for several months, it often produces dramatic results.

Flavonoids have other health benefits as well. They reduce allergies, fight inflammation, and destroy hepatotoxins (substances that are toxic to the liver).

Flavonals. In addition to their powerful antioxidant activity, these select flavonoids strengthen collagen, the most abundant protein in the body. Collagen literally holds your body together: Intertwined strands of the stuff make up soft tissues, tendons, ligaments, and bones. Flavonals provide structural support for collagen by increasing the number of cross-links, or bridges, that connect neighboring collagen molecules to each other. This strengthens your support system and keeps you from sagging.

One subgroup of flavonals, the proanthocyanidins, are second only to melatonin in terms of their antioxidant potency. Proanthocyanidins are extracted from the bark of the maritime pine or Landes pine (as pycnogenol) as well as from grape seeds. They have enjoyed great commercial success because they relieve the subjective fatigue and related symptoms experienced by people under excessive oxidative stress (depletion of the body's antioxidant supply by free radicals). The range of conditions benefited by proanthocyanidins is enormous: These flavonals ease arthritis and allergies, lower cholesterol, strengthen capillaries, and promote healthy skin.

No matter what their form—the currently trendy pycnogenol or the equally effective grape seed extract—proanthocyanidins increase the efficacy of other antioxidants such as vitamins C and E. Specifically, proanthocyanidins recycle spent antioxidants by giving them back their lost electrons, so they can go right back to the front line and neutralize more free radicals. (As you'll recall from chapter 2, an antioxidant gives up its spare electron in order to stabilize a free radical.)

Isoflavones. Isoflavones—the best known are daidzein and genistein—exert weak estrogenic activity. They prevent cancer by loosely binding to estrogen receptor sites on cells, blocking them so that more powerful cancer-causing estrogen molecules can't dock there. Breast and uterine cancers are rare among women who consume traditional diets rich in soy foods. (Likewise, prostate cancer is uncommon among men who eat lots of soy foods.)

Like other phenols, isoflavones effectively block enzymes that promote tumor growth. And they inhibit new blood vessel growth (called angiogenesis), so tumors and metastases can't spread.

Isoflavones are found primarily in soybeans as well as other beans. Getting more soy into your diet from sources such as tofu and soy milk is a brilliant strategy for reducing your risk of cancer.

Catechins and gallic acid. Green tea, black tea, and even coffee contain phenolic antioxidants that have been shown to lower cholesterol and prevent cancer.

Chemically, catechins look like flavonoids. They share the protective properties of flavonoids. The most common catechins—epicatechin, epicatechin gallate, and epigallo-catechin gallate—are found in green tea.

Gallic acid can inhibit the formation of nitrosamines and other carcinogens. It's also anti-mutagenic, that is, it prevents genetic mutation. Gallic acid is a component of coffee.

Thiols

Members of this class of phytochemicals contain sulfur. The allylic sulfides mentioned above are one example. Thiols come from garlic and cruciferous vegetables.

Glucosinolates. Cruciferous vegetables contain glucosinolates, potent little molecules that perform a variety of functions. The glucosinolates in your bok choy, broccoli, cabbage, or cauliflower stimulate the production of cytokines. Cytokines are hormonelike messenger molecules that choreograph your immune defenses, ensuring a smooth and accurate response to foreign invaders and free radicals.

Glucosinolates also switch on your liver's detoxification enzymes, which are your blood's garbage removal system. And they activate scavenging white blood cells, which remove foreign and toxic debris.

But glucosinolates don't stop there. They can biochemically "morph" into a variety of other protective molecules, including dithiolthiones, isothiocyanates, and sulforaphane. Each of these compounds protects specific tissues. And each packs an anti-cancer wallop, blocking enzymes that promote tumor growth in the esophagus, breasts, lungs, stomach, liver, colon, and elsewhere. Sulforaphane, in particular, has enjoyed more than its 15 minutes of fame. This unassuming molecule, found in abundance in broccoli, has garnered a lot of attention for its aggressive anti-cancer activity.

Allylic sulfides. Allylic sulfides, a subgroup of the phytochemicals known as thiols, safeguard your cells against oxidative damage by free radicals. These compounds protect the cardiovascular and immune systems, prevent cancer, and thwart genetic mutation. Specifically, they lower cholesterol; reduce the stickiness of blood platelets, which form blood clots; act as natural antibiotics against viruses, bacteria, fungi, and parasites; and block tumor growth.

You get allylic sulfides from chives, garlic, leeks, onions, and shallots. When you cut or smash one of these plants, the damaged cells release enzymes, which then activate the allylic sulfides. Take garlic as an example: The enzyme allicinase activates allicin, garlic's allylic sulfide.

Indoles. Despite intimidating names like 3,3-dindolyl-methane, indole-3-carbinol, and indole-3-acetonitrite, indoles are actually friendly phytochemicals. Add them to your list of anti-cancer allies. They increase your production of enzymes that inactivate food toxins and carcinogens while also increasing production of glutathione, one of your principal free radical scavengers.

You get a healthy dose of indoles every time you eat a member of the *Brassica* (crucifer) family, which includes bok choy, broccoli, brussels sprouts, cabbage, cauliflower, collard greens, kale, mustard greens, rutabaga, and turnips. Because indoles are easily destroyed during cooking, either steam your crucifers or eat them raw.

Tocopherols

What you probably know as vitamin E actually is a group of structurally similar phytochemicals that includes d-alpha, d-beta, d-gamma, and d-delta tocopherols. Together these compounds form the vitamin E complex.

Vitamin E is among the premier protectors of cell membranes. Way back in chapters 2 and 3, I explained that these membranes are made from fatty acid molecules lined up alongside each other in rows. Because the membranes safeguard cells and organelles, keeping them healthy is key to a longer life. This is where vitamin E comes in. Like a sentinel, it stands guard over cell membranes, ready to grab and dispatch would-be invaders.

Remember the galloping hordes of free radical Huns that would storm the Great Wall of your membranes and invade your cells and organelles? Well, think of vitamin E as the Great Defender. It waits, hidden in the fatty acid matrix of a membrane. Then when a free radical approaches the membrane, the vitamin E molecule grabs it and neutralizes it by giving it an electron (as any antioxidant would do).

Of course, once vitamin E gives up its electron, it becomes oxidized. But within a few nanoseconds, a beta-carotene, coenzyme Q_{10}, glutathione, or vitamin C molecule comes along and donates its spare electron to vitamin E. Once recycled, the vitamin E molecule can grab and neutralize another marauding free radical.

Tocopherols occur naturally in seeds, nuts, soybeans, wheat germ, and whole grains. But you cannot get optimum amounts from diet alone. So be sure that your personal anti-aging supplement program includes 400 to 1,600 international units per day of mixed tocopherols from natural (not synthetic) sources. (Look for the phrases "mixed tocopherols" and "natural sources" on the supplement label.) D-alpha tocopherol alone, whether synthetic or natural, will not suffice. Nor will products containing the "l" form of tocopherol, which is an ineffective mirror image molecule.

Note: People who are taking blood thinners should consult their doctors before taking supplemental vitamin E.

Isoprenoids

Isoprenoids attach themselves to the fatty membranes surrounding your cells and their internal organelles such as the mitochondria. Like microscopic Venus flytraps, these crafty molecules lie in wait, poised to grab passing free radicals. Upon handcuffing a free radical, the isoprenoid turns it over to a more mobile antioxidant molecule, such as coenzyme Q_{10}, glutathione, or vitamin C. Isoprenoids come from grains, nuts, and seeds.

SUPERSTAR FOOD SOURCES

Because thousands of different phytochemicals exist, and because each one contributes to your health in its own unique way, consuming a variety of these compounds is absolutely essential. You can get them only from plant-derived foods—grains, legumes, fruits, and vegetables. Conveniently enough, these are the stars of the New Four Food Groups, which form the foundation of the Anti-Aging Diet.

In terms of phytochemical content, the following plant-derived foods stand out as especially healthful.

Garlic and Onions

Garlic and onions as well as chives, leeks, scallions, and shallots belong to the *Allium* family. These nutritional powerhouses contain upward of 200 phytochemical compounds, including daillyl disulfide, one of the most potent tumor suppressors known.

The list of benefits provided by the *Allium* family is very long. Garlic, onions, and their relatives boost immunity, block atherosclerosis (hardening and clogging of the arteries), prevent just about every type of cancer, fight infection, and serve as a virtual launching pad for Renewal. (You can find out more about the therapeutic powers of garlic in chapter 28.)

For a tasty anti-aging treat, place a few cloves of garlic in a coffee cup and drizzle a very small amount of olive oil over the top. Cover the cup and microwave for five seconds per clove. This softens the garlic so it pops right out of its shell. You can eat it as is or add it to a salad or just about any other dish.

Soybeans

Simple but superb, the soybean is nothing less than a phytopharmaceutical warehouse stocked with Renewal-enhancing nutrients. No other food contains as many different anti-aging compounds. No other food contains as many different anti-cancer compounds. No other food, with the possible exception of garlic, prevents as many different diseases. No other plant-derived food contains all of the essential amino acids: Like meat, soy is a complete protein.

Soy's ability to safeguard the heart and prevent heart attacks and strokes has been known for more than 80 years. The isoflavone compounds in soy lower total cholesterol, LDL cholesterol, and triglyceride levels, while raising "good" high-density lipoprotein (HDL) cholesterol.

Isoflavones such as daidzein, genistein, and glycetein also inhibit the development of cancer. Of these, genistein is probably the best known. Since its discovery 10 years ago, several hundred papers have appeared documenting its anti-cancer effects.

Genistein suppresses the growth of every kind of cancer cell. It can even rehabilitate cancer cells, restoring them to a normal, precancerous state. Plus, genistein and other isoflavones are phytoestrogenic. In other words, they act like weak estrogens, blocking estrogen receptor sites on cells so that they can't be occupied by cancer-causing molecules.

Isoflavones have even more weapons in their anti-cancer arsenal. They influence the synthesis of tumor proteins, slow the growth of malignant cells, block pro-cancer enzymes, and inhibit the growth of blood vessels that nourish tumors.

Phytates, another compound in soybeans, defend against cancer by controlling abnormal cell growth and chelating excess iron, an oxidizing agent that encourages cancer as well as heart disease. And phytates act as antioxidants, helping to scavenge cell-damaging (and cancer-causing) free radicals. Studies have shown that people who eat soy regularly have lower rates of just about every type of cancer. This includes cancers of the lung, stomach, prostate, colon, and rectum.

Soybeans are rich in protease inhibitors. These compounds have been in the news lately as an effective treatment for HIV. And like isoflavones and phytates, protease inhibitors help to prevent cancer by deactivating certain cancer-promoting proteins.

Soybeans are also among the best sources of antioxidant, anti–heart disease, anti-cancer tocopherols. In fact, supplement manufacturers use soy to make vitamin E capsules.

As a food, soy is as versatile as it is healthful. Many stores carry baked marinated tofu, which you can eat as is, blend into a stir-fry, or use as filling for a tasty sandwich. (You can also make your own baked tofu, using the recipe on page 577.) Tempeh, a fermented soy product that is high in protein and an excellent source of genistein, has a meaty texture that makes it especially suitable for casseroles and stir-fries. Miso, a salty paste made from fermented soybeans, makes a great soup base. Just dissolve it in hot water and add other soup ingredients. You can also use miso to flavor salad dressings, sauces, and stews.

Other suggestions: Try prepared burgers made from tofu, tempeh, or textured soy protein. Add soy cheese to sandwiches, pizza, and soy burgers. Substitute soy milk for cow's milk on your cereal. (It probably will taste strange at first, but give it a chance. I needed a couple of weeks to adjust to soy milk, but now I prefer it to cow's milk.) You can buy all of these soy products in health food stores and some grocery stores.

Admittedly, soy foods can take some getting used to. But I strongly encourage you to open up your diet to tofu, tempeh, miso, and other soy products. I recommend consuming at least one serving of soy per day. That's about three ounces of tofu, ½ cup of tempeh or miso, or 1 cup of soy milk.

Personally, I don't eat soy at every meal. But I do average at least one serving a day. Believe me, it's worth it.

Cruciferous Vegetables
They've been described as wonder drugs cleverly disguised as vegetables. And no wonder: The crucifers—which include arugula, bok choy, broccoli, brussels sprouts, cabbage, cauliflower, collards, kale, kohlrabi, mustard greens, rutabaga, turnips, and watercress—are blessed with an astounding abundance of phytochemicals and other important nutrients.

All crucifers contain potent anti-cancer antioxidant compounds such as indole-3-carbinol, isothiocyanates, and sulforaphane. They also have folic acid, which helps maintain heart health and blocks the development of colon cancer and polyps. Throw in their oversize helpings of vitamins A and C, beta-carotene, and fiber, and you have a winning nutritional combination that boosts immunity, fends off tumors and infections, and fights aging.

Orange, Red, and Yellow Fruits and Vegetables
What creates the rainbow of colors that fruits and vegetables are famous for? Carotenoids—more than 600 of them and still counting.

The most extensively researched category of phytochemicals, carotenoids defend DNA against free radical damage, enhance the immune system, improve intellectual functioning, and protect aging eyes from the oxidative stress that usually manifests itself as cataracts or macular degeneration (a condition characterized by cellular breakdown in the retina that leads to vision loss). Carotenoids also prevent every conceivable type of cancer. In fact, some can even reverse cancer once it has started.

A complete listing of all of the carotenoids, along with

all of the fruits and vegetables that contain each one, would be extremely long. So here's an abbreviated version, just to whet your appetite to the possibilities.

- Alpha-carotene: apples, carrots, corn, green peppers, leafy greens, peaches, potatoes, squash, and watermelons
- Beta-carotene: apricots, carrots, green peppers, leafy greens, spinach, squash, and sweet potatoes
- Capsanthin: sweet red peppers
- Cryptoxanthin: apples, apricots, corn, green peppers, lemons, oranges, papayas, and persimmons
- Lutein:carrots, corn, potatoes, spinach, and tomatoes
- Lycopene: apricots, carrots, green peppers, pink grapefruit, and tomatoes
- Zeaxanthin: corn and spinach

Whole Grains

Whether they're common (corn, oats, rice, and wheat) or exotic (amaranth, kamut, quinoa, and spelt), grains pack in the nutrients. They offer abundant supplies of the B-complex vitamins, including folic acid; vitamin E; minerals such as calcium, iron, magnesium, and zinc; amino acids and essential fatty acids; and, of course, fiber.

Fiber is arguably the most beneficial of all the compounds in grains. It lowers cholesterol and blood pressure, helping to protect against heart disease. It also prevents colon cancer, Type II diabetes, and obesity. (You'll read more about fiber in chapter 30.)

Grains supply an array of phytochemicals as well. Phenolic acids, for example, protect DNA from free radical assault. Phytates put the kibosh on breast cancer in its earliest stages, before it gets a foothold. Flavonoids and lignans also inhibit the development of cancer.

Unfortunately, processing robs a grain of all of its Renewal-enhancing nutrients. All of the goodies are stripped away, leaving a pale, starchy shadow in their wake.

In a six-year study of 65,000 women, researchers at the Harvard School of Public Health found that those who ate refined grains (white breads, white rice, and pasta made from refined flour) had 2½ times the risk of developing Type II diabetes compared with those who ate whole-grain breads, rice, and pasta. Why? Digestive enzymes quickly convert refined grains into sugar. And without fiber to slow it down, sugar gets absorbed too rapidly and raises blood sugar too quickly. This triggers the pancreas to produce excess insulin. Eventually, the overworked pancreas and the overstimulated insulin receptors in the liver and muscles fail, resulting in diabetes.

Make sure that the pastas, cereals, breads, and other baked goods you eat come from whole, unprocessed grains. In the Smith household, we avoid white flour, white rice, and processed grains like the plague. All of our pastas, cereals, breads, crackers, and flours are whole grain and organic.

Citrus Fruits

If you haven't already decided that I'm a little nutty, this may convince you: When I eat my daily orange or grapefruit, I thoroughly chew the seeds and then swallow them. Not only that, I also gnaw on and ingest the fluffy white stuff between the orange or grapefruit pulp and the rind.

Why? Well, the seeds and the rind (but not the pulp) contain limonoids, powerful phytochemicals that deactivate carcinogens. And the pith—the fluffy white stuff found in all citrus fruits (grapefruit has the most)—is jam-packed with flavonoids.

Citrus fruits are among the most potent and most tasty cancer-fighting foods around. Beyond vitamin C and fiber, at least 60 anti-cancer phytochemicals lurk beneath those shiny rinds—more than in any other food.

To benefit from these nutrients, though, you must eat fresh citrus fruits. Any type of processing removes virtually all of the phytochemicals, essential nutrients, and fiber, leaving behind a blend of sugar and water. This goes for canned fruits as well as canned, cartoned, and bottled fruit juices.

Miscellaneous Fruits

I've already discussed the stellar phytochemical content of citrus fruits. But truth be told, you can't go wrong with any fruit: All are packed with phytochemicals and other healing nutrients. Here's just a sampling.

- Apricots and cantaloupes are rich in carotenoids and vitamin C.

- Bananas supply pectin fiber, which stabilizes blood sugar, and magnesium and potassium, which foster heart and circulatory health.
- Kiwifruit, papayas, and pineapples contain bromelain, an anti-inflammatory enzyme that enhances immunity and fights allergies and autoimmune diseases such as arthritis.
- Mangoes supply carotenoids and flavonoids.
- Strawberries contain ellagic acid and lycopene, both potent cancer fighters.
- Tomatoes are the number one source of lycopene.

Legumes

While no food is perfect, legumes sure come close. The soybean earns the highest honors (you'll read more about it in a bit). But any of its cousins certainly qualifies as a close runner-up.

Legumes—including adzuki beans, black beans, brown beans, chickpeas, kidney beans, lentils, mung beans, navy beans, pinto beans, red beans, and split peas—provide a bounty of Renewal-enhancing phytochemicals. Legumes protect against cancer, thanks to their high contents of phytoestrogenic lignins and isoflavonoids, proteases, and phytates. They lower total cholesterol and "bad" low-density lipoprotein (LDL) cholesterol, dramatically reducing the risk of heart disease. And they stabilize blood sugar levels, helping to prevent obesity and Type II (non-insulin-dependent) diabetes.

Besides their outstanding phytochemical content, legumes are low in fat, high in complex carbohydrates and protein, loaded with soluble and insoluble fiber, and chock-full of essential fatty acids. In short, they're the ideal anti-aging food.

Tomatoes

Tomatoes taste so good that you may have a hard time believing they're healthy. Yet these juicy, red *pommes d'amours*—"love apples," as the French call them—are perhaps your best all-round insurance policy against degenerative disease and premature death.

Though loaded with anti-aging nutrients such as vitamins A and C and the powerful antioxidant glutathione, tomatoes may be best known for their exceptional levels of lycopene. One of 600-plus carotenoids, lycopene is a very powerful antioxidant that blocks cancer formation and slows cancer progression once it has a foothold. It is particularly adept at preventing and reversing prostate cancer, although it works against all types of cancer. One Harvard University study showed that regular tomato consumption can slash cancer risk in half.

While the whole story is not yet clear, research suggests that lycopene safeguards against cancer in a number of ways. First, as a more potent antioxidant than alphacarotene and beta-carotene, lycopene neutralizes singlet oxygen, one of the nastiest free radicals of all. Second, lycopene suppresses cancer cell growth by inhibiting DNA synthesis in cancer cells. Third, lycopene totally blocks insulin-like growth factor-1, and it may have a similar effect on other tumor growth factors. In short, the lycopene in tomatoes whips your body's cancer defenses into overdrive.

Tomatoes are fruits, so eat them as you would apples. I love them au naturel. You can also drizzle a small amount of olive oil over them and bake them with basil, cut them into salads, or turn them into salsa. The cherry tomato is just as healthful as larger varieties and, in the words of Miss Manners (Judith Martin), is "a marvelous invention, producing as it does a satisfactorily explosive squish when bitten."

Unlike many phytochemicals, lycopene holds up nicely when exposed to heat. So concentrated tomato products such as sauces and pastes have significantly higher concentrations of lycopene than ripe tomatoes. (Of course, processing blasts the B vitamins and vitamin C to smithereens.) Try whole-grain pastas topped with tomato sauce, and soups, stews, and casseroles with tomato bases.

Tomatoes go well with garlic, another anti-aging superfood. One of my favorite dishes is the pizza my wife, Dellie, cooks up every couple of weeks: tomato paste, garlic, a touch of olive oil, onions, and other chopped vegetable toppings on a whole-grain crust. Yum.

As part of my anti-aging strategy, I make sure to eat at least one whole tomato (or the equivalent in tomato sauce or paste) just about every day. I urge you to do the same.

Oriental Mushrooms

The enoki, oyster, reishi, shiitake, and tree ear varieties of oriental mushrooms contain compounds that lower cholesterol and block cancer. They're also rich in beta-glucan, an immune system stimulant that can ward off viral infections if taken soon after exposure and that treats all immunological disorders. (I prescribe beta-glucan in capsule form to patients with chronic fatigue immune dysfunction syndrome and others with compromised immune systems as well as to anyone who wants to avoid colds and flu.)

The basic white mushrooms that you find in the produce section of most supermarkets do not have the same therapeutic properties as the oriental mushrooms. In fact, the most common varieties contain high levels of carcinogenic hydrazines, corrosive compounds that have been used as fuel for jet engines.

Chili Peppers

These hot little numbers contain capsaicin, a phenol that has gotten a lot of press lately for its pain-relieving properties. It also protects DNA from oxidative damage, thins blood to protect against heart attack and stroke, and thins mucus to ease congestion.

Tumeric

Tumeric gives prepared mustard its distinctive yellow color. It also happens to be a powerful antioxidant.

Tumeric protects against heart disease by lowering total cholesterol, raising HDL cholesterol, and preventing abnormal blood clotting. When volunteers were given one-half gram of tumeric daily, their HDL levels rose by 29 percent in just one week. Meanwhile, their serum lipid peroxides—a measure of free radical activity in damaging blood fats—plummeted by 33 percent.

That's not all. Tumeric neutralizes dietary carcinogens and blocks cancer in all three stages: initiation, promotion, and progression. The spice also fights infection and inhibits replication of HIV.

DEBUNKING ZOONUTRIENTS

You'll notice that all of the foods above come from plants. That's because only plants contain phytochemicals. True, researchers haven't zeroed in on animal-derived foods, but that's because they already know what they would find: nothing. To borrow from American writer Gertrude Stein, "There is no there there."

Phytochemicals draw a very clear line between the plant kingdom (intrinsically mundane but healthful to eat) and the animal kingdom (fun to look at—in zoos, at least—but age-accelerating when eaten). Oblivious to the compelling consistency of this line and unable to let go of their cravings for fat and protein, some hard-core carnivores remain convinced that since plants have protective ingredients, animals must have them as well. And so they've coined the term *zoonutrient*, a scientific non sequitur that's intended to parallel the phytochemical concept.

While plants contain thousands of different protective nutrients, all that has ever been identified in animals is fish oil (which contains docosahexaenoic acid and eicosapentanoic acid, both omega-3 fatty acids). In exchange for this token benefit of eating fish, you expose yourself to a fusillade of toxins—including brain-addling methylmercury, concentrated pesticides, and bacteria—as well as to a hefty dose of cholesterol. Eating fish to get healthier is like stepping in front of a moving bus to pick up a quarter.

What about the report that Eskimos, who eat large quantities of omega-3-rich fish, have lower rates of heart disease? That infamous fish story has been thoroughly debunked. Harvard University researchers—aware that eating fish doesn't lower cholesterol but curious as to whether the omega-3 fatty acids in fish offer any heart protection—followed more than 44,000 male health professionals for six years. As the researchers reported in the *New England Journal of Medicine*, the men who ate the most fish had the most heart attacks. This proved to be the coup de grâce for an idea that was flawed from the get-go.

So let's keep fish in the disease-promoting column where it belongs. Get your omega-3's from flaxseed oil and soy oil as well as from beans and vegetables. Plant-derived foods provide the nutritional goods with no negative trade-offs.

WHAT YOU EAT (AND DON'T EAT) CAN HURT YOU

You already know that animal-derived foods undermine your health and hasten your demise. But steering clear of these foods is only half of the health equation. The other half? Fortifying your protective and healing systems with a low-fat vegan diet based on the New Four Food Groups: grains, legumes, fruits, and vegetables. The discovery of phytochemicals dramatically illustrates the importance of doing so.

Every time you eat a health-eroding animal-derived food, you deprive yourself of a health-enhancing plant-derived food. Nutritionally, you're taking two steps backward. I'm not saying that a single serving of roast beef, Swiss cheese, or rocky road ice cream is enough to do you in. But the more you indulge, the more the damage adds up, as cells struggle to survive against escalating numbers of free radicals.

This raises another important point: Animal-derived foods not only lack phytochemicals, they actually deplete your reserves of the nutrients. Your body has to dip into its phytochemical and antioxidant stores in order to process animal-derived food. So really, you're taking three steps backward. Catching up requires major effort—at the very least, several days of enlightened eating.

By now you can see why consuming animal-derived foods on a daily basis can pave the way to heart disease, cancer, osteoporosis, arthritis, cataracts, and a host of other degenerative ills. Think of it in terms of the following equation:

Plant Foods ÷ Animal Foods = Health and Longevity

In other words, the more plant-derived foods you eat, and the fewer animal-derived foods you eat, the better your chances of achieving optimum health and maximum life span.

MAXIMIZING PHYTOCHEMICAL CONSUMPTION

The Anti-Aging Diet presented in part 2 of this book shifts your eating focus from animal-derived foods to plant-derived foods. Follow the diet, and you'll naturally increase your intake of grains, legumes, fruits, and vegetables—the foods that supply phytochemicals. Remember, the more phytochemicals you consume, the stronger your protection against disease and aging.

No single plant food contains all of the phytochemicals. So get in the habit of varying your diet—within the realm of the New Four Food Groups, of course. If you're unsure of where to start, turn to page 535. There you will find a two-week menu plan, along with meal ideas and recipes. Use these to broaden your culinary horizons.

For extra protection, I recommend taking one or two capsules of a phytochemical supplement every day. Look for a product that combines 17 different fruits and vegetables.

DISEASE-"PHYTERS" AT WORK

In case you're not yet sold on the importance of phytochemicals to long-term health, perhaps the story of Karen, one of my patients, can persuade you. A registered nurse, Karen was the victim of a malfunctioning immune system. She felt tired all the time. She suffered from multiple allergies—to foods, inhalants, and environmental chemicals such as perfumes and car exhaust. She had yeast syndrome (or candidiasis), recurrent infections, and ongoing gastrointestinal problems.

Karen had been following a low-fat vegan diet, supplementing essential nutrients and antioxidants, and using other immune-enhancing therapies. Still, she wasn't getting better.

Suspecting that Karen may have a free radical overload, I ordered an oxidative stress panel. This test includes three measures of free radical activity: hydroxyl free radical level; serum lipid peroxide level, which indicates the extent to which blood fats and cell membranes are being oxidized; and glutathione level. These measures show whether free radicals are depleting a patient's antioxidant supply.

Karen's test revealed severe oxidative stress. Her hydroxyl free radical level and serum lipid peroxide level were quite high, while her glutathione level was quite low.

Based on Karen's test results, my next step was to determine the source of her oxidative stress. I ordered an antioxidant profile, which evaluates blood levels of several key antioxidants: vitamins A and C, coenzyme Q_{10}, alpha-carotene, beta-carotene, alpha-tocopherol, gamma-tocopherol, and lycopene. A deficiency of even one of these nutrients would weaken the entire antioxidant protective network. They can run low for any number of reasons, including insufficient amounts in the diet, poor absorption in the intestines, and excessive numbers of free radicals.

Karen's antioxidant profile disclosed that while her levels of vitamins A and C and gamma-tocopherol were within the normal range, her levels of coenzyme Q_{10}, alpha-carotene, beta-carotene, alpha-tocopherol, and lycopene were dangerously low. The depleted antioxidants fit her symptom picture of immune deficiency, fatigue, allergies, and frequent infections.

I explained to Karen that her antioxidant protective armor had developed holes, which left her cells vulnerable to free radical damage. This was driving her health problems. To help her replace the missing antioxidants, I developed a list of top-notch food sources. I advised her to eat lots of tomatoes for lycopene and orange, red, and yellow fruits and vegetables for carotenoids. I also prescribed a mixed carotenoid supplement and a coenzyme Q_{10} supplement (because no food supplies significant amounts of this nutrient). This program would repair Karen's antioxidant protective armor, thus allowing her body—and, in particular, her immune system—to heal.

When Karen returned two months later for her follow-up exam, her symptoms were much improved. She felt more energetic, her allergies had diminished, her candidiasis had subsided, and her gastrointestinal tract was back on track. She had even begun exercising, something she couldn't manage before. A repeat antioxidant profile indicated that her nutritional program had successfully elevated the levels of all the key antioxidants to within normal range.

I would follow this same protocol to detect and correct oxidative stress in anyone who wants maximum protection against free radicals. It's the most efficient and effective way to optimize Renewal and extend life span.

LOOKING TO THE FUTURE

The discovery of the phytochemicals underscores the nutritional importance of plant-derived foods while pounding another nail in the coffin of animal-derived foods. These supernutrients will dominate nutritional news in the twenty-first century, as new information emerges about their contributions to health and longevity.

Scientific exploration of the vast phytochemical terrain has only just begun. But even at this early stage, one thing is absolutely certain: Only foods from the plant kingdom contain these healing nutrients. Better to head for these greener pastures than to venture into the animal kingdom's nutritional wasteland.

Yes, changing your dietary direction may pose some challenges. On the other hand, isn't it exciting to know that you can increase both the quantity and quality of your life simply by eating more plant-derived foods?

With their amazing anti-aging properties, herbs are a natural choice for the Anti-Aging Supplement Program. In the next three chapters, I profile what I consider to be the cream of the herbal crop: ginseng, ginkgo, and garlic. This trio has shown the most promise in terms of protecting against degenerative disease and staving off the effects of aging. First on deck: ginseng.

Ginseng: The King
of Tonics

*To hear the claims made for ginseng is to be thrust into
one of two positions: either a romantic awe of this God-
given root which is a most amazing panacea or a total
cynicism concerning a root which symbolizes man's
capacity to make a fool of himself.*
—STEPHEN FULDER, PH.D.,
  THE TAO OF MEDICINE

"This is a 48-year-old gentleman with headaches, nasal
congestion, lower back pain..." I began.

"Symptoms, schmymptoms," my mentor, Dr. Tang, interrupted.

He said it authoritatively, but with a kindly twinkle in
his eye. He delighted in doing this. It was his way of getting
me back on track.

Once again, as so often happened in my early days of
studying Chinese traditional medicine, I had made the mistake of presenting a patient's case the way that I had
learned in medical school: by starting with the symptoms.

"Take the pulse," Dr. Tang instructed. "Examine the
tongue. Find the source of disharmony. If you cure the root
cause of the problem, all of those symptoms that you're
preoccupied with will take care of themselves. Your
patient's headaches might come from an energy distur-
bance in the gallbladder or kidneys or liver or somewhere
else. You must find the cause, Dr. Tim."

He was right, of course. He was always right.

Dr. Tang was a seventh-generation Chinese doctor whose
practice spanned five decades. Taoist medicine was in his

genes. He would take a patient's pulse, examine a patient's eyes, tongue, face, skin, tone of voice—everything, including subtle essences that defy description. His objective: to divine the disharmonies in energy that had instigated the patient's illness. Sure, he kept track of symptoms. But like most Chinese doctors, he viewed them in the context of the whole person, not in isolation.

Early in my studies, I realized that Chinese traditional medicine espoused a totally different perspective of illness than mainstream Western medicine. With Dr. Tang's gentle prodding, I learned how to recognize aberrant energy patterns, the essence of Chinese diagnosis.

I also learned that "symptoms, schmymptoms" was Dr. Tang's way of saying, "Look, you have a choice. You can focus on the symptoms and prescribe powerful drugs to suppress them. Or you can use the subtler methods that I'm teaching you to diagnose the energy imbalance underlying the symptoms so you can isolate the root cause of illness. The symptoms may change, but the root cause will not. If you focus on just symptoms, you'll never discover the cause. And if you never treat the cause, your treatments will ultimately fail. Sooner or later, new symptoms will pop up to replace the old ones you suppressed. Use herbs and acupuncture to gently nudge the body's energy back into balance. Then the body will keep itself healthy."

Dr. Tang would usually underscore his message by quoting from the *Nei Ching*, the world's oldest medical textbook: "Only the inferior doctor treats the symptoms. The superior doctor understands the cause of the symptoms and restores harmony."

After more than two decades of studying and practicing Chinese traditional medicine, I know this principle holds true. And it can be taken one step further: With experience, a Chinese doctor can diagnose an energy imbalance before the symptoms have manifested themselves. Then he can prescribe preventive therapies to correct the imbalance and keep the patient healthy.

In ancient China, a patient paid his doctor for services only if he didn't get sick. The best doctor—the "superior doctor"—detected and corrected any disharmony of energy before it produced symptoms.

ELIXIR FROM THE EAST

Over the course of several thousand years, practitioners of Chinese traditional medicine have developed an arsenal of powerful herbal remedies. The Chinese expect much more from a remedy than we Westerners do: It must go far beyond relieving symptoms to correcting the energy imbalance that drives the symptoms. It must also restore internal harmony while strengthening the body. And it absolutely cannot have toxic properties.

No herb meets these stringent requirements better than ginseng. Chinese doctors consider ginseng one of their premier prescriptives for keeping people healthy. In fact, they recommend ginseng more than any of the 1,500 other Chinese herbal remedies.

In Asian countries, where people rely on herbs for health and healing, ginseng reigns as the most prized plant of all. Millions take the herb daily for its rejuvenating, anti-stress, and anti-aging properties.

These days, Westerners are discovering the numerous benefits of ginseng for themselves. As our bodies endure the nonstop assault of stress, environmental toxins, poor diet, and other hazards of modern life, we need a natural restorative that fosters internal harmony while building resistance to disease before it appears. Ginseng fills the bill perfectly.

HOMEGROWN HEALING

Two species of ginseng exist. One, *Panax quinquefolius* (or American ginseng), grows naturally in cool woodlands from the Canadian provinces of Quebec and Manitoba to Alabama, Arkansas, Florida, and Louisiana. The other, *Panax ginseng* (or Asian ginseng), is native to Manchuria (a region of northeast China) and to North and South Korea. Nowadays, you'd be hard-pressed to find the herb growing naturally anywhere in Asia, since residents there have virtually picked the forests clean.

Because of worldwide demand, virtually all Panax ginseng is commercially grown in Canada, China, Japan, North Korea, Russia, South Korea, and the United States. After thorough drying, most of the American crop is exported to Hong Kong and from there distributed throughout Asia and the world.

A small perennial, Panax ginseng requires rich soil and shade to grow. A quality plant takes five to seven years to mature from seed. The older the plant, the more potent—and thus the more valuable—it becomes.

Be wary of so-called Siberian ginseng, or *Eleutherococcus senticosus*. This herbal imposter is often passed off as the equivalent of Panax ginseng. Truth be told, Siberian ginseng isn't ginseng at all. It has a fraction of the potency of the real thing. Chinese herbalists have known about Siberian ginseng for hundreds of years. They don't hold it in the same high regard as Panax ginseng.

AN HERB FOR THE AGES

The name *ginseng* comes from the Chinese *jen-shen*—*jen* meaning "human" or "person," and *shen* meaning "essence" or "spirit." The Chinese believe that the ginseng root contains a human's essence because its branches look like arms and legs. In fact, the more the root resembles a human, the greater its therapeutic powers.

For more than 5,000 years, the Chinese have revered and coveted Panax ginseng. For them, the herb symbolizes health, strength, and long life. Indeed, the Chinese emperor Shen Nung anointed ginseng number one among the hundreds of herbs in use when he compiled the *Pen Tsao Ching*, the oldest existing record of herbal remedies.

In this country, Native Americans taught early American settlers about ginseng's medicinal properties. By the 1700s, enterprising settlers were shipping the herb to China. In 1773, the sloop Hingham sailed out of Boston Harbor for the Far East with 55 tons of ginseng root on board. In 1862, more than 600,000 pounds of the herb were exported, with almost all of the shipment going to China.

Ginseng farming took off in the United States between 1895 and 1903. Spurred by foreign demand for the herb, profiteers formed companies to grow ginseng on a massive scale. In 1904, a ginseng leaf disease devastated many plantations, bringing a burgeoning industry to its knees.

By all accounts, the boom is on again. Farmers from Canada to Alabama are growing huge quantities of high-quality ginseng and sending it to Asian countries. Buyers from Hong Kong size up North American crops and purchase the rights to them years before they're mature enough to harvest.

Much of the ginseng on ·the global market has been grown in the United States. Ironically, the ginseng that's available in the United States is, for the most part, imported from Asia.

THE SECRET INGREDIENTS

Ginseng contains many biologically active substances, the most notable of which are the ginsenosides. These compounds enable the body to better respond to stress and to better resist the effects of external stressors, be they physical, emotional, chemical, or environmental. Scientists have so far identified at least 13 distinct ginsenosides in ginseng, each with unique pharmacological activity. The higher the herb's total ginsenoside content, the higher its quality and potency.

Because the active ingredients in ginseng help the body adapt to whatever life throws its way, herbalists classify ginseng as (appropriately enough) an adaptogen. A universal remedy, the herb provides broad-spectrum support to improve physical and mental performance, strengthen immunity, increase resistance to disease, and thus promote all-over health. (The Latin *Panax* means "all-healing," as in panacea.)

Labels aside, ginseng does have a knack for reversing conditions characterized by exhaustion and a lack of zest for life. Chinese doctors often recommend the herb to people who are facing stressful situations or events. It helps to minimize and even prevent the cumulative damage that is bound to result from long-term stress. Those who have been subjected to prolonged physical or mental exertion—such as the Russian cosmonauts, who routinely use the herb on space missions—praise ginseng's anti-stress effects.

As an herbal remedy, ginseng has proven effective in treating insomnia and depression as well as hangovers and other conditions of overindulgence. Some folks take the herb as a natural upper to raise their spirits, foster a more positive outlook, and enhance memory, alertness, and concentration.

These days, ginseng is attracting a lot of attention

because of its potential as an anti-aging agent. A growing body of scientific evidence supports the widely held belief that ginseng can not only promote health and vitality but also prolong life.

Nature's Anti-Aging Ace

For thousands of years, folks in the Far East have relied on ginseng to keep them healthy and young. Do they know something that we don't? Yes . . . but we're slowly catching on. Through extensive scientific research, we're learning that ginseng does indeed fight disease and slow the aging process. Here's how.

- Enhances brain and central nervous system function
- Enhances sugar metabolism
- Hinders cancer cell reproduction
- Improves digestion
- Improves sexual desire and performance
- Improves stress tolerance
- Increases resistance to infection
- Lowers "bad" low-density lipoprotein cholesterol
- Lowers total cholesterol
- Lowers triglycerides
- Neutralizes free radicals
- Promotes protein synthesis and inhibits protein breakdown
- Protects against carcinogens
- Protects against physical and mental fatigue
- Protects the liver against toxin exposure
- Protects tissues against radiation exposure
- Purifies the blood
- Raises "good" high-density lipoprotein cholesterol
- Stimulates circulation
- Stimulates the adrenal glands

Ginseng has earned a place in the Anti-Aging Supplement Program because of its profound Renewal-promoting effects. The herb acts as an all-around restorative and fortifier: It stimulates activity in the immune and endocrine (hormone-producing) systems. It combats stress, anxiety, and fatigue. It revitalizes the blood vessels, thus improving circulation. It boosts brain health. It protects against heart disease and cancer. And in women, it minimizes menopausal discomfort.

In Asian countries, people who can afford ginseng usually take the herb every day. They believe that ginseng protects against degenerative disease and extends life span.

MINING FOR SCIENTIFIC FINDINGS

Demanding scientific proof that ginseng works seems like something of a double standard. For five millennia before science wielded its seal of approval, billions of people took ginseng simply because they felt rejuvenated by it. That's more proof than any prescription or over-the-counter drug can claim. In his book *Light of Asia*, noted traveler and author Sir Edwin Arnold sums up ginseng's dilemma nicely: "According to the Chinese, Asiatic ginseng is the best and most potent of all cordials, stimulants, tonics, stomachics, cardiacs, febrifuges, and above all, will best renovate and invigorate failing forces. It fills the heart with hilarity, while its occasional use will, it is said, add a decade to human life. Can all the generations of Orientals who have praised heaven for ginseng's manly benefits have been totally deceived? Was humanity ever quite mistaken when half of it believed in something never puffed and never advertised?"

Nevertheless, thanks to decades of scientific scrutiny, the previously "unsubstantiated" anecdotal and empirical claims about ginseng now have mounds of research to back them up. This is especially welcome news for those in the medical and scientific communities, who tend to prefer hard evidence to softer claims such as "invigorates failing forces," "strengthens the vital spirit," "fortifies the beast," and "dissolves pituitous tumors."

Put under even the most powerful microscope, ginseng passes muster. We now have unequivocal proof that the herb benefits the body in numerous ways. In addition to the Renewal-promoting effects mentioned in the previous section, ginseng stimulates protein synthesis, which speeds healing; revives blood cells after exposure to radiation;

safeguards the liver against exposure to toxins; improves metabolism of carbohydrates; lowers blood cholesterol and triglyceride levels, which helps prevent heart disease; and supports functioning of the central nervous system.

Much of the scientific examination of ginseng has focused on six specific areas: immune enhancement, cancer prevention and treatment, protection against radiation, heart disease prevention and treatment, brain health, and stress tolerance. Let's look at each of these areas in turn.

A PROVEN IMMUNE BOOSTER

For those of us interested in slowing the aging process and maximizing longevity, the positive impact of ginseng on the immune system holds the greatest promise. Hundreds of studies have shown that the combination of chemical compounds in ginseng enhances immunity in a variety of ways.

In one study conducted at the Central Drug Research Institute and King George's Medical College in Lucknow, India, researchers infected two groups of mice with a lethal virus. One group had received ginseng for 5½ days prior to viral exposure, while the other did not. Treatment continued for 3½ days after viral exposure. Thirty-five percent of the ginseng-takers survived, compared with none of the non-ginseng-takers. What's more, the ginseng-takers were later found to have developed immunity to the virus.

This study suggests that long-term consumption of ginseng can inhibit age-related immune decline. The herb provides a significant degree of protection against the infectious diseases to which older individuals are especially susceptible.

COMBATING THE KILLER C

Ginseng makes a potent cancer-fighter as well, and not just because of its immune-boosting power. As a team of South Korean researchers found, the herb can also defuse the effects of carcinogens.

In their study, the researchers divided 600 mice into six groups. Two groups were exposed to one of the following common carcinogens: aflatoxin (a mold commonly found on peanuts) and urethane (found in convenience-food and fast-food containers). Another two groups were exposed to one of the same carcinogens, but these mice also received ginseng. The remaining two groups served as controls.

After 6 to 12 months, a time that simulates long-term carcinogen exposure in humans, the researchers counted and measured the tumors in each mouse. The mice that received ginseng consistently developed fewer tumors than the mice that didn't receive ginseng. What's more, the tumors in the ginseng-takers were 20 to 25 percent smaller than the tumors in the non-ginseng-takers. These results validated the researchers' hypotheses that long-term supplementation of ginseng increases resistance to cancer and that ginseng can successfully inhibit the incidence and invasiveness of cancer.

In a similar study conducted at Kyung Hee University in Seoul, South Korea, researchers applied dimethylbenzanthracene—a highly carcinogenic substance—to the cheeks of 40 hamsters. Then 20 of the animals received ginseng in their drinking water (one gram of herb per liter of water), while the other 20 did not. Again, the ginseng-takers had smaller, slower-growing tumors than the non-ginseng-takers.

Japanese researchers have uncovered evidence that certain chemical compounds in ginseng, called saponins, not only inhibit the growth of cancer cells but actually cause them to revert to their normal state.

ARRESTING THE EFFECTS OF RADIATION

A series of studies conducted by the department of medicine and hygiene of the Radiation Center of Osaka, Japan, has conclusively demonstrated that ginseng protects against damage caused by radiation exposure. Ginseng extracts almost completely prevent internal hemorrhaging and stimulate the recovery of red blood cells, white blood cells, and blood platelets. The herb's proven ability to promote protein synthesis, which in turn speeds healing, also contributes to its protective effects.

In one of the Osaka studies, researchers exposed two groups of mice to lethal doses of radiation. One group also received injections of purified ginseng extract, while the other group received injections of a saline solution. Among the ginseng-takers, the 30-day survival rate varied depending upon how much of the herb was given and when it was given. The mice that received the largest dose of ginseng had the highest survival rate—82 percent. Likewise, the mice that received the herb beginning 24 hours before radiation exposure and continuing for 2½ hours after exposure fared best. Among the mice that received the saline solution, none survived. Administering the herb just one day after radiation exposure did nothing to improve survival rate.

TUNING UP THE TICKER

Japanese experiments involving both animals and humans indicate that ginseng lowers total cholesterol, low-density lipoprotein cholesterol (the bad kind), and triglycerides, while elevating high-density lipoprotein cholesterol (the good kind). By shaping up a person's blood-lipid profile in this way, ginseng effectively reduces the risk of heart disease.

Incidentally, hospital emergency rooms throughout China use ginseng as part of the standard protocol for treating shock induced by heart attack or hemorrhage. Extensive research has shown that, in such cases, the herb can restore blood pressure and normalize heart function.

MAXIMIZING MIND POWER

Scientists seem especially intrigued by ginseng's influence over brain function. Italian researchers, for instance, have concluded that the herb enhances an array of cognitive qualities and skills: It extends attention span, increases math aptitude, sharpens deductive reasoning, and shortens decision-making and auditory reaction times.

Japanese researchers have found that rats perform tasks better and make fewer mistakes when given ginseng. And Bulgarian researchers report that, in humans, the herb delays the onset of mental and physical fatigue. It accomplishes this through its actions on the immune system, the central nervous system, and other components of the body.

YOUR STRESS DEFENSE

Ginseng strengthens the body's resistance to stress by acting on what physiologists call the pituitary-adrenal axis.

The ginsenosides in the herb trigger the release of adrenocorticotropic hormone (ACTH) from the pituitary gland, which is located at the base of the brain. ACTH travels through the bloodstream to the adrenal glands, which are perched atop the kidneys, and instructs them to manufacture and release corticosteroid hormones. The greater the availability of corticosteroids in the bloodstream, the greater the body's ability to withstand the effects of stress.

When researchers at the University of Buenos Aires in Argentina subjected mice to high heat and electric shock, they found that the rodents that were predosed with ginseng were less likely to die from exposure to the extreme stressors.

A similar experiment performed by Indian researchers showed that rats given ginseng better tolerated cold temperatures and high altitudes. Thankfully, more humane experiments involving both animals and humans have confirmed ginseng's ability to stave off stress.

In my medical practice, I often see patients who have extreme physical or emotional stress. As a result, their adrenal glands don't secrete enough corticosteroid hormones to sustain normal function (a condition known as hypoadrenocorticism). I usually prescribe ginseng, along with a combination of pantothenic acid (a B vitamin), potassium-magnesium aspartate, and adrenal extract. I also advise people to wean themselves from caffeine and sugar, which artificially stimulate the adrenal glands. Invariably, these patients report that they feel less tired and tense and more energized. Their bodies are better able to handle the effects of stress.

THE ANTI-AGING APHRODISIAC?

More than a few ginseng aficionados contend that the herb enhances sexual desire and performance. While science has yet to delve deeply into this delicate subject, history offers testaments of its own.

Ancient Vedic scriptures contain hymns that graphically describe ginseng's legendary libido-stimulating properties: "Ginseng aids in bringing forth the seed that is poured into the female that forsooth is the way to bring forth a son. . . . The strength of the horse, the mule, the ram, even the strength of the bull, ginseng bestows on him. This herb will make thee so full of lusty strength that thou shall, when thou art excited, exhale heat as a thing on fire." Whoa.

Of course, some have cast doubt on whether ginseng really acts as an aphrodisiac. Perhaps William Byrd, an eighteenth-century plantation owner, captured the critics' viewpoint best when he wrote, "(Ginseng) will make a man live a great while, and very well while he does live . . . however, 'tis of little use in feats of love, as a great prince once found, who hearing of its invigorating quality, sent as far as China for some of it, though his ladies could not boast of any advantage thereby."

Indeed, early indications are that science will ultimately prove Byrd right. Ginseng may improve sexual desire and performance simply by virtue of enhancing overall health. If the herb has any libido-boosting properties, they're modest at best.

THERE'S MORE IN STORE

Other areas of ginseng research show great promise as well. Researchers at Harvard Medical School, for example, have discovered that ginseng stimulates the synthesis of DNA, RNA, and protein in humans. This breakthrough may help to explain why ginseng slows the aging process, since DNA and RNA regulate the synthesis of the enzymes that control all of the body's biochemical reactions. Plus, by stimulating the synthesis of DNA, ginseng may promote DNA repair and thus minimize free radical damage.

For women who are going through or past menopause, ginseng may provide a natural, gentle antidote to declining estrogen levels. In studies, ginseng exhibits mild phytoestrogenic activity, making it an ideal antidote for the hot flashes, mood swings, and other symptoms associated with declining estrogen production. I often prescribe Panax ginseng extract, along with soy products and other sources of natural estrogen, to female patients who have such symptoms. Ginseng's mildness provides a sharp contrast to the toxic estrogenic blast from unnatural hormones such as Premarin.

SAFE . . . AND THEN SOME

Like most herbs, ginseng is eminently safe. All nations permit its unrestricted sale. In the United States, ginseng has even earned GRAS (generally regarded as safe) status from the Food and Drug Administration—and it is one of the few substances truly deserving of the honor.

Efforts to determine a toxic dose for ginseng have instead reaffirmed the herb's harmlessness. Perhaps the most extensive investigation of ginseng's safety and effectiveness has been orchestrated by I. I. Brekhman, director of the pharmacology and experimental therapy laboratory at the Institute of Biologically Active Substances in Vladivostok, Russia. Brekhman has published seven volumes of reports and findings on ginseng, the culmination of 15 years of research.

In his attempt to establish a toxic dose for the herb, Brekhman made a remarkable discovery. Mice that were not given ginseng survived an average of 660 days, while mice that were given a supposedly lethal dose of the herb survived an average of 800 days before succumbing to an overdose. Even the lethal dose had extended the lives of the test animals. Brekhman's findings suggest that if a person took too much ginseng, he'd still fare better in the long run than if he hadn't taken the herb at all.

Toxicity aside, ginseng can produce harmless, reversible side effects in highly sensitive people. Signs of overstimulation include irritability, insomnia, and elevated blood pressure and can be exaggerated if the herb is taken with another stimulant—most notably, caffeine.

QUALITY, NOT QUANTITY

While toxicity isn't an issue with ginseng, choosing the right supplement is. Walk by the supplement display at your local health food store or drugstore, and you'll likely see an array of ginseng products: whole root, sliced root, powdered root, capsules, tinctures, teas, chewing gum, candy, snuff, and even cigarettes.

As I mentioned earlier, the United States exports most of its home-grown ginseng to Hong Kong. From there, the herb is distributed throughout Asia and the world. Most of the ginseng sold in this country comes from South Korea, where it has been cultivated for more than 1,000 years. The Korean people take great pride in their ginseng, and their government regulates its production. Korean Red, a Panax ginseng, carries the government seal—a symbol of purity and potency that's recognized and respected around the world. Unfortunately, counterfeit knock-offs have shown up on the market.

While Panax ginseng contains a variety of active compounds, including vitamins, minerals, and flavonoids (a group of phytochemicals), its potency is measured by its ginsenoside content. High-quality whole ginseng root weighs in with about 4 percent ginsenoside compounds. The most active of these compounds, and therefore the one that's used for standardization, is the highly prized ginsenoside Rg1. A standardized ginseng product retains less active, but nonetheless very important, ginsenoside compounds in direct relative proportion to Rg1. In other words, the more Rg1 in a product, the greater the quantities of the "supporting" ginsenosides.

Nothing but the Root

With ginseng root, tracking daily dosage can prove something of a challenge. This is why I usually recommend capsules of standardized ginseng extract. But if you really prefer the root, the following two dosage methods should put you within the recommended range of 500 to 6,000 milligrams per day.

By the cup: Place ⅛ ounce of ginseng root and 3 cups water in a saucepan. Bring the water to a boil, then let it continue cooking until the 3 cups is reduced to 1 cup. Allow the tea to cool before drinking it. The average "dosage" is one cup of tea per day.

By the slice: Steam the ginseng root to soften it, then cut it into slices about ½ inch thick. Chew one or two slices per day.

Commercial ginseng products vary greatly in ginsenoside content. When tested, many show little or no ginsenoside activity. They're made with the lowest-grade ginseng root, then diluted and blended with inert ingredients so that virtually none of the active ginsenoside compounds remain.

The only surefire way to know a quality ginseng product from an inferior one is through pharmacological analysis—

not exactly a do-it-yourself endeavor. You could ask a store employee for a recommendation, but unless he's aware of the variations in potency, he may unintentionally steer you toward something worthless.

Of all of the ginseng products on the market, your best bets are whole root and capsules of standardized extract. These forms surpass the others in terms of availability, practicality, and effectiveness.

With whole roots, potency varies widely. Older roots tend to have the highest ginsenoside concentrations, but they also tend to be prohibitively expensive. The most prized root of all, called Tung-Pei Wild Imperial Ginseng, is at least 100 years old and costs about $20,000. That's per root.

For every root of Tung-Pei Wild Imperial Ginseng, you'll find plenty of roots that are less expensive but are of poor quality. Selecting the right specimen requires professional assistance. I recommend that you consult a Chinese doctor, an herbalist, or another trained and trustworthy herbal practitioner who can help you find the perfect root. (Some say that the Chinese know ginseng like the French know wine: Neither can be fooled by an inferior-grade product.)

Your other option—and, in my opinion, the better option—is capsules of standardized ginseng extract. A standardized extract guarantees potency as well as a dependably consistent dose.

How do you know that you're getting a quality ginseng product? Read the label. It should say something like this: "Panax ginseng. Standardized to contain X percent (for example, 5 to 20 percent) saponins calculated as ginsenoside Rg1." It should also specify the dose per capsule, as in "100 milligrams (or mg.)." These phrases tell you exactly what you're getting in each capsule, so you don't have to guess whether you're hitting the mark in terms of your optimum intake.

THE IDEAL DOSAGE

The usual recommended dosage for capsules of standardized ginseng extract is 25 to 75 milligrams of ginsenoside Rg1 per day. You may have to do some simple calculations, using information provided on a product's label, to determine how much Rg1 you're getting per capsule. All you have to do is multiply milligrams of standardized extract by percent Rg1.

Suppose, for example, you have a capsule that contains 100 milligrams of standardized ginseng extract and 7 percent ginsenoside Rg1. Multiply 100 by 0.07, and you get 7. So each capsule contains 7 milligrams of Rg1. Taking two such capsules twice each day adds up to 28 milligrams of Rg1 daily, which falls at the low end of the dosage range.

If you're taking pure ginseng root, the recommended dosage is 500 to 6,000 milligrams daily (see "Nothing but the Root"). Again, ginsenoside content can vary greatly from one root to another, so you're not assured of a consistent potency.

No matter whether you choose capsules of standardized ginseng extract or pure ginseng root, keep in mind that exceeding the recommended dosage won't bolster the herb's therapeutic benefits. A little does the job; more just wastes money.

How often you take ginseng depends upon your age. Generally, the older you are, the more the herb can benefit you. My recommendations:

- If you are over age 60 or have a chronic illness, take ginseng every day.
- If you are between ages 40 and 60, take ginseng for one to two months, stop for one month, then repeat.
- If you're under age 40, take ginseng as needed—when you're under considerable stress, for example.

In fact, regardless of your age, you can use ginseng at any time as a natural stimulant to combat the effects of fatigue or stress. You may also want to tap into the herb's immune-enhancing properties during the fall and winter months, when resistance to disease runs low. (Most Chinese doctors advise against taking ginseng while you have a fever, a cold, or the flu. You can resume use of the herb once your symptoms subside, to rebuild your immune system.)

As we've seen, ginseng can do wonders for mental function. But it can't compete with ginkgo. In fact, no substance—manmade or nature-made—can match ginkgo for revitalizing and maximizing mental performance. You'll read all about this anti-aging herb in the next chapter.

Ginkgo: Nature's Brain Booster

When I think of an herbal remedy that is a perfect example of the marriage of folklore and modern science, ginkgo biloba comes to mind.
—DONALD J. BROWN, N.D., *HERBAL PRESCRIPTIONS FOR BETTER HEALTH*

The ginkgo tree stands as a living monument to the potential and miracle of longevity. Fossil records indicate that the tree's botanical family, *Ginkgoaceae*, has been around for some 200 million years. The ginkgo tree itself has a life expectancy of up to 4,000 years. In fact, *Ginkgo biloba* is the oldest surviving species of tree on the planet, a distinction that has earned it the nickname "the living fossil."

Of course, the ginkgo tree would likely have become extinct long ago were it not for its remarkable resiliency and resistance to environmental stressors such as insects, pollutants, viruses, and fungi. For proof of the species' hardiness, consider that a ginkgo tree actually survived the atomic bomb blast that leveled Hiroshima, Japan, in 1945. The tree still stands today near the epicenter of the explosion.

Each leaf of the ginkgo tree supplies a broad spectrum of substances that exist nowhere else in nature. These tongue-twisting chemical compounds—flavonoids, terpenes, and other organic compounds collectively called ginkgo-flavone glycosides—work together to produce an astounding range of therapeutic effects.

As an anti-aging herb, ginkgo supports Renewal in a variety of ways. It scavenges disease-causing free radicals and strengthens cell membranes. It boosts production of adenosine triphosphate (ATP), a chemical that supports cellular metabolism. It regulates the "stickiness" of platelets, the blood cells that cling together to form clots. In this way, ginkgo helps to prevent the arterial clogging that can lead to heart attack and stroke.

Despite all of these benefits, however, ginkgo remains best known as a brain booster. For centuries, Eastern herbalists have prescribed ginkgo to prevent and reverse memory loss and other symptoms of mental decline. Now Western scientists know why: Their research has shown that the herb not only enhances communication between nerve cells but also increases blood flow to the brain (as well as to the eyes, ears, and extremities). These factors combine to keep the mind sharp.

A LONG HISTORY OF HEALING

According to ancient Chinese medical texts, ginkgo has been used as a healing agent for at least 5,000 years. But for the Chinese, the herb had both medicinal and spiritual significance. Buddhist monks regarded the ginkgo tree as holy, anointing it the elder statesman of trees.

While most people think of the ginkgo tree as native to Asian countries, it may at one time have grown on European soil as well. Evidence suggests that the European ginkgos fell victim to advancing glaciers during the Ice Age. So Westerners didn't "discover" the majestic trees until the 1600s, when European explorers began traveling to China and Japan.

One European who apparently was quite taken with the ginkgo tree was Engelbert Kämpfer, a German doctor and botanist. In 1690, Kämpfer journeyed to Japan, where he encountered his first *Ginkgo biloba*. From that point on, he devoted a great deal of time and energy to the study of the ginkgo tree. Historically, Kämpfer is said to have coined the name *ginkgo*, a variation on the original Japanese *ginkyo*.

The "biloba" of *Ginkgo biloba*—the ginkgo tree's botanical name—was contributed by the Swedish botanist Carolus Linnaeus. The term refers to the two lobes of the ginkgo leaf.

The shape of the ginkgo leaf so captivated the German poet Johann Wolfgang von Goethe that he immortalized it with the following verse.

> *The leaf of this tree*
> *Brought to my garden from the East*
> *Holds a secret meaning—*
> *But only for those who can divine:*
> *Is it one living being*
> *That grew divided in itself?*
> *Or are they two who chose each other,*
> *Wishing to be known as one?*
>
> *The answer to these deep questions*
> *Is very clear to me:*
> *Can you feel from my poem*
> *That I could one—or both—be?*

The ginkgo tree's natural beauty and hardiness led to its cultivation as an ornamental plant not just in Western countries but also throughout the world. Only recently has the therapeutic value of the ginkgo leaves begun to receive the scientific attention that it deserves.

BONANZA FOR THE BRAIN

Mother Nature seems to have crafted ginkgo specifically as an antidote to aging. The herb has a remarkable ability to invigorate the body's circulatory and nervous systems, slowing and even reversing their age-related breakdown. In this way, ginkgo protects against heart attacks, strokes, and a whole host of brain disorders, not the least of which is senility.

Just like other organs and tissues of the body, the brain relies on blood to deliver a steady supply of oxygen and nutrients. When circulation is impaired, the brain doesn't get as much blood as it should. This condition leads to the mental deterioration that we so often associate with "growing old."

By enhancing blood flow to the brain (and throughout the body), ginkgo protects and even improves mental function. The herb offers great hope to anyone who has already begun to show signs of diminished mental performance—

as well as to anyone who simply wants to boost his brain power.

GO WITH THE FLOW

When the arteries that feed the brain harden and clog, blood has a hard time reaching its destination. This condition, known as cerebral ischemia, deprives the brain of the oxygen and nutrients it needs. Over time, cerebral ischemia produces common symptoms of mental decline: agitation, confusion, depression, disorientation, fatigue, forgetfulness, impaired hearing and vision, lack of coordination, poor concentration, tinnitus (ringing in the ears), and vertigo. Cerebral ischemia can even lead to transient ischemic attacks, or mini-strokes.

The oxygen deprivation that results from cerebral ischemia causes a dangerous accumulation of free radicals in the brain. Of all the cells in the body, brain cells are among the most vulnerable to free radical damage, primarily because of their high concentrations of fat. (You'll recall from chapter 2 that fat molecules are easily damaged by free radicals, which snatch their electrons.) Injury to a brain cell's protective membranes interferes with cell function and eventually leads to cell death.

Both cerebral ischemia and cerebral hypoxia (the medical term for oxygen deficiency in the brain) become more common with advancing age. But unlike a full-fledged stroke, which causes often irreversible brain damage, cerebral ischemia and cerebral hypoxia are highly treatable. Restoration of optimum blood flow to the brain is key.

More than 40 scientific studies have found that ginkgo dramatically improves blood circulation to the brain. With its circulatory system operating at peak capacity, the brain gets all of the oxygen and nutrients that it needs to function. Cerebral ischemia and cerebral hypoxia go into remission, and their symptoms subside. Mental performance returns to normal—in fact, it may be sharper and stronger than ever.

It is in this context—in the arena of improved circulatory and nervous system function—that ginkgo's restorative effects seem downright amazing. Equally important for those of us who want to extend our life spans is ginkgo's protective effects. Daily supplementation with the herb inhibits the relentless forward progress of aging of the brain, central nervous system, and cardiovascular system.

NEURAL NETWORKING

Ginkgo also enhances brain function by improving communication between nerve cells. For starters, the herb increases the availability of neurotransmitters, the chemicals that enable nerve cells to "talk" to one another. It supports the production of new neurotransmitters and facilitates the recycling of used ones. The greater the number of these chemical messengers, the more efficient the message transmission between nerve cells.

In addition, ginkgo increases the number of neurotransmitter receptor sites on nerve cells. This enables the nerve cells to send and receive more messages. To visualize how this works, think of a nerve cell as a phone system. The more lines that it has, the more calls it can handle at one time. The cell's productivity—and with it your ability to process, store, and retrieve information—increases exponentially.

As nerve cells fire messages back and forth, they create various patterns of electrical activity. These brain waves, as they're called, serve as a good indicator of brain function. They can be measured with the help of an electroencephalogram, or EEG.

At least one study has suggested that ginkgo positively influences brain wave activity. In the study, older people who had displayed symptoms of mental deterioration were given ginkgo supplements. Their EEGs showed increased alpha waves, which are associated with alertness, and decreased theta waves, associated with a sleeplike mental state.

THANKS FOR THE MEMORIES

Other research has provided evidence that large doses of ginkgo can have positive short-term effects on intellectual processes, memory, mood, and sociability. In one study, half of a group of healthy female volunteers took a single large dose of *Ginkgo biloba* extract. The rest of the volunteers took a placebo. None of the women knew which pill they had been given. (For that matter, neither did the researchers overseeing the experiment.)

The ginkgo-takers experienced immediate and significant improvement in short-term memory, compared with the placebo-takers. Keep in mind that ginkgo does not act as a stimulant. Instead, it sharpens memory through a combination of improved blood circulation and enhanced nerve cell communication.

I often take a combination of ginkgo and ginseng before sitting down to a long session of writing. It removes the cobwebs and helps me to think with greater clarity. I've also recommended ginkgo to several of my patients who needed a brain boost—students taking exams, professionals with business reports due, and others who needed their short-term intellectual capacity to be at its peak. They've told me that the herb helped them, too.

Several studies of the effects of ginkgo on Alzheimer's disease have also yielded encouraging results. Although the herb cannot cure Alzheimer's, it may slow the progression of the disease or delay its onset. Alzheimer's patients who were given ginkgo showed significant improvement in mood and mental sharpness.

THE BETTER TO SEE YOU WITH, MY DEAR

By virtue of its role as a circulatory aid, ginkgo has proven effective as a treatment and preventive for an assortment of age-related health problems. For instance, the herb has been used to correct age-related sensory disorders such as vision and hearing loss.

Ginkgo boosts blood flow to the numerous tiny vessels that feed the eyes and ears—vessels that gradually deteriorate with advancing age. For the eyes, the combination of improved circulation and enhanced nerve cell communication helps to delay and even prevent vision impairment and loss. Ginkgo safeguards eyesight against conditions directly caused by compromised circulation, such as cataracts, diabetic retinopathy (deterioration of the retina associated with diabetes), and macular degeneration (a condition characterized by cell breakdown in the retina that leads to vision loss).

For the ears, improved circulation—courtesy of ginkgo—can mean relief from the ringing and other "background noise" associated with tinnitus. It can also put an end to balance and equilibrium problems such as dizziness, lightheadedness, and vertigo.

BACK IN CIRCULATION

By delivering blood to the arms and legs, ginkgo can ease the symptoms of peripheral arterial insufficiency—a fancy name for poor circulation to the extremities. These symptoms can include cold hands and feet, tingling sensations (paresthesias) in the arms and legs, muscle cramps, leg pain upon exertion (intermittent claudication), and sores on the arms and legs that won't heal. All of these symptoms respond well to ginkgo therapy.

In studies, people who took ginkgo supplements for poor circulation had warmer extremities, experienced fewer nighttime leg cramps, and walked farther without pain. Since exercise is key to longevity, the enhanced exercise tolerance afforded by ginkgo may rank among the herb's most important anti-aging effects.

And let's not overlook the link between ginkgo and another "extremity." The herb has a good track record in the treatment of impotence caused by insufficient blood flow.

OUTWITTING THE KILLERS

As I mentioned at the beginning of the chapter, ginkgo offers superior protection against heart attack and stroke. Specifically, it inhibits the inappropriate formation of blood clots by platelets.

Platelets are very small blood cells with a very big responsibility. When a blood vessel becomes injured—by a cut, for example—platelets swarm to the site and plug up the hole in the vessel wall. They do this by sticking together to form a clot. Without the platelets' speedy repair work, blood would continue leaking out of the vessel. Uncontrolled hemorrhaging could lead to death.

Sometimes, however, the clotting mechanism goes awry. Platelets become more sticky than normal, causing them to cling to the blood vessel wall or to each other for no apparent reason. The resulting clot may remain attached to the vessel wall (if it does, it's called a thrombus). Or it may break free and float around the bloodstream until it encounters a vessel that it can't pass through (in which case, it is known as an embolus).

Wherever the embolus lodges, it wreaks havoc. In the brain, it causes a stroke; in the lungs, a pulmonary embolism; in the heart, a heart attack. No matter which way you look at it, the outcome is disastrous.

By preventing platelets from becoming excessively sticky, ginkgo can substantially reduce the likelihood that any of these scenarios will ever play out. Consider the herb your longevity insurance policy.

GINKGO EVERY DAY

With daily supplementation of ginkgo, "inevitable" age-related changes in health no longer seem quite so inevitable. Most notably, your circulatory and nervous systems remain strong, and your mind retains the agility of youth.

Globally, millions of people are already taking advantage of ginkgo's remarkable anti-aging benefits. In European and Asian countries, consumers spend more than $500 million annually on over-the-counter ginkgo products. Physicians in France and Germany routinely recommend standardized ginkgo extracts to their patients. Physicians around the world write more than 10 million prescriptions for ginkgo every year.

THE SUPPLEMENT OF CHOICE

Perhaps the hardest part about taking ginkgo is choosing the right supplement. A great many commercial ginkgo products are available—but they're not all created equal.

All of the definitive studies of ginkgo used a 24 percent standardized extract. This is what I recommend to my patients. Such a product should have the phrase "24 percent standardized extract" clearly marked on the label. The "24 percent" refers to the amount of flavone glycoside, the primary active ingredient in ginkgo, that the supplement contains. "Standardized" means that the amount of flavone glycosides was verified against an approved laboratory measure.

Nonstandardized supplements can vary greatly in potency. With these products, you never know just how much of ginkgo's active ingredient you're getting. You may be getting a therapeutic dose, or you may not.

All Systems Go

Ginkgo helps keep your circulatory and nervous systems in good working order. In the process, the herb fends off all of the following conditions.

Circulatory Problems
Angina pectoris (chest pain)
Congestive heart failure
Deep-vein thrombosis (formation of a blood clot, often in a leg vein)
Diabetes-related disorders

Nervous System Problems
Age-related cognitive decline
Alzheimer's disease
Anxiety
Cerebral circulatory disorders
Decreased alertness
Decreased reaction time
Depression
Headache
Memory impairment or loss
Poor concentration
Senility

Sensory Problems
Cataracts
Diabetic retinopathy (deterioration of the retina associated with diabetes)
Macular degeneration (cell breakdown in the retina that leads to vision loss)
Tinnitus (ringing in the ears)
Vertigo

My advice: Use only standardized products. Steer clear of all non-standardized products, whether liquid extracts, tinctures, freeze-dried supplements, or fresh leaves.

THE RIGHT DOSE

For disease prevention and life extension, I suggest taking one or two 60-milligram capsules of 24 percent standardized ginkgo extract twice daily (for a total of 120 to 240 milligrams a day). To treat any of the conditions listed in "All Systems Go," increase your dosage to 180 to 360 milligrams daily.

Ginkgo is amazingly well-tolerated by the body. Besides the fact that ginkgo has been safely used in Chinese traditional medicine for more than 5,000 years, extensive scientific studies have proven the herb to be completely nontoxic and free of side effects—even in dosages much larger than those I recommend here. And it has no known interactions with nutrients or drugs.

Once you start taking ginkgo supplements, give them time to work. A trial period of at least three months is appropriate, especially if you're using the herb to treat a specific condition. For significant improvement, expect to wait six months or more.

Garlic has gotten a lot of attention of late for its ability to lower cholesterol. But the so-called stinking rose has a multitude of other talents, too. In the next chapter, you'll meet this natural medicinal marvel and find out just what it can do for you.

Garlic: The Most Amazing Herb of All

Garlic doth have power to save from death
Bear with it though it maketh unsavory breath,
And scorn not garlic like some that think
It only maketh men wink and drink and stink.
—SIR JOHN HARINGTON (1561–1612),
  ENGLISH AUTHOR

Folklore has long extolled garlic for its ability to ward off disease, evil spirits, and even vampires. While scientists can't vouch for the herb's supernatural powers, they have begun investigating its purported health benefits. Their findings so far have been nothing short of remarkable.

Hundreds of studies unequivocally confirm what ancient herbalists empirically divined: Garlic is among the most potent preventive and therapeutic agents around. The odorous bulb contains literally hundreds of compounds that defend cells against attack by marauding free radicals and block the development of heart disease, cancer, and numerous other life-shortening ailments.

MEDICINE FROM NATURE

Garlic is a member of the lily family, a group of plants that also includes onions, shallots, leeks, and chives. There are at least 88 species of garlic worldwide, 68 of which can be found in the United States. The herb goes by the botanical name *Allium .sativum* (meaning, appropriately, "all

An Aromatic Rx

If you've shied away from garlic because of its pungent odor, consider this: The compounds that make garlic smell also give the herb some of its most potent disease-fighting powers. In studies, garlic has proven effective in preventing and treating a range of ailments, including the following ones.

- Arthritis
- Asthma
- Atherosclerosis (hardening and clogging of the arteries)
- Athlete's foot
- Bronchitis
- Cancer (prevention only)
- Chronic candidiasis (a type of yeast infection)
- Cold
- Cough
- Diabetes

pungent"), but aficionados simply refer to it as the stinking rose.

When cut, grated, pressed, crushed, or chewed, fresh garlic releases enzymes that in turn trigger a cascade of chemical reactions. This results in the formation of more than 200 phytochemical compounds, each of which possesses impressive medicinal powers.

Garlic seems especially adept at curtailing the cellular damage inflicted by air pollutants, pesticides, and other toxins. Part of the credit goes to those antioxidant phytochemicals, which can neutralize any free radicals generated by the toxins. But just as important are garlic's sulfur-containing amino acids. Cysteine is one. It latches onto substances such as cadmium, lead, and mercury and ushers them out of the body. In doing so, cysteine stops these poisons from overburdening the liver, which is responsible for detoxifying the blood.

Arginine is another amino acid—though not the kind that contains sulfur—found in abundance in garlic. Arginine supports Renewal in several ways. It stimulates the release of growth hormone, which has been shown to

- Dysentery (severe diarrhea)
- Flu
- Fungal infections
- Heart attack
- Heavy metal poisoning (such as lead or cadmium)
- Herpes simplex (oral and genital)
- High blood pressure
- High cholesterol
- Pneumonia
- Radiation exposure
- Respiratory allergies (including hay fever)
- Senile dementia
- Sinus infections
- Skin ulcers
- Stroke
- Tuberculosis
- Vaginal yeast infection
- Viral infections
- Whooping cough

extend life span; it strengthens the immune system; and it helps remove ammonia, a toxic by-product of protein metabolism. Nutrition-minded doctors may prescribe arginine to treat liver disease and increase sperm production.

REDISCOVERING AN ANCIENT REMEDY

Garlic can claim a long and varied history as an herbal remedy. Over the course of 6,000 years, the herb has been used to treat an incredible array of conditions ranging from the common cold to atherosclerosis (hardening and clogging of the arteries).

According to records dating back to 3748 B.C., Egyptian slaves—in what must have been one of the world's first labor strikes—refused to continue building the Great Pyramid of Cheops until they received their daily ration of garlic. The Romans believed that garlic increased strength and so gave it to both slaves and soldiers. Physicians in India and China used the herb for cleaning wounds and treating headache, fever, dysentery, and cholera. The

Phoenicians and Vikings carried it on their sea voyages as medicine for a variety of ills.

A Life-Preserving Herb

Garlic helps you achieve maximum life span by protecting your body against disease. The herb contains literally hundreds of compounds that stimulate and reinforce your body's natural defenses in a variety of ways, some of which I've listed here.

Cardiovascular Benefits
Lowers blood pressure
Lowers total cholesterol, low-density lipoprotein cholesterol, and triglycerides
Prevents abnormal blood clotting
Prevents and reverses atherosclerosis (hardening and clogging of the arteries)
Raises high-density lipoprotein cholesterol

Immune System Benefits
Has antibiotic, anti-inflammatory, and antiseptic properties
Inactivates harmful toxins
Neutralizes free radicals
Protects against the harmful effects of radiation
Stimulates immune cell activity

Other Benefits
Counteracts fatigue
Helps protect against the effects of stress

The Greek physician Hippocrates prescribed garlic as an antibiotic for pneumonia and skin infections. The Roman poet Virgil, in his *Second Idyll*, suggested that garlic be used for snakebite. And the Roman scholar Pliny, in his *Historica Naturalis*, recommended garlic for tumors, asthma, convulsions, gastrointestinal disorders, madness, consumption (tuberculosis), scorpion stings, and dog bites.

Other historical documents credit garlic for providing protection against the ravages of the bubonic plague. In France in 1721, four condemned criminals who were ordered to bury victims of the plague surprised everyone, including themselves, by not succumbing to the disease. Their enhanced immunity was attributed to their regular consumption of garlic steeped in wine. The French folk remedy *vinaigre des quatre voleurs*, or four thieves vinegar, is named in their honor.

In 1858, French chemist and microbiologist Louis Pasteur found that garlic juice killed bacteria when applied to microbes in culture dishes. He reported on garlic's antibacterial effects in the medical literature of the day. Decades later, during World Wars I and II, physicians employed garlic as an antibiotic to prevent soldiers' wounds from becoming gangrenous. And French physician Albert Schweitzer used the herb to treat dysentery during his missionary work in Africa.

THE HERB FOR A HEALTHY HEART

Pasteur's and Schweitzer's work with garlic finally brought the herb some recognition and legitimacy in the eyes of the Western medical community. Time and scientific study would ultimately validate garlic's diverse medicinal uses.

For instance, modern research has confirmed the claim made by ancient Greek physician Pedanius Dioscorides that "garlic doth clear the arteries." Indeed, garlic, along with onions and other members of the lily family, imposes a spectacular spectrum of beneficial effects on the cardiovascular system.

When fatty deposits, or plaque, remain on arterial walls, they narrow the vessels to the point where blood can no longer pass through. The combination of plaque and blood clots, or thromboses, effectively shuts off the blood supply. Blockage of an artery that feeds the heart muscle causes a heart attack. If the obstructed artery feeds the brain, the result is a stroke.

The actual symptoms in people who suffer heart attacks, strokes, and other so-called vascular incidents arise not from the blockage itself but rather from the lack of blood supply to tissues downstream from the blockage. Doctors use the term *ischemia* to describe the obstructed blood supply and accompanying oxygen deprivation that occur in these sorts of medical emergencies.

In healthy individuals, garlic prevents the fatty buildup that leads to atherosclerosis. And in those who already have atherosclerosis, garlic—reinforced by a diet free of animal-derived foods and by a comprehensive supplement program and regular aerobic exercise—accelerates the removal of fatty deposits from arterial walls and actually reverses arterial damage.

ARE YOU AT RISK?

The arterial plaque that sets the stage for heart attacks and strokes comes from cholesterol. Cholesterol comes from two sources: your body, which manufactures it, and animal-derived foods. But most people—including most physicians—fail to realize one important fact: While dietary cholesterol and saturated fat raise blood cholesterol levels, so do sugar, alcohol, and excessive numbers of calories.

Still, cholesterol levels are at best imprecise indicators of atherosclerosis risk. In fact, they can be highly misleading. A person who has a "healthy" total cholesterol reading may develop a false sense of security and indulge in unhealthy behaviors, such as eating animal-derived foods and becoming sedentary. Even though high cholesterol increases the likelihood of developing atherosclerotic diseases, low cholesterol does not guarantee immunity. Heart attacks, strokes, and the hardened arteries of senile brain disease affect millions of people with "healthy" total cholesterol levels. About half of all people who experience heart attacks have cholesterol readings deemed normal by medical standards.

What I'm driving at here is this: If you adopt preventive measures such as eating garlic, you have an excellent chance of defying atherosclerosis and living longer than you ever thought possible. Conversely, if you choose to indulge in unhealthy behaviors, your risk of atherosclerosis certainly increases, whether or not your total cholesterol level does.

DEFENSE ON ALL FRONTS

Garlic offers broad-spectrum protection against atherosclerosis and the heart attacks, strokes, and other vascular incidents that usually result from it. What amazes me about the herb—and convinces me of its potential to preserve cardiovascular health—is its positive influence on all of the major risk factors associated with atherosclerosis.

Among garlic's known benefits: It lowers total cholesterol, "bad" low-density lipoprotein (LDL) cholesterol, and triglycerides (another type of blood fat). It raises "good" high-density lipoprotein (HDL) cholesterol. It discourages platelets, the blood cells that support coagulation, from becoming sticky. As long as platelets remain slippery, they won't participate in the abnormal clotting that leads to arterial blockages. Garlic also inhibits clot formation by increasing what doctors call fibrinolytic activity. Fibrin is a blood protein that aggregates into threads, which then form a clot. Fibrinolytic activity is the breakdown of a clot before it gets big enough to cause trouble by obstructing arterial blood flow.

Research has suggested that garlic blocks clot formation more effectively than aspirin, which many doctors recommend as a heart attack preventive. The herb also helps the body dissolve existing clots—something that aspirin can't do. Garlic has other advantages over aspirin: It is a natural food substance, not a drug; it doesn't cause stomach irritation; and it protects the heart and blood vessels in a variety of ways rather than providing just one basic benefit.

SCRUBBING ARTERIES CLEAN

Given the choice between preventing atherosclerosis and treating it, I'd take prevention any day. Keeping blood vessels healthy in the first place is clearly preferable to mopping up the mess after atherosclerosis sets in.

Still, garlic does a miraculous job of salvaging damaged arteries. In fact, if consumed daily over a period of several months, garlic can actually reverse atherosclerosis. This benefit alone makes garlic worthy of inclusion in the Anti-Aging Supplement Program, especially when you consider that atherosclerosis is responsible for more premature deaths than any other disease.

In one study, researchers made rabbits' arteries atherosclerotic by feeding them large quantities of cholesterol and fat. The researchers found that they could reduce the amount of arterial hardening in the rabbits by feeding them the human equivalent of a one- to two-ounce garlic bulb every day. By the end of the study, the garlic-fed rabbits had less than half as many plaques in their arteries as a group of rabbits that hadn't been fed garlic.

Of course, rabbits are animals. Could garlic have the same effect in humans? According to another study, yes.

In this study, Indian researchers divided 432 post–heart attack patients into two groups. One group received daily garlic supplements, while the other received placebos. Over three years, the garlic-takers experienced 60 percent fewer heart attacks than the placebo-takers and enjoyed lower blood pressures and blood cholesterol levels. By the end of the study, twice as many placebo-takers had died.

Members of the garlic group not only lived longer but also felt better, too. They reported enhanced energy, increased libido, greater exercise tolerance, and less joint pain. Since garlic's benefits became more pronounced the longer the patients took supplements, the researchers concluded that the herb worked by dissolving atherosclerotic blockages in the coronary arteries.

Garlic stops the formation of new blockages, and thus holds atherosclerosis at bay, by keeping blood cholesterol levels in check. Some of the most provocative research into the relationship between garlic and cholesterol has been conducted by Benjamin Lau, M.D., Ph.D., professor of immunology at Loma Linda University School of Medicine in California.

In one study, Dr. Lau selected 32 people with significant elevations in their cholesterol levels (which ranged from 220 to 440 milligrams per deciliter of blood) and divided them into two groups. One group received four capsules of aged garlic per day, while the other group received placebos. The study subjects had their cholesterol and triglycerides measured monthly.

After two months, the garlic-takers' readings had actually increased, much to Dr. Lau's surprise and dismay. Another month went by before their readings began to drop. Finally, after six months, most of the garlic-takers had cholesterol and triglyceride levels in the "normal" range. The placebo-takers showed no changes in their cholesterol and triglyceride readings, as expected.

In a subsequent study, Dr. Lau focused on low-density lipoprotein and very low density lipoprotein (VLDL) cholesterol, both of which are considered risk factors for atherosclerosis. A similar pattern emerged: People who took garlic supplements initially showed increases in their LDL and VLDL levels, then significant drops three months later. (Levels of HDL, which protects against atherosclerosis, gradually rose over the six months.)

After considerable reflection, Dr. Lau realized that for the first two months of each study, garlic had been dissolving arterial plaques and moving the cholesterol that they contain into the bloodstream. This process caused temporary rises in cholesterol levels. With time, the fatty slough was removed from the bloodstream, so cholesterol levels finally declined. The lesson from all this: Garlic supplements won't improve your cholesterol profile overnight. Months may pass before you see results.

Research has also shown that the more garlic you take, the greater the change in your cholesterol reading. In one study, Indian researchers compared three groups of vegetarians with essentially identical diets. The group that consumed large amounts of garlic had an average total cholesterol level of 159, the lowest of all three groups. The group that ate small amounts of garlic had an average total cholesterol level of 172—higher, but still acceptable. The group that consumed no garlic at all had the highest average cholesterol level: 208. Those who spurned garlic were also most prone to blood clots, another risk factor for atherosclerosis.

UNPARALLELED PROTECTION AGAINST CANCER

Garlic's disease-fighting ability extends beyond atherosclerosis. For instance, the herb has proven quite effective at defending the body against a broad spectrum of cancers, including those of the breasts, colon, rectum, bladder, skin, and esophagus.

Note: While garlic helps prevent cancer, it does not cure the disease and should not be used as a treatment.

Research suggests that garlic thwarts the development of cancer in several ways. For instance, studies at the M.D. Anderson Cancer Center in Houston, Pennsylvania State University, and other major U.S. medical centers indicate that certain compounds in garlic block the action of carcinogens within the body. Other studies suggest that the herb inhibits the transformation of normal cells into cancer cells and prevents already formed cancer cells from replicating. Still other studies postulate that garlic stimulates natural killer cells, immune cells that attack and destroy cancer cells.

Then, too, garlic contains abundant supplies of an array of antioxidant phytochemicals. These compounds neutralize free radicals before they have an opportunity to inflict damage on cells and, in particular, on the DNA housed in a cell's nucleus. As you'll recall from chapter 3, fractured DNA can lead to genetic mutation and uncontrolled cell division—the precursors to cancer.

CHEMICAL WEAPONS

Government scientists have taken a great interest in garlic's anti-cancer effects. A team at the National Cancer Institute is working to isolate the compounds that make the herb such a potent preventive.

Among those compounds is germanium, a mineral that has gained fame, at least in nutritional circles, for its immune-enhancing properties. Garlic contains an abundant supply of germanium: 754 parts per million.

In the body, germanium stimulates the production of interferon, a powerful immune-enhancing chemical. Interferon improves the function of immune cells called T-lymphocytes (which destroy free radical–forming substances) and B lymphocytes (which manufacture antibodies). It also boosts the activity of natural killer cells. All of these cells work together to block the growth of cancer as well as viruses.

POTENT PROTECTION

While government scientists put garlic under the microscope, other scientists in this country and around the world are turning up equally persuasive evidence of the herb's protective effects.

Here in the United States, for example, researchers at the Akbar Clinic and Research Institute in Panama City, Florida, found that regular garlic consumption stepped up the destruction of cancer cells. Volunteers who ate garlic every day for three weeks had 1½ times as much cancer cell–killing activity in their blood when the study ended. The dramatic increase is important because the human body constantly produces cancer cells that must be destroyed by natural killer cells.

In China, researchers found that regions of the country in which people consumed garlic regularly had one-tenth as many cases of gastric cancer as regions in which people consumed no garlic. Why the difference? One possible explanation: Garlic stops the transformation of nitrates into highly carcinogenic nitrosamines.

BETTER THAN MEDICINE?

Garlic's benefits don't end with atherosclerosis reversal and cancer prevention, although they alone make for an impressive résumé. The herb also fends off all kinds of disease-causing microorganisms, including viruses, bacteria, fungi, and parasites. In fact, garlic has been referred to as Russian penicillin because the Russian people use it as an antibiotic to treat infections of all sorts.

Garlic works especially well against fungal infections. In my practice, I usually prescribe garlic supplements to patients with intestinal candidiasis, a yeast infection that is caused by the fungus *Candida albicans* and that suppresses immune function. *C. albicans* can also take up residence in the skin, the vaginal area, and the mouth (a condition known as thrush).

Athlete's foot is another type of fungal infection. It, too, responds well to garlic therapy. Simply apply garlic oil directly to the affected areas.

Besides killing "bad bugs," garlic increases the body's natural resistance to infection by reinforcing the immune system. In my family, which plays host to a seemingly endless succession of viruses unintentionally brought home by two young children, all of us take lots of garlic (both as a food and as deodorized capsules) as well as extra vitamin C and liberal doses of the herb echinacea (which has antibiotic, immune-boosting properties). The combination has done wonders for us. Most times we completely escape the cold and flu epidemics that run through the rest of the community. And on those rare occasions when we do get sick, we experience a much milder version of the illness compared with our neighbors.

GETTING THE MOST FROM GARLIC

In this chapter, I've discussed using garlic in both its fresh and supplement forms. Use whichever form you find most convenient. Both are entirely safe and nontoxic.

To prevent atherosclerosis, cancer, and other life-shortening diseases, I recommend consuming two to four cloves of fresh garlic or taking two to eight 250-milligram garlic capsules daily. If you're incorporating fresh garlic into your meals, keep in mind that steaming and microwaving preserve the herb's phytochemicals better than cooking at higher temperatures.

To treat infections like colds or the flu in the early, acute phase, increase your dosage to 12 cloves a day or four capsules three or even four times a day. Dosing garlic in this way quickly boosts tissue levels of the herb's healing compounds. You may also want to try teaming up garlic with vitamin A, vitamin C, zinc, and echinacea. They work synergistically with the herb to produce immune-stimulating and antibiotic effects.

SELECTING A SUPPLEMENT

These days, health food stores and many drugstores carry an array of garlic supplements. Which one should you choose? Well, that depends on whom you ask. Nutrition experts continue to debate whether aged garlic extracts (such as Kyolic) are superior to standardized high-allicin extracts (such as Garlicin Pro).

Aging is a method of preserving garlic. It was developed thousands of years ago by Chinese herbalists, who found that "steeping" garlic in vinegar for a few years actually increased the herb's potency. A Japanese company reinvented the process in the 1950s. In the modern version, organically grown garlic is placed in large vats of vinegar for two years. Proponents say that aging the garlic in this way enhances the herb's antioxidant properties, prevents the rapid deterioration of important compounds, and removes the odor as well as irritants that might cause stomach upset.

Indeed, if you're concerned about garlic breath, an aged extract or enteric-coated tablet is the way to go. If you're treating an infection of some kind, a standardized high-allicin extract is the better choice. Aging destroys garlic's antibiotic properties.

And if your main concern is preventing heart disease or cancer, you can choose either an aged extract or a high-allicin extract. Both work equally well. How can you tell the difference between these two types of garlic supplements? Read the labels—products should be clearly marked.

Now that you're familiar with the anti-aging herbs, let's move on to the next category of the Anti-Aging Supplement Program: the brain nutrients.

CHAPTER 29

Age-Proofing Your Brain:
Smart Pills and
Neuronutrients

Of all the things I've lost, I miss my mind the most.
—FROM A BUMPER STICKER SPOTTED IN
BERKELEY, CALIFORNIA

Medical school, as I remember it, was a seemingly end-less blur—a procession of days crammed full of powerful images of disease and healing, life and death. One day you'd be in surgery, holding retractors during a coronary bypass; the next might find you administering electroen-cephalograms (EEGs) or delivering babies. It was sort of like a marathon showing of *ER* reruns, except these episodes were all too real. You'd catch a little sleep, then jump right back into the maelstrom as the succession of intense dramas started all over again.

Of all the images that bombarded my senses during my medical school years, one remains indelibly etched in my memory. I want to share it with you because it so vividly illustrates why a healthy brain is indispensable for all else that life has to offer.

It happened during my junior year. After two years of basic science courses, my classmates and I had finally begun our clinical training. At last, we were seeing real live patients rather than reading about them in textbooks.

My first assignment happened to be the neurology serv-ice. Rounds were usually held on the university hospital's neurology ward, but on one appropriately gloomy wintry day, we assembled at a chronic care facility far removed from the main campus. I'm sure we looked for all the world like a flock of eager ducklings as we trundled along behind Bob Townsend, M.D., our neurology professor.

After looking in on an assortment of chronic neurological patients, Dr. Townsend stopped abruptly in front of the closed door to a private room. "Please don't talk while we're in this room. I'll explain later." Then he held open the door, and one by one, we quietly filed in.

Inside, the scene was surreal—and depressing. The room was darkened and eerily quiet. A gaunt old man in a white hospital gown lay flat in the bed, passive and motionless. His head was propped up on a pillow, and he stared, expressionless, in the general direction of a television set that was turned on but had no picture or sound—just the fuzz you get when a channel isn't tuned in.

He didn't react to our presence. No body movement, no utterance, no blink—just a sunken, glassy gaze. The darkened room, the lifeless yet living man, Dr. Townsend's secrecy—all of it gave me the willies. My classmates also suspected something unusual was up. They began shooting furtive glances back and forth, as if to say, "This is weird. What gives here?" Though the man was clearly alive, he was, in a sense, more dead than alive.

Obviously not in a mood to linger, Dr. Townsend performed one of the fastest and most perfunctory neurological exams I've ever seen. Almost as soon as we had entered the room, we were back outside in the hall.

Dr. Townsend quickly slipped into teaching mode, grilling our eager little group on comas and strokes and brain syndromes. We weren't the first group of would-be clinicians he'd seen, nor would we be the last. He rapidly moved us through a series of questions designed to help us understand what living brains do, what dead—or dying—brains cannot do, and how all this applied to the patient we had just seen.

Dr. Townsend then explained that this gentleman had totally lost his cognitive functioning as a result of cerebrovascular disease. In effect, atherosclerosis had choked off the blood supply in the arteries feeding his brain. He had been totally unresponsive for years. "Because he is unable to respond, we don't know whether he can see, hear, smell, or think. That is why I asked you not to talk. It is possible, though rather unlikely, that he could regain those functions.

"Only his cognitive centers are affected—not the vegetative ones, which control bodily functions like heart rate and digestion," Dr. Townsend continued. "His vital signs are normal. It is possible that he could perceive or experience stimuli, like our conversation. But because he is totally unable to react to stimuli by initiating voluntary motor behavior, he has absolutely no way of responding. So we don't really know whether he is thinking and, if he is, what he's thinking about."

When we were just about to move along to the next room, Dr. Townsend—almost as an afterthought, in a tone that seemed to seek immunity for him and the rest of us from a similar, cruel fate—quietly revealed the man's identity: "Gentlemen, that was Theodore Jenkins."

What a shock. We all knew the name, but no one had recognized him. That shell of a man was none other than the recently retired president of the university. He had been a mental giant, a man of the most impeccable intellectual credentials. His brain had served him well.

On the way home, a profound sadness came over me. I wondered how such a fate could befall such an intelligent, accomplished man. To be alive without a functioning brain seemed a horrendous fate. Why did his physical body have to live out its life span when his brain had already checked out? To see him incapacitated that way triggered a cascade of strong feelings and a myriad of questions about life and death.

Beyond these ponderables, certain facts were clear. Dr. Jenkins was a victim of medical ignorance. He had suffered the consequences of cerebral atherosclerosis (hardening and clogging of the arteries that feed the brain) and age-related cognitive decline in the days before we knew that these conditions could be prevented through diet, supplementation, and exercise. Deprived of these protections, the arteries feeding his brain had gradually narrowed, choking off the blood supply to his brain cells. Free radicals took over, clobbering his brain cells into oblivion.

Thanks to what we've learned in the 30 or so years since this scenario played out, we now have the ability to dramatically improve cerebral health and age-proof the brain.

The information in this chapter can help you protect that vital resource between your ears so you can keep your mind's fires burning as brightly as possible for as long as possible.

A CHANGING MIND

Have you ever felt as if your brain has turned into a huge sieve with really large holes? Or maybe a great big bowl of oatmeal? Well, you're not alone.

Most of us, by the time we reach age 40 or so, have begun to experience at least a few of the early signs of what neuroscientists call age-related cognitive decline (ARCD). About the time that the gray hair and wrinkles appear, the lights upstairs start dimming a bit as well. It's not as if we've suddenly become stupid. Our minds simply aren't as nimble as they used to be.

ARCD is the loss of cerebral function caused by the death or dysfunction of nerve cells (neurons) in an aging brain. It causes us to forget names and phone numbers, misplace keys, and enter rooms without remembering why.

ARCD occurs as a result of cumulative free radical damage to nerve cells—or, more specifically, to the cells' membranes. The less antioxidant protection you have, the faster ARCD progresses. You can beef up your free radical defenses by eating plenty of antioxidant-rich foods and avoiding all free radical–promoting foods. Supplementing antioxidants such as coenzyme Q_{10}, glutathione, vitamin E, and the essential fatty acids is especially important for protecting brain cells from harm. (Dosages of these nutrients are listed in "The Program at a Glance" on page 296.)

Maintaining optimum brain health for as long as possible is the highest priority of anti-aging medicine. When you stop to think about it, brain aging determines overall age: You can literally be no younger than your brain. For all practical purposes, when your brain goes, you go with it.

Of course, occasional memory lapses are an inevitable aspect of life with a brain. But these embarrassing moments happen more often with age, as one by one those irreplaceable brain cells sputter and fail. Gradually, the slowing of mental function becomes global, affecting everything from reaction time to learning rate to recall speed.

THE BRAIN REBORN

Now for the good news: Age-related declines in thinking, learning, concentration, memory, and overall cerebral function are not inevitable. Cognitive enhancers—what I call smart pills or neuronutrients—can put the kibosh on ARCD, jet-propel your thinking, elevate your IQ, hot-wire your memory, and age-proof your brain. These are breathtaking and life-saving discoveries.

Cognitive enhancers are for real, and they are here to stay. Advances in neurochemistry, molecular biology, and cell biology have unraveled profound secrets of nerve cell structure and function, culminating in astonishing and historic breakthroughs. The "smart supplements" described in this chapter can speed the transmission of messages between nerve cells, amplify mental clarity, increase intellectual process, and upgrade memory. In most cases, ARCD can be prevented and in some cases even reversed, restoring the brain power that's so important to long-term health and vitality.

Best of all, the cognitive enhancers are safe, naturally occurring, food-derived nutrients that meet all of our requirements for Renewal. They protect brain cells from free radical damage. And when protection fails, they facilitate the repair of injured cells. The result is rejuvenation of the central nervous system. Flagging functions are restored to normal, bestowing heightened cleverness and creativity and improved intellect—in short, more cerebral pizzazz. The result: a brain and central nervous system that age much more slowly.

ANATOMY OF THE BRAIN

The brain is unique. It serves as the chief executive officer of your central nervous system, which uses electrical and chemical impulses to send and receive messages in a body-wide communications network. Without it, you'd be in a pickle.

Your brain has trillions of nerve cells. One cubic centimeter of brain tissue, about the size of a sugar cube, contains several million cells.

While every type of cell is amazing in its own way, nerve cells are especially remarkable. Why? Because they carry the messages that contain our thoughts, our emotions, our impulses, our perceptions, and the sights, sounds, smells, tastes, and textures of the world around us.

Though the architecture is decidedly different, each nerve cell has the same parts as other cells: an outer cell membrane; internal structures, or organelles (including the all-important energy-generating mitochondria), which are themselves surrounded by membranes; and a nucleus with DNA. Nerve cells perform all of the housekeeping functions that other cells do, such as nutrient absorption, energy production, protein and membrane synthesis, and waste removal.

Nerve cells are very efficiently designed to accomplish the job of rapid communication. They are very long and thin, like wires (which isn't too surprising, since they also function like wires). They're arranged in cablelike bundles called nerves, which carry messages around the body.

A nerve cell delivers its electrical message along a thin structure called an axon. If the body of a nerve cell were the size of a basketball, the axon would extend several blocks. A message travels along the axon at speeds of up to 300 miles per hour. That's fast.

The end of the axon splits into branches. Each branch ends with a terminal bud, or synaptic nob. This is where chemicals called neurotransmitters are manufactured and released. Once a message reaches the axon's terminal bud, it triggers the release of a neurotransmitter. The neurotransmitter travels across a gap (called the synaptic cleft) to a "receiver" (called a dendrite) on the next nerve cell. There, the neurotransmitter triggers another electrical message, which whizzes off along the nerve cell. This chain reaction continues from one nerve cell to the next, until the message finally reaches its destination. The axon of each nerve cell has many branches, so it can establish contact with many dendrites on neighboring nerve cells. In fact, an axon may have connections to the dendrites of 150,000 or more nerve cells downstream.

THOSE AMAZING MEMBRANES

Membranes are the sifters and the winnowers of your biochemical soup. They decide what gets into and what goes out of cells.

In the nervous system, the synaptic cleft—the gap between an axon branch of one nerve cell and a dendrite of another nerve cell—is where the action is. The area is dominated by membranes that play important roles in message transmission between nerve cells. For example, the terminal bud—itself a membrane—also contains large numbers of membrane-walled mitochondria. These mitochondria supply the energy necessary for the production of neurotransmitters. Likewise, membrane-bound sacks called vesicles hold neurotransmitters prior to their release. And on the other side of the synaptic cleft, a membrane covers the dendrite that receives the neurotransmitter molecules.

When a nerve cell fires, the vesicle containing the neurotransmitter migrates to the inside of the terminal bud membrane and merges with it. The vesicle releases its neurotransmitter to the outside, spilling the molecules into the synaptic cleft. The molecules quickly hop across the gap to the dendrite membrane's receptor proteins on the other side. The spent neurotransmitter molecules are broken down by enzymes in the dendrite, and the fragments are sent back to the axon from which they came. There the fragments are reassembled into another neurotransmitter molecule.

Because membranes act as the nerve cells' doors and walls, keeping them healthy is a potent strategy for enhancing brain function. Phosphatidylserine, acetyl-L-carnitine, and ginkgo all assist in membrane maintenance. I'll tell you more about these neuronutrients in a bit.

SOUPED-UP CEREBRAL FUNCTION

As an ambitious, fact-hungry young medical student, I fantasized about a pill that I could take to supercharge my brain. I wanted a mental edge so I could get better grades while cutting back on study time.

Back then there was no such miracle medicine. Thirty years later, there is. And none too soon for me, since I'm entering my mid-fifties, when mental decline begins.

As their understanding of ARCD has evolved, scientists have identified structures and molecules that become injured or depleted as we get older. Far-fetched as it may seem, we no longer have to watch helplessly as brain function—and with it character, personality structure, and joie de vivre—deteriorate with age. We can apply the quantum-leap scientific advances to improve mental performance and extend "brain span."

The nutrients discussed in this chapter renew the brain and slow the cumulative damage that causes ARCD. They do this by:

- Enhancing message transmission capacity
- Enhancing the energy production of nerve cells
- Facilitating neurotransmitter production and release
- Improving the synthesis of eicosanoid molecules, which carry hormonal messages to nearby cells
- Increasing reservoirs of the raw material from which neurotransmitters are synthesized
- Reducing the wear and tear of brain cells so that they last longer
- Strengthening the membranes of nerve cells
- Supporting the multiple functions of critical membrane-based proteins

I've devoted the bulk of this chapter to the four nutrients that top my list of potent brain-boosters: phosphatidylserine (a fatty acid), acetyl-L-carnitine (an amino acid), pregnenolone (a hormone), and ginkgo (an herb). Hundreds of studies have shown that these nutrients improve intellectual function while age-proofing your brain. They nurture brain Renewal by protecting cells from damage and promoting cell repair.

As you read about these brain-nourishing supplements, keep in mind that they work best in the context of the complete Renewal Anti-Aging Program: the Anti-Aging Diet, the Anti-Aging Supplement Program, and the Anti-Aging Exercise Program. It has long been known that optimum levels of vitamins, minerals, essential fatty acids, and amino acids are necessary to support basic nervous tissue health. Think of these brain nutrients as the icing on the cake. Without the cake—that is, diet, supplements, and exercise—they are useless.

PHOSPHATIDYLSERINE: GUARDING AGAINST COGNITIVE DECLINE

To grow older is to experience gradual cognitive erosion—a nibbling around the edges of brain power. We can lose up to half of our everyday memory, thinking, and reasoning capacities in the course of "normal" aging.

Phosphatidylserine (PS) is an exciting new development in the study of brain function. A soy-derived supplement, PS renews aging brain cells and improves overall mental performance. It also plays important roles in brain energy, memory, and alertness. In effect, PS switches on a lightbulb in your brain.

Doctors experienced in nutrition and/or anti-aging medicine prescribe PS as a treatment for ARCD. The nutrient can also be used as a preventive, to enhance mental processes in otherwise healthy individuals. PS supplementation helps regenerate stressed-out or damaged nerve cells, actually reversing defects in nerve cell message transmission. This is the quintessence of Renewal.

PS benefits many brain functions that tend to decline with age: memory, learning, vocabulary skills, concentration, mood, alertness, and sociability. Students, professionals, seniors—practically anyone interested in maintaining and maximizing their mental abilities can benefit from taking PS. Clinical research indicates that PS is a premier candidate for inclusion in any program aimed at supporting cognitive function.

HOW DOES IT WORK?

PS is a naturally occurring "good fat"—technically, a phospholipid (a fat with a phosphate group attached). A youthful brain makes sufficient amounts of PS on its own, but production declines with advancing age. The brain is particularly sensitive to low levels of PS. An older person with impaired mental function and depression almost certainly has a PS deficiency.

PS can be found in the membranes of all cells, but it is especially concentrated in the nerve cells of the brain. A cell's outer and inner membranes are comprised of a double layer of phospholipid molecules derived from essential fatty acids and other nutrients. PS is one of these vital phospholipids.

In nerve cells, PS plays several important roles. As an essential building block of cell membranes, PS enhances membrane integrity and stimulates membrane repair. It also supports the functions of several important membrane proteins. These large protein molecules station themselves like sentries along the phospholipid wall, where they perform a variety of important functions necessary for nerve cell message transmission. For example, they process enzymatic and hormonal signals from outside the cell. They catalyze the nerve cell's mitochondrial energy production. They facilitate the release of neurotransmitters. And they support the functions of the proteins in the neurotransmitter receptors of dendrites.

PS itself assists in neurotransmitter synthesis, release, and activity. It also serves as a reservoir of raw material for the manufacture of eicosanoid (prostaglandin) molecules, which carry hormonal messages to nearby cells.

PS has a phenomenal ability to boost learning rate, concentration, and memory. Though PS produces even stronger benefits when combined with other neuronutrients (such as acetyl-L-carnitine, pregnenolone, and ginkgo), some researchers feel that it's the single best bet for the treatment and prevention of ARCD.

WHAT SCIENCE SAYS

Research focusing on PS has yielded results that are nothing short of astonishing. This miraculous nutrient rejuvenates just about every function controlled by the central nervous system. Several clinical trials involving thousands of subjects have demonstrated that PS fine-tunes the brain's biochemical environment. It effectively halts and even reverses the cognitive degeneration that results in ARCD and senility. It restores memory (informational, visual, and numeric), boosts concentration, improves mood, and quickens reflexes.

In one U.S. study, volunteers between the ages of 50 and 75 with ARCD took 100 milligrams of PS three times a day for three months. The nutrient reversed the decline in name-face recognition skills by a statistical 12 years. In other words, the average scores attained by 64-year-olds rose to match the average scores attained by 52-year-olds. The people taking PS showed significant reductions in memory impairment, with those who had the worst memory lapses improving the most.

Depression in older people and depressive mood changes during the fall and winter months (seasonal affective disorder) are particularly responsive to PS therapy. The nutrient also improves cerebral functioning in people with Alzheimer's disease or Parkinson's disease (although it won't cure either condition).

Several studies have noted that the benefits of PS supplementation, even at levels as low as 200 milligrams per day, could persist for up to three months after people discontinue it. Your brain is not stupid, you know: It knows a good thing when it sees it. So when PS comes down the pike, your brain latches onto it, stores it, and even recycles it. That's why its effects linger.

GUIDELINES FOR SUPPLEMENTATION

Research has shown PS to be a remarkably safe nutritional supplement, noting no serious side effects. Why would there be? After all, PS is a friendly molecule. Your body makes its own, and the supplemental form comes from a natural source: soybean phospholipids.

To start, take 200 to 300 milligrams of PS per day in divided doses—that is, 100 milligrams two or three times per day. Then after one month, switch to a maintenance dose of 100 to 200 milligrams per day.

Because it's a food product, PS is compatible with all other foods and supplements. It does work best when used as part of a comprehensive anti-aging program that also includes proper diet, regular exercise, and supplementation of other brain nutrients.

Your body has the genetic program to synthesize PS from these nutrients. But because synthesis involves several steps and consumes quite a bit of energy, it generates only modest amounts of PS. Supplementation is a more efficient means of achieving optimum levels of the nutrient.

You can enhance the effects of PS by taking the nutrient's precursors: vitamin B_{12} (at least 1,000 micrograms daily), vitamin C (675 to 3,000 milligrams daily), folic acid (800 to 2,000 micrograms daily), and omega-3 and omega-6 fatty acids (from flaxseed and borage oils—2,000 to 10,000 milligrams and 250 to 500 milligrams, respectively). You'll get these doses just by following the Anti-Aging Supplement Program.

Can you get PS directly from soy foods? Unfortunately, no. The amount of PS in soy is so small that you'd never be able to consume enough foods to reach therapeutic levels.

When you start taking PS supplements, give them a chance to work. After all, rebuilding brain cells takes time. You won't turn into Einstein overnight. PS requires about a month to improve memory and several months to achieve peak results. (Let's hope that during the wait you won't forget why you're taking it.)

If you stop taking PS, any memory enhancement that you've experienced will gradually fade after several months.

ACETYL-L-CARNITINE: ENERGIZING YOUR BRAIN

As you get older, your mental processes gradually decelerate. You think slower, write slower, drive slower, take longer to fill out forms, start losing to the kids at Scrabble. You want to hang on to as much brain power as possible for as long as possible.

For protecting the brain from aging, nothing tops acetyl-L-carnitine (ALC). This stuff is incredible. Your body makes its own ALC. But as with phosphatidylserine and other key anti-aging nutrients, production drops off with age. For optimum brain health, you need to maintain ALC at pre-decline levels. Studies indicate that in people over 40, ALC supplementation dramatically slows and even reverses cerebral aging. It resuscitates nerve cells and enhances memory, alertness, and learning. It restores mental vitality.

According to one researcher, "We don't know how much brain life extension we can get out of taking ALC, because nobody has been taking it supplementally for long enough to find out. But if animal studies are correct, we can expect a lot of extra 'brain years.'"

THE MULTIPURPOSE NEURONUTRIENT

ALC is remarkably versatile. An inventory of the nutrient's beneficial functions reads like a Renewal wish list.

Acetyl-L-carnitine supercharges energy production in the mitochondria. In nerve cells, the mitochondria are concentrated in the terminal buds because this is where energy is needed for neurotransmitter synthesis. ALC literally loads up fat molecules in the cell's cytoplasm (the viscous substance inside the cell), hauls them through the mitochondrial membrane into the inside of the power plant, and drops them off right where they are burned to release energy. Like a train hauling coal to a power plant, ALC shuttles fuel to the furnaces of your brain.

ALC also assists in the production of acetylcholine, one of your body's main neurotransmitters. Acetylcholine production declines with age, causing memory loss and cognitive decline. (The "acetyl" portion of acetylcholine comes from acetyl-L-carnitine. The "choline" portion comes from another neuronutrient, called phosphatidylcholine.)

But ALC goes beyond merely enhancing and maximizing brain energy and neurotransmitter production. For starters, it prevents age-related loss of nerve cells by shoring up brain structure. How does it do this? Once again, those all-important cell membranes loom large.

As you age, your cell membranes go through certain changes, such as losing fluidity and elasticity because of free radical damage. These changes have long been considered irreversible. For a nerve cell, that's bad news. Because unlike all other types of cells, nerve cells can't replicate. You're born with a certain number of them, and once they're gone, they're gone.

In chapters 2 and 3, I explained how the largest and potentially the most destructive free radicals are unleashed in the mitochondria during energy production, sort of like sparks from a fire. Since these particular free radicals hover right next to the mitochondrial membranes, they can easily oxidize the fats in these membranes—a process called lipid peroxidation—unless they are rapidly and efficiently snuffed out. (You can find out the rate at which lipid peroxidation occurs in your body by having your serum lipid peroxide level checked. This blood test can be performed at your local laboratory, but it requires a prescription.)

The job of protecting the mitochondrial membranes falls to coenzyme Q_{10} and glutathione. These two nutrients position themselves near the mitochondria, ready and able to neutralize free radicals. ALC serves as an able assistant to coenzyme Q_{10} and glutathione. A potent free radical scavenger in its own right, ALC protects nerve cells against oxidative stress and defends them against lipid peroxidation. With a helping hand from ALC, coenzyme Q_{10} and glutathione molecules are under much less stress. They're free to protect your body elsewhere. That's what I call antioxidant protection with a capital P.

ALC supports the mitochondria in another way as well: It repairs their run-down, worn-out membranes. In fact, ALC maintains the membranes of all nerve cell structures, including the terminal buds.

The presence of optimum amounts of ALC in the body translates into a host of benefits for the brain. Scientists say that ALC "promotes membrane stability," "improves neuronal energetics," "improves neuronal repair mechanisms," and "restores age-related membrane changes." We can simply call it age-proofing the brain.

THE RESEARCH VERDICT

Many population studies have substantiated the brain-boosting powers of acetyl-L-carnitine. In one study, for example, Italian researchers gave 20 senile patients 500 milligrams of ALC three times a day for 40 days. Another 20 patients received placebos. Intellectual performance—the ability to think and remember—improved significantly in the ALC-takers.

Of course, this was a relatively short experiment. A longer one would almost certainly produce even better results. For maximum benefit, I suggest a trial period of at least 60 and preferably 90 days.

In another study, a group of senile patients took 1,500 milligrams of ALC daily for six months. They improved significantly in all parameters studied, including cognitive ability, motor activity, behavioral performance, and self-sufficiency. According to the researchers, patients achieved "an effective recovery of . . . quality of life and improved participation in family and social life."

Other research has shown that ALC is highly effective at treating depression in older people, particularly those with senility. It also slows (but doesn't reverse) the progressive deterioration associated with Alzheimer's disease.

Does ALC have any benefit for younger people? To investigate the nutrient's ability to enhance attention span and reflex velocity, 17 men and women between the ages of 22 and 27 took 1,500 milligrams of ALC every day for a month. Ten of the study participants were involved in competition-level sports, while the remaining seven were sedentary. The researchers used special devices to evaluate reaction time to an auditory stimulus as well as learning time, as measured by speed and error rate in getting out of a video game maze. For comparison, the researchers also tested a second group of young people who had not taken ALC.

The ALC-takers not only reacted faster but also solved the maze faster, and with a fraction of the number of errors. Their overall performance scores far surpassed those of the non-ALC-takers.

WHO SHOULD TAKE IT?

I consider ALC an invaluable addition to the Anti-Aging Supplement Program. Anyone interested in improving their mental performance can benefit from ALC. This includes older people as well as students, businessmen and businesswomen, and people who are under stress or experiencing depression. The usual dose is 500 to 1,500 milligrams once or twice daily. (I take 1,000 to 2,000 milligrams a day.)

In my practice, I recommend ALC to patients with ARCD, Alzheimer's disease, dementia, post-stroke amnesia, memory loss, Parkinson's disease, depression, and chronic fatigue syndrome. The dose is the same as above.

PREGNENOLONE: THANKS FOR THE MEMORIES

At a party not long ago, one of my more outrageous colleagues sidled over to me, looked me square in the eye, and said: "Ever since I started taking three-alpha-hydroxy-five-beta-pregnen-twenty-one, I've been able to remember its name. I tried stopping once, but then I forgot it."

After pausing to give me time to wonder whether he had finally lost it, he laughingly explained that this is the chemical name for pregnenolone (which I didn't know). Then he proceeded to remind me of pregnenolone's ability to rejuvenate flagging neurotransmitter receptors in the brain, amplifying memory, alertness, concentration, learning, and mood (which I did know).

Pregnenolone stands at the head of the class as arguably the most powerful intelligence- and memory-enhancing nutrient yet discovered. A superpotent brain hormone, it has powerful effects on the brain.

If you're in the market for a memory upgrade, pregnenolone may be your single best bet. Research conducted by Eugene Roberts, Ph.D., a neurobiologist at the City of Hope Medical Center in Los Angeles, and his colleague James Morley, M.D., a biologist at the St. Louis Veterans Administration Medical Center, found that pregnenolone is several hundred times more potent than any previously tested memory booster. In an article published in the *Proceedings of the National Academy of Sciences*, Roberts and Morley report that pregnenolone effectively reverses age-related declines in memory, restoring levels back to normal. They note that in laboratory animals, extremely tiny doses of the nutrient—fewer than 200 molecules—improved memory.

I have taken 100 to 200 milligrams of pregnenolone on an almost daily basis for more than three years, both for the nutrient's mind-sharpening effects (it made writing this book easier) and for a longer life. Not that I could memorize the entire New York City phone directory. But I find myself better able to mentally manage the nonstop information overload. Thoughts flow more readily, details are accessed more easily, creativity seems more fertile. I have a heightened awareness of visual stimuli, a longer attention span, and generally a better mood. My energy level has increased as well.

Chapter 33 offers a more detailed discussion of pregnenolone's anti-aging properties, complete with dosage information. You'll find out how pregnenolone can help both your brain and your body last longer.

GINKGO: PLANT FOOD FOR THOUGHT

Although a relative newcomer to the American nutritional medicine scene, *Ginkgo biloba* has been used in Europe for decades and in China for centuries. The Chinese were brewing tea from ginkgo leaves to treat brain

394 The Renewal Anti-Aging Supplement Program

and circulatory ailments long before neurochemists figured out how the herb works—in fact, thousands of years before neurochemistry even existed.

We now know that ginkgo increases blood flow throughout the body and especially in the brain. In this way, the herb improves memory, concentration, alertness, and overall cerebral functioning. Numerous studies have demonstrated ginkgo's ability to exert a positive influence on human cognitive skills and mental performance.

You'll find dosage recommendations for ginkgo in chapter 27.

ON THE HORIZON

The four nutrients profiled above represent the most promising and most potent of the known brain rejuvenators. A number of other supplements have shown potential for restoring and preserving brain function. These include DMAE, 5-hydroxytryptophan, ginseng, St.-John's-wort (hypericum), L-glutamine, L-tyrosine, phosphatidylcholine, pyroglutamic acid, and B_6, B_{12}, and other B-complex vitamins.

I've already incorporated a few of these into my personal anti-brain-aging program, which I outline below. Expect to read and hear more about this new wave of neuronutrients in the months and years ahead.

A GAME PLAN FOR YOUR BRAIN

The nutritional cognitive enhancers presented here are not panaceas for all brain disease, but they do slow the progression of disease and salvage brain function. In clinical trials, even patients suffering from degenerative neurological disorders have shown improvement when given supplements of these neuronutrients. But you needn't suffer from ARCD or any brain disease to benefit from neuronutrients. In fact, prevention is one of the most compelling reasons for beginning an anti-brain-aging program.

The beauty of the natural neuronutrients is that they don't just suppress symptoms to create the illusion that all is well, which is how fluoxetine hydrochloride (Prozac) and its chemical cousins operate. You're actually supplying the exact substance that an ailing brain needs to heal itself, simultaneously solving—at least in part—the puzzle of cognitive dysfunction. To age-proof my own brain, I've devised the following supplement program.

- Phosphatidylserine: 100 milligrams one to three times daily
- Acetyl-L-carnitine: 500 to 1,000 milligrams once or twice daily
- Pregnenolone: 100 milligrams twice daily
- Ginkgo: 30 to 60 milligrams (as 24 percent standardized extract) twice daily
- B-complex vitamins: especially 50 to 250 milligrams of B_6 daily and 500 to 2,000 micrograms of B_{12} daily (my multivitamin supplies these)
- Vitamin E: 1,600 international units daily
- Essential fatty acids: 6,000 milligrams of flaxseed oil daily and 500 milligrams of borage oil
- Ginseng: 25 to 75 milligrams (as standardized to ginsenoside Rg1)
- Phosphatidylcholine: 250 to 1,000 milligrams once or twice daily
- DMAE (dimethylaminoethanol): 250 to 500 milligrams once or twice daily

Just how much of each supplement I take each day depends on a variety of factors—how stressed I feel, for example, or how much exercise or sleep I've gotten. As you become accustomed to these supplements, you'll learn to adjust your daily dosages, too.

In addition to the supplement program, I adhere to a low-fat vegan diet and exercise daily. Eating only plant-derived foods reduces my exposure to oxidized fat molecules. These free radicals cause atherosclerosis in the cerebral blood vessels—the primary causative factor behind ARCD and senility. Regular workouts keep me mentally sharp, preserve my reaction time, and improve my memory. Physical gymnastics support mental gymnastics.

The neuronutrients improve the odds that my brain will not give out before my body. This in itself makes them worth taking. But I also value the clarity of thought and the heightened consciousness that they sometimes provide. As Rollo May writes in his book *The Courage to Create*:

"Genuine creativity is characterized by an intensity of awareness, a heightened consciousness."

I don't always experience this, mind you. After all, real life still has its ups and downs. But there are days when a state of pure joy reigns. I'm spending much more of my time in this delicious realm. By taking the neuronutrients, so can you.

Now that you know how to take care of your brain, let's move south to your intestinal tract. That's where nutrients get absorbed into your bloodstream. If your intestinal tract isn't in the pink, chances are that the rest of your body isn't, either.

So how do you keep it healthy? Fill up on fiber, for starters. The next chapter gives you the details.

Fiber: Zen Food and Internal Cleanser

I am convinced digestion is the great secret of life.
—SYDNEY SMITH (1771–1845),
   BRITISH CLERGYMAN AND AUTHOR

Few issues in medicine and nutritional science evoke general consensus among the experts. Fiber is one of the exceptions.

Fiber plays an essential role in overall good nutrition and is necessary to achieve optimum health. It helps to prevent a broad range of diseases, including the two responsible for most deaths: heart disease and cancer. A fiber deficiency, on the other hand, contributes to a multiplicity of common health problems—several of which can deprive you of maximum life span.

Most folks in the United States consume far too little fiber. For starters, the standard American diet still emphasizes foods of animal origin. Meat, poultry, fish, dairy products, and eggs contain no fiber whatsoever. Then, too, our diet features an abundance of packaged foods, which have had their fiber stripped away. Like vitamins, minerals, and essential fatty acids, fiber is often a casualty of modern refining and processing.

Actually, the practice of removing fiber from foods has its roots in the earliest years of nutritional science. Back then, nutritionists deemed fiber expendable because it con-

The Risks of Insufficient Roughage

Constipation may be the most immediate consequence of a low-fiber diet. But it's not the only consequence—nor the most serious. Research has linked poor fiber intake to a surprising array of health problems, including the following ones.

Cardiovascular Problems
Angina
Deep-vein thromboses and thrombophlebitis (formation of blood clots, often within leg veins)
Heart attack
Heart disease
High blood pressure
High cholesterol
Kidney failure
Pulmonary embolism (a blood clot that travels to the lungs)
Varicose veins

Gastrointestinal Problems
Appendicitis
Colitis and ulcerative colitis (inflammation of the colon)
Colon cancer

tains no nutrients, has no calories, and is indigestible. Fiber, they believed, does nothing.

Of course, they couldn't have been more wrong. As any student of Zen knows, even doing nothing amounts to doing something. Such is the case with fiber.

Nutritionists now realize that fiber quickly ushers noxious chemicals and other waste products from the intestinal tract. This benefits not just the digestive system but the entire body in a variety of ways, which I'll discuss a bit later.

The combination of a high-fiber diet and daily fiber supplements fosters a cleaner, healthier internal environment. It primes your insides to withstand the life-shortening ravages of toxins and time.

Crohn's disease (inflammation of the ileum, a segment of the small intestine)

Diarrhea

Diverticulosis and diverticulitis (the formation and infection of small pouches in the intestinal wall)

Hemorrhoids

Hiatal hernia (a hernia formed by the protrusion of the stomach through the diaphragm, the muscle that separates the chest from the abdomen)

Inguinal hernia (a hernia in the groin region)

Irritable bowel syndrome

Metabolic Problems

Diabetes

Gallstones

Gout

Kidney stones

Obesity

Other Problems

Autoimmune disorders (when immune cells attack healthy tissues)

Dermatological disorders

Multiple sclerosis

Tooth decay

A CHECKERED PAST

For a substance that can do the body so much good, fiber has generated its share of controversy. Perhaps the first to cast doubt on the substance's value was the Greek physician Hippocrates, who stated that "white bread is more nutritious, as it makes less feces." The Father of Medicine, being a hygiene-oriented guy, equated more feces with more filth and therefore with less health. He apparently failed to realize that abundant bowel movements actually keep the intestinal tract clean. In doing so, he set the tone for the debate that was to come.

Centuries later, American Sylvester Graham (of graham cracker fame) challenged Hippocrates' pronouncement by launching a campaign in support of whole-grain foods. Although he failed to persuade folks on this side of the Atlantic, he did make a believer out of Britain's Queen Victoria. She switched to whole-grain bread in 1847, at age 28. She lived 54 more years, to age 82—quite remarkable for those times.

None of this persuaded the American Medical Association, which in 1936 officially condemned the use of bran. The organization's move effectively stifled fiber research for three decades. When John Harvey Kellogg—who "invented" dry breakfast cereals with his brother, Will—began preaching the health benefits of whole grains and bran, the American Medical Association condemned him, too.

It wasn't until the 1960s that fiber once again became the center of attention in medical and scientific circles. This time, several investigators announced that they had observed striking health differences between populations who consumed high-fiber diets and those who didn't. In affluent Western countries, where people ate mostly refined and processed foods, degenerative conditions—including heart disease, colon and rectal cancer, diverticulitis, appendicitis, gallstones, hemorrhoids, hiatal hernias, and varicose veins—had reached epidemic proportions. These ailments were almost unheard of in Third World countries, where people ate primarily whole (unprocessed) foods.

Based on their findings, the investigators speculated about a possible link between a low intake of fiber and the development of disease. They noted that the refined and processed foods common in Western diets were made with fiberless white flour. Plus, fiber-rich plant-derived foods—the whole-food staples of Third World diets—were all but gone from Western diets, having been replaced by fiber-poor animal-derived foods.

Soon after, Denis Burkitt, M.D.—a British surgeon best known for his discovery of Burkitt's lymphoma, a cancer associated with the Epstein-Barr virus—corroborated the investigators' theory with his own findings. During his 20 years of practicing medicine in Africa, Dr. Burkitt observed that the people there seldom developed the degenerative conditions prevalent in Western countries. He, too, attributed the disparity to the lack of fiber in Western diets. Because his reputation was firmly established,

Dr. Burkitt persuaded others in the medical and scientific communities to rethink their position on fiber.

Dr. Burkitt's work had been limited to Africa's rural populations. When other populations were studied, however, the same general pattern emerged. Countries in which the typical diet was high in fiber, low in fat, and devoid of refined and processed foods had the lowest rates of degenerative disease.

Subsequent research uncovered yet another interesting phenomenon: When people move from a country in which refined and processed foods are scarce to one in which these foods are standard fare, their risk of degenerative disease rises considerably. For example, Japanese citizens who move to the United States and adopt American eating habits are much more likely to develop heart disease, cancer, and other health problems than Japanese citizens who remain in their homeland.

FIBER DEMYSTIFIED

Fiber—or the lack of it—clearly has a profound influence on your health. So just what is the stuff, and how does it work in your body?

The term *fiber* actually encompasses an array of substances: celluloses, gums, hemicelluloses, lignins, mucilages, and pectins. All are remnants of plant cell walls, and all resist the action of digestive enzymes and so move through your system unaltered.

Each of the various types of fiber falls into one of two general categories, based on its solubility in water. The natural gel-forming fibers—gums, mucilages, and pectins as well as certain hemicelluloses—are soluble. The structural fibers—celluloses, lignins, and the remaining hemicelluloses—are insoluble.

Plant-derived foods contain various combinations of soluble and insoluble fibers. (Remember, animal-derived foods have no fiber at all.) Often, either the soluble or insoluble types are dominant. Oats, for example, supply an abundance of soluble fibers, while wheat offers mostly the insoluble variety.

Once inside your body, soluble and insoluble fibers perform different but complementary functions. Soluble fibers act like tiny sponges, sopping up water as well as toxins that would otherwise irritate the intestinal lining or be absorbed into the bloodstream. Insoluble fibers act like tiny brooms, sweeping away stagnant waste and keeping the intestinal environment clean. Together, the fibers police your intestines, making sure that toxins and other waste vacate the premises as quickly as possible. Otherwise, these poisons can slip through the intestinal wall and into your bloodstream, along with food and water. Once there, they contaminate your blood and can travel anywhere in your body.

A DIAMOND IN THE ROUGHAGE

You may not think of it this way, but your intestinal tract serves as an internal containment system. It protects the rest of your body from the toxic soup that it holds. Its highly selective mucous membrane lining allows only nutrients and water to pass through the intestinal wall and into your bloodstream.

Should the toxins become excessive or should their journey through the intestines slow considerably, they're more likely to slip into your bloodstream. They then place an extra burden on your liver and kidneys, the organs responsible for cleansing your blood.

You can easily prevent this sort of toxic overload just by following a high-fiber diet. Toxins simply don't stand a chance in the presence of optimum amounts of fiber.

For starters, fiber promotes peristalsis, the muscular contractions along the intestinal wall that move waste through the intestines. Here's what happens: Soluble fiber absorbs water in the intestines, causing it to swell to several times its original size. As the fiber expands, it adds bulk to the waste. Stools become larger and softer, exerting a gentle pressure on the intestinal wall that prompts the muscles of the wall to contract. (An interesting fact: Populations that consume high-fiber diets have an average fecal weight of 500 grams, compared with 100 grams for populations that consume low-fiber diets.)

What's more, the combination of increased bulk and enhanced peristalsis shortens the amount of time required to digest food and process waste—what the experts call transit time. In population studies, high-fiber diets consistently produce rapid transit times of 24 to 36 hours, while low-fiber diets produce much slower transit times of 72 to 96 hours.

Of course, the faster waste moves through your system, the less opportunity toxins have to irritate the intestinal wall or to escape through the wall and into the bloodstream. Allowing toxins to linger in your body any longer than absolutely necessary is not to your advantage. In populations with slow average transit times, colon and rectal cancers rank second only to lung cancer in frequency. But colon and rectal cancers are almost unheard of in populations with rapid average transit times.

The fast transit time associated with a high-fiber diet has another benefit as well. It limits the exposure of the beneficial bacteria that live in your intestinal tract to toxins. As long as these "good bugs" are plentiful and healthy, they prevent disease-causing bacteria and fungi from making themselves at home. (You'll learn more about your intestinal ecosystem and its inhabitants in chapter 31.)

HIDDEN ASSETS

Fiber certainly does an outstanding job of keeping your intestinal tract healthy. But its benefits extend far beyond gut level. In fact, the relationship between fiber intake and disease risk is so strong that nutrition-minded doctors routinely prescribe high-fiber diets and fiber supplements as preventive and therapeutic measures.

To be honest, nutrition researchers have just barely scratched the surface in understanding the effects of fiber on human health. Here are some of the conditions that they have found fiber to be helpful in combating so far.

Cardiovascular diseases. Atherosclerosis—the hardening and clogging of arteries that leads to heart attacks, strokes, and other so-called vascular incidents—usually begins with high cholesterol. According to at least one study, fiber and prescription drugs work equally well in lowering cholesterol. People who took 60 to 90 grams of oat bran a day showed just as much improvement in their cholesterol readings as people taking medication. But fiber costs much less, and it produces no side effects.

Other research suggests that fiber influences cholesterol

levels in several ways. It nabs saturated fat and cholesterol in the intestines, before they get absorbed into the bloodstream. (Saturated fat, you'll recall, is converted into cholesterol by the body.) It binds with bile acids, substances that are synthesized from cholesterol by the liver and that eventually excrete into the small intestine, and prevents them from getting absorbed, too. (If the bile acids get into the bloodstream, they can be used to make more cholesterol.) It reduces "bad" low-density lipoprotein cholesterol and raises "good" high-density lipoprotein cholesterol, thus improving your total cholesterol profile.

Fiber also blocks atherosclerosis by escorting toxins from the body. Otherwise, these poisons can pass through the intestinal wall and into the bloodstream, where they generate free radicals. And when free radicals attack arterial cells, the damage results in artery-hardening plaque.

Cancer. A Dutch study, published in the British medical journal *Lancet*, found that death rates from all types of cancer were three times higher among men with poor fiber intakes than among men with optimum fiber intakes. Once again, fiber moves cancer-causing compounds out of the body before they can do any harm—either in the intestines or elsewhere.

The Anti-Aging Diet, with its emphasis on organically grown plant-derived foods, can substantially reduce your body's carcinogen load. But it can't eliminate carcinogens completely. Nothing can. That's because cancer-causing compounds occur naturally, as by-products of your body's routine processes.

During digestion, for example, the gallbladder releases stored bile acids from the liver into the small intestine. These acids emulsify fats to make them more absorbable. If the acids are not promptly removed from the small intestine once they've done their job, they're transformed into cancer-promoting substances by harmful intestinal bacteria. The likelihood of actually developing cancer from these substances, regardless of their source, increases both with their concentration and with the duration of their contact with the intestines.

You can keep concentration and "contact time" from exceeding safe limits simply by following a high-fiber diet (like the Anti-Aging Diet) and supporting it with daily fiber supplements. This nutritional one-two punch minimizes your cancer risk.

Blood sugar problems. White sugar, white flour, and other refined grains have simple molecular structures that allow them to be rapidly digested and absorbed. When consumed, these so-called simple carbohydrates cause blood sugar to rise rapidly. In response, the pancreas releases large quantities of the hormone insulin, which clears the excess blood sugar by storing it in the liver and muscles. Just like that, blood sugar dips downward.

This roller-coaster effect—blood sugar skyrocketing, then plummeting—is known as rebound hypoglycemia. It reaches its lowest point two to four hours after a meal. When it does, you start to feel hungry. And if you happen to eat a simple carbohydrate such as white sugar or white flour, the roller-coaster ride starts all over again. Over time, fluctuating blood sugar can contribute to a host of health problems, including atherosclerosis and diabetes (the result of pancreatic burnout).

Complex carbohydrates—whole grains, legumes, potatoes, and the like—help the body to regulate its own blood sugar level. The starches in these fiber-rich foods have complicated molecular structures, so they take longer to be broken down into simple sugars. Plus, the fiber slows the rate at which the simple sugars are absorbed. As a result, insulin is released in a slow and controlled manner. This prevents rebound hypoglycemia as well as post-meal hunger pangs. In other words, no more roller-coaster ride.

No wonder a high-fiber diet has such great value in the treatment of hypoglycemia as well as Type II (non-insulin-dependent) diabetes. As one of my patients put it, "I don't get hungry between meals anymore—and my sweet tooth has disappeared, too."

Overweight. Although many people consider overweight an issue of appearance, it is in fact a serious, life-shortening health problem. It affects more folks in the United States than in any other country in the world.

One of the reasons we Americans tend to weigh too much is that we eat too much. Overeating is the most common nutritional disorder in the United States. That's because our diet features lots of fiberless refined and processed foods, which require little "chew time" and fail to fill us up.

A high-fiber diet, on the other hand, supports weight loss. Fiber-rich foods take longer to chew, so they do a better job of stimulating the flow of digestive juices in the mouth and stomach. You can eat less and still feel satisfied. And as the fiber absorbs water and expands, it delays emptying of the stomach. This creates a sense of fullness and contentment while buying time for more thorough digestion in the stomach.

Constipation. Proper elimination is of vital importance to every aspect of health. Indeed, we Americans spend millions of dollars each year on the more than 700 laxative products now on the market—all in an effort to keep things moving, so to speak.

But laxatives treat only the symptoms of constipation, not its cause: a low-fiber diet based on animal-derived foods and refined grains, which increase transit time and generate huge quantities of toxins. The feelings of stuffiness, fuzzy-headedness, and general ill health that accompany constipation are physical manifestations of internal toxicity.

The immobilizing effects of a low-fiber diet can be compounded by inactivity. Some scientists have concluded that lack of exercise, rather than old age per se, causes the constipation common among the elderly. Walking, jogging, tennis, and other activities stimulate the abdominal and back muscles to literally massage the intestines, which increases peristalsis.

When the intestines must struggle and strain to push through hard, dry stools, weak areas along the intestinal wall can bulge out over time. The tiny pouches that form signal the onset of diverticulosis. Should these pouches become infected, diverticulosis turns into diverticulitis, an extremely painful abdominal condition.

Both diverticulosis and diverticulitis are entirely preventable. In countries where the traditional diet consists primarily of fiber-rich plant-derived foods, people just plain don't get these diseases.

Hemorrhoids, varicose veins, and hiatal hernias. Without sufficient fiber to hold water, the contents of the intestines become dry and compacted. The resulting stool moves along very slowly and is difficult to pass. Straining to expel the hardened feces forces blood downward, engorging blood vessels in the lower body.

When you repeatedly strain to pass stool, the stress produces bulges in the rectal veins—what you may know as hemorrhoids. The extreme downward pressure can also damage the leg veins, causing the familiar swelling and distention of varicose veins. Any upward pressure created by straining may contribute to a hiatal hernia (when part of the stomach protrudes through the diaphragm, the muscular wall that separates the chest from the abdomen).

Tooth decay and periodontal disease. Refined carbohydrates—fiberless foods such as sugar and white flour—are key players in the development of cavities. They provide nourishment for the bacteria that foster tooth decay and dental plaque. And because refined carbs contain no vitamins or minerals, they contribute to nutrient deficiencies, which further encourage cavity formation.

Complex carbohydrates, on the other hand, are vitamin and mineral powerhouses. And they're rich in fiber, which means that they require more chewing. In these ways, complex carbs help keep teeth and gums healthy and strong. (Incidentally, both tooth decay and periodontal disease are rare in Third World countries, where diets consist primarily of whole, unprocessed, unrefined foods.)

GETTING YOUR FILL

Of course, to reap all the health benefits of fiber, you need to make sure that you're getting enough of the stuff. A person following the typical American diet consumes 5 to 15 grams of fiber daily. Although no Recommended Dietary Allowance exists for fiber, health organizations such as the American Cancer Society, the American Diabetes Association, the American Heart Association, the National Cancer Institute, and the American Medical Association agree that this intake is woefully inadequate. Optimum intake from all sources—foods and supplements—ranges from 40 to 60 grams daily.

This doesn't mean that you have to tally every gram of fiber you eat over the course of a day. In fact, I advise you not to even try it, since it's a frustratingly difficult task. Besides, you automatically maximize your dietary fiber intake just by adopting the Anti-Aging Diet. Based on the New Four Food Groups—grains, legumes, fruits, and vegetables—the Anti-Aging Diet is naturally high in fiber and low in calories.

To ease into the diet and notch your fiber intake upward, begin by cutting back on (and eventually eliminating) fiberless foods: red meat, poultry, fish, dairy products, eggs, baked goods made with white or enriched flour, and anything containing sugar. Then gradually add in high-fiber foods such as almonds, apples, beans, broccoli, corn, oatmeal, prunes, raspberries, spinach, whole oats, and whole wheat.

You can also increase the fiber content of meals and snacks by substituting one food for another. Some examples: Choose whole-grain cereals over toaster pastries, brown rice over white, popcorn (sans butter) over potato chips, whole fruits over juices, and hummus or bean dip over sour cream dip.

SUPPLEMENTS FOR INSURANCE

Even a healthy diet like the Anti-Aging Diet can vary in the quantity and quality of fiber that it supplies from one day to the next. Then, too, diet alone cannot provide the amount of fiber required for maximum disease prevention. For both of these reasons, I recommend daily fiber supplementation.

If you are over age 30 and have been consuming the standard American diet for most of your life, I suggest you start by supplementing with two to five grams of fiber once or twice daily to clean and restore your intestinal tract. (One gram of fiber equals two 500-milligram capsules.) Then, after a few months, you can cut back to one to three grams daily as a maintenance dosage—a sort of fiber insurance policy. Trial and error is the best way to determine the exact amount of fiber you need.

You'll find many excellent fiber supplements on the market. The one I prefer is Yerba Prima's Daily Fiber, which contains psyllium, oat bran, apple pectin, guar gum, and rice bran. Everyone is different, however, so you may want to try a few different products until you find one that you like.

Steer clear of any product that contains sugar, fructose, or aspartame.

Some people experience intestinal discomfort, bloating, or gas when they first increase their fiber intakes. These symptoms occur as the fiber is fermented by gas-forming bacteria in the intestines. Don't take these symptoms as a sign that a high-fiber diet and fiber supplements are not for you. Your intestines just need time to adjust. Eventually, the gas-forming "bad bugs" will die off and be replaced by beneficial bacteria.

If you're bothered by symptoms, reduce your fiber supplementation to a dosage that you can better tolerate. Give your body a chance to get used to the supplements. After a while, you can try increasing your dosage again, but do it very gradually.

If your symptoms continue despite these measures, you may be allergic to psyllium, oat bran, or another ingredient in your fiber supplement. In this case, I suggest discontinuing the mixed-fiber product and trying each type of fiber as a single supplement until you find the one that best agrees with you.

As you increase your fiber intake, be sure to increase your fluid intake, too. Fiber needs water to do its job in the intestines. Plus, water is necessary for efficient detoxification and elimination. Most experts recommend drinking at least eight eight-ounce glasses of H_2O a day.

A FRIEND FOR LIFE

Fiber is just one ingredient in the Renewal "recipe." But without it, the Renewal process would collapse. You need fiber to soak up and sweep away damaging toxins and to keep your insides clean.

There are other ways that you can limit your exposure to toxins. For instance, you can choose only organically grown foods, drink only chemical-free water, and take other daily supplements in addition to fiber (as recommended in the Anti-Aging Supplement Program). Together, these strategies can safeguard your cells against toxic contamination.

Remember: The cleaner the cellular environment, the healthier the cells. And healthy, long-lived cells translate into a healthy, long-lived you.

* * *

Fiber has a partner in protecting your intestinal wellness. It's called acidophilus, which is a fancy name for a supplement that may contain not one but several different types of bacteria. Don't worry, though: These bacteria are actually good guys. And as the next chapter explains, you'll want to have plenty of them around.

CHAPTER 31

Acidophilus: Protection
That Grows on You

I have finally come to the conclusion that a good reliable set of bowels is worth more to a man than any quantity of brains.
—HENRY WHEELER SHAW (1818–85), AMERICAN
  HUMORIST

The intestines figure prominently in the Renewal process. They're responsible for extracting nutrients from the foods you eat and moving those nutrients into your bloodstream. To carry out this all-important task as efficiently as possible, the intestines rely on multitudes of beneficial bacteria.

About 400 species of these "good bugs" inhabit the intestines. Their total population is somewhere in the quadrillions—100 times the number of cells in your body. Remarkably, these microorganisms peacefully coexist in a carefully balanced internal ecosystem. As long as they flourish, they prevent pathogenic (disease-causing) bacteria and fungi from colonizing. In this way, beneficial bacteria help keep you healthy.

If the delicate intestinal environment is somehow disrupted, pathogenic bacteria, parasites, and fungi—unsavory critters with names like clostridia, salmonella, staphylococcus, *Blastocystis hominis*, and *Candida albicans*—waste no time in taking advantage of the situation. They move in, multiply, and overrun the beneficial bacteria.

Once pathogenic bacteria and fungi make themselves at home, they can be very difficult to roust. So avoid rolling out the welcome mat in the first place. How? By taking acidophilus supplements. These supplements, which I sometimes refer to as probiotics (*pro* meaning "supporting" and *biotic* meaning "life"), contain a variety of beneficial microorganisms. They increase the population of friendly flora in your intestines and thus maintain a Renewal-supporting environment.

Protecting Your Internal Ecosystem

Acidophilus supplements do a tremendous job of protecting your digestive health. They supply the beneficial bacteria that create a thriving, hospitable intestinal environment. In this way, acidophilus defends against a variety of intestinal ailments, including the following:

- Candidiasis (a yeast infection of the gastrointestinal tract, skin, respiratory tract, or vagina; usually caused by *Candida albicans*)
- Constipation
- Diarrhea
- Diverticulosis and diverticulitis (the formation and infection of small pouches in the intestinal wall)
- Flatulence
- Intestinal infections (bacterial, fungal, parasitic)
- Irritable bowel syndrome
- Ulcerative colitis (ulceration of the colon's mucous membrane lining)

MICROBES WITH A MISSION

The good bugs don't just float around in your gut. Instead, they cling to the mucous membrane lining of your intestines. Actually, this lining covers your entire gastrointestinal tract. If it were spread out flat, its surface area would exceed that of two tennis courts.

The intestinal lining's carpetlike surface is suffused with

nutrients, as if it were fertile soil. It provides an abundance of food and a warm, nurturing environment in which beneficial bacteria can thrive. Ecologically balanced with each other and with you, the bacteria form a protective coating for the lining.

The symbiotic relationship between the bacteria and the intestinal lining ultimately benefits Renewal as well. As I mentioned earlier, the friendly flora facilitate the digestion of food and the absorption of nutrients. But that's not all.

Beneficial bacteria support the synthesis of certain vitamins, including biotin, folic acid, niacin, pantothenic acid, riboflavin, thiamin, vitamin B_6, vitamin B_{12}, and vitamin K. The bacteria also break down dietary proteins into amino acids, which are then reconfigured into "new" proteins that the body can use. Bacteria even keep a lid on the amount of toxic material in your intestines, making sure that poisons get flushed out of your system (via the stool) rather than absorbed into your bloodstream.

Just as important, beneficial bacteria promote immune health. They stimulate activity in the thymus (the immune system's master gland) and spleen (another key immune system organ). They prompt your body to manufacture natural antibodies. Certain acidophilus strains even defend against the formation of tumors and promote production of interferon, a hormone that protects against cancer.

NASTY NEIGHBORS

As expansive as the intestinal lining is, it provides only so much real estate for microorganisms. The objective, then, is to make sure the good bugs occupy all of the available properties. Because once they start moving out—which can happen for a variety of reasons, as I explain a bit later—the bad bugs settle into the vacated space. And believe me, they can make life miserable.

Fortifying themselves with the nutrients intended for the beneficial bacteria, pathogenic bacteria and fungi quickly seize control of as much intestinal territory as they can. Initially, they may produce only mild symptoms such as gas, bloating, diarrhea, constipation, and cramps. But as they continue their rampage, they create and release an unsavory stew of toxins: amides, ammonia, hydrogen sulfide, indole, methane, methylated amines, and phenol mercaptans. These chemicals can irritate the intestines' mucous membrane lining, causing or aggravating abdominal symptoms. An inflamed lining allows large, incompletely digested food molecules (called macromolecules) to pass through the intestinal wall and into the bloodstream, where they are targeted by immune cells as invaders. The resulting allergic reaction can cause symptoms ranging from "just not feeling right" to headaches, arthritis-like pain, fatigue, depression, and confusion.

But wayward macromolecules aren't the only problem to arise from the proliferation of unfriendly flora. The chemicals that these bad bugs produce can escape from the intestines, as toxin-laden liquid gets absorbed from fecal matter through the intestinal wall and into the bloodstream. Once there, these chemicals increase internal free radical load and damage cells. They must also be reprocessed by the liver and kidneys, thus increasing the workload of these detoxifying organs. The resulting backlog blocks cellular Renewal and ultimately accelerates the aging process.

Pathogenic bacteria and fungi also manufacture enzymes that convert harmless compounds into chemical carcinogens. These enzymes, which go by names such as nitroreductase, azoreductase, and beta-glucuronidase, can pass through the intestinal wall and into the bloodstream. There, they have the freedom to travel anywhere in the body, potentially raising your risk of cancer in the process.

A VANISHING ACT

Clearly, unfriendly flora can cause all sorts of trouble within your body. But remember, they're opportunists: They run amok only when the friendly types are depleted.

So what drives the good bugs out of your intestines? At the top of the list of offenders is a diet that includes animal-derived foods (meats, poultry, fish, dairy products, and eggs), processed or preserved foods, sugar, or alcohol. Any of these offenders increase your exposure to free radicals and toxins, creating a hostile internal environment in which beneficial bacteria struggle to survive.

Then there are antibiotics, which can decimate much of your intestinal population of beneficial bacteria. With the good bugs gone, the intestines become especially vulnerable to bad bugs such as staphylococcus and *C. albicans* (the latter of which is more commonly known as yeast). Other prescription drugs—namely, oral contraceptives and immunosuppressants (such as steroids)—have similar adverse effects on the intestinal ecosystem.

FINDING BALANCE

Regular supplementation with acidophilus repopulates your intestinal tract with benevolent bugs. These microorganisms restore and maintain balance within your internal ecosystem while at the same time displacing noxious bacteria and fungi. They also increase the acidity of the intestinal environment, which good bugs love (acidophilus literally means "love of acid") and bad bugs hate.

By making the intestines less hospitable to malevolent microorganisms, acidophilus supplements have another benefit: They reduce the amounts of toxic chemicals floating around your system. (Pathogenic bacteria and fungi, you'll recall, produce their own toxins.) At a local level, this helps minimize your risk of colon cancer. On a larger scale, it protects your entire body and improves overall health.

Acidophilus supplements are widely available in health food stores as well as drugstores. Indeed, choosing from among the numerous "something-dophilus" products that line store shelves may seem like a daunting task. Read their labels, and you'll discover a variety of good bugs—not just *Lactobacillus acidophilus* but also *Bifidobacterium bifidum, Lactobacillus bulgaricus, Streptococcus faecium*, and others. Some products may contain fructo-oligosaccharides, sugars that nourish beneficial bacteria to make them colonize faster. All of these "ingredients" are acceptable, and any combination of them works well.

Keep in mind that acidophilus supplements contain living organisms, so freshness is critical. Purchase a product well before its expiration date—in fact, make sure it has an expiration date. Once you open the supplements, keep them refrigerated. And toss them out once they're more than six months old. At that point, they're dead.

As for dosage, it varies from one product to another. Your best bet is to follow the instructions on the label.

A final bit of advice: If your doctor puts you on antibiotics, which at times is absolutely necessary, make sure you double each dose of acidophilus. Take the supplements a couple of hours before or after the antibiotics so the microorganisms aren't destroyed by the medication.

There's one more element of the Anti-Aging Supplement Program that we need to discuss: the anti-aging hormones. Strictly speaking, they're not nutritional supplements, but they're every bit as important to Renewal. The next section profiles all of the anti-aging hormones, so you can decide which are right for you.

PART 5
The Anti-Aging Hormones

CHAPTER 32

Natural Hormone Replacement Therapy: A Powerful Means of Reversing Aging

Honey, you need to get yourself some hormones.
—FROM THE MOVIE *FRIED GREEN TOMATOES*
  (1991)

At least since the dawn of recorded time, humans have searched for the elixir of youth. Shamans sought the magical potion; herbalists, the miracle plant. Spanish explorer Juan Ponce de León pursued his quest halfway around the world, to what is now Florida. But he needn't have traveled so far from home. As modern-day "explorers" of medicine and science know, the real fountain of youth has been inside the human body all along.

What has the power to keep us youthful and disease-free for a lifetime? Human hormones, the substances naturally produced by various components of the endocrine system: the adrenal glands, ovaries, pineal gland, pituitary gland, testicles, and thyroid gland. Understanding how changing levels of hormones influence the aging process—for better or for worse—gives us tremendous leverage in our bid to slow down and even turn back the hands of time.

By maintaining optimum amounts of certain hormones in the bloodstream, hormone replacement therapy has genuine potential to put the brakes on aging. Already, millions of folks have begun tapping into the anti-aging effects of dehydroepiandrosterone (DHEA) and melatonin, which include enhanced energy, better sleep, improved stress tolerance, and an overall healthier body. And millions of women who are going through or past menopause have discovered the benefits of natural estrogen and progesterone replacement, a risk-free alternative to synthetic hormone replacement.

To some, hormone therapy may seem unproven or even dangerous. Indeed, hormones are powerful substances that must be used properly and carefully. But when taken in amounts that exactly match the body's shortfall—no more, no less—natural hormones catapult out of the questionable quagmire of synthetic hormones and into the realm of safe, scientifically sound preventive medicine.

CHAIRMEN OF THE BOD

Biochemically speaking, hormones operate differently from vitamins, minerals, and other essential nutrients. Hormones oversee and regulate the complex dance of metabolic activity within your body, while essential nutrients do the actual work (as antioxidants, catalysts, and structural components). If your body were a Fortune 500 company, all of its hormones would sit on the board of directors, while essential nutrients would man the assembly lines. Hormones make the top-level decisions about what will get done, how, when, and by whom. And like top executives, they are quite effective even in small numbers.

Detecting and correcting hormone deficiencies can pay huge dividends in terms of longevity. Maintaining hormone levels comparable to those of our twenties and thirties not only slows aging but also makes us healthier and improves our quality of life. In the next several chapters, you'll discover how hormone replacement can prevent and reverse the physical and mental changes that we usually view as "normal" consequences of getting older: impaired immunity, brittle bones, fragile blood vessels, atrophied muscles, loss of memory, insomnia, weakness, fatigue, and loss of libido.

Can hormone replacement really accomplish all this? Absolutely. By supporting the Renewal process, it helps your body to heal itself faster and protect itself better. So you become healthier—and you live longer.

GIVING NATURE A HAND

The phrase *hormone replacement* implies that hormones are missing. They don't actually disappear. Your body simply makes fewer of them.

Once you reach your thirties, your body begins a long—and hopefully slow—decline. Driving this gradual deterioration is the diminished output of hormones by the various glands and organs of the endocrine system. The drop in productivity doesn't just happen, by the way. It is programmed into your genes.

As hormone production slows down, the aging process speeds up. In fact, the rate at which hormone production decreases (or the steepness of the curve, as we scientists say) directly determines the rate of aging. Your body makes less of these crucial anti-aging hormones as you get older.

- DHEA and pregnenolone
- Melatonin
- The sex hormones—estrogen, progesterone, and testosterone
- Thyroid hormone

By restoring these hormones to pre-decline levels, you can slow and even reverse the aging process. Research has shown that hormone replacement combats disease, revitalizes the body, and primes you for extra decades of life.

Of course, each type of hormone performs a very specific set of tasks within your body. DHEA has perhaps the most profound influence on the aging process. In fact, DHEA therapy alone may extend life span, according to some experts. Melatonin governs the body's sleep-wake cycle and, in supplement form, makes an excellent sleeping aid and jet lag remedy. The hormone also scavenges free radicals, which fights the effects of stress, inhibits the development of cancer, and controls the body's aging clock. Natural estrogen and progesterone combine to ease a woman's passage through menopause as well as to safeguard her health after menopause—without increasing her risk of cancer, as synthetic sex hormones do.

Based on my own research and experience, I'm thoroughly convinced that natural hormone replacement therapy plays an essential part in human health and maximum life span. I count myself among the thousands of doctors around the world who prescribe natural hormone replacement therapy to patients. We use natural hormones in two ways: first, as treatment for specific symptoms (such as estrogen for hot flashes, testosterone for low libido, and thyroid hormone for fatigue); and second, as preventive medicine to compensate for declining hormone production, which forestalls the aging process.

Natural hormone replacement therapy comes with two simple but important rules for its safe and effective use. First, a hormone supplement must have the exact same molecular structure as the hormone that your body produces naturally. Not similar, but identical. Second, the supplement dosage should raise the level of hormone just enough to match the amount that floated around your bloodstream prior to age 30. This is called a physiologic dose, and it's what your body is accustomed to. When hormone therapy backfires, it's because one of these two rules has been violated.

ONLY NATURAL WILL DO

Close may count in horseshoes, but not in hormone replacement. Your body desires, expects, and deserves the real thing. It cannot be reprogrammed to accept anything less, especially not in such an intimate role.

Synthetic hormones have some of the same benefits as natural hormones. But they also have some undesirable effects. Most notably, the lookalikes upset your finely tuned endocrine system.

Hormone receptors located on the surface of every single cell are designed to recognize and lock onto the hormones that your own body makes. But if a synthetic hormone approaches an empty receptor, the impostor can just as easily attach. There's a price to be paid for this transgression. First, with the lookalike occupying the receptor site, the real hormone cannot hook up with the cell. Second, the lookalike doesn't behave as it should. Like a party crasher, it shows up uninvited and disrupts the action.

The indiscriminate use of synthetic hormones is responsible for some of the most profoundly shocking and woeful chapters in the history of medicine. Fake estrogen and progesterone, for example, have already caused far too many women to develop cancer and to die prematurely. Years before these hormones gained notoriety, diethylstilbestrol (DES)—a synthetic hormone with a molecular structure similar to progesterone—was linked to uterine cancer. In this case, however, the cancer affected the daughters of women who took DES during pregnancy to prevent miscarriage.

Then, too, farmers continue to spray tons of hormone-mimicking pesticides on the public food supply. The pesticide molecules can trigger inappropriate hormonal reactions and the uncontrolled formation of cancer cells.

Lookalike hormones are to blame for a great deal of needless human suffering. Just take a look at the package insert or the *Physicians Desk Reference* listing for any synthetic hormone. Pay special attention to the sections labeled "Adverse Reactions," "Precautions," and "Contraindications," where you'll find long lists of side effects. These are your body's way of saying, "What is this stuff? I'm not sure how to use it."

If synthetic hormones are so detrimental to human health and longevity, then why do they stay on the market? Because their natural counterparts, while more effective, are also much less profitable. You see, drug companies cannot patent natural compounds. So they spend millions of dollars on research to develop patentable fakes. Basically, they're trying to reinvent the wheel, but their versions amount to the endocrinological equivalent of wobbling. Second-guessing nature, as the drug companies have, is bound to produce second-rate compounds that are unsafe and more likely to cause adverse reactions. These wannabe hormones are not the same as real hormones, nor will they ever be.

Nature has already done the research to determine precisely which hormones you need. These are the substances that your body is genetically programmed to make. They have sustained you for this long, and they will continue to do so. They simply can't be improved upon.

No amount of experimentation can disprove nature's research or improve upon the hormones that she has created. A little synthetic embellishment of nature's original "recipe" can make a hormone patentable and profitable—as well as toxic. This, we now know, is an invitation to disaster.

Natural hormone replacement supplies exact replicas of the compounds that are manufactured by your body. It offers the same benefits as synthetic hormone replacement, but with none of the inherent risks.

The point is this: Your body has gotten really attached to the hormones and other molecules that it makes for itself. It doesn't like surprises, and it doesn't appreciate substitutes. This is why synthetic lookalikes produce unwanted effects. The real thing never has and never will.

QUANTITY COUNTS, TOO

For natural hormone replacement to work as it should, the dosage should closely approximate the maximum hormone level maintained by the body. This amount, the physiologic dose, is just what the body needs, as determined by nature over tens of thousands of generations. (A higher amount, called a pharmacological dose, is used to achieve a druglike effect.)

This underscores an important point: Hormone replacement, when administered properly, only restores a hormone to its optimum level. The therapy never advocates taking more of a substance than the body can actually use. Such an overdose could actually create more health problems than it treats or prevents.

THE RIGHT DOC FOR THE JOB

In the following chapters, I'll be profiling each of the anti-aging hormones and offering some guidelines for supplementation. But because determining the right hormone dosage is so critical, I urge you to consult a doctor who has experience with natural hormone replacement therapy. He can help you set up your own hormone replacement program, monitor its effectiveness, and recommend adjustments as necessary.

Finding the right doctor can be a bit of a challenge. From what I've observed, physicians' attitudes toward hormones can range from skeptical to schizophrenic. For example, many mainstream doctors espouse hormone replacement therapy for women at or past menopause. (Unfortunately, they usually prescribe synthetic hormones such as Premarin, an "estrogen" that's extracted from horse urine, and Provera, a fake progesterone.) But these same doctors express serious reservations about DHEA, pregnenolone, and melatonin—even though these natural hormones are much safer and better tolerated than the synthetic stuff they're giving to their female patients. "We want more proof," these doctors say. "We want more studies."

Of course, estrogen and progesterone are not the only hormones that decline with age. Nor does diminished hormone output affect only women. So if physicians can embrace estrogen and progesterone replacement, why can't they accept other types of hormone replacement as well?

If your doctor seems reluctant or uncomfortable when discussing natural hormone replacement therapy, you may need to look for someone else. For a referral, see Resources and References on page 591.

Now that you understand the basic principles of natural hormone replacement therapy, let's take a closer look at each of the anti-aging hormones. First up: DHEA and pregnenolone, the dynamic duo that may do more than any other substances to slow and reverse the aging process.

DHEA and Pregnenolone: The Anti-Aging Superhormones

Old age must be resisted and its deficiencies restored.
—MARCUS TULLIUS CICERO (106–43 B.C.),
ROMAN STATESMAN AND AUTHOR

It happened in the Las Vegas airport. I was heading home from the Fourth Annual International Conference of the American Academy of Anti-Aging Medicine, a gathering of more than 2,000 doctors and researchers—one of the most exciting events on my professional calendar. I had spent three fascinating days attending lectures on cutting-edge developments in anti-aging medicine and schmoozing . . . er, I mean exchanging valuable new clinical data with colleagues from around the world. Several of the presentations had focused on dehydroepiandrosterone (DHEA), and the overwhelming consensus was that the hormone holds great promise in enhancing health and slowing aging.

Now if you've ever been there, you know that the airport in Las Vegas is unlike any other. Where else do you encounter slot machines beckoning to you inches from where you board your plane? In that setting, I suppose I should have expected anything. Still, I couldn't help but be surprised when I saw DHEA sitting on the counter where I purchased my newspaper. That really made me do a double take.

Prior to that experience, I thought I knew a lot about

DHEA. I had been taking it for several years and prescribing it to my patients for three years. I knew that millions of people were using it. But when a product finds its way out of health food stores and into airport concession stands . . . well, I knew something had shifted, and not so subtly.

A HORMONE LIKE NO OTHER

Imagine a natural substance that creates feelings of well-being and slows the aging process to boot. Would you take it?

I would. In fact, I do. If I could take only one supplement, I'd choose DHEA. Not just because it will extend my life span (which I'll get to in a moment) but also because it makes me feel good.

DHEA is "the superstar of the superhormones," suggests William Regelson, M.D., an oncologist at the Medical College of Virginia in Richmond, in his book *Superhormone Promise*. He contends that DHEA rejuvenates virtually every organ system, so it "actually makes you look, feel, and think better."

A growing body of research suggests that DHEA can prevent or reverse the diseases that anti-aging experts have identified as the most prominent markers of accelerated aging: atherosclerosis (hardening and clogging of the arteries), cancer, diabetes, and reduced immunity. Moreover, mounting evidence indicates that the level of DHEA in a person's blood is an excellent predictor not only of these age-related health problems but also of aging itself. "DHEA is undeniably one of the most crucial predictive factors in diagnosing aging-related diseases," according to Ronald Klatz, D.O., president of the American Academy of Anti-Aging Medicine.

There is no question that DHEA extends the life spans of animals and holds promise as a defense against the degenerative diseases of aging. But can the hormone actually extend human life span? While the research literature strongly supports this claim, it remains unproven.

The definitive answer should come soon. Formerly relegated to a position of minor importance by the scientific establishment, DHEA has become the subject of intense scrutiny. A flurry of research is underway, underwritten by the National Cancer Institute, the National Institutes of Health, the National Institute on Aging, and the American Cancer Society. These and other major agencies are investigating DHEA as a potential treatment for chronic fatigue syndrome, depression, Epstein-Barr virus, herpes, lupus and other autoimmune diseases, menopausal symptoms, osteoporosis, and even AIDS.

What can the average healthy person expect from DHEA? Although everyone's experience differs, people report that they have more energy, handle stress more easily, think more clearly, and generally feel better. Other benefits include enhanced immunity (stronger resistance to colds, flu, and the like) and lower cholesterol.

THE AGE-OLD QUESTION

Your adrenal glands are responsible for manufacturing DHEA. Actually, the cascade of adrenal hormones starts with cholesterol, from which the brain hormone pregnenolone is made. Pregnenolone is then transformed into DHEA. And DHEA serves as the raw material from which all other important adrenal hormones—including the sex hormones estrogen, progesterone, and testosterone and the stress hormone cortisol—are synthesized.

DHEA is the most abundant hormone in your body. But production peaks at around age 20. From then on, your DHEA level decreases with age. By the time you reach 40, your body makes about half as much DHEA as it used to. By 65, output drops to 10 to 20 percent of optimum; by age 80, it plummets to less than 5 percent of optimum.

Because DHEA has such broad-spectrum effects, declining production makes itself known in every system, every organ, and every tissue of your body. The immune system is especially sensitive to diminishing DHEA output, opening the door not just to viruses, bacteria, and other microbes but also to free radicals and the Pandora's box of degenerative diseases they cause.

If levels of DHEA decline with age, can replacing the hormone reverse aging in humans? Nobody knows for sure. In studies, laboratory animals given DHEA supplements live up to 50 percent longer than normal. But we humans metabolize DHEA differently than animals, so these results don't necessarily apply to us.

A host of studies suggest that the lower a person's level of DHEA, the greater his risk of death from age-related disease. DHEA levels in 242 men between the ages of 50 and 79 were tracked for 12 years in a study by noted hormone researcher Elizabeth Barrett-Connor, M.D., professor and chairperson of the department of preventive medicine at the University of California, San Diego. The study found a close correlation between higher DHEA levels and reduced risk of death from all causes. The men who survived had three times the DHEA levels of the men who died.

Research has pinpointed low DHEA levels as a marker for many degenerative diseases and accelerated aging. The hormone has been implicated as a contributing factor in a host of health problems, including Alzheimer's disease, autoimmune disease and other immunological disorders, cancer, chronic fatigue syndrome, diabetes, heart disease, high cholesterol, memory problems, obesity, osteoporosis, and stress disorders.

What's more, the collective indirect evidence from more than 5,000 published studies overwhelmingly supports DHEA's anti-aging role. Scientists now have proof that DHEA:

- Enhances immunity
- Decreases the risk of heart disease
- Defends against some cancers
- Improves blood sugar control, decreasing the risk of diabetes
- Reverses the age-accelerating effects of the stress hormone cortisol
- Prevents and reverses osteoporosis

How could any substance that protects us from virtually every major degenerative disease not protect us from aging as well?

LIVING BETTER THAN EVER

Whether or not DHEA extends life span, it undoubtedly improves quality of life. Most people who take DHEA do so because the hormone helps them deal better with stress, gives them more pizzazz, and makes them feel young again. My patients on DHEA almost invariably report that they just plain feel better. This is not a placebo effect. Research has shown that DHEA levels in the bloodstream correlate highly with general health and vitality, sense of well-being, and increased stress tolerance.

In 1994, the *Journal of Clinical Endocrinology and Metabolism* published the first placebo-controlled human study examining the therapeutic effects of DHEA replacement therapy. ("Placebo-controlled" means that some participants received DHEA, while others received fake pills.) The DHEA-takers had more energy, slept better, and handled stress better than the placebo-takers. The researchers concluded that "DHEA will improve the quality of life over a longer period and will postpone some of the unpleasant effects of aging, such as fatigue and muscle weakness."

In another study, researchers at the University of California, La Jolla, gave people 50 milligrams of DHEA every day for six months. Sixty-seven percent of the men and 84 percent of the women reported improvements in energy, sleep, mood, feelings of relaxation, and ability to handle stress—overall, a remarkable increase in subjective experience of physical and psychological well-being.

MAXIMIZING IMMUNITY

Does DHEA rejuvenate immune function? You bet. It boosts antibody production; enhances the activity of monocytes, immune cells that attack cancer cells and viruses; activates natural killer cells, immune cells that attack and destroy viruses and other foreign invaders; and maximizes the anti-cancer function of immune cells known as T lymphocytes. In aging laboratory animals, DHEA restores youthful levels of cytokines (immune chemicals involved in protection and healing) and reduces the production of autoantibodies (antibodies that attack healthy tissues). When administered concurrently with a flu vaccine, DHEA dramatically improved the effectiveness of the vaccine in aging mice and in older humans.

DHEA's power to invigorate the immune system is closely linked to its potential to fight aging. Remember, heightened immunity translates directly into protection against oxidation, which in turn translates directly into protection against degenerative disease. So anything that strengthens your immune system also has the capacity to lengthen life. Immune deterioration with age is accompanied by increased incidence of atherosclerosis, autoimmune diseases, cancer, cataracts, and infections—all evidence of accelerated aging.

An important study conducted by leading DHEA researcher Samuel Yen, M.D., of the University of California, San Diego, underscores the hormone's age-opposing activation of immune function. After measuring baseline immune parameters in healthy older men (average age 63), Dr. Yen put the men on a program of 50 milligrams of DHEA per day. After 20 weeks, the men showed dramatic improvement in all markers of immune function, including an average of 45 percent increases in monocytes, 29 percent increases in antibody-making B lymphocytes, 20 percent increases in T lymphocyte activation, 40 percent increases in T lymphocyte anti-cancer response, and 22 to 37 percent increases in natural killer cells.

Perhaps most significant of all, DHEA increases production of insulin-like growth factor-1 (IGF-1), a hormonelike molecule that is used to measure levels of another potent anti-aging compound called human growth hormone. (Because it is not yet widely available, is administered by injection, and is very costly—$10,000 a year—human growth hormone exceeds the scope of this book.)

STOPPING STRESS IN ITS TRACKS

DHEA protects your body from the hormone cortisol and the stress that triggers its production. Like DHEA, cortisol is secreted by the adrenal glands. If oversecreted, cortisol injures your body's tissues.

When you're under stress, your adrenal glands release large amounts of cortisol. People under chronic stress have high cortisol levels (unless their adrenal glands have already burned out, in which case their cortisol levels are low). The presence of too much cortisol leads to age-accelerating damage. As stress accumulates over decades, cortisol levels tend to rise as well. Many people over age 40 have elevated cortisol.

DHEA and cortisol have an inverse, or adversarial,

relationship. When you're faced with prolonged stress, your cortisol/DHEA ratio—a measure of health status and aging—can rise by a factor of 5. This means that the excess cortisol is battering DHEA's protective shield. DHEA supplementation increases your stress tolerance, lowers your cortisol/DHEA ratio, and protects you against cortisol-induced cellular damage.

MENDING A BROKEN HEART

The cardiovascular research community is abuzz about DHEA's potential to conquer America's number one killer, heart disease. Several studies examining the role of DHEA in heart disease have produced intriguing findings.

Research has shown that depleted DHEA is a more accurate predictor of heart attack than elevated cholesterol. DHEA levels were significantly lower in men who died of heart attacks than in men who were healthy.

DHEA level was shown to correlate with the degree of atherosclerosis in 200 men and women undergoing coronary angiography, in a study by David Herrington, M.D., of Bowman Gray School of Medicine of Wake Forest University in Winston-Salem, North Carolina, which was published in the *Journal of the American College of Cardiology*. He found that as DHEA levels went up, coronary artery disease (as measured by the frequency and severity of arterial lesions) went down.

A follow-up study showed that the degree of development of atherosclerosis in 63 heart transplant patients was inversely correlated with DHEA levels. In other words, the higher the heart recipient's DHEA level, the lower his likelihood of developing post-transplant atherosclerosis. What's more, the heart recipients with high DHEA had a much better five-year survival rate (87 percent) than the heart recipients with low DHEA (65 percent).

That's not all. In people undergoing angioplasty (a procedure in which a balloon is used to open a clogged blood vessel), DHEA reduced the rate of restenosis—a treated vessel closes off again—from 68 percent to 28 percent. In healthy males given a clot-promoting substance (arachidonic acid, found in abundance in meat), DHEA blocked an increase in clotting. (An increased tendency to clot is a risk factor for heart attack and stroke.) In men, DHEA lowered total cholesterol and "bad" low-density lipoprotein cholesterol better than and more safely than the "statin" drugs such as clofibrate and gemfibrozil. DHEA is also nontoxic.

Animal studies are producing similar promising results. When researchers gave DHEA to rabbits with atherosclerotic arteries, the hormone produced a 50 percent decline in arterial plaques.

The bottom line in all of this: Age-related DHEA declines may leave us vulnerable to atherosclerosis, while DHEA replacement therapy appears to offer potent protection.

BEATING CANCER

Can DHEA prevent cancer? While scientists don't yet know for certain, the early reports are encouraging.

Low DHEA predicts breast cancer more accurately than any other known marker. Women with breast cancer consistently have lower-than-normal DHEA readings. DHEA may help protect against breast cancer by inhibiting glucose-6-phosphate dehydrogenase, an enzyme required for cancer growth. Also, because DHEA has antioxidant properties, the hormone probably defends against free radical cancer initiators.

In animal studies, DHEA has provided dramatic protection against tumors of the breasts, colon, liver, lungs, lymphatic vessels, prostate, and skin. Of course, what happens in animals doesn't necessarily translate to humans. This is especially true with DHEA because very little of the hormone is found in the bloodstreams of rodents.

So despite a general feeling among anti-aging experts that DHEA may well inhibit cancer formation, the jury remains out on the DHEA-cancer link—at least for the time being.

GOOD TO YOUR BONES

Osteoporosis is like a football game. Build a strong offense, and you're bound to gain yardage—that is, bone. Make do with a weak offense, and the opposing team will push you back for a serious loss.

Certain dietary and lifestyle factors give the opponent a

distinct advantage: too little calcium; too much protein; preservative-rich processed foods; alcohol and other drugs; and lack of exercise. You can retain control of the ball by recruiting the following players for your bone-building team: regular exercise, a low-protein vegan diet, vitamins (A, B_6, C, D_3, K, and folic acid), minerals (boron, copper, magnesium, manganese, silicon, zinc—and, of course, calcium), and hormones.

Among the anti-aging hormones, DHEA stands out as a multitalented star with amazing ways of outsmarting osteoporosis. DHEA is the only hormone that can both inhibit bone breakdown and stimulate bone formation. Plus, DHEA is a precursor to estrogen, progesterone, and testosterone, all of which prevent bone loss in their own rights.

Bone cells convert DHEA to estrone, a type of estrogen that in turn increases the activity of bone-making cells called osteoblasts. DHEA's transformation into estrone depends on the presence of vitamin D_3. (Likewise, D_3 requires DHEA to stimulate osteoblasts. It can't do the job alone.)

Japanese researchers found a positive correlation between DHEA levels and bone density in women over age 50. The higher the women's DHEA, the denser their bones. When the same researchers gave DHEA to "post-menopausal" rats (actually, the animals had had their ovaries removed), the rats' bone density increased.

As DHEA levels decline with age, osteoporosis may appear. People with osteoporosis have significantly lower DHEA levels than people without the disease. When osteoporotic lab animals are given DHEA, their bones remineralize—that is, their bones become stronger. Although human studies have yet to be done, DHEA supplementation would in all likelihood increase our bone density as well.

MEDICINE FOR THE MIND

Don't be surprised if, in the next few years, you start seeing reports that DHEA is being used to treat Alzheimer's disease and other degenerative brain diseases. (You can say you read it here first.) While DHEA is no cure for Alzheimer's, strong evidence exists that the hormone is essential for maintaining healthy brain cells.

DHEA levels sink to markedly low levels later in life, when the incidence of degenerative brain disease is much higher. DHEA levels in people who have Alzheimer's are much lower than in people who don't have the disease. Studies show that even very small doses of the hormone reduce amnesia while improving long-term memory.

When researchers gave 30 to 90 milligrams of DHEA a day to depressed middle-aged patients, they saw significant evidence not only of reduced depression but of improved memory as well.

THE LUPUS LINK

Systemic lupus erythematosus is a chronic autoimmune disease in which the immune system manufactures autoantibodies, which attack healthy tissues. In effect, the body turns on itself. Blood vessels, connective tissues, joints, kidneys, the nervous system, and skin may be affected.

Lupus is commonly treated using immunosuppressive steroids and cancer chemotherapy agents. The treatment damages the immune system and thus undermines the healing process. Its side effects can be worse than the disease itself.

Aware of DHEA's immune-enhancing effects, researchers at Stanford University gave DHEA to 57 women with lupus. About two-thirds of the women reported some alleviation of their symptoms, including reduced frequency and severity of joint pain, headaches, rashes, and fatigue. Many also reported better exercise tolerance and improved concentration. Impressed with these findings, the Food and Drug Administration is supporting clinical trials to evaluate DHEA's efficacy as an alternative to conventional lupus therapy.

TAKING DHEA

DHEA replacement therapy offers powerful health benefits and is virtually risk-free. People have taken doses as high as 1,600 milligrams daily for a month with no adverse reactions.

In my practice, I test the DHEA levels of all of my patients over age 40. If the results indicate a deficiency (as they invariably do), I usually recommend DHEA replacement therapy. I provide informative articles about DHEA, and the patient and I reach a decision together.

The recommended daily dose range is 10 to 50 milligrams for women, 25 to 100 milligrams for men. (Women need less DHEA than men.) I usually start my patients—women and men—at 25 milligrams once or twice daily. The initial dose is determined by gender and baseline DHEA level (the lower the level, the higher the starting dose).

After one month, I retest. I increase the dose until the patient's DHEA level matches that of a 30-year-old of the same gender: between 200 and 300 micrograms per deciliter of blood for women, and between 300 and 400 micrograms per deciliter of blood for men. Once the patient's DHEA level stabilizes within the desired range, testing can be done semiannually.

Though most people take DHEA without the benefit of knowing their blood levels of the hormone, routine monitoring is a really good idea. How else can you know whether you are taking the optimum amount? Many insurance plans, including Medicare, cover DHEA testing if it's ordered by a physician.

If you are not a patient of a physician who can order testing, you can monitor your level of DHEA (and certain other hormones) at home with a simple, inexpensive saliva test. (For more information about the test, refer to Resources and References on page 591.) Because you don't want to undershoot or overshoot the desirable DHEA range (taking too much won't harm you—it's simply a waste of supplements), check your DHEA level one to two months after each change in dose. Once you find your optimum dose, retesting every six months is adequate.

The ideal anti-aging strategy is to supplement both DHEA and its precursor, pregnenolone (which I'll discuss in a bit). Since your body will convert some of the pregnenolone to DHEA, any increase in the dosage of pregnenolone may result in a higher level of DHEA. (The opposite does not hold true, however: Your body doesn't convert DHEA to pregnenolone.) The rate at which pregnenolone is converted to DHEA varies from one person to the next. So monitor levels of both hormones every few months and adjust your doses until both are within their respective desired ranges.

Many hormones, including cortisol and thyroid hormone, are controlled by a feedback loop system that shuts off production when levels get high. Not so with DHEA and pregnenolone: Your body will keep right on making these hormones in the same amounts as before you began supplementation. In other words, taking supplements of DHEA and pregnenolone won't suppress your body's production of these hormones or cause adrenal atrophy.

For most people, the purpose of DHEA replacement therapy is to improve quality and quantity of life. But it may be prescribed for certain medical conditions, including Alzheimer's disease and other organic brain diseases, chronic fatigue syndrome, depression, diabetes, heart disease, immune deficiency syndromes, lupus and other autoimmune diseases, osteoporosis, and stress-related disorders. Patients who, because of family history or other factors, are at higher risk for any of these conditions can benefit from DHEA as preventive therapy.

Who shouldn't take DHEA? People under age 35 and people who have normal DHEA levels ("normal" being the level typical of a 29-year-old). They simply don't need it. Men with prostate cancer and women with reproductive cancers should consult their doctors before taking DHEA, even though no adverse effects have been reported.

DHEA does stimulate hair follicles and sebaceous (oil) glands, so it may cause facial hair growth in women or transient acne. (An article in the *New England Journal of Medicine* linked teenage acne to the rise in DHEA that takes place near puberty.) These side effects are rare. If they do occur, they'll disappear with dose reduction or discontinuation.

BEWARE THE WANNABES

Commercial DHEA products are made from diosgenin, an extract from the Mexican wild yam of the *Dioscorea* family. Biochemists can convert diosgenin to DHEA by engineering a series of chemical conversions.

The market is flooded with encapsulated yam products claiming to be "DHEA precursors" or "natural DHEA." Unfortunately, the human body—or any living system, for that matter—cannot convert diosgenin to DHEA. It happens only in the laboratory.

The ingestion of *Dioscorea* plant extracts can't possibly

lead to the formation of DHEA in the body, according to prominent DHEA expert Seymour Lieberman, Ph.D., of St. Luke's–Roosevelt Hospital Center in New York City. Products containing Mexican yam or unconverted diosgenin may produce other beneficial hormonal effects, but they will not raise DHEA levels.

The research studies revealing DHEA's therapeutic effects were all done with real hormone, not yam extracts. Read labels and insist on 99 percent pharmacologically pure DHEA.

EXPERT OBSERVATIONS

Clearly, much remains to be learned about DHEA. Among the experts, opinions about the hormone range from cautious optimism to enthusiastic endorsement.

When best-selling author Ray Sahelian, M.D., asked several of the world's leading DHEA researchers "Should I take DHEA?" he got an interesting mix of responses. Here's just a sampling, from Dr. Sahelian's book *DHEA: A Practical Guide.*

• Michael Bennett, M.D., of the department of pathology at the University of Texas Southwestern Medical Center at Dallas: "Many strains of mice have lived longer with DHEA. I'm 60 years of age. If my blood test showed that my level was low, I would consider taking low doses such as 25 milligrams to raise my levels."

• Etienne-Emile Baulieu, M.D., Ph.D., of the department of hormonal research of the Institut National de la Santé et de la Recherche Medicale in Paris: "We are studying the possible beneficial effects of reestablishing a 'young' level of DHEA in people over 60 years of age. The comparison to estrogen replacement therapy after menopause is a good one. However, we need long-term studies to make sure there are no negative effects on hormone-responsive tumors such as prostate and breast. . . . I would consider taking 25 to 50 milligrams daily if my blood levels were found to be low."

• Ward Dean, M.D., medical director of the Center for Bio-Gerontology in Pensacola, Florida, and co-author of *Smart Drugs and Nutrients* and *Smart Drugs II*: "This steroid is absolutely appropriate for hormone replacement therapy. I start my patients in their forties, at a dose of 25 milligrams taken in the morning. DHEA is highest in the morning, and giving it at that time would follow the normal circadian rhythm."

• Alan Gaby, M.D., researcher, author, and past president of the American Holistic Medical Association: "DHEA, without a doubt, has a role to play in hormone replacement therapy. I have treated at least 300 patients and find this steroid to be helpful for anti-aging purposes, as far as increasing muscle strength, better density of bone, and improved skin color."

PREGNENOLONE: THE FEEL-GOOD HORMONE

What hormone can outperform DHEA? Quite possibly DHEA's "mother": pregnenolone.

Notice that I said "possibly." Less is known about pregnenolone than DHEA because, until recently, research interest in it has not been as intense.

Pregnenolone has finally captured scientists' attention because of its structural and functional similarities to DHEA. Perhaps even more intriguing, pregnenolone alone is the precursor to more than 150 human steroid hormones, including DHEA. When the studies are done and the results are in, pregnenolone may well outshine DHEA as an anti-aging hormone.

In the meantime, pregnenolone has amply demonstrated its potent rejuvenative effects on the body and brain. It boosts energy, elevates mood, and improves memory and mental performance. It creates a sense of well-being while improving the ability to tolerate stress.

For me, pregnenolone has lived up to its reputation. It has improved my mood and my mental sharpness. And by keeping me clear-headed, alert, and focused, it has helped me to write this book.

ALL IN THE FAMILY

I like to call pregnenolone the grandmother hormone. Perched atop the adrenal family tree, it is the stuff from which all other steroid hormones are made.

Your adrenal glands manufacture pregnenolone from cholesterol (yes, the same cholesterol that has a knack for breaking hearts). Your body either uses pregnenolone as is or converts it to one of its two "daughter hormones": DHEA and progesterone. These, in turn, spawn dozens of "granddaughter hormones," the most important and prevalent of which are the three estrogens (estriol, estrone, and estradiol), testosterone, and cortisol.

Pregnenolone's de facto position at the very top of the hormone heap confers upon it certain unique powers. As the ultimate precursor, ready and willing to be converted to any of more than 150 adrenal steroids, pregnenolone can participate in every biochemical action that every steroid hormone is party to.

Thus, pregnenolone influences cerebral function, energy level, the female reproductive cycle, immune defenses, inflammation, mood, skin health, sleep patterns, stress tolerance, wound healing, and much, much more. This is one hormone that knows where the action is and loves to take part.

As with DHEA and other anti-aging hormones, the production of pregnenolone declines with age. Research will almost certainly prove that pregnenolone replacement therapy can slow the aging process. Many scientists and doctors, including yours truly, believe that restoring pregnenolone to youthful levels is a powerful anti-aging strategy for both body and brain.

Pregnenolone supplementation is natural and physically harmonious, according to Eugene Roberts, Ph.D., a neurobiologist at the City of Hope Medical Center in Los Angeles. Because of the hormone's role as a precursor, pregnenolone has the unique ability to bring all of the other hormones into balance. It stimulates production of those other hormones, but only when they're needed. Taking pregnenolone therefore normalizes and rejuvenates the entire adrenal cascade.

Let's examine some of pregnenolone's key benefits a bit more closely.

THE BEST AGAINST STRESS

When you get right down to it, stress is what kills us. It takes many forms: oxidative stress from free radicals, chemical stress from toxins, trauma, and emotional stress. Your ability to tolerate stress is directly linked to your health and longevity.

Responsibility for coping with all of this stress falls to your adrenal glands—or, more specifically, to the hormones they make. Pregnenolone is a powerful anti-stress hormone in its own right, and it provides the raw material for all of the other anti-stress hormones.

In the 1940s, famed researcher Hans Selye—the "father of stress"—performed some of the earliest studies on pregnenolone. He concluded that the hormone reduces stress and fatigue and elevates energy.

Like its daughter DHEA, pregnenolone blocks and reverses all of the age-accelerating effects of excess cortisol. Cortisol, you'll recall, is a pro-aging hormone. (It is also a granddaughter of pregnenolone and the only adrenal steroid hormone that increases with age.) Normally the adrenal glands produce small amounts of cortisol to protect you from stress. This is okay, at least in the short run. Prolonged overproduction of cortisol brought on by excessive, unrelenting stress, however, causes an array of damaging effects: brain dysfunction, accelerated skin aging, impaired wound healing, excess fluid retention, depression, and poor sleep quality. All of these shift the aging process into overdrive.

Pregnenolone also protects you against chemical stress. Your liver contains enzyme systems that are responsible for removing toxins from your body. By protecting these enzymes from cortisol, which degrades them, pregnenolone reinforces your body's detox power.

MENTAL MOXIE

As I first mentioned in chapter 29, pregnenolone is a potent neuronutrient that improves memory, concentration, and mood. It supercharges your brain by facilitating the transmission of nerve impulses so brain cells can communicate with each other more easily. Humans given pregnenolone became more productive on the job, felt better, and coped with stress better.

Many neuroscientists now believe that pregnenolone is the most potent known memory-enhancer, perhaps many times more powerful than any other memory-enhancer. Unbelievably small doses boosted memory in animals. Rats fed pregnenolone whizzed through their mazes.

Pregnenolone fights depression, too. In one study, peo-

ple who were not depressed had twice the amount of pregnenolone circulating in their bloodstreams as people who
were depressed.

TAKING AIM AT ARTHRITIS

In the late 1940s, pregnenolone attracted considerable
scientific interest as a potential anti-inflammatory agent
for the treatment of arthritis and related conditions. Several studies, including one published in the *Journal of the
American Medical Association*, described the hormone's
effectiveness in reducing the swelling and pain of rheumatoid arthritis. It also established pregnenolone's safety and
freedom from side effects. The effective dose was fairly
high by today's standards: 500 milligrams daily. Other
reports told of pregnenolone's success as a therapy for
lupus, psoriasis, and scleroderma.

Back then, these findings attracted little attention. Pharmaceutical companies dismissed pregnenolone because
they couldn't turn a profit by manufacturing it. (Since it's a
natural substance produced by the body, it couldn't be
patented.) When the superpotent steroid drug cortisone
came along, pregnenolone was left in the dust.

Now the hormone is making a comeback, as more and
more people experience the adverse effects of anti-inflammatory steroids like prednisolone. In my practice, I've
found pregnenolone to be extremely effective against
arthritis and other inflammatory disorders.

THE PREGNENOLONE PRESCRIPTION

Pregnenolone is extremely, amazingly safe. In researching this chapter, I could find no references to adverse reactions or side effects. Scientists consistently comment on the
hormone's virtual absence of toxicity.

In laboratory experiments, mice tolerated doses of five
grams per kilogram of body weight, which, in human
terms, translates to ¾ pound per day. People have taken
doses as high as 500 milligrams daily for several months
with no ill effects.

Though long-term toxicity studies have yet to be done,
pregnenolone in modest doses should prove nothing but
beneficial. The Food and Drug Administration must agree

with this assessment, since the agency has designated pregnenolone a natural food product and therefore does not regulate it.

As with DHEA, I measure pregnenolone in all of my patients over age 40. If test results indicate a shortage of the hormone, I recommend pregnenolone replacement therapy. I'll continue to monitor the patient with follow-up testing until the pregnenolone level matches that of a 29-year-old.

Monitoring is the best way to ensure that you're achieving the optimum, anti-aging level of the hormone, although it isn't absolutely necessary at doses below 200 milligrams per day. You can check your pregnenolone level at home with a self-administered saliva test. (For more information, refer to Resources and References on page 591.)

You'll find pregnenolone in health food stores and some drugstores. Make certain that you are getting a pharmacologically pure product, not a yam-derived "precursor." A very safe dose is between 25 and 200 milligrams per day. (Unlike DHEA, the dose range for pregnenolone is the same for men and women.)

If you are taking both pregnenolone and DHEA, you'll probably need less of the latter. As I explained earlier, your body will convert some of the pregnenolone to DHEA. Conversion rates differ from one person to the next, so monitor your levels of both hormones for a few months and adjust their doses until you are within the desired ranges.

Melatonin has a reputation as a natural tranquilizer. But as the next chapter explains, the hormone is much more versatile than previously believed—especially in the anti-aging arena.

Melatonin: Medical Megamarvel or Magnificent Myth?

Whatever gets you through the night . . . it's all right, it's all right.
—JOHN LENNON, "WHATEVER GETS YOU THROUGH THE NIGHT"

"**W**hat I have here is an amazing little pill that can add decades—that's right, decades—to your life. Who among you wants to live for 120 years? Step right up . . ."

Even those street-corner medicine men of a century or so ago couldn't have dreamed up a miracle elixir like melatonin. For starters, it promises longevity—extra years of youthful vitality. Then it throws in some mighty impressive health benefits as part of the bargain: immune system enhancement, cancer protection, stress reduction, and sound sleep.

And guess what? This stuff is for real.

Bolstered by two *Newsweek* cover stories extolling its virtues, melatonin has become one hot hormone. Consumers are scarfing melatonin tablets by the billions, making the hormone one of the best-selling products of its kind. (It's cheap, too—about 10 cents a tablet.)

Most people take melatonin for its sleep-inducing effects. Granted, there's a lot to be said about the benefits of deep, restorative slumber. But the hormone offers so much more than just a trendy new cure for insomnia, especially in the anti-aging arena.

We know, for example, that melatonin is a potent—perhaps the most potent—scavenger of those marauding molecules known as free radicals. It thwarts the cellular degeneration that leads to heart disease, cancer, and other debilitating health problems.

Even more exciting for us Renewal-seekers is the discovery of melatonin's ability to reset the body's biological clock, which determines how quickly we age. This breakthrough prompted the following observation from Russell Reiter, Ph.D., a cellular biologist at the University of Texas Health Science Center at San Antonio and co-author with Jo Robinson of *Melatonin: Your Body's Natural Wonder Drug*: "I want to die young as late in life as possible, and I think this hormone could help."

YOUR INTERNAL ALARM CLOCK

Manufacturing and secreting melatonin is the responsibility of the pineal gland, a sunflower seed–size structure located deep within your brain. The gland evolved from primitive eye tissue, and like a third eye, it monitors the day/night cycle and regulates your body's rhythms. When daylight reaches the pineal gland—traveling by way of the retinas and optic nerves in your eyes and the nerve cells in your brain—it shuts down production of melatonin. Darkness, on the other hand, stimulates production.

Blood levels of melatonin remain relatively low (around 10 picograms per milliliter) during waking hours. Then just before bedtime, between 9:00 and 10:00 P.M. for most people, the gland begins releasing melatonin into the bloodstream. By about 2:00 A.M., levels of the hormone peak at around 100 picograms per milliliter of blood. By about 7:00 or 8:00 A.M., levels return to their low daytime state. There they stay until nightfall, when the cycle begins all over again.

Although nighttime levels of melatonin run about 10 times higher than daytime levels, neither quantity is exactly humongous. A picogram is just one-trillionth of a gram, an amount that's invisible to the naked eye. Melatonin is so potent, though, that even microscopic specks of the stuff can send you to dreamland for hours.

KEEPING TIME FOR A LIFETIME

Longevity researchers now believe that the pineal gland does more than regulate your 24-hour, sleep/wake clock. It may house your aging clock, the one that drives the aging process.

As you get older, the pineal gland produces less melatonin. A growing body of scientific literature strongly suggests—but has yet to prove—that restoring and maintaining optimum levels of melatonin turns back the aging clock. In this way, the hormone may extend life span.

Some of the most exciting research on this subject has been conducted by Walter Pierpaoli, M.D., Ph.D., an immunologist at the Biancalana-Masera Foundation for the Aged in Ancona, Italy. When Dr. Pierpaoli gave melatonin to old mice, the hormone reversed age-related shrinkage in the animal's thymus glands, which in turn revitalized the animals' immune systems. Intrigued by his findings, Dr. Pierpaoli teamed up with Vladimir A. Lesnikov of the Institute of Experimental Medicine in St. Petersburg, Russia, to transplant the pineal glands of young mice into old mice. The old mice were rejuvenated, their life spans extended by one-third.

Dr. Pierpaoli and Lesnikov then flip-flopped the experiment, transplanting the pineal glands of old mice into young mice. The results of the experiment flip-flopped as well: This time, the life spans of the young mice were shortened by one-third.

From these studies, Dr. Pierpaoli concluded that human aging begins in the pineal gland. He also demonstrated that melatonin could counterbalance the aging process. As he explains, "We should think of the pineal as the aging clock and melatonin as a means by which it translates its time-keeping pulses into body changes."

FENDING OFF FREE RADICALS

Scientific understanding of melatonin has certainly come a long way since the hormone's discovery in the 1950s. Back then, cell biologists assumed that melatonin's sole function was the regulation of the sleep/wake (or diurnal) cycle. Today, of course, we know better.

With anti-aging medicine turning the spotlight on free radical biochemistry, melatonin has stolen the show because of its super-powerful antioxidant properties. Indeed, researchers have concluded that the pineal gland produces melatonin not only to induce sleep and regulate the body's hormonal systems but also to protect itself from free radical damage.

Of course, a properly fed body already has an ample supply of antioxidant nutrients, including vitamins A, C, and E, coenzyme Q_{10}, and the antioxidant phytochemicals. What can melatonin do that these other antioxidants cannot?

Back in chapter 24, I explained how each antioxidant nutrient specializes in servicing a particular area, or compartment, of the body. Well, melatonin is an exception to the rule. Its small molecular size allows the hormone to travel anywhere within the body—even to the brain. So it provides unequaled broad-spectrum protection against free radicals.

Melatonin is not only more versatile but also more potent than its fellow antioxidants. The hormone appears to have a far greater capacity for neutralizing free radicals than even the most powerful of the known naturally occurring antioxidants. "We've tested melatonin in every conceivable system that we can assemble," says Dr. Reiter. "It continues to perform as well as or better than any other antioxidant." This makes sense, biochemically speaking. It means the gland that regulates the aging process also produces the strongest defenders against free radical attack.

Because of its antioxidant properties, melatonin may play a leading role in the prevention and treatment of the chronic degenerative conditions caused by the cumulative effects of oxidative stress. (Oxidative stress, you'll recall, refers to the catastrophic cellular breakdown that occurs when free radicals overwhelm antioxidants.) Among the conditions linked to oxidative stress are Alzheimer's disease, atherosclerosis (hardening and clogging of the arteries), cancer, diabetes, multiple sclerosis, Parkinson's disease, and rheumatoid arthritis.

RETHINKING AGING

As melatonin has gained fame, it has also revolutionized our understanding of the aging process. In chapter 1, I described how most anti-aging experts subscribe either to program theories or to damage theories. Program theorists maintain that we humans are genetically destined to die at a certain age. Damage theorists contend that the cellular wear-and-tear caused by free radicals speeds up the aging process and eventually kills us.

The boundaries between these two schools of thought became blurred when melatonin burst onto the scene. In their effort to explain how the hormone turns back the clock, experts on both sides have forged a new perspective on aging that combines both program and damage theories.

According to the researchers, melatonin protects the pineal gland—and the gland's preprogrammed aging clock—from free radical damage. But as with all other hormones, melatonin production declines with age. The resulting melatonin shortage leaves the pineal gland vulnerable to free radical attack. The combination of decreasing melatonin production and increasing free radical damage accelerates aging and precipitates physical and mental decline.

Restoring melatonin to optimum levels protects the pineal gland and its aging clock from free radical damage. This is how melatonin reduces oxidative stress and extends life span.

TURNING BACK THE CLOCK

The body's melatonin production peaks while we're in our twenties, then begins a long and slow decline. The goal of melatonin replacement therapy is to reinstate the hormone levels of youth.

Scientists have yet to determine precisely how much melatonin is necessary to produce optimum anti-aging effects and prolong life. But given the intense research attention that melatonin—and natural hormone therapy in general—has been getting lately, I expect that we'll have some definitive answers within the next few years.

In the meantime, dosage recommendations can vary considerably. I have two friends—one a physician, the other a research scientist—who have published work on the subject of melatonin. One takes 1 milligram of the hormone nightly; the other, 30 milligrams nightly. Go figure.

So how much should you take? My advice is to stay

within the range of 0.5 to 10 milligrams per day, even though the hormone has tested safe in much higher doses. If you're between ages 40 and 60, aim for the low end of the range (say, 0.5 to 3 milligrams). If you're over 60, you may want to take a tad more (2 to 6 milligrams). Within the appropriate range, try different doses until you find one that you feel comfortable with.

I usually don't recommend melatonin to people under 40 solely for its anti-aging benefits. Their bodies' production of the hormone has not yet dropped off all that dramatically.

THE IMMUNE SYSTEM STIMULANT

Melatonin can recharge an immune system undermined by age-related decline. As you get older, your thymus gland, spleen, and bone marrow—all key immune system players—begin to atrophy. In studies, all appear to recoup their former functionality with the help of melatonin replacement therapy.

Interestingly, scientists have discovered melatonin receptor sites on the surfaces of the thymus gland, spleen, and bone marrow cells. All of these tissues appear to be revived with added melatonin. What's more, the lymphocytes in bone marrow have melatonin receptor sites. Research has shown that melatonin reverses age-related declines in lymphocyte antibody production.

Melatonin also appears to protect lymphocytes against the effects of radiation. In one study, lymphocytes that were treated with melatonin sustained 70 percent less damage from ionizing radiation than those that were not treated. People who require diagnostic x-rays or who are undergoing radiation therapy may be able to protect their healthy tissues from radiation exposure by taking a dose of melatonin beforehand.

If the findings of several animal studies hold up for humans, melatonin may rejuvenate and protect the immune system in myriad other ways. Here's a sampling of what these studies have turned up so far.

- Mice given melatonin produced more antibodies when exposed to an antigen. (An antigen is any substance that induces an immune response.)

- Mice given melatonin produced more interferon and interleukin-2, potent immune system chemicals that protect against viral and bacterial infections.
- Mice given melatonin had twice as much immunity to an encephalitis virus as mice not given the hormone.
- Rats injected with melatonin before and after exposure to paraquat, a toxic herbicide, showed none of the devastating lung and liver damage experienced by unprotected rats.

FIGHTING CANCER ON ALL FRONTS

Given its immune-enhancing and antioxidant properties, melatonin has the makings of a natural cancer-fighter. Indeed, the hormone appears to inhibit development of the disease, though perhaps in some surprising ways.

For instance, melatonin may protect against breast cancer and other hormone-dependent cancers by regulating the release of estrogen. The longer a woman is exposed to estrogen over the course of her lifetime, the greater her risk of developing a hormone-dependent cancer. Factors that increase exposure include early onset of puberty, use of oral contraceptives, not bearing children, late onset of menopause, and non-natural estrogen replacement therapy.

Population studies have shown that women in countries with high breast cancer rates have low melatonin outputs. (Melatonin output is measured by the degree of calcification—that is, calcium salt deposits—in the pineal gland.) The opposite also holds true: Women in countries with low breast cancer rates have high melatonin outputs.

Breast cancer rates also tend to be high among women who've lost their vision. Scientists theorize that the women's pineal glands receive minimal light stimulation, which reduces their melatonin production.

Animal studies suggest that melatonin may block the formation of cancerous tumors. In one such study, cancer-prone mice received nightly doses of melatonin equivalent to human doses of one to three milligrams. After one year, only 23 percent of the hormone-treated mice had developed tumors, compared with 62 percent of untreated mice.

Beyond prevention, melatonin may someday prove useful as a cancer therapy. In test tube experiments, the hormone takes direct lethal action against breast cancer cells and impedes the growth of prostate cancer cells. Researchers have launched trials involving cancer patients to evaluate the hormone's effectiveness as a treatment.

Patients with a metastatic (spreading) form of lung cancer were given nightly 10-milligram doses of melatonin in a study conducted by Dr. Paoli Lissoni and his colleagues at Geraldo Hospital in Milan, Italy. The patients' one-year survival rate rose. Impressed with this result, the researchers then added melatonin to the interleukin-2 being given to patients with various types of cancer. (Interleukin-2 is often used as an anti-cancer drug to increase levels of T lymphocytes, immune cells that destroy cancer cells.) In the presence of melatonin, interleukin-2 was effective in a dramatically smaller dose—a godsend for the patients since the side effects of interleukin-2 can be horrendous.

Researchers have also used melatonin as a pretreatment for breast cancer cells. They found that the hormone increased by 100-fold the inhibitory effects of the breast cancer drug tamoxifen.

NUMBER ONE FOR SLUMBER

As a sleep aid, melatonin works even better than synthetic sedatives such as barbiturates and benzodiazepenes. For starters, melatonin is effective in small doses and produces no side effects. Plus, the hormone preserves the normal architecture of sleep, including the timing and duration of dream phases characterized by rapid eye movement (REM).

Anyone of any age who suffers from insomnia can benefit from melatonin. The hormone is especially appropriate for older people. These folks may have trouble getting a good night's sleep because their pineal glands have cut production of melatonin.

You needn't be a floor-pacing, sheep-counting, hardcore insomniac to benefit from melatonin. For people like me, who sleep okay but not always as soundly as possible, the hormone can encourage deeper, more restorative slumber. You feel much more refreshed the next day.

Melatonin supplements facilitate sleep by raising blood

concentrations of the hormone from daytime levels of 10 picograms per milliliter to nighttime levels of 100 picograms per milliliter. The supplement dose required to achieve this increase varies from one person to the next. "Normal" doses range from 0.3 to 6.0 milligrams, although in my experience, some stubborn cases of insomnia have required doses as high as 20 milligrams. Your best bet is to begin at the lower end of the range—say, 1 to 3 milligrams—and gradually increase your dose until you find what works for you.

The type of insomnia you have determines the time you should take melatonin for maximum effect. For instance, if you have trouble falling asleep but no problem staying asleep, take regular melatonin a half-hour before bedtime. If you fall asleep easily but then sleep shallowly or even wake up in the wee hours of the morning (between 2:00 and 5:00 A.M.), you may get better results from taking timed-release melatonin right at bedtime.

Some people have both types of insomnia. If you're one of them, you may want to experiment with a combination of regular and timed-release melatonin supplements.

When you first start taking melatonin, you may feel vaguely disoriented or fuzzy-headed for the first few hours after you wake up. This sensation should go away after a few nights of melatonin use. If it persists, you likely need to cut back your dose.

TROUBLE-FREE TIME TRAVEL

The Spanish king Alfonso the Wise (1221–84) once said, "Had I been present at the Creation, I would have given some helpful hints." Now I don't know what he may have had in mind. But I'd cast my vote for a body better suited to travel across time zones.

We humans are not designed for rapid transit from one spot on the globe to another. It leaves us with the familiar symptoms of jet lag: fatigue, insomnia, irritability, and poor concentration. Nothing terribly serious—but enough to spoil travel plans, whether for business or for pleasure.

Crossing time zones catches your pineal gland off guard. The gland expects the sun to set at more or less the same time every day. When you change time zones, it continues secreting melatonin on the same schedule as if you were back home. Since melatonin controls so many of the body's internal cycles, the body is thrown into temporary turmoil. Left to its own devices, the pineal gland requires a few days to reset its 24-hour clock to the new time zone.

Until melatonin supplements came along, the only real recourse against jet lag was to tough it out until the pineal gland made the necessary adjustments. The more time zones crossed, the greater the discombobulation, and the longer the pineal gland needed to acclimate.

I am very sensitive to jet lag. Before melatonin supplements came along, I'd arrive at my destination and wander around like a zombie for a couple of days. I had to allow extra time in my travel schedules to recover from my flights.

If you're prone to jet lag, melatonin supplements can help reset your pineal gland when you travel from one time zone to another. My advice: The first night that you're in the new time zone, take a dose of melatonin at bedtime. The size of the dose is not set in stone. Try different amounts until you determine what works best for you. Some experts recommend taking one milligram of melatonin for each time zone that you cross. When I travel to the East Coast from my home in northern California, I add five milligrams to my regular nightly dose of melatonin. I take this larger dose at bedtime on my first night in my destination city.

Is there any advantage to starting melatonin supplementation a few days before you travel? No. In fact, researchers found that people who took melatonin ahead of time actually experienced more severe jet lag symptoms. They felt even worse than people who took placebos.

MAXIMIZING MELATONIN'S BENEFITS

The title of this chapter asks whether melatonin is a "medical megamarvel" or "magnificent myth." Based on the information presented here, I'd say that the hormone lands squarely in the former category. Of course, much research remains to be done to determine whether melatonin actually lives up to expectations.

Right now, one absolute certainty about melatonin is its safety. When researchers attempted to determine the lethal dose of melatonin for 50 percent of a group of mice (the

LD-50, in scientific speak), they couldn't do it. Not a single mouse succumbed, no matter how much of the hormone it was given. (As an animal rights advocate, I can say that I like this kind of experiment.) The mice were, however, very well rested.

In a study involving humans, a whopping 6,000 milligrams of melatonin—that's 1,000 times the average effective dose—failed to produce more than occasional stomach upset or mild foggy-headedness when taken every night for a month. Even 250 milligrams of melatonin, administered intravenously on a nightly basis, caused no short-term or long-term toxic reaction. Gram for gram, ordinary table salt is more toxic than melatonin.

I've been taking melatonin for several years now. I've prescribed it to hundreds of patients as well. Not once have I heard of a person having an adverse reaction to the hormone.

There are a few rules of thumb for using melatonin effectively. First, always take the hormone just before bedtime. If you take it earlier in the day, it can disrupt your sleep/wake cycle, which you definitely don't want.

How close the dose is to bedtime really depends on you. Earlier in the chapter, I made specific recommendations for insomnia and jet lag. In general, people seem to feel that melatonin works best when taken a half-hour before bedtime. Some folks extend that window to one or even two hours to achieve the desired effects. (If you work at night, take melatonin at your regular bedtime, whenever that is.)

Second, if you have a serious illness of any kind—especially leukemia, lymphoma (cancer of the lymph tissue), an autoimmune disorder (in which immune cells attack healthy tissues), or major depression—you should consult a doctor before beginning melatonin supplementation. The same rule applies if you're taking any prescription medication, particularly an immune-suppressing drug such as prednisone or cyclosporine. Melatonin is not recommended for anyone on antidepressant medication, especially serotonin reuptake inhibitors such as paroxetine (Paxil), fluoxetine (Prozac), and sertraline (Zoloft) and monoamine oxidase inhibitors.

Third, if you're a woman who is pregnant or nursing, absolutely do not take melatonin.

ONLY NATURAL, PLEASE

The magic of melatonin is that it achieves its anti-aging effects without poisoning any of the body's organs and systems in the process. The hormone fosters internal harmony rather than undermining it, as so many prescription and over-the-counter drugs do. With melatonin, there is no toxicity, no risk of dependency or overdose, no adverse reaction.

Melatonin supplementation underscores the ultimate wisdom of using "friendly molecules" to the greatest extent possible in the treatment and prevention of disease. There are two types of friendly molecules: the one that your cells make, and the one that comes from the foods you eat. (Remember, the structure and dose must be identical.) When your biochemical machinery—genes, enzymes, and cell membranes and receptor sites—encounters friendly molecules, it accepts them without question. It knows that these substances belong.

When taken in the appropriate physiologic dose (that is, the dose that matches the amount produced by the body), a natural hormone such as melatonin is incapable of causing a toxic reaction. The same cannot be said of synthetic hormones, drugs, and other unfriendly molecules. When your cells encounter these frauds, they go into alarm/damage control/detoxification mode—the metabolic equivalent of dialing 911. This puts your body through a tremendous amount of stress. And stress accelerates aging.

FINDING HOPE IN A HORMONE

As an anti-aging strategy, melatonin replacement therapy works because it targets causes of age-related decline rather than merely masking symptoms. The road to longevity must be paved with nontoxic, health-enhancing therapies like melatonin and other natural hormones.

In their groundbreaking best-seller *The Melatonin Miracle*, Dr. Pierpaoli and William Regelson, M.D., eloquently summarize this point of view:

"We want you to understand that 'senescence,' the downward spiral that is now the hallmark of aging, is not inevitable and that aging is neither irresistible nor irreversible. It is possible to retain our strength, sexual vigor, and love of life for all of our decades.

"The miracle of melatonin is not just that it can extend your life and preserve your health and vigor. The true miracle of melatonin is the wider impact that it will have on our generation and on generations to come. We are embarking on an adventure together. We are the first generation to have the power to prevent the disease and the debility that have come to typify 'normal' aging. For the first time, we have the power to preserve our youthfulness and to stay vital and vigorous for our entire lives. For the first time, not only are we able to prevent the physical decline associated with aging but we're actually able to slow down and even reverse the aging process itself. This is truly the melatonin miracle."

Amen.

The sex hormones, estrogen, progesterone, and testosterone, are probably the best known of the anti-aging hormones. They're also probably the most controversial. The next chapter sorts through all of the conflicting information to help you decide whether any of these hormones is right for you.

CHAPTER 35

The Sex Hormones: Natural Estrogen, Progesterone, and Testosterone

How old would you be if you didn't know how old you was?
—LEROY "SATCHEL" PAIGE (1906–82), AFRICAN-AMERICAN BASEBALL PLAYER

Ever since the first endocrinology lecture I attended in medical school, I've found hormones and hormone replacement therapy to be one of the most complex and difficult-to-understand areas of medicine. I know I'm not alone. We've all heard the conflicting reports.

Women, especially if they are in their forties or beyond, understand the poignant dilemma of hormone replacement therapy: Using it alleviates menopausal symptoms, protects against heart disease and osteoporosis . . . but increases the risk of cancer. Every few months, another study appears proving once and for all that hormones do—or don't—cause cancer. Women who are entering or past menopause struggle mightily with the decision of whether to take or not to take, and they find their doctors hedging recommendations in terms of risk-benefit ratios. Understandably, women are confused.

Through the 1970s and 1980s, so many health problems were associated with hormone replacement therapy (not the least of which was cancer) that my blanket recommendation to patients was "Avoid it until we know more." I maneuvered around the problem by treating menopausal symptoms with acupuncture therapy as well as Chinese traditional herbs, Western herbs, homeopathic remedies, and other nutritional medicines. I continue to prescribe these on occasion, but I've found natural hormone replacement therapy to be far more effective for most women.

Over the past 10 years, with a growing body of evidence in support of an anti-aging role for estrogen, progesterone, and testosterone, these hormones have become increasingly difficult for me to ignore. As with the other anti-aging hormones (dehydroepiandrosterone, or DHEA; pregnenolone; melatonin; and thyroid), levels of the sex steroid hormones decline with age. Restoration to youthful levels promotes optimum health and may well extend life span.

Because public consciousness of these hormones has been relatively high, most people have preformed opinions about them. This is especially true of unnatural estrogen, which most doctors and the general public don't realize is a far cry from natural human estrogen.

A MATCH MADE IN A LABORATORY

My reluctance to prescribe hormones changed when leading alternative physicians began saying that cancer and other health problems associated with hormone replacement therapy might not be caused by the therapy per se. Rather, the doctors theorized, these problems arise from failure to use an exact replica of a molecule of human hormone and failure to maintain balance among the various hormones.

You see, when it comes to hormones, imitations—even very good imitations—don't work as well. Your body is incredibly sensitive to minor structural alterations. Tinker with the molecular makeup by rearranging even just one oxygen atom, and the body knows. In the short run, side effects may appear. In the long run, if hormone replacement therapy is used for several years, cancer risk may rise.

Why isn't an exact replica used? Because even though natural estrogen and progesterone can easily be obtained from plant sources—thousands of plants make phytosteroids—drug companies can't patent naturally occurring compounds. To make money, they had to develop patentable synthetic lookalikes—products that resemble but don't exactly match the real thing. These impostor hormones have been extremely profitable. But in the process, they've caused untold human suffering.

Problems also arise when the balance of hormones is wrong. Take estrogen as an example. The human body produces not one but three principal estrogenic hormones: estrone, estradiol, and estriol. If you replace one but not the others, you upset their delicate balance. What's more, estrone or estradiol alone promotes cancer, while estriol alone protects against cancer. Unfortunately, many synthetic hormone replacement products contain only estradiol. Maximum protection requires replacing all three estrogens in physiologic proportions, that is, in proportions the body is accustomed to.

Hormonal imbalance can likewise occur when estrogen is unopposed—in other words, it isn't paired off with progesterone. Estrogen and progesterone balance each others' effects in a woman's body. Too much estrogen (unnatural or otherwise) relative to progesterone leads to breast and uterine cancers. For this reason, estrogen and progesterone should always be taken together.

So the great hormone debate boils down to two basic issues: mismatched molecules and unbalanced hormones. This is where the difference between natural and unnatural hormone replacement becomes so critical. I'm convinced that natural hormones, prescribed with attention to overall balance, support optimum health and likely lengthen life span. Unnatural hormones do just the opposite: They undermine health and shorten life span.

MENOPAUSE: BRACING FOR THE CHANGE

Before getting into the specifics of hormone replacement therapy, let's spend a few moments on the subject of menopause. Understanding the mechanics of "the change" may help clarify why hormone replacement becomes necessary at this stage of a woman's life.

The onset of menopause, or climacteric, signals the end of a woman's reproductive years. True menopause begins with a woman's last period. It marks the culmination of several years of gradually declining hormone output, usually starting when a woman is in her late forties or early fifties. During this time, known as perimenopause, the ovaries decrease their production of estrogen and proges-

terone. Fluctuating and declining levels of these two hormones cause major physical and emotional changes, not all
of which are desirable.

Menopause affects every woman differently. Some
women breeze through with nary a hot flash; others feel as
though they've been banished to a living hell. Most women
fall somewhere in the middle, experiencing the classic
menopausal symptoms: hot flashes, night sweats, bladder
control problems, mood swings, memory problems, vaginal
dryness, and decreased sex drive. Since most of these
symptoms result from declining ovarian hormone production, restoring hormones to premenopausal levels provides
relief and has a rejuvenating, anti-aging effect on the entire
body.

Once menses (menstruation) ends permanently and
wildly fluctuating hormones stabilize, women enter a
longer-term phase in which they can no longer depend
upon estrogen and progesterone to keep their bones
strong and their blood vessels pliable. The loss of bone
density increases vulnerability to osteoporosis. The hardening of blood vessels, caused by rising levels of total cholesterol and "bad" low-density lipoprotein (LDL)
cholesterol, elevates the risk of heart disease.

BAD NEWS FOR BONES

In osteoporosis, bones become porous, brittle, and exceptionally vulnerable to fracture—all because their mineral
content has declined. They start losing minerals even before
menopause, as hormone output gradually slows. But the
process speeds up at menopause, when estrogen and progesterone levels take a nosedive. At that point, estrogen and
progesterone receptors on the surface of bone-forming cells
(called osteoblasts and osteoclasts) are no longer being stimulated.

Osteoporosis is by no means rare. Without long-term
estrogen replacement therapy, postmenopausal women
have a one-in-four chance of serious bone loss and fracture. The risk of moderate bone loss and spinal deformity is
even higher. A study conducted at the Mayo Clinic in
Rochester, Minnesota, found that 18 percent of women
over age 50 had at least one vertebral fracture due to
osteoporosis. One in three women will suffer hip fractures

at some point in their lifetimes, and half of these women will no longer be able to live independently. About one in six will die as a result of their injuries.

No one questions that estrogen replacement can decrease the risk of osteoporosis by preserving bone density. It doesn't stimulate the growth of new bone, however. It just saves the bone you already have. Another caveat: It takes at least seven years to work.

Conventional treatment for osteoporosis usually consists of unnatural estrogen supplements, calcium supplements, and exercise. The problem with this approach, beyond its use of unnatural hormone, is its focus on estrogen. The ovaries make two hormones, both of which decline in menopause. Why replace just one? To treat and prevent osteoporosis, menopausal women need progesterone and estrogen. Progesterone (along with DHEA and testosterone) stimulates osteoblasts, the cells that lay down new bone. This means osteoporotic bones can heal.

Signs of the Times

Menopause announces itself with a bang in some women, a whimper in others. It can manifest itself in myriad ways. Here are some of the most common signs of "the change."

- Irregular menstruation
- Depression, irritability, and mood swings
- Hot flashes
- Night sweats
- Loss of bladder control
- Frequent or urgent urination
- Forgetfulness and loss of concentration
- Reduced libido
- Sleep disturbances
- Vaginal dryness and painful intercourse
- Heart palpitations
- Aches and pains in joints and muscles

A VULNERABLE HEART

Estrogen softens blood vessels, lowers LDL cholesterol, increases "good" high-density lipoprotein (HDL) cholesterol, and decreases the likelihood of clot formation. Thanks to these protective effects, women have a very low risk of heart disease prior to menopause. Of course, when the ovaries go out of business, this "estrogen advantage" is lost. The average woman enters full menopause at age 50. By 65, she is just as vulnerable to heart disease as a man of the same age.

Among women in the United States, the epidemic of heart disease dwarfs the epidemic of cancer. More than 10 times as many women succumb to heart disease, stroke, and other cardiovascular disorders as to breast cancer. One hundred times as many women die of cardiovascular disease as of uterine cancer.

Natural or unnatural, estrogen does indeed cut heart disease risk. Data from a 10-year study of more than 48,000 nurses reveal that replacing estrogen slashes the rate of fatal heart attacks by half. As is the case with osteoporosis prevention, the hormone must be taken for several years to achieve heart-protective effects.

Premarin, a commonly prescribed unnatural estrogen (I'll tell you more about it in a bit), was found to reduce the rate of heart attacks among women who are post-menopausal. The news gave proponents of unnatural estrogen replacement the perfect rationale to recommend it as standard therapy.

Unfortunately, in the process of protecting against heart disease, Premarin was contributing to uterine cancer. So doctors began pairing Premarin with synthetic progesterone (Provera) to prevent the uterine cancer. Guess what? Heart disease risk rose once again.

Fortunately, natural progesterone doesn't pose this problem. According to a large-scale study reported in the *Journal of the American Medical Association*, combining Premarin with natural micronized progesterone (a form of progesterone that can be taken orally) reduced heart disease risk to almost the same level as when Premarin was taken alone. You have to wonder whether risk would have dropped even further if both natural estrogen and natural progesterone had been used.

ESTROGEN: CURE-ALL OR CATASTROPHE?

In his 1966 book *Feminine Forever*, Robert A. Wilson, M.D., postulated the now-quaint notion that menopause is an "estrogen deficiency disease." Deprived of their femininity-enhancing hormones, women would become barren, sexless creatures—in Dr. Wilson's words, "caricatures of their former selves" and "the equivalents of eunuchs."

The cure? Why, estrogen, of course. Estrogen replacement would dispel the specter of asexuality, vanquish that nasty eunuch lurking within, and cure the dreaded menopause disease. With new hormones, women could live happily ever after, secure in their unchallenged femininity.

And sure enough, for many women, estrogen fulfills the promise—or seems to. It eases or eliminates flushing, night sweats, vaginal atrophy, and depression. It preserves the skin's youthful appearance. It even lifts "brain fog."

For others, however, estrogen causes lethargy, fatigue, and premenstrual symptoms. More than half of all women who start taking it stop within a year. Many experience both positive and negative effects. They go on and off the hormone, trapped between the devilish side effects and the need for relief, not to mention longer-term protection from bone loss and heart disease.

IT JUST ISN'T NATURAL

Estrogen, one of the most powerful hormones in the human body, produces an extensive array of effects. It stimulates the ovaries to produce mature eggs. It tells the endometrium, the lining of the uterus, to proliferate in preparation to receive a fertilized egg. It affects many other parts of the body as well, including the brain, breasts, kidneys, liver, blood vessels, and bones.

As I explained earlier, estrogen is not a single hormone but a trio of hormones working together to perform a complex network of tasks. For a healthy, young adult female, the typical mix is 10 to 20 percent estrone, 10 to 20 percent estradiol, and 60 to 80 percent estriol. This ratio is not accidental. Mother Nature herself personally sorted through the possibilities over the millennia and came up with this, the optimum combination for women.

For estrogen replacement, conventional medicine has relied on two approaches, neither of which qualifies as natural. The first consists solely of estradiol. Your body does make its own estradiol, but it also balances the hormone with estrone and estriol. When unaccompanied by its sister hormones, estradiol causes cancer.

The second approach involves Premarin, a combination of estrogenic compounds extracted from the urine of pregnant mares (Premarin—get it?). Premarin contains 5 to 19 percent estradiol, 75 to 80 percent estrone, 6 to 15 percent equilin (strictly a horse hormone and possibly a human carcinogen), plus trace amounts of other horse hormones. These equine hormone molecules make a lousy match for those produced by the human female body. They may be great for horses, but in humans, they transform the tightly choreographed and highly complex "dance of the sex steroids" into a chaotic free-for-all.

Estrogen replacement with Premarin (not to mention estradiol and similar products) is fraught with risks. Experts have long debated its safety. Next time you're in the mood for some scary reading, check out the fine print on the package insert for Premarin (or read the hormone's entry in the *Physicians Desk Reference*). You'll find a very long litany of what can go wrong when mismatched molecules are tossed into your finely tuned endocrine system.

One of my patients, Margaret, didn't believe me when I told her that the estrogen she had been taking for nearly 15 years was actually horse urine in pill form. When she found out that I was right, she went ballistic. And she got even madder when I told her the rest of the story.

You see, drug companies couldn't make any money by selling natural estrogen, because it isn't patentable. So they had no interest in funding research for it or in developing products containing it. This is despite the fact that their synthetic estrogen is unsafe, less effective, and almost certainly responsible for many serious health problems.

When you stop to think about it, the situation is appalling. On the one hand, we have an undeniably toxic drug that causes a vast array of side effects and adverse reactions and for which there is a safe, natural alternative.

On the other hand, we have drug companies that control the research (through funding) and the marketplace (through advertising and education for physicians) to protect their bottom lines. Those bottom lines are very large: Female replacement hormones are one of the biggest money-makers in the history of the pharmaceutical industry.

Surely the drug-makers know that natural hormone replacement would prevent the carnage. But because they can't profit from it, they have zero interest in exploring its use. If ever there was a Catch-22, this is it.

And don't even get me started on the 80,000 pregnant mares that "manufacture" Premarin for the pharmaceutical industry. They're confined to tiny stalls (to prevent them from lying down) and deprived of exercise, with urine collection devices strapped to their underbellies to collect their "product." If this barbaric practice were justifiable in terms of alleviating human disease, perhaps the ethics issues could be rationalized away. But we have natural, medically preferable alternatives available.

WHERE'S THE EVIDENCE?

Incredibly, natural estrogen replacement has never been studied. We have absolutely no scientific data on the actual hormone molecules that all women make throughout their lives. All of those media reports about estrogen—indeed, the whole debate about the benefits and risks of female hormone replacement—concern only the unnatural types. Apparently, nobody ever questioned whether using horse estrogen instead of human estrogen mattered. It's a case of apples being passed off as bananas.

One of the first to notice this problem was leading nutritional physician Jonathan V. Wright, M.D., of Kent, Washington, who describes the problem this way: "We need to take the last 40 years' worth of study on so-called estrogen, jam it in the wastebasket, and start over. All of those studies involved giving human beings horse estrogen. The next time I see a menopausal horse, I will be happy to prescribe Premarin, a horse estrogen! But for menopausal people, we need people hormones.

"There has been not one, not a single . . . well-controlled long-term study of the use of estrogens that are actually identical to human estrogen as replacement therapy for women. Without that kind of study, the best thing we can say is that we don't know anything. We've wasted 40 years in studying horse hormones in humans, and it's about time to start studying *human* hormones in humans. Then maybe we'll know something. But right now we know nothing scientifically, and we have to fly by common sense and the seat of our pants until we get the real human studies done."

THE CANCER CONNECTION

Premarin and other unnatural estrogen replacement products enjoyed a sunny outlook until reports that they contribute to cancer began to cloud the horizon. To make a long (two-decade) story short, unnatural estrogen stimulates hormonally sensitive tissues, raising the risk of breast, uterine (endometrial), and ovarian cancers. Women taking unnatural estrogen are at least four times more likely to develop endometrial cancer. Similarly, taking unnatural estrogen for at least six years produces a 40 percent increase in women's risks of developing the almost uniformly fatal ovarian cancer.

Of greatest concern is the link between unnatural estrogen replacement and breast cancer, which has already reached epidemic proportions in the United States. In an article published in the *New England Journal of Medicine*, researchers at Harvard Medical School reported that women who used unnatural estrogen replacement for five or more years after menopause were 30 to 40 percent more likely to develop breast cancer than those who did not.

As I said before, all of these studies and statistics are based on unnatural estrogen-like compounds. Amazingly, nobody ever bothered to examine real estrogen to see whether it would have similar effects.

This information presented women and their doctors with a dilemma. Do you try unnatural estrogen replacement and risk getting cancer? Or do you forgo replacement therapy and risk heart disease and osteoporosis, not to mention menopausal symptoms?

Most doctors buy into the former option, and they feel justified in recommending it to their patients. Their argument: Unnatural estrogen is better than no estrogen, because eight times as many women die of heart attacks as of breast cancer. Plus, unnatural estrogen reduces osteo-porosis risk.

"Basically, you are presenting women with the possibil-ity of increasing the risk of getting breast cancer at 60 in order to prevent a heart attack at 70 and a hip fracture at 80," says Isaac Schiff, M.D., chief of obstetrics and gynecol-ogy at Massachusetts General Hospital in Boston. His statement is clever, but it doesn't tell the whole story. First, unnatural estrogen increases risk of uterine and ovarian cancers as well as breast cancer. Second, women can pro-foundly decrease the probability of heart disease and osteoporosis simply by making dietary and lifestyle changes. Third, cancer is more devastating at an earlier age.

ESTRIOL: THE REAL MCCOY

Earlier in the chapter, I mentioned that estrogen con-tains both pro- and anti-cancer compounds. Specifically, estradiol and estrone promote cancer, while estriol pre-vents it.

For women in menopause, doctors usually prescribe either estradiol or Premarin. Both increase lifetime expo-sure to the pro-cancer types of estrogen. The unnatural, horse urine–derived compounds in Premarin are con-verted by the body primarily to estrone, the estrogen impli-cated in cancers of the breasts and uterus.

The fact that estriol prevents cancer was revealed by research conducted by H. M. Lemon, M.D., in the late 1960s. Women with breast cancer make less estriol and so are presumably more vulnerable to the disease. Women who are cancer-free have high estriol levels.

Estriol presents none of the health hazards associated with estradiol and Premarin. It protects against cancer by blocking the action of estrone.

In Europe, estriol has been in use for more than 20 years. European clinical studies have shown that estriol safely and effectively relieves menopausal symptoms. In one major German study conducted by 22 gynecologists from 11 large hospitals, more than 900 women were given estriol and monitored over a five-year period. The estriol proved very effective at relieving menopausal symptoms, was well-tolerated, and produced no significant side effects.

Why hasn't this safe and preferable alternative to unnatural estrogen become standard therapy in the United States? Blame the power of the pharmaceutical and advertising industries and the medical profession's resistance to change.

In 1978, the *Journal of the American Medical Association* published an article by Alvin H. Follingstad, M.D., in which he called for doctors to switch to estriol as a safer form of estrogen replacement. He argued that while estriol prevents cancer, the other two naturally occurring estrogens—estradiol and estrone—increase risk. He cited the problem-free use of estriol in Europe and reported that the hormone stopped the spread of metastatic breast cancer in 37 percent of a group of women who were past menopause. Sadly, Dr. Follingstad's admonitions fell on deaf ears.

With the advantage of hindsight, we in the medical community now know how right Dr. Follingstad was. Sometime in the 1960s, we got on the wrong track, prescribing unnatural estrogen that caused millions of potentially preventable cancers. Now that we're aware of the mistake we made, don't we have a scientific—if not a moral—obligation to go back, start over, and do it right?

We can now state with certainty that unnatural estrogen causes cancer. We have no proof that natural estrogen does not cause cancer. But is there any reason why it would? After all, women have been manufacturing estriol, estradiol, estrone, and progesterone all their lives. So if we're going to replace these hormones, let's use the exact same molecules that the female body produces on its own.

GOING NATURAL

Going back to the drawing board, Dr. Wright sought to create the most-natural possible estrogen replacement by emulating the estrogen balance within the female body. His research led to the formulation of triple estrogen, a natural, physiologically balanced form of hormone replacement therapy. Triple estrogen consists of a combination of the three human estrogens in the proportions in which they occur naturally: 10 percent estrone, 10 percent estradiol, and 80 percent estriol. Triple estrogen is the closest approximation to the natural spectrum and balance of hormones that the female body makes (or would make, if it has already stopped).

Triple estrogen has become standard therapy among alternative and nutritional medical doctors. It is available by prescription from any compounding pharmacy (that is, a pharmacy that can mix medications to a doctor's specifications). The usual starting dose is 2.5 milligrams per day, which equals 0.625 milligram of Premarin. Every woman is different, however. You may need more or less. Work with your doctor to find the best dose for you. (To find the compounding pharmacy nearest you, refer to Resources and References on page 591.)

Because balancing the sex steroid hormones is so important, and because unopposed estrogen is undesirable, I usually start my patients on triple estrogen along with micronized progesterone capsules (100 to 200 milligrams per day) or progesterone cream (one-half to one teaspoon daily). Both hormones should be stopped altogether for the first 7 to 10 days of the menstrual cycle or for one week each month if menstruation has stopped.

Some women experience a return of their menopausal symptoms when they abruptly change over from estradiol or Premarin to triple estrogen. This does not mean the natural version isn't working. With unnatural estrogen replacement, the body is subjected to—and adjusts to—long-term exposure to unfriendly molecules. These molecules bind with the hormone receptor sites on cells differently than natural molecules. The return of menopausal symptoms simply means that the body needs time to adjust to the natural molecules.

If you're already taking estradiol or Premarin, you can avoid menopausal symptoms by making the switch to natural estrogen gradually. Each month, decrease your dosage of estradiol or Premarin by one-third and increase your dosage of natural estrogen by an equivalent one-third.

To make this process easy, I recommend the following: Take Premarin (or another drug hormone) on days one and two and triple estrogen on day three. Continue this dosage pattern for one month (or cycle). Then during the second month, take Premarin only on day one and triple estrogen on days two and three. By the third month, the transition to triple estrogen is complete. If the changeover still causes menopausal symptoms, you can slow the pace even more.

Don't give up if your initial attempt to make the switch doesn't seem to work. Hormone pathways are complex and quirky. If you've been jamming them with molecules that look funny and communicate in scrambled tongues, don't expect your body to adjust immediately. Give it the time it needs to relearn the proper hormone language.

PROGESTERONE: ESTROGEN'S PARTNER IN PROTECTION

My ideas about hormones and hormone replacement therapy began changing in 1994, on a family vacation to Maui. Since it didn't take up much space, I packed a copy of *Natural Progesterone: The Multiple Roles of a Remarkable Hormone* by John Lee, M.D.—just a tidbit to glance at if my compulsion to read medical journals reared its ugly head.

A few days into our vacation, I picked up the book at bedtime, fully expecting to be bored to sleep. But when I started reading that little gem, I was so fascinated that I couldn't put it down. I was introduced to "unopposed estrogen" and the "dance of the steroids"; I discovered why unnatural hormones are dangerous and how osteoporosis can be reversed. What Dr. Lee said spoke directly to my heart as well as my mind: Clearly we shared a commitment to finding nontoxic and natural approaches to medicine.

Every free moment over the next few days, I lay on the beach, lost in Dr. Lee's book, my kids bouncing beach balls off my head and spraying wet sand on the pages. My wife was appalled: "We're supposed to be on vacation, Tim. You need to get away from your work. Why don't you read Grisham or at least *some* kind of fiction?" But her words came too late. I was hooked.

In a small but significant way, that book would change my life. For the first time in my career, I felt a glimmer of hope that I could understand hormones.

FINDING THE RIGHT BALANCE

One of Dr. Lee's principal messages was that balancing female hormones does not stop at replacing estrogen. Citing the failure of unnatural estrogen to safely address menopausal symptoms, he helped focus attention on natural progesterone, the other side of the female hormone replacement equation.

In a premenopausal female body, estrogen is always in balance with progesterone. These hormones work together to keep a woman healthy. Unopposed estrogen, even when it's natural, can lead to problems.

For instance, unnatural estrogen replacement is known to increase a woman's risk of endometrial cancer. Adding progesterone to the mix eliminates this risk.

The good news is that the idea of hormonal balance has finally taken hold—sort of. The bad news is that doctors have traditionally prescribed unnatural forms of both hormones: estrogen from horse urine (Premarin) and synthetic progesterone (Provera).

PREVENTION IN A PILL

If any one individual is responsible for raising consciousness about progesterone, it is Dr. Lee. His name has become synonymous with natural progesterone replacement for treating menopausal symptoms, reversing osteoporosis, and preventing cancer, among other ailments.

In the 1970s, Dr. Lee attended a lecture at a meeting of the San Francisco Orthomolecular Society in which biochemist Ray Peat, Ph.D., chided doctors for replacing estrogen after menopause without prescribing progesterone as well. This concept intrigued Dr. Lee. And so over the next several months, he read everything he could get his hands on about progesterone. He concluded that Dr. Peat was absolutely right. Progesterone's importance had been underestimated, and unopposed estrogen—that is, estrogen without progesterone—was responsible for numerous diseases, not the least of which was cancer.

Dr. Lee began using natural progesterone as a last resort in treating patients who had osteoporosis but could not take estrogen (because they had a history of cancer or another condition that contraindicates its use). For more than six years, he monitored the bone status of 63 patients with osteoporosis using regular dual photon bone absorptiometry (a highly sensitive measure of bone mineral density). To his amazement, instead of the expected 4.5 percent bone loss, the patients registered remarkable increases—an average of 15.4 percent. Their bones were remineralizing. His discovery was all the more amazing because stimulating new bone growth is unheard of. Estrogen only slows bone loss—it cannot reverse it.

What's more, these patients reported reversals of many other symptoms that had been bothering them. Their energy levels and sleep patterns improved, their skin appeared healthier, their libidos increased, and they lost weight more easily.

To educate women and their doctors about natural progesterone replacement, Dr. Lee and Virginia L. Hopkins co-authored the pioneering book *What Your Doctor May Not Tell You about Menopause*—a must-read for menopausal women. In the introduction, Dr. Lee describes how his discoveries slammed into conventional medicine's wall of resistance:"I talked to my colleagues and gave talks at our hospital staff meetings. The reception was warm, but their looks of perplexity led me to understand that I had hit what others have called cognitive dissonance. While unable to dispute my work, my colleagues could not understand how the knowledge I presented was missing from their own education and the textbooks (and the pharmaceutical advertising) on which they relied. In their minds, the file marked 'progesterone' was filled with advertising about synthetic progestins, which are not the same thing."

SUPPLEMENTATION PLUS

I recommend natural progesterone replacement, either micronized progesterone in capsules or progesterone cream, to all of my patients who are taking estrogen or are at risk for osteoporosis.

If you choose the cream, rub one-half to one teaspoon (one teaspoon contains 80 to 100 milligrams of natural progesterone) into your skin—on your breasts, abdomen, buttocks, or thighs—daily from the second through fourth weeks of your menstrual cycle. Take the first week off. If you are no longer menstruating, designate the first day of the calendar month as day one of your "cycle." Then take the first week off each month.

For progesterone capsules, the starting dose is 100 milligrams daily for the last three weeks of the menstrual cycle. If you're no longer menstruating, follow the same "cycle" as for progesterone cream.

Beyond natural progesterone replacement, a low-protein diet is absolutely necessary to prevent bone loss. Processed foods, sugar, alcohol, caffeine, and carbonated beverages also steal calcium from your bones. Calcium supplementation is crucial, too—but taking the mineral alone won't do any good. You need the bone-building nutritional complex that only a broad-spectrum multivitamin/mineral supplement can provide: boron, copper, magnesium, potassium, vitamin K, and zinc.

And by all means, stay on a regular exercise program. Nothing stops bone loss and maintains bone health as effectively as exercise. Walk for at least 30 minutes every day. And for your upper body, try strength training. If you have special fitness needs, you may wish to consult a personal trainer, who can set up a workout routine for you.

TESTOSTERONE: NOT FOR MEN ONLY

In the movie *Liar, Liar*, an attorney falls under a spell that not only prevents him from lying but transforms him into an embarrassingly honest individual. When a judge asks him, more or less rhetorically, "And how are we today?" the lawyer, unable to hide the truth, replies, "Fine, except I had a disappointing sexual encounter last night." The judge quips, "As you get older, you'll find that happens more and more." This may be a funny line for a film. But from the perspective of anti-aging medicine, it's definitely the wrong message. Men don't want to have this kind of experience as they get older. Nor do women. Testosterone can prevent and correct a loss of libido—and it works for both sexes.

AN EQUAL OPPORTUNITY DEPLOYER

Both men and women make the entire spectrum of sex steroid hormones. Only the ratios differ. Testosterone—the principal androgen (male sex hormone)—is made by the testes in men, by the ovaries in women, and by the adrenal glands in both sexes.

At puberty, testosterone output in males increases dramatically. The hormone has masculinizing effects: It deepens the voice, increases muscle mass and strength, improves the muscle-to-fat ratio, regulates the maturation of the male sex glands, and boosts sex drive. As men get older, testosterone production gradually declines, resulting in an ill-defined syndrome now dubbed andropause—male menopause. The transition is slower and smoother than with menopause.

Postpubescent females continue to make testosterone, too, but in much smaller amounts than males. Then at menopause, female testosterone production declines in tandem with the other sex steroid hormones. More than 50 percent of women past menopause report declines in sexual desire. Some women with reduced testosterone output have weaker sexual urges, and their fantasies—once libido-enhancing—now fall flat. Their orgasms are non-events: shorter, less intense, more localized. Estrogen/progesterone replacement alone cannot correct the lack of sexual desire caused by a testosterone deficiency.

The physical changes, lethargy, and lack of libido that accompany menopause and andropause are usually attributed to aging itself rather than to declining hormone production. Doctors tell patients who experience these symptoms to just "live with it." My advice: Don't.

If testosterone production is declining, hormone replacement can be powerful anti-aging medicine. Its rejuvenating effects go well beyond generating stronger and more frequent libidinal impulses. For men and women, testosterone energizes the entire body, instilling a heightened sense of well-being. It increases lean muscle mass, reversing the fat accumulation and muscular atrophy that accompany aging. Like estrogen and progesterone, it fights osteoporosis. And testosterone improves cardiovascular functioning and protects against heart disease.

Hormone replacement therapy makes just as much sense for men at andropause as for women at menopause. It has anti-aging effects, restoring testosterone to the level of a 30- to 40-year-old male. Unfortunately, doctors rarely consider such treatment for men.

WHAT'S LOVE GOT TO DO WITH IT?

Because it regulates sexual attraction and sex drive, testosterone has been dubbed the love hormone. A declining libido signals a declining testosterone level. When this happens, hormone replacement can make all the difference for both men and women.

Take the case of Jenny and Mark Alexander, patients of mine whom I've known for more than two decades. Happily married with two kids in college, they came to me with a problem. Jenny was the first to bring it up.

"I've lost that old romantic spark," she told me. "We used to have a great sex life, but I'm just not interested anymore. I don't even think about it. Mark has slowed down a little in the past few years, but even so, I still can't seem to keep up with him. And when we do make love, I don't get aroused the way I used to. Those Roman candle orgasms are a thing of the past. What's wrong with me? I've been taking the natural estrogen and progesterone you prescribed, but they don't seem to help."

I suggested that Jenny add a small dose of supplemental testosterone to her hormone replacement program. It worked like a charm. "All of a sudden, I'm interested in sex again," Jenny reported. "My orgasms are back, too. In fact, now Mark can't keep up with me." That was easily solved: Mark began using hormone replacement as well.

MAKING HEART DISEASE HISTORY

Beyond restoring libido, testosterone may protect men from heart disease in the same way that estrogen and progesterone protect women. A team of physicians at Columbia University found that men with low testosterone levels were much more likely to have arteries narrowed by atherosclerosis than men with higher testosterone levels. Several other studies have found a correlation between low testosterone and unhealthy blood lipid profiles: elevated total cholesterol, LDL cholesterol, and triglycerides, and low HDL cholesterol. There's some evidence, too, that a testosterone deficiency may contribute to high blood pressure and an increased risk of diabetes.

MAKING UP FOR LOST HORMONE

Blood levels of testosterone normally range from 15 to 100 milligrams per deciliter in women and from 300 to 1,200 milligrams per deciliter in men. Testosterone replacement may prove beneficial for women whose blood levels are below 60 and for men whose blood levels are below 900. Although the hormone can be administered by injection, oral forms (tablets, capsules, and lozenges) and skin patches are much more convenient.

If a testosterone deficiency is the sole cause of a diminished sex drive, as is typically the case for women at menopause and men at andropause, then testosterone replacement is worth a try. If psychological factors such as depression are playing a role, however, testosterone replacement probably won't help much. In these cases, despite diminished sexual desire, orgasms will remain normal. I've found that trial supplementation of the natural antidepressant St.-John's-wort (hypericum) often works wonders. I usually prescribe 330 milligrams three times daily. If you try it, use a standardized extract only. Give it at least a month to work.

Although there is no indication that testosterone supplementation causes prostate cancer, men with a history of the disease should not use testosterone replacement. All men over age 50 should have an annual prostate-specific antigen (PSA) screening, whether or not they are on testosterone. Testosterone replacement can cause slight, transient elevations in PSA level. This is not an indication of cancer, but normal stimulation of the prostate gland's activity.

Older males often experience increased frequency and urgency of urination, especially at night. Supplementation with extract of the herb saw palmetto (*Serenoa repens*) relieves these symptoms—collectively called prostatic hypertrophy—by preventing the conversion of testosterone into dihydrotestosterone. Dihydrotestosterone causes prostatic hypertrophy.

THE CHOICE IS YOURS

Hormone replacement is a complex issue with many questions and few definitive answers. Any decision to take or not take hormones, natural or otherwise, must be based on individual circumstances and should be made with the counsel of a physician. All options should at least be considered before a choice is made.

More and more physicians are recognizing the importance of natural hormone replacement therapy. If your doctor is not among them, you may want to consult with one who is. The American College for the Advancement of Medicine can refer you to a physician in your area who has experience in natural hormone replacement. Refer to Resources and References on page 591 for more information.

Hypothyroidism is among the most insidious age-accelerators around. Many people who have it don't even know it. In the next chapter, you'll find out how this condition speeds the aging process—and how natural thyroid hormone brings it under control.

CHAPTER 36

Thyroid Hormone: Deficiency Drives the Signs of Aging

Thousands upon thousands of persons have studied disease. Almost no one has studied health.
—ADELLE DAVIS, *LET'S EAT RIGHT TO KEEP FIT*

Of all the problems that can block Renewal, undermine health, and accelerate the aging process, none is more common—or more likely to be overlooked—than an underactive thyroid gland. And if your thyroid doesn't work right, the rest of your body doesn't, either.

Hypothyroidism, the medical term for an underactive thyroid, has such an unbelievably broad range of subtle symptoms that it is often undiagnosed or misdiagnosed. Experts estimate that undetected hypothyroidism has reached epidemic proportions in the United States, affecting between 25 and 40 percent of the nation's population.

Because a malfunctioning thyroid can thwart your bid to achieve maximum life span, you owe it to yourself to make sure that your gland is in good working order. A simple, 10-minute at-home test can tell you whether you have subclinical hypothyroidism ("subclinical" means that it displays no obvious, clearly defined symptoms). If you do, you can treat the condition safely, effectively, and inexpensively with thyroid hormone replacement.

A GRAND LITTLE GLAND

The thyroid gland sits in the front of your neck, just below and to either side of your Adam's apple. In size and shape, the gland resembles a butterfly. Its rather diminutive size—it weighs less than an ounce—belies its importance.

The hormone produced by your thyroid travels through your bloodstream to receptor sites on each and every cell in your body. Once it "docks," the hormone sets the rate of cellular metabolism. In other words, it tells the cell how fast to work.

The amount of thyroid hormone that is available in your bloodstream determines each cell's metabolic rate. If the hormone is in short supply, cells behave sluggishly. Their impaired performance can translate into any of a number of health problems, depending on the types of cells involved.

If a thyroid hormone deficiency affects nerve cells, for example, thinking may slow down, or depression may set in. If it affects muscle cells, strength declines. If it affects intestinal cells, the digestion of food and absorption of nutrients may be compromised. If it affects skin cells, acne, eczema, hair loss, and other dermatologic disorders may occur.

The immune system is especially vulnerable to low levels of thyroid hormone. White blood cell production slows down, and lymphocytes lose the aggressiveness with which they usually attack and remove infectious and allergenic invaders.

Because thyroid hormone regulates metabolic activity within the endocrine system, a hormone deficiency obstructs the functioning of the system's glands and organs. (The thyroid itself is part of the endocrine system.) These components, which also include the thymus gland, adrenal glands, pancreas, ovaries, and testicles, may be unable to maintain their own hormone outputs at optimum levels. This decline in hormone production can lead to an array of physical symptoms: fatigue (adrenal glands), digestive dysfunction (pancreas), infertility and menstrual irregularities in women (ovaries), and infertility in men (testes).

SIGNS OF A SHORTFALL

Hypothyroidism is a great masquerader, with vague symptoms that can mimic those of scores of other ailments. Many people who have the condition don't even realize it. In fact, the American Association of Clinical Endocrinologists estimates that only half of those afflicted have actually been diagnosed. No wonder hypothyroidism was dubbed the unsuspected illness by pioneering endocrinologist Broda Barnes, M.D., Ph.D. Dr. Barnes's pioneering work has brought greater understanding of the thyroid gland's pivotal role in human health.

The symptoms of hypothyroidism usually arise from the sluggish behavior of another organ or system within the body. Without thyroid hormone to give it marching orders, the organ or system simply doesn't know quite what to do. Nothing is whipping it into action. As a result, the organ or system just languishes, a victim of hormone deficiency.

The single most common complaint among people with underactive thyroids is low energy. But since the condition can cause any organ or system to function below par, symptoms can include heart palpitations, high cholesterol, digestive problems, constipation, circulatory problems, anemia, allergies, frequent infections, sleep disturbances, fatigue, muscle weakness, hair loss, dry skin, acne, eczema, infertility, premenstrual syndrome, memory loss, depression, difficulty losing weight, and intolerance of extreme heat or cold. All of these are physical manifestations of the metabolic slowdown that accompanies thyroid hormone deficiency. You can see why doctors so often fail to suspect hypothyroidism. They're dealing with a condition that takes many forms.

An underactive thyroid can contribute to more serious health problems as well, including heart disease, immune disorders, nervous system disorders, and the like. In such cases, treating the presenting symptoms—the obvious, outward signs of illness—won't be effective unless the underlying thyroid imbalance is corrected as well.

AN UNUSUAL SUSPECT

Most people go to their doctors with some idea of what's wrong with them—"My neck hurts," "This wart won't go away," "My allergies are acting up." But I've yet to have a patient say to me, "Dr. Smith, my thyroid gland is bothering me." It's always something else.

Signs of Trouble

Hypothyroidism can manifest itself as any of the following conditions. If even one of them applies to you, then you may have an underactive thyroid.

- Allergies
- Anemia
- Angina
- Atherosclerosis (hardening and clogging of the arteries)
- Brittle nails
- Chronic or frequent infections
- Cold hands and feet
- Constipation
- Depression
- Difficulty losing weight
- Digestive problems
- Dry skin
- Fatigue
- Hair loss
- Headaches
- Heart rhythm disturbances
- High cholesterol
- Immune dysfunction
- Infertility
- Irregular menstrual periods
- Lethargy
- Loss of appetite
- Loss of libido
- Low resistance to colds and flu
- Memory problems
- Mental sluggishness
- Muscle weakness and atrophy
- Slowness of movement
- Slow wound healing
- Stiff joints

One of my patients, Ellen, said that she felt cold all the time. Herb had high blood pressure. Mary complained of constant fatigue. Joe's eczema drove him crazy. Sue couldn't lose weight. Al suffered from chronic headaches. Elizabeth struggled with severe premenstrual syndrome.

Mel lost all interest in sex. Jenny couldn't get pregnant (and no, she isn't married to Mel). Jeff couldn't shake his allergies. Carol was plagued by recurrent infections. Michael didn't have any symptoms at all—just elevated cholesterol. When tested, every one of these people had an underactive thyroid.

I've found that certain symptoms serve as fairly accurate predictors of hypothyroidism. I usually test for the condition whenever a patient has one or more of the following: high cholesterol, anemia, allergies, fatigue, infertility, premenstrual syndrome, chronic infection or illness, or temperature intolerance.

THE AGE FACTOR

Age plays a part in hypothyroidism. While anyone can develop the condition, it is especially common in people over 50. In fact, it is the most often overlooked diagnosis in this age group.

As you get older, thyroid function declines. The gland's once-abundant hormone output dwindles to a mere trickle. (This phenomenon affects all of the glands and organs that produce anti-aging hormones, not just the thyroid.) The resulting hormone deficiency can speed up aging. And—here's the real kicker—it can produce physical and mental changes that mimic the aging process itself.

Just think of the sorts of ailments normally associated with growing old: fatigue, circulatory problems (feeling cold), dry skin, depression, digestive problems, memory loss, muscle weakness. Every one of these can result from a thyroid hormone deficiency.

The distinction may not seem important until you consider this: When a person over 50 experiences some type of physical or mental decline, both doctor and patient may write it off as "normal aging." They may not even discuss treatment. Yet thyroid hormone replacement could make all the difference in the world.

This brings to mind a patient of mine by the name of Sam Goodwin. A retired business executive in his seventies, Sam had been healthy all of his life. But then he started to experience a puzzling array of symptoms. He felt cold and tired most of the time. He had trouble remembering things. He no longer cared about sex. His entire body seemed to be shutting down. He mentioned all of this to his doctor, who simply replied, "You're getting up there, Sam. What do you expect?"

Testing Yourself for Hypothyroidism

Many doctors believe that basal metabolic temperature (BMT) is the most sensitive and accurate measure of thyroid function. You can check your own BMT at home, using an ordinary oral thermometer (the liquid-in-glass type, not digital). Just follow the instructions below.

Note: If you have an infection of any kind, you should wait until it clears up before performing the test. Otherwise, your elevated body temperature will skew the results.

1. Before going to sleep, shake down an oral thermometer and place it within reach of your bed. (Shaking down the thermometer in the morning, when you wake up, can raise your temperature and invalidate the test.)
2. When you wake up in the morning, place the thermometer in your armpit and leave it there for 10 minutes. Lie as still as possible—avoid getting up or moving around. Doing so increases your metabolic rate and raises your temperature.
3. After 10 minutes, read and record your temperature. Repeat this process for at least three consecutive days.

If your BMT consistently falls below 97.8°F, you likely have an underactive thyroid. BMT normally ranges from 97.8° to 98.2°F.

Needless to say, the doctor's remark didn't sit well with Sam. That's when he came to see me. All of his laboratory tests checked out fine. But his basal metabolic temperature was running about ½°F low, a good indicator of hypothyroidism. (I'll explain basal temperatures a bit later in the chapter.)

I started Sam on a trial dose of thyroid hormone. Within a few weeks, he reported noticeable improvements in his stamina, his memory, and his libido. I continued to monitor Sam's treatment for a few months, adjusting the hormone dose a couple of times. Within six months, his initial symptoms had all but disappeared.

Clearly, Sam's problems had nothing to do with "normal aging." They were the handiwork of an underactive thyroid gland. And Sam is not alone: Millions of folks suffer from hypothyroidism. Unfortunately, the majority of them have not been tested or treated for the condition.

DIAGNOSING HYPOTHYROIDISM

If you have any of the conditions listed in "Signs of Trouble" on page 481, you may very well have an underactive thyroid gland. In that case, check your basal metabolic temperature (BMT), using the guidelines presented in "Testing Yourself for Hypothyroidism." If your temperature is consistently below 97.8°F, you probably have an underactive thyroid. Report your findings to your doctor, along with any other symptoms you've been experiencing.

You want your doctor to perform two blood tests. One test measures your baseline level of thyroid-stimulating hormone (TSH), a substance secreted by the pituitary gland that instructs the thyroid to produce and release its own hormone. The other, called an antithyroid antibody panel, determines whether your immune system is manufacturing antibodies that may attack your thyroid. Positive results on these tests, along with low BMT and typical symptoms, confirm the diagnosis of an underactive thyroid.

Most doctors, myself included, look at the overall symptoms and correlate them with the test results. Often, the lab tests come back normal, even though the patient's BMT and symptom profile point to hypothyroidism. In such a situation, the doctor may prescribe a low dose of natural thyroid hormone on a trial basis. For a patient who has no serious illness, such a trial poses little risk, and its potential benefits are enormous.

What if your doctor dismisses your symptoms as "normal aging" and nothing more? Then you need to find another doctor who will take your concerns seriously. It may take a bit of legwork on your part—but hey, we're talking about your health and longevity here. (If you're not sure where to begin your search, you may want to consult one of the organizations listed in Resources and References on page 591.)

DETERMINING DOSAGE

Once you and your doctor agree to try thyroid hormone replacement, he must figure out the proper dosage. He must also monitor your treatment and adjust your dosage as necessary. (This is another reason why having a doctor whom you feel comfortable with and trust is so critical.)

Your level of thyroid-stimulating hormone is the best indicator of the effectiveness of hormone replacement. As thyroid hormone rises, thyroid-stimulating hormone falls. Ideally, however, thyroid-stimulating hormone should drop no lower than 0.5 to 1.0 international unit per milliliter. If it does, then your thyroid hormone dosage is too high. (BMT doesn't necessarily return to normal with hormone replacement, so it isn't a very good tool for assessing whether a dosage is adequate.)

When I put a patient on thyroid hormone replacement, I check her level of thyroid-stimulating hormone every month for the first two or three months. Then once I've established the optimum dosage, I check the level of thyroid-stimulating hormone three or four times a year. Finding that optimum dosage is absolutely essential. Undertreatment can allow deficiency-related disease to get a foothold. Overtreatment can raise the patient's risk of osteoporosis.

Just as dosage is important, so, too, is the type of hormone you take. I prescribe only natural thyroid hormone replacement for my patients. You should insist on the same. The synthetic stuff does not replace the full spectrum of thyroid hormones that your body produces. Natural hormone supplements do.

Natural thyroid hormone is available only by prescription. Don't confuse it with over-the-counter thyroid glandular support formulas. These support thyroid function, but they can't correct a hormone deficiency. In fact, these products have had all of the active thyroid hormone removed.

PERSONAL PROOF

Regardless of whether you need thyroid hormone replacement, you can take other steps to ensure that your thyroid gland operates at peak efficiency. The nutrients provided by the Anti-Aging Diet and the Anti-Aging Supplement Program help keep your thyroid in tip-top condition.

Hormone replacement gives a reluctant thyroid a much-needed boost. In doing so, it makes a dramatic difference in how you feel and perform. I know, because I speak from firsthand experience.

A couple of years ago, I developed fatigue that I just couldn't seem to shake. At first, I chalked it up to a hectic schedule. But when the tiredness persisted, I decided to check my BMT. Much to my surprise, my temperature was more than 1°F below normal—a clear indication of hypothyroidism.

After a blood test to determine my baseline level of thyroid-stimulating hormone, I began taking a small dose of natural thyroid hormone every morning. Initially, the treatment didn't seem to help (which, by the way, is fairly typical). But after a month, I felt better. And after two months, my fatigue completely disappeared. The improvement was so gradual, though, that I barely noticed it.

If you are among the large percentage of the population with hypothyroidism, you, too, may be amazed at how much younger you feel once thyroid health is restored. Thyroid hormone replacement does work slowly, however. You need to give it at least three months. Just be patient. The results are well worth the wait.

We have one final component of the Renewal Anti-Aging Program to cover. What is it? Why, exercise, of course. Renewal simply can't take place without it. The next chapter explains why.

PART 6
The Renewal Anti-Aging Exercise Program

Exercise as if Your Life Depends on It . . . It Does

Git along little dogies.
—FROM AN OLD WEST FOLK SONG

Carole, a college professor in her sixties, came to her initial consultation colorfully dressed but quite downhearted—literally and figuratively. Her heart had begun to fail seven years before, requiring increasingly stronger drugs to keep it under control. Then she was diagnosed with Type II (non-insulin-dependent) diabetes, which required another medication for blood sugar control. To top that off, she was 95 pounds overweight. She handed me a list of the 12 medications that she was taking: two heart drugs, three diuretics, and an assortment of other medicines.

An intelligent woman, she was perplexed. "Dr. Smith, the doctors I see at the HMO don't seem to have any overall plan to get rid of this. They just keep giving me more medicines, and every time I go back they tell me I have to stay on these for the rest of my life. I don't want to take all these drugs. I want to get well, get off of the drugs, and get on with my life."

Her previous doctors had diagnosed Carole with cardiomyopathy (a heart muscle disorder), high blood pressure, diabetes, edema (fluid accumulation), kidney failure, and hypothyroidism. But the one condition they missed—the one that had gone unaddressed and would surely kill her—was couch potato-ism. Her activity level was virtually nil, and her excess weight reflected this. She was consuming far more calories (mostly from junk foods) than she was burning off, thus accumulating the extra weight that was putting an excessive burden on her heart and slowly robbing her of her health.

We could address the heart problems and diabetes naturally with a combination of nutritional supplements, acupuncture, and other natural therapies. What Carole desperately needed, however, was an exercise program. Without one, she would never truly get better.

Though she was curable, Carole had been given the impression that she was terminally ill. Her doctors prescribed increasingly stronger medications with the admonition that she'd have to take them until she died. Predictably, this robbed Carole of any hope and gave her the feeling that she was indeed dying. One by one, the specialists had instituted appropriate mainstream treatments for the various diseased organs—the failing heart and kidneys, the diabetic pancreas and liver—but none had looked at the larger picture of her overall lifestyle. Carole's inactivity was killing her, plain and simple. An exercise program would be her only cure.

I explained to Carole how exercise would affect each of her health problems and why it would work when even the best drugs had failed. She agreed to gradually increase her level of activity, following a program that we would develop together.

She stuck with it, and the results were nothing short of miraculous. As expected, progress was slow. Success was measured in terms of small accomplishments rather than meeting perhaps unrealistic goals. After six months, Carole was able to get rid of half of her medications. After a year, she was 25 pounds lighter, she was off almost all of her medications, and she felt like she was getting her life back. Her heart was healing. Her blood sugar was returning to normal. She was right on track for getting back to her ideal weight in three or four more years. We'd come this far together, and we both knew she'd make it.

Get a Move On

Need a good reason to exercise? Here are 20 of them. Regular physical activity supports the Renewal process in the following ways.

- Enlarges coronary arteries for better blood circulation
- Improves the heart's pumping action
- Improves the body's ability to dissolve blood clots
- Improves immunity
- Improves insulin response
- Increases reaction time
- Improves stress tolerance
- Increases activity of anti-aging enzymes
- Increases cardiac output
- Increases levels of endorphins (the body's natural pain relievers)
- Increases maximum oxygen intake
- Increases physical work capacity
- Prevents anxiety, depression, and insomnia
- Prevents cancer
- Prevents constipation
- Reduces blood pressure
- Reduces body fat and facilitates weight control
- Reduces resting heart rate
- Slows neuromuscular aging
- Strengthens bones

A NATURAL ELIXIR

Why did this approach work when the best pharmacological treatments held little hope for a normal life for Carole? Because her exercise program did things drugs cannot do. It healed her heart, lowered her blood pressure, and brought her cardiovascular system back from the edge of collapse. It was controlling her diabetes by correcting her body's insulin response. It strengthened her immune system and restored her endocrine (hormone) system. And the exercise-induced release of growth hormone, endorphins, enzymes, cytokines, and other healing chemicals helped her feel so much better that she found it easy to stay on the program.

The health benefits of exercise are legion. It is just as important to your Anti-Aging Program as to Carole's treatment program. The human body is designed to be active, and things just don't work right if it isn't. With regular exercise, the body produces an array of age-retarding chemicals. Production of antioxidants, anti-aging hormones (especially age-reversing growth hormone), immune factors, and other age-retarding biochemicals is enhanced. Renewal is promoted. Regular exercise will lower your blood pressure and heart rate and slow down age-related bone deterioration while strengthening the arterial, neuromuscular, endocrine, and immune systems. A program of regular workouts, as described in the following pages, dramatically reduces your risk of death from degenerative diseases. The same Renewal enhancement that literally saved Carole's life can prolong yours, too.

INACTIVITY IS TO DIE FOR

Question: What's twice as likely to kill you as a high cholesterol level?

Answer: A sedentary lifestyle.

Inactivity is a luxury that those who would like to live longer (not to mention look and feel better) just plain can't afford. As a result of several decades of research examining lifestyles, certain risk factors have been identified as associated with increased probability of death from heart disease. These risk factors include high cholesterol, high blood pressure, obesity, diabetes, smoking, and sedentary lifestyle.

In a huge, federally funded study of more than 55,000 people, researchers at the Centers for Disease Control and Prevention examined risk factors with respect to exercise. They found that couch potatoes are more likely to die from heart disease because of their inactivity than because of any other risk factor, including high cholesterol. An inactive lifestyle was defined as one that does not include at least 20 minutes of vigorous physical activity three times a week. Amazingly, a vegetative behavior pattern was twice as likely to shorten life span as its closest competitor, elevated cholesterol.

Much research evidence, not to mention common sense, supports the notion that inactivity shortens life span. When researchers divided rats into two otherwise identical groups and gave one group access to an exercise wheel while depriving the other, they found that the exercised rats lived considerably longer: 19 percent longer for the males, and 11.5 percent for the females. Presumably, these rats had no added incentive to exercise other than the presence of the equipment.

How many of us have, in a moment of pure motivation, purchased that exercise cycle, stairclimber, or treadmill—the one that's now collecting dust and creating seemingly endless guilt? Rodents aside, many of us humans apparently do need motivating factors that go beyond the mere joy of exercise—like fear of flab, or the intellectual knowledge that you will be healthier.

Okay, big deal. So rats who work out live longer, I hear you saying. What about humans? There is no reason to believe that rats are any different from humans . . . when it comes to exercise, that is. But for those humans who prefer human studies, a Finnish study of 7,700 men and women found that those with low levels of physical activity had four times the death rate (that is, they were four times as likely to die in any given year) as those in the high activity group.

Further, a study examining the lifestyles of more than 4,000 healthy men, published in the *New England Journal of Medicine*, concluded that "a lower level of physical fitness is associated with a higher risk of death from coronary heart disease and cardiovascular disease in clinically healthy men, independent of conventional coronary risk factors."

A BODY IN MOTION LASTS LONGER

The more physically fit you are, the longer you will live, concludes the largest study yet to examine the effects of fitness on life span. More than 13,000 men and women were followed over an 11-year period at the Institute for Aerobics Research in Dallas. Each participant received a fitness score (low, moderate, or high) based on how long he or she could keep walking during a treadmill exercise test. All were followed for several years. To make sure participants were capable of fitness and not likely to die of a preexisting disease, only healthy people were allowed into the study.

The results: The least physically fit people were three times more likely to die (of all causes) during the study period than the most fit. And the least fit were eight times more likely to die of heart or cardiovascular disease than the most fit.

Why does a sedentary lifestyle shorten life span? There are many answers to this question, and I'll get to them later, but we must start with the cardiovascular system. Aging happens faster—much faster—if your body isn't properly fed. We were designed to move, and if we don't, the heart and blood vessels get lazy and weak, and they literally shrink. Their muscular walls atrophy, and the capillary beds get smaller, so each supplies a smaller area. Exercise is like the road crew for your vascular highway system. Activity tells blood vessels to heal, stay strong, and to be prepared to carry some heavy traffic. If they fall into disrepair, the vessels can't deliver the stuff (nutrients, hormones, enzymes) your cells need to Renew. Literally every organ, tissue, and cell in your body is dependent on the blood vessels. If they are sick, you are sick. Exercise keeps them healthy.

Nowhere is the old adage "use it or lose it" more true than when applied to physical conditioning of the heart and blood vessels. Most of us don't think of blood vessels as muscular, but they are. Our bodies contain thousands of miles of blood vessels, the walls of which contain tiny muscles.

Unused muscles in any part of your body become loose and flabby. If they happen to be in your belly, the result of your sedentary lifestyle is merely poor appearance. When those teensy little muscles in your arteries go without exercise, though, they become flabby and clogged, and you have much more than a cosmetic problem. You have a roadblock to Renewal, because the nutrients can't get to where they are needed, and metabolic debris can't be properly removed.

The bottom line with exercise and life extension is this: A body can be no healthier than its cardiovascular system. It comes down to a simple matter of distributing supplies and removing waste. The supply side is the arterial network, which provides nourishment to all tissues and organs in the form of blood carrying oxygen, amino acids, glucose, vitamins, and a wealth of other healing and nourishing substances needed for cellular renewal. The veins are your waste removal system, which drain away the cellular garbage generated by trillions of cells buzzing with metabolic activity. (The waste goes primarily to the liver and kidneys, which excrete it.)

To understand why couch potatoes tend to have shorter life expectancies, imagine a large city under siege, in which the food supply routes have been cut off by 50 percent. (We're talking about atherosclerosis, weak arterial muscles, a flabby heart, and impaired circulation.) Gradual starvation would ensue. Imagine further that half the garbage removal personnel went on strike. Now we would really have a mess on our hands. Like the city under siege, a body slowly starved and then forced to wallow in its own excrement just can't survive for long.

Below I discuss the three keys to a successful exercise program: aerobics, strength training, and stretching. Each is important, but aerobics stands out because it alone provides critical cardiovascular conditioning. You can—and should—train for strength and stretch for flexibility, but without those aerobic workouts, you won't add much to your life expectancy.

THE ROLE OF EXERCISE IN RENEWAL

At the risk of pushing the limits of redundancy, I'll say it again: Exercise buffs up your circulatory system, so more nutrient-rich blood can access more areas of your body. Your body will have developed that more-powerful heart and those sleek, muscle-bound jumbo vessels to service those large, hungry, churning leg and trunk muscles. But guess what? From brain to big toe, the entire body, literally every cell, is the beneficiary of this abundance. Protection is strengthened, repair is more rapid. Healing is enhanced and accelerated. Let me share some examples.

The brain can send and receive nerve and hormone signals faster. The hypothalamus gland (which regulates hunger, thirst, and sex drive) and the pineal gland (which regulates sleep and waking, stress, and immunity) can send out more accurate signals to the rest of the body, which can respond more promptly and effectively to them. The thyroid and adrenal glands, which regulate metabolic activity levels, can make sure you have enough energy. The digestive organs will digest, absorb, and deliver nutrients better. The liver can process blood with greater efficiency, and the kidneys use the extra flow to clean house better. The hormones of the endocrine system go to their target tissue destinations more rapidly and give more appropriate feedback messages. I could go on and on, but you get the point: Everything works better.

Now let's look at some specific benefits of exercise.

Enhanced antioxidant activity. Since exercise, by raising the level of metabolism, is known to cause increased free radical production, one might reasonably wonder—especially after all the negative comments I've made about free radicals—how this could be desirable. In a scenario similar to that with the blood vessels that rise to the occasion, exercise also teaches your body to expect more radicals. Even when you are not exercising, the added antioxidant protection remains, so you have better overall long-term protection. This is attested to by the following study.

In mice given voluntary wheel training (the rodent equivalent of a treadmill), levels of all three internally produced free radical scavengers (glutathione peroxidase, catalase, and superoxide dismutase) increased, while antioxidant protection (as measured by lower levels of oxidized fats in the blood) improved. These findings show that even though exercise increases free radical production, it simultaneously trains the body to improve its free radical scavenging capacity, ultimately improving antioxidant protection. This added capacity for reduction of free radicals adds another dimension to Renewal, and it provides yet another mechanism to explain the anti-aging and life-extending effects noted for regular exercise in humans.

Beefed-up production of anti-aging chemicals. To me, two of the most interesting effects of exercise are that it encourages our bodies to produce more of certain powerful anti-aging chemicals, among which are human growth hormone (HGH) and L-glutamine.

Growth hormone is a potent anti-aging hormone made by your pituitary gland. Though pricey, it is widely administered by anti-aging physicians as a rejuvenative. You can increase your supply of growth hormone for free simply by working out.

The other substance, L-glutamine, is the most prevalent amino acid in the body. It is manufactured by the muscles, and the more muscles you have, the more of the chemical you make. L-glutamine is necessary for optimum immune functioning, and higher levels are associated with both increased immunity and longer life. Thus a powerful connection exists between the atrophying muscles and weakened immunity of old age. With regular strength-training exercises, you will maintain greater muscle mass, which increases L-glutamine production, improves immune system health, and reverses aging.

Better brainpower. Your ability to think, concentrate, solve problems, process information, and remember depends on healthy brain cells. Flabby, cholesterol-laden, clogged-up arteries can't deliver oxygen and nutrients to brain cells, which weakens them and accounts for the gradual faltering of thinking power that is characteristic of aging. When brain cells starve, they can't generate and carry electrical signals as fast, which slows thoughts and blocks access to memory.

Exercise age-proofs the brain by improving the health of the brain's blood vessels, which, when kept vitalized, are then able to continue to properly nourish the brain itself and efficiently remove carbon dioxide and other waste matter.

Augmenting the brain's rations of oxygen- and nutrient-rich blood improves information-processing capability, memory, concentration, and virtually all other aspects of mental performance.

Though all of the nutrients play a role in brain health and Renewal, the most important ones are the B-complex vitamins (especially B_6, B_{12}, choline, riboflavin, and thiamin) and vitamins C and E; the minerals calcium, magnesium, manganese, potassium, and zinc; and the amino acids carnitine, glutamine, phenylalanine, taurine, tryptophan, and tyrosine. A compromised cerebral blood supply would also impede access to the brain by acetyl-L-carnitine, coenzyme Q_{10}, garlic, ginkgo, ginseng, phosphatidylserine, pregnenolone, and other brain nutrients. Suboptimum supplies of these nutrients encourage the development of senile

brain disease, the symptoms of which are subtle and insidious at first, but later gather momentum: forgetfulness, disorientation, and confusion.

One group of researchers demonstrated the power of
exercise to improve mental vigor in a group of previously
sedentary 55- to 70-year-olds who were put on a program
of brisk walking. Striking increases in short-term memory,
ability to reason, and reaction time were observed in virtually all of the participants.

Those who achieved aerobic fitness showed the most
improvement. A host of similar experiments has been
done, showing improved brain function with exercise.

Quicker reflexes. The benefits of physical activity go way
beyond the brain. Exercise is a general tonic for the entire
nervous system. Physically active people have quicker
reflexes than sedentary types. And remarkably, aerobic
exercise speeds up those delayed reaction times that "normally" occur with aging. Maybe membership in a fitness
club should be a prerequisite for driver's license renewal
after a certain age?

Improved mood. Ever wonder why you feel so darn good
after a workout (and generally, when working out regularly)? Or why you no longer feel like the beach wimp in
those Charles Atlas ads (you know, the guy who always got
sand kicked in his face)? Or why some people seem
addicted to exercise?

It's because a workout tells your cells to synthesize the
natural (and legal) opiate beta-endorphin. This biochemical is structurally and pharmacologically similar to mor-
phine: It reduces pain, stimulates feelings of well-being,
and supplies a natural high.

Elevated endorphins explain why physical conditioning
relieves depression, lowers anxiety levels, and increases
self-esteem. Fit people feel (and are) more relaxed and
self-assured, have fewer mood swings, less fatigue, and
improved sleep patterns. So exercise not only helps you
stay young longer, it helps you feel younger. In my medical
practice, I often prescribe regular exercise for depression
and insomnia. The results are so uniformly successful that I
have come to regard exercise as one of the best tranquilizers and antidepressants there is.

Stronger bones. Bones need calcium. Physical inactivity causes osteoporosis, the loss of calcium that makes bones brittle and fracture-prone. An individual confined to bed will lose up to 4 percent of bone mass within a month.

A few years ago, on the evening news, we witnessed the return to earth of a Soviet cosmonaut who had been stranded in space for almost a year because the Soviet Union and its space program had disintegrated while he was away. Although certainly a paragon of physical fitness prior to his departure, through inactivity his musculoskeletal system had so weakened that he was unable to stand unassisted when removed from his capsule.

This was a dramatic demonstration of the necessity of weight-bearing exercise to maintain health.

Like the cosmonaut (though not so dramatically, because we live in a gravitational field), if you lead a sedentary lifestyle, your bones will gradually weaken. Bones respond to regular weight-bearing exercise by taking on more calcium, thus adding strength. In other words, when it comes to bones, you either use them or lose them.

Protection against cancer. Virtually every study examining the link between cancer and exercise has confirmed the notion that exercise helps prevent cancer. No one is sure why, though, which gives us license to theorize. My theory is that in fit people, blood-borne antioxidants and immune cells can better penetrate to areas where cancer might be gaining a foothold, reversing it before it expands to irreversibility.

Exercise specifically reduces colon cancer risk. How? Regular activity and toned abdominal muscles massage your intestines, stimulating the peristaltic action that produces increased frequency and regularity of bowel movements. When the bowels are sluggish, carcinogens in the stool sit around and irritate the intestinal wall, eventually causing cancer there. Exercise in combination with a high-residue vegan diet will be far more effective at preventing all types of cancer than exercise alone, however.

Blood sugar regulation. Exercise helps control diabetes and hypoglycemia in people like Carole by increasing the efficiency of carbohydrate utilization. This improves blood sugar control and decreases insulin requirements by making insulin work more efficiently. In fact, Type II diabetes will always be helped just by exercise.

Weight loss and maintenance. Exercise is essential for healthy weight control. Exercise reduces body fat but also turns up your metabolic thermostat, so you're burning extra calories up to 15 hours or more after you have stopped exercising.

AEROBIC EXERCISE: THE BEST FOR LONGEVITY

Based on exercise type, who would you expect to live longest: Arnold Schwarzenegger, Mikhail Baryshnikov, or Carl Lewis?

Though the number of ways to exercise your body approaches infinity, experts generally recognize three aspects of any fitness regimen. The first is strength: how heavy a weight you can lift. (Think of Schwarzenegger here.) The second is flexibility: well-stretched muscles, ligaments, and tendons move more smoothly and with greater range of motion (Baryshnikov). And third is endurance: the ability to exercise over a long period of time (Lewis).

Although each of the three elements of fitness is important, endurance is clearly the champ in terms of Renewal and a longer life. Aerobics has been proven to lengthen life expectancy, while the other two types, weight training and stretching—though vital components of an exercise program—have not.

Specifically, cardiovascular endurance, unattainable without aerobics, is the most potent anti-aging weapon in the exercise arsenal. So it is important to make a distinction between long-term aerobic endurance training and non-aerobic exercises.

Now the correct answer to my riddle is obvious. It's Carl Lewis, because his exercise form emphasizes endurance over strength and flexibility. Obviously, there is some overlap among these three. A stronger body, for example, will have greater flexibility and endurance; endurance training increases strength and flexibility.

At the start of any exercise, there is enough oxygen stored·in the muscles to supply the temporarily increased demand. This, then, is anaerobic exercise, because it requires no additional oxygen. About three minutes into a workout, when your reserve oxygen supply is exhausted, the aerobic form of exercise kicks in. Forced to consume extra oxygen, you begin to huff and puff to extract more oxygen from the air. Your heart begins beating harder and faster, and your blood vessels dilate to carry more blood. The exercise has now become aerobic.

With aerobic exercise you strengthen several kinds of muscles. Your heart is obviously a muscle, and increasing its work load strengthens it. But what about your lungs? Are they muscles? No, but they are surrounded by muscles that force them open and shut to pump air like a bellows. Aerobic exercise strengthens these respiratory muscles. And finally, there are the muscles in the walls of your blood vessels, which also get larger.

Your blood vessels also do something else that's interesting: They multiply. With regular aerobic exercise, you are conditioning your vascular system to expect extra loads and to improve its efficiency. Like adding new lanes and even new side streets to a freeway system, your body's far-flung network of blood vessels grows, forming a thicker network of supply lines. Through a process called vascularization, new networks of vessels grow into all the muscles in anticipation of the next aerobic workout. Your heart, respiratory muscles, skeletal muscles, and even the muscles in the walls of the blood vessels (which are supplying blood to all those other muscles) get extra supply lines. Your payoff for those workouts is a body that has made great leaps in efficiency of operation.

Aerobic exercise is any activity that involves repetitive muscular movements and that raises heart rate to 75 to 80 percent of its maximum for at least 20 minutes. (I recommend 30 minutes.) Although there are many types of aerobic activity, running, jogging, brisk walking, cycling, aerobic dancing, and swimming are the most popular. Aerobic exercises develop cardiovascular endurance, rather than speed, strength, or flexibility. The common goal of all aerobic exercises is to increase the rate at which oxygen is processed by the body. This is called aerobic capacity. The Big, Bad Wolf has nothing on you: If you're huffing and puffing, you're in the aerobic zone.

Physicians and fitness specialists agree that although stretching for flexibility and weight training for strength have their places, aerobic exercise is the most important type of exercise in any fitness program. Other exercises like stretching, toning, weight training, movement, dance, and yoga will lift your spirits, improve neuromuscular coordination, develop specific muscle groups, develop strength, and/or remove flab from unwanted areas like buttocks and bellies. But these can't impart the powerful life-extending properties offered by aerobics, because they don't require the sustained heart rate elevation necessary to develop collateral vessels. Non-aerobic exercises are important, too, but not as a substitute. Aerobics is the sine qua non for life extension.

THE BENEFITS OF AEROBIC ACTIVITY

A regular, moderate aerobic workout cures depression, improves self-esteem, and elevates mood. It gives you increased energy, stamina, and agility. On a metabolic level, it stabilizes your blood sugar levels, reduces cholesterol, and improves fat metabolism. By strengthening the heart and arteries and reducing blood pressure, aerobic exercise dramatically reduces your chances of succumbing to a heart attack, and so provides added protection against those nasty cardiovascular degenerative diseases that kill three out of every four people. By increasing your overall metabolic rate, aerobics improves biochemical functioning of the body, rendering it more resistant to disease.

Endurance conditioning makes for strong, sturdy bones by halting the loss of bone mass responsible for the osteoporosis that plagues so many older people. It strengthens the entire body, stimulates the immune system, assists in weight control by reducing appetite and burning off extra calories, relieves constipation, reduces stress, cures insomnia, quickens reflexes, and helps you look and feel younger.

All this, and it's free, too—or at least not very expensive. Unless you feel you need designer athletic wear to perform at your very best, that is.

PUMP UP YOUR HEART MUSCLE

As mentioned above, aerobic exercise strengthens the heart muscle, allowing it to pump more blood per beat and thus to circulate more blood with fewer beats. Because it can do the same work at a slower rate, your heart can rest longer between beats, which allows it more time to replenish its oxygen and nutrient supplies. A rate reduction of only 10 beats per minute—easily attained on a moderate exercise program—adds up to 14,400 fewer beats per day, and 5,256,000 beats per year. So, paradoxical though it may seem, increasing your activity level actually rests your heart. Bottom line: a happy, efficient heart which will keep on ticking a lot longer.

Aerobics improves the blood lipid picture by increasing protective high-density lipoprotein cholesterol levels, while decreasing low-density lipoprotein cholesterol and triglycerides, all of which are associated with decreased risk of hardened arteries and cardiovascular disease. Regular exercise increases your body's efficiency at processing fats, so that rather than sticking around and plastering themselves to the insides of your arteries, they are rapidly eliminated, lowering your risk of vascular disease. Exercise's fat-lowering effect is independent of the amount of fat eaten at any given meal, which, in any event, should be kept at a minimum.

And, as if all that weren't sufficient, aerobics also augments the body's ability to dissolve blood clots in the arteries, further reducing the risk of heart attack and stroke.

DIET COUNTS, TOO

Although prevention is clearly preferable, there is also hope for those whose hearts are already giving them messages that all is not well. A person who has angina or who has had a heart attack can still benefit from aerobic exercise. Experiments in which dye was injected into the coronary arteries revealed that regular exercise can slow down the development of coronary artery disease. Of course, strict supervision is crucial here: For individuals whose cardiac function is already compromised, there is an extremely fine line between too little exercise and too much. The postmyocardial infarction patient must be careful not to overexert his unconditioned heart muscle. This situation requires supervision by a physician trained in exercise physiology.

If you are among those who believe that exercise can compensate for a high-fat diet, excess sugar consumption, alcohol use, or other dietary transgressions, please disabuse yourself of this notion now. As good as it is for you, exercise alone will not protect you from heart disease.

Consider the tragic case of James F. Fixx, author of *The Complete Book of Running*, one of the most successful books on the subject. The premier running advocate, Fixx practiced what he preached: He ran 80 miles per week for the last 15 years of his life. Fixx's arteries were blocked with atherosclerotic plaque, but so strong was his belief that exercise (and the collateral circulation it generates) would protect him that he ignored expert advice about lowering the fat content of his diet. This recommendation emanated from, among others, Nathan Pritikin, director of the Pritikin Longevity Center in Santa Monica, California.

Fixx figured that the American Heart Association's diet, which limits fat intake to 30 percent of calories and cholesterol to 300 milligrams daily, would protect him. But the seven-year, $115 million, 12,000-person Multiple Risk Factor Intervention Trial (MRFIT) resoundingly demonstrated that there is no difference in total deaths between the American Heart Association's 30 percent diet and the higher-fat standard American diet. Others have shown that for meaningful protection you have to get fat intake down to 10 percent.

Like many runners, Fixx also thought that he could "run through" his coronary blockage, healing it in the process. For this miscalculation, Fixx paid the ultimate price: He died of a massive heart attack while running alone on a country road in Vermont.

In his 1985 book *Diet for Runners*, Pritikin described a conversation with Fixx: "About six months before his death this year, Jim Fixx phoned me and criticized the chapter 'Run and Die on the American Diet' in *The Pritikin Promise*. In that chapter, I documented my thesis that running is not protective against heart disease. I said that many runners on the average American diet have died and will continue to drop dead during or shortly after long-distance events or training sessions. Jim thought the chapter was hysterical in tone and would frighten a lot of runners. I told him that was my intention. I hoped it would frighten them into changing their diets. I explained that I think it is better to be hysterical before someone dies than after. Too many men, I told Jim, had already died because they believed that anyone who could run a marathon in under four hours and who was a nonsmoker had absolute immunity from having a heart attack."

Allow me to burst the bubble on a couple of other common misconceptions. First, a normal electrocardiogram (EKG), coupled with a running program, is no protection against a heart attack. Coronary vessels can be significantly clogged, and the EKG—even a stress EKG—can be normal. Another delusion is that a high level of HDL cholesterol can protect you from a heart attack, especially if you work out. It won't, and many are those who've lost their lives by mistakenly adhering to this belief. A high HDL can be achieved through healthy activities like exercise, or unhealthy ones, like drinking. Normal levels are 30 to 60 milligrams per deciliter of blood. Fixx's was an incredible 87 milligrams per deciliter.

Heart disease can be reversed by adhering strictly to the Renewal Anti-Aging Program. The only hope for meaningful long-term prevention or reversal of coronary vessel disease is the Renewal approach: a low-fat vegetarian diet, nutritional supplements, and a program of daily aerobic exercise. In fact, Dean Ornish, M.D., founder and director of the Preventive Medicine Research Institute in Sausalito, California, has demonstrated reversal of coronary artery lesions in patients who adhered to a strict regimen that included exercise, a low-fat, high-complex carbohydrate, vegetarian diet, and a stress management program.

ANYTHING CAN BE AEROBIC
(WELL, ALMOST ANYTHING)

Because they're inherently ideal for sustained activity, walking and jogging are the best forms of aerobic exercise. But they're not for everyone. It's important to find an exercise you enjoy, because that's the one you'll be most likely to stick with. The only real requirement is that your exercise be a daily aerobic workout of 30 minutes at your target heart rate. Certain sports, like baseball, bowling, golf, horseshoes, and volleyball, are difficult to turn into an aerobic workout. This is because the nature of these activities is inherently intermittent and therefore the sustained activity level requirement is difficult or impossible to meet. (Can you imagine a horseshoe game in which your heart rate would go over 100 for 30 minutes?)

But any activity, done vigorously enough to satisfy the sustained heart rate requirement, would qualify. Here is a real opportunity to be creative. For example, I have attained and sustained my target rate for 30 minutes, at various times in my aerobics career, by pushing a stroller with a baby in it, jogging in place in front of the television while watching half of *60 Minutes*, and even pushing a lawn mower. However, most days I either run three to five miles or swim for 30 minutes.

AIM FOR THE TARGET

For any exercise activity, heart rate is the best indicator for determining whether the activity is vigorous enough to qualify as aerobic. A generally accepted norm is that your exercise should raise and sustain your heart rate to 70 to 85 percent of your maximum rate for at least 20 minutes.

The formula for determining your maximum and target heart rates is as follows: First, determine maximum rate by subtracting your age from 220. (My age is 55, so my maximum rate is 165.) But you don't want to exercise flat out at 100 percent maximum—that would do damage very quickly. The experts have therefore determined that 70 to 85 percent of maximum is best. So multiply your maximum rate by 0.70 and 0.85 (or use the chart that follows) to determine your target heart rate range. Mine is: 0.70×165 = 115 (the low end) and 0.85×165 = 140 (the high end).

When I exercise, I stop occasionally to take my pulse rate, and if it's below 115, I pick up the pace a bit. Actually, I aim for the middle of my target range, which is about 130. Because my tendency (and most likely yours as well) is to go slower rather than faster than necessary, reducing my activity level has never been a problem. I've never gone above my maximum rate of 165, and I wouldn't recommend it. Getting in shape takes time and commitment, and pushing your limits won't speed up the process, but it can cause an injury.

Heart rate can be measured by taking the carotid pulse in the neck or the radial pulse at the base of the thumb in the wrist. Take a 20-second reading, then multiply by 3 to get the rate per minute. Don't attempt to take your pulse while you are in motion; stop to do it. If you like new age technology and don't want to stop to take your pulse, you can purchase an electronic pulse rate indicator, which can be worn during exercise and will give continuous readings while you are moving.

Like me, you may discover that, after initial frequent pulse readings, you gradually begin to learn what it feels like to be at (or near) your target rate. Then you won't need to take your pulse as often.

CHOOSE THE RIGHT TARGET

To get a good aerobic workout, you must exercise within your target heart rate range. The following chart can help you determine your personal range. Simply locate your age in the left-hand column, then refer to the corresponding numbers in the right-hand column. These numbers indicate how many times your heart should beat per minutes during your workout.

Age	Target Heart Rate Range
25–29	135–164
30–34	132–161
35–39	129–157
40–44	126–153
45–49	124–150
50–54	122–148
55–59	119–144
60–64	117–142
65–69	114–138

Regardless of the type, or combination of types, of exercise you choose, it is crucial to learn to use your target heart rate as your guide. Because it adjusts automatically to your level of fitness, no matter whether you are just starting out or are already in excellent condition, your pulse rate will always tell you whether you are working out at an aerobic fitness level. As your level of aerobic conditioning improves, your resting pulse rate will become slower at any given activity level.

Achieving a moderate level of fitness would provide most of the life-extending benefits exercise has to offer. An average adult can achieve these by jogging or brisk walking for at least 30 minutes, at target heart rate, three days a week. An optimum jogging or brisk walking level would be three to four miles, five to six days per week. Older people might need a little less; younger a little more.

STRENGTH TRAINING: MUSCLE IN ON LONGEVITY

Not long ago, muscle strengthening exercises were generally thought to be important only for narcissistic Incredible Hulk–like Neanderthals. Now, most fitness experts agree that strength training, though not as important as aerobics, is an essential component of any well-balanced complete exercise program. Why? Because though aerobics does add some strength, it mainly develops cardiovascular endurance and burns off calories. Strength training adds . . . well, strength. This does not mean the ability to lift 400 pounds; it has to do with stronger muscles—all over your body.

Strength training induces the development of additional new muscle cells and more resilient tendons, ligaments, and muscles. Added strength improves neuromuscular control, which in turn protects you from injury. Strength training is especially important for the back, since lower-back pain is often caused by weakness of the abdominal and/or back muscles.

By adding pure strength, strength training adds depth to your exercise program. Most of the best aerobic exercises—like jogging, brisk walking, or cycling—work primarily on the lower body, which can become overdeveloped in relation to the upper.

This is a recent revelation for yours truly. Until about two years ago, I thought I was doing everything I needed to do by getting out there and running my little heart out three or four times a week—aerobically, of course. Oh, I did some occasional upper-body stuff, but I never really got systematic about it. Then, in the course of researching this chapter, I learned that people like me who just jog have grossly underdeveloped upper body musculature, and this is not good. Strength training with hand weights can balance things out. So I got myself some hand weights: one-pound ones to do arm exercises with while I am running, and five-pound ones to do other stationary upper-body exercises with. I also do pushups and pullups, and crunches (those modified partial situps) to strengthen my midsection. What can I say? I've developed some muscles I didn't know I had.

It's beyond the scope of this book to provide specific strength-training exercises. Trainers at health and fitness clubs can help, and your local bookstore has many excellent books on fitness that can help you design your personal program.

STRETCHING: MAINTAIN RANGE OF MOTION

Flexibility diminishes with age. Muscle fibers shorten. Connective tissue loses elasticity. Stretching slows these changes, integrates the other aspects of a conditioning program, and improves the flexibility of muscles, tendons, ligaments, and joint tissues and protects them from injury. Ballet, tai chi, and yoga all increase flexibility. But just doing stretching exercises will suffice.

VARIETY IS THE SPICE OF FITNESS

Let's talk about cross-training. From the previous sections, it must be becoming clear that no one exercise does it all. We need to seek variety in our workouts. Cross-training is any fitness program that systematically incorporates a variety of activities to promote balanced fitness. Instead of just running or just swimming or just bicycling or just aerobics classes or just anything, cross-training is participating in several different exercise activities.

Your muscles have memory. They learn. Just like driving a car or adding up long lists of numbers, you'll become very efficient at doing anything you do repeatedly. Whether it is jogging or calypso dancing, if you do the same old thing over and over again, your muscles will get very good at it, and it will no longer feel like exercise.

When you think about it, the possibilities are endless.

JUST DO IT

As much as I dislike plugging a huge corporation, you have to admit this is a great slogan. It sums up in three words the resistance many of us have to exercising. Lack of time is the "reason" we all use to procrastinate about exercise. Is it reassuring to know that even elite world-class athletes use this excuse? In this modern era, it is easy to let the pressures of work, family, and all those other commitments push exercise time right out of the picture. Don't. Because you'll live longer, and you'll end up with even more time.

With two kids, a busy medical practice, teaching, writing, and keeping up with new research, I admit it's an ongoing struggle to find time to exercise. My search for a few free minutes sometimes leads me to look like a moron, like when I do leg stretches and jumping jacks while my gas tank is filling up. I take work breaks and shoot baskets. At home, I have a Health Rider and a treadmill. I make up activity games with my kids—or we just chase each other around the house. This is not exactly easy for a grown man to admit, but I've even jumped on my daughter's pogo stick.

BUT DON'T OVERDO IT

Start out slowly and increase your activity level gradually. The importance of this cannot be overemphasized. Although it is never too late to start, one can't make up for a lifetime of inactivity in one month. It takes time. I've seen many a patient who scorned his body's need to adjust gradually to the stress of exercise and paid the price by sustaining an injury. Then often comes the illogical conclusion that "Exercise is not for me."

Moderate activity is best. Some zealots operate on the assumption that if a little is good, a lot must be better. Unfortunately, this is not true. Sustained overexercising can cause damage at a rate faster than the body's ability to heal. This will wear you out prematurely. Not only is there no upside to excessive training but by generating more free radicals than the body is prepared to scavenge, overtraining actually weakens the immune system and increases susceptibility to degenerative disease. Consistency is far more important than intensity.

The early warning signs of overexercise are first fatigue, then pain. If either occurs, the message is clear: Slow down. Another advantage to using target heart rate as a guide to activity level is that it will help protect against overexercise injury. A newly reformed couch potato, when initiating an aerobics program, will require very little activity to achieve target rate. But as he gradually becomes more fit, it takes more and more vigorous workouts to achieve the same rate.

And finally, be sure to exercise as far from traffic and pollution as you can. You don't want to undo exercise's health benefits by exposure to carbon monoxide, ozone, oxides of sulfur and nitrogen, particulate matter, and hundreds of other toxic chemicals. Increased depth and rate of breathing during aerobic exercise magnifies the detrimental effects of polluted air. I am always amazed to see joggers running along heavily traveled city streets, where exhaust fumes are concentrated and air quality is poor. They could just as easily be in the cleaner air of the side streets nearby. Be sure to exercise in a location as far away from traffic as you can get.

Now that you're familiar with all of the components of the Renewal Anti-Aging Program, your next step is to incorporate them into your lifestyle. Chapter 38 will show you how.

PART 7
Renewal for Life

CHAPTER 38

Implementing the Renewal Anti-Aging Program

A light heart lives long.
—WILLIAM SHAKESPEARE

This is an exciting time to be alive—the dawning of a new era in medicine. Respected researchers are engaged in serious discussions about the prospects for living longer than ever thought possible. The disorders once viewed as inevitable consequences of "normal" aging—including cancer, heart disease, high blood pressure, Type II (non-insulin-dependent) diabetes, stroke, autoimmune disorders, and osteoporosis—have now been shown to be preventable and, with early detection, even reversible. The challenge has become to either flat-out prevent these age-related degenerative diseases or to detect them, through aggressive testing, in those early stages when they can still be reversed by natural and nutritional therapies.

All the information I've presented in the previous pages is about being healthier now, not just living longer. Optimum health and longevity are inseparable. They are opposite sides of the same coin. Through Renewal, you can grow old—very old—and remain healthy and happy and vital until the end.

Armed with all of the information in this book, you are now ready to design your personal Anti-Aging Program.

After that, in the following section, I'll show you how to monitor your program's effectiveness.

WINNING THE BATTLE WITHIN

In chapters 2 and 3, I described in detail the lifelong battle raging within each of us: the free radicals versus the antioxidants. We are very fortunate. No other generation in human history has been granted access to the incredible molecular biological window through which we can view the hand-to-hand, molecule-to-molecule combat being waged in our cells between the friendly, protective antioxidant molecules and those belligerent free radicals, hell-bent on causing disease and destroying us. Never before has it been possible to make enlightened and systematic choices that shift the balance in this battle in our favor. Now we can.

By following the Renewal Anti-Aging Program, you are supporting your natural healing systems, preventing free radical oxidation, fortifying your organ and energy systems, and protecting your cells. You're enhancing Renewal and setting the stage for a longer, healthier life span.

THE ANTI-AGING DIET

You already know that the Anti-Aging Diet is a low-fat, vegan eating plan based on the New Four Food Groups: grains, legumes, fruits, and vegetables. Beginning on page 535, you'll find a 14-day menu plan, more than 30 recipes, and meal ideas galore—all created to help you make the Anti-Aging Diet part of your lifestyle.

The quickest, simplest way to pack the maximum quantities of health-supporting, phytochemical-rich, antioxidant-bearing nutrients into your diet is to make juices, smoothies, soups, and salads. I recommend investing in a large blender—one with a motor that's powerful enough to shred—and using it every day to make fresh fruit and vegetable juices. This way of juicing preserves the phytochemicals in fruits and vegetables, most of which are heat-sensitive.

The phytochemicals in grains, legumes, and onions, garlic, squash, yams, potatoes, and other starchy vegetables are fairly heat-stable. Use these foods to make pots of simple, wholesome soups.

THE ANTI-AGING SUPPLEMENT PROGRAM

For optimum health, even a fantastic diet requires supplementation. As you customize the Anti-Aging Supplement Program to meet your particular needs, keep in mind the basic premises of Renewal. First, you are protecting your cells from damage. Second, you are promoting cellular repair. Third, you are encouraging cellular regeneration.

Always start with the basics: the essential nutrients. Be sure your program includes all of the vitamins, minerals, essential fatty acids, and coenzyme Q_{10}. This can be accomplished by taking a high-quality multivitamin/mineral formula, a flaxseed oil/borage oil combination supplement, and a coenzyme Q_{10} capsule. (The recommended doses are provided in chapter 23.) The essential nutrients are essential for a reason: Without them, your body can't perform the most fundamental operations of cellular Renewal.

Next, add the anti-aging hormones. If you are over age 40 and want to safely extend your life span, then tap into the astonishing harvest of health benefits provided by the superhormones dehydroepiandrosterone (DHEA) and pregnenolone. Production of these hormones declines with age, while higher levels are closely linked to freedom from degenerative diseases and longer life spans. A reasonable starting dose for DHEA is 15 milligrams twice daily for women and 25 milligrams twice daily for men. For pregnenolone, 50 milligrams twice daily is a conservative starting dose for both men and women.

After a couple of months, you might want to test your DHEA and pregnenolone levels. This can be done using either saliva or serum. (See Resources and References on page 591.) Optimum levels for both hormones are those of a 30-year-old. Though not absolutely essential, testing will give you feedback to help fine-tune your dose. Although a consultation with an alternative-minded physician might prove helpful, it is not necessary. Both hormones and tests are available without a prescription.

You also won't want to miss out on the anti-aging benefits of melatonin. You can purchase this anti-insomnia, antioxidant, anti-aging, stress-reducing superhormone at just about any pharmacy or health food store. Take mela-

---

Powering Up Your Supplement Program

The chapters on anti-aging supplements provide information about the nutrients, herbs, internal cleansers, and hormones you need. Here are a few more tips to help you get the most from your supplement program.

Set your own schedule. The optimum dosing regimen is not set in stone. Figure out what schedule works best for you, then follow it. Having prescribed hundreds of supplement programs to my patients, I have found that the level of complexity is inversely proportional to the rate of compliance. (In plain English: If it gets too complicated, people won't do it.) I usually recommend twice-a-day dosing: morning (with breakfast or lunch) and evening (with dinner or at bedtime). You can spread out your supplements even more, if you like. But it's usually not necessary.

Replace pills with foods. To reduce the total number of pills that you're taking each day, try getting certain nutrients from foods. For example, use liquid essential

---

tonin only at bedtime—0.5 to 1 milligram if you sleep soundly, more if you need help with sleep.

If you are a woman and a candidate for hormone replacement therapy, consider taking natural estrogen and natural progesterone. This must be done in cooperation with your physician.

Women and men over 40 who are losing libido may want to consider testosterone replacement therapy. Patches or pills are available by prescription only. This hormone can safely revitalize your sex life.

Hypothyroidism is widespread. As much as 40 percent of the population may have it. Replacement therapy with natural thyroid hormone, when appropriate, can work miracles. You'll need the help of a nutritional medicine physician here.

Because we need them to protect us in our ongoing war against the degenerative diseases of aging, the anti-aging antioxidants, phytochemicals, and herbs will further improve your chances of reaching that goal of 120 years—

fatty acids—flaxseed oil and borage oil—as butter substitutes on your morning toast. (I've been doing this for years and I love it.) Add fresh garlic to foods rather than taking garlic capsules. Chew on a slice of ginseng root, or steep it in boiling water for a tea.

Replace pills with drinks. Certain supplement formulations can be mixed with water or juice to create a pleasant-tasting drink. For availability information, refer to Resources and References.

Take your supplements in cycles. Stretch a recommended dosage over a longer period of time. Instead of squeezing 10 500-milligram tablets of vitamin C into one day, spread them out over a day and a half. You'll start a new supplement "cycle" every other day. (This technique is not appropriate for hormones, which should be taken daily in the prescribed doses.)

Go slowly. If your body has never before had the luxury of an abundance of Renewal-promoting nutrients, you'll need to give it time to adjust to supernutrition. Add one supplement at a time, starting with the smallest possible dose and increasing gradually.

or beyond. Each of these offers a unique spectrum of benefits—and they enhance each other's effectiveness. So consuming a wide variety is advisable.

Are your levels of antioxidants high enough to protect you against the free radicals in your body? Testing will answer this question. (The antioxidant profile and oxidative stress panel are described a bit later in the chapter.) This information is of more than academic interest. Assessing antioxidant levels and degree of free radical damage not only translates directly into rate of aging but also provides exactly the information you need to take corrective action.

Armed with the results of these tests, supplementation can be targeted to replace deficient nutrients, thus plugging the holes in the antioxidant protective armor. For antioxidants already at optimum levels, more needn't be taken. But if vitamins E or C or coenzyme Q_{10} is low, you can supplement each to improve antioxidant protection, support Renewal, and slow aging.

Fiber and acidophilus supplementation is optional. More than one-third of the U.S. population has intestinal parasites and/or an overgrowth of "bad bacterial bugs." These critters alter the milieu in your intestinal tract. If you have digestive symptoms such as gas, bloating, cramps, indigestion, constipation, or diarrhea, you probably need fiber and acidophilus.

The brain nutrients (phosphatidylserine, acetyl-L-carnitine, pregnenolone, and ginkgo) can be used to help slow down the progression of brain disease in persons who—regardless of cause—are already experiencing memory loss or cognitive decline. If you are over age 50, these nutrients can help protect against age-related cognitive dysfunction. And at any age, used on a short-term basis, they'll help sharpen your wits and improve your IQ. At school or at work, if you use your brain in what you do, these cognitive enhancers can help improve your intellectual performance.

Supplements vary tremendously in quality, from very good to very bad. Likewise, prices for the same nutrient differ from one supplement supplier to the next. Certain companies specialize in highest-purity, highest-quality nutrients. (See Resources and References on page 591 for a list of the best companies and products.)

THE ANTI-AGING EXERCISE PROGRAM

This is both the easiest and the hardest part of the program. Unlike diet and supplements, which can be complicated, it's easy to understand what good exercise consists of. Actually doing it—setting aside the time and building a workable program into your life—is what's hard. If you are having difficulty, consider joining a gym and/or getting some help from a personal trainer.

Combine aerobics and strength training. Stretch. Go for variety. And remember, couch potatoes are guaranteed losers in the longevity game.

HOW DO YOU KNOW IT'S WORKING?

Once you've been on the Anti-Aging Program for a few months, you'll feel better—a lot better. But as the months and years roll by, how will you know whether you are achieving optimal results?

Well, you'll have more energy. Your skin will look healthier; and you'll notice that cuts and bruises heal faster. (Though you can't see it, this is happening on the inside as well.) You'll observe that even though you are not immune to colds and flus, they'll be less frequent, less severe, and shorter-lived. At times, you'll even escape a bug that everyone else seems to be catching. There'll be a sparkle in your step and a twinkle in your eye.

People will notice these changes. They'll say things like "You look better," "You seem happier," and "What are you doing?" By all means, tell them.

BIOMARKERS: THE BEST MEASURE OF SUCCESS

These subjective observations are perfectly valid. But laboratory testing can add a valuable dimension that will provide the objective information you need to fine-tune your program.

Keeping your Anti-Aging Program on track is like finding your way to an unfamiliar part of town: You need a road map. Testing is your road map to longevity. It will tell you whether you're headed in the right direction, and if you get lost, it will help you get back on track.

Tests—technically called biomarkers of aging—identify biochemical, hormonal, immunologic, or metabolic changes that are linked with aging. Testing provides a sine qua non for those who wish to live as long and healthy a life as possible. Because tests provide a special window through which to view your body's subtlest inner workings, they facilitate identification of treament choices and can be used to monitor the effectiveness of your treatment program.

Although your innards may seem astonishingly complex, they're not beyond comprehension. Do you remember that scene in *The Wizard of Oz* when Dorothy and her friends confronted the Wizard? Actually a kindly man, the Wizard had succeeded in fooling and intimidating everyone into believing he was utterly omnipotent. Then Toto blew his cover by pulling back the curtain he was hiding behind. Once exposed, the demystified Wizard didn't seem so scary, and a hopeless predicament was suddenly infused with possibilities.

Medical testing pulls back a similar curtain, revealing an

intimate view of your inner workings and opening up previously inaccessible therapeutic avenues. Testing can reveal whether, for example, free radicals are having a field day beating up on your antioxidants, or whether your thyroid or DHEA are low, or whether heart disease or osteoporosis is developing, or whether you have nutrient deficiencies.

EARLY DETECTION REQUIRES TESTING

Alternative and anti-aging medicines assume a spectrum of possible levels of wellness, maintained by your healing systems. Disease happens when these healing systems malfunction. By shifting the focus to earlier in the disease process, to the transitional zone of dysfunction that lies between wellness and overt pathology, we can detect a disease in the making. Then natural treatments can be used to get the body's healing systems back on track, to slow down the disease or reverse it before more serious pathology—requiring more toxic treatments—emerges.

Earlier detection (hopefully before the point of irreversibility) is the driving idea behind a new approach called "functional" testing. Functional testing searches out causative factors, be they digestive, infectious, physiological, biochemical, metabolic, hormonal, organic, or nutritional. Often multiple systems are involved, and often digestive dysfunction and nutrient deficits exacerbate the patient's condition. Rather than ignoring the problem or using symptom-suppressive drug therapies, functional testing attempts to identify dysfunctional tendencies and correct them before they have evolved into distinct pathological entities.

The information that testing provides is tremendously empowering. It supports Renewal in three ways. First, testing provides a means for early detection of any metabolic imbalances that you might have, which, unchecked, would eventually lead to overt or more serious disease. Second, testing produces empowering information you can use to design your Anti-Aging Program. Third, repeat testing provides feedback about the effectiveness of your program, so you can fine-tune it.

Chances are, unless you have an exceptional doctor, he will be unaware of this new approach. Most doctors have not been schooled in alternative and preventive methods, and they may not be familiar with some of the tests commonly used in alternative medical practices. For help in finding doctors familiar with these approaches, refer to Resources and References on page 591.

Getting Tested

Doctors in the fields of alternative and anti-aging medicine often use the following tests to check the body's various systems and uncover any imbalances that may lead to disease. This list doesn't include all of the diagnostic techniques currently available. Your doctor can help you determine which, if any, of these tests you need.

Antioxidant profile. Measures the most important antioxidant nutrients: vitamin A, vitamin C, vitamin E (alpha-tocopherol and gamma-tocopherol), coenzyme Q_{10}, alpha-carotene, beta-carotene, lycopene, and glutathione.

Comprehensive digestive stool analysis. Useful for assessing digestive function, as are the hepatic detoxification profile and intestinal permeability profile.

Dual photon absorptiometry. Detects the gradual loss of bone density that leads to osteoporosis, as does the N-telopeptide urine test.

Food allergy test. A blood test that identifies 100 antibodies produced by the body in response to specific food allergens.

HeartScan. Detects atherosclerotic plaque, which can lead to arterial hardening and clogging.

Oxidative stress profile. Assesses the degree of free radical damage in the body by measuring levels of glutathione and of oxidized fats. Glutathione is the main antioxidant produced by the body to protect cells against free radical attack. Oxidized fats (also known as serum lipid peroxides) are fatty acid molecules that have been altered by free radicals. If glutathione is low and/or oxidized fats are high, your body's protective shield has been breached, and free radicals are running rampant.

Prostate-specific antigen test. Detects prostate cancer.

FINAL THOUGHTS

I make a lot of recommendations in this book. No one could follow them all. It is important, however, to take a minute or two to write down what you are willing to do. Everyone has a different starting point: You may already be a vegetarian, but you may not be taking supplements—or vice versa. Write down the diet you plan to follow, the exact supplements you are going to start with, and the exercise program you are willing to commit to. Don't be overly ambitious: You can always increase what you are doing later, after you've established a baseline.

You have plenty of time to make these changes. Don't feel overwhelmed or give up in desperation. Integrating all my recommended changes into your daily life is not easy. It's not necessary to change abruptly to the Anti-Aging Program. We are creatures of habit, and change—meaningful change—doesn't happen overnight. Give yourself all the time you need. First make the changes that are easy for you. Save the hard stuff for later. If you make the commitment and work at it, you'll get there.

You can do all or any part of this program. Although positive changes will produce positive results at any age, the sooner you start, the better. And remember: *The extent to which you follow the Renewal Anti-Aging Program determines the extent to which you'll benefit from it.*

Epilogue

Youth has no age.
—PABLO PICASSO (1881–1973)

Completion has always been difficult for me. This book was no exception. Having finished writing drafts of all of the chapters, I wanted to compose an eloquent epilogue that consolidated and integrated the book's diverse array of concepts. I wanted my final words to provide some practical advice about how to get started on the Renewal Anti-Aging Program and how to monitor its effectiveness. And finally, I wanted to send you off with just enough enlightened self-confidence that you'd know you could succeed.

Having studied, practiced, and taught Chinese traditional medicine for more than a quarter-century, I've come to appreciate the Taoist philosophy upon which it is based. Over the years, whenever I was in trouble, or needed advice or inspiration, or was unsure how to handle a difficult situation, I would consult the *I Ching* (*Book of Changes*), the Taoist Chinese oracle.

After I had written—and discarded—a few drafts of this epilogue, I knew it was time to ask for some sage advice, so I brought out my dog-eared copy of the *I Ching*. I threw my ancient Chinese *I Ching* coins, asking the oracle to provide me with some kind of conceptual framework for viewing this final chapter.

I asked: "What final words of wisdom can I leave my readers with?"

The answer came back loud and clear.

The first hexagram (representing a judgment of what is happening now) was number seven: *Shih*, or the Army. *Shih* is a symbol for the internal strength one stores up for protection and for potential use against an enemy. The *I Ching* was encouraging me to reemphasize the importance of creating a strong healing system—an internal army— with which to accomplish the goals of Renewal: protection from damage, repair, and regeneration. This army uses weapons such as essential nutrients and antioxidants to help you win your lifelong war against free radicals.

I can't imagine a better image to characterize the goals of the Anti-Aging Program than an army. An army has strength, discipline, cohesion, and a reluctance to fight. It preserves peace by virtue of its strength. In order to become an effective disease-fighting force, your internal army must also be organized (that is, you need an Anti-Aging Program) and disciplined (you need to actually follow the program).

When a hexagram has changing lines, as mine did, the *I Ching* makes a second judgment—its prediction for the future. To my astonishment and delight, the hexagram changed to number 14: *Ta Yu*, Possession in Great Measure. The text for *Ta Yu* reads, "The time is favorable—a time of strength within, clarity and culture without. Power is expressing itself in a graceful and controlled way. This brings supreme success and wealth." This means that if you create a strong internal army by following the Anti-Aging Diet, Anti-Aging Supplement Program, and Anti-Aging Exercise Program, you can expect to achieve Possession in Great Measure—a longer, richer, healthier life.

A CHANGING MEDICAL PARADIGM

The Renewal Anti-Aging Program advocates personal change. On a grander scale, it fosters a changing vision of health and healing—and a new way of practicing medicine.

The day will soon arrive when physicians must consider a heart attack or a stroke not a call to therapeutic action but a failure of traditional medical methodology. Mainstream medicine's Johnny-come-lately interventions are no longer acceptable. We must find a way to encourage doctors to teach prevention. We need a shift toward earlier diagnosis. And we need to replace drugs and surgery with a gentler approach in which natural therapies restore balance and harmony, enabling the body to heal itself.

Doctors of the future will focus on early detection, utilizing diagnostic testing that surveys the biological terrain and identifies nutritional, hormonal, functional, and metabolic imbalances. These imbalances will be corrected, perhaps even before symptoms appear, with the help of natural therapies and health-promoting lifestyle changes that nurture the body's healing systems.

Physicians specializing in alternative, nutritional, and anti-aging medicine are well ahead of the curve. They already use these principles in their practices.

CAN PATIENTS SAVE THEIR DOCTORS?

Those of us alternative physicians who have been in the trenches, dodging flak from the mainstreamers for decades, can thank our lucky stars for emerging grassroots support of our "cause." A growing number of Americans have embraced the wisdom of natural and holistic medical models. And they haven't been afraid to tell their mainstream doctors that a naturopathic physician, a nutritional doctor, an herbalist, a homeopath, an osteopath, or an acupuncturist helped them when orthodox medicine failed.

Thank goodness for you, the patient. Left to the medical establishment, the government, and the drug industry (what I call the medical-industrial complex), the new medical paradigm would have been torpedoed long ago. Alternative medicine and optimum health are increasingly preferred by the average person. "Wellness" has become a household word. Having suffered two decades of rejection by the medical establishment, alternative medicine is now on the verge of going mainstream—if it hasn't already.

Some encouraging signs: The *New England Journal of Medicine* has reported that more people are making more visits to alternative practitioners than to mainstream doctors. Recent sales graph trajectories for the health foods and supplements industry resemble the liftoff of the space shuttle: The industry's gross income topped $9 billion last year. And the National Institutes of Health has established an Office of Alternative Medicine, earmarking $40 million for natural healing research.

In 1994, Congress passed the Dietary Health and Supplement Education Act—despite intense lobbying against it by the Food and Drug Administration and the drug industry. The new law redefines supplements as foods (which puts their use in the hands of the public) rather than as drugs (which places them under FDA control). In other words, it encourages people to take responsibility for their own health.

The massive outpouring of public support for what is popularly known as the Health Freedom Act is a measure of the timeliness of the new medical paradigm. And it happened before alternative health guru Andrew Weil, M.D., made the cover of *Time* magazine.

We new-paradigm doctors are deeply indebted to the millions of patients who courageously called their elected officials to fight for these changes. But it is not a good sign that, on average, patients discover the importance of natural medicine long before their doctors. The former are now further burdened with the task of dragging the latter, kicking and screaming, into the medicine of the twenty-first century.

To its credit (I guess), the American Medical Association has now adopted a "We can't beat 'em (and don't think we haven't tried, but they refuse to go away), so we'd better join 'em" attitude. Even though mainstream doctors know that alternative medicine is an idea whose time has come, they are challenged by the paradigm shift required to comprehend its essence.

I've emphasized the importance of nurturing your healing systems and avoiding foods, chemicals, and other practices that interfere with them. Please support a medicine of the future in which the importance of Renewal is appreciated and doctors prescribe natural and preventive therapies that support our bodies' healing systems.

HEADING FOR HOME

Shortly after completing the manuscript for this book, I found myself homeward bound on a flight from a conference I had attended. With the pressure of writing deadlines behind me for the first time in many months, I settled back in my seat, relishing—finally—a chance to pause and reflect.

It was an exceptionally clear day, and as the plane headed south toward the San Francisco Bay Area, I spotted Mount Rainier. It reminded me of the year I'd just completed—writing in solitude, spending too much time away from my wife and daughters, completing this massive project. I felt for all the world like I had climbed a mountain.

A little later, as we followed the Pacific coastline southward, the great redwood forests appeared in my window. They reminded me of how fragile our ecosystems can be, both internal and external—and the importance of protecting our health and that of our planet.

Then as my plane continued south over the fertile farmlands of my home in Sonoma County, I thought about my wonderful wife and of our hopes and dreams for the health and welfare of our two daughters, and of how much I'd missed them all during the past year.

When we circled over Berkeley, where I have practiced for 30 years, I thought of the many patients who have benefited from the Renewal Anti-Aging Program. I thought about my good friend Steve, who reversed his collision course with a heart attack by going on the program. I thought of Linda, who went on the program following a lumpectomy. She has gone 10 years now without a recurrence, is far healthier than before her malignancy, and is considered "cured." I thought about Madge, whose arthritis was so crippling that she limped into my office. She now walks her dog and plays golf every day. I thought about Jean, who was crippled by chronic fatigue syndrome but has now returned to work.

And I thought about my mother, Elizabeth, who has been on the Renewal Anti-Aging Program longer than anyone else. At age 85, Mom is healthier than many 50-year-olds. She is the most dramatic example of what the

Renewal Anti-Aging Program can do. In great shape, she is going strong—an inspiration to us all. She has no disease and requires no medications. A retired author and English professor, she has remained mentally sharp as a tack—with the assistance of brain nutrients. She published a medical journal article last year and is now working on a new play. She jogs, walks her dog, and does aerobics every day. She became a vegetarian 15 years ago and takes most of the supplements I recommend in this book (though not all of them every day).

As we banked to the west, then back north, I looked out over the Pacific Ocean. Dazzled by the sun's reflection on the water, I thought about my return to "real life"—no longer a sequestered author, back to practicing medicine full-time and spending more time playing with my kids and hiking in the woods with my wife.

As we made our final approach to the airport, my thoughts turned to this book and all the people who would read it, and I wondered whether it would make a difference in their lives. I wondered whether I had succeeded in my attempts to turn some daunting biochemistry into user-friendly information. I wondered whether it was presumptuous of me to be telling folks that if they followed my advice they could live longer. But then I remembered all of the hundreds of patients, like Steve and Linda and Madge, who had benefited.

And as the plane touched down, I realized that all my life as a physician, I've been blessed with a career in which I've had the opportunity to make a real difference in people's lives. Until I wrote this book, however, it was pretty much one person at a time. Now I've been granted the great good fortune of this opportunity to make a difference in many people's lives.

My hope—my dream—is that this book will help you to transform your life, that it will provide wings with which you can soar through a life that is not only longer but healthier and happier as well. Writing it will have been amply rewarded if these ideas help you—and those you love—to achieve the bold promise of the *I Ching*: Possession in Great Measure.

Anti-Aging Medicine is a new and rapidly evolving medical specialty. For research updates and a free copy of my quarterly newsletter, information about my exclusive nutrient formulations, and referrals to anti-aging doctors in your area, please contact me.

Timothy J. Smith, M.D.
2635 Regent St.
Berkeley, CA 94704
Phone: (510) 548-8022

Anti-Aging Medicine Center of Northern California
321 South Main Street, PMB 41
Sebastopol, CA 95472
Phone: (800) 555-1459 or (707) 824-0110
Fax: (707) 824-0111

Please visit my web site at www.renewalnow.com.

Tools for Renewal

Renewal 14-Day
Menu Plan

To ease your transition to the Renewal Anti-Aging Diet—a low-fat, vegan diet based on the New Four Food Groups—here's a simple 14-day menu plan for you to follow. The plan will familiarize you with appropriate food choices for the Anti-Aging Diet. It will also introduce you to dozens of exciting new dishes that you can prepare for yourself and your family.

As you read through the menu plan below, you'll notice that some of the food suggestions have page numbers following them. These refer you to either the Renewal Meal Ideas (beginning on page 541) or the Renewal Recipes (beginning on page 550). There you'll find specific instructions for the preparation of each dish. For beverage suggestions, refer to page 252.

As you become accustomed to eating for Renewal, you can make substitutions in the menus below or develop your own weekly plans. As long as you stick with the New Four Food Groups—grains, legumes, fruits, and vegetables—you can't go wrong.

Day 1

Breakfast
Fruit or fruit smoothie
Cold cereal with soy or
rice milk

Whole-Wheat Pancakes
(page 552)
Hot beverage (herbal
tea or grain beverage)

Lunch
    Roll-up with hummus
    and vegetables (page
    544) or sandwich (page
    544)
    Raw or steamed veg-
    etables

Dinner
    Bean and Corn Enchi-
    ladas (page 579)
    Salsa Fresca (page 564)
    Green salad with dress-
    ing
    Berry Banana Sorbet
    (page 588) or fruit

Day 2

Breakfast
    Orange slices
    Hot organic whole-
    grain cereal with soy or
    rice milk
    Whole-grain toast with
    almond butter and/or
    fruit spread
    Hot beverage

Lunch
    Baked potato topped
    with canned vegetarian
    chili, beans, or other
    creative topping (page
    543)
    Green salad with dress-
    ing
    Fruit or fruit smoothie

Dinner
    Vegetable curry (page
    583)
    Steamed brown rice
    Raw vegetables with
    Vegetable and Herb
    Tofu Dip (page 563) or
    green salad with dress-
    ing
    Fruit or fruit smoothie

Day 3

Breakfast
    Cold cereal with sliced
    bananas and soy or rice
    milk
    Applesauce-Oat
    Muffins (page 556)
    Hot beverage

Lunch
    Leftover Vegetable
    Curry in a whole-wheat
    tortilla or pita
    Green salad with
    dressing, or raw veg-
    etables
    Fruit or fruit smoothie

Dinner
    Crackers or bread with
    Freeke's Eggplant
    Caviar (page 560)
    Pasta with tomato
    sauce
    Green salad with Del-
    lie's Delicious Dressing
    (page 575)
    Fruit salad or frozen
    fruit sorbet

Day 4

Breakfast
Hot seven-grain cereal
with fruit and soy or
rice milk
Whole-grain toast
Hot beverage

Lunch
Tofu burger on a bun
with lettuce, tomatoes,
and condiments
Low-fat corn chips and
salsa
Carrot sticks
Fruit or fruit smoothie

Dinner
Shepherd's Pie (page
585)
Steamed seasonal veg-
etables
Green salad with dress-
ing
Hot whole-grain bread
or muffin
Cinnamon-Baked
Apples (page 590)

Day 5

Breakfast
Cold cereal with fruit
and soy or rice milk
Whole-grain toast or
muffin
Hot beverage

Lunch
Baked sweet potato
Rice crackers or low-
fat chips with Zesty
Bean Spread (page 561)
Fruit or fruit smoothie

Dinner
Minestrone (page 568)
Steamed seasonal veg-
etables
Green salad with dress-
ing
Cornbread (page 557)
Spicy Fruit Compote
(page 589)

Day 6

Breakfast
Cold cereal with fruit
and soy or rice milk
Nabolom's Raisin Bran
Muffins (page 554) or
toast
Hot beverage

Lunch
Leftover Minestrone or
sandwich
Raw carrots, cauli-
flower, and celery with
Vegetable and Herb
Tofu Dip (page 563)
Whole-grain bread

Dinner
Stuffed Winter Squash
(page 582)
Steamed vegetables
and/or green salad with
dressing
Pumpkin Bread (page
558)

Day 7

Breakfast
Warmed Pumpkin
Bread (page 558) or
toast
Cold cereal with
banana slices and rice
or soy milk
Hot beverage

Lunch
Miso Vegetable Soup
(page 566) or tofu dog
in whole-grain bun
Whole-grain bread or
rice crackers
Applesauce

Dinner
Polenta with Rata-
touille (page 584)
Green salad with dress-
ing
Gingerbread (page 559)

Day 8

Breakfast
Hot cereal with fruit
and soy or rice milk
Whole-grain toast or
muffin
Hot beverage

Lunch
Sandwich made with
almond butter and fruit
spread
Raw vegetables and
Creamy Hummus Dip
(page 562)
Fruit smoothie

Dinner
Savory Baked Tofu
(page 577)
Baked potato
Asian Coleslaw (page
574) or green salad
with dressing
Cinnamon-Baked
Apples (page 590) or
fresh fruit or fruit
smoothie

Day 9

Breakfast
Hot seven-grain cereal
with berries or banana
slices and soy or rice
milk
Whole-grain toast
Hot beverage

Lunch
Sandwich made with
Savory Baked Tofu
(page 577)
Carrot sticks
Pretzels
Applesauce or fresh
fruit or fruit smoothie

Dinner
Gazpacho (page 565)
Steamed seasonal veg-
etables
Tricolor Pasta Salad
(page 573)
Cornbread (page 557)
or whole-grain bread
Low-fat juice cookies

Day 10

Breakfast
One-half grapefruit
Cold cereal with soy or
rice milk
Whole-grain toast or
muffin
Hot beverage

Lunch
Lentil Soup (page 569)
with whole-grain bread
or soy cheese sandwich
Orange slices

Dinner
Middle Eastern Chick-
pea Stew (page 567)
Whole-wheat couscous
Green salad with dress-
ing
Melon-Peach Sorbet
(page 588)

Day 11

Breakfast
Kiwifruit or one-half
grapefruit
Banana Muffins (page
555)
Hot beverage

Lunch
Middle Eastern Chick-
pea Stew (page 567)
rolled in a tortilla or
pita or veggie burger on
a bun with condiments
Steamed or raw broc-
coli and carrots
Fruit or fruit smoothie

Dinner
Red Rice with Corn
and Black Beans (page
581)
Salsa Fresca (page 564)
Warm corn tortillas
Jicama, Orange, and
Cilantro Salad (page
574)
Low-fat juice cookies
or sorbet

Day 12

Breakfast
Orange slices
Larry's Famous Oat-
meal (page 551)
Hot beverage

Lunch
Leftover Red Rice with
Corn and Black Beans
(page 581) in a whole-
wheat tortilla with let-
tuce and tomatoes
Grapes or other sea-
sonal fruit

Dinner
Teriyaki Tofu and Broc-
coli (page 576)
Steamed brown rice
Green salad with dress-
ing
Berry Banana Sorbet
(page 588)

Day 13

Breakfast
Waffle made from
organic low-fat mix,
topped with fruit
Hot beverage

Lunch
Potato-Leek Soup (page
570) or ramen with
tofu and vegetables
Whole-grain bread or
rice crackers
Fruit or fruit smoothie

Dinner
Quick Burritos (page
578)
Green salad with dress-
ing
Sebastopol Apple Crisp
(page 587)

Day 14

Breakfast
Tofu and Oven Pota-
toes (page 553)
Whole-grain toast or
muffins
Hot beverage

Lunch
Quinoa with steamed
vegetables or soy
cheese sandwich
Carrot sticks
Fruit or fruit smoothie

Dinner
Healthy pizza (page
547)
Confetti Rice Salad
(page 572)
Fruit sorbet

Renewal Meal Ideas

Maybe you have only a few minutes to get a meal on the table. Or maybe you simply don't want to spend a lot of time in the kitchen. Either way, let the following meal ideas come to your rescue. They're fast and easy to prepare, and they fit perfectly in the Anti-Aging Diet. They make ideal substitutions for the foods in the 14-day menu plan beginning on page 535.

BREAKFAST: SIMPLE STARTS

Many people skip breakfast because they're convinced that they don't have time to eat. The following selections can be ready to go when you are.

Cereals. On cold winter mornings, nothing warms you up like a bowl of hot cereal. Choose oatmeal, seven-grain, rice, or cream of wheat. Top it with raisins, dates, or sliced fruit and rice milk or soy milk.

Among ready-to-eat cereals, whole-grain varieties are your healthiest choices. Some examples include fat-free granola or muesli, flaked cereals, puffed cereals, and shredded wheat. Add berries, sliced bananas, or other fruit and rice milk or soy milk.

Speaking of soy milk . . . if you tried it in the past but couldn't stand the chalky taste, I have some good news: Soy milk isn't what it used to be. Manufacturers have improved the taste tremendously. Even kids love it—and if you start them on it early, they'll grow up free of the health-eroding, immunity-suppressing dairy addiction so prevalent among youngsters today.

Personally, I've also become an aficionado of rice milk. It goes great on cereal, hot or cold.

Fresh fruits. Apples, bananas, berries, grapefruit, kiwifruit, melons, oranges—take your pick. If fresh fruit isn't readily available, opt for frozen and thaw it in the microwave.

Fruit juices. Fresh-squeezed is best. If you prefer bottled for convenience, make sure it's organic.

Fruit smoothies. These blender drinks whip up fast. Make them from whatever fruits (fresh or frozen) you have on hand. Add rice or soy milk for creaminess.

Muffins. Low-fat, dairy-free vegan muffins are not always easy to find. If you do come across them, buy several and freeze them. Try low-fat, lightly sweetened bran or wheat muffins. Or if you have time, you can bake your own using one of the delicious recipes beginning on page 554.

Pancakes and waffles. Look for an organic mix to which you can add rice milk or soy milk for delicious pancakes and waffles. Top them with fruit spread or a little maple syrup for a real breakfast treat.

Soy Foods. There is no law that says you can eat only traditional breakfast fare. Why not have hot miso soup or rice and tofu for breakfast?

Toast. By "toast," I mean bread that is warmed, not browned or burned. (Browning and burning, you'll recall, generate oodles of free radicals.) As for spreads, use your imagination. Try a small amount (a level teaspoon or less) of almond butter, topped with berries or pureed fresh fruit. Or try applesauce—especially the fruit-flavored varieties. The kind with cherries is positively delicious. Other suggestions: organic fruit puree or fruit conserves, apple butter, mashed bananas, and flaxseed oil.

LUNCH: MIDDAY MEALS IN MINUTES

You can use the following dishes as basic building blocks for a variety of meals. Just vary the ingredients and seasonings.

Baked potatoes with toppings. Potatoes are rich in vitamins B and C, iron, and protein. Just one makes a complete meal. Like tofu, a potato goes with just about anything and takes on the flavors of whatever it's paired with. So the possibilities for toppings are truly endless. Here are a few personal favorites.

- Baked beans (from a can)
- Dijon mustard mixed with fresh lemon juice
- Mango chutney
- Organic tomato pasta sauce (from a jar)
- Salsa
- Steamed broccoli, carrots, green or sweet red or yellow peppers, or other vegetables
- Stewed tomatoes sprinkled with an herb vinegar
- Stir-fried vegetables
- Sweet-and-sour sauce with pineapple and vegetables
- Tofu cubes marinated in garlic, ginger, soy sauce, and vinegar
- Tofu sour cream (mashed tofu mixed with lemon juice and a dash of soy sauce)
- Vegetable curry
- Vegetable stew
- Vegetarian chili (from a can)
- Zucchini stewed with onions and tomatoes

Burgers. Replace those greasy hamburgers with soy burgers, tempeh burgers, and veggie burgers. For a fast-food–style burger without all the fat and calories, try this simple "recipe": Cook a veggie burger according to the package instructions, then put it in a warmed organic whole-grain bun. Add lettuce or cabbage, tomatoes, red onions, sprouts, pickle or pickle relish, and your favorite condiments.

Burritos. You'll find vegan burritos, along with other low-fat ready-made entrées and à la carte items, in the frozen foods section of your health food store. For a complete lunch, just microwave a burrito and serve it with carrots or a baked potato and applesauce or a piece of fresh fruit.

Hot dogs. Tofu hot dogs make superb substitutes for nitrate-laden regular hot dogs. Store them in the freezer, and when you're hungry for one, just pop one in the microwave. You can serve the frank in a whole-grain bun, on a slice of whole-grain bread, or in a tortilla. Top it with lettuce, tomatoes, mustard, ketchup, or other low-fat toppings, and you have a great-tasting, wholesome lunch.

You can also pair tofu hot dogs with canned vegetarian baked beans or vegetarian chili. Be sure to read labels, though: These canned products can be high in fat.

Roll-ups with hummus and vegetables. Start with a whole-wheat tortilla. Add hummus, grated carrots, grated cabbage, chopped tomatoes, and chopped lettuce. Drizzle with a little low-fat dressing and roll it up.

Salads. Here's an opportunity to exercise your culinary creativity. First, prepare a basic salad by combining your choice of the following ingredients: lettuce, spinach, cabbage, bok choy, carrots, celery, scallions, tomatoes, cucumbers, and sprouts of all kinds. Then experiment. Maybe you have some leftover pasta, rice, or steamed vegetables to toss into your salad. Some cooked beans, steamed potatoes, or marinated tofu chunks to mix with the other ingredients. Or some broccoli stalks or raw beets to grate over top. Add low-fat dressing as well as a few sunflower seeds or walnuts for extra crunch. There you have it—a veritable green feast.

Sandwiches. Use whole-wheat, oat, or multigrain bread or whole-wheat pita bread. For filling, use your imagination. You might try a microwaved tofu burger, baked tofu (you can make your own using the recipe on page 577), soy cheese, canned beans (such as vegetarian baked beans) mashed into a tasty pâté, or leftovers from dinner the night before. Then for crunch and moisture, add lettuce, tomato slices, cucumber slices, shredded carrots, sprouts, or spinach leaves.

You can even put a new, healthy spin on the classic peanut butter and jelly sandwich. Trade in the peanut butter for almond butter, which has a better essential fatty acid profile. (But it's still high in fat, so use it sparingly.) Instead of jelly, use fruit conserves or a small amount of honey.

Soups. You can turn virtually any combination of ingredients into a soup. To make it as nutritionally complete as possible, be sure to include a grain and/or beans as well as vegetables. You can choose from the following or come up with your own: barley or rice, bay leaf (remove before serving the soup), carrots, diced potatoes, leeks, onions, pasta, sliced zucchini, small navy beans or other beans, soy sauce, tomatoes, and your favorite seasonings. You can even toss in several cloves—or an entire bulb—of garlic.

To get acquainted with the basics of soup-making, try this quick and easy starter recipe: Cook ramen noodles in boiling water according to the package directions, adding your choice of fresh or frozen chopped vegetables. (Make sure the noodles aren't fried—read labels.) When the noodles and vegetables are done, add chunks of tofu for extra body and protein. Serve the soup with low-fat wheat crackers.

For an even simpler soup, add quick-cooking vegetables and a leftover starchy food—pasta, potatoes, or rice—to vegetable broth. Cook until the veggies are done.

Tortillas. In my household, tortillas are a staple. We use them several times a week to make quick and healthy meals. Simply heat a corn or whole-wheat tortilla in a skillet (without oil) or in the microwave. Fill the warmed tortilla with almost anything: beans, rice, tofu, leftovers from the night before. Top the filling with lettuce, tomatoes, or other vegetables of your choice. Spoon on salsa or drizzle with soy sauce, and you have a tasty meal. For variety, use chapati (a bread from India that's similar to a tortilla) or pita bread instead of tortillas.

DINNER: PLATE EXPECTATIONS

Most of us were raised to believe that dinner just isn't dinner unless it features some form of meat. And vegetables belong on the side, bit players to meat's starring role.

To eat for Renewal, you may have to change your perception of the evening meal. It could consist of several complementary dishes, all of which get equal billing on the plate. And of course, these dishes consist of only plant-derived foods—no meats or other animal-derived foods allowed.

Any of the lunch suggestions above will work equally well for dinner. You may also want to sample some or all of the following items.

Basic stir-fry. Prepared properly, a stir-fry is positively packed with vitamins and minerals. You can use almost any combination of vegetables. (At our house, we often make stir-fries in order to use up the leftover veggies hiding in the crisper bins and at the back of the refrigerator.) The trick is to heat the ingredients while minimizing the browning and burning that generates scads of free radicals.

When you make a stir-fry, begin by steaming the grain, because it takes the longest. You can try different grains to vary the taste and texture of the dish. Whole-grain organic brown rice is a good choice, but at my house we also occasionally use basmati rice, bulgur wheat, couscous, or quinoa.

Next, chop onions and garlic. Figure on half of an average-size onion and four cloves of garlic per person. Place these ingredients in a nonstick skillet or wok with enough olive oil or soybean oil to just cover the surface of the pan (a teaspoon or two should suffice). Slowly cook the onions and garlic until they're translucent. You want the temperature high enough that cooking doesn't take all day but not so high that browning occurs. Medium-high heat often works well.

Now you can begin chopping the rest of the vegetables for the stir-fry. Start with the firmest veggies, such as cauliflower and carrots, which take longer to cook. Other good candidates for stir-frying include (but are not limited to) bamboo shoots, bean sprouts, bok choy, broccoli, cabbage, chard, eggplant, green beans, green peppers, kale, spinach, sugar snap peas, sweet red peppers, and zucchini.

As soon as the onions and garlic are soft and translucent, begin adding the remaining vegetables to the pan—again, firmest ones first. You want the veggies to cook fast, so keep the heat fairly high. Add a little water or vegetable broth if you hear sizzling, which indicates too much heat. (The liquid reduces the temperature to boiling.) When the vegetables are crisp-tender, or al dente, remove the pan from the heat. Add soy sauce to taste.

For me, the most difficult part of preparing a stir-fry is getting each vegetable to cook to the proper consistency. But I'm pleased to report that my technique is gradually improving. (I know this because the broccoli doesn't disintegrate like it used to.)

Serve your magnificent creation over the steamed grain. Add a tossed salad for a complete longevity-supporting meal.

Healthy pizza. Spread a whole-wheat crust (which you can purchase ready-made) with tomato sauce or tomato paste. Then add generous amounts of your choice of toppings: green or sweet red or yellow peppers, broccoli, diced veggie burgers, garlic, onions, shiitake mushrooms, pineapple, spinach, tofu slices, tomatoes, zucchini. Be creative.

If you want cheese on your pizza, soy cheese makes a good substitute for mozzarella. It's now widely available in health food stores. Bake the pie according to the package instructions for the crust.

Pasta. Pasta dishes are not only delicious but also fast and easy to prepare. Simply bring a pot of water to a boil, add whole-grain noodles, cook, and drain. Serve the pasta topped with spaghetti sauce (many organic sauces now come in jars). Add a tossed salad and broccoli, carrots, or another steamed vegetable, and you have a complete, nutritious, satisfying meal.

Potatoes. Earlier in this chapter, I alluded to the potato's exceptional nutritional value and versatility. Eat them often—baked, boiled, microwaved, or steamed, but never, ever fried.

Instead of french fries, try my recipe for home fries: Thinly slice potatoes and place the slices on a baking sheet lightly coated with nonstick cooking spray. Add a sprinkle of salt and bake at 400°F for 15 minutes, turning once, until the potatoes are lightly browned and tender. If you want, you can top the potatoes with ketchup made from organic tomatoes and other natural ingredients. (Several brands are available in health food stores.)

These home fries taste great. You can eat them anytime—for breakfast, lunch, or dinner or as a healthy snack.

Rice and beans. Rice and beans go well with a wide range of foods. Cook up more than you need and store the leftovers in the refrigerator or freezer. Then all you have to do is reheat them.

Serve rice and beans with a stir-fry or with steamed vegetables such as broccoli or carrots. Wrap them in a tortilla or chapati, or stuff them in pita bread with lettuce, tomatoes, and steamed vegetables. Add a little soy sauce, ginger, and garlic to give them an Asian flavor; a little curry powder for a taste of India; or some salsa to send them south of the border.

And of course, if you're in a hurry, you can eat your rice and beans plain.

Steamed vegetables. You can build an entire meal around steamed vegetables. And they cook up fast and easy. All you have to do is boil water. Be sure to use a stainless steel steamer rather than an aluminum one. (Aluminum has been linked to Alzheimer's disease.) Add your veggies from firmest to softest: carrots and potatoes first, broccoli next, and squash last.

Tofu. Soy is one of the few plant-derived foods that contains complete protein. Tofu, a soy product, makes a great meat substitute. And it's so versatile that it can blend with the ingredients of almost any dish. Try lightly sautéing it with soy sauce, ginger, garlic, and onions. Serve it with rice and/or vegetables.

SNACKS: SMART MUNCHING

Snacks certainly have their place in the Anti-Aging Diet. In fact, they can contribute tò your daily intake of vitamins, minerals, and other important nutrients—provided you make healthful choices. Any of the following foods will satisfy between-meal hunger pangs without a lot of fat and calories.

Applesauce. I like the kind with added fruit, such as apricots and raspberries. Scrumptious!

Corn chips. Make sure they're made with little or no added fat. Sample different brands until you find your favorite.

Fresh fruits. They're the ideal snack—nutritious, naturally sweet, and portable. Stock up on whatever is in season: apples, berries, grapes, kiwifruit, melons, oranges, peaches, and pears.

Juice pops. Make your own with pure organic fruit juice, embellished with chunks of real fruit (if you prefer). Or instead of juice, use a smoothie. You can buy plastic ice-pop trays in discount stores and some grocery stores.

Juice-sweetened cookies. Read the label before buying. Some brands are very high in fat.

Potato chips. Grocery stores and health food stores now carry several brands of low-fat, baked potato chips. If you prefer, you can make your own "chips" by baking or microwaving thinly sliced potatoes. Serve them with ketchup, salsa, or a dash of soy sauce.

Pretzels. These treats supply lots of crunch without lots of fat or calories. Look for organic varieties, preferably whole-wheat.

Rice cakes and crackers. Many delicious flavors are now available. Look for a brand that is made with organic rice. Enjoy these snacks with one of the dips or spreads beginning on page 560.

Wheat crackers. Make sure that they are whole-grain and additive-free. Watch out for added fat.

Renewal Recipes

Vegetarian cooking has a reputation as a costly and time-consuming venture that produces nothing but flavorless, textureless fare. I hope that the recipes presented here will convince you otherwise. They were developed by my wife, Dellie, and our close friend Larry Needleman, in accordance with the basic principles of the Renewal Anti-Aging Diet. Many are featured in the 14-day menu plan presented on page 535.

Think of these recipes as an introduction to eating for Renewal. Once you become accustomed to the ingredients and cooking techniques that are available, feel free to do some experimenting. You can create new dishes or simply modify your old favorites. You can also invest in a new cookbook or two with recipes that fit into the Renewal program. (I've listed some of my favorite cookbooks in Resources and References on page 594.)

A note about the nutritional analyses that accompany the recipes: The amount of each nutrient has been calculated using the smallest quantity of each ingredient. For example, if a recipe calls for one-quarter to one-half cup soy milk, the nutritional analysis is based on one-quarter cup. If you decide to use more than one-quarter cup, the nutrient content of the dish will vary accordingly (though not by much).

BREAKFASTS

A healthful morning meal stokes your body's calorie-burning furnace and gives you a head start in meeting your daily quota of many Renewal-promoting nutrients. Even if you're a dyed-in-the-wool breakfast-skipper, I'm wagering that you'll find the following creations too delectable to resist.

Larry's Famous Oatmeal

Makes 6 servings

Start your day with a bowl of stick-to-your-ribs goodness. You can freeze the cooked oatmeal in single containers and microwave it later for fast, nonfat breakfasts.

4½	cups water
½	teaspoon salt
2	cups rolled oats
½	cup raisins
¼	cup honey
1	tablespoon blackstrap molasses
½	teaspoon vanilla
¼	teaspoon ground cinnamon
⅛	teaspoon ground cloves

In a medium pot (at least 6 cups), bring the water and salt to a boil. Reduce the heat to low and stir in the oats. The oats will start to foam, so stir until the foaming stops. Simmer, uncovered, for 25 minutes, occasionally stirring to the bottom to prevent sticking.

Remove the pot from the heat. Stir in the raisins, honey, molasses, vanilla, cinnamon, and cloves, and serve.

Per serving: 192 calories, 1.8 g. fat, 4.7 g. protein, 41 g. carbohydrates, 1.9 g. fiber, 0 mg. cholesterol, 189 mg. sodium

Note: The thickness of the oatmeal is determined by the ratio of water to dry oats. Experiment until you get it the way you like it best. Also, the honey adds liquid, so the oatmeal will be slightly thinner after you add the honey.

Whole-Wheat Pancakes

Makes 12

Cornmeal gives these pancakes a delightful crunch. Another type of flour, such as soy or barley, can be substituted for the rice flour. Serve the pancakes with maple syrup, fruit spread, or fresh fruit.

1	cup whole-wheat flour
½	cup rice flour
½	cup cornmeal
1	teaspoon baking soda
⅛	teaspoon salt
1¼ to 1½ cups soy milk	
1	tablespoon vinegar
1	tablespoon honey

In a large bowl, combine the whole-wheat flour, rice flour, cornmeal, baking soda, and salt. In a small bowl, combine the soy milk, vinegar, and honey. Add the soy milk mixture to the flour mixture and mix just until well-blended.

Coat a large nonstick skillet with nonstick spray. Warm over medium-high heat until a drop of water dropped into the skillet sizzles. Using a ⅓-cup measuring cup as a ladle, scoop out ⅓ cup of batter for each pancake. (If the batter is too thick, add more soy milk.) Drop the batter onto the skillet, being careful not to crowd the pancakes.

Cook for 2 to 3 minutes, or until small bubbles appear on the top of each pancake. Turn the pancakes over and cook for 1 to 2 minutes, or until golden. Remove to a warm platter.

Take the skillet off the heat and coat it with more nonstick spray. Continue until all the batter is used.

Per 2 pancakes: 180 calories, 2.1 g. fat, 5.8 g. protein, 36.3 g. carbohydrates, 4.6. g. fiber, 0 mg. cholesterol, 153 mg. sodium

Tofu and Oven Potatoes

Makes 6 servings

This dish is delicious topped with salsa. For variety, replace the vegetables listed in the recipe with other favorites. Some suggestions: mung bean sprouts, tomatoes, and zucchini.

3	large potatoes, scrubbed and cut into ½" chunks
½	onion, chopped
1	sweet red or green pepper, chopped
5	cloves garlic, minced
1½	teaspoons olive oil
½	teaspoon salt
2	scallions, chopped
2	ribs celery, finely chopped (optional)
4–6	shiitake mushrooms, sliced (optional)
12	ounces soft tofu, crumbled
1	teaspoon soy sauce
½	teaspoon turmeric powder
½	teaspoon curry powder
½	teaspoon dried dill weed

Preheat the oven to 450°F.

Place the potatoes in a steamer basket placed over 1" simmering water. Steam the potatoes for 10 minutes, or until just tender. Remove the potatoes to a baking sheet with half the onion, half the pepper, and two-thirds of the garlic. Add 1 teaspoon of the olive oil and the salt and toss well. Bake for 10 to 15 minutes or until lightly browned, turning occasionally with a spatula.

Meanwhile, heat the remaining ½ teaspoon olive oil in a nonstick skillet over medium-high heat. Add the remaining onion, pepper, and garlic, and the scallions. Add the celery and mushrooms (if using). Cook, stirring frequently, for 3 to 4 minutes. Add the tofu, soy sauce, turmeric powder, curry powder, and dill weed and cook, stirring, for 3 minutes, or until the tofu is heated through.

Per serving: 116 calories, 3.2 g. fat, 6.6 g. protein, 16.8 g. carbohydrates, 1.9 g. fiber, 0 mg. cholesterol, 245 mg. sodium

BAKED GOODS

By themselves, these muffins and breads are excellent for breakfast. Or they can be served at lunch or dinner, as substitutes for traditional sliced breads. Either way, they taste great. And as a bonus, they have just a fraction of the fat and calories of traditional baked goods.

Nabolom's Raisin Bran Muffins

Makes 12

This is a version of a muffin from my wife's days in a collective bakery in Berkeley, California. These chewy muffins get you going on cold mornings or are equally delicious served with baked beans at dinner.

1½	cups soy milk
1	tablespoon vinegar (I use apple cider vinegar)
1½	cups wheat bran
¾	cup whole-wheat flour
¾	cup whole-wheat pastry flour
1	teaspoon baking soda
½	teaspoon salt
¼	cup blackstrap molasses
¼	cup honey
½	cup raisins

Preheat the oven to 350°F. Coat a 12-cup muffin tin with nonstick cooking spray.

In a small bowl, mix the soy milk and vinegar and set aside.

In a large bowl, combine the wheat bran, whole-wheat flour, whole-wheat pastry flour, baking soda, and salt. Add the molasses, honey, raisins, and soy milk mixture to the flour mixture. Mix until just well-blended. Divide mixture into the prepared muffin tin. (The batter will seem rather thin.)

Bake for 20 minutes, or until a toothpick inserted in the center of one of the muffins comes out clean. Remove from

the muffin tin and allow to cool slightly on a wire rack.
Serve slightly warm.

Per muffin: 133 calories, 0.9 g. fat, 3.9 g. protein, 31.8 g. carbohydrates, 3.3 g. fiber, 0 mg. cholesterol, 177 mg. sodium

Banana Muffins

Makes 12

*These muffins are very easy to whip up on a morning
when you've got just a little extra time. They are best right
out of the oven. They can be frozen and quickly reheated for
a breakfast treat.*

2½	cups whole-wheat pastry flour
2	teaspoons baking powder
1	teaspoon baking soda
⅔	cup silken tofu
½	cup soy milk
¼	cup honey
1	teaspoon vanilla
1	cup mashed bananas
½	cup chopped walnuts (optional)

Preheat the oven to 350°F. Coat a 12-cup muffin tin with
nonstick cooking spray.

In a large bowl, combine the flour, baking powder, and
baking soda. Place the tofu, soy milk, honey, and vanilla in
a food processor or blender and process until smooth.

Combine the tofu mixture, bananas, and the nuts (if
using) with the flour mixture, and mix until just blended.
Divide the mixture into the prepared muffin tin.

Bake for 20 minutes, or until a toothpick inserted in the
center of one of the muffins comes out clean. Remove from
the muffin tin and allow to cool slightly on a wire rack.
Serve slightly warm.

Per muffin: 130 calories, 0.9 g. fat, 4.6 g. protein, 27.8 g. carbohydrates, 3.4 g. fiber, 0 mg. cholesterol, 135 mg. sodium

Applesauce-Oat Muffins

Makes 12

My family lives in Gravenstein apple country, and from August through October abandoned apples dangle from many a tree along our road. When time allows, my wife, Dellie, collects these and makes fresh applesauce for these muffins. Even when she uses the ready-made applesauce, the smell of these muffins baking still reminds me of the rich fall bounty where we live.

1½	cups whole-wheat pastry flour
½	cup rolled oats
2	teaspoons baking powder
½	teaspoon baking soda
½	teaspoon salt
1	teaspoon ground cinnamon
¼	teaspoon ground cloves
½	teaspoon ground nutmeg
2	tablespoons honey
2	tablespoons walnut oil
1½	cups applesauce
½	cup currants (optional)

Preheat the oven to 350°F. Coat a 12-cup muffin tin with nonstick cooking spray.

In a large bowl, combine the flour, oats, baking powder, baking soda, salt, cinnamon, cloves, and nutmeg. Add the honey, oil, applesauce, and the currants (if using), and mix until just blended. Divide the mixture into the prepared muffin tin.

Bake for 20 minutes, or until a toothpick inserted in the center of one of the muffins comes out clean. Remove from the muffin tin and allow to cool slightly on a wire rack. Serve slightly warm.

Per muffin: 110 calories, 2.8 g. fat, 2.7 g. protein, 19.8 g. carbohydrates, 2.5 g. fiber, 0 mg. cholesterol, 180 mg. sodium

Cornbread

Makes 8 servings

This cornbread can be whipped up in minutes and makes an excellent addition to a meal of soup and salad.

1	cup whole-wheat pastry flour
¾	cup cornmeal
1½	teaspoons baking powder
½	teaspoon baking soda
½	teaspoon salt
1¼	cups soy milk
1¼	tablespoons apple cider vinegar
1	tablespoon honey or maple syrup

Preheat the oven to 350°F. Coat an 8" × 8" glass baking dish with nonstick cooking spray.

In a large bowl, combine the flour, cornmeal, baking powder, baking soda, and salt. In a small bowl, combine the soy milk, vinegar, and honey or syrup. Add the soy milk mixture to the flour mixture, and mix until just blended.

Place in the prepared baking dish, and bake for 20 minutes, or until a toothpick inserted in the center comes out clean.

Per serving: 115 calories, 1 g. fat, 3.6 g. protein, 24.4 g. carbohydrates, 3.8 g. fiber, 0 mg. cholesterol, 225 mg. sodium

Pumpkin Bread

___

Makes 8 servings

Enjoy this delicious and moist quick bread for breakfast, dessert, or a snack.

2	cups whole-wheat pastry flour
1	teaspoon baking powder
1	teaspoon baking soda
1½	teaspoons ground cinnamon
½	teaspoon ground nutmeg
¼	teaspoon ground cloves
½	teaspoon salt
1	cup canned pumpkin puree
¼	cup honey
½	cup soy milk
2	tablespoons vegetable oil
½	cup raisins or currants (optional)

Preheat the oven to 350°F. Coat a 9" × 5" loaf pan with nonstick spray.

In a large bowl, combine the flour, baking powder, baking soda, cinnamon, nutmeg, cloves, and salt; set aside.

In a medium bowl, combine the pumpkin, honey, soy milk, and oil. Add the pumpkin mixture and the raisins or currants (if using) to the flour mixture. Mix until just well-blended. Transfer to the prepared loaf pan, and bake for 45 minutes, or until a toothpick inserted in the center comes out clean. Cool in the pan for 5 minutes. Remove to a wire rack to cool completely.

Per serving: 182 calories, 4.4 g. fat, 4.9 g. protein, 33.6 g. carbohydrates, 4.4 g. fiber, 0 mg. cholesterol, 283 mg. sodium

Gingerbread

Fill your kitchen with the enticing aroma of this moist, flavorful cake. It makes a great dessert or snack. Try it warm out of the oven, topped with sliced strawberries and rice milk.

1	cup whole-wheat pastry flour
½	cup whole-wheat flour
1	teaspoon baking powder
1	teaspoon baking soda
½	teaspoon salt
1	tablespoon ground ginger
½	teaspoon ground cinnamon
¼	teaspoon ground cloves
¾	cup applesauce
¼	cup blackstrap molasses
1	tablespoon honey
2	tablespoons walnut oil
¼	cup soy or rice milk

Preheat the oven to 350°F. Coat an 8" × 8" glass baking dish with nonstick cooking spray.

In a large bowl, combine the flours, baking powder, baking soda, salt, ginger, cinnamon, and cloves.

In a small bowl, combine the applesauce, molasses, honey, oil, and soy or rice milk. Add the applesauce mixture to the flour mixture and mix just until blended.

Place the batter in the prepared baking dish and bake for 25 minutes, or until a toothpick inserted in the center comes out clean.

Per serving: 154 calories, 3.9 g. fat, 2.8 g. protein, 27.5 g. carbohydrates, 1.7 g. fiber, 0 mg. cholesterol, 289 mg. sodium

Note: To make measuring the honey and molasses easier, first coat the measuring cup and spoon with nonstick cooking spray. The honey and molasses will just slip out without sticking.

APPETIZERS AND SNACKS

Uh-oh . . . company's coming. You want to dazzle them with delectable treats, but you don't want to abandon the principles of eating for Renewal. The following recipes rise to the occasion. They're guaranteed to win raves from your guests—and keep your eating habits on track.

Freeke's Eggplant Caviar

Makes 6 servings

My mother-in-law has made a similar version of this delicious dish for many years. She also created this low-fat version. It is delicious as a dip for crackers, or spread on bread. It can also be eaten cold as a side dish.

1	teaspoon olive oil
2	large onions, chopped
4	cloves garlic, minced
2	large green peppers, chopped
1	large eggplant (about 1½ pounds), cut into 1" chunks
1	can (6 ounces) tomato paste
2	tablespoons chopped fresh basil or 2 teaspoons dried basil
	Salt and ground black pepper

In a large saucepan, heat the oil over medium-high heat. Add the onions and garlic and cook for 5 minutes, stirring frequently until the onions are soft. (Add a tablespoon of water if they stick.) Add the green peppers and cook for 7 minutes, or until the vegetables are tender.

Meanwhile, in a medium saucepan, cook the eggplant and ½ cup water over medium heat until soft, about 5 minutes.

Stir the eggplant, tomato paste, and basil into the saucepan with the onions and peppers. Over medium heat, bring to a boil. Reduce heat to low, cover, and simmer for 15 minutes. Season with the salt and a generous amount of black pepper. Refrigerate until ready to serve.

Per serving: 90 calories, 1.2 g. fat, 3.4 g. protein, 19.2 g. carbohydrates, 2.6 g. fiber, 0 mg. cholesterol, 326 mg. sodium

Roasted Soy Nuts

Makes 6 servings

This easy-to-make crunchy treat tastes like dry roasted nuts, but provides all the health benefits of soy.

1	cup dried soybeans
	Salt or organic soy sauce

Place the soybeans in a large bowl and cover with water. (They will more than double in volume, so make sure there is adequate room in the bowl for the expansion and adequate water to keep them covered.) Refrigerate the soaking soybeans overnight.

Drain the soybeans in a colander and spread them between layers of paper towels to dry. Refrigerate for at least 1 hour.

Preheat the oven to 250°F. Divide the soybeans onto two baking sheets. Roast for 1 hour or until lightly browned, turning occasionally with a spatula.

Place the roasted soybeans in a large bowl and stir in the salt or soy sauce, to taste, while still hot.

Per serving: 129 calories, 6.2 g. fat, 11.4 g. protein, 9.4 g. carbohydrates, 0 g. fiber, 0 mg. cholesterol, 178 mg. sodium

Note: For extra flavor, try sprinkling the soy nuts with onion or garlic powder or any favorite seasoning in addition to the salt or soy sauce.

Zesty Bean Spread

Makes 8 servings

Of all the dips and spreads, this is the quickest one to prepare. It takes only about 5 minutes to make a delicious, healthy dip for chips or vegetables. It could also be spread on warm corn tortillas with lettuce and sprouts to make an easy lunch.

1	can (15 ounces) nonfat refried beans
1	small red onion, finely chopped

½	green or sweet red pepper, finely chopped
½	teaspoon chili powder
½	teaspoon ground cumin
¾	teaspoon soy sauce
1	small tomato, finely chopped (optional)
2	tablespoons chopped fresh cilantro (optional)

In a medium bowl, combine the beans, onion, pepper, chili powder, cumin, soy sauce, and tomato and cilantro (if using). Mix until well-blended.

Per serving: 48 calories, 0.1 g. fat, 2.5 g. protein, 9.3 g. carbohydrates, 2.1 g. fiber, 0 mg. cholesterol, 287 mg. sodium

Note: For an even easier bean spread, you could simply add ⅓ to ½ cup of your favorite salsa to the can of refried beans and use as a dip for chips or vegetables.

Creamy Hummus Dip

Makes 8 servings

Hummus makes a delicious dip for fresh vegetables. It also can be used in sandwiches or roll-ups or spread on bread or crackers. The color and flavor can be varied with the use of either of the optional ingredients. The roasted red pepper makes a wonderful orange spread.

1	can (15 ounces) chickpeas, rinsed and drained
2	scallions, chopped into large pieces
4	cloves garlic
1	tablespoon tahini paste
¾	teaspoon ground cumin
	Juice of ½ lemon
2	teaspoons soy sauce
½	cup roasted red pepper or 2 tablespoons fresh cilantro (optional)

Place the chickpeas, scallions, garlic, tahini, cumin, lemon juice, soy sauce, and roasted red pepper or cilantro (if using) in a blender or food processor. Puree until smooth.

Per serving: 56 calories, 2 g. fat, 2.4 g. protein, 7.6 g. carbohydrates, 2.2 g. fiber, 0 mg. cholesterol, 244 mg. sodium

Vegetable and Herb Tofu Dip

Makes 1 pint

Serve this dip with baked tortilla chips or raw or blanched vegetables. Or use it as a sandwich filling: Spread it on whole-grain bread or stuff it in a pita, then top it with lettuce, tomatoes, and sprouts.

1	pound tofu (any but nigari firm, which is very dense)
1	tablespoon finely chopped yellow onion
1	tablespoon chopped fresh parsley
1½	teaspoons dried basil
1	teaspoon salt
1	teaspoon organic soy sauce
1	teaspoon onion powder
½	teaspoon garlic powder
¼	teaspoon ground cumin
¼	teaspoon ground thyme
	Pinch ground red pepper
1	rib celery, finely chopped
1	carrot, finely chopped
1	green, sweet red, or yellow pepper or any favorite raw vegetable, finely chopped (optional)

In a food processor or blender, blend the tofu until smooth (about 10 seconds). Add the onion, parsley, basil, salt, soy sauce, onion powder, garlic powder, cumin, thyme, and ground red pepper. Process on pulse until just combined, about 5 seconds.

Place in a plastic container and stir in the celery, carrot, and pepper or other vegetable (if using). Cover and refrigerate overnight to allow flavors to meld. Before serving, add more seasoning to taste because tofu continues to absorb flavor as it sits.

Per serving: 26.8 calories, 1.4 g. fat, 2.5 g. protein, 1.8 g. carbohydrates, 0.3 g. fiber, 0 mg. cholesterol, 161 mg. sodium

Salsa Fresca

Makes 6 servings

This fresh salsa makes a great dip for chips and a flavorful condiment for Mexican dishes such as enchiladas, burritos, tacos, and rice and beans. One mouthful of this pico de gallo, and you'll be transported south of the border.

3–4	ripe tomatoes, diced or finely chopped
3	cloves garlic, minced
1	small red onion, finely chopped
1	jalapeño pepper, seeded and diced (wear plastic gloves when handling)
½	cup cilantro leaves, chopped
	Juice of 1 lime
	Salt

In a medium bowl, combine the tomatoes, garlic, onion, pepper, cilantro, and lime juice. Season with salt to taste. Refrigerate until ready to serve.

Per serving: 26 calories, 0.3 g. fat, 1 g. protein, 5.8 g. carbohydrates, 1.2 g. fiber, 0 mg. cholesterol, 96 mg. sodium

SOUPS AND STEWS

Most folks think of soups and stews as cold-weather foods. But the ones presented here are so simple and satisfying that they're perfect year-round. Enjoy them as meals unto themselves, or serve them as appetizers or accompaniments.

Gazpacho

This soup is delicious on a hot summer day when the garden or farmers' market is overflowing with tomatoes and peppers. You could substitute fresh cilantro for the basil and add a chopped jalapeño pepper to get a Mexican flavor.

3	pounds fresh tomatoes or 1 can (28 ounces) whole or chopped tomatoes with juice
3–4	cloves garlic, minced
1	cucumber, peeled, seeded, and chopped
½	sweet red pepper, chopped
½	green pepper, chopped
¼	cup chopped fresh basil
½	medium red onion, finely chopped
1	tablespoon lime juice
1	tablespoon balsamic or rice vinegar
	Salt

If using fresh tomatoes, first core and peel them. Peel by dropping them about 3 at a time for 10 seconds into a small pot of boiling water. Remove them from the boiling water and put them immediately into cold water. After a minute or so in the cold water, the skins should slip off easily.

Put about two-thirds of the tomatoes in a food processor or blender with the garlic and half the cucumber, and puree. Chop the remaining tomatoes (if whole) and mix in a bowl with the pureed tomatoes, the remaining cucumber, and the red and green pepper, basil, onion, lime juice, and vinegar. Season with the salt, to taste. Refrigerate until ready to serve.

Per serving: 68 calories, 0.9 g. fat, 2.6 g. protein, 15.2 g. carbohydrates, 3.8 g. fiber, 0 mg. cholesterol, 112 mg. sodium

Miso Vegetable Soup

Makes 6 servings

You can make this hearty, flavorful soup in just minutes.

2	cups water
2	cloves fresh garlic, minced
3–5	coin-size pieces of fresh ginger
6	ounces tofu, cubed
2	teaspoons tamari or 1 tablespoon organic soy sauce
3	shiitake mushrooms, sliced
2	large chard leaves, or any other vegetable leaf
1½	tablespoons miso
1	scallion, sliced
¼	teaspoon toasted sesame oil (optional)
¾	cup cooked rice or noodles

In a medium pot, bring the water to a boil. While the water is heating, add the garlic, ginger, tofu, and tamari or soy sauce.

When the water boils, cover the pot, lower the heat, and simmer for 5 minutes.

Add the mushrooms and chard (or other vegetable leaf) to the pot and simmer for another 5 minutes, or until vegetables are tender.

Meanwhile, in a heat-resistant serving bowl, dissolve the miso in 2 tablespoons of broth from the pot. Add the scallion and the sesame oil (if using).

Remove the pot from the heat and carefully transfer the contents to the serving bowl. Add the cooked rice or noodles and serve.

Per serving: 253 calories, 8.9 g. fat, 19 g. protein, 29.4 g. carbohydrates, 3.1 g. fiber, 0 mg. cholesterol, 1,036 mg. sodium

Note: For a tasty variation, substitute your favorite stock for the water. When adding the vegetables, use any other favorite, fast-cooking vegetables, such as zucchini, onions, bean sprouts, snow peas, or chopped cabbage.

Middle Eastern Chickpea Stew

Makes 4 servings

This delicious dish is most authentic when served over whole-wheat couscous or in a whole-wheat pita. It's less authentic—but equally delectable—served over brown or basmati rice or any other grain.

1	medium onion, chopped
4	cloves garlic, minced
4	tablespoons vegetable broth or water
1	teaspoon ground cinnamon
2	teaspoons ground cumin
1	teaspoon ground coriander
1	can (15 ounces) chopped tomatoes with juice
1	large sweet potato, peeled and cut into 1" chunks
1	green or sweet red pepper, chopped
1	medium zucchini, cut into 1" chunks
1	can (15 ounces) chickpeas, drained and rinsed or 1½ cups cooked chickpeas
¼	cup raisins (optional)
2	tablespoons lemon juice
	Salt and ground black pepper

In a large nonstick saucepan over medium-high heat, cook the onion and garlic in 2 tablespoons of the broth or water for 3 minutes. Add the cinnamon, cumin, and coriander with the remaining 2 tablespoons broth or water. Cook for 3 minutes, stirring constantly. Add the tomatoes, sweet potato, pepper, and zucchini. Bring the mixture to a boil. Reduce the heat to low, cover, and simmer for 15 minutes, or until the vegetables are tender.

Stir in the chickpeas, raisins (if using), and lemon juice. Cook for 3 minutes, or until the beans are heated through. Season with salt and pepper to taste.

Per serving: 169 calories, 2.2 g. fat, 6.9 g. protein, 33.6 g. carbohydrates, 7.4 g. fiber, 0 mg. cholesterol, 663 mg. sodium

Minestrone

This is a soup that cries out for creativity and variation. It is basically a tomato-based soup with beans, pasta, and vegetables. The variety of bean, shape of pasta, and mixture of vegetables can all vary depending on the season and availability in your garden or pantry. The garlic, if used in larger quantities, becomes your daily dose of this Anti-Aging nutrient. Start with 4 to 6 cloves and add more each time you make the soup, until you reach the perfect amount for you.

1	medium onion, chopped
4–24	cloves garlic, minced
2	ribs celery, chopped
½	cup sliced shiitake mushrooms (optional)
6½	cups water or vegetable broth
2	green, sweet red, or yellow peppers (or a mixture of the three), chopped
1	carrot, chopped
1½	cups summer squash, chopped (a mixture of green and yellow is nice)
1	cup eggplant, cubed (or carrots, green beans, potatoes, or rutabaga)
1½	cups chopped fresh tomatoes or 1 can (15 ounces) chopped tomatoes
½	teaspoon oregano
1	teaspoon dried basil or 1 tablespoon fresh chopped basil
¼	cup red wine or nonalcoholic red wine (optional)
1½	cups cooked or drained and rinsed canned beans, such as kidney beans, red beans, or chickpeas
½	cup small pasta such as orzo, elbows, or shells
2	cups spinach or chard leaves, chopped (optional)
	Salt and ground black pepper

In a large saucepan over medium heat, cook the onion, garlic, celery, and mushrooms (if using) in 2 tablespoons of the water or broth. Cook for 5 to 7 minutes, or until tender, stirring occasionally and adding water or broth as needed to prevent burning.

Add 6 cups of the water or broth, the peppers, carrot, squash, eggplant, tomatoes, oregano, basil, and wine (if using). Turn the heat to high and bring to a boil. Reduce the heat to low, cover, and simmer for 10 minutes.

Add the beans, pasta, and spinach or chard (if using). Simmer for 10 minutes, or until the pasta is cooked. Season with salt and black pepper to taste.

Per serving: 128 calories, 0.7 g. fat, 6.6 g. protein, 25.6 g. carbohydrates, 2.2 g. fiber, 0 mg. cholesterol, 121 mg. sodium

Lentil Soup

Makes 8 servings

This hearty soup is quite easy to prepare and can be ready to eat in under an hour. The recipe can be halved if desired or the whole recipe can be made and part put in the freezer to be available for another meal. This soup is even better the day after it's made.

2½	quarts water
2	cups dry lentils, rinsed
1	can (28 ounces) crushed tomatoes
1	large onion, chopped
3–4	cloves garlic, minced
¼	cup Bragg's Liquid Aminos, organic soy sauce, or bouillon
1	tablespoon dried basil
1	tablespoon ground cumin
1	tablespoon balsamic vinegar
3	medium potatoes, peeled and diced

In a large stockpot over high heat, bring the water to a boil. Add the lentils, tomatoes, onion, garlic, liquid aminos or soy sauce or bouillon, basil, cumin, and vinegar. Return to a boil, reduce the heat to low, and simmer, uncovered,

for 30 minutes. Add the potatoes and continue simmering
for 45 minutes, or until lentils and potatoes are tender.

**Per serving: 198 calories, 0.9 g. fat, 12.8 g. protein, 37.3 g. carbo-
hydrates, 6 g. fiber, 0 mg. cholesterol, 179 mg. sodium**

Potato-Leek Soup

Makes 6 servings

*Many soups benefit from adding a homemade vegetable
stock rather than water. The stock can be easily made from
potatoes, carrots, onions, and greens and can include vegetable parts that are otherwise thrown away, such as potato
skins, leek greens, or the stalks of shiitake mushrooms. You
must be careful not to add a large amount of cruciferous
vegetables, as they will give the stock a strong flavor. The
stock can be simmering while other parts of the soup are
cooking and can be added later. This soup is still tasty without the stock, but you get added nutrients and flavor with the
stock.*

Stock

6	cups water
3–4	leek greens, cut into 1–2" pieces
2	ribs celery, chopped
2	carrots, chopped
2	cloves garlic, crushed
1	medium potato, scrubbed and cut into 1" chunks

Soup

2	teaspoons olive oil
3–4	leeks, white portion only
4	cloves garlic
1	rib celery
¼	cup sliced fresh shiitake mushrooms or 1 ounce dried (optional)
6	cups stock or water
3	large potatoes, scrubbed and chopped into 1" chunks
	Salt and ground black pepper

To make the stock: In a large saucepan over high·heat, combine the water, leek greens, celery, carrots, garlic, and potato, and bring to a boil. Reduce the heat to low, cover, and simmer for 1 hour. Strain the stock and discard the vegetables.

To make the soup: Heat the oil in a large nonstick saucepan over low heat. Add the leeks, garlic, celery, and mushrooms (if using) and cook slowly, stirring frequently, for 10 minutes, or until very tender. (If necessary, add 1 to 2 tablespoons of the stock or water to prevent the vegetables from burning.)

Add the potatoes and 2 cups (or enough to cover the potatoes) of the stock or water. Bring to a boil over high heat. Reduce the heat to low, cover, and simmer for 20 minutes, or until the potatoes are very tender.

Remove from the heat, uncover, and let sit for 5 minutes. Place the vegetable mixture in batches in a food processor or blender and process until smooth. Return the mixture to a large saucepan and add the remaining stock or water, 1 cup at a time, until the desired consistency is reached. Over high heat, bring the mixture to a boil. Reduce the heat to low, cover, and simmer for 3 minutes. Season with salt and pepper to taste.

Per serving: 120 calories, 1.8 g. fat, 3.8 g. protein, 24.2 g. carbohydrates, 1.4 g. fiber, 0 mg. cholesterol, 410 mg. sodium

SALADS AND DRESSINGS

At some restaurants, a salad consists of nothing more than some lettuce and a few slices of tomato. Sorry, but that just doesn't cut it. A salad should exploit all the tastes, textures, and colors that plant-derived foods have to offer. And with the right combination of ingredients, it can pack a serious nutritional punch. Now here are some *real* salads.

Confetti Rice Salad

Makes 8 servings

   The vegetables in this cooked salad should be finely chopped so that they resemble grains of rice. The job goes quickly with a food processor. The salad has a wonderful fresh vegetable flavor that's even better the next day.

4	cups water
1½	teaspoons salt
2	cups short-grain brown rice
3	tablespoons organic soy sauce
2	tablespoons extra-virgin olive oil
3	tablespoons rice vinegar
4–8	cloves garlic, minced
½	red cabbage (8 ounces), finely chopped
2	medium carrots, finely chopped
1	medium red onion, finely chopped
1	bunch parsley, minced

   In a large saucepan over high heat, bring the water and salt to a boil. Stir in the rice. Reduce the heat to low, cover, and simmer for 45 minutes. Remove from the heat and allow the rice to cool.
   Meanwhile, in a large bowl, whisk together the soy sauce, oil, vinegar, and garlic. Add the cabbage, carrots, onion, parsley, and cooled rice. Stir until well-blended. Taste and add more soy sauce if desired. Refrigerate until ready to serve.

Per serving: 172 calories, 4.8 g. fat, 5.5 g. protein, 42.6 g. carbohydrates, 1.8 g. fiber, 0 mg. cholesterol, 920 mg. sodium

Tricolor Pasta Salad

Makes 6 servings

The colorful array of crunchy vegetables in this salad brings summer sunshine to your table. This dish is great for picnics.

12	ounces short, chunky whole-grain pasta, such as shells, elbows, or penne
2	tablespoons balsamic vinegar
1½	tablespoons olive oil
2	tablespoons lemon juice
3–4	cloves garlic, minced
1	tablespoon soy sauce
1	small zucchini, chopped
1	small yellow squash, chopped
1	sweet red, yellow, and/or green pepper, chopped
1	small red onion, finely chopped
1	large tomato, chopped
¼	cup sun-dried tomatoes, soaked and chopped (optional)
15	kalamata olives, pitted and chopped
¼	cup chopped fresh basil
	Salt and ground black pepper

In a large saucepan, cook the pasta according to the package directions. Drain and rinse with cold water; set aside.

In a large bowl, whisk together the vinegar, oil, lemon juice, garlic, and soy sauce. Add the zucchini, squash, sweet pepper, onion, tomato, sun-dried tomatoes (if using), olives, and basil. Let marinate for 15 to 30 minutes. Stir in the pasta and add the salt and black pepper to taste. Refrigerate until ready to serve.

Per serving: 407 calories, 11.4 g. fat, 12.9 g. protein, 68.9 g. carbohydrates, 3.6 g. fiber, 0 mg. cholesterol, 740 mg. sodium

Jicama, Orange, and Cilantro Salad

Makes 8 servings

This unusual vegetable and fruit mixture makes a salad so special that you could serve it for a holiday dinner. Plus, it's a phytonutrient bonanza.

½	**cup fresh-squeezed orange juice**
1	**tablespoon extra-virgin olive oil**
2	**teaspoons rice vinegar**
	Salt and white pepper
1	**medium jicama (approximately 1½ pounds), peeled and julienned**
½	**medium red onion, cut into thin wedges**
½	**cup cilantro leaves**
2	**large oranges, peeled and segmented**
8	**large lettuce leaves**

In a large bowl, whisk together the orange juice, oil, and vinegar. Add salt and pepper to taste. Add the jicama, onion, cilantro, and oranges. Toss well to coat. Refrigerate for at least 1 hour, tossing occasionally.

To serve, line each of 8 salad plates or bowls with a lettuce leaf, then divide the salad onto the leaves.

Per serving: 79 calories, 2 g. fat, 2 g. protein, 14.3 g. carbohydrates, 1.3 g. fiber, 0 mg. cholesterol, 74 mg. sodium

Asian Coleslaw

Makes 8 servings

Our children get tired of lettuce salads. They like crunch. This creation has become one of their favorites.

¼	**cup rice vinegar**
¼	**cup soy sauce**
½	**teaspoon sesame oil**
3	**cloves garlic, minced**
1	**teaspoon grated fresh ginger**

2–3	cups shredded cabbage
2	carrots, shredded
1	cup mung bean sprouts
½	sweet red pepper, thinly sliced
2	scallions, chopped
½	cup cilantro leaves, chopped
2	tablespoons toasted sesame seeds (optional)

In a large bowl, whisk together the vinegar, soy sauce, sesame oil, garlic, and ginger. Add the cabbage, carrots, sprouts, pepper, scallions, and cilantro. Toss well to coat. Just before serving, sprinkle with the sesame seeds (if using).

Per serving: 27 calories, 0.4 g. fat, 1.5 g. protein, 5.6 g. carbohydrates, 1.3 g. fiber, 0 mg. cholesterol, 525 mg. sodium

Dellie's Delicious Dressing

Makes about ¾ cup

Flaxseed oil bolsters kids' (and adults') immune systems—but only if you can get them to eat it. This oil has a distinctive flavor that our seven-year-old did not like. So my wife, Dellie, created this dressing, which turns out to be a great way to make flaxseed oil acceptable to those who don't appreciate it au naturel. Try it. You may discover a much less expensive way than capsules to take this important Anti-Aging supplement.

6	tablespoons flaxseed oil
3	tablespoons balsamic vinegar
4	tablespoons lemon juice
1	teaspoon Dijon mustard
2	cloves garlic, minced
1	tablespoon minced fresh basil leaves, or ½ teaspoon dried basil

Place the oil, vinegar, lemon juice, mustard, garlic, and basil in a medium jar with a tight-fitting lid. Shake well to blend thoroughly. Refrigerate until ready to use.

Per serving: 216 calories, 21.1 g. fat, 0.2 g. protein, 4.6 g. carbohydrates, 0 g. fiber, 0 mg. cholesterol, 21 mg. sodium

MAIN DISHES

Can a meal without meat be satisfying? The answer is an
emphatic yes. Granted, if you're accustomed to eating meat
at almost every meal, your tastebuds may need some time to
adjust. But with entrées as hearty as the ones presented
here, you'll never again wonder, "Where's the beef?"

Teriyaki Tofu and Broccoli

Makes 4 servings

*This dish utilizes a process sometimes known as water
sautéing or braising. It involves no fat, but instead uses a
small amount of water to keep food from burning or sticking.*

1	bunch broccoli florets (see note)
1	pound tofu, cut into ¾" cubes
1	small yellow onion, sliced
1	clove garlic, minced
1	piece (about ½") fresh ginger, peeled and minced
¼	cup water
¼	cup organic soy sauce
1	tablespoon cornstarch
1½	teaspoons honey
2	cups cooked brown rice

In a large covered skillet over high heat, cook the broccoli, tofu, onion, garlic, and ginger in 2 tablespoons of the
water for about 5 minutes, or until crisp-tender. Stir occasionally while the ingredients are cooking and add another
2 tablespoons of water if they are sticking.

In a small bowl, combine the soy sauce, cornstarch, and
honey, stirring until the cornstarch is completely dissolved.
Add the soy sauce mixture to the skillet and cook, stirring
constantly, for 3 minutes, or until thickened.

Serve over the brown rice.

Per serving: 256 calories, 6.7 g. fat, 15.6 g. protein, 37.6 g. carbohydrates, 4.6 g. fiber, 0 mg. cholesterol, 1,068 mg. sodium

Note: Try peeling the raw broccoli stems and eating them while preparing the meal. If they're fresh, they'll be crisp and sweet. Kids usually love them, too. They are also good grated and added to salads.

Savory Baked Tofu

Makes 6 servings

This recipe produces tofu that costs a tiny fraction of the product sold commercially and is far superior in flavor and texture.

2	packages (1 pound each) firm tofu
3	cloves garlic
1	piece (about 1") fresh ginger, sliced
1	small onion, quartered
⅔	cup organic soy sauce
½	teaspoon olive oil
¼–½	teaspoon ground star anise or five-spice powder (optional)

Open the tofu package and drain and rinse the tofu.

Cut the tofu into 16 uniform slices, each approximately ⅜" thick. Wrap the tofu slices in a clean dish towel by placing 1 row along the short end of the towel and rolling the towel once to cover them. Add another row to the pile and roll once more. Continue until all are wrapped with one layer of toweling between each layer. Place the wrapped tofu in a shallow pan.

Put the tofu in the refrigerator to drain for 1 to 2 hours. (Draining the tofu this way pulls water out so that the tofu will absorb the marinade.)

In a blender or food processor, combine the garlic, ginger, onion, soy sauce, oil, and ground star anise or five-spice powder (if using). Place in a bowl. Cover and refrigerate for 1 to 2 hours, while the tofu is draining.

Remove the tofu from the toweling. Place in a 13" × 9" glass baking dish, stacking 2 slices on top of each other to

create 8 stacks. Coat with the marinade. Cover the baking
dish with plastic wrap and refrigerate for 1 to 3 hours
(depending on how strongly flavored you'd like the tofu).
Turn the tofu once or twice during this time.

Preheat the oven to 400°F. Place the tofu on two baking
sheets. Place in the oven and immediately reduce the heat
to 325°F.

Bake for 30 to 45 minutes, turning the tofu once during
this time. (Use the shorter time if tender texture is desired,
the longer if chewy texture is desired.)

If you are not serving it immediately, allow the tofu to
cool, place it in an airtight container, and refrigerate it for up
to a week.

**Per serving: 250 calories, 13.7 g. fat, 25.9 g. protein, 11.6 g. car-
bohydrates, 2.1 g. fiber, 0 mg. cholesterol, 1,850 mg. sodium**

Quick Burritos

Makes 6 servings

*These burritos have innumerable variations, depending
on your family's tastes. You can make your own refried
beans. You can add almost any chopped raw or steamed
vegetable. You can even use corn tortillas and make soft
tacos.*

2	cans nonfat organic refried beans (or 3 cups cooked and mashed kidney or black beans)
2	cups cooked brown rice
1	teaspoon chili powder
1½	cups chopped tomatoes
6	whole-wheat tortillas (10"–12" in diameter) or 12 corn tortillas (6" in diameter)
1½	cups chopped lettuce
1	cup bean sprouts (optional)
	Salsa
½	cup chopped cilantro (optional)
1	cup grated soy cheese (optional)

Place the beans in a small saucepan over medium-low heat and cook for 5 minutes, stirring frequently, until heated through. (Alternately, the beans can be warmed in a microwave oven. Place them in a bowl and cook on medium for 3 minutes or until heated through, stirring twice.)

In another saucepan over medium heat, combine the rice, chili powder, and tomatoes. Cook for 5 minutes, stirring frequently, until heated through and well-combined. (This, too, can alternately be heated in a microwave oven. Place the mixture in a bowl and cook on medium for 3 to 5 minutes, stirring twice, until heated through.)

Meanwhile, warm the tortillas by placing them between 2 plates and cooking them in the microwave on high for 1 minute. If you don't have a microwave, they can be warmed on a griddle or in a skillet with a lid.

Divide the beans and the rice mixture evenly among the tortillas. Top each with the lettuce, sprouts (if using), salsa, and cilantro and cheese (if using). Roll to enclose the filling.

Per serving: 298 calories, 3.8 g. fat, 11.6 g. protein, 62.2 g. carbohydrates, 11.7 g. fiber, 0 mg. cholesterol, 998 mg. sodium

Bean and Corn Enchiladas

Makes 4 servings

I knew these delicious enchiladas were a success when our two young daughters wanted second and third helpings. Fresh corn, if available, will make this dish especially irresistible.

1	teaspoon olive oil
1	onion, finely chopped
4	cloves garlic, minced
1	green or sweet red pepper, chopped
1	cup fresh or frozen and thawed corn kernels
1	cup zucchini or yellow squash, cut into 1" chunks
1	tomato, cut into ½" chunks

1	teaspoon chili powder
1	teaspoon ground cumin
½	teaspoon salt
¼	cup water
1½	cups cooked beans (kidney, pinto, black, or chili or one 15-ounce can, rinsed and drained)
12	corn tortillas (6" diameter)
2	cups enchilada sauce

Preheat the oven to 350°F.

Heat the oil in a large nonstick skillet over medium-high heat. Add the onion and cook for 5 minutes, stirring occasionally. Add the garlic and pepper and cook for 3 minutes. Add the corn, zucchini or squash, tomato, chili powder, cumin, and salt. Add the water, cover the skillet, and cook for 10 minutes, stirring occasionally. Add the beans and cook for 3 minutes, or until heated through.

Meanwhile, warm the tortillas by placing them between two plates and heating them in the microwave on high for 1 minute. If you don't have a microwave, they can be warmed on a griddle or in a skillet with a lid.

Pour about a third of the enchilada sauce in a 13" × 9" baking dish. Heap about 3 tablespoons of filling in the middle of each tortilla and roll it up. Place the enchiladas close together in the baking pan. When they are all filled, you can put any extra filling around the edges. Pour the remaining sauce on top of the enchiladas. Cover the dish with aluminum foil and bake for 15 minutes, or until bubbly.

Per serving: 403 calories, 8.4 g. fat, 15.6 g. protein, 76.9 g. carbohydrates, 8.4 g. fiber, 0 mg. cholesterol, 957 mg. sodium

Note: If enchilada sauce is not available, you can substitute 2 cups of tomato sauce seasoned with ½ teaspoon chili powder and ½ teaspoon ground cumin. It will not be exactly the same but will still make a tasty dish.

Red Rice with Corn and Black Beans

Makes 8 servings

This dish takes very little time to prepare. It can be eaten as is or rolled up in tortillas.

2	cups brown rice
1	tablespoon olive oil
2	cloves garlic, chopped
¼	medium onion, chopped
1	medium tomato, quartered
¼	cup Bragg's Liquid Aminos, soy sauce, or bouillon
3½	cups water
1	tablespoon dried basil
1	can (15 ounces) corn kernels, drained
1	can (15 ounces) black beans, rinsed and drained
½	cup salsa

In a medium saucepan, combine the rice, oil, garlic, and onion. Cook over medium-low heat, stirring frequently, for about 5 minutes, or until the rice is lightly browned.

Combine the tomato, liquid aminos or soy sauce or bouillon, and 1 cup of the water in a blender or food processor, and blend on low speed or pulse until just blended. Add enough of the remaining water to the mixture to make a total of 4 cups of liquid. Stir in the basil.

Add the blended liquid to the rice. Increase the heat to high and bring to a boil while stirring. Reduce the heat to low, cover, and simmer for 45 minutes. Remove the pan from the heat and allow it to sit for 5 minutes. Uncover and fluff the rice with a fork. Stir in the corn, beans, and salsa. Return to the heat and cook, stirring constantly, until heated through.

Per serving: 260 calories, 2.6 g. fat, 8.1 g. protein, 53 g. carbohydrates, 3.7 g. fiber, 0 mg. cholesterol, 321 mg. sodium

Note: If Bragg's Liquid Aminos is not available (you'd most likely find it in a health food store), you may substitute your favorite bouillon cube or powder.

Stuffed Winter Squash

Makes 4 servings

This dish is quite easy to prepare and makes a wonderful meal for a holiday or for any day. The cooking time varies with the size of squash that is used.

1	large (about 2½–3½ pounds) kabocha squash or 4 small sweet dumpling squash
1	teaspoon olive oil
2	medium onions, chopped
2	ribs celery, chopped
1	green or sweet red pepper, chopped
3–5	cloves garlic, minced
2	cups cooked brown rice
1	apple, cored and chopped
⅓	cup currants or dried cranberries (optional)
⅓	cup chopped walnuts or sunflower seeds (optional)
1	tablespoon fresh chopped parsley
1	teaspoon dried oregano
½	teaspoon salt
½	cup apple juice or vegetable broth

Preheat the oven to 350°F. Cut the top(s) off of the squash and remove the seeds and pulp. Place the tops back on the squash. Place the squash in a 9" × 9" baking dish. Fill the dish with 1" of water. Bake for 30 minutes.

Meanwhile, heat the oil in a large nonstick skillet over medium heat. Add the onions, celery, pepper, and garlic. Cook for 5 minutes, stirring frequently. Add the rice, apple, currants or cranberries (if using), walnuts or sunflower seeds (if using), parsley, oregano, salt, and juice or broth. Cook for 2 to 3 minutes, or until heated through.

Remove the squash from the oven and take off the top(s). Fill with the rice mixture. (If there is any remaining rice mixture, place it in a baking dish, cover, and bake along with the squash.) Put the top(s) back on. Bake for 30 minutes, or until the squash is tender and the rice mixture is heated through.

Per serving: 288 calories, 2.6 g. fat, 5.9 g. protein, 65.4 g. carbohydrates, 4.3 g. fiber, 0 mg. cholesterol, 301 mg. sodium

Vegetable Curry

Makes 4 servings

Serve this curry over brown rice or another whole grain, such as quinoa or couscous. Be sure to start cooking the grain early enough that it will be done with the curry.

1	teaspoon olive oil
1	tablespoon curry powder
2	teaspoons black mustard seeds (optional)
1	teaspoon fennel seeds, crushed
1	teaspoon grated fresh ginger
½	teaspoon ground turmeric
1	medium onion, chopped
1	rib celery, chopped
1½	cups water
3	potatoes, cut into 1" chunks
½	head cauliflower, cut into florets
1	large carrot, chopped
1	medium zucchini, chopped
1	green pepper, chopped
1	cup fresh or frozen and thawed peas
½	teaspoon salt
½	teaspoon ground red pepper (optional)
	Raisins and chutney (optional)

Heat the oil in a large nonstick skillet over medium-high heat. Add the curry powder, mustard seeds (if using), fennel seeds, ginger, and turmeric. Cook for 1 minute. Add the onion, celery, and ½ cup of the water. Cook for 5 minutes, or until the vegetables are tender, stirring frequently.

Add the potatoes, cauliflower, carrot, and remaining 1 cup water. Over high heat, bring to a boil. Reduce the heat to low, cover, and simmer for 15 minutes. Add the zucchini, pepper, peas, salt, and ground red pepper (if using).

Cook for 10 minutes longer, or until the vegetables are tender.

To serve, garnish with the raisins and chutney (if using).

Per serving: 171 calories, 2 g. fat, 6.7 g. protein, 34.6 g. carbohydrates, 3.5 g. fiber, 0 mg. cholesterol, 303 mg. sodium

Polenta with Ratatouille

Makes 6 servings

*If you don't have time to make the ratatouille, serve the
polenta with plain tomato sauce, pesto sauce, or steamed
veggies. By itself, the ratatouille can be eaten cold, ladled
over rice or pasta, or rolled up in tortillas.*

Ratatouille

2	large onions, chopped
6	cloves garlic, minced
¼–½	cup water or vegetable broth
8	shiitake mushrooms, sliced (optional)
2	cups eggplant, cubed
2	cups zucchini and/or yellow squash, cubed
1	large green, sweet red, or yellow pepper, chopped
2½	cups crushed or chopped fresh tomatoes or 27 ounces canned chopped tomatoes
¼	cup red wine or nonalcoholic red wine (optional)
½	teaspoon dried oregano
¼	cup chopped fresh basil or 1 tablespoon dried basil
2	tablespoons chopped fresh parsley
1	tablespoon soy sauce
	Dash of ground black pepper

Polenta

6	cups water
2	cups polenta or coarse yellow cornmeal
½	teaspoon salt
⅛	teaspoon ground black pepper
	Soy Parmesan cheese (optional)

To make the ratatouille: In a large nonstick skillet, cook the onions and garlic in 2 to 3 tablespoons of the water or broth for about 5 minutes. Add the mushrooms (if using) and cook for 3 to 4 minutes.

Add the eggplant, zucchini or squash, green or sweet pepper, tomatoes, wine (if using), and oregano. Cover and simmer for 20 minutes, or until the vegetables are tender. Add the basil, parsley, soy sauce, and black pepper to taste.

To make the polenta: In a large saucepan over high heat, bring the water to a boil. Slowly add the polenta while stirring with a whisk. Add the salt and pepper. Reduce the heat to low and simmer for 25 minutes, stirring frequently.

Serve a large dollop of polenta on each plate. Top with the ratatouille and a small amount of the Parmesan (if using).

Per serving: 211 calories, 2 g. fat, 6.2 g. protein, 45.3 g. carbohydrates, 8.8 g. fiber, 0 mg. cholesterol, 541 mg. sodium

Shepherd's Pie

Makes 6 servings

This dish is somewhat involved but well worth the effort. Instead of the vegetables listed in the recipe, you can use 3 cups of whatever mix you have available. The method of preparing tofu that is described here can be used for other dishes such as chilis and casseroles.

4	large all-purpose potatoes, peeled and cubed
½	cup soy or rice milk
½	teaspoon salt
1	large onion, chopped
½	cup vegetable broth or water
3–4	cloves garlic, minced
2	ribs celery, chopped
1	large carrot, chopped
1	cup peas, fresh or frozen and thawed
1	medium zucchini, chopped
¾	cup fresh or frozen and thawed cut green beans or corn

½	teaspoon dried basil
½	teaspoon dried oregano
1	pound tofu, prepared for recipe (see note)
1½	tablespoons soy sauce

Preheat the oven to 350°F. Coat a 13" × 9 " baking dish with nonstick spray.

Place the potatoes in a large saucepan and cover with water. Over high heat, bring to a boil. Reduce heat to low, cover, and simmer for 15 minutes or until tender. Drain the potatoes and place in a bowl with the soy or rice milk and salt. Mash with an electric mixer or potato masher. Set aside.

Meanwhile, coat a large nonstick skillet with nonstick cooking spray. Cook the onion in 2 tablespoons of the broth or water over medium heat for 5 minutes, or until soft.

Add the garlic, celery, carrot, peas, zucchini, green beans or corn, basil, and oregano. Cook for 5 minutes, adding more broth or water if necessary.

Add the remaining broth or water and the tofu and soy sauce. Reduce the heat to low, cover, and cook for 5 minutes, or until the vegetables are tender. Pour the mixture into the prepared baking dish. Spread the mashed potatoes on top of the vegetables. Bake for 25 minutes, or until lightly browned.

Per serving: 187 calories, 3.9 g. fat, 11.6 g. protein, 29.6 g. carbohydrates, 4.3 g. fiber, 0 mg. cholesterol, 494 mg. sodium

Notes: Here are two ways to prepare tofu for recipes. The first method is to freeze the tofu. This is an excellent way to remove the water from the tofu, making it more dense and chewy. Drain the tofu and place in a plastic food storage bag or plastic wrap. Freeze overnight, or for at least 10 hours. Remove the tofu from the freezer and place it in warm water for 10 minutes. Then remove the tofu from the water, discard the plastic, and place the tofu in a dish towel or cheesecloth. Hold it over the sink, between the palms of your hands, and press until all of the water is released.

A second method is to crumble the tofu and drop it into a pot of boiling water. After boiling for 1 minute, pour the tofu and water into a colander lined with cheesecloth. Twist and squeeze the cheesecloth to remove as much liquid as possible.

DESSERTS

Dinner without dessert? Perish the thought. In fact, you can end any meal sweetly with one of the following treats. They're guaranteed to please even the sweetest of sweet tooths.

Sebastopol Apple Crisp

Makes 8 servings

Sebastopol, where our family lives, is known throughout northern California as apple country. We find the aroma of apples filling our kitchen quite irresistible. The ground walnuts give this dessert an added richness while providing extra omega-3 fatty acids.

1½	cups rolled oats
1	cup whole-wheat pastry flour
1	teaspoon ground cinnamon
¼	teaspoon salt
½	cup walnuts, finely ground
2	tablespoons soy or walnut oil
⅓	cup maple syrup
4	cups sliced apples
	Juice of one lemon
½	cup water

Preheat the oven to 350°F.

In a large bowl, combine the oats, flour, cinnamon, salt, and walnuts. Add the oil and maple syrup and mix well.

Place half the apples in a 9" pie pan or 8 " × 8" baking dish. Pour half the lemon juice over them and top with half the oat mixture. Place the remaining apples and lemon juice over the oat mixture. Sprinkle with the remaining oat mixture. Pour the water over the crisp. Bake for about 30 minutes, or until the apples are tender when pierced by a fork.

Per serving: 241 calories, 7.7 g. fat, 5.9 g. protein, 40.8 g. carbohydrates, 4.3 g. fiber, 0 mg. cholesterol, 82 mg. sodium

Berry Banana Sorbet

Makes 4 servings

We keep frozen bananas and berries (organic, of course) on hand so we can quickly whip up this treat for an after-dinner sweet tooth attack. The creamy texture of the sorbet belies the fact that it contains no dairy products and almost no fat.

2	**frozen bananas**
2	**cups frozen berries**
2	**tablespoons soy or rice milk, or juice**

Remove the bananas from the freezer and let sit for about 5 minutes, until they begin to thaw a little. Cut the bananas into chunks. Place in the food processor with the berries and milk or juice. Process until smooth.

Per serving: 54 calories, 0.3 g. fat, 0.7 g. protein, 13.5 g. carbohydrates, 1.9 g. fiber, 0 mg. cholesterol, 2 mg. sodium

Melon-Peach Sorbet

Makes 4 servings

For variety, try using mango chunks, berries, or pineapple chunks in place of the peaches or melon. Add a little bit of grated lemon or orange peel for an extra-tangy flavor.

3	**tablespoons honey or frozen juice concentrate**
½	**cup hot water**
1	**cup peeled, sliced peaches**

1   **cup melon chunks, such as honeydew or cantaloupe**

Dissolve the honey or juice concentrate in the hot water.

Combine the peaches and melon in a blender or food processor and puree. Place in a 13" × 9" baking dish. Stir in the honey or juice mixture. Place in the freezer for at least 4 hours.

To serve, cut the frozen mixture into 1½" pieces. Place in the blender or food processor and process until smooth.

Per serving: 82 calories, 0.1 g. fat, 0.5 g. protein, 21.4 g. carbohydrates, 1.1 g. fiber, 0 mg. cholesterol, 6 mg. sodium

Spicy Fruit Compote

Makes 6 servings

Fruity and intensely seasoned, this compote provides the perfect antidote to a craving for sweets. Its flavors seem especially appropriate for fall and winter.

1	orange, quartered
2	cups apple cider
1	teaspoon ground cinnamon
½	teaspoon ground nutmeg
¼	teaspoon ground ginger
⅛	teaspoon ground cloves
4	dried, pitted prunes + ½ cup
1	apple, cored and cut into chunks
1	cup fresh or canned and drained pineapple chunks
2	fresh peaches, cut into slices, or 2 cups frozen and thawed peach slices
½	cup nonfat plain yogurt (optional)

Chop one quarter of the orange, including the peel. Put the chopped orange, apple cider, cinnamon, nutmeg, ginger, cloves, and 4 prunes in a blender or food processor and process until smooth.

Peel and coarsely chop the remaining 3 orange quarters. In a large saucepan over high heat, bring the blended mixture, chopped orange, apple, and remaining prunes to a boil. Reduce the heat to low, cover, and simmer for 5 minutes, stirring occasionally.

Add the pineapple and peaches to the pan and remove from the heat. Serve hot or refrigerate to serve cold. Top with a dollop of yogurt (if using).

Per serving: 131 calories, 0.4 g. fat, 1.1 g. protein, 26.4 g. carbohydrates, 3.2 g. fiber, 0 mg. cholesterol, 1 mg. sodium

Cinnamon-Baked Apples

Makes 4

These baked apples make a perfect ending to most any meal. They're easy to make, too: Pop them in the oven before you sit down to eat, and by the time you're done, they will be, too.

4	**large apples, cored**
4	**tablespoons raisins**
1	**teaspoon ground cinnamon**
½	**cup apple juice or water**

Preheat the oven to 350°F.

Place the apples in an 8" × 8" baking dish. Put 1 tablespoon of the raisins in the hollowed core of each apple. Sprinkle with the cinnamon and pour the juice or water over the apples. Cover with a lid and bake for 40 minutes, or until the apples are tender when pierced with a fork.

Per apple: 124 calories, 0.6 g. fat, 0.6 g. protein, 32.4 g. carbohydrates, 3.6 g. fiber, 0 mg. cholesterol, 3 mg. sodium

Resources and References

RESOURCES

All of the following organizations offer information and services that will help you to implement the Renewal Anti-Aging Program. Only addresses are listed here. If you prefer to contact a particular organization by phone, you can obtain a toll-free number by calling 800 directory assistance.

Anti-Aging Medical Organizations

American Academy of Anti-Aging Medicine (A4M)
1341 West Fullerton, Suite 111
Chicago, IL 60614

International College for Advanced Longevity Medicine (ICALM)
1407 North Wells Street
Chicago, IL 60610

Life Extension Foundation
P.O. Box 229120
Hollywood, FL 33022

Alternative Medical Organizations

American Academy of Medical Acupuncture (AAMA)
5820 Wilshire Boulevard,
Suite 500
Los Angeles, CA 90036
Physicians who practice medical acupuncture.

American Association of Naturopathic Physicians
601 Valley Street, Suite 105
Seattle, WA 98109

American College for the Advancement of Medicine (ACAM)
23121 Verdugo Drive, Suite 204
Laguna Hills, CA 92653
Physicians who practice preventive and nutritional medicine.

American Holistic Medical Association (AHMA)
4101 Lake Boone Trail, Suite 201
Raleigh, NC 27607

National Center for Homeopathy
801 North Fairfax Street,
Suite 306
Alexandria, VA 22314

Physicians Committee for Responsible Medicine (PCRM)
5100 Wisconsin Avenue NW,
Suite 104
Washington, DC 20016
Promotes preventive medicine, vegan nutrition, ethical research practices, and compassionate medical policy.

Anti-Aging Nutritional Supplements, Programs, and Products

Renewal Research
(800) 555-4810
Web site address: www.renewal-now.com
Provides products featuring the author's exclusive formulations of the nutritional supplements discussed in this book—including vitamins, minerals, essential fatty acids, amino acids, antioxidants, herbs, phytochemicals, acidophilus, fiber, neuronutrients, and anti-aging hormones.

Anti-Aging Medicine Center of Northern California
321 South Main Street, PMB 41
Sebastopol, CA 95472
Phone: (800) 555-1459 or (707) 824-0110
Provides individualized anti-aging programs, telephone consultation service, quarterly newsletter (sample issue free), and referrals to anti-aging doctors in your area.

Laboratories and Testing

Aeron Lifecycles
1933 Davis Street, Suite 310
San Leandro, CA 94577
Saliva testing for hormone levels. No doctor's prescription needed for DHEA, melatonin, progesterone, estradiol, and testosterone. Prescription

required for estriol, estrone, and cortisol.

Genox Corporation
1414 Key Highway
Baltimore, MD 21230
The Genox Oxidative Stress Profile measures antioxidant protection and free radical activity.

Great Smokies Diagnostic Laboratory
63 Zillicoa Street
Asheville, NC 28801
Oxidative Stress (free radical activity) Panel, Hormone Profiles, Detoxification Profile, Comprehensive Digestive Stool Analysis, Intestinal Permeability, and other useful tests.

Immunosciences Lab, Inc.
8730 Wilshire Boulevard, #305
Beverly Hills, CA 90211

Meridian Valley Clinical Laboratory
515 West Harrison Street
Kent, WA 98042
Comprehensive hormone profiles and food allergy testing.

Metametrix Laboratories
5000 Peachtree Industrial Boulevard,
Suite 110
Norcross, GA 30071

Pantox Laboratories
4622 Santa Fe Street
San Diego, CA 92109
Pantox Antioxidant Profile: a serum assay of over 20 determinants of antioxidant defense system status.

Coronary Atherosclerosis

HeartScan Imaging

389 Oyster Point Boulevard,
Suite 5
South San Francisco, CA 94080
*Ultrafast computed tomography
(CT) scan imaging of the heart
detects atherosclerotic plaque in
the coronary arteries that can
lead to a heart attack. Contact for
a referral to a center in your area.*

Hypothyroidism

Broda O. Barnes, M.D., Research Foundation

P.O. Box 98
Trumbull, CT 06611

The Thyroid Institute

Stephen E. Langer, M.D.
3031 Telegraph Avenue,
Suite 230
Berkeley, CA 94705

Osteoporosis

*Dual photon absorptiometry is a
sensitive measure of bone density.
The N-Telopeptide (NTx) is a protein released by bone loss that
can be detected in a urine sample. Elevated NTx indicates
increased rate of bone loss.
Available at any local laboratory.*

Prostate Cancer

*Prostate Specific Antigen (PSA)
detects marker present in early
stages of prostate cancer. Available at any local laboratory.*

Compounding Pharmacies

College Pharmacy

833 North Tejon Street
Colorado Springs, CO 80903
Mail order from anywhere.

Dollar Drug

1055 West College Avenue
Santa Rosa, CA 95401
Mail order from anywhere.

Hopewell Pharmacy and Compounding Center

1 West Broad Street
Hopewell, NJ 08525
Mail order from anywhere.

International Academy of Compounding Pharmacists (IACP)

P.O. Box 1365
Sugar Land, TX 77487
*Provides referrals to a com-
pounding pharmacy near you.*

Professional Compounding Centers of America, Inc. (PCCA)

9901 South Wilcrest
Houston, TX 77099
*Provides referrals to a com-
pounding pharmacy near you.*

Women's International Pharmacy

5708 Monona Drive
Madison, WI 53716
Mail order from anywhere.

Vegetarian Organizations

American Natural Hygiene Society

12816 Race Track Road
Tampa, FL 33625

American Vegan Society

501 Old Harding Highway
Malaga, NJ 08328

North American Vegetarian Society

P.O. Box 72
Dolgeville, NY 13329

Vegetarian Nutrition Dietetic Practice Group

c/o American Dietetic Association

216 West Jackson Boulevard,
Suite 800
Chicago, IL 60606

Vegetarian Resource Group
P.O. Box 1463
Baltimore, MD 21203

Vegetarian Cookbooks

Carroll, Mary, with Straus, Hal. *The No Cholesterol (No Kidding!) Cookbook* (Emmaus, Pa.: Rodale Press, 1991).

Chelf, Vicki Rae. *Cooking with the Right Side of the Brain* (Garden City, N.Y.: Avery Publishing Group, 1991).

Diamond, Marilyn. *The American Vegetarian Cookbook from the Fit for Life Kitchen* (New York: Warner Books, 1990).

Grogan, Bryanna Clark. *The (Almost) No-Fat Cookbook: Everyday Vegetarian Recipes* (Summertown, Tenn.: Book Publishing Company, 1994).

McDougall, John A., and McDougall, Mary. *The McDougall Quick and Easy Cookbook* (New York: Dutton, 1997).

McDougall, John A., and McDougall, Mary. *The New McDougall Cookbook* (New York: Plume, 1997).

Messina, Virginia, and Messina, Mark. *The Vegetarian Way* (New York: Crown Trade Paperbacks, 1996).

Moosewood Collective, *The Moosewood Restaurant Low-Fat Favorites: Flavorful Recipes for Healthful Meals* (New York: Clarkson Potter, 1996).

Ornish, Dean. *Everyday Cooking with Dr. Dean Ornish: 150 Simple Seasonal Recipes for Family and Friends* (New York: Harper-Collins Publishers, 1996).

Raymond, Jennifer. *The Peaceful Palate* (Calistoga, Calif.: Heart and Soul Publications, 1992).

Robbins, John. *May All Be Fed: Diet for a New World* (New York: William Morrow and Company, 1992).

Siegel, Robert. *Fat-Free and Delicious* (Pacifica, Calif.: Pacifica Press, 1996).

Stepaniak, Joanne. *The Uncheese Cookbook* (Summertown, Tenn.: Book Publishing Company, 1994).

Wagner, Lindsay, and Spade, Ariane. *The High Road to Health* (New York: Simon and Schuster, 1990).

References

Chapter 1

Ames, B. N., Shigenaga, M. K., and Hagen, T. M. "Oxidants, Antioxidants, and the Degenerative Diseases of Aging." *Proceedings of the National Academy of Sciences of the United States of America* 90 (1993): 7915–22;18: 1–29.

Bjorksten, J. "Crosslinkage and the Aging Process." In *Theoretical Aspects of Aging* (New York: Academic Press, 1974).

Bjorksten, J. "The Crosslinkage Theory of Aging: Clinical Implications." *Comprehensive Therapy* II (1976): 65.

Campbell, N. A. *Biology* (Menlo Park, Calif.: The Benjamin/Cummings Publishing Company, 1987).

Cutler, R. G., "The Molecular and Evolutionary Aspects of Human Aging and Longevity." In *Anti-Aging Medicine* (Larchmont, N.Y.: Mary Ann Liebert Publishers, 1996).

Harman, D. "Free Radical Theory of Aging: Effect of Free Radical Reaction Inhibitors on the Mortality Rate of Male LAF Mice." *Journal of Gerontology* 23 (1968): 476.

Harman, D. "Free Radical Theory of Aging: Origin of Life, Evolution, and Aging." *Age* 3 (1980): 100.

Hayflick, L. *How and Why We Age* (New York: Ballantine Books, 1994).

Hayflick, L. "Theories of Aging." In *Fundamentals of Geriatric Medicine* (New York: Raven Press, 1983).

Klatz, R., and Goldman, R. *Stopping the Clock* (New Canaan, Conn.: Keats Publishing, 1996).

Mann, J. A. *Secrets of Life Extension* (Berkeley, Calif.: And/Or Press, 1980).

Orten, J., and Neuhaus, O. *Human Biochemistry* (St. Louis: Mosby Year-Book, 1986).

Passwater, R. A. *Supernutrition* (New York: Simon and Schuster, 1975).

Pierson, D., and Shaw, S. *Life Extension: A Practical Scientific Approach* (New York: Warner Books, 1983).

Rosenfeld, Albert. *Prolongevity II* (New York: Alfred A. Knopf, 1985).

Walford, R. L. *Maximum Life Span* (New York: W. W. Norton, 1983).

Chapter 2

Bendlich, A. "Vitamin E and Immunity." *Nutrition Report* 5 (3) (1987): 16, 20, 24.

Bierenbaum, M. et al. "Modification of Lipid Peroxidation Risk by Vitamin E Supplementation." *Clinical Research* 39 (1991): A395.

Bolton-Smith, C. et al. "Dietary Antioxidant Vitamins and Odds Ratios for Coronary Heart Disease." *Federation of American Societies for Experimental Biology Journal* 5 (1991): A715.

Bray, T., and Bettger, W. "The Physiological Role of Zinc as an Antioxidant." *Free Radical Biology and Medicine* 8 (1990): 281–91.

Chuaqui, C. A., and Petkau, A. "Chemical Reactivity and Biological Effects of Superoxide Radicals." *Physical Chemistry* 30 (5/6) (1987): 365–73.

Cranton, E., and Frackelton, J. "Free Radical Pathology in Age-Associated Diseases: Treatment with EDTA Chelation, Nutrition, and Antioxidants." *Journal of Holistic Medicine* 6 (1) (Spring/summer 1984).

Cutler, R. G. "Aging and Oxygen Radicals." In *Physiology and Oxygen Radicals.* Clinical Monograph Series. Bethesda, Md.: American Physiological Society (1986): 251–85.

Cutler, R. G. "Human Longevity and Aging: Possible Role of Reactive Oxygen Species." *Annals of the New York Academy of Sciences* 621 (1991):1–28.

Davies, S., Underwood, S., Wickens, D. et al. "Systematic Pattern of Free Radical Generation during Coronary Bypass Surgery." *British Heart Journal* 64 (1990): 236–40.

Floyd, R. "Role of Oxygen Free Radicals in Carcinogenesis and Brain Ischemia." *Federation of American Societies for Experimental Biology Journal* 4 (1990): 2587–597.

Harman, D. "Aging: A Theory Based on Free Radical and Radiation Chemistry." *Journal of Gerontology* 11 (1956a): 298–300.

Harman, D. "Free Radical Theory of Aging: Effect of Free Radical Reaction Inhibitors on the Mortality Rate of Male LAF Mice." *Journal of Gerontology* 23 (1968): 476.

Harman, D. "Free Radical Theory of Aging: Origin of Life, Evolution, and Aging." *Age* 3 (1980): 100.

Jacques, P., Chylack, L., McGandy, R. et al. "Antioxidant Status in Persons with and without Senile Cataract." *Archives of Ophthalmology* 106 (1988): 337–40.

Kappus, H. *Oxidative Stress* (Orlando, Fla.: Academic Press, 1985).

Kok, F. et al. "Do Antioxidants and Polyunsaturated Fatty Acids Have a Combined Association with Coronary Atherosclerosis?" *Atherosclerosis* 86 (1991): 85–90.

Korthius, R. J., and Granger, D. N. "Reactive Oxygen Metabolites, Neutrophils, and the Pathogenesis of Ischemic-Tissue/Reperfusion." *Clinical Cardiology* 16 (Apr. Suppl. 1) (1993): 1–19.

Levine, S., and Kidd, P. *Antioxidant Adaptation: Its Role in Free Radical Induced Pathology* (San Francisco: Biocurrents Press, 1985).

Levine, S., and Kidd, P. "Beyond Antioxidant Adaptation: A Clonal Selection Theory of Cancer Causation." *Journal of Orthomolecular Psychiatry* (1985).

Lin, D. J. *Free Radicals and Disease Prevention: What You Must Know* (New Canaan, Conn.: Keats Publishing, 1993).

Marx, J. L. "Oxygen Free Radicals Linked to Many Diseases." *Science* 235 (1987): 529–31.

McCord, J. M. "Oxygen-Derived Free Radicals in Postischemic Tissue Injury." *New England Journal of Medicine* 312 (3) (1985): 159–63.

Meydani, S., Barklund, M., Liu, S. et al. "Vitamin E Supplementation Enhances Cell-Mediated Immunity in Healthy Elderly Subjects." *American Journal of Clinical Nutrition* 52 (1990): 557–63.

Moriguchi, S., Kobayashi, N., Kishino, Y. "High Dietary Intakes of Vitamin E and Cellular Immune Functions in Rats." *Journal of Nutrition* 120 (1990): 1096–1102.

Proctor, P. H., and Reynolds, E. S. "Free Radicals and Disease in Man." *Physiological Chemistry and Physics* (1984); 16, 175.

Pryor, W. A. "Free Radicals in Biological Systems." In *Readings from Scientific American: Organic Chemistry of Life* (San Francisco: W. H. Freeman).

Rosenfeld, A. *Prolongevity II* (New York: Alfred A. Knopf, 1985).

Sangeetha, P., Das, U., Koratkar, R. et al. "Increase in Free Radical Generation and Lipid Peroxidation Following Chemotherapy in Patients with Cancer." *Free Radical Biology and Medicine* 8 (1990): 15–19.

Sato, K., Niki, E., Shimasaki, H. "Free Radical Mediated Chain Oxidation of Low Density Lipoprotein and Its Synergistic Inhibition by Vitamin E and Vitamin C." *Archives of Biochemistry and Biophysics* 279 (1990): 402–5.

Somer, E. "The Role of Free Radicals in Atherogenesis: More Than Just Speculation." *Nutrition Report* (Aug 1990): 58.

Southorn, P. A. "Free Radicals in Medicine 1. Chemical Nature and Biologic Reactions." *Mayo Clinic Proceedings* 63 (1988): 381–89.

Southorn, P. A. "Free Radicals in Medicine 2. Involvement in Human Disease." *Mayo Clinic Proceedings* 63 (1988): 390–408.

Steinbrecher, U., Zhang, H., Lougheed, M. "Role of Oxidatively Modified LDL in Atherosclerosis." *Free Radical Biology and Medicine* 9 (1990): 155–68.

Walford, R. L. *The Immunologic Theory of Aging* (Baltimore: Williams and Wilkins, 1969).

Walford, R. L. *Maximum Life Span* (New York: W. W. Norton, 1983).

Wartanowicz, M., Panczenko-Kresowska, B., Ziemlanski, S. et al. "The Effect of Alpha-Tocopherol and Ascorbic Acid on the Serum Lipid Peroxide Level in Elderly People." *Annals of Nutrition and Metabolism* 28 (1984): 186–91.

Wefers, H., and Sies, H. "The Protection of Ascorbate and Glutathione against Microsomal Lipid Peroxidation Is Dependent on Vitamin E." *European Journal of Biochemistry* 174 (1988): 353–57.

Wood, M. "Vitamin C Shortage Undermines Antioxidant Defense System." *Agricultural Research* (June 1992).

Yuting, C., Rongliang, Z., Zhongjian, J. et al. "Flavonoids As Superoxide Scavengers and Antioxidants." *Free Radical Biology and Medicine* 9 (1990): 19–21.

Chapter 3

Ames, B. N., Gold, L. S., and Willett, W. C. "The Causes and Prevention of Cancer." *Proceedings of the National Academy of Sciences of the United States of America* 92 (1995): 5258–65.

Ames, B. N., Shigenaga, M. K., and Hagen, T. M. "Oxidants, Antioxidants, and the Degenerative Diseases of Aging." *Proceedings of the National Academy of Sciences of the United States of America* 90 (1993): 7915–22.18: 1–29.

Bland, J. "Chronological Age versus Biological Age: How *Old* Are You?" *Let's Live* (Oct. 1995).

Block, G., Patterson, B., and Subar, A. "Fruit, Vegetables, and Cancer Prevention: A Review of the Epidemiologic Evidence." *Nutrition and Cancer* (1992).

Boobis, A., Fawthrop, D., Davies, D. "Mechanisms of Cell Death." *Trends in Pharmacological Sciences* (1989): 10.

Campbell, N. A. *Biology* (Menlo Park, Calif.: The Benjamin/Cummings Publishing Company, 1987).

Cutler, R. G. "The Molecular and Evolutionary Aspects of Human Aging and Longevity." In *Anti-Aging Medicine* (Larchmont, N.Y.: Mary Ann Liebert Publishers, 1996).

Cutler, R. G., Packer, L., Bertram, J., Mori, A., eds. *Oxidative Stress and Aging* (Basel; Boston: Birkhauser Verlag, 1995).

Halliwell, B. "Antioxidants in Health and Disease." *Annual Review of Nutrition* 16 (1996): 33–50.

Korthius, R. J., and Granger, D. N. "Reactive Oxygen Metabolites, Neutrophils, and the Pathogenesis of Ischemic-Tissue/Reperfusion." *Clinical Cardiology* 16 (Apr. Suppl. 1) (1993): 1–19.

Marx, J. L. "Oxygen Free Radicals Linked to Many Diseases." *Science* 235 (1987): 529–31.

Mehta, J., Yang, B., and Nichols, W. "Free Radicals, Antioxidants, and Coronary Heart Disease." *Journal of Myocardial Ischemia* 5 (8) (1993): 31–41.

Miquel, J. "Theoretical and Experimental Support for an 'Oxygen Radical-Mitochondrial Injury' Hypothesis of Cell Aging." In *Free Radicals, Aging, and Degenerative Diseases* (New York: Aland R. Liss, 1986), 51.

Plotnick, G. D., Coretti, M. C., and Vogel, R. A. "Effect of Antioxidant Vitamins in the Transient Impairment of Endothelium-Dependent Brachial Artery Vasoactivity Following a Single High-Fat Meal." *Journal of the American Medical Association* 278 (1997): 1682–86.

Sheffy, B. E., and Schultz, R. D. "Influence of Vitamin E and Selenium on Immune Response Mechanisms." *Federation Proceedings* 38 (1979): 2139–43.

Shigenaga, M. K., Hagen, T. M., and Ames, B. N. "Oxidative Damage and Mitochondrial Decay in Aging." *Proceedings of the National Academy of Sciences of the United States of America* 91 (1994): 10771–778.

Tamkins, T. "Antioxidants Appear to Work in Nutritional Concert." *Medical Tribune* (Jan. 11, 1996).

Tappel, A. "Vitamin E Spares the Parts of the Cell and Tissues from Free Radical Damage." *Nutrition Today* 8 (1973): 4.

Thomas, C. A. "Assessing the Individual's Antioxidant Status." In *Anti-Aging Medicine* (Larchmont, N.Y.: Mary Ann Liebert Publishers, 1996).

Veith, I. *The Yellow Emperor's Classic of Internal Medicine* (Berkeley: University of California Press, 1972).

Weitzman, S. A., and Stossel, T. A. "Effects of Oxygen Radical Scavengers and Antioxidants on Phagocyte-Induced Mutagenesis." *Journal of Immunology* 128 (1982): 1770.

Woodhead, A. D., Blackett, A. D., and Hollaender, A., eds. *Molecular Biology of Aging* (New York: Plenum Press, 1985).

Chapter 5

Barnard, N. D. *Eat Right, Live Longer* (New York: Harmony Books, 1995).

Barnard, N. D. *Food for Life: How the New Four Food Groups Can Save Your Life* (New York: Harmony Books, 1993).

Barnard, N. D. *The Power of Your Plate: A Plan for Better Living* (Summertown, Tenn.: Book Publishing Company, 1990).

Barnard, N. D. "The Pyramid Crumbles: Rewriting, U.S. Dietary Guidelines." *Good Medicine* 4 (2) (Summer 1995): 16–18.

Cooper, R. K., and Cooper, L. L. *Low-Fat Living* (Emmaus, Pa.: Rodale Press, 1996).

Diamond, M. *The American Vegetarian Cookbook* (New York: Warner Books, 1990).

Erasmus, U. *Fats and Oils: The Complete Guide to Fats and Oils in Health and Nutrition* (Vancouver: Alive Publishing, 1986).

Garrison, R. H., and Somer, E. *The Nutrition Desk Reference* (New Canaan, Conn.: Keats Publishing, 1985).

Haas, E. *Staying Healthy with the Seasons* (Berkeley, Calif.: Celestial Arts, 1981).

Leonard, J., Hofer, J. L., and Pritikin, N. *Live Longer Now: The First One Hundred Years of Your Life* (New York: Charter Books, 1974).

"Low-Fat, High-Fiber Diet Improves Post-Breast Cancer Immune Function." *Family Practice News* (Feb. 1, 1995): 21.

McDougall, J. *The McDougall Plan* (Clinton, N.J.: New Win, 1983).

McDougall, J. *McDougall's Medicine* (Clinton, N.J.: New Win, 1985).

Messina, V., and Messina, M. *The Vegetarian Way* (New York: Random House, 1996).

Ornish, D. *Dr. Dean Ornish's Program for Reversing Heart Disease* (New York: HarperCollins, 1993).

Ornish, D. et al. "Can Lifestyle Changes Reverse Coronary Heart Disease? The Lifestyle Heart Trial." *Lancet* 336 (1990): 129–33.

Packer, L. "Health Effects of Nutritional Antioxidants." *Free Radical Biology and Medicine* 15 (1993): 685–86.

Pritikin, N., and McGrady, P. M. *The Pritikin Program for Diet and Exercise* (New York: Grosset and Dunlap, 1979).

Quillan, P. *Safe Eating* (New York: M. Evans and Company, 1990).

Rath, M. *Eradicating Heart Disease* (San Francisco: Health Now, 1993).

Robbins, J. *Diet for a New America* (Walpole, N.H.: Stillpoint Publishing, 1987).

Robbins, J. *May All Be Fed: Diet for a New World* (New York: William Morrow and Company, 1992).

Steinman, D. *Diet for a Poisoned Planet* (New York: Ballantine Books, 1990).

Wasserman, D., and Mangels, R. *Simply Vegan* (Baltimore: The Vegetarian Resource Group, 1991).

Chapter 6

Allen, L. "Protein-Induced Hypercalciuria: A Longer Term Study." *American Journal of Clinical Nutrition* 32 (1979): 741.

American Dietetic Association. "Position of the American Dietetic Association on Vegetarian Diets." *Journal of the American Dietetic Association* 93 (1993): 1317–19.

Anderson, J. W., and Johnstone, B. M. "Meta-Analysis of the Effects of Soy Protein Intake on Serum Lipids." *New England Journal of Medicine* 333 (1995): 276–82.

Barnard, N. D. *Eat Right, Live Longer* (New York: Harmony Books, 1995).

Barnard, N. D. *The Power of Your Plate* (Summertown, Tenn.: Book Publishing Company, 1990).

Barnard, N. D. "The Pyramid Crumbles: Rewriting U.S. Dietary Guidelines." *Good Medicine* 4 (2) (Summer 1995).

Brenner, B. "Dietary Protein Intake and the Progressive Nature of Kidney Disease: The Role of Hemodynamically Mediated Glomerular Injury in the Pathogenesis of Progressive Glomerular Sclerosis in Aging, Renal Ablation and Intrinsic Renal Disease." *New England Journal of Medicine* 307 (1982): 652.

Brockis, J. "The Effects of Vegetable and Animal Protein Diets on Calcium, Urate, and Oxalate Excretion." *British Journal of Urology* 54 (1982): 590.

Carpenter, B. "Investigating the Next Silent Spring: Why Are Sperm Counts Falling So Precipitously?" *U.S. News and World Report* 120 (10) (Mar. 11, 1996): 50.

Check, W. "Switch to Soy Protein for Boring but Healthful Diet." *Journal of the American Medical Association* 247 (1982): 3045–46.

Diamond, H., and Diamond, M. *Fit for Life* (New York: Warner Books, 1985).

Garrison, R. H., and Somer, E. *The Nutrition Desk Reference* (New Canaan, Conn.: Keats Publishing, 1985).

Kushi, M. *The Book of Macrobiotics* (Japan Publications, 1977).

Lappé, F. M. *Diet for a Small Planet* (New York: Ballantine Books, 1975).

Leonard, J., Hofer, J. L., and Pritikin, N. *Live Longer Now: The First One Hundred Years of Your Life* (New York: Charter Books, 1974).

Liebman, B. "Are Vegetarians Healthier Than the Rest of Us?" *Nutrition Action Health Letter* (Dec. 1988).

Marsh, A. G. "Cortical Bone Density of Adult Lacto-Ovo-Vegetarian and Omnivorous Women." *Journal of the American Dietetic Association* (Feb. 1980): 148–51.

Masterson, M. "The Poison Within: A Special Report." Phoenix: *Arizona Republic*, Jan. 29–Feb. 3, 1989.

McDougall, J. *The McDougall Plan* (Clinton, N.J.: New Win, 1983).

McDougall, J. *McDougall's Medicine* (Clinton, N.J.: New Win, 1985).

Mott, L., and Snyder, K. *Pesticide Alert* (San Francisco: Sierra Club Books, 1988).

Quillan, P. *Safe Eating* (New York: M. Evans and Company, 1990).

Rath, M. *Eradicating Heart Disease* (San Francisco: Health Now, 1993).

Robbins, J. *Diet for a New America* (Walpole, N.H.: Stillpoint Publishing, 1987).

Robbins, J. *May All Be Fed: Diet for a New World* (New York: William Morrow and Company, 1992).

Sacks, F. M. et al. "Effect of Ingestion of Meat on Plasma Cholesterol of Vegetarians." *Journal of the American Medical Association* 246 (1981): 640–44.

Sanchez, I. V. et al. "Bone Mineral Mass in Elderly Vegetarian Females." *American Journal of Roentgenology* 131 (1978): 542.

Sirtori, C. R., Even, R., and Lovati, M. R. "Soybean Protein Diet and Plasma Cholesterol: From Therapy to Molecular Mechanisms." *Annals of the New York Academy of Sciences.* 676 (1993): 188–201.

Steinman, D. *Diet for a Poisoned Planet* (New York: Ballantine Books, 1990).

Steinman, D. "Gender-Bending Foods." *Natural Health* 27 (1) (Jan.–Feb. 1997): 48ff.

Steinmetz, K. A. "Vegetables, Fruit, and Cancer." *Epidemiology. Cancer Causes Control* 2 (5) (1991): 325–57.

Warrick, Pamela. "Where's the Beef? Not on Dr. Spock's List." *Los Angeles Times*, Feb. 3, 1995.

Wehrbach, M. *Nutritional Influences on Illness* (Tarzana, Calif.: Third Line Press, 1987).

Yuesheng, Z. et al. "A Major Inducer of Anticarcinogenic Protective Enzymes from Broccoli: Isolation and Elucidation of Structure." *Proceedings of the National Academy of Sciences of the United States of America*, 1992.

Chapter 7

Aro, A. et al. "Adipose Tissue Isomeric Trans-Fatty Acids and Risk of Myocardial Infarction in Nine Countries: The EURAMIC Study." *Lancet* 345 (1995): 273–78.

Bicknell, F. Chemicals in Food and in Farm Produce: Their Harmful Effects (London: Faber and Faber, 1960).

Bougnoix, P. et al. "Alpha-Linolenic Acid Content of Adipose Breast Tissue: A Host Determinant of the Risk of Early Metastasis in Breast Cancer." British Journal of Cancer 21 (1994): 103–11.

Braly, J., and Torbet, F. Dr. Braly's Optimum Health Program (New York: Times Books, 1985).

Brazg, R. et al. "Effects of Dietary Antioxidants on LDL Oxidation in Noninsulin-Dependent Diabetics." Clinical Research 40 (1992): 103A.

Cooper, R. K., and Cooper, L. L. Low-Fat Living (Emmaus, Pa.: Rodale Press, 1996).

Deschrijver, R., and Privett, O. S. "Energetic Efficiency and Mitochondrial Function in Rats Fed Trans-Fatty Acids." Journal of Nutrition 114 (1984): 1183–91.

"Diet May Affect Tumor Recurrence." Family Practice News (Feb. 1, 1995): 21.

Erasmus, U. Fats and Oils: The Complete Guide to Fats and Oils in Health and Nutrition (Vancouver: Alive Publishing, 1986).

Erasmus, U. Fats That Heal; Fats That Kill: The Complete Guide to Fats, Oils, Cholesterol, and Human Health (Vancouver: Alive Publishing, 1993).

Goldstrich, J. D. The Cardiologist's Painless Prescription for a Healthy Heart and a Longer Life (Dallas: 9-HEART-9 Publishing, 1994).

Hubbard, R., and Sanchez, A. "Oxidized Cholesterol in the Foods You Eat." Nutrition Report 8 (1990): 56, 64.

Jialal, I. "Micronutrient Modulation of Nonconventional Risk Factors for CAD." In The Role of Diet in Reducing the Risk of Heart Disease (Minneapolis: McGraw-Hill, 1997).

Leonard, J., Hofer, J. L., and Pritikin, N. Live Longer Now: The First One Hundred Years of Your Life (New York: Charter Books, 1974).

"Low-Fat Diet's Role in Breast Cancer Risk Reduction Addressed." Family Practice News (Feb. 1, 1995): 21.

McDougall, J. The McDougall Plan (Clinton, N.J.: New Win, 1983).

McDougall, J. The McDougall Program: Twelve Days to Dynamic Health (New York: NAL Books, 1990).

McDougall, J. McDougall's Medicine (Clinton, N.J.: New Win, 1985).

McKeigue, P. "Trans-Fatty Acids and Coronary Heart Disease: Weighing the Evidence against Hardened Fat." Lancet 345 (1995): 269–70.

Ornish, D. Dr. Dean Ornish's Program for Reversing Heart Disease (New York: HarperCollins, 1993).

Ornish, D. Everyday Cooking with Dr. Dean Ornish (New York: HarperCollins, 1996).

Pritikin, N., and McGrady, P. M. The Pritikin Program for Diet and

Exercise (New York: Grosset and Dunlap, 1979).

Roberts, T. L. et al. "Trans Isomers of Oleic and Linoleic Acids in Adipose Tissue and Sudden Cardiac Death." *Lancet* 345 (1995): 278–82.

Rudin, D. O., and Felix, C. *The Omega-3 Phenomenon* (New York: Rawson Associates, 1987).

Simon, J. A. "Vitamin C and Heart Disease." *The Nutrition Report* (Aug. 1992).

Chapter 8

Behan, P. O., Behan, W. B. H., and Horrobin, D. F. "Effect of High Doses of Essential Fatty Acids on the Postviral Fatigue Syndrome." *Acta Neurologica Scandinavica* 82 (1990): 209.

Biagi, P. L., Bordoni, A., Hrelia, S., Celadon, M., and Horrobin, D. F. "Gamma-Linolenic Acid Dietary Supplementation Can Reverse the Aging Influence on Rat Liver Microsome Delta 6-Desaturase Activity." *Biochimica et Biophysica Acta* 1083 (1991): 187–92.

Budwig, J. *Das Fettsyndrom (The Fat Syndrome)* (Frieburg, West Germany : Hyperion Verlag, 1959).

Budwig, J. *Die Elementare Funktion der Atmung in Iher Beziehung zu Autoxydasblen Nahrungstoffen* (*The Basic Function of Cell Respiration in Its Relationship to Autooxidizable Nutrients*) (Frieburg, West Germany: Hyperion Verlag, 1953).

Budwig, J. *Fettfibel (Fat Notebook)* (Frieburg, West Germany: Hyperion Verlag, 1979).

Cameron, N. E., Cotter, M. A., and Robertson, S. "Essential Fatty Acid Diet Supplementation. Effects on Peripheral Nerve and Skeletal Muscle Function and Capillarization in Streptozocin-Induced Diabetic Rats." *Diabetes* 40 (1991): 532–39.

Chase, H. P. et al. "Intravenous Linoleic Acid Supplementation in Children with Cystic Fibrosis." *Pediatrics* 64 (1979): 207–13.

Erasmus, U. *Fats and Oils: The Complete Guide to Fats and Oils in Health and Nutrition* (Vancouver: Alive Publishing, 1986).

Erasmus, U. *Fats That Heal; Fats That Kill: The Complete Guide to Fats, Oils, Cholesterol, and Human Health* (Vancouver: Alive Publishing, 1993).

Galland, L., with Buchman, D. D. *Superimmunity for Kids* (New York: Dutton, 1988).

Hill, E. G. et al. "Perturbations of the Metabolism of EFA by Dietary Partially Hydrogenated Vegetable Oil." *Proceedings of the National Academy of Sciences of the United States of America* 79 (1982):953–57.

Horrobin, D. F. *Clinical Uses for Essential Fatty Acids* (St Albans, Vt.: Eden Press, 1983).

Horrobin, D. F. "Essential Fatty Acids: A Review." In *Clinical Uses of Essential Fatty Acids* (London: Eden Press, 1982).

Horrobin, D. F. "Essential Omega-6 and Omega-3 Fatty Acids in Medicine: A Practical Guide." *Journal of Advancement in Medicine* 3 (1990).

Johnston, I. M., and Johnston, J. R. *Flaxseed (Linseed) Oil and the Power of Omega-3. How to Make Nature's Cholesterol Fighters Work for You* (New Canaan, Conn.: Keats Publishing, 1990).

Kelley, D. S. "Alpha-Linolenic Acid and Immune Response." *Nutrition* 8 (1992): 215–17.

Kremer, J. M. et al. "Effects of Manipulation of Dietary Fatty Acids on Clinical Manifestations of Rheumatoid Arthritis." *Lancet* 1 (1985): 184–87.

Leaf, A., and Weber, P. C. "Cardiovascular Effects of n-fatty Acids: An Update." *New England Journal of Medicine* 318 (1988): 549–57.

Rudin, D. O. "Omega-3 Essential Fatty Acids in Medicine." In *1984–85 Yearbook of Nutritional Medicine* (New Canaan, Conn.: Keats, 1985).

Rudin, D. O. "On Essential Fatty Acids: An Interview." In *Health News and Review* (July–Aug. 1984).

Rudin, D. O. "The Dominant Diseases of Modernized Societies as Omega-3 Essential Fatty Acid Deficiency Syndrome: Substrate Beriberi." *Medical Hypotheses* 8 (1982): 17–47.

Rudin, D. O. "The Three Pellagras." *Journal of Orthomolecular Psychiatry* 12 (2) (1983): 91–110.

Rudin, D. O., and Felix, C. *The Omega-3 Phenomenon* (New York: Rawson Associates, 1987).

Serraino, M., and Thompson, L. U. "The Effect of Flaxseed on Early Risk Markers for Mammary Carcinogenesis." *Cancer Letters* 60 (1991):135–42.

Serraino, M., and Thompson, L. U. "Flaxseed Supplementation and Early Markers of Colon Carcinogenesis." *Cancer Letters* 63 (1992): 159–65.

Simopoulos, A. P. "Omega-3 Fatty Acids in Health and Disease and in Growth and Development." *American Journal of Clinical Nutrition* 54 (1991): 438–63.

Chapter 9

Barnard, N. D. *Eat Right, Live Longer* (New York: Harmony Books, 1995).

Cooper, R. K., and Cooper, L. L. *Low-Fat Living* (Emmaus, Pa.: Rodale Press, 1996).

Erasmus, U. *Fats and Oils: The Complete Guide to Fats and Oils in Health and Nutrition* (Vancouver: Alive Publishing, 1986).

Garrison, R. H., and Somer, E. *The Nutrition Desk Reference* (New Canaan, Conn.: Keats Publishing, 1985).

Grogan, B. C. *The (Almost) No Fat Cookbook: Everyday Vegetarian Recipes* (Summertown, Tenn.: Book Publishing Company, 1994).

Kurzweil, R. *The 10 Percent Solution for a Healthy Life* (New York: Crown Publishers, 1993).

Leonard, J., Hofer, J. L., and Pritikin, N. *Live Longer Now: The First One Hundred Years of Your Life* (New York: Charter Books, 1974).

McDougall, J. *McDougall's Medicine* (Clinton, N.J.: New Win, 1985).

McDougall, J. *The McDougall Program: Twelve Days to Dynamic Health* (New York: NAL Books, 1990).

McDougall, J. A., and McDougall, M. *The McDougall Quick and Easy Cookbook* (New York: Dutton, 1997).

McDougall, J. A., and McDougall, M. *The New McDougall Cookbook* (New York: Dutton, 1993).

Messina, V., and Messina, M. *The Vegetarian Way* (New York: Random House, 1996).

Ornish, D. *Dr. Dean Ornish's Program for Reversing Heart Disease* (New York: HarperCollins, 1993).

Ornish, D. *Everyday Cooking with Dr. Dean Ornish* (New York: HarperCollins, 1996).

Pritikin, N., and McGrady, P. M. *The Pritikin Program for Diet and Exercise* (New York: Grosset and Dunlap, 1979).

Whitaker, J. *Banish Fat at Every Meal* (Potomac, Md.: Philips Publishing, 1996).

Chapter 10

Anderson, J. W., and Johnstone, B. M. "Meta-Analysis of the Effects of Soy Protein Intake on Serum Lipids." *New England Journal of Medicine* 333 (1995): 276–82.

Bosch, J. P. et al. "Renal Functional Reserve in Humans: Effect of Protein Intake on Glomerular Filtration Rate." *American Journal of Medicine* 75 (1983): 943–50.

Brenner, B. M. et al. "Dietary Protein Intake and the Progressive Nature of Kidney Disease." *New England Journal of Medicine* 307 (11) (1982): 52–59.

Brenner, B. M. et al. "The Role of Hemodynamically Mediated Glomerular Injury in the Pathenogenesis of Progressive Glomerular Sclerosis in Aging, Renal Ablation, and Intrinsic Renal Disease." *New England Journal of Medicine* 307 (1982): 652–59.

Breslau, N. A. et al. "Relationship of Animal Protein-Rich Diet to Kidney Stone Formation and Calcium Metabolism." *Journal of Clinical Endocrinology and Metabolism.*

Committee on Diet, Nutrition, and Cancer of the National Research Council. *Diet, Nutrition, and Cancer.* Washington, D.C. (1982).

El Nalas, A. M., and Coles, C. A. "Dietary Treatment of Chronic Renal Failure: Ten Unanswered Questions." *Lancet* (Mar. 15, 1986): 597–600.

Hegsted, D. M. "Calcium and Osteoporosis." *Journal of Nutrition* 116 (1986): 2316–19.

Hegsted, D. M. et al. "Urinary Calcium and Calcium Balance in Young Men as Affected by Level of Protein and Phosphorus Intake." *Journal of Nutrition* 111 (1981): 553–62.

Jones, M. G. et al. "The Effect of Dietary Protein on Glomerular Filtration Rate in Normal Subjects." *Clinical Nephrology* 27 (2) (1987): 71–75.

Koury, S. D., and Hodges, R. E. "Soybean Proteins for Human Diets?" *Journal of the American Diabetic Association* 52 (1968): 480–84.

Lappé, F. M. *Diet for a Small Planet* (New York: Ballantine Books, *1975*).

Lee, C. J. et al. "Nitrogen Retention of Young Men Fed Rice with or without Supplementary Chicken." *American Journal of Clinical Nutrition* 24 (1971): 318–23.

Linkswiler, H. M. et al. "Protein-Induced Hyper-Calciuria." *Federation Proceedings* 40 (1981): 2429–33.

McDougall, J. *The McDougall Plan* (Clinton, N.J.: New Win, 1983).

McDougall, J. *McDougall's Medicine* (Clinton, N.J.: New Win, 1985).

Meinertz, H. et al. "Soy Protein and Casein in Cholesterol-Enriched Diets: Effects on Plasma Lipoproteins in Normolipidemic Subjects." *American Journal of Clinical Nutrition* 50: 785–93.

Messina, V., and Messina, M. *The Vegetarian Way* (New York: Random House, 1996).

"Position of the American Dietetic Association: Vegetarian Diets." *Journal of the American Dietetic Association* 88 (1988): 351–55.

"Protein: Exploding the Myths." *Physicians Committee for Responsible Medicine Guide to Healthy Eating* (Sept.–Oct. 1990).

Robertson, P. J. et al. "The Effect of High Animal Protein Intake on the Risk of Calcium Stone Formation in the Urinary Tract." *Clinical Science* 57 (1979): 285–88.

Walker, R. M., and Linkswiler, H. M. "Calcium Retention in the Adult Human Male as Affected by Protein Intake." *Journal of Nutrition* 102 (1972): 1297–1302.

Zemel, M. B. "Calcium Utilization: Effect of Varying Level and Source of Dietary Protein." *American Journal of Clinical Nutrition* 48 (1988): 880–83.

Chapter 11

Bashin, B. J. "The Freshness Illusion: A Few Good Words for Frozen Food and Some Serious New Questions about the Content of Supermarket Produce." *Harrowsmith* (Jan.–Feb. 1987).

Begley, S. "The Great Impostors: Do Chemical Companies Produce Substances That Dangerously Mimic Human Hormones?" *Newsweek* 127 (12) (Mar. 18, 1996): 48.

"Cancer-Causing Pesticides Abound in Supermarkets' Bounty." *Health News and Review* (Summer 1995): 14.

Carpenter, B. "Investigating the Next 'Silent Spring': Why Are Sperm Counts Falling So Precipitously?" *U.S. News and World Report* 120 (10) (Mar. 11, 1996): 50.

Carson, R. *Silent Spring* (Boston: Houghton Mifflin Company, 1962).

Colburn, T., Dumanoski, D., and Myers, J. P. *Our Stolen Future: Are We Threatening Our Fertility, Intelligence, and Survival? A Scientific Detective Story* (New York: Dutton, 1996).

"Consumers Win New Pesticide Regulations." *Environmental Nutrition* 19 (9) (Sept. 1996): 1.

Dadd, D. L. *Nontoxic, Natural, and Earthwise* (Los Angeles: Jeremy P. Tarcher, 1990).

Dadd-Redalia, D. L. *Sustaining the Earth: Choosing Consumer Products That Are Safe for You, Your Family, and the Earth* (New York: Hearst Books, 1994).

Durner, P. "How Safe Are the Pesticides on Food?" *Organic Gardening* (June 1987): 69–76.

Garrison, R. H., and Somer, E. *The Nutrition Desk Reference* (New Canaan, Conn.: Keats Publishing, 1985).

Goldbeck, N., and Goldbeck, D. *The Goldbeck's Guide to Good Food* (New York: NAL Books, 1987).

Goldman, L. R. "EPA Seeks Public Health Views on New Pesticide Law." *Public Health Reports* 111 (6) (Nov.–Dec. 1996): 512 (3).

Herman, P. "Breast Cancer and the Environment: The Deadly Link with Widespread Pesticides: (How the Environment Affects Our Health and What We Can Do about It)." *Health News and Review* (Winter 1995): 9.

Hunter, B. T. *Fact Book on Food Additives and Your Health* (New Canaan, Conn.: Keats Publishing, 1972).

Isaac, K., and Gold, S. *Eating Clean*. Center for the Study of Responsive Law, Washington, D.C., 1987.

Jacobson, M. *The Complete Eater's Digest and Nutrition Scoreboard* (Garden City, N.Y.: Doubleday and Company, 1985).

Kermode, G. O. *Food Additives in Human Nutrition: Reading from Scientific American* (San Francisco: W. H. Freeman and Company, 1978).

Lee, J. *What Your Doctor May Not Tell You about Menopause* (New York: Warner Books, 1996).

Long, C. "Chemical Combinations 1,000 Times As Deadly! (Residues of Pesticides and PCBs Affect Human Endocrine System." *Organic Gardening* 44 (1) (Jan. 1997): 18.

Malakoff, D. "Breast Cancer and Pesticides, What's the Connection?" *Pesticides and You* 13 (3 and 4): 16–25.

Marwick, C. " 'Provocative' Report Issued on Use of Pesticides." *Journal of the American Medical Association* 275 (12) (Mar. 27, 1996): 899(2).

McKelway, B., ed. "Guess What's Coming to Dinner." Americans for Safe Food, Washington, D.C.: Center for Science in the Public Interest (1987).

Mott, L., and Snyder, K. *Pesticide Alert* (San Francisco: Sierra Club Books, 1988).

Murray, M. T. "Male Infertility: A Growing Concern." *American Journal of Natural Medicine* (Apr. 1997): 6–15.

Null, G. *Clearer, Cleaner, Safer, Greener: A Blueprint for Detoxifying Your Environment* (New York: Villard Books, 1990).

"Protein: Exploding the Myths." *Physicians Committee for Responsible Medicine Guide to Healthy Eating* (Sept.–Oct. 1990).

Quillan, P. *Safe Eating* (New York: M. Evans and Company, 1990).

Raloff, J. "Estrogen Pairings Can Increase Potency. (Synergistic Estrogenic Effects Observed among the Pesticides Endosulfan, Dieldrin, and Chlorodanehare.)" *Science News* 149 (23) (June 8, 1996): 356.

Robbins, J. *Diet for a New America* (Walpole, N. H.: Stillpoint Publishing, 1987).

Saifer, P., and Zellerbach, M. *Detox* (New York: Ballantine Books, 1984).

Schrader, E. "A Giant Spraying Sound: Since NAFTA, Mexican Growers Are Spraying More Toxic Pesticides on Fruits, Vegetables—And Workers." *Mother Jones* 20 (1) (Jan.–Feb. 1995): 34(6).

Sewell, B., and Whyatt, R. *Intolerable Risk: Pesticides in Our Children's Food* (San Francisco: Natural Resources Defense Council, Feb. 1989).

Steenland, K. "Chronic Neurogical Effects of Organophosphate Pesticides: Subclinical Damage Does Occur, but Longer Follow-Up Studies Are Needed." *British Medical Journal* 312 (7042) (May 25, 1996): 1312.

Steinman, D. *Diet for a Poisoned Planet* (New York: Ballantine Books, 1990).

Steinman, D. "Gender-Bending Foods: Common Pesticides in Our Foods Are Threatening to Give Women Cancer and Make Men Sterile. Here's How to Reduce Your Risk." *Natural Health* 27 (1) (Jan.–Feb. 1997): 48.

"The Wax Cover-Up: What Consumers Aren't Told about Pesticides on Fresh Produce." Washington, D.C.: Center for Science in the Public Interest, 1989.

Weir, D., and Schapiro, M. *Circle of Poison* (San Francisco: Institute for Food and Development Policy, 1981).

Winter, R. *A Consumer's Dictionary of Food Additives* (New York: Crown Publishers, 1989).

Zamm, A. V., with Gannon, R. *Why Your House May Endanger Your Health* (New York: Simon and Schuster, 1980).

Chapter 12

Adlercreutz, H. "Diet and Breast Cancer." *Acta Oncologica* 31 (2) (1992): 175–81.

Alabaster, O. *The Power of Prevention* (Georgetown, Washington, D.C.: Saville Books, 1989).

Ames, B. N., Gold, L. S., and Willett, W. C. "The Causes and Prevention of Cancer." *Proceedings of the National Academy of Sciences of the United States of America* 92 (1995): 5258–65.

Barnard, N. D. *The Power of Your Plate* (Summertown, Tenn.: Book Publishing Company, 1990).

Block, G., Patterson, B., and Subar, A. "Fruit, Vegetables, and Cancer Prevention: A Review of the Epidemiologic Evidence." *Nutrition and Cancer* (1992).

Block, G., Patterson, B., and Subar, A. *Nutrition and Cancer* 18 (1992): 1–29.

Bogoch, S., and Bogoch, E. "Early Detection of Cancer with the Antimalignin Antibody in Serum (AMAS) Test." In *Advances in Anti-Aging Medicine* (Larchmont, N.Y.: Mary Ann Liebert Publishers, 1996): 109–25.

Cerutti, P. A. "Pro-Oxidant States and Tumor Promotion." *Science* 227 (1985): 375–81.

De Luca, L. et al. "Retinoids in Differentiation and Neoplasia." *Scientific American: Science and Medicine* (July–Aug. 1995): 28–37.

Dreher, Henry. *Your Defense against Cancer* (New York: Harper and Row, 1988).

Garrison, R. H., and Somer, E. *The Nutrition Desk Reference* (New Canaan, Conn.: Keats Publishing, 1985).

Goldberg, B. *Alternative Medicine: The Definitive Guide* (Puyallup, Wash.: Future Medicine Publishing, 1993).

Holm, L. E. "Treatment Failure and Dietary Habits in Women with Breast Cancer." *Journal of the National Cancer Institute* 85 (1) (1993): 32–36.

Howe, G. E. "Dietary Factors and Risk of Breast Cancer: Combined Analysis of 12 Case-Controlled Studies." *Journal of the National Cancer Institute* 82 (7) (1990): 561–69.

Kandaswami, C. "Cancer Prevention by Nutritional intervention." In *Advances in Anti-Aging Medicine* (Larchmont, N.Y.: Mary Ann Liebert Publishers, 1996): 109–25.

Kok, F. J., Martin, R. F., Mervyn, L. et al. "Selenium, Cancer Foe." *Better Nutrition for Today's Living* (Nov. 1990).

Lijinsky, W., and Shubik, P. "Benzopyrene and Other Polynuclear Hydrocarbons in Charcoal Broiled Meats." *Science* (145) (1964): 53.

Lubin, F. "Consumption of Methylxanthine-Containing Beverages and the Risk of Breast Cancer." *Cancer Letter* 53 (2–3) (1990): 81–90.

Plum, F., and Bennett, J. C., eds. *Cecil Textbook of Medicine* (Philadelphia: W. B. Saunders, 1996):1004–77.

Quillan, P. *Beating Cancer with Nutrition* (Tulsa: Nutrition/Times Press, 1994).

Simone, C. B. *Cancer and Nutrition* (New York: McGraw-Hill, 1983).

Singh, Vishwa N., and Gaby, Suzanne K. "Premalignant Lesions: Role of Antioxidant Vitamins and Beta-Carotene in Risk Reduction and Prevention of Malignant Transformation." In *American Journal of Nutrition: Supplement 2* "Antioxidants and Beta-Carotene in Disease Prevention" 52 (1) (Jan. 1991): 386S–390S.

Steinman, D. *Diet for a Poisoned Planet* (New York: Ballantine Books, 1990).

Varmus, H., and Weinberg, R. A. *Genes and the Biology of Cancer* (New York: Scientific American Library, 1993).

Wasserman, M. "Organochlorine Compounds in Neoplastic and Adjacent Apparently Normal Breast Tissue." *Bulletin of Environmental Contamination and Toxicology* 15 (1976): 478–84.

Weisburger, J. H. "Nutritional Approach to Cancer Prevention with Emphasis on Vitamins, Antioxidants, and Carotenoids." *American Journal of Clinical Nutrition* 53 (1991): 226S–237S.

Werbach, M. R. *Nutritional Influences on Illness: A Sourcebook of Clinical Research* (Tarzana, Calif.: Third Line Press, 1987).

Chapter 13

Adlecreutz, H. "Phytoestrogens: Epidemiology and a Possible Role in Cancer Protection." *Environmental Health Perspectives* 103 (Suppl. 7) (Oct. 1995): 103–12.

Babbs, C. "Free Radicals and the Etiology of Colon Cancer." *Free Radical Biology and Medicine* 8 (1990): 191–200.

Barnes, S. "Soybeans Inhibit Mammary Tumors in Models of Breast Cancer." *Progress in Clinical and Biological Research* 347 (1990): 239–53.

Berkowitz, K. F. "Will Designer Foods Fortified with Phytochemicals Fight Cancer?" *Environmental Nutrition* (Mar. 1993): 1–2.

Block, G. "Fruit, Vegetables, and Cancer Prevention: A Review of the Epidemiological Evidence." *Nutrition and Cancer* 18 (1992):1–29.

Bresnick, E. "Reduction in Mammary Tumorigenesis in the Rat by Cabbage and Cabbage Residue." *Carcinogenesis* 11 (7) (1990): 1159–63.

Brevard, P., Anderson, L., and Magee, A. "In Vitro Effects of Retinoids on the Histological Changes in Human Adenomas and Adenocarcinomas." *Nutrition Report* 35 (1987): 219–31.

Cameron, E., and Pauling, L. *Cancer and Vitamin C* (Menlo Park, Calif.: Linus Pauling Institute of Science and Medicine, 1979).

Caragay, A. B. "Cancer-Preventive Foods and Ingredients." *Food Technology* 46 (1992): 65–68.

Colditz, G. et al. "Increased Green and Yellow Vegetable Intake and Lowered Cancer Death in an Elderly Population." *American Journal of Clinical Nutrition* 41 (1985): 1.

Connett, J. E. et al. "Relationship between Carotenoids and Cancer. The Multiple Risk Factor Intervention Trial (MRFIT) Study." *Cancer* 64 (1989): 126–34.

"Foods 'Designed' to Prevent Cancer." *American Institute for Cancer Research Newsletter* Issue 35 (Spring 1992).

"Green Tea: Drink to Your Health?" *American Institute for Cancer Research Newsletter* Issue 39 (Spring 1993).

Hall, S. S. "Fruits and Vegetables Fight Cancer." *Hippocrates* (May 1997).

Henson, D. E. "Ascorbic Acid: Biological Functions and Relation to Cancer." *Journal of the National Cancer Institute* 83 (8) (1991): 547–50.

"Inhibition of Breast Cancer Progression with Omega-3 Fatty Acids." *Cancer Biotechnology Weekly* (Apr. 17, 1995): 10.

Khackik, F. et al. "Lutein, Lycopene, and Their Oxidative Metabolites in Chemoprevention of Cancer." *Journal of Cellular Biochemistry* (Suppl. 22): 236–46.

King, M., and McCay, P. "Modulation of Tumor Incidence and Possible Mechanisms of Inhibition of Mammary Carcinogenesis by Dietary Antioxidants." *Cancer Research* 43 (1983): 2485–90.

Knight, D. C., and Eden, J. A. "A Review of the Clinical Effects of Phytoestrogens." *Obstetrics and Gynecology* 87 (5 pt. 2) (May 1996): 897–904.

Lau, B. H. S. "Garlic Components Modulate Macrophage and T-Lymphocyte Functions." *Molecular Biotherapy* 3 (1991): 103–7.

Liebman, B. "Carrots against Cancer?" *Nutrition Action Health Letter* Dec. 1988.

Lin, R. I. S. "First World Congress on the Health Significance of Garlic and Garlic Constituents." Aug. 1990.

"Linking Plants to People." *American Institute for Cancer Research Newsletter* Issue 46 (Winter 1995).

McKeown, L. A. "Diet High in Fruit and Vegetables Linked to Lower Breast Cancer Risk." *Medical Tribune* (July 9, 1992): 14.

Messina, M. "Soybeans and Cancer." *Guide to Healthy Eating* (Washington, D.C.: The Physicians Committee for Responsible Medicine, Jan.–Feb. 1991): 5.

Messina, M. "The Role of Soy Products in Reducing the Risk of Cancer." *Journal of the National Cancer Institute* 83 (8) (1991): 541–46.

Meyskens, F. L., Jr. "Coming of Age: The Chemoprevention of Cancer." *New England Journal of Medicine* 23 (12) (Sept. 20, 1990): 825–26.

Newmark, H. L. "A Hypothesis for Dietary Components as Blocking Agents of Chemical Carcinogenesis: Plant Phenolics and Pyrolle Pigments." *Nutrition and Cancer* 6 (1984): 58–70.

Newmark, H. L. "Plant Phenolics as Inhibitors of Mutational and Precarcinogenic Events." *Canadian Journal of Physiology and Pharmacology* 65 (1987): 461–66.

Passwater, R. *Selenium as Food and Medicine* (New Canaan, Conn.: Keats Publishing, 1980).

"Phytochemicals: First Line against Disease." *Patient Care* (Nov. 15, 1995).

Probhala, R., Garewal, H., Meyskens, F. et al. "Immunomodulation in Humans Caused by Beta-Carotene and Vitamin

A." *Nutrition Research* 10 (1990): 1473–86.

Salaman, M. K. "The Prevention of Cancer through Diet: Beyond Theory." *Total Health* (Oct. 1996): 14–16.

Schardt, D. "Phytochemicals: Plants against Cancer." *Nutrition Action Healthletter* (Apr. 1994): 1–4.

Schwartz, J. L. "Beta Carotene and/or Vitamin E as Modulators of Alkylating Agents in SCC-25 Human Squamous Carcinoma Cells." *Cancer Chemotherapy and Pharmacology* 29 (3) (1992): 207–13.

Stahelin, H. B. et al. "Cancer, Vitamins, and Plasma Lipids: Prospective Base Study." *Journal of the National Cancer Institute* 73: 1463–68.

Stavrit, B. "Antimutagens and Anti-Carcinogens in Foods." *Food and Chemical Toxicology* 32 (1) (1994): 79–90.

Temple, N. J., and Basu, T. K. "Does Beta-Carotene Prevent Cancer? A Critical Appraisal." *Nutrition Research* 8 (1988): 685–701.

Wattenberg, L. W. "Inhibition of Carcinogenesis by Minor Nutrient Constituents of the Diet." *Proceedings of the Nutrition Society 1990*; 49 (2): 173–83.

Yu, S., Mao, B., Xiao, P. et al. "Intervention Trial with Selenium for the Prevention of Lung Cancer among Tin Miners in Yunnan, China: A Pilot Study." *Biological Trace Element Research* 24 (1990): 105–9.

Zhang, Y. "A Major Inducer of Anticarcinogenic Protective Enzymes from Broccoli: Isolation and Elucidation of Structure." *Proceedings of the National Academy of Sciences of the United States of America* 89 (1992): 2339–2403.

Ziegler, R. G. "Vegetables, Fruits, and Carotenoids and the Risk of Cancer." *American Journal of Clinical Nutrition* 53 (1991): 251S–259S.

Chapter 14

Andrews, E. L. "United States Wins Beef with Europeans." *New York Times* (May 9, 1997).

Barnard, N. D. *Eat Right, Live Longer* (New York: Random House, 1995).

Barnard, N. D. *The Power of Your Plate* (Summertown, Tenn.: Book Publishing Company, 1990).

Erasmus, U. *Fats and Oils: The Complete Guide to Fats and Oils in Health and Nutrition* (Vancouver: Alive Publishing, 1986).

Goldberg, B. *Alternative Medicine: The Definitive Guide* (Puyallup, Wash.: Future Medicine Publishing, 1993).

Lappé, M. *Germs That Won't Die: Medical Consequences of the Misuse of Antibiotics* (Garden City, N.Y.: Anchor Press/Doubleday, 1982).

Masters, W. H. "Sex Steroid Influences on the Aging Process." *American Journal of Obstetrics and Gynecology* (Oct. 1957).

McKelway, B., ed. "Guess What's Coming to Dinner." Americans for

Safe Food, Washington, D.C.: Center for Science in the Public Interest (1987).

National Research Council. *Meat and Poultry Inspection—The Scientific Basis of the Nation's Program* (Washington, D.C.: National Academy Press, 1985).

Puzo, D. "Animal Rights Group Claims Poor Treatment of Calves, Calls for Boycott." *Los Angeles Times*, 793qw2 (June 22, 1989).

Quillan, P. *Safe Eating* (New York: M. Evans and Company, 1990).

Rifkin, J. *Beyond Beef: The Rise and Fall of the Cattle Culture* (New York: Dutton, 1992).

Robbins, J. *Diet for a New America* (Walpole, N.H.: Stillpoint Publishing, 1987).

Robbins, J. *May All Be Fed: Diet for a New World* (New York: William Morrow and Company, 1992).

Schell, O. *Modern Meat: Antibiotics, Hormones, and the Pharmaceutical Farm* (New York: Random House, 1984).

Steinman, D. *Diet for a Poisoned Planet* (New York: Ballantine Books, 1990).

Zuckerman, S. *Nutrition Action Healthletter* (Jan. 1985).

Chapter 15

Anthan, G. "Contamination Rate Reaches 80 Percent at Some U.S. Poultry Plants." *Des Moines Register* (Apr. 12, 1987).

Anthan, G. "Poultry Firms Allowed to Vacuum Away Pus, U.S. Inspectors Say." *Des Moines Register* (June 16, 1987).

Anthan, G. "Salmonella Poisoning: More Than an Upset Stomach." *Des Moines Register* (Apr. 13, 1987).

Cohen, M., and Tauxe, R. "Drug-Resistant Salmonella in the United States: An Epidemiologic Perspective." *Science* 234 (Nov. 21, 1986): 964–69.

Livingston-Wheeler, V. with Addeo, E. G. *The Conquest of Cancer: Vaccines and Diet* (New York: Franklin Watts, 1984).

"Loss of Tainted Chickens Won't Hurt Prices: Analyst." *Supermarket News* (Mar. 20, 1989).

Nicholson, Andrew. "Chicken Is Not a Health Food." *Good Medicine* III (4) (Autumn 1994).

"Poultry Affected by Salmonella Enteritidis." *Federal Register* 55 (33) (Feb. 16, 1990).

"Risk from Chicken (The U.S. Agriculture Department Reported That 3,000 People Die Every Year from Contaminated Meat and Poultry)." *Maclean's* 109 (13) (Mar. 25, 1996): 33.

Robbins, J. *Diet for a New America* (Walpole, N.H.: Stillpoint Publishing, 1987).

Robbins, J. *May All Be Fed: Diet for a New World* (New York: William Morrow and Company, 1992).

Schell, O. *Modern Meat: Antibiotics, Hormones, and the Pharma-*

ceutical Farm (New York: Random House, 1984).

Steinman, D. *Diet for a Poisoned Planet* (New York: Ballantine Books, 1990).

"USDA Recalls Processed Chicken from Schools." *Cancer Weekly Plus* (Sept. 8, 1997): 17–18.

Zuckerman, S. "The Overuse of Antibiotics in Animal Feed." *Nutrition Action* (Jan.–Feb. 1985).

Chapter 16

Castleman, M. "On the Hook (Contamination of Fish by Toxic Pollutants)." *Sierra* 79 (2) (Mar.–Apr. 1994): 34.

Committee on Evaluation of the Safety of Fishery Products, Institute of Medicine. *Seafood Safety* (Washington, D.C.: National Academy Press, 1991).

Craig, C. P. "It's Always the Big Ones That Should Get Away." *Journal of the American Medical Association* 244 (1980): 272.

Foster, D. "You Are What You Eat: A Glowing Report on Radioactive Waste in the Sea." *Mother Jones* (July 1981).

Gerhard, G., Patton, B. D. et al. "Comparison of Three Species of Dietary Fish: Effects on Serum Concentrations of Low-Density-Lipoprotein Cholesterol and Apolipoprotein in Normotriglyceridemic Subjects." *American Journal of Clinical Nutrition* 54 (1991): 334–39.

Gossett, R., Wikholm, G., Ljubenkov, J., Steinman, D. "Human Serum DDT Levels Related to Consumption of Fish from the Coastal Waters of Los Angeles." *Environmental Toxicology and Chemistry* 8 (1989): 951–55.

Grandjean, P., Weihe, P., Jorgensen, P. J. et al. "Impact of Maternal Seafood Diet on Fetal Exposure to Mercury, Selenium, and Lead." *Archives of Environmental Health* 47 (1992): 185–95.

Haas, E. et al. "The Great American Fish Scandal: Health Risks Unchecked." *Public Voice for Food and Health Policy*, Washington, D.C. (1986): 27.

Hokama, Y. "Detection of Ciguatoxin and Related Polyethers in Fish Tissues Associated with Ciguatera Poisoning by the Stick Enzyme Immunoassay." Paper presented before the National Academy of Sciences Committee on Evaluation of Safety of Fishery Products, Woods Hole, Mass. (July 26, 1989).

Hughes, J. M., and Merson, M. H. "Fish and Shellfish Poisoning." *New England Journal of Medicine* 295 (1976): 1117.

Hughes, J. M., Merson, M. H., and Gangarosa, E. J. "The Safety of Eating Shellfish." *Journal of the American Medical Association* 237 (1977): 1980.

"Is Our Fish Fit to Eat?" *Consumer Reports* 57 (Feb. 1992): 103–14.

McKelway, B., ed. "Guess What's Coming to Dinner." Americans for Safe Food, Washington, D.C.: Center for Science in the Public Interest (1987).

"Minamata: Mercury's Crippling Legacy." *Multinational Monitor* (Apr. 1987): 16–17.

Oskarsson, A., Schutz, A., Skerfving, S., Hallen, I. P., Ohlin, B., and Lagerkvist, B. J. "Total and Inorganic Mercury in Breast Milk and Blood in Relation to Fish Consumption and Amalgam Filling in Lactating Women." *Archives of Environmental Health* 51 (3) (May–June 1996): 234(8).

Raloff, J. "Mercurial Risks from Acid's Reign: Tainted Fish May Pose a Serious Human Health Hazard." *Science News* 139 (Mar. 9, 1991): 152 (5).

"Seafood Poisoning." *Scientific American Medicine* 4 (1) (Jan. 1981).

"Seafood Safety: Present and Future." Presentation made by U.S. Food and Drug Administration at the Institute of Food Technologists meeting in Chicago (June 1989).

Skerfving, S. "Mercury in Women Exposed to Methylmercury through Fish Consumption and in Their Newborn Babies and Breast Milk." *Bulletin of Environmental Contamination and Toxicology* 41 (1988): 475–82.

Vreeland, L. "How Safe Is Our Fish?" *Ladies' Home Journal* 109 (May 1992): 196–97.

Wastes in Marine Environments (Washington, D.C.: U.S. Office of Technology Assessment, Apr. 1987).

Wender, R., and Patton, B. D. "Comparison of Three Species of Fish Consumed as Part of a Western Diet: Effects on Platelet Fatty Acids and Function, Hemostasis, and Production of Thromboxane." *American Journal of Clinical Nutrition* 54 (1991): 326–33.

Wilcox, F. "Multiple Exposures." In *Chronicles of the Radiation Age,* by Catherine Caulfield. *Amicus Journal* (Fall 1989): 53–54.

Williams, G. "What's Wrong with Fish? It's Usually the Last Meat Vegetarians Give Up. Maybe It Should Be the First." *Vegetarian Times* (Aug. 1995): 54.

Young, B. B. "Mercury: Pregnant and Nursing Women Take Heed." *Nutrition Action* (Sept. 1984).

Zied, E. S. "How Risky Is Eating Fish? EN's Guide to Eating Seafood Safely." *Environmental Nutrition* 21 (3) (Mar. 1998): 1–2.

Chapter 17

Alcohol

"Alcohol Intake and Coronary Heart Disease." *Nutrition Research Newsletter* 16 (11–12) (Nov.–Dec. 1997): 11(2).

"Beer Drinking and the Risk of Rectal Cancer." *Nutrition Reviews* 42 (1984): 244.

Bikle, D. D. et al. "Bone Disease in Alcohol Abuse." *Annals of Internal Medicine* 103 (1985): 42–48.

"Can a Drink a Day Keep a Heart Attack Away?" *Archives of Internal Medicine* (Feb. 27, 1995).

Fortmann, S. P. et al. "The Association of Blood Pressure and Dietary Alcohol: Differences by Age, Sex, and Estrogen Use." *American Journal of Epidemiology* 118 (4) (1983): 497–507.

"Going for the French Factor." *Prevention* 47 (8) (Aug. 1995): 74(6).

Haskell, W. et al. "The Effect of Cessation and Resumption of Moderate Alcohol Intake on Serum High-Density Lipoprotein Subfractions." *New England Journal of Medicine* 310 (1984): 805–10.

Horrobin, D. "A Biochemical Basis for Alcoholism and Alcohol-Induced Damage Including the Fetal Alcohol Syndrome and Cirrhosis: Interference with Essential Fatty Acid and Prostaglandin Metabolism." *Medical Hypotheses* 6 (1980): 929–42.

Kaufman, D. W. et al. "Alcoholic Beverages and Myocardial Infarction in Young Men." *American Journal of Epidemiology* 121 (1985): 548–54.

Kissin, B., and Begleiter, H., eds. *The Biology of Alcoholism, Volume 3: Clinical Pathology* (New York: Plenum Press, 1974).

Mark, V. "The Reversible Causes of Dementia." In *Advances in Anti-Aging Medicine, Volume 1* (Larchmont, N.Y.: Mary Ann Liebert Publishers, 1996).

"Nonpharmacological Approaches to the Control of High Blood Pressure. Final Report of the Subcommittee on Nonpharmacological Therapy of the 1984 Joint National Committee on Detection, Evaluation, and Treatment of High Blood Pressure." *Hypertension* 8 (5) (1986): 444–67.

"Red Wine and Lipid Peroxidation." *Nutrition Research Newsletter* 14 (4) (Apr. 1995): 45(1).

Rosenberg, L. et al. "Breast Cancer and Alcoholic Beverage Consumption." *Lancet* 1 (1982): 267.

Saville, P. D. "Changes in Bone Mass with Age and Alcoholism." *Journal of Bone and Joint Surgery* 47A (1965): 492–99.

"60 Minutes Skews the Facts Again (About Wine's Effects on the Body)." *Tufts University Diet and Nutrition Letter* 13 (10) (Dec. 1995): 1(2).

Caffeine

Barnard, N. D. *Eat Right, Live Longer* (New York: Harmony Books, 1995).

Forde, O. H. et al. "The Tromso Heart Study: Coffee Consumption and Serum Lipid Concentrations in Men with Hypercholesterolaemia: A Randomised Intervention Study." *British Medical Journal* 290 (1985): 893–95.

Haas, E. *The Detox Diet* (Berkeley, Calif.: Celestial Arts Publishing, 1996).

Haffner, S. M. et al. "Coffee Consumption, Diet, and Lipids." *American Journal of Epidemiology* 122 (1) (1985): 1–12.

Heaney, R. P., and Recker, R. R. "Effects of Nitrogen, Phosphorus, and Caffeine on Calcium Balance in Women." *Journal of Laboratory and Clinical Medicine* 99 (1982): 46–55.

Kark, J. et al. "Coffee, Tea, and Plasma Cholesterol: The

Jerusalem Lipid Research Clinic Prevalence Study." *British Medical Journal* 291 (6497) (1985): 699–704.

LaCroix, A. Z. et al. "Coffee Consumption and the Incidence of Coronary Heart Disease." *New England Journal of Medicine* 315 (16) (1986): 977–82.

Massey, L. K., and Berg, T. A. "The Effect of Dietary Caffeine on Urinary Excretion of Calcium, Magnesium, Phosphorus, Sodium, Potassium, Chloride, and Zinc in Healthy Males." *Nutrition Research* 5 (1985): 1281–84.

Morck, T. A. et al. "Inhibition of Food Iron Absorption by Coffee." *American Journal of Clinical Nutrition* 37 (3) 1 (1983): 416–20.

Shirlow, M. J. et al. "A Study of Caffeine Consumption and Symptoms: Indigestion, Palpitations, Tremor, Headache, and Insomnia." *International Journal of Epidemiology* 14 (2) (June 1985): 239–48.

Steinman, D. *Diet for a Poisoned Planet* (New York: Ballantine Books, 1990).

Wilcox, A., Weinberg, C., and Baird, D. "Caffeinated Beverages and Decreased Fertility." *Lancet* 7 (Dec. 24, 1988): 1473–76.

Williams, P. T. et al. "Caffeine Intake and Elevated Cholesterol and Apolipoprotein B Levels in Men." *Journal of the American Medical Association* 253 (10) (1985): 1407–11.

Yeh, J. K. et al. "Caffeine Increases Urinary Ca Excretion by Acceleration?" *Journal of Nutrition* 116 (2) (1986): 273–80.

Sugar

Bernstein, J. et al. "Depression of Lymphocyte Transformation Following Oral Glucose Ingestion." *American Journal of Clinical Nutrition* 30 (1977): 613.

Carper, J. *Jean Carper's Total Nutrition Guide* (New York: Bantam Books, 1987): 26–33.

Crook, W. *The Yeast Connection* (New York: Vintage Books, 1986).

Dadd, D. L. *Nontoxic, Natural, and Earthwise* (Los Angeles: Jeremy P. Tarcher, 1990): 116–20.

Duffy, W. *Sugar Blues* (New York: Warner, 1976).

Erasmus, U. *Fats and Oils: The Complete Guide to Fats and Oils in Health and Nutrition* (Vancouver: Alive Publishing, 1986): 25–28.

"Fructose Risk for High-Fat Diners?" *Science News* 133 (13) (Mar. 26, 1988).

Reiser, S. "Effect of Dietary Sugars on Metabolic Risk Factors Associated with Heart Disease." *Nutrition and Health* 3 (1985): 203–16.

Saifer, P., and Zellerbach, M. *Detox* (New York: Ballantine Books, 1984): 39–41.

Sanchez et al. "Role of Sugars in Human Neutrophilic Phagocytosis." *American Journal of Clinical Nutrition* 26 (1973): 180.

Szanto, S., and Yudkin, J. "Dietary Sucrose and the Behaviour of

Blood Platelets." *Proceedings of the Nutrition Society* 29 (1) (Suppl. 3A) (1970).

Temple, N. J. "Coronary Heart Disease: Dietary Lipids or Refined Carbohydrates?" *Medical Hypotheses* 10 (4) (1983): 425–35.

Winitz, M., Graff, J., and Seedman, D. A. "Effect of Dietary Carbohydrate on Serum Cholesterol Levels." *Archives of Biochemistry and Biophysics* 108 (1964): 576–79.

Yudkin, J. "Report of the COMA Panel on Dietary Sugars in Human Disease: Discussion Paper." *Journal of the Royal Society of Medicine* 83 (Oct. 1990): 627–28.

Yudkin, J. *Sweet and Dangerous* (New York: Peter W. Hayden, 1972).

Yudkin, J. et al. "Effects of High Dietary Sugar." *British Medical Journal* 281 (1980): 1396.

Yudkin, J., Edelman, J., and Hough, L., eds. *Sugar: Chemical, Biological, and Nutritional Aspects of Sucrose* (Hartford, Conn.: Daniel Harvey).

Yudkin, J., and Szanto, S. "The Relationship between Sucrose Intake, Plasma Insulin, and Platelet Adhesiveness in Men with and without Occlusive Vascular Disease." *Proceedings of the Nutrition Society* 29 (1) (Suppl. 2A–3A) (1970).

Chapters 19–22

Abbey, M., Nestel, P. J., and Baghurst, P. "Antioxidant Vitamins and Low-Density Lipoprotein Oxidation." *American Journal of Clinical Nutrition* 58 (1993): 525–32.

Ames, B., Shigenaga, M., and Hagen, T. "Oxidants, Antioxidants, and the Degenerative Diseases of Aging." *Proceedings of the National Academy of Sciences of the United States of America* 90 (Sept. 1993): 7915–22.

Beisel, W. R. "Single Nutrients and Immunity." *American Journal of Clinical Nutrition* 35 (Suppl.) (1982): 417.

Benowicz, R. J. *Vitamins and You* (New York: Berkley Books, 1981).

Bhaskaram, C., and Reddy, V. "Cell-Mediated Immunity in Iron- and Vitamin-Deficient Children." *British Medical Journal* 3 (1975): 522.

Block, G. et al. "Vitamin Supplement Use, by Demographic Characteristics." *American Journal of Epidemiology* 127 (1988): 297–309.

Block, G. "Vitamin C and Cancer Prevention: The Epidemiologic Evidence." *American Journal of Clinical Nutrition* 53 (1991): 270S–282S.

Blot, W. J. et al. "The Linxian Trials: Mortality Rates by Vitamin-Mineral Intervention Group." *American Journal of Clinical Nutrition* 62 (Suppl. 6) (1995): 1424S–1426S.

Blot, W. J. et al. "Nutrition Intervention Trials in Linxian, China: Supplementation with Specific Vitamin/ Mineral Combinations, Cancer Incidence, and Disease-Specific Mortality in the General

Population." *Journal of the National Cancer Institute* 85 (1993): 1483–91.

Bordia, A. K. "The Effect of Ascorbic Acid on Blood Lipids, Fibrinolytic Activity, and Platelet Adhesiveness in Patients with Coronary Artery Disease." *Atherosclerosis* 35 (1980): 181–87.

Bush, M. J., and Verlangieri, A. J. "An Acute Study on the Relative Gastrointestinal Absorption of a Novel Form of Calcium Ascorbate." *Research Communications in Chemical Pathology and Pharmacology* 5 (1) (1987).

Chandra, R. J. et al. "Vitamins for the Elderly." *Lancet* 340 (1993): 1124–27.

Chandra, R. K. "Immunocompetence Is a Sensitive and Functional Barometer of Nutritional Status." *Acta Paediatrica Scandinavica* (Suppl. 374) (1991): 129–32.

Cheraskin, E. *Vitamin C: Who Needs It?* (Birmingham, Ala.: Arlington Press, 1993).

Cherniske, S. *The DHEA Breakthrough* (New York: Ballantine Books, 1996).

Clarke, R. "Lowering Blood Homocysteine with Folic Acid Based Supplements: Meta-Analysis of Randomised Trials." *British Medical Journal* 316 (7135) (Mar. 21, 1998): 894(5).

Cousins, N. *Anatomy of an Illness* (New York: Bantam Books, 1974).

Cutler, R. G. "Carotenoids and Retinol: Their Possible Importance in Determining Longevity of Primate Species." *Proceedings of the National Academy of Sciences of the United States of America* 81 (1984): 7627–31.

Dobson, H. M. et al. "The Effect of Ascorbic Acid on the Seasonal Variations in Serum Cholesterol Levels." *Scottish Medical Journal* 29 (3) (1984): 176–82.

Fidanza, D. A. et al. "Vitamin C and Atherosclerosis." *Alimentazione Nutrizione Metabolismo* (1981) 23169–82.

First Health and Nutrition Examination Survey (HANES I), 1971–1974. U.S. Department of Health, Education, and Welfare, Public Health Service, National Center for Health Statistics (79–1657) (1979).

Frei, B., England, L., and Ames, B. N. "Ascorbate Is an Outstanding Antioxidant in Human Blood Plasma." *Proceedings of the National Academy of Sciences of the United States of America* 86 (1989): 6377–81.

Fried, J. *Vitamin Politics* (Buffalo, N.Y.: Prometheus Books, 1984): 220.

Gaby, S. K., and Machlin, L. J. "Vitamin E." *Vitamin Intake and Health: A Scientific Review* (New York: Marcel Dekker, 1991): 72–89.

Gey, K. F., and Puska, P. "Plasma Vitamins E and A Inversely Correlated to Mortality from Ischemic Heart Disease Cross-Cultural Epidemiology." *Annals of the New York Academy of Sciences* 570 (1989): 268–82.

Gey, K. F. et al. "Inverse Correlation between Plasma, Vitamin E, and Mortality from Ischemic Heart Disease in Cross-Cultural Epidemiology." *American Journal of Clinical Nutrition* 53 (1991): 326S–344S.

Giles, T. D. "Magnesium Deficiency: An Important Cardiovascular Risk Factor." *Advances in Cardiology* 1 (5) (1990).

Good, R. A., and Lorenz, E. "Nutrition and Cellular Immunity." *International Journal of Immunopharmacology* 14 (3) (1992): 361–66.

Hallfrisch, J. et al. "High Plasma Vitamin C Associated with High Plasma HDL and HDL Cholesterol." *American Journal of Clinical Nutrition* 60 (1994): 100–105.

Hartz, S. C., Otradovec, C. L., McGandy, R. B. et al. "Nutrient Supplement Use by Healthy Elderly." *Journal of the American College of Nutrition* 7 (2) (1988): 119.

Hennekens, C. H., and Gaziano, J. M. "Antioxidants and Heart Disease: Epidemiology and Clinical Evidence." *Clinical Cardiology* 16 (Suppl. 1) (1993): 10–15.

Hodis, H. N., Mack, W. J. et al. "Serial Coronary Angiographic Evidence That Antioxidant Vitamin Intake Reduces Progression of Coronary Artery Atherosclerosis." *Journal of the American Medical Association* 273 (23) (June 21, 1995): 1849–54.

Jacob, R. et al. "Vitamin C Status and Nutrient Interactions in a Healthy Elderly Population." *American Journal of Clinical Nutrition* 48 (1988): 1436–42.

Jialal, I., and Fuller, C. J. "Effect of Vitamin E, Vitamin C and Beta Carotene on LDL Oxidation and Atherosclerosis." *Canadian Journal of Cardiology* 11 (Suppl. G) (Oct. 1995): 97G–103G.

Kanter, M. M., Nolte, L. A. et al. "Effects of an Antioxidant Vitamin Mixture on Lipid Peroxidation at Rest and Postexercise." *Journal of Applied Physiology* 74 (2) (1993): 965–69.

Katakity, M., Webb, J. F., and Dickerson, J. W. T. "Some Effects of a Food Supplement in Elderly Hospital Patients: A Longitudinal Study." *Human Nutrition. Applied Nutrition* 37A (1983): 85.

Kennedy, S. H. "Vitamin Supplements Win New-Found Respect." *Modern Medicine* 60 (1992): 15–18.

Kok, F. J. et al. "Low Vitamin B_6 Status in Patients with Acute Myocardial Infarction." *American Journal of Cardiology* 63 (1989): 513–16.

Krinsky, N. I. "Antioxidant Function of Carotenoids." *Free Radical Biology and Medicine* 7 (1989): 627–35.

Leevy, C. M., Cardi, L., Frank, O. et al. "Incidence and Significance of Hypovitaminemia in a Randomly Selected Municipal Hospital Population." *American Journal of Clinical Nutrition* 17 (1965): 259.

Losonczy, K. G., Harris, T. B., and Havlik, R. J. "Vitamin E and

Vitamin C Supplement Use and Risk of All-Cause and Coronary Heart Disease Mortality in Older Persons: The Established Populations for Epidemiologic Studies of the Elderly." *American Journal of Clinical Nutrition* 64 (2) (Aug. 1996).

Murakoshi, M. et al. "Potent Preventive Action of Alpha-Carotene against Carcinogenesis." *Cancer Research* 52 (1992): 6583–87.

Murray, M. T. *Encyclopedia of Nutritional Supplements* (Rocklin, Calif.: Prima Publishing, 1996).

National Research Council. *Diet and Health: Implications for Reducing Chronic Disease Risk* (Washington, D.C.: National Academy Press, 1989).

National Research Council. *Recommended Dietary Allowances*, 10th ed. (Washington, D.C.: National Academy Press, 1989).

Packer, L. "Health Effects of Nutritional Antioxidants." *Free Radical Biology and Medicine* 15 (1993): 685–86.

Paolisso, G. et al. "Chronic Intake of Pharmacological Doses of Vitamin E Might Be Useful in the Therapy of Elderly Patients with Coronary Heart Disease." *American Journal of Clinical Nutrition* 61 (1995): 848–52.

Paolisso, G. et al. "Pharmacologic Doses of Vitamin E Improve Insulin Action in Healthy Subjects and Non-Insulin-Dependent Diabetic Patients." *American Journal of Clinical Nutrition* 57 (1993): 650–56.

Passwater, R. A. "Measuring Your Antioxidant Status: An Interview with Dr. Charles A. Thomas." *Whole Foods* (June 1995): 50–54.

Platzman, A. D. "Folic Acid: Once Overlooked, Now a Nutrient on the Brink of Stardom." *Environmental Nutrition* 21 (1) (Jan. 1998): 1(2).

Princen, H. M. G. et al. "Supplementation with Low Doses of Vitamin E Protects LDL from Lipid Peroxidation in Men and Women." *Arterioscler Thromb Vasc Biol* 15 (1995): 325–33.

Rath, M. *Eradicating Heart Disease* (San Francisco: Health Now, 1993).

Reynolds, R. "Vitamin Supplements: Current Controversies." *Journal of the American College of Nutrition* 13 (2) (1994): 118–26.

Rimm, E. B. et al. "Vitamin E Consumption and the Risk of Coronary Heart Disease in Men." *New England Journal of Medicine* 328 (1993): 1450–56.

Ringsdorf, W. M., Jr., and Cheraskin, E. "Vitamin C and Wound Healing." *Oral Surgery* 53 (3) (1982): 231–36.

Robinson, K. et al. "Hyperhomocysteinemia and Low Pyridoxal Phosphate." *Circulation* 92 (1995): 2825–30.

Rudin, D. O. "The Dominant Diseases of Modernized Societies as Omega-3 Essential Fatty Acid Deficiency Syndromes: Substrate Beri-Beri." *Medical Hypotheses* 8 (1982): 17–47.

Rudin, D. O. "A New Diagnostic Entity: Synergistic Malnutrition from Interacting Food Modifications." *Journal of Orthomolecular Medicine* 2 (1) (1987): 3–14.

Semba, R. D. "Vitamin A, Immunity, and Infection." *Clinical Infectious Diseases* 19 (1994): 489–99.

Simone, Charles B. *Cancer and Nutrition* (New York: McGraw-Hill, 1983).

Skerrett, P. J. "Mighty Vitamins." *Medical World News* 34 (1) (1993): 24–32.

Spake, A. "Vitamin Sense: The Institute of Medicine Recommends That Adults Increase Their Folic Acid Intake to 400 Micrograms." *U.S. News and World Report* 124 (15) (Apr. 20, 1998): 70(1).

Stampfer, M. J. et al. "Vitamin E Consumption and the Risk of Coronary Disease in Women." *New England Journal of Medicine* 328 (1993): 1444–49.

Street, D. A. et al. "Serum Antioxidants and Myocardial Infarction." *Circulation* 90 (1994): 1154–61.

Taylor, P. R., Wang, G. Q., Dawsey, S. M. et al. "The Effect of Nutrition Intervention on Intermediate Endpoints in Esophageal and Gastric Carcinogenesis." *American Journal of Clinical Nutrition* 62 (Suppl.) (1995): 1420S–1423S.

Taylor, T. V. et al. "Ascorbic Acid Supplementation in the Treatment of Pressure Sores." *Lancet* 2 (1974): 544–46.

Ten State Nutrition Survey, 1968–1970. U.S. Department of Health, Education, and Welfare, Health Services and Mental Health Administration, Centers for Disease Control, Atlanta (HSM 72 8130–34), 1972.

Thomas, C. A. "Assessing Your Antioxidant Defense System." *Nutrition Journal* 18 (1 and 2) (June 1994): 1.

Van Goot et al. "Review, Cobalamin Deficiency and Mental Impairment in Elderly People." *Age and Aging* 24 (1995): 536–42.

Wehrbach, M. *Nutritional Influences on Illness* (Tarzana, Calif.: Third Line Press, 1987).

Whitaker, Julian. *Dr. Whitaker's Guide to Natural Healing* (Rocklin, Calif.: Prima Publishing, 1995).

Williams, R. J. *Nutrition in a Nutshell* (Garden City, N.Y.: Doubleday and Company, 1962).

Williams, R. J. "On Your Startling Biochemical Individuality." *Executive Health* 12 (8) (May 1976).

Wittler, A. J. et al. "Nutrient Density—Evaluation of Nutritional Attributes of Food." *Journal of Nutrition Education* 9 (1977): 26–30, 198.

Chapter 24

Alabaster, O., Blumberg, J., Stampfer, M. J., and Stavric, B. "Do Antioxidants Really Prevent Disease?" *Patient Care* (Nov. 15, 1995): 18–32.

Alleva, R. et al. "The Roles of Coenzyme Q_{10} and Vitamin E on the Peroxidation of Human Low

Density Lipoprotein Subfractions." *Proceedings of the National Academy of Sciences of the United States of America* 92 (1995): 9388–91.

Ames, B. N., Shigenaga, M. K., and Hagen, T. M. "Oxidants, Antioxidants, and the Degenerative Diseases of Aging." *Proceedings of the National Academy of Sciences of the United States of America* 90 (1993): 7915–22.

Beyer, R. "An Analysis of the Role of Coenzyme Q_{10} in Free Radical Generation and as an Antioxidant." *Biochemistry and Cell Biology* 70 (1992): 390–403.

Bland, J. "Chronological Age versus Biological Age: How *Old* Are You?" *Let's Live* (Oct. 1995).

Bliznakov, E. G., and Hunt, G. L. *The Miracle Nutrient: Coenzyme Q10* (New York: Bantam Books, 1987).

Block, G. "Fruit, Vegetables, and Cancer Prevention: A Review of the Epidemiological Evidence." *Nutrition and Cancer* 18 (1992): 1–29.

Blumenthal, M. "Pycnogenol and Grapeseed Extract: Oligomeric Procyanidins and Polyphenols; The Dietary Supplement Industry's New World Order." *Whole Foods* (Aug. 1996): 32–36.

Burton, G. W. "Beta-Carotene: An Unusual Type of Antioxidant." *Science* 224 (1984): 569–73.

Carper, J. *Stop Aging Now* (New York: HarperCollins, 1995).

Cutler, R. G. "The Molecular and Evolutionary Aspects of Human Aging and Longevity." In *Anti-Aging Medicine* Vol. 1 (Larchmont, N.Y.: Mary Ann Liebert Publishers, 1996).

Cutler, R. G., Packer, L., Bertram, J., Mori, A., eds. *Oxidative Stress and Aging* (Basel; Boston: Birkhauser Verlag, 1995).

Di Mascio, P., Murphy, M. E., and Sies, H. "Antioxidant Defense Systems: The Role of Carotenoids, Tocopherols, and Thiols." *American Journal of Clinical Nutrition* 53 (Suppl.) (1991): 194S–200S.

Folkers, K., ed. *Biomedical and Clinical Aspects of Coenzyme Q10* Vol. 3. (Amsterdam: Elsevier, 1981).

Frei, H., England, L., and Ames, B. N. "Ascorbate Is an Outstanding Antioxidant in Human Blood Plasma." *Proceedings of the National Academy of Sciences of the United States of America* 86 (1989): 6377–81.

Gilligan, D. M., Sack, M. N. Guetta, V. et al. "Effect of Antioxidant Vitamins on Low-Density Lipoprotein Oxidation and Impaired Endothelium-Dependent Vasodilation in Patients with Hypercholesterolemia." *Journal of the American College of Cardiology* 24 (1994): 1611–17.

Greenberg, S. M., and Frishman, W. H. "Coenzyme Q10: A New Drug for Cardiovascular Disease." *Journal of Clinical Pharmacology* 30 (1990): 596–608.

Greenberg, S. M., and Frishman, W. H. "Coenzyme Q10: A New Drug for Myocardial Ischemia?" *Medical Clinics of North America* 72 (1) (1988): 243–58.

Halliwell, B. et al. "Free Radicals, Antioxidants, and Human Disease: Where Are We Now?" *Journal of Laboratory and Clinical Medicine* 119 (1992): 598–620.

Jacques, P. F., and Chylack, L. T. "Epidemiological Evidence of a Role for the Antioxidant Vitamins and Carotenoids in Cataract Prevention." *American Journal of Clinical Nutrition* 53 (1991): 352S–355S.

Khackik, F. et al. "Lutein, Lycopene, and Their Oxidative Metabolites in Chemoprevention of Cancer." *Journal of Cellular Biochemistry* (Suppl. 22) (1995): 236–46.

Knekt, P. "Serum Vitamin E Level and the Risk of Female Cancers." *International Journal of Epidemiology* 17 (1988): 281–88.

Kumar, C. T. et al. "Dietary Supplementation of Vitamin E Protects Heart Tissue from Exercise-Induced Oxidant Stress." *Molecular and Cellular Biochemistry* 111 (1992): 109–15.

Linder, M. C., ed. *Nutritional Biochemistry and Metabolism with Clinical Applications* 2nd ed. (Norwalk, Conn.: Appleton and Lange, 1991): 156.

Lockwood, K., Moesgaard, S. et al. "Partial and Complete Regression of Breast Cancer in Patients in Relation to Dosage of Coenzyme Q10." *Biochemical and Biophysical Research Communications* 199 (1994): 1504–8.

"Of Radicals and Scavengers: How Antioxidants Work." *Patient Care* (Nov. 15, 1995).

Ozhogina, O. A., and Kasaikina, O. T. "Beta-Carotene as an Interceptor of Free Radicals." *Free Radical Biology and Medicine* 19 (1995): 573–81.

Passwater, R. A., and Kanddaswami, C. *Pycnogenol, The Super "Protector" Nutrient* (New Canaan, Conn.: Keats Publishing, 1994).

Plotnick, G. D., Coretti, M. C., and Vogel, R. A. "Effect of Antioxidant Vitamins in the Transient Impairment of Endothelium-Dependent Brachial Artery Vasoactivity Following a Single High-Fat Meal." *Journal of the American Medical Association* 278 (1997): 1682–86.

Rimm, E. B. et al. "Vitamin E Consumption and the Risk of Coronary Heart Disease in Men." *New England Journal of Medicine* 328 (1993): 1450–56.

Ronzio, R. "Antioxidants, Nutraceuticals and Functional Foods." *Townsend Letter for Doctors and Patients* (Aug./Sept. 1996): 30–33.

Schalch, W. "Carotenoids in the Retina: A Review of Their Possible Role in Preventing or Limiting Damage Caused by Light and Oxygen." *Experientia. Supplementum* 62 (1992): 280–98.

Shambhu, V. D. "Scientific Basis for Medical Therapy of Cataracts by Antioxidants." *American Journal of Clinical Nutrition* 53 (1991): 335S–345S.

Sics, H. et al. "Antioxidant Functions of Vitamins." *Annals of the New York Academy of Sciences* 669 (1992): 7–20.

Slater, T. F., and Block, G. "Antioxidant Vitamins and B-Carotene in Disease Prevention." *American Journal of Clinical Nutrition* 53 (1991): 189S–396S.

Stahelin, H. B. et al. "Cancer, Vitamins, and Plasma Lipids. Prospective Base Study." *Journal of the National Cancer Institute* 73 (1984): 1463–68.

Stich, H. F. et al. "Remission of Precancerous Lesions in the Oral Cavity of Tobacco Chewers and Maintenance of the Protective Effect of Beta-Carotene or Vitamin A." *American Journal of Clinical Nutrition* 53 (1991): 298S–304S.

Tamkins, T. "Antioxidants Appear to Work in Nutritional Concert." *Medical Tribune* (Jan. 11, 1996).

Temple, N. J., and Basu, T. K. "Does Beta-Carotene Prevent Cancer? A Critical Appraisal." *Nutrition Research* 8 (1988): 685–701.

Thomas, C. A. "Assessing the Individual's Antioxidant Status." In *Anti-Aging Medicine* Vol. 1, (Larchmont, N.Y.: Mary Ann Liebert Publishers, 1996).

Tribble, D. L. et al. "Oxidative Susceptibility of Low-Density Lipoprotein Subfactions Is Related to Their Ubiquinol-10 and Alpha-Tocopherol Content." *Proceedings of the National Academy of Sciences of the United States of America* 91 (1994): 1183–87.

Wood, M. "Vitamin C Shortage Undermines Antioxidant Defense System." *Agricultural Research* (June 1992).

Yuting, C., Rongliang, Z., Zhongjian, J. et al. "Flavonoids as Superoxide Scavengers and Antioxidants." *Free Radical Biology and Medicine* 9 (1990): 19–21.

Ziegler, R. G. "Vegetables, Fruits, and Carotenoids and the Risk of Cancer." *American Journal of Clinical Nutrition* 53 (1991): 251S–259S.

Chapter 25

Adlercreutz, H. "Phytoestrogens: Epidemiology and a Possible Role in Cancer Prevention." Department of Clinical Chemistry, University of Helsinki, Finland. *Environmental Health Perspectives* (U.S.) 103 (Suppl. 7) (Oct. 1995): 103–12.

Arjmandi, B. H., Alekel, L., Hollis, B. W., Amin, D., Stacewicz-Sapuntzakis, M., Guo, P., and Kukreja, S. C. "Dietary Soybean Protein Prevents Bone Loss in an Ovariectaomized Rat Model of Osteoporosis." Department of Human Nutrition and Dietetics, University of Illinois at Chicago *Journal of Nutrition* 126 (1) (Jan. 1996): 161–67.

Carper, J. *Food: Our Miracle Medicine* (New York: HarperCollins, 1993).

Colditz, G. et al. "Increased Green and Yellow Vegetable Intake and Lowered Cancer Death in an Elderly Population." *American Journal of Clinical Nutrition* 41 (1985): 1.

Coles, L. S. "Take Your Phytomins: Your Mother Was Right When She Told You to Eat Your Vegetables." *Journal of Longevity Research* 1 (8) (1995).

Di Mascio, P., Kaiser, S., and Sies, H. "Lycopene as the Most Efficient Biological Carotenoid Singlet Oxygen Quencher." *Archives of Biochemistry and Biophysics* 274 (1989): 532–38.

Dorant, E. et al. "Garlic and Its Significance for the Prevention of Cancer in Humans: A Cultural Review." *British Journal of Cancer* 67 (1993): 424–29.

Ebnother, C. "The Phytochemical Miracle." *Journal of Longevity Research* 2 (5) (1996): 9–12.

"Epidemiologic Correlations between Diet and Cancer Frequency." *Cancer Research* 41 (1981): 3685–89.

First World Congress on the Health Significance of Garlic and Garlic Constituents. Washington, D.C.: Willard Hotel, Aug. 28–30, 1990.

Graf, F., and Eaton, J. W. "Suppression of Colonic Cancer by Dietary Phytic Acid." *Nutrition and Cancer* 19 (1993): 11–19.

Hertzog, M. G., Feskens, E. J., Hollman, P. C. et al. "Dietary Antioxidant Flavonoids and Risk of Coronary Heart Disease: The Zutphen Elderly Study." *Lancet* 342 (1993): 1007–11.

"Inhibition of Breast Cancer Progression with Omega-3 Fatty Acids." *Cancer Biotechnology Weekly* (Apr. 17, 1995): 10.

Knight, D. C., and Eaton, J. A. "Phytoestrogens—A Short Review." Royal Hospital for Women, New South Wales, Australia. *Maturitas* 22 (3) (Nov. 1995): 167–75.

Knight, D. C., and Eden, J. A. "A Review of the Clinical Effects of Phytoestrogens." Royal Hospital for Women, New South Wales, Australia. *Obstetrics and Gynecology* 87 (May 1996): 897–904.

Lim, B. P., Nagao, A., Terao, J. et al. "Antioxidant Activity of Xanthophyls on Peroxyl Radical-Mediated Phospholipid Peroxidation." *Biochimica et Biophysica Acta* 1126 (1992): 178–84.

Messina, M., and Messina, V. *The Simple Soybean and Your Health* (New York: Avery Publishing Group, 1994).

Murray, M. T. *The Healing Power of Herbs* (Rocklin, Calif.: Prima Publishing, 1992): 223–30.

Newmark, H. I. "A Hypothesis for Dietary Components as Blocking Agents of Chemical Carcinogenesis: Plant Phenolics and Pyrolle Pigments." *Nutrition and Cancer* 6 (1984): 58–70.

Newmark, H. I. "Plant Phenolics as Inhibitors of Mutational and Precarcinogenic Events." *Canadian Journal of Physiology and Pharmacology* 65 (1987): 461–66.

"Phytochemicals: First Line against Disease." *Patient Care* (Nov. 15, 1995).

Pool, R. "Wresting Anticancer Secrets from Garlic and Soy Sauce." *Science* 257 (1992): 1349.

"Some Mushroom Varieties Sprout More Than Just Good Taste." *Environmental Nutrition* 17 (1994): 75.

Sonai, K. B. et al. "Effect of Oral Curcumin Administration on

Serum Peroxides and Cholesterol Levels in Human Volunteers." *Indian Journal of Physiology and Pharmacology* 36 (1992): 272–93.

Srinavasa, L. et al. "Turmerin: A Water-Soluble Antioxidant Peptide from Turmeric." *Archives of Biochemistry and Biophysics* 292 (2) (1992): 617–23.

Srivastava, K. C. "Effects of Aqueous Extracts of Onion, Garlic, and Ginger on Platelet Aggregation and Metabolism of Arachidonic Acid in the Blood Vascular System: In Vitro Study." *Prostaglandins, Leukotrienes, and Medicine* 13 (1984): 227–29.

Stravric, B. "Antimutagens and Anticarcinogens in Foods." *Clinical Biochemistry* 27 (1994): 319–32.

Turner, L. "Food for the Next Millennium: Top 10 Super Foods." *Let's Live* (Jan. 1997): 64–68.

Turner, L. *Meals That Heal* (Rochester, Vt.: Healing Arts Press, 1996).

Tyler, Varro E. *Herbs of Choice: The Therapeutic Use of Phytochemicals* (New York: Pharmaceutical Products Press, 1994).

Werbach, M. et al. *Botanical Influences on Illness* (Tarzana, Calif.: Third Line Press, 1994): 23, 25.

Yang, C. S. et al. "Tea and Cancer." *Journal of the National Cancer Institute* 85 (1993): 13, 1038.

Chapter 26

Bombardelli, E., Cirstoni, A., and Leitti, A. "The Effect of Acute and Chronic (Panax) Ginseng Saponins Treatment on Adrenal Function: Biochemical and Pharmacological." Proceedings, Third International Ginseng Symposium, 1980: 9–16.

Brekhman, I. I. *Pharmacology of Oriental Plants*. (New York: Pergamon Press, 1963): 97–102.

Brekhman, I. I. "Pharmacological Investigations of Glycosides from Ginseng and Eleutherococcus." *Lloydia* XXXII (Mar. 1969): 46–51.

Brekhman, I. I., and Dardymov, I. V. "New Substances of Plant Origin Which Increase Non-Specific Resistance." *Vladivistok USSR Annual Review of Pharmacology* vol. IX (1968): 415–30.

Chen, X. "Experimental Study on the Cardiovascular Effects of Ginsenosides." *Chung Hua Hsin Hsueh Kuan Ping Tsa Chih* 10 (2) (1982): 147–50.

D'Angelo, L., Grimaldi, R., Caravaggi, M. et al. "A Double-Blind Placebo Controlled Clinical Study on the Effects of a Standardized Ginseng Extract on Psychomotor Performance in Healthy Volunteers." *Journal of Ethnopharmacology* 16 (1986): 15–22.

Dolby, V. "Java Aside—Jump Start Your Day with a Jolt from Ginseng." *Better Nutrition for Today's Living* 59 (4) (Apr. 1997): 26.

Foster, S. "Ginseng: Get to the Root of Health." *Better Nutrition for Today's Living* 57 (3) (Mar. 1995): 66 (3).

Fulder, S. J. "Ginseng and the Hypothalamic-Pituitary Control of Stress." *American Journal of Chinese Medicine* 9 (1981): 112–18.

Fulder, S. J. *The Tao of Medicine: Oriental Remedies and the Pharmacology of Harmony* (Rochester, Vt.: Destiny Books, 1987).

"Ginseng: The Anti-Stress Therapy." *Anti-Aging News* (Oct. 1983): 111.

Harriman, S. *The Book of Ginseng* (Pyramid Publishing, Harcourt, 1976).

Heffern, R. *The Complete Book of Ginseng* (Milbrae, Calif.: Celestial Arts, 1976).

Hiai, S., Yokoyama, H., and Oura, H. "Features of Ginseng Saponin-Induced Corticosterone Secretion." *Endocrinologia Japonica* 26 (1979): 737–40.

Hiai, S., Yokoyama, H., Oura, H., and Kawashima, Y. "Evaluation of Corticosterone Secretion-Inducing Effects of Ginsenosides and Their Prosapogenins and Sapogenins." *Chemical and Pharmaceutical Bulletin* 31 (1983): 168–74.

Hiai, S., Yokoyama, H., Oura, H., and Yano, S. "Stimulation of Pituitary-Adrenocortical System of Ginseng Saponin." *Endocrinologia Japonica* 26 (6) (1979): 661–65.

Hu, S-Y. "A Contribution to our Knowledge of Ginseng." *American Journal of Chinese Medicine* 5 (1) (1977): 1–23.

Hu, S-Y. "The Genus Panax Ginseng in Chinese Medicine." *Economic Botany* 30 (Jan.–Mar. 1976): 11–28.

Iljutjecok, R. J., and Tjaplygina, S. R. "The Effects of a Preparation of Eleutherococcus Senticosus on Memory in Mice." The Department of Physiology, Academy of Sciences of the Soviet Union, Novosibirsk, 1978.

Kim, C. et al. "Influence of Ginseng on the Stress Mechanism." *Lloydia* 33 (1970): 43–48.

Lee, K-D., and Huemer, R. "Antitumoral Activity of Panax Ginseng Extracts." *Japanese Journal of Pharmacology* XXI (1970): 299–302.

Liberti, L. E., and Marderosian, A. D. "Evaluation of Commercial Ginseng Products." *Journal of Pharmaceutical Sciences* 67 (1978): 1487–89.

McCaleb, R. S. "Ginseng for Vigor." *Better Nutrition for Today's Living* (Nov. 1990): 23–25.

Mowrey, D. B. "Ginseng: The World's Best Anti-Stress Tonic." In *Next-Generation Herbal Medicine* (New Canaan, Conn.: Keats Publishing, 1990).

Mowrey, D. B. *The Scientific Validation of Herbal Medicine* (New Canaan, Conn.: Keats Publishing, 1990).

Pelton, R., and Pelton, T. C. *Mind Food and Smart Pills* (Garden City, N.Y.: Doubleday and Company, 1989).

Petkov, V. "Effect of Ginseng on the Brain Biogenic Monoamines and 3'.5'-AMP System. Experiments in Rats." *Arzneimittel-Forschung/ Drug Research* 28 (1978): 388–93.

Petkov, V. "Effects of Standardized Ginseng Extract on Learning, Memory and Physical Capabilities." *American Journal of Chinese Medicine* 15 (1) (1987): 19–29.

Petkov, V. "Pharmacological Studies of the Drug P. Ginseng." *Arzneimittel-Forschung* 9 (1959): 305–11.

Petkov, V., and Staneua, S. "The Effect of an Extract of Ginseng on the Adrenal Cortex." Proceedings of the Second International Pharmacology Meeting. Prague, 1963. Vol. 7 (New York: Pergamon Press): 39–45.

Petkov, V., and Staneua, S. "The Effect of an Extract of Ginseng (Panax Ginseng) on the Function of the Adrenal Cortex." *In Pharmacology of Oriental Plants* (New York: Pergamon Press, 1965): 39–50.

Pizzomo, J. E., and Murray, M. T. "Panax Ginseng." In *A Textbook of Natural Medicine* (Seattle: JBC Publications, 1987).

Singh, V. K., Agarwal, S. S., and Gupta, B. M. "Immunomodulatory Activity of Panax Ginseng Extract." *Planta Medica* 50 (6) (Dec. 1984): 462–65.

Takeda, A., Katoh, N., and Yonezawa, M. "Restoration of Radiation Injury by Ginseng. XVII. Enhanced Recovery of Blood Figure by Ginseng in Comparison with Krestin in Irradiated Rats." *Journal of Radiation Research* 26 (abstr. 2-C-19) (Mar. 1985): 44.

Takeda, A., Yonezawa, M., and Katoh, N. "Restoration of Radiation Injury by Ginseng. I. Responses of X-Irradiated Mice to Ginseng Extract." *Journal of Radiation Research* 22 (1981): 323–35.

Theonen, H. et al. "Potentiation of NG7-Medicated Nerve Fiber Outgrowth by Ginsenoside Rb1." *Japanese Journal of Pharmacology* 27 (3) (June 1997): 445–62.

Voskersarsky, T. et al. "Effect of Eleutherococcus and Ginseng on the Development of Free-Radical Pathology." Proceeding of the Second International Symposium of Eleutherococcus. Moscow, 1985: 141–45.

Wang, B. X., Cui, J. C., Lui, A. J., and Wu, S. K. "Studies on the Anti-Fatigue Effect of the Saponins of Stems and Leaves of Panax Ginseng." *Journal of Traditional Chinese Medicine* 3 (2) (1983): 89–94.

Yamamoto, M., Uemura, T., Nakama, S., Uemiya, M., and Kumagi, A. "Serum HDL-Cholesterol Increasing and Fatty Liver Improving Actions of Panax Ginseng in High-Cholesterol Diet Fed Rats with Clinical Effect on Hyperlipidemia in Man." *American Journal of Chinese Medicine* 11 (1–4) (1983): 96–101.

Yun, T-K., Yun, Y. S., and Han, I. W. "Anti-carcinogenic Effect of Long-Term Oral Administration of Red Ginseng on Newborn Mice Exposed to Various Chemical Carcinogens." *Cancer Detection and Prevention* 6 (1983): 515–25.

Zhong-Qi, L., and Rice, J. F. "Ginseng Extract Inhibits Protein in Degradation and Stimulates Protein Synthesis in Human Fibroblasts." *Biochemical and Biophysical Research Communications* 126 (1985): 636–40.

Chapter 27

Allain, H., Raoul, P., Lieury, A. et al. "Effect of Two Doses of Ginkgo Biloba Extract (EGb 761) on the Dual-Coding Test in Elderly Subjects." *Clinical Therapeutics* 15 (1993): 549–58.

Bauer, U. "6-Month Double-Blind Randomized Clinical Trial of Ginkgo Biloba Extract versus Placebo in Two Parallel Groups in Patients Suffering from Peripheral Arterial Insufficiency." *Arzneimittel-Forschung/Drug Research* 34 (1984): 716–21.

Bergner, P. "Ginkgo Biloba: Tonic for the Ailments of Old Age." *Townsend Letter for Doctors* (Apr. 1998).

Brown, D. J. "Ginkgo Biloba—Old and New." *Let's Live* (Apr. 1992): 8–9.

Chatterjee, S. S., and Gabard, B. "Studies on the Mechanism of Action of an Extract of Ginkgo Biloba, a Drug for the Treatment of Ischemic Vascular Diseases." *Naunyn-Schmiedeberg's Archives of Pharmacology* 320 (1982): R52.

Clostre, F. "From the Body to Cell Membranes: The Different Levels of Action of Ginkgo Biloba Extract." *La Presse Medicale* 15 (1986): 1529–38.

Dean, W., and Morgenthaler, J. *Smart Drugs and Nutrients* (Santa Cruz, Calif.: B and J Productions, 1990).

DeFeudis, F. V., ed. *Ginkgo Biloba Extract (EGb 761): Pharmacological Activities and Clinical Applications* (Paris: Elsevier, 1991).

Gaby, A. "Ginkgo Biloba Extract: A Review." In *Alternative Medicine Review* 1 (4) (1996): 236–42.

Gessner, B., Voelp, A., and Klasser, M. "Study of the Long-Term Actions of Ginkgo Biloba Extract on Vigilance and Mental Performance as Determined by Means of Quantitative Pharmeco-EEG and Psychometric Measurements." *Arzneimittel-Forschung/Drug Research* 35 (1985): 1459–65.

Haguenauer, J. P. et al. "Treatment of Disturbances of Equilibrium with Ginkgo Biloba Extract. A Multicentre, Double-Blind Drug versus Placebo Study." *La Presse Medicale* 15 (1986): 1569–72.

Hindmarch, I., and Subhan, Z. "The Psychopharmacological Effects of Ginkgo Biloba in Normal Healthy Volunteers." *International Journal of Clinical Pharmacology Research* 4 (1984): 89–93.

Hitzenberger, G. "The Effect of Ginkgo Biloba Special Extract (EGb 761, Tebofortan). *Wiener Medizinische Wochenschrift* 142 (1992): 371–79.

Hobbs, C. *Ginkgo: Elixir of Youth* (Capitola, Calif.: Botanica Press, 1991).

Hofferberth, B. "Effect of Ginkgo Biloba Extract on Neurophysiological and Psychometric Measurement in Patients with Cerebro-Organic Syndrome. A Double-Blind Study versus Placebo." *Arzneimittel-Forschung/ Drug Research* 39 (1989): 918–22.

Hopfenmuller, W. "Proof of the Therapeutical Effectiveness of a Ginkgo Biloba Special Extract— Meta-Analysis of 11 Clinical Trials in Aged Patients with Cerebral Insufficiency." *Arzneimittel Forschung/Drug Research* 44 (1994): 1005–13.

Itil, T., and Martorano, D. "Natural Substances in Psychiatry (Ginkgo Biloba in Dementia)." *Psychopharmacology Bulletin* 31 (1995): 147–58.

Kanowski, S., Herrmann, W. M., Stephan, K. et al. "Proof of Efficacy of the Ginkgo Biloba Special Extract EGb 761 in Outpatients Suffering from Mild to Moderate Primary Degenerative Dementia of the Alzheimer Type or Multi-Infarct Dementia." *Pharmacopsychiatry* 29 (1996): 47–56.

Kleijnen, J., and Knipschild, P. "Ginkgo Biloba." *Lancet* 340 (1992): 1136–39.

Kleijnen, J., and Knipschild, P. "Ginkgo Biloba for Cerebral Insufficiency." *British Journal of Clinical Pharmacology* 34 (1992): 352–58.

Luthringer, R., d'Arbingy, P., and Macher, J. P. "Ginkgo Biloba Extract (EGb 761) and Event Related Potentials Mapping Profile." In *Advances in Ginkgo Biloba Extract Research, volume 4, Effects of Ginkgo Biloba Extract (EGb 761) on Aging and Age-Related Disorders* (Paris: Elsevier, 1995): 107–18.

Michel, P. F. "The Oldest Tree: Ginkgo Biloba" *La Presse Medicale* 15 (1986): 1450–54.

Michel, P. F., and Hosford, D. "Ginkgo Biloba: From 'Living Fossil' to Modern Therapeutic Agent." In *Ginkgolides, volume I* (Barcelona: J. R. Prous, 1988): 1–8.

Mowrey, D. *Next-Generation Herbal Medicine* (Cormorant Books, 1988).

Oberpichler, H. et al. "Effects of Ginkgo Biloba Constituents Related to Protection against Brain Damage Caused by Hypoxia." *Pharmacological Research Communications* 20 (1988): 349–68.

Pincemail, J., Dupris, M. et al. "Superoxide Anion Scavenging Effect and Superoxide Dismutase Activity of Ginkgo Biloba Extract." *Experimentia* 45 (1989): 708–12.

Pincemail, J. et al. "Anti-Radical Properties of Ginkgo Biloba Extract." *La Presse Medicale* 15 (1986): 1475–79.

Rai, G. S., Shovlin, C., and Wesnes, K. A. "A Double-Blind, Placebo Controlled Study of Ginkgo Biloba Extract ('Tanakan') in Elderly Out-Patients with Mild to Moderate Memory Impairment." *Current Medical Research and Opinion* 12 (1991): 350–55.

Schneider, B. "Ginkgo Biloba Extract in Peripheral Arterial Diseases. Meta-Analysis of Controlled Clinical Studies." *Arzneimit-tel-Forschung/Drug Research* 42 (1992): 428–36.

Shen, J. G., and Zhou, D-Y. "Efficiency of Ginkgo Biloba Extract (EGb 761) in Antioxidant Protection against Myocardial Ischemia and Reperfusion Injury." *Biochemistry and Molecular Biology International* 35 (1995): 125–34.

Vorberg, G. "Ginkgo Biloba Extract (GBE): A Long-Term Study of Chronic Cerebral Insufficiency in Geriatric Patients." *Clinical Trials Journal* 22 (2) (1985): 149.

Wilford, J. N. "Ancient Tree Yields Secrets of Potent Healing Substance." *New York Times* (Mar. 1, 1988).

Winter, E. "Effects of an Extract of Ginkgo Biloba on Learning and Memory in Mice." *Pharmacology, Biochemistry, and Behavior* 38 (1991): 109–14.

Chapter 28

Adamu, I. et al. "Hypolipidemic Action of Onion and Garlic Unsaturated Oils in Sucrose-Fed Rats over a Two-Month Period." *Experientia* 38 (1982): 899–901, 1982.

Apitz-Castro, R., Escalante, J. et al. "Ajoene, the Major Antiaggregatory Compound Derived from Garlic, Potentiates the Inhibitory Effect of PG, Indomethacin, Dipyridamole, and ASA on Human Blood Platelets." *Thrombosis and Haemostasis* 54 (1) (1985): 126.

Baghurst, K. I. et al. "Onions and Platelet Aggregation." *Lancet* (Jan. 8, 1977).

Belman, S. "Onion and Garlic Oil Inhibit Tumor Growth." *Carcinogenesis* 4 (8) (1983): 1063–65.

Block, E. "The Chemistry of Garlic and Onions." *Scientific American* 252 (3) (Mar. 1985): 114–19.

Blot, W. J. "Garlic in Relation to Cancer in Human Populations." First World Congress on the Health Significance of Garlic and Garlic Constituents, Washington, D.C., Aug. 28–30, 1990.

Bobbo, A. et al. "Hypolipidemic Effects of Onion Oil and Garlic Oil in Ethanol-Fed Rats." *Indian Journal of Biochemistry and Biophysics* 21 (1984): 211–13.

Bordia, A. "Effect of Garlic on Blood Lipids in Patients with Coronary Heart Disease." *American Journal of Clinical Nutrition* 34 (1981): 2100–2103.

Bordia, A. "Effect of Garlic on Human Platelet Aggregation in Vitro." *Atherosclerosis* 30 (1978): 355.

Bordia, A. K. et al. "Effect of Garlic Oil on Fibrinolytic Activity in Patients with CHD." *Atherosclerosis* 28 (1977): 155–59.

Bordia, A., and Verma, S. K. "Effect of Three Years' Treatment with Garlic on the Rate of Reinfarction and Mortality in Patients with Coronary Artery Disease." First World Congress on the Health Significance of Garlic and Garlic Constituents, Washington, D.C., Aug. 28–30, 1990.

Bordia, A., Verma, S. K., Vyas, A. K. et al. "Effect of Essential Oil of Onion and Garlic on Experimental Atherosclerosis in Rabbits." *Atherosclerosis* 26 (1977): 379–86.

Brody, J. "After 4,000 Years, Medical Science Considers Garlic." *New York Times* (Sept. 4, 1990).

Doullin, D. J. "Garlic as a Platelet Inhibitor." *Lancet* 1 (1981): 776–77.

Jain, A. K. et al. "Can Garlic Reduce Levels of Serum Lipids? A Controlled Clinical Study." *American Journal of Medicine* 94 (1993): 632–35.

Kidd, P. M. "Germanium-132 (Ge-132): Homeostatic Normalizer and Immunostimulant, a Review of Its Preventive and Therapeutic Efficacy." *International Clinical Nutrition Review* 7 (1980): 11–20.

Kleijnen, J. et al. "Garlic, Onions, and Cardiovascular Risk Factors: A Review of the Evidence from Human Experiments with Emphasis on Commercially Available Preparations." *British Journal of Clinical Pharmacology* 28 (1989): 535–44.

Kroning, F. "Garlic as an Inhibitor for Spontaneous Tumors in Mice." *Acta Unio. Intern. Contra Cancrum* 20 (3) (1964): 855.

Lau, B. H. S. *Garlic for Health* (Wilmot, Wis.: Lotus Light Publications, 1988).

Lau, B. H. S. *Garlic Research Update* (Vancouver: Odyssey Publishing Company, 1991).

Lau, B. H. S., Adetumbi, M. A., and Sanchez, A. "Allium Sativum (Garlic) and Atherosclerosis: A Review." *Nutrition Research* 43 (1983): 119–28.

Lau, B. H. S., Lam, F., and Wang-Cheng, R. "Effect of an Odor-Modified Garlic Preparation on Blood Lipids." *Nutrition Research* 7 (1987): 139–49.

Mader, F. H. "Treatment of Hyperlipidemia with Garlic Powder Tablets." *Arzneimittel-Forschung/Drug Research* 40 (1990): 1111–16.

Nishino, H. "Inhibition of Tumorigenesis by Garlic Constituents." First World Congress on the Health Significance of Garlic and Garlic Constituents, Washington, D.C., Aug. 28–30, 1990.

Pasteur, L. *Ann. Chim. Phys. Ser.* 1858 (S2): 404.

Rotzch, W. et al. "Postprandial Lepaemia under Treatment with Allium Sativum. Controlled Double-Blind Study in Healthy Volunteers with Reduced HDL-2 Cholesterol Levels." *Arzneimittel-Forschung/Drug Research* 42 (1992): 1223–27.

Sainani, G. S., Desai, D. B., Gorhe, N. H., Natu, S. M., Pise, D. V., and Sainani, P. G. "Dietary Garlic, Onion, and Some Coagulation Parameters in Jain Community." *Journal of the Association of Physicians of India* 27 (1979): 707.

Sainani, G. S., Desai, D. B., Gorhe, N. H., Natu, S. M., Pise, D. V., and Sainani, P. G. "Effect of Dietary Garlic and Onion on Serum Lipid Profile in Jain Community." *Indian Journal of Medical Research* 69 (1979): 776.

Sainani, G. S., Desai, D. B., and More, K. N. "Onion, Garlic and Atherosclerosis." *Lancet* 1 (1976): 575.

Shoeten, A. et al. "Hypolipidemic Effects of Garlic Oil in Rats Fed Ethanol and a High Lipid Diet." *Experientia* 40 (3) (1984): 261–63.

Simons, P. *Garlic* (San Francisco: Thorsons Publishers, 1980).

Srivastava, K. C. "Aqueous Extracts of Onion, Garlic and Ginger Inhibit Platelet Aggregation and Alter Arachidonic Acid Metabolism." *Biomedica Biochimica Acta* 43 (8/9) (1984).

Steiner, M. et al. "A Double-Blind Crossover Study in Moderately Hypercholesterolemic Men That Compared the Effect of Aged Garlic Extract and Placebo Administration on Blood Lipids." *American Journal of Clinical Nutrition* 64 (1996): 866–70.

Warshafsky, S., Kamer, R. S., and Sivak, S. L. "Effect of Garlic on Total Serum Cholesterol." *Annals of Internal Medicine* 119 (1993): 599–605.

Chapter 29

"The Aging Brain: Cognitive Decline and Phosphatidylserine." *Total Health* 18 (3) (June 1996).

Albano, C. "Evaluation of the Activity of Acetyl-L-Carnitine in the Senile Dementia Alzheimer Type." Abstract of Fourth World Congress of Biological Psychiatry, Philadelphia (1985): 106.

Allegro, L., Favaretto, V., and Ziliotto, G. "Oral Phosphatidylserine in Elderly Subjects with Cognitive Deterioration—An Open Study." *Clinical Trials Journal* 24 (1987): 104–8.

Amaducci, L. "SMID Group. Phosphatidylserine in the Dosing of Alzheimer's Disease: Results of a Multicenter Study." *Psychopharmacology Bulletin* 24 (1988): 130–34.

Atkins, R. "The Smart Fat for Feeding Your Head." *Dr. Robert Atkins' Health Revelations* (Apr. 1996).

Bella, R., Biondi, R., Raffaele, R., and Pennisi, G. "Effect of Acetyl-L-Carnitine on Geriatric Patients Suffering from Dysthymic Disorders." *International Journal of Clinical Pharmacology Research* 10 (1990): 355–60.

Benninger, Jon. "Understanding Phosphatidylserine." *Health Supplement Retailer* (Oct. 1996).

Bodis-Wollner, I. et al. "Acetyl-Levo-Carnitine Protects against MPTP-Induced Parkinsonism in Primates." *Journal of Neural Transmission* 3 (1991): 63–72.

Bonavita, E. "Study of the Efficacy and Tolerability of L-Acetylcarnitine Therapy in the Senile Brain." *Journal of Clinical Pharmacology, Therapy, and Toxicology* 24 (1986): 511–16.

Bossoni, G., and Carpi, C. "Effect of Acetyl-L-Carnitine on Conditioned Reflex Learning Rate and Retention in Laboratory Animals." *Drugs under Experimental and Clinical Research* (1986): 911–16.

Cacinotta, D. et al. "Clinical Experience with Acetyl-L-Carnitine in the Treatment of Signs and Symptoms of Senile Mental Deterioration in the Aged." Fifth Capo Boi Conference on Neuroscience (1987) (abstr.).

Caffarra, P., and Santamaria, V. "The Effects of Phosphatidylserine in Patients with Mild Cognitive Decline. An Open Trial." *Clinical Trials Journal* 24 (1) (1987): 109–14.

Calvani, M. et al. "Action of Acetyl-L-Carnitine in Neurodegeneration and Alzheimer's Disease." *Annals of the New York Academy of Sciences* 663 (1992): 483–86.

Calvin, W. H., and Ojemann, G. A. *Inside the Brain: An Enthralling Account of the Structure and Workings of the Human Brain* (New York: New American Library, 1980).

Carta, A. et al. "Acetyl-L-Carnitine and Alzheimer's Disease: Pharmacological Considerations beyond the Cholinergic Sphere." *Annals of the New York Academy of Sciences* 695 (1993): 324–26.

Cenacchi, B., Baggio, C., and Palin, E. "Human Tolerability of Oral Phosphatidylserine Assessed through Laboratory Examinations." *Clinical Trials Journal* 24 (1987): 125–30.

Cenacchi, B. et al. "Cognitive Decline in the Elderly. A Double-Blind, Placebo-Controlled, Multicenter Study on Efficacy of Phosphatidylserine Administration." *Aging—Clinical and Experimental Research* 5 (1993): 123–33.

Cipolli, C., and Chiari, G. "Effects of L-Acetylcarnitine on Mental Deterioration in the Aged: Initial Results." *Clinica Terapeutica* 132 (1990): 479–510.

Cocito, L. et al. "GABA and Phosphatidylserine in Human Photosensitivity: A Pilot Study." *Epilepsy Research* 17 (1994): 49–53.

Cohen, S. A., and Mueller, W. E. "Age-Related Alterations in NMDA-Receptor Properties in the Mouse Forebrain: Partial Restoration by Chronic Phosphatidylserine Dosing." *Brain Research* 584 (1992): 174–80.

Crayhon, R. "Carnitine: An Extraordinary Nutrient with Many Applications." *Total Health* (Oct. 1996): 30–31.

Crook, T. H. et al. "Effects of Phosphatidylserine in Age-Associated Memory Impairment." *Neurology* 41 (1991): 644–49.

Crook, T. H. et al. "Effects of Phosphatidylserine in Alzheimer's Disease." *Psychopharmacology Bulletin* 28 (1992): 61–66.

Dean, W., and Morgenthaler, J. *Smart Drugs and Nutrients* (Santa Cruz, Calif.: B and J Productions, 1990).

Dean, W., Morgenthaler, J., and Fowkes, S. W. *Smart Drugs II* (Menlo Park, Calif.: Health Freedom Press, 1993).

Delwaide, P., Gyselynck-Mambourg, A. M., Hurlet, A., and

Ylieff, M. "Double-Blind Randomized Controlled Study of Phosphatidylserine in Senile Demented Patients." *Acta Neurologica Scandinavica* 73 (1986): 136–40.

Engel, R. R. et al. "Double-Blind Crossover Study of Phosphatidylserine versus Placebo in Subjects with Early Cognitive Deterioration of the Alzheimer's Type." *European Neuropsychopharmacology* 2 (1992): 149–55.

"First the Rage Was Antioxidants, Now It's the Hormone Therapy Revolution." *Life Enhancement* 33 (1997): 7–15.

Fowkes, S. W. "Natural Substances to Make Us Smarter." *Nutrition and Healing* (Mar. 1996).

Funfgeld, E. W. et al. "Double-Blind Study with Phosphatidylserine (PS) in Parkinsonian Patients with Senile Dementia of Alzheimer's Type (SDAT)." *Progress in Clinical and Biological Research* 317 (1989): 1235–46.

Gecele, M., Francesetti, G., and Meluzzi, A. "Acetyl-L-Carnitine in Aged Subjects with Major Depression: Clinical Efficacy and Effects on the Circadian Rhythm of Cortisol." *Dementia* 2 (1991): 333–37.

Ghirardi, O. et al. "Long-Term Acetyl-L-Carnitine Preserves Sp Learning in the Senescent Rat." *Progress in Neuro-Psychopharmacology and Biological Psychiatry* 12 (1–2) (1989): 237–45.

Granata, Q., and DiMichele, J. "Phosphatidylserine in Elderly Patients. An Open Trial." Clinical *Trials Journal* 24 (1987): 99–103.

Guarnaschelli, C. et al. "Pathological Brain Aging: Evaluation of the Efficacy of a Pharmacological Aid." *Drugs under Experimental and Clinical Research* 14 (11) (1988): 715–18.

Kidd, P. M. *Phosphatidylserine (PS), a Remarkable Brain Cell Nutrient* (Lucas Meyer, 1995).

Klinkhammer, P., Szelies, B., and Heiss, W. D. "Effect of Phosphatidylserine on Cerebral Glucose Metabolism in Alzheimer's Disease." *Cognitive Deterioration* 1 (1990): 197–201.

Latorraca, S. et al. "Effects of Phosphatidylserine on Free Radical Susceptibility in Human Diploid Fibroblasts." *Journal of Neural Transmission* 6 (1993) 73–77.

Lino, A. et al. "Psycho-Functional Changes in Attention and Learning under the Action of L-Acetylcarnitine in 17 Young Subjects. A Pilot Study of Its Use in Mental Deterioration." *Clinica Terapeutica* 140 (1992): 569–73.

Maggioni, M. et al. "Effects of Phosphatidylserine Therapy in Geriatric Subjects with Depressive Disorders." *Acta Psychiatrica Scandinavica* 81 (1990): 265–70.

Manfredi, M. et al. "Clinical Results with Phosphatidylserine Therapy in 40 Women Suffering from Psychosomatic Disorders, at Climacteric and Senile Ages." *La Clinica Terapeutica*, I 120 (1987): 33–36.

Masturzo, P. et al. "TSH Circadian Secretions in Aged Men and

Effect of Phosphatidylserine Dosing." *Chronobiologia* 17 (1990): 267–74.

Monteleone, P. et al. "Blunting by Chronic Phosphatidylserine Administration of the Stress-Induced Activation of the Hypothalamo-Pituitary-Adrenal Axis in Healthy Men." *European Journal of Clinical Pharmacology* 41 (1992): 385–88.

Monteleone, P. et al. "Effects of Phosphatidylserine on the Neuroendocrine Response to Physical Stress in Humans." *Neuroendocrinology* 52 (1990): 243.

Nerozzi, D. et al. "Fosfatidilserine disturbidelli memoria nell 'anziano." *La Clinica Terapeutica* 120 (1987): 399– 404.

Nishizuka, Y. "Turnover of Inositol Phospholipids and Signal Transduction." *Science* 225 (1984): 1365–70.

Nunzi, M. G. et al. "Therapeutic Properties of Phosphatidylserine in the Aging Brain." In *Phospholipids: Biochemical, Pharmaceutical, and Analytical Considerations* (New York: Plenum Press, 1990).

Nunzi, M. G., Milan, F., Guidolin, D., Toffano, G. "Dendritic Spin Loss in Hippocampus of Aged Rats. Effect of Brain Phosphatidylserine Administration." *Neurobiology of Aging* 8 (1987): 501–10.

Palmieri, G. et al. "Double-Blind Controlled Trial of Phosphatidylserine in Subjects with Senile Mental Deterioration." *Clinical Trials Journal* 24 (1987): 73–83.

Parnetti, L. et al. "Multicentre Study of L-Alpha-Glyceryl-Phosphorylcholine versus ST200 among Patients with Probable Senile Dementia of Alzheimer's Type." *Drugs and Aging* 3 (1993): 159–64.

Pettegrew, J. W. et al. "Clinical and Neurochemical Effects of Acetyl-L-Carnitine in Alzheimer's Disease." *Neurobiology of Aging* 16 (1) (1995): 1–4.

Pettorossi, V. E., Brunetti, O., Carobi, C., Della Torre, G., and Grassi, S. "L-Acetyl-Carnitine Enhances Functional Muscle Re-Innervation." *Drugs under Experimental and Clinical Research* 17 (2) (1991): 119–25.

Puca, F. M. et al. "Exploratory Trial of Phosphatidylserine Efficacy in Mildly Demented Subjects." *Clinical Trials Journal* 24 (1987): 94–98.

Rai, G. et al. "Double-Blind, Placebo Controlled Study of Aceytl-L-Carnitine in Patients with Alzheimer's Dementia." *Current Medical Research and Opinion* 11 (1990): 638–47.

Ransmayr, G. et al. "Double-Blind Placebo-Controlled Trial of Phosphatidylserine in Elderly Subjects with Arteriosclerotic Encephalopathy." *Clinical Trials Journal* 24 (1987): 62–72.

Rosadini, G. et al. "Phosphatidylserine: Quantitative Effects in Healthy Volunteers." *Neuropsychobiology* 24 (1991): 42–48.

Sinforiani, E. et al. "Cognitive Decline in Aging Brain. Therapeutic Approach with Phosphatidylserine." *Clinical Trials Journal* 24 (1987): 115–24.

Sinforiani, E. et al. "Neuropsychological Changes in Demented Patients Treated with Acetyl-L-Carnitine." *International Journal of Clinical Pharmacology Research* 10 (1990): 69–74.

Spagnoli, A. et al. "Long-Term Acetyl-L-Carnitine Treatment in Alzheimer's Disease." *Neurology* 41 (1991): 1726–32.

Tempesta, E. et al. "L-Acetylcarnitine in Depressed Elderly Subjects. A Cross-Over Study versus Placebo." *Drugs under Experimental and Clinical Research* 13 (1987): 417–23.

Toffano, G. "The Therapeutic Value of Phosphatidylserine Effect in the Aging Brain." In *Lecithin: Technological, Biological, and Therapeutic Aspects* (New York: Plenum Press, 1987): 137–46.

Villardita, C. et al. "Multicentre Clinical Trial of Brain Phosphatidylserine in Elderly Subjects with Mental Deterioration." *Clinical Trials Journal* 24 (1987): 84–93.

Walker, M. "Phosphatidylserine: Memory Enhancer." *Health Foods Business* (Oct. 1996).

Whitaker, J. "Alert Body, Alert Mind." *Let's Live* (Sept. 1992): 80.

See pages 628 and 641 for ginkgo and pregnenolone references.

Chapter 30

Aldercreutz, H. "Does Fiber-Rich Food Containing Animal Lignin Precursors Protect Against Both Colon and Breast Cancer? An Extension of the Fiber Hypothesis." *Gastroenterology* 86 (1984): 761–66.

Anderson, J. W., Deakins, D. A., Floore, T. L., Smith, B. M., and Whitis, S. E. "Dietary Fiber and Coronary Heart Disease." *Critical Reviews in Food Science and Nutrition* 29 (1990): 95–147.

Anderson, J. W., Gustafson, N. J., Bryant, C. A., and Tielyen-Clark, J. "Dietary Fiber and Diabetes: A Comprehensive Review and Practical Application." *Journal of the American Dietetic Association* 87 (1987): 1189–97.

Anderson, J. W., Story, L., Sieling, B., and Chen, W.-J. L. "Hypocholesterolemic Effects of High-Fiber Diets Rich in Water-Soluble Plant Fibres." *Journal of the Canadian Dietetic Association* 45 (1984): 140–48.

Bell, L. et al. "Cholesterol-Lowering Effects of Psyllium Hydrophilic Mucilloid." *Journal of the American Medical Association* 261 (23) (1989): 3419–23.

Blackburn, G. L. "The Right Way to Fiber Up." *Prevention* (Dec. 1989): 25–32.

Burkitt, D. P. "Economic Development—Not All Bonus." *Nutrition Today* 11 (1976): 6–13.

Burkitt, D. P. "Some Diseases Characteristic of Modern Western Civilization." *British Medical Journal* 1 (1973): 274–78.

Burkitt, D. P. "The Link between Low-Fiber Diets and Disease." *Human Nature* (Dec. 1978).

Burkitt, D. P., and Trowell, H. *Western Diseases: Their Emergence and Prevention* (Cambridge, Mass.: Harvard University Press, 1981).

Cleave, T. L., Campbell, G. D., and Painter, N. S. *Diabetes, Coronary Thrombosis and the Saccharine Disease* (Bristol, England: John Wright, 1966).

Cummings, J. H. "Health and the Large Intestine." In *Nutrition and Health: A Perspective* (New York: Alan R. Liss, 1982).

Heaton, K. W. "The Epidemiology of Gallstones and Suggested Aetiology." *Clinics in Gastroenterology* 2 (1973): 67–83.

Heaton, K. W. "Food Fiber as an Obstacle to Energy Intake." *Lancet* 2 (1973): 1418–21.

Jenkins, D. et al. "Decrease in Postprandial Insulin and Glucose Concentrations by Guar and Pectin." *Annals of Internal Medicine* 86 (1977): 20–23.

Kinosian, B. P., and Eisenberg, J. M. "Cutting into Cholesterol: Cost-Effective Alternatives to Treating Hypercholesterolemia." *Journal of the American Medical Association* 259 (15) (1988): 2249–54.

Kirby, R. et al. "Oat-Bran Intake Selectively Lowers Serum Low-Density Lipoprotein Cholesterol Concentrations of Hypercholesterolemic Men." *American Journal of Clinical Nutrition* 34 (1981): 824–29.

Khaw, K. T., Barrett-Connor, E. "Dietary Fiber and Reduced Ischemic Heart Disease Mortality Rates in Men and Women: A 12-Year Prospective Study." *American Journal of Epidemiology* (1987): 1093–1102.

Kromhout, D., Borschieter, E. B., Coulander, C. D. L. "Dietary Fiber and Ten-Year Mortality from Coronary Heart Disease, Cancer, and All Causes: The Zutphen Study." *Lancet* 2 (1982): 518–21.

Kushi, L. H., Lew, R. A., Stare, F. J. et al. "Diet and 20-Year Mortality from Coronary Heart Disease: The Ireland-Boston Diet-Heart Study." *New England Journal of Medicine* 312 (1985): 811–18.

Liu, K., Stamler, J., Trevisan, M., and Moss, D. "Dietary Lipids, Sugar, Fiber, and Mortality from Coronary Heart Disease." *Arteriosclerosis* 2 (1982): 221–27.

"Low-Fat, High-Fiber Diet Improves Post-Breast Cancer Immune Function." *Family Practice News* (Feb. 1, 1995): 21.

Painter, S. S. "Pressures in the Colon Related to Diverticular Disease." *Proceedings of the Royal Society of Medicine* 63 (1970): 144–45.

Pechter, K. "The Amazing Benefits of the New Fiber Supplements." *Prevention* (Oct. 1982): 26–32.

"Pectin May Reduce Cholesterol, Colon Cancer Incidence." *Cardiology World News* (Sept. 8, 1991).

Reddy, B. S. "Dietary Fiber and Colon Cancer." *Canadian Medical Association Journal* 123 (1980): 850–56.

Selvendran, R. R. "The Plant Cell Wall as a Source of Dietary Fiber: Chemistry and Structure." *American Journal of Clinical Nutrition* 39 (1984): 320–37.

Trowell, H. "Definition of Dietary Fiber and Hypothesis That It Is a Protective Factor in Certain Diseases." *American Journal of Clinical Nutrition* 29 (1976): 417–27.

Trowell, H. *Non-Infective Diseases in Africa* (London: Edward Arnold, 1960): 217–22.

Vahouny, G., and Kritchevsky, D. *Dietary Fiber in Health and Disease* (New York: Plenum Press, 1982).

Walker, A. R. P. "Dietary Fiber and the Pattern of Diseases." *Annals of Internal Medicine* 80 (1974): 663.

Chapter 31

Aso, Y. et al. "Preventive Effect of a Lactobacillus Casei Preparation on the Recurrence of Superficial Bladder Cancer in a Double-Blind Trial. The BLP Study Group." *European Urology* 27 (2) (1995): 104–9.

Bartlett, J. G., Finegold, J. M., Gosbach, S. L., Wilson, S. E. "Bacteriology of the Gut and Its Clinical Implications." *New England Journal of Medicine* 121 (1974): 390–403.

Bezkorovainy, A., and Miller-Catchpole, R. *Biochemistry and Physiology of Bifidobacteria* (Boca Raton, Fla.: CRC Press, 1989).

Black, F. et al. "Effect of Lactic Acid Producing Bacteria on the Human Intestinal Microflora during Ampicillin Treatment." *Scandinavian Journal of Infectious Diseases* 23 (2) (1991): 247–54.

Chaitow, L., and Trener, N. *Probiotics* (London: Thorsons, 1990).

Collins, E. B., and Hardi, P. "Inhibition of Candida Albicans by Lactobacillus Acidophilus." *Journal of Dairy Science* 63 (1979): 830–32.

De Simone, C. et al. "Effect of Bifidobacterium Bifidum and Lactobacillus Acidophilus on Gut Mucosa and Peripheral Blood B Lymphocytes." *Immunopharmacology and Immunotoxicology* 14 (1–2) (1992): 331–40.

Donaldson, R. M. "Normal Bacterial Populations of the Intestine and Their Relation to Intestinal Function." *New England Journal of Medicine* 270 (1964): 938–45.

Draser, B. S., and Hill, M. J. *Human Intestinal Flora* (New York: Academic Press, 1974): 36–42.

Friend, B. A., and Shahani, K. M. "Antitumor Properties of Lactobacilli and Dairy Products Fermented by Lactobacilli." *Journal of Food Protection* 47 (9): 717–28.

Friend, B. A., and Shahani, K. M. "Nutritional and Therapeutic Aspects of Lactobacilli." *Journal of Applied Nutrition* 36 (2) (1984): 125.

Gillard, S. E., and Speck, M. L. "Antagonistic Action of Lactobacillus Acidophilus toward Intestinal and Foodborne Pathogens in Associative Cultures." *Journal of Food Protection* 40 (12) (1977): 829–33.

Goldin, B. R. et al. "Effect of Diet and Lactobacillus Acidophilus

Supplements on Human Fecal Bacterial Enzymes." *Journal of the National Cancer Institute* 64 (1980): 255–61.

Isolauri, E. et al. "Oral Bacteriotherapy for Viral Gastroenteritis." *Digestive Diseases and Sciences* 39 (12) (1994): 2595–2600.

Kaila, M. et al. "Enhancement of the Circulating Antibody Secreting Cell Response in Human Diarrhea by a Human Lactobacillus Strain." *Pediatric Research* 32 (2) (1992): 141–44.

"Lactobacilli May Form Natural Defense against Nitrosamines in Intestine." *Food Product Development* 14 (2) (1980): 12.

Ling, W. H. et al. "Lactobacillus Strain GG Supplementation Decreases Colonic Hydrolytic and Reductive Enzyme Activities in Healthy Female Adults." *Journal of Nutrition* 124 (1) (1994): 18–23.

Metchnikoff, E. *Prolongation of Life* (New York: G. P. Putnam and Sons, 1908).

Nester et al. *Microbiology, Molecules, Microbes and Man* (Holt, Reinhart and Winston, 1973).

Oksanen, P. L. et al. "Prevention of Travellers' Diarrhea by Lactobacillus GG." *Annals of Medicine* 22 (1) (1990): 53–56.

Rasic, J., and Kurmann, J. *Bifido Bacterium and Their Role* (Boston: Birkhauser, 1983).

Sardine, W. E. "Lactic Acid Bacteria in Food and Health: A Review with Special Reference to Enteropathogenic E. Coli as Well as Certain Enteric Diseases and Their Treatment with Antibiotics and Lactobacillus." *Journal of Milk and Food Technology* 35: 691–702.

Shahani, K. M., and Chandan, R. "Nutritional and Healthful Aspects of Cultured and Culture-Containing Dairy." *Journal of Dairy Science* 62 (1979): 1685–94.

Shahani, K. M. et al. "Natural Antibiotic Activity of Lactobacillus Acidophilus and Bulgaricus." *Cultured Dairy Products Journal* 1262 (1977): 8.

Vincent, J. G., Veomott, R. C., and Riley, R. F. "Anti-Bacterial Activity Associated with Lactobacillus Acidophilus." *Journal of Bacteriology* 78 (1959): 477–84.

Chapter 33

DHEA

Barrett-Connor, E., and Goodman-Gruen, D. "The Epidemiology of DHEAs and Cardiovascular Disease." *Annals of the New York Academy of Sciences* 774 (1995): 259–70.

Barrett-Conner, E., Khaw, K. T., and Yen, S. S. "A Prospective Study of Dehydroepiandrosterone Sulfate, Mortality, and Cardiovascular Disease." *New England Journal of Medicine* 315 (1986): 1519–24.

Bednarek-Tupikowska, G., Kossowska, B., Bohdanowics-Pawlak, A., and Sciborski, R. "The Influence of DHEA on Serum Lipids, Insulin and Sex Hormone Levels in Rabbits with Induced Hypercholesterolemia." *Gynecological Endocrinology* 9 (1995): 23–28.

Bird, C. E. et al. "Dehydroepiandrosterone: Kinetics of Metabolism in Normal Men and Women." *Journal of Clinical Endocrinology and Metabolism* 47 (1978): 818–22.

Boggs, C. "DHEA: The Youth Hormone Can Now Be Added Back to the Body with Full Rejuvenating Potential." *Journal of Longevity Research* 1 (1) (1994).

Braverman, E. R. "DHEA and Adrenopause: A New Sign of Aging and a New Treatment." *Total Health* 16 (1) (Feb. 1994).

Calabrese, V. P. et al. "DHEA in Multiple Sclerosis: Positive Effects on the Fatigue Syndrome in Non-Randomized Study." In *The Biologic Role of DHEA* (New York: Walter De Gruyter, 1990): 95–100.

Carey, B. "Hooked on Youth." *Hippocrates* (1996): 37–44.

Cherniske, S. A. *The DHEA Breakthrough* (New York: Ballantine Books, 1996).

Dilman, V. M., and Ward, D. *The Neuroendocrine Theory of Aging and Degenerative Disease* (Pensacola, Fla.: The Center for Bio-Gerontology, 1992).

Drucker, M. D., Blumberg, J. M., Gandy, H. M., David, R. R., and Verde, A. L. "Biologic Activity of DHEAs in Man." *Journal of Clinical Endocrinology and Metabolism* 35 (54) (1972): 48–54.

Ebeling, P., and Veikko, A. K. "Physiological Importance of Dehydroepiandrosterone." *Lancet* 343 (8911) (June 11, 1994).

Fettner, A. G. "DHEA Gets Respect." *Harvard Health Letter* 19 (9) (July 1994).

"First the Rage Was Antioxidants, Now It's the Hormone Therapy Revolution." *Life Enhancement* 33 (1997): 7–15.

Flood, J. F., Smith, G. E., and Roberts, E. "Dehydroepiandrosterone and Its Sulfate Enhance Memory Retention in Mice." *Brain Research* 447 (1988): 269–78.

Gaby, A. R. "Dehydroepiandrosterone: Biological Effects and Clinical Significance." *Alternative Medicine Review* 1 (2) (July 1996): 60–69.

Gordon, G. et al. "Reduction of Atherosclerosis by Administration of Dehydroepiandrosterone." *Journal of Clinical Investigation* 82 (2) (Aug. 1988): 712–20.

Herrington, D. "DHEA and Coronary Atherosclerosis." *Annals of the New York Academy of Sciences* 774 (1995): 271–80.

Hoagland, H. "Adventures in Biological Engineering." *Science* 100 (1944): 63–67.

Hornsby, P. "Biosynthesis of DHEAs by the Human Adrenal Cortex and Its Age-Related Decline." *Annals of the New York Academy of Sciences* 774 (1995): 29–46.

Khorram, O., Vu, L., and Yen, S. S. "Activation of Immune Function by Dehydroepiandrosterone

(DHEA) in Age-Advanced Men." *Journals of Gerontology. Series A: Biological Sciences and Medical Sciences* 52 (1997): 1–7.

Lohman, R., Yowell, R., Barton, S., Araneo, B., and Siemionow, M. "Dehydroepiandrosterone Protects Muscle Flap Microcirculatory Hemodynamics from Ischemia/Reperfusion Injury: An Experimental In Vivo Study." *Journal of Trauma* 42 (1997): 74–80.

Majewska, M. D. "Neuronal Actions of DHEAs: Implications for Aging." Dehydroepiandrosterone (DHEA) and Aging, New York Academy of Sciences Meeting, June 17–19, 1995.

Morales, A. J., Nolan, J. J., Nelson, J. C., and Yen, S. S. "Effects of Replacement Dose of Dehydroepiandrosterone in Men and Women of Advancing Age." *Journal of Clinical Endocrinology and Metabolism* (U.S.) 78 (6) (June 1994): 1360–67.

Nyce, J. W. et al. "Inhibition of 1.2 Dimethylhydrazine-Induced Tumorigenesis in Mice by DHEA." *Carcinogenesis* 5 (184): 57–62.

Regelson, W., and Colman, C. *The Superhormone Promise* (New York: Simon and Schuster, 1996).

Regelson, W., and Kalimi, M. *The Biologic Role of Dehydroepiandrosterone (DHEA)* (Berlin: Walter de Gruyter, 1990).

Regelson, W., Loria, R., and Kalimi, M. "Hormonal Intervention: 'Buffer Hormones' or 'State Dependency.' The Role of Dehydroepiandrosterone (DHEA), Thyroid Hormone, Estrogen and Hypophysectomy in Aging." *Annals of the New York Academy of Sciences* 521 (1988): 260–73.

Sahelian, R. *DHEA: A Practical Guide* (Garden City Park, N.Y.: Avery Publishing Group, 1996).

Schwartz, A. G., and Pashko, L. L. "Cancer Chemoprevention with the Adrenocortical Steroid Dehydroepiandrosterone and Structural Analogs." *Journal of Cellular Biochemistry* (Suppl. 17G) (1993): 73–79.

Schwartz, A. G., and Pashko, L. L. "Cancer Prevention with Dehydroepiandrosterone and Nonandrogenic Structural Analogs." *Journal of Cellular Biochemistry* (Suppl. 22) (1995): 210–17.

Schwartz, A. G., and Pashko, L. L. "Mechanism of Cancer Preventive Action of DHEA." *Annals of the New York Academy of Sciences* 774 (1995): 180–86.

Schwartz, A. G., Whitcomb, J. M., Nyce, J. W., Lewbart, M. L., and Pashko, L. L. "Dehydroepiandrosterone and Structural Analogs: A New Class of Cancer Chemopreventive Agents." *Advances in Cancer Research* 51 (1986): 391–424.

Whitcomb, J. M. "Inhibition of Tumor Development by Dehydroepiandrosterone and Related Steroids." *Toxicologic Pathology* 14 (3) (1986): 357–62.

Wolkowitz, O. M., Reus, V. I., Roberts, E., Manfredi, F., Chan, T., Ormiston, S., Johnson, R., Canick, J., Brizedine, L., and Weingartner, H. "Antidepressant and Cognition-Enhancing Effects of DHEA in Major Depression." Dehydroepiandrosterone (DHEA) and Aging, New York Academy of Sciences Meeting, June 17–19, 1995.

Yen, S. S., Morales, A. J., and Khorram, O. "Replacement of DHEA in Aging Men and Women." *Annals of the New York Academy of Sciences* 774 (1995): 128–42.

Yen, T. T., Allan, J. A., Pearson, V., Acton, J. M., and Greenberg, M. M. "Prevention of Obesity in Avy/A Mice by Dehydroepiandrosterone." *Lipids* 12 (1977): 409–13.

Pregnenolone

Davison, R. et al. "Effects of Delta-5-Pregnenolone on Rheumatoid Arthritis." *Archives of Internal Medicine* 85 (1950): 365–88.

Flood, J. F., Morley, J. E., and Roberts, E. "Memory-Enhancing Effects in Male Mice of Pregnenolone and Steroids Metabolically Derived from It." *Proceedings of the National Academy of Sciences of the United States of America* 89 (1992): 1567–71.

Flood, J. F., Morley, J. E., and Roberts, E. "Pregnenolone Sulfate Enhances Post-Training Memory Processes When Injected in Very Low Doses into Limbic System Structures: The Amygdala Is by Far the Most Sensitive." *Proceedings of the National Academy of Sciences of the United States of America* 92 (1995): 10806–10.

Freeman, H. et al. "Therapeutic Efficacy of Delta-5-Preg-nenolone in Rheumatoid Arthritis." *Journal of the American Medical Association* 143 (1950): 338–44.

George, M., Guidotti, A., Rubinow, D., Pan, B., Mikalauskas, K., and Post, R. "CSF Neuroactive Steroids in Affective Disorders: Pregnenolone, Progesterone, and DBI." *Biological Psychiatry* 35 (10) (1994): 775–80.

Guth, L., Zhang, A., and Roberts, E. "Key Role for Pregnenolone in Combination Therapy That Promotes Recovery after Spinal Cord Injury." *Proceedings of the National Academy of Sciences of the United States of America* 91 (25) (1994): 12308–12.

Henderson, E., Weinberg, M., and Wright, W. "Pregnenolone." *Journal of Clinical Endocrinology and Metabolism* 10 (1950): 455–74.

Isaacson, R., and Varner, J. "The Effects of Pregnenolone Sulfate and Ethylestrenol on Retention of a Passive Avoidance Task." *Brain Research* 689 (1995): 79–84.

Mathis, C., Vogel, E., Cagniard, B., Criscuolo, F., and Ungerer, A. "The Neurosteroid Pregnenolone Sulfate Blocks Deficits Induced by a Competitive NMDA Antagonist in Active Avoidance and Lever-Press Learning Tasks in Mice." *Neuropharmacology* 35 (1996): 1057–64.

McGavack, T., Chevalley, J., and Weissberg, J. "The Use of Pregnenolone in Various Clinical Disorders." *Journal of Clinical Endocrinology and Metabolism* 11 (1951): 559–77.

Morfin, R., and Courchay, G. "Pregnenolone. and DHEA as Precursors of Native 7-Hydroxylated Metabolites Which Increase the Immune Response in Mice." *B Steroid Biochem Mol Bio* 50 (1–2) (1994): 91–100.

Pincus, G., and Hoagland, H. "Effects of Administered Pregnenolone on Fatiguing Psychomotor Performance." *Journal of Aviation Medicine* 15 (1944): 98–115.

Roberts, E. "Pregnenolone from Selye to Alzheimer and a Model of the Pregnenolone Sulfate Binding Site on the GABA Receptor." *Biochemical Pharmacology* 49 (1995): 1–16.

Sahelian, R. "The Promise of Pregnenolone." *Life Enhancement* 36 (1997): 3–11.

Selye, H., Clarke, E. "Potentiation of a Pituitary Extract with Pregnenolone and Additional Observations Concerning the Influence of Various Organs on Steroid Metabolism." *Rev Can Biol* 2 (1943): 319–28.

Steiger, A., Trachel, L., and Guldner, J. "Neurosteroid Pregnenolone Induces Sleep EEG Changes in Man Compatible with Inverse Agonistic GABA Receptor Modulation." *Brain Research* 615 (1993): 267–74.

Wu, E., Gibbs, T., and Farb, D. "Pregnenolone Sulfate: A Positive Allosteric Modulator at the N-Methyl-D-Aspartate Receptor." *Molecular Pharmacology* 40 (1991): 333–36.

Chapter 34

Barchas, J. D., Da Costa, F., and Spector, S. "Acute Pharmacology of Melatonin." *Nature* 214 (1967): 919–20.

Caroleo, M., Frasca, D., Nistico, G., and Doria, G. "Melatonin as Immunomodulator in Immunodeficient Mice." *Immunopharmacology* 23 (1992): 81–89.

Claustrat, B., Brun, J., David, M. et al. "Melatonin and Jet Lag: Confirmatory Result Using a Simplified Protocol." *Biological Psychiatry* 32 (1992): 705–11.

Cowley, G. "Melatonin." *Newsweek* (Aug. 7, 1995): 46–49.

Dollins, A. B., Zhdanova, I. V., Wurtman, R. J. et al. "Effect of Inducing Nocturnal Serum Melatonin Concentration in Daytime on Sleep, Mood, Body Temperature, and Performance." *Proceedings of the National Academy of Sciences of the United States of America* 91 (1994): 1824–28.

El Domeiri, A. A. H., and Das Gupta, T. K. "Reversal by Melatonin of the Effect of Pinealectomy on Tumor Growth." *Cancer Research (USA)* 33 (11) (1973): 2830–33.

"First the Rage Was Antioxidants, Now It's the Hormone Therapy Revolution." *Life Enhancement* 33 (1997): 7–15.

Grad, B. R., and Rozencwaig, R. "The Role of Melatonin and Serotonin in Aging: Update." *Psychoneuroendocrinology* 18 (1993): 283–95.

Haimov, I., Laudon, M., Zisapel, N., Souroujon, M., Nof, D., Shlitner, A., Herer, P., Tzischinsky, O., and Lavie, P. "Sleep Disorders and Melatonin Rhythms in Elderly People." *British Medical Journal* 309 (1993): 167.

Harma, M., Laitinen, J., Partinen, M., and Suvanto, S. "The Effect of Four-Day Round Trip Flights over 10 Time Zones on the Circadian Variation of Salivary Melatonin and Cortisol in Airline Flight Attendants." *Ergonomics* 37 (1993): 1479–89.

Hughes, P. "The Hormone Whose Time Has Come." *Hippocrates* (July–Aug. 1994).

Kent, S. "How Melatonin Combats Aging." *Life Extension Magazine* (Dec. 1995): 10–27.

Kloeden, P. "Does a Centralized Clock for Aging Exist?" *Gerontology* 36 (1990): 314–22.

Lesnikov, V. A., Pierpaoli, W. "Pineal Cross-Transplantation (Old-to-Young and Vice Versa) as Evidence for an Endogenous 'Aging clock.' " *Annals of the New York Academy of Sciences* 719 (1994): 456–60.

Lissoni, P., Ardizzoia, A. et al. "Amplification of Eosinophilia by Melatonin during the Immunotherapy of Cancer with Interleukin-2." *Journal of Biological Regulators and Homeostatic Agents* 7 (1993): 34–36.

Lissoni, P., Barni, S., Tancini, G., Ardizzoia, A., Brivio, F. et al. "Therapeutic Use of the Pineal Hormone Melatonin in Human Neoplasms: Update Results." *Acta Neurobiologiae Experimentalis* 54 (Suppl.) (1994): 127–28.

Lissoni, P., Barni, S., Tancini, G., Rovelli, F., Ardizzoia, A., Conti, A., and Maestroni, G. J. M. "A Study of the Mechanisms Involved in the Immunostimulatory Action of Pineal Hormone in Cancer Patients." *Oncology (Switzerland)* 50 (6) (1993): 399–402.

Lissoni, P., Mergalli, S., Barni, S., and Frigerio, F. "A Randomized Study of Immunotherapy with Low-Dose Subcutaneous Interleukin-2 Plus Melatonin versus Chemotherapy with Cisplatin and Etoposide as First-Line Therapy for Advanced Non-Small-Cell Lung Cancer." *Tumori* 80 (1994): 464–67.

Maestroni, G., Conti, A., and Pierpaoli, W. "Pineal Melatonin, Its Fundamental Immunoregulatory Role in Aging and Cancer." *Annals of the New York Academy of Sciences* 521 (1988): 140–48.

Maestroni, G., Conti, A., and Pierpaoli, W. "Role of the Pineal Gland in Immunity. Circadian Synthesis and Release of Melatonin Modulates the Antibody Response and Antagonizes the Immunosuppressive Effect of Corticosterone." *Journal of Neuroimmunology* 3 (1986): 19–30.

Nair, N., Hariharasubramanian, N., Pilapil, C., Isaac, I., and Thavundayil, J. "Plasma Melatonin—An Index of Brain Aging in Humans?" *Biological Psychiatry* 21 (1986): 141–50.

Petrie, K., Dawson, A., Thompson, L., and Brook, R. "A Double-Blind Trial of Melatonin as a

Treatment for Jet Lag in International Cabin Crew." *Biological Psychiatry* 33 (1993): 526–30.

Pierpaoli, W., and Regelson, W. "Pineal Control of Aging: Effect of Melatonin and Pineal Grafting on Aging Mice." *Proceedings of the National Academy of Sciences of the United States of America* 91 (1994): 787–91.

Pierpaoli, W., and Regelson, W., with Colman, C. *The Melatonin Miracle* (New York: Simon and Schuster, 1995): 29–30.

Pierpaoli, W., Regelson, W. et al. "The Aging Clock: The Pineal Gland and Other Pacemakers in the Progression of Aging and Carcinogenesis." *Annals of the New York Academy of Sciences* 719 (1994).

Regelson, W., and Pierpaoli, W. "Melatonin: A Rediscovered Anti-Tumor Hormone? Its Relation to Surface Receptors, Sex Steroid Metabolism, Immunologic Response and Chronobiologic Factors in Tumor Growth and Therapy." *Cancer Investigation* 5 (4) (1987): 379–85.

Reiter, R. J. "Oxidative Processes and Antioxidative Defense Mechanisms in the Aging Brain." *Federation of American Societies for Experimental Biology* 9 (1995): 526–33.

Reiter, R. J. "The Pineal Gland and Melatonin in Relation to Aging: A Summary of the Theories and of the Data." *Experimental Gerontology* 30 (1995): 199–212.

Reiter, R. J. "The Role of the Neurohormone Melatonin as a Buffer against Oxidative Damage." *Neurochemistry International* 2 (1995): 453–60.

Reiter, R. J. et al. "A Review of the Evidence Supporting Melatonin's Role as an Antioxidant." *Journal of Pineal Research* 18 (1) (Jan. 1994): 1–11.

Reiter, R. J., and Robinson, J. *Melatonin* (New York: Bantam Books, 1995).

Rozencwaig, R., Grad, B. R., and Ochoa, J. "The Role of Melatonin and Serotonin in Aging." *Medical Hypotheses* 23 (1987): 337–52.

Sahelian, R. *Melatonin: Nature's Sleeping Pill* (Marina Del Rey, Calif.: Be Happier Press, 1995).

Sahelian, R. "Melatonin: The Natural Sleep Medicine." *Total Health* 17 (4) (Aug. 1995): 30 (3).

Zhdanova, I. V., Wurtman, R. J., and Schomer, D. L. "Sleep-Inducing Effects of Low Doses of Melatonin Ingested in the Evening." *Clinical Pharmacology and Therapeutics* 57 (1995): 552–58.

Chapter 35

Aldercreutz, H. et al. "Dietary Phytoestrogens and Menopause in Japan." *Lancet* 339 (1992): 1233.

Barnard, N. D. "Natural Progesterone: Is Estrogen the Wrong Hormone? An Interview with John R. Lee, M.D." *Good Health* (Spring 1994).

Bates, B. "Libido Decline May Signal Low Testosterone." *Family Practice News* (July 15, 1997): 40.

Burger, H. et al. "Effect of Combined Implants of Oestradiol and Testosterone on Libido in Postmenopausal Women." *British Medical Journal* 294 (Apr. 11, 1987): 936–37.

"Do You Need the Hormone of Desire?" *Prevention* 49 (8) (Aug. 1997): 73.

"Effects of Estrogen or Estrogen/Progestin Regimens on Heart Disease Risk Factors in Postmenopausal Women." The Postmenopausal Estrogen/Progestin Intervention (PEPI) Trial. *Journal of the American Medical Association* 273 (3) (Jan. 18, 1995): 199–208.

"Estrogen Deficiency and Risk of Alzheimer's Disease in Women." *American Journal of Epidemiology* 140: 256–61.

Ettinger, B., Friedman, G. D., Bush, T., and Quesenberry, C. P., Jr. "Reduced Mortality Associated with Long-Term Postmenopausal Estrogen Therapy." *Obstetrics and Gynecology* 87 (1996): 6–12.

Follingstad, A. H. "Estriol, the Forgotten Estrogen?" *Journal of the American Medical Association* 239 (1) (Jan. 2, 1978): 29–30.

Folsom, A. R., Mink, P. J., Sellers, T. A., Hong, C. P., Zheng, W., and Potter, J. D. "Hormonal Replacement Therapy and Morbidity and Mortality in a Prospective Study of Postmenopausal Women." *American Journal of Public Health* 85 (1995): 1128–32.

Gaby, A. R. *Preventing and Reversing Osteoporosis* (Rocklin, Calif.: Prima Publishing, 1994).

Genant, H. K., Baylink, D. J., and Gallagher, J. C. "Estrogens in the Prevention of Osteoporosis in Postmenopausal Women." *American Journal of Obstetrics and Gynecology* 161 (6) (1989): 1842, cited in *Office Nurse*: 8.

Goldzieher, J. W. "Postmenopausal Androgen Therapy." *The Female Patient* 22 (Apr. 1997): 10–12.

Grady, D., Rugin, S., and Petitti, D. "Hormone Therapy to Prevent Disease and Prolong Life in Postmenopausal Women." *Annals of Internal Medicine* 117 (1992): 1016–37.

Halberstam, M. J. "If Estrogens Retard Osteoporosis, Are They Worth the Cancer Risk?" *Modern Medicine* 45 (1977): 9, 15.

Hargrove, J. T., Maxson, W. S., and Wentz, A. C. "Absorption of Oral Progesterone Is Influenced by Vehicle and Particle Size." *American Journal of Obstetrics and Gynecology* 161 (4) (Oct. 1989): 948–51.

Hargrove, J. T., Maxson, W. S., Wentz, A. C., and Burnett, L. S. "Menopausal Hormone Replacement Therapy with Continuous Daily Oral Micronized Estradiol and Progesterone." *Obstetrics and Gynecology* 73 (1989): 606–12.

Kamen, B. *Hormone Replacement Therapy, Yes or No?* (Novata, Calif.: Nutrition Encounter, 1993).

Keough, C., ed. *The Complete Book of Cancer Prevention* (Emmaus, Pa.: Rodale Press, 1988): 131–34.

Lee, J. R. "Is Natural Progesterone the Missing Link in Osteoporosis Prevention and Treatment?" *Medical Hypothesis* 35 (1991): 316–18.

Lee, J. R. *Natural Progesterone: The Multiple Roles of a Remarkable Hormone* (Sebastopol, Calif.: B.L.I. Publishing, 1993).

Lee, J. R. "Osteoporosis Reversal. The Role of Progesterone." *International Clinical Nutrition Review* 10 (3) (July 1990): 384–91.

Lee, J. R. "Osteoporosis Reversal with Transdermal Progesterone (Letter)." *Lancet* 336 (1990): 1327.

Lee, J. R. "Successful Menopausal Osteoporosis Treatment Restoring Osteoclast/ Osteoblast Equilibrium." *Townsend Letter for Doctors* (1994): 133–34, 900–905.

Lee, J. R. *What Your Doctor May Not Tell You about Menopause* (New York: Warner Books, 1996).

Lee, J. R., and Wright, J. "The Many Clinical Benefits of Natural Progesterone." *Life Enhancement* 30 (Feb. 1997): 4–11.

Lemon, H. M. "Estriol Prevention of Mammary Carcinoma Induced by 7,12-Dimethylbenzanthrocene and Procarbazine." *Cancer Research* 35 (1975): 1341–53.

Lemon, H. M. "Pathophysiologic Considerations in the Treatment of Menopausal Patients with Oestrogens; the Role of Oestriol in the Prevention of Mammary Carcinoma." *Acta Endocrinologica. Supplementum* 233 (1980): 17–27.

Lemon, H. M. et al. "Reduced Estriol Excretion in Patients with Breast Cancer Prior to Endocrine Therapy." *Journal of the American Medical Association* 196 (1966): 1128–34.

Matsumoto, A. M. "Andropause— Are Reduced Androgen Levels in Aging Men Physiologically Important?" *Western Journal of Medicine* 159 (5) (Nov. 1993): 618–20.

Mayeaux, E. J., and Johnson, C. "Current Concepts in Postmenopausal Hormone Replacement Therapy." *Journal of Family Practice* 43 (1) (July 1996).

McKeown, L. A. "Diet High in Fruits and Vegetables Linked to Lower Breast Cancer Risk." *Medical Tribune* (July 9, 1992): 14.

Phillips, G. B. et al. "The Association of Hypotestosteronemia with Coronary Artery Disease in Men." *Arteriosclerosis and Thrombosis* 14 (5) (May 1994): 701–6.

Physicians Desk Reference (PDR) (Montvale, N.J.: Medical Economics Data).

Prior, J. C. "Progesterone as a Bone-Trophic Hormone." *Endocrine Reviews* 11 (1990): 386–98.

Scarbeck, K. "Androgens Can Add to the Benefits of HRT."

Family Practice News (July 15, 1997): 41.

Stampfer, M. J., and Colditz, G. A. "Estrogen Replacement Therapy and Coronary Heart Disease: A Quantitative Assessment of the Epidemiologic Evidence." *Preventive Medicine* 20 (1) (1991): 47, cited in *Office Nurse*: 7.

Stampfer, M. J., Colditz, G. A. et al. "Postmenopausal Estrogen Therapy and Cardiovascular Disease: Ten-Year Follow-Up from the Nurses Health Study." *New England Journal of Medicine* 325 (11) (1991): 756, cited in *Office Nurse*: 10.

Tenover, J. "Effects of Testosterone Supplementation in the Aging Male." *Journal of Clinical Endocrinology and Metabolism* (1992): 1092–98.

Tenover, J. S. "Androgen Administration to Aging Men." *Clinical Andrology* 23 (4) (Dec. 1994): 877–87.

Voigt, L. F., Weiss, N. S. et al. "Progestagen Supplementation of Exogenous Oestrogens and Risk of Endometrial Cancer." *Lancet* 338 (8762) (1991): 274, cited in *Office Nurse*: 8.

Wallis, C. "The Estrogen Dilemma." *Time* (June 26, 1995): 48–53.

Weiss, R. "Prescription for Passion." *Hippocrates* (Oct. 1995): 55–62.

Whitaker, J. *Dr. Julian Whitaker's Health and Healing* 3 (3) (Mar. 1993): 3.

Wilcox, G. et al. "Oestrogenic Effects of Plant Foods in Postmenopausal Women." *British Medical Journal* 301 (Oct. 1990): 905.

Williams, D. J. "The Forgotten Hormone." *Alternatives for the Health Conscious Individual* 4 (6) (Dec. 1991): 42–51.

Wilson, R. A. *Feminine Forever* (New York: M. Evans and Company, 1996).

Chapter 36

Banovac, K., Zakarija, M., and McKenzie, J. M. "Experience with Routine Thyroid Function Testing: Abnormal Results in 'Normal' Populations." *Journal of the Florida Medical Association* 72 (1985): 835–39.

Barnes, B. O., and Barnes, C. W. *Heart Attack Rareness in Thyroid-Treated Patients* (Springfield, Ill.: Charles C. Thomas, 1972).

Barnes, B. O., and Barnes, C. W. *Solved: The Riddle of Heart Attacks* (Fort Collins, Colo.: Robinson Press, 1976).

Barnes, B. O., and Galton, L. *Hypothyroidism: The Unsuspected Illness* (New York: Thomas Crowell, 1976).

Bennett, J. C., and Plum, F., eds. *Cecil Textbook of Medicine* 20th ed., vol. 2 (Philadelphia: W. B. Saunders Company, 1996).

Bennett, J. C., Plura, F. et al. *Cecil Textbook of Medicine*. 20th ed., vol. 2 (Philadelphia: W. B. Saunders): 1227–45.

Brayshaw, N. D., and Brayshaw, D. D. "Thyroid Hypofunction in

Premenstrual Syndrome." *New England Journal of Medicine* 315 (1986): 1486–87.

Cooper, D. S. "Thyroid Hormone Treatment: New Insights into an Old Therapy." *Journal of the American Medical Association* 261 (18) (May 12, 1989): 2684–95.

Drinka, P. J., and Nolten, W. E. "Review: Subclinical Hypothyroidism in the Elderly: To Treat or Not to Treat?" *American Journal of the Medical Sciences* 295 (1988): 125–28.

Gaby, A. R. "Treatment with Thyroid Hormone" (Letter to Editor) *Journal of the American Medical Association* 252 (13) (Oct. 6, 1989): 1774.

Galton, L. "Low Thyroid: Is It Sapping Your Energy?" *Family Circle* (Oct. 1973).

Gold, M. et al. "Hypothyroidism and Depression, Evidence from Complete Thyroid Evaluation." *Journal of the American Medical Association* 245 (1981): 1919–22.

Harby, K. "New Practice Guidelines Urge Thyroid Screening." *Medical Tribune* (Jan. 19, 1995).

Jennings, I. W. *Vitamins in Endocrine Metabolism* (Springfield, Ill.: Charles C. Thomas, 1970).

Kountz, W. B. *Thyroid Disease and Its Possible Role in Vascular Degeneration* (Springfield, Ill.: Charles C. Thomas, 1951).

Langer, S. E., and Scheer, J. F. *Solved: The Riddle of Illness* 2nd ed. (New Canaan, Conn.: Keats Publishing, 1995).

Levey, G. S. "Hypothyroidism: A Treacherous Masquerader." In *Acute Care Medicine* (May 1984).

Rosenthal, M. J., Hunt, W. C., Garry, P. J., and Goodwin, J. S. "Thyroid Failure in the Elderly: Microsomal Antibodies as Discriminate for Therapy." *Journal of the American Medical Association* 258 (1987): 209–13.

Spencer, J. G. C. "The Influence of Thyroid in Malignant Disease." *British Journal of Cancer* 8 (1954): 393.

Wiczyk, H. P. "Recognizing Thyroid Disease." *The Female Patient* 23 (Mar. 1998): 9–22.

Wren, J. C. "Thyroid Function and Coronary Thrombosis." *Journal of the American Geriatric Society* 16 (1968): 696–704.

Chapter 37

Abdo, J. "Creating Ourselves." *Life Extension* (Apr. 1998).

Alession, H. M., and Goldfarb, A. H. "Lipid Peroxidation and Scavenger Enzymes during Exercise: Adaptive Response to Training." *Journal of Applied Physiology* 64 (1988): 1333–36.

American College of Sports Medicine. *Guidelines for Exercise Testing and Prescription* (Philadelphia: Lea and Febiger, 1986).

Barry, D. *Stay Fit and Healthy Until You're Dead* (Emmaus, Pa.: Rodale Press, 1985).

Blair, S. N., Kohl, H. W., Paffenbarger, R. S. et al. "Physical Fitness and All-Cause Mortality." *Journal of the American Medical Association* 262 (1989): 2395–401.

Bloch, G. B. *Cross-Training: The Complete Handbook and Training Guide for All Sports* (New York: Simon and Schuster, 1992).

Caine, W., and Garfinkel, P. et al. *The Male Body: An Owner's Manual* (Emmaus, Pa.: Rodale Press, 1996).

Cooper, K. H. *Dr. Kenneth H. Cooper's Antioxidant Revolution* (Nashville: T. Nelson Publishers, 1994).

Cooper, K. H., and Cooper, M. *New Aerobics for Women* (New York: Bantam Books, 1973).

De Rosa, G., and Suarez, N. R. "Effect of Exercise on Tumor Growth and Body Composition of the Host." *Federation of American Societies for Experimental Biology Journal* (1980): 1118.

Ekelund, L.-G. et al. "Physical Fitness as a Predictor of Cardiovascular Mortality in Asymptomatic North American Men." *New England Journal of Medicine* 319 (Nov. 24, 1988): 1379–84.

Evans, W., and Rosenberg, I. H. *Biomarkers: The Ten Keys to Prolonging Vitality* (New York: Fireside, 1991).

Fixx, J. F. *The Complete Book of Running* (New York: Random House, 1977).

Gilmore, C. P., and the Editors of Time-Life Books. *Exercising for Fitness* (Alexandria, Va.: Time-Life Books, 1981).

Goldman, R. "Sports Training for the Senior Athlete." In *Advances in Anti-Aging Medicine* (Larchmont, N.Y.: Mary Ann Liebert Publishers, 1996): 141–49.

Goodrick, C. L. "Effects of Long-Term Voluntary Wheel Exercise on Male and Female Wistar Rats." *Gerontology* 26 (1980): 22–23.

Griffin, K. "An Active Life Makes for a Longer Life." *Hippocrates* (May 1997).

Gutfeld, G. "Muscle Up Your Metabolism." *Prevention* (Aug. 1991).

Kaufman, L. "Healing Power." *Hippocrates* (Nov. 1997).

Kramsch, D. M., Aspen, A. J., Abramowitz, B. M. et al. "Reduction of Coronary Atherosclerosis by Moderate Conditioning Exercise in Monkeys on an Atherogenic Diet." *New England Journal of Medicine* 305 (1981): 1483–89.

LaPerriere, A. et al. "Exercise and Psychoneuroimmunology." *Medical Science Sports Exercise* (Feb. 26, 1994).

"Lowering Cholesterol Can Reverse CHD Lesions." *Family*

Practice News 3 (Feb. 1–14, 1990): 1.

Merrill, J. et al. "Hyperlipidemic Response of Young Trained and Untrained Men after a High-Fat Meal." *Arteriosclerosis* 9 (1989): 217–22.

Milvy, P., ed. "The Marathon: Physiological, Medical, Epidemiological, and Psychological Studies." *Annals of the New York Academy of Sciences* 301 (1977): 519–49.

"Moderate Exercise Slows CAD." *Medical World News* (Aug. 10, 1987): 26–27.

Paffenbarger, R. S., Hyde, R. T., Wing, A. L. et al. "Physical Activity, All-Cause Mortality, and Longevity of College Alumni." *New England Journal of Medicine* 314 (1986): 605–13.

Paffenbarger, R. S., Jr. et al. "The Association of Changes in Physical Activity Level and Other Lifestyle Characteristics with Mortality among Men." *New England Journal of Medicine* 328 (8) (Feb. 25, 1993).

Parkhouse, W. S., Willis, P. E., and Zhang, J. "Hepatic Lipid Peroxidation and Antioxidant Enzyme Responses to Long-Term Voluntary Physical Activity and Aging." *Age* 18 (1995): 11–17.

Perlmutter, C. "Can You Walk Your Way to Maximum Immunity?" *Prevention* (Apr. 1990).

Prior, J. C., Vigna, Y., Sciarretta, D., Alojado, N., and Schulzer, M. "Conditioning Exercise Decreases Premenstrual Symptoms: A Prospective, Controlled Six-Month Trial." *Fertility and Sterility* 47 (1987): 402–8.

Pritikin, N. *Diet for Runners* (New York: Simon and Schuster, 1985).

Rose, C. L., and Cohen, M. L. "Relative Importance of Physical Activity for Longevity." In "The Marathon: Physiological, Medical, Epidemiological, and Psychological Studies." *Annals of the New York Academy of Sciences* 301 (1977): 671–97.

Salonen, J. T. et al. "Physical Activity and Risk of Myocardial Infarction, Cerebral Stroke, and Death: A Longitudinal Study in Eastern Finland." *American Journal of Epidemiology* 115 (4) (1982): 526–37.

Sandvik, L. et al. "Physical Fitness as a Predictor of Mortality among Healthy Middle-Aged Norwegian Men." *New England Journal of Medicine* 328 (8) (Feb. 25, 1993).

Sheehan, G. A. *Dr. Sheehan on Running* (Cleveland: World Publications, 1975).

Sinatra, S. "Exercise, Aging, Nutrition, and the Heart." In *Advances in Anti-Aging Medicine* (Larchmont, N.Y.: Mary Ann Liebert Publishers, 1996): 151–62.

Spirduso, W. W. "Physical Fitness, Aging, and Psychomotor Speed: A Review." *Journal of Gerontology* 35 (1980): 850.

Sylvester, R., Camp, J., and Sanonarco, M. "Effects of Exercise Training on Progression of Documented Coronary Arteriosclerosis in Men." *Annals of the New York Academy of Sciences* 301 (1977): 495.

"U.S. Surgeon General's Report on Physical Activity and Health." Centers for Disease Control and Prevention, Atlanta (July 11, 1996).

White, T. P., and the Editors of the University of California at Berkeley Wellness Letter. *The Wellness Guide to Lifelong Fitness* (New York: Random House, 1993).

Index

Underscored page references indicate boxed text. **Boldface** references indicate illustrations.

Underscored page references indicate boxed text. **Boldface**
references indicate illustrations.

Underscored page references indicate boxed text. **Boldface** references indicate illustrations.

Underscored page references indicate boxed text. **Boldface** references indicate illustrations.

Underscored page references indicate boxed text. **Boldface** references indicate illustrations.

Underscored page references indicate boxed text. **Boldface** references indicate illustrations.

<u>Underscored</u> page references indicate boxed text. **Boldface**
references indicate illustrations.

<u>Underscored</u> page references indicate boxed text. **Boldface** references indicate illustrations.

Underscored page references indicate boxed text. **Boldface**
references indicate illustrations.

Underscored page references indicate boxed text. **Boldface** references indicate illustrations.

Underscored page references indicate boxed text. **Boldface** references indicate illustrations.

Underscored page references indicate boxed text. **Boldface** references indicate illustrations.

Underscored page references indicate boxed text. **Boldface** references indicate illustrations.

Underscored page references indicate boxed text. **Boldface** references indicate illustrations.

<u>Underscored</u> page references indicate boxed text. **Boldface** references indicate illustrations.

Underscored page references indicate boxed text. **Boldface**
references indicate illustrations.

<u>Underscored</u> page references indicate boxed text. **Boldface** references indicate illustrations.

Underscored page references indicate boxed text. **Boldface**
references indicate illustrations.

Underscored page references indicate boxed text. **Boldface**
references indicate illustrations.

<u>Underscored</u> page references indicate boxed text. **Boldface**
references indicate illustrations.

Underscored page references indicate boxed text. **Boldface** references indicate illustrations.

<u>Underscored</u> page references indicate boxed text. **Boldface** references indicate illustrations.

About the Author

Timothy J. Smith, M.D., has been studying and practicing alternative and conventional healing principles for more than 25 years. A 1970 graduate of the University of Cincinnati College of Medicine, he completed his internship at the Pacific Medical Center in San Francisco and his residency at the University of California, San Francisco, Medical Center. He subsequently established a general family practice in Berkeley, California, where he continues to treat and counsel patients using an array of Eastern and Western medical techniques. Dr. Smith consults by telephone with patients around the world, specializing in difficult diagnoses and designing alternative treatment programs for a wide variety of medical problems.

A longtime student and advocate of Chinese traditional medicine, Dr. Smith was instrumental in introducing acupuncture to the American medical community. In 1972, he founded the first publicly funded acupuncture clinic in the United States. He gained national recognition for his use of acupuncture therapy in treating opiate withdrawal syndrome.

Because of his extensive work with acupuncture, Dr. Smith was invited to join the first delegation of American physicians practicing Chinese traditional medicine to visit the People's Republic of China. One of the highlights of his visit was being invited to present a lecture to the faculty of the prestigious Shanghai College of Chinese Medicine.

In addition to his medical practice in Berkeley, Dr.

Smith has served as a lecturer on Chinese medicine at the University of California, San Francisco, College of Medicine; at the University of California, Berkeley; and at the University of California, Los Angeles.

Dr. Smith is a Founding Member of the American Academy of Medical Acupuncture and past vice president of the American Acupuncture Association. He is a member of numerous professional organizations, including the American Academy of Anti-Aging Medicine, the Physicians Committee for Responsible Medicine, and the American College for the Advancement of Medicine.

Dr. Smith resides in Sebastopol, California, with his wife, Dellie, and two daughters.